The Great Book of
Birds

The Great Book of
Birds

John Gooders

Foreword by
Roger Tory Peterson

The Dial Press
New York 1975

Other books by John Gooders

Birds of the World (Nine volumes Editor)
Where to Watch Birds
Where to Watch Birds in Europe
The Wildlife Paradises of the World
Wildlife Photography (with Eric Hosking)

For Children

How and Why of Birds
How and Why of the Spoilt Earth

Originally published in Great Britain under the title
Birds: an illustrated survey of the
bird families of the world by
The Hamlyn Publishing Group Limited
London · New York · Sydney · Toronto
Astronaut House, Feltham, Middlesex, England
Copyright © 1975 by The Hamlyn Publishing Group Limited

Library of Congress Cataloging in Publication Data

Gooders, John.
    The great book of birds.

    1. Birds. 2. Birds—Pictorial works. I. Title.
QL673.G58   598.2   74–23534
ISBN 0–8037–3110–8

Manufactured in Italy

First Dial printing, 1975

Foreword

Of all the varied productions of nature, birds are the most admired, the most studied – and the most defended. They appeal to the senses – musically and visually. Because they can fly where they want to when they want to they symbolize freedom (even though they are as subject to natural laws as we are – or more so). Many of us would almost give our souls to have their mobility and, indeed, as air travellers or tourists we may strive to emulate them.

This book will be welcomed by the new breed of birdwatcher that has evolved and multiplied during recent years; the kind of person who has seen most of the birds of his own area and is curious about the avifauna of the rest of the world. He may be merely an armchair traveller, or he may deliberately plan his vacations so as to add new species to his 'life list.'

The number of birds in the world is usually calculated to be between 8,600 and 8,700 species, give or take a few score, depending on one's taxonomic views. New species are still being discovered, especially in the deep tropics and on islands, but at a very slow yearly rate. These additions to the world total are being cancelled out by extinctions and also by the revisionary work of systematists who are 'lumping' more and more so-called species, reducing them to the rank of subspecies.

Birds outnumber all other vertebrates except fishes and are distributed virtually everywhere throughout the world except the heart of the Antarctic continent – and even there the occasional wandering skua has been reported. They have adapted to the sterile concrete canyons of our largest cities, the driest deserts, the most humid jungles, and the highest mountains. All of the millions of square miles of sea are traversed by birds at some time or other, from the Antarctic iceshelf to the uttermost iceleads near the North Pole. Some birds, such as the oilbirds and swiftlets, even live in caves so dark that they must employ a kind of vocal sonar to guide them. Loons (divers) and some sea ducks pursue their finny prey to depths that man cannot reach without special diving equipment.

It would seem quite impossible for any birder, no matter how much time and money he has at his disposal, to seek out all 8,600+ species during his lifetime. In fact, I know of only one person, Stuart Keith, who has observed more than half of all the world's birds. His total tally recently passed the 4,500 mark and will, I am sure, eventually top 5,000.

To see even a representative of each bird family would be no mean feat. It would require visiting every continent except Antarctica and also some islands. Take the Kagu, for example, the sole representative of a monotypic family. Nocturnal, surviving in only a few patches of mountain forest in New Caledonia, it is in grave danger of extinction. I once tried to find it in its mysterious haunts without success. However, I was able to examine two of these birds in a small aviary in nearby Noumea. And therein lies one of the best functions of a good zoo or aviary – to act as a holding operation; to breed endangered species and eventually return them to the wild.

Leaf through the pages of this book, compiled so skillfully by John Gooders, and you will be enthralled by the variety of avian shapes, colours and patterns. What functions are served by all these adornments? Is their survival value not obvious to us, or is beauty its own reason for being? Certainly some birds signal with their plumage as well as by their movements and voices, but it is not clear why a Peacock should be so much more elegant than a sparrow. Natural selection has undoubtedly decreed it and a million years from now, after a million generations of Peacocks have displayed aggressively and their hens have made their choices, Peacocks may have become even more gorgeous. Certainly at this point in time, the world is blessed with a breathtaking galaxy of birds. Few are as bizarre as Peacocks or birds of paradise, but all are worthy of our attention and our study.

Some years ago, my friend the late James Fisher, the gifted British ornithologist, commented: 'The observation of birds may be a superstition, a tradition, an art, a science, a sport, a pleasure, a hobby, or a bore; this depends entirely on the nature of the observer.' To me, the pursuit of birds has been many-faceted, but never a bore. As a schoolboy, I developed an obsession for drawing and photographing them and from this obsession I have never freed myself.

Those of us who watch birds – what should we call ourselves? 'Ornithologists'? Perhaps that presumes too much. 'Bird-lovers'? I believe the term is inappropriate because loving (in the usual sense) invites reciprocation and birds simply do not reciprocate. 'Birdwatchers'? This is better, a catch-all term that can include bird-oriented people of practically every hue and stripe, from the watcher at the window to the academic. To be more specific, 'bird-listers' well describes the tally-hunters, those who tick off their finds on little white check lists. Usually, they are simply called 'birders'.

As I have stated elsewhere, birds are far more than robins, thrushes and finches to brighten the suburban garden, ducks and grouse to fill the sportsman's bag, or rare waders and warblers to be ticked off on the birder's check list. They are indicators of the environment – a sort of 'ecological litmus paper.' Because of their high rate of metabolism and furious pace of living, they reflect changes in the environment rather quickly; they warn us of things out of balance. They send out signals when there is a deterioration of the ecosystem. Inevitably, the intelligent person who watches birds (or mammals or fish or butterflies) becomes an environmentalist. He may be called an 'eco-freak' by those who are biologically illiterate, but he is dedicated to the preservation of the living world on which we depend ultimately for our own survival.

Roger Tory Peterson

Roger Tory Peterson
Old Lyme, Connecticut   October 1974

Contents

7

Introduction

When I was asked to edit the nine volume encyclopedia *Birds of the World* two thoughts flashed through my mind, 'Marvellous' and 'Oh dear!' 'Marvellous' because of the immense scope given by 2,688 pages, and 'Oh dear' because even with a work of that size there was a need to leave something out. It was a quandary that hours of thought and discussion never fully resolved. In the end the result was, like so many, a compromise. Well over a quarter of the world's birds were fully described by the experts with examples

Left Deep among the coniferous woodlands of Eurasia Wood Sandpipers usually nest beside some marshy forest pool. But they are resourceful birds and will happily take to an old Redwing's nest placed high on a lofty branch among the tangle of hanging lichens and broken branches.

Below The family of cranes has suffered a sharp decline in fortunes. Large and obvious birds, they have proved consistently unable to withstand the pressures of hunting and persecution, although changing land-use is perhaps a more important factor. These are Siberian White Cranes over Bharatpur, India.

chosen from every family and a majority of genera. Or, if you prefer, nearly three-quarters of the world's birds were omitted or, at most, barely mentioned. We could have detailed every bird in the world, but this would have cut space seriously and prevented authors from really getting into their subjects. It would also have resulted in one of the most eminently unreadable books ever to have been produced and, no doubt, would have had little appeal to a circulation-conscious partwork publisher.

Thus when the present publisher approached me to write another book on the birds of the world, I was able to live again and fill the obviously vacant niche. This book covers all of the birds family by family. It is not a new concept, but our knowledge of birds and their lives has changed remarkably since *Birds of the*

World by Oliver L. Austin Jnr. and Arthur Singer appeared in 1961. While I have an immense admiration for the paintings of Arthur Singer, there can be no doubt that a new generation of bird photographers has hit the unphotographed list for six over the last fourteen years. Certainly over half of the approximately 8,600 species of birds have now been recorded on colour film, and to illustrate a bird book, other than a field guide, without photographs is virtually unthinkable.

Against the light of the setting sun, Pink-backed Pelicans stand as silhouetted sentinels over Kenya's Lake Naivasha. Here, among dead and dying trees, vast papyrus swamps and entwining waterlilies, can be found one of the greatest of all concentrations of waterbirds.

Fourteen years ago most birdwatchers were thinking on a national scale, with only a privileged minority able to contemplate even the avifauna of the continent on which they lived. Today birdwatching knows no bounds. Eyes have been opened to the wealth of species found beyond the national boundaries, and what were once highly organized and professionally planned expeditions are now simply holidays. Tours and books covering every part of the world proliferate, but there is still a need, I believe, for the summarizing survey that I have produced here. If it is less

concerned with basic data about egg size and coloration, incubation and fledging periods, I make no apology. Most birdwatchers are concerned with birds – living, eating, fighting, flying birds. I am, and I hope it shows in the pages that follow.

To write such a book requires help and I am grateful to the host of ornithological writers that have paved my way. Many are listed in the Bibliography, but most are unaware of my reading their papers in journals and magazines. Indeed it is often difficult to acknowledge pieces of information that have been assimilated over the years, sometimes even difficult to decide whether or not an idea is one's own or someone else's. As editor I read every word that appeared in the nine volume *Birds of the World*. I have re-read much of it with interest again and I am indebted to the hundreds

A male Dotterel feigns injury in an attempt to draw the photographer from its nest. Role reversal between the sexes is well established in this and several other waders – a great benefit in the short Arctic breeding season.

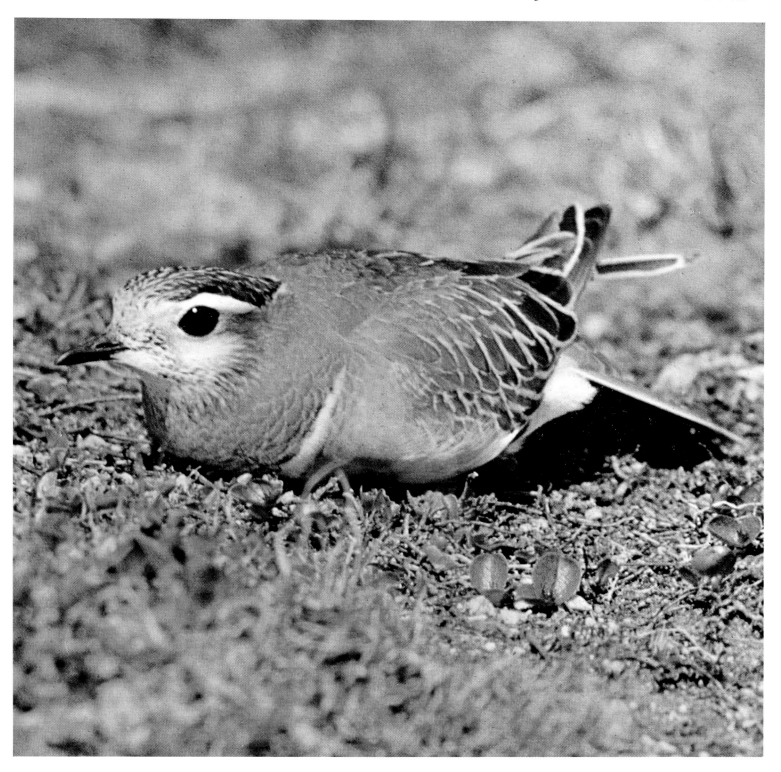

of authors who contributed articles to the work.

Watching birds is best done with companions and I have been fortunate enough to meet many experts during my travels. Most have suffered a local beginner gladly, giving of their time and expertise in the most generous fashion. But then birdwatchers are like that. Perhaps it is an investment for their trips to my part of the world, although in practice it is a matter of everyone helping everyone else with the swings and roundabouts roughly evening out.

I could thank a whole host of friends for their help and encouragement while this book was in preparation, but as every writer knows the process is ultimately a solo one. Seasons have passed while my hours were spent below ground level where, without distractions, I find my best working environment. From the virtually illegible manuscript that emerged Hazel Cooper has produced as mistake-proof a typescript as anyone could wish. I hope that she will feel the effort worthwhile. The publishers have been as helpful and encouraging as one could desire, and my wife and children enjoyed a husbandless and fatherless life to which I hope they have not become too accustomed.

John Gooders
Sussex, England.   June 1974

The two groups of vultures are similar in appearance but have different ancestries. The New World have distant affinities to storks and cormorants whereas the Old World probably had an eagle-like ancestor. This is the European Black Vulture.

A history of birds

Archaeopteryx lithographica, the first bird, is known only from a few fossilized specimens found in the Jurassic limestone of Bavaria. The tail, wing structure and teeth resemble a small dinosaur, but the fine deposits have preserved the impression of the wing and tail feathers.

Because of the frailty of the skeletons and feathers of birds, many stages in their evolution have yet to be discovered. Birds doubtless originated from reptiles like the lizard *Kuhneosaurus*, which was able to glide from tree to tree on a membrane extending from the sides of its body.

Hesperornis lived during the Cretaceous period and resembled nothing more than an overlarge diver. Unlike its modern equivalent it boasted a fine set of teeth, well adapted to gripping slippery fish, a feature surprisingly absent from most modern fish catchers apart from the mergansers or saw-bill ducks.

The more closely related 'Proto-bird' was an intermediate stage between the flying lizard and *Archaeopteryx*. Scales extended from the forearms and tail in the manner of birds and it is comparatively simple to envisage the gradual increase in length and decrease in weight so that over a period of time scales became feathers.

Prophaeton was a large version of the present day tropicbirds and had the light, gull-like flight and extended tail feathers of those birds. It lived during the Eocene, by which time many modern families of birds could be found.

Above The flightless auk *Mancalla* evolved in the Northern Hemisphere during the Pliocene period and is a forerunner of the Great Auk. Unlike that species, however, it lived among the shallow seas and sandbars of California rather than the Atlantic, and the structure of the flippers more closely resembled that of the penguins.

Left By the Miocene period the ancestors of many modern species were in existence, including the flamingo-like *Palaeolodus*. Although lacking the fine gracefulness of flamingoes, it apparently occupied a similar niche to modern members of that family.

Below Examples of the enormous *Teratornis*, ancestor perhaps of the modern condors of North and South America, have been discovered in the deposits of California's Rancho La Brea tar pits. They no doubt became engulfed during their scavenging operations on the carcasses of other animals that had become trapped.

The beginnings of birds go back some 225 to 180 million years to the Triassic period when they evolved from the same basic stock as the dinosaurs. Yet while dinosaurs of all shapes and sizes are unearthed every year, the fossil record for birds is notably incomplete. In view of their structure, with their fragile bones and a covering of even more flimsy feathers, this is not perhaps so surprising, but it does make it difficult to pick out an exact line of descent. What is more, palaeontologists have been far more concerned with studying the line of progression from fish to mammals, rather than with the side track that led to birds.

No doubt birds descended from forest-dwelling reptiles that evolved the capacity to glide from tree to tree, or from ground dwellers that jumped or flew into trees for safety. The reptilian scales gradually lengthened and modified to form feathers, and other changes gradually adapted these animals to an aerial existence.

Fortunately, conditions in Bavaria during the Upper Jurassic period were ideally suited to laying down a fine tilth of limestone. During the nineteenth century this rock was widely used for lithographic reproduction and intensively quarried as a result. In 1861 a fossil feather was discovered and named *Archaeopteryx lithographica*. A skeleton was discovered soon afterwards confirming the existence of a reptile-like animal with feathers in the Jurassic period. *Archaeopteryx*, while clearly a bird, was unlike any of today's species. It had a true tail which was feathered along its considerable length. It possessed a strong row of teeth and retained claws at the bend of the wing. It did not fly very well and probably

Species tend to die out slowly in nature, but the demise of the Great Auk can be attributed directly to man. His need for food on the high seas, plus his superstitious nature, led to the last birds being killed in 1844.

lived among waterside trees.

The special conditions found in Jurassic Bavaria preserved the *Archaeopteryx*, but thereafter the evolution of birds becomes a blank until the Cretaceous period some 135 to 70 million years ago. Here about twenty species of birds have been discovered and, while dinosaurs still dominated the earth, several modern bird families had their origins. Tern-like birds, as well as some bearing strong resemblances to divers, grebes and wildfowl, were quite widespread from England to Australia.

Hesperornis of the Upper Cretaceous deposits of North America was a 6 feet long, diver-like bird that was incapable of flight. It certainly had teeth and, like some modern birds, it could raise and lower the upper mandible as well as the lower one. The exact significance of this ability in birds is not understood, indeed some authorities have considered it purely fortuitous. The fact that *Hesperornis* had a quite distinct method of managing this cranial kinesis, as it is called, casts doubt on the fortuitous theory.

Fossils of birds become more abundant as we progress towards modern times, but there seems a quite significant rush of species during the Eocene period. These new birds show clear affinities with modern families, while older and more primitive birds rapidly disappear. At the same time the dinosaurs disappeared and their place was taken by mammals. This helps perhaps to explain the rise of the Diatrymiformes, a group of huge, ratite-like birds related to the modern Ostrich and Emu. These birds did not have the ungulate-like foot of modern ratites, but they possessed reduced wings and grew to over 7 feet in height. *Diatryma steini* from Wyoming, the most complete of the skeletons so far discovered, had a huge bill that may have been used rapaciously or, alternatively, for cutting vegetation.

By the Oligocene period, some 40 to 25 million years ago, a quarter of modern bird families had evolved, while by the Miocene, 25 to 12 million years ago, over a third of the birds are sufficiently close to modern birds as to be placed in the same genera. Herons, bustards, owls, parrots, woodpeckers and finches can all be recognized. By the Pliocene, some 12 to 3 million years ago, seventy-five per cent of species can be assigned to modern genera, and several fossils have been identified as belonging to modern species.

By the Ice Age the avifauna was essentially modern in character, but the fluctuations in temperature and vegetation must have had a considerable effect on the birds of the time. Many populations must have moved southwards where, pushed to the very edges of continents and on to islands, they evolved distinct characters and became full species. Certainly the basic north-south migration pattern of many birds evolved during this period, and some species still show a breeding range that can only be explained by the limitations imposed on them by the effects of glaciation.

At the same time a remarkable number of giant birds developed, including the huge *Teratornis* vultures of the famous Rancho La Brea tar pits in California, which had a wing span of some 14 feet. Best known of these huge birds are the moas of New Zealand, which stood up to 12 feet in height. Moas were persecuted by the invading Maoris, but they survived until modern times. The elephant-birds of Madagascar never grew to such heights, but lived for almost the same period.

The process of evolution is a dynamic one. Species are evolved and others disappear. With the coming of man the process of destruction increased, however, and a great many birds have become extinct within historical times. Voyages of exploration, colonization and the changing of landscape have had their effects on every part of this planet. Indeed many birds, protected by isolation for millions of years, were no sooner seen than dead. The case of the

Above An Ancient Egyptian wildfowler among his quarry in a papyrus marsh. The painting of the waterfowl is accurate enough for species to be identified.

Above Throughout the world, primitive man painted animals on the walls and ceilings of his caves and shelters. These are partly signs of his dependence on the animals for food, but often they also have a semi-religious significance and many displays of birds have been integrated into tribal dances.

Right A mounted specimen of the Passenger Pigeon photographed in a museum. Museums are the only places where this once numerous species can still be seen. Never before or since have so many birds been shot in such a short time as on the plains of North America during the last half of the nineteenth century.

Dodo *Raphus cucullatus* is a classic. This giant flightless pigeon was first discovered in 1599 and thereafter was hunted for food by mariners. Pigs and monkeys were introduced to the island of Mauritius and because of the disturbance the Dodos were soon unable to breed. By 1681 they were extinct. Similar fates befell many other birds, particularly those that had evolved on the protective isolation of islands.

The Great Auk *Pinguinus impennis* of the North Atlantic was exterminated by sailors in 1844. This flightless, 30-inch bird was the northern equivalent of the penguins and lived a similar existence. Vulnerable only on its breeding grounds, it was suspected of witchcraft but was nevertheless a welcome item of food to

scurvy-ridden sailors on long, monotonous voyages.

Perhaps no story of man's senseless slaughter matches that of the extermination of the Passenger Pigeon *Ectopistes migratorius*. No doubt when the first white men arrived in America, the Passenger Pigeon was the most numerous bird on earth. Breeding colonies could often be measured in miles, and flocks darkened the sky and passed by all day long. Millions of birds were involved. By the middle of the nineteenth century thousands of professional hunters earned their living from shooting the birds. Within a couple of generations the flocks were no more, and the last wild individual was seen in 1907. Martha, a captive female, died in Cincinnati Zoo in 1914, the last of her line.

Man has, and will continue to have, an ever-increasing effect on the birds and other animals that share this planet. As his numbers increase more and more of the earth's surface will be changed. Forests will disappear and along with them the more specialized forms of life. Only those species that are able to adapt to the newly created conditions will survive, but they may well survive in increasing numbers perhaps to reach pest proportions. Perhaps the actual numbers of birds in the world will increase, but the number of species will decline. In 1,000 years we may still awake to the chirp of the House Sparrow and the scream of the Starling, while a birdwatcher may have a big day if he sees ten species.

Living birds

Birds are found in practically every part of the world. Only the extreme conditions around the poles fail to provide them with a livelihood, although even in these regions several bird species manage to breed within a few hundred miles of the earth's axis. The ability to occupy almost every productive zone, every little niche, shows the extraordinary success that birds have enjoyed since they first appeared on the scene some 150 million years ago during the Late Jurassic period. Yet, despite occupying such a diversity of life zones, birds are a remarkably homogeneous class of animals. No one, I would venture, would have any problem in picking out almost every bird in the world as being a bird, and not a mammal, reptile, fish or any other animal. This similarity is due to a variety of factors, the most important of which is the sustained ability to fly.

All but a handful of the world's birds can fly. Some fly well, while others do little more than flap their way from one tree to the next. Only the Ostrich, Flightless Cormorant and a few others have totally abandoned flight, and enjoy the immense adaptive freedom that this allows. It is, then, the need to fly that limits the diversity of size, shape and structure that birds can enjoy, but it is this ability that has enabled them to colonize almost every part of the globe.

The largest flying birds are small when compared with other classes of higher animals. The Wandering Albatross may have a wing span of 11 feet, but it weighs only a fraction of a Mute Swan or Great Bustard, the two contenders for the title 'heaviest flying bird'. This size restriction is a matter of aerodynamics and is dependent on the density of the air at the altitudes that birds live. Not surprisingly, the majority of birds are small creatures, and the most accomplished fliers are the tiniest of all. Like rock climbers, it is the strength to body weight ratio that is of crucial importance.

Every aspect of the structure of a bird is geared to flight. Consider the strength of a feather in relation to its weight. Flight and body feathers both serve their functions in the most economical manner. Eiderdown, plucked from her own breast by the duck Eider to line her nest, is one of the most efficient of insulators. Pound for pound it is beyond compare. Like a thermos flask it insulates against extremes of temperature, and yet a down quilt weighs a fraction of a blanket made from sheep's wool. Despite modern technology we still have not invented an equivalent artificial or synthetic substitute.

Body feathers insulate birds against cold and heat, but also serve a variety of other functions. Their colours help birds to recognize one another; they serve as warnings; help birds to hide, and in some species are remarkably efficient wet suits. The lightness of feathers has enabled them to become adapted almost to the bizarre in the form of nuptial plumes which, in some cases, quite definitely hinder the birds. Here the disadvantage to the individual is offset by the advantage to the species as a whole. The train of a male Peacock, for example, is to say the least extravagant, yet it is a significant factor

in enabling these jungle birds to meet and reproduce successfully. Despite its size, the weight of the feathers is tiny in proportion to that of the bird.

Body, or contour feathers as they are known, do not grow continuously over the body. They are produced along well-defined tracts which extend lengthwise down the body. Flight feathers also grow in tracts and they too serve a variety of functions. The Pennant-winged Nightjar, for example, has long streamers extending from its wings which, while of great value in attracting a mate, do little to improve the bird's air power. Many other species boast tail streamers that serve a similar function. Not surprisingly these are often broken or worn by the end of the breeding season, when their function has been served.

The major flight feathers are appropriately called primaries and form the outer part of the extended wing. They vary in number from nine to twelve, and this variation is generally regarded as a significant factor in deciding a bird's taxonomic relationship. The inner wing is composed of six to thirty-seven secondary feathers. While the primaries are the major source of propulsion, the secondaries give lift, and it is not surprising that the albatrosses, so dependent on lift from the winds that scour their oceanic homes, have the longest wings and largest number of these feathers. Tail feathers too provide lift, but also act as an efficient rudder and air-brake. They vary in number between eight and twenty-four.

The flight feathers consist of a hollow shaft with narrow barbs growing on either side. Each barb is lined with barbules which interlock to form a vane held in place by barbicels. While remaining flexible, each feather is immensely strong.

The primary wing feathers are positioned to overlap and form a solid area on each down-stroke. On the up-stroke they twist to allow the air to pass easily between them. Thus as the bird flies the wings are continually opening and closing like a series of valves.

Opposite A selection of the different forms of bill and foot structure to be found in the bird world, showing the diverse ways in which the structure can be modified for function. Bills in particular are extremely variable, reflecting the diversity of ecological niches to which birds have adapted.

BILLS
1. Curve-billed Scythebill
2. Wilson's Warbler
3. Avocet
4. Hawfinch
5. Chilean Flamingo
6. Olive Oropendola
7. Two-barred Crossbill
8. Shoebill
9. Scarlet Macaw
10. Spoonbill
11. Fulmar
12. Lettered Aracari
13. Pink-eared Duck

FEET
14. Jacana
15. Ostrich
16. Tawny Owl
17. Oystercatcher
18. Skylark
19. Kingfisher
20. Three-toed Woodpecker
21. Golden eagle
22. Cuckoo
23. Swift
24. Great Crested Grebe
25. Cormorant

A Wood Pigeon dissected to show the main flight muscles. Note the size of the pectoral muscles, which provide the main power for flight.

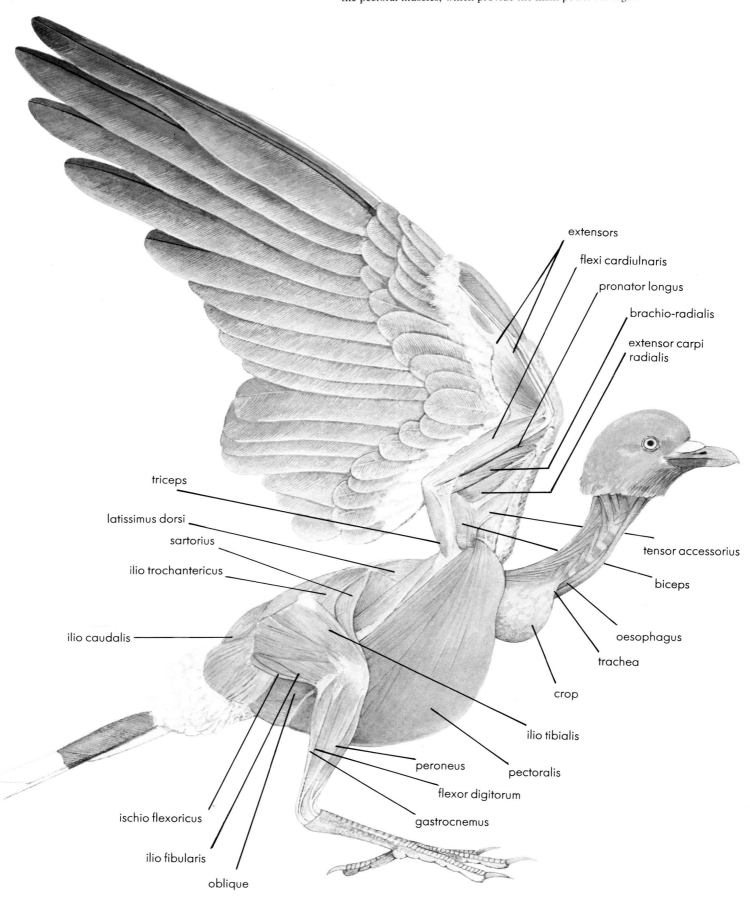

extensors

flexi cardiulnaris

pronator longus

brachio-radialis

extensor carpi radialis

triceps

latissimus dorsi

sartorius

ilio trochantericus

ilio caudalis

tensor accessorius

biceps

oesophagus

trachea

crop

ilio tibialis

peroneus

pectoralis

flexor digitorum

gastrocnemus

ischio flexoricus

ilio fibularis

oblique

All flying machines maintain height by propulsion. If forward motion is too slow they stall and they must increase speed, usually by diving, to regain control. Various devices have been used to allow aircraft to fly slowly, particularly when taking off and landing. Modern jets have flaps that extend their wing areas, but birds have their own anti-stall device. This consists of a special growth of stiff feathers that grow from the vestigial thumb known as the bastard wing. When landing the bastard wing is raised to smooth the passage of air over the extended wing, thus reducing the stalling speed by maintaining lift during the slow flight.

With their curious, spatulate bills, Spoonbills are adapted in a unique way to sifting food from water. They are found on every significant land mass in the world and are threatened only by man and his draining of wetlands. They are marshland birds frequenting fresh and salt water lagoons.

The tail feathers in most birds are an efficient air-brake. When landing they are spread to offer the largest possible surface area to the air, but in some species this is insufficient, and crash landings are common occurrences. Many seabirds are better adapted to diving into the sea than they are to performing a perfect landing. This is one of those delicate balances of advantage that are so common in the natural world. Shearwaters regularly land on their breasts with a thump, while gannets spread their large webbed feet as additional air-brakes to compensate for the inadequate braking force of the tail.

Birds fly in a variety of ways, but each is ideally suited to a particular mode of existence. Albatrosses fly on the long wings of a glider. For hour after hour they follow boats with barely a movement of their wings, relying on the updraughts of air produced by the waves to keep them aloft. In a totally different manner birds of prey soar on still wings, utilizing the hot air that rises in thermals from the land. Doubtless if they could find an easy method of getting airborne, as gliders and albatrosses do in their different ways, the birds of prey too would have adapted long narrow wings. But, of course, their life style is not suited to such modifications.

Feathers are not, however, the only adaptation to flight. The structure of a bird is totally geared to saving weight. Bones are hollow or, where necessary, honeycombed for strength. Muscles are very much reduced and, as anyone who has eaten chicken will know, the best meat is found either side of the breast bone or sternum. In a strong, flying bird, over fifty per cent of its weight may consist of these breast muscles, which are those used for flying. These are the bird's engine room. The larger outer muscles pull the wings downwards in the propulsive stroke, while the inner ones raise the wing ready for the next.

Birds are adapted to weight saving in other ways. Their digestive system is speeded up remarkably so that food is turned into fuel with the minimum of delay. The laying of eggs into a nest is another such adaptation, for while mammals grow fat when carrying their young, birds can afford no such luxury. Many small passerines lay their own weight in eggs and, while no doubt they could still fly, their efficiency would be very much reduced by such an extra burden.

All birds, except the flightless ones, share these characteristics that have adapted them to an aerial existence. In other ways they

The Hawaiian Goose, or Néné, saved from certain extinction by an intensive campaign of breeding in captivity at the Wildfowl Trust centre at Slimbridge, England. Now the emphasis is on reintroducing the bird to its native Pacific islands where it was all but extinct by 1950.

Top An Audouin's Gull perches on its rocky island home in the eastern Mediterranean. Although apparently facing few natural dangers the species is now a considerable rarity and exhibits what can only be called a relict distribution.

Above Because the vast majority of birds incubate their own eggs and rear their own young, birds like the Eurasian Cuckoo have been able to adopt a parasitic breeding routine in which the care of eggs and young is left to another species.

Left On the verge of extinction, the California Condor slowly declines in number year by year. No more than fifty birds remain in the coastal ranges near Los Angeles and there seems little chance of their escaping the fate of the Dodo.

differ enormously. In no respect is this more obvious than in the structure of their bills and feet. From a glance at these 'soft parts' of a bird, as they are often called, it is possible to predict fairly accurately how a bird lives. It may have a thick seed-cracking bill like a finch or a delicate thin probe like a godwit; a sifter bill like a spoonbill or a flesh-tearing one like a hawk. All shapes and sizes of bills including the most colourful and grotesque can be found.

Feet and legs too vary enormously from the tiny, clinging feet of swifts to the great hoof of the Ostrich, which bears a strong resemblance to that of the ungulates with which it shares the open African plains. Eagles have grasping talons; lily-trotters long, weight-spreading toes; and waterbirds effectively webbed paddles. All are suited to a particular life style.

These variations among birds arouse great curiosity among ornithologists in the field of systematics. For while some birds have little in common, others are quite clearly closely related. All birds are placed in the class Aves. Within this broad grouping they are subdivided into twenty-nine distinct orders, the members of which share various characteristics. Thus the order Charadriiformes, for instance, includes all the gulls, terns and wading birds. Each order is further subdivided into the families that form the backbone of this book, 154 in all. Some families have been divided into subfamilies, while others have only a single member and are

referred to as monotypic. Within the family the next division is the genus, within which all birds are quite clearly related. There are some 2,100 genera in all. Below that level come the species, nearly 8,600 of them.

It is the function of the systematist to arrange the birds in correct relationships in the light of the most recent knowledge of their structure, distribution and behaviour. Thus species are constantly

Below Families of birds evolve to take advantage of a variety of food sources. Although we think of owls as being rapacious nocturnal hunters of mammals, the Little Owl thrives on a diet of insects and invertebrates and is often active by day.

Opposite The Eurasian Kingfisher is a master fisherman, but many other kingfishers live in the manner of shrikes and even inhabit the arid, waterless areas beloved of those birds.

1

2

4

5

The development of a bird. Once the ovum has been fertilized the nucleus begins dividing to form the blastoderm. The next stage in the development is the formation of a cavity between the blastoderm and the yolk; at this point the blastoderm is composed of endoderm and ectoderm. The so-called 'primitive streak' then forms in the ectoderm, and from this cells bud off and migrate to form the mesoderm. All these processes are completed within about the first twenty hours of incubation, when the three germal layers have developed. The ectoderm will give rise to the skin and nervous system, the endoderm to the guts and allied organs and the mesoderm to the muscles and bones. **1.** Chick at twelve hours. The pale spot on the surface of the yolk is a flat disc of blastoderm cells, from which the embryo will develop. (At this stage the 'primitive streak' – forerunner of the notochord – is forming, but cannot be seen.) 2. Chick at seventy-two hours. Embryo *in situ*. The main blood vessels are visible, spreading over the surface of the yolk. Blood is carried to and from the yolk sac via the vitelline arteries and veins, which also carry nourishment back to the developing embryo. This embryo has an enlarged front region, due to early development of the brain and eyes. 3. Chick at five days. Embryo lying on its side *in situ*, surrounded by a network of blood vessels bringing nourishment from the yolk. The head lies to the left, and one eye and the

3

On sharply angled wings the world's longest distance migrant, the Arctic Tern, flies from Arctic to Antarctic and back every year. Such journeys are fraught with danger, but are of advantage to the terns allowing them to enjoy more hours of daylight than any other animal.

being changed from one group to another at all levels. To the layman and birdwatcher this is an intensely frustrating process, for it eliminates any possibility of a permanent and stable list of birds. Even the scientific names themselves may be changed, involving moving a bird from one genus to another. These changes are important and significant and, by the nature of the process, cannot be halted. Besides which, most systematists feel that arranging birds in a list is, in itself, an artificial device and one that serves little purpose. For these reasons there is much to be said for standardizing vernacular and English names of birds. There are, for instance, a host of birds around the world called 'robin'. If each were given an appropriate English name, then systematists could go about their business arranging and rearranging at all levels, and even changing the scientific name daily, without confusing the birdwatcher who simply wants a handy label by which he can refer to a specific bird. Unfortunately no such list exists at present, although I understand that an American computer has produced one.

To a bird nothing is more important than ensuring its place in the sun, and many of the aspects of its life that we find so appealing are dedicated to this end. Some birds migrate from one end of the earth to the other so that they can breed in the few short, but rich, weeks of the Arctic summer. Indeed, wherever food is available, whether in the sea or on land, some species of bird will have adapted to take advantage of it. Long journeys are dangerous and wasteful of life but, from the viewpoint of the survival of a species, they have their value. Without long, migratory flights large areas of the world would be uninhabited by birds. Individuals die along the way, but this must be offset by the benefits to those that survive. This is another of those balances of pros and cons in nature.

Birdsong, so appealing to our ears, proclaims a bird's territory and advertises for a mate. In general, the more colourful the bird the less it has need of a distinctive song and, it is not, therefore, surprising that the Nightingale is a rather drab, brown bird. The

6

rudimentary limbs are visible. 4. Chick at seven days. The embryo has been removed from the egg for clarity, and although it is still contained inside the amniotic cavity, the blood vessels were unavoidably cut during dissection. At this stage the head forms half the total body size, and the eyes and brain can be clearly seen. 5. A ten-day-old embryo removed from the shell. The head and limbs are well developed and the feathers are beginning to show. 6. Chick at fifteen days. This embryo has been isolated and the surrounding membrane removed to show the reduced size of the yolk sac. Note the closed eyes, the obvious feathers, and the claws on the curled, soft feet. The chick is ready to hatch at twenty days.

Above While some birds suffer at the hand of man, others, like the Collared Dove, have benefited from his wastage. The extraordinary spread of this species across Europe is one of the most interesting ornithological phenomena of the present century.

Left Migration brings vast numbers of birds to the Mediterranean every year where, exhausted, they are pursued by 'sportsmen'. The slaughter, particularly in spring, may have a significant influence on the populations of many European birds. These are Turtle Doves and Golden Orioles.

Top left and right A remarkable example of convergent evolution exists between the meadowlarks of North America and the longclaws of Africa. Both inhabit open grassland and the Yellow-throated Longclaw (right) is almost identical to the Eastern (left) and Western Meadowlarks, although they belong to widely separated families. Both have yellow breasts marked with horseshoes of black, and also share many structural features.

territories of birds spread them out through whatever habitat is appropriate to them. They enable birds to rear a family in peace and without interference from their neighbours. Even seabirds, clustered on some stack or seacliff, have tiny territories, often only as large as they can reach with their bills, and from which they will drive intruders. Very few birds live totally communal lives. Most sing, fight and breed within their territory – their place in the sun.

Birds communicate by song and by their various call notes. Almost anyone can recognize an alarm call when they hear one, but birds utter a great variety of other calls. Some fifty-seven distinct calls of the Great Tit have been isolated, for example. Whether each one can be recognized and understood by other Great Tits we do not know, but it is reasonable to suppose that such a variety of calls would serve some purpose in communication.

Birds communicate in a variety of other ways: indeed they are comparatively simple animals and their behaviour is often triggered by stimulae. At times this simple stimulus-response behaviour may make them appear stupid. The foster parents of the Cuckoo, for instance, like other birds, react to an open mouth in their nest by feeding it. The larger the mouth the greater the stimulus to feed. They are not to know that the young Cuckoo is not their own offspring, even when it grows to twice their own size. If a nest of tiny chicks has another nest of older chicks of the same species placed next to it, the parents will turn their feeding attention to the larger brood.

A gull will recognize its own egg if it is placed a short distance from the nest and roll it back into place. If a huge, but similarly patterned egg is placed the same distance away the gull will react to this super-stimulus in the same way. But if its own egg is placed at a greater distance it will not be recognized, and may well be eaten by the bird.

If much bird behaviour is so simply explained it does little to diminish its appeal. Throughout the world there is a growing awareness of the appeal of birds and a growth of birdwatching as a leisure activity. Instead of shooting and egg collecting there is a boom in field identification, comparative studies, distributional research and ethology. That such studies should be adding to the

factors that aid the work of systematists, progressively more concerned with the ways birds live rather than their basic anatomical peculiarities, is all to the good. More important perhaps is the optimism generated by mass interest in ensuring that birds survive in what is essentially a hostile world. More birdwatchers equals more conservationists, more conservationists equals more money to protect birds and other endangered wildlife. While at present, conservation, especially when backed by money, tends to be somewhat parochial, there is a glimmer of light that shows that those interested in nature are becoming more international in outlook. Provided priorities are examined and arranged and that money and educational efforts are correctly directed to where they are most needed, then the outlook for the birds of the world is bright. Let us have no more examples of fascinating birds disappearing from the face of the earth, like the New Zealand wattlebirds, before anyone has time to study them. The history of birds leads one to pessimism, but the growth of birdwatching as a recreation is potentially a source of optimism.

Confined to a small number of well-defined and traditional breeding sites the Grey Heron is an ideal subject for census. In Britain its numbers are counted every year giving a most accurate picture of the fluctuations experienced by a wild bird population.

Overleaf Once thought extinct, the Takahe was recently rediscovered in a remote area of New Zealand's South Island. The destruction caused by introducing an alien element to an island fauna is well shown by the rarity of this and other New Zealand species.

The families of birds

Ostriches Struthionidae

The Ostrich *Struthio camelus*, sole member of the Struthionidae, is the world's largest living bird. A male will weigh anything up to 340 pounds and stand up to 8 feet tall. With such stature it is not surprising that Ostriches have lost the power of flight; the energy required to lift a bird of that weight simply cannot be produced in a viable form. Instead the Ostrich is perfectly adapted to a mode of

life that depends on running to escape predators. It has even evolved a cloven hoof consisting of only two toes, similar to that of the other animals that share its plain's existence. An Ostrich has been seen to pass an antelope in full gallop at 40 miles per hour, a feat which places it among the fastest of all the birds, in spite of the fact that it does not fly.

This dependence on speed worked very well until the automobile and high-power rifle came into widespread use. Then, within a matter of five years, the Ostrich was exterminated from North Africa and the Middle East. Today it survives in a belt that extends through the open country south of the Sahara, southwards into East Africa and Zambia. Birds found in southern Africa are descended from the feral stock that was introduced during the great Ostrich-farming boom at the end of last century. Several distinct forms have been recognized – the Somali, the Masai, etc., – but all are usually regarded as belonging to the single species.

Having abandoned flight the Ostrich has lost the strong, stiff feathers of the wing and tail that mark aerial species. Instead, a growth of soft plumage, with almost the warmth of down, acts as an insulation against the harsh temperature endured by Ostriches throughout their arid range. The soft feathers of the wings and tail were formerly much in demand for the boas sported by fashionable Victorian ladies. It was this trade that lead to the establishment of farms, a few of which continue to operate in South Africa.

Ostriches are polygamous. The male gathers around him a harem of three, sometimes up to five, females all of which lay their eggs in the same nest. Thus a clutch of between fifteen and fifty eggs is produced. The eggs are almost spherical in shape, about six inches long and equivalent in volume to about twenty hens' eggs. Such a clutch laid on open ground presents a significant meal to a jackal, the dominant predator. Egyptian Vultures have also learned to break Ostrich eggs by cracking them with large stones, a habit that is spreading. Since the time of the ancient Egyptians the shells of Ostrich eggs have been used as vessels and bowls.

The completed clutch is incubated by the male, with some assistance from the dull-coloured hens, and the chicks run about within minutes of hatching. Only their cryptic colouring, and an elaborate distraction display of the adults, protects them from the many predators that share their living zone.

Like the other plains' game animals that live in the bush, Ostriches are nomadic, wandering wherever food is most readily available.

Large, flightless birds like the Ostrich were once found in many parts of the world. They have adapted to a terrestrial life style and rely on their fleetness of foot rather than flight to escape the unwelcome attentions of predators.

Rheas Rheidae

The two species of rhea are the South American equivalents of the Ostrich, although both are considerably smaller than the African bird. The Common Rhea *Rhea americana* stands 5 feet in height and weighs a mere 50 pounds, compared with the male Ostrich at 8 feet and 340 pounds. It also lacks a bold, black and white plumage, being a dull grey in colour with a dark base to the neck in the male, and its feathers have never been of any significant commercial value. The Common Rhea is found in the pampas of South America and was formerly more widespread than today. The inevitable advance of agriculture has pushed it to the more remote areas although it mixes freely with cattle if not persecuted. Darwin's Rhea *Pterocnemia pennata* is a smaller bird with white tips to the wings. It is found among the eastern ranges of the Andes.

Rheas are flightless, fast-running birds with three strong toes, and have the ability to change course violently with a flurry of wings that effectively throws off pursuers. Although rheas have larger wings than the other ratite birds – Ostriches, Emus and cassowaries – they are not sufficient for flying.

Rheas live in groups of ten to thirty birds for most of the year, but during the breeding season the dominant males chase out younger males and fight each other for control of a harem. They bite and kick each other, but little serious damage is done. The winner becomes master of four or five, sometimes as many as eight, hens and a breeding territory often near water. It is the male that constructs the nest and leads the hens to it after he has displayed and mated them. Unlike the Ostrich, the rhea has a considerable vocal repertoire, although the grunts produced sound more like a mammal than a bird.

Each hen lays up to eighteen eggs, but is not desperately concerned whether they are in the nest or not. Eggs are often laid quite indiscriminately, and although the male will roll nearby ones into his nest, many are wasted. Some hens lay in a nest belonging to a different male from the one with which they mated. Once the clutch is complete (anything from ten to eighty eggs) the male chases off all intruders and many more eggs then go to waste as they are laid by the hen. The male performs all the incubation and leads the grey and black striped youngsters away soon after they hatch. Many chicks are lost and join other families, so that parties of young rheas can vary in age quite considerably.

Rheas inhabit the grassy plains of the Argentinian pampas and are the New World equivalent of the Ostrich. Like the Ostrich they have long, strong legs for running and a keen eye for the approach of danger.

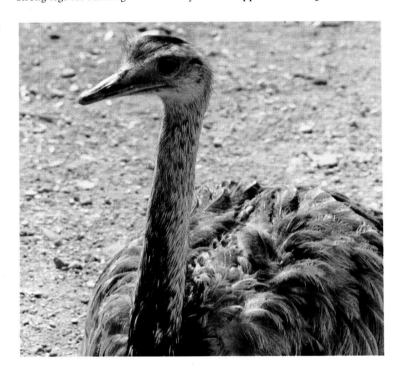

Cassowaries Casuariidae

Cassowaries are large, flightless ratite birds found in north-eastern Australia and the adjacent parts of New Guinea, as well as the nearby islands of Aru, Ceram, Jobi and New Britain. This geographical isolation has lead to the development of many distinct forms, but all are now grouped into three species exhibiting many subspecies.

Cassowaries may stand up to 5 feet in height and weigh over 100 pounds. Unlike the other ratites the female is larger than the male, and they are not known to be polygamous. Like the others, the male alone incubates, but both sexes care for the attractively striped chicks. This striping is an effective camouflage in the mottled light of their forest home.

Like the kiwis and unlike the other ratites, cassowaries are birds of thick forest. Their feathers consist of long quills which have the consistency of thick hair, and which form a fine protection against thorns and other snags as they run through the undergrowth. In addition the wings boast several strong, stout quills that act as fenders, and the head has a prominent horned casque that is held forward to break a way through the jungle. It has been estimated that cassowaries can run through undergrowth at speeds up to 30 miles per hour. The legs are strong and the bird defends itself

The Cassowary is unusual among ratite birds in being an inhabitant of dense jungle. The prominent horn on the head is used as a buffer as it forces its way at speed through thick vegetation.

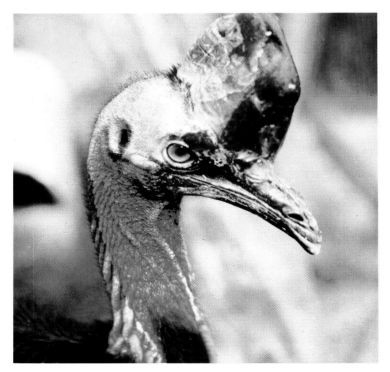

by kicking violently and inflicting nasty wounds with its sharp talon-like nails. Many natives in New Guinea have been killed in encounters with cassowaries, and a European boy was killed in Queensland.

Cassowaries are black in colour and two species boast large red and blue wattles on the face and neck. The third species, the smaller and more dull Bennett's Cassowary *Casuarius bennetti*, is found in New Britain. Only the two-wattled Australian Cassowary *C. casuarius* occurs in Australia, while the One-wattled Cassowary *C. unappendiculatus* is confined to New Guinea.

The three to six large, green eggs may be up to five and a half inches in length, and are laid in a forest clearing. The male incubates the eggs and cares for the young which remain with the parents for up to five months.

Emu Dromaiidae

The sole surviving member of its family, the Emu *Dromaius novaehollandiae*, is second in size only to the Ostrich among living birds. It is widespread throughout Australia (now extinct in Tasmania) except for in the tropical rainforests of the north-east, where it is replaced by its nearest relative the Australian Cassowary. Although such a large and obvious bird, and in spite of hunting pressure from the early settlers and an organized 'Emu-War' in 1932, the Emu has survived the settlement and taming of that continent. Settlers claimed that its meat tasted like beef, and their wives found they could feed a whole family on a single egg. The Emu was beaten back but only slowly. Farming interests raised so much commotion, however, that on 2nd November 1932 a machine gun unit was sent to Western Australia to thin out the 20,000 Emus that were breaking down fences and eating crops. After a month of significant failure the Royal Australian Artillery was withdrawn, and the farmers settled for Emu-proof fences. Even today Western Australia pays a bounty on the bill of an Emu and thousands are killed every year.

Like the cassowaries, Emus have hair-like feathers but lack the other adaptations to forest living of those birds. They also lack the aggressive claws and instincts of that species, and are often quite tame and approachable when left unmolested. Emus run well when alarmed and usually spend their time in small bands roaming in search of food, which consists of fruits and other vegetable matter as well as insects. They spend most of their time feeding their huge bulk – males may stand 6 feet in height and weigh 120 pounds.

The nest is usually made in the shade of a tree, but invariably on open ground where the sitting bird can spot approaching danger. The eight to ten eggs (up to sixteen have been recorded) are about five and a half inches long and dark green in colour. They are much sought after as they can be carved in the manner of an artist's scraper board.

The male alone incubates the clutch for some sixty days, and broods and cares for the young for a similar period after hatching.

Emus live in the open areas of Australia and form large flocks which frequently raid farmland in their search for food. Despite attempts at control and frequent persecution they continue to prosper.

Moas Dinornithidae and Anomalopterygidae

The two families of moas, consisting of seventeen distinct species, are extinct birds that were confined to New Zealand. Without exception they were large birds and quite incapable of flight. The largest of all moas, *Dinornis maximus*, stood 10 feet in height. Despite popular opinion, moas are not myths. When the Maoris arrived in New Zealand from Polynesia about 1,000 years ago, they found moas in plenty and used them as a readily available source of food. Many of the bones of these great birds have been collected from middens, although even larger numbers have been found in circumstances that suggest natural deaths.

The name moa is a Maori word adopted by the earliest European settlers who found only the bones or fossil bones of the birds. There seems little doubt that the last moas survived into the seventeenth century, but it is just possible that one of the smaller species *Megalapteryx* of South Island may have survived into the nineteenth century, and have been seen by at least a few European

settlers, although its accepted date of extinction is 1773. The best that ornithologists have to work on are a plentiful supply of bones, a few pieces of skin and feathers, a few eggs and a lot of eggshell pieces. There are also Maori rock paintings at Craigmore and Pareora that depict moas. From these sources we can establish that moas must have closely resembled the emus of Australia; that they had a vegetarian diet; that they were most common in the foothills; that the females were larger than the males; and that the latter performed the incubation. The eggs, which are huge, are nevertheless similar in structure to those of other birds.

It is not unreasonable that such a huge bird could have survived in New Zealand, with its total lack of large predators, for such a long time after other monster birds had become extinct. Deposits are not ancient (the earliest bone is dated as mid-Pliocene, about five million years ago) but there is some evidence of other large birds inhabiting the islands about the same time.

Kiwis Apterygidae

Kiwis are, at one and the same time, among the most familiar and least known birds in the world. Almost everything we know about their lives has been gleaned from the study of captive birds in zoos, and while the visitor to their native New Zealand would count himself extraordinarily fortunate to see a kiwi, he would be more likely to join the vast majority of New Zealanders to whom the bird is an unseen symbol. Kiwis – there are three distinct species – have their home among the huge evergreen forests of three of the New Zealand islands. Perhaps more than many other birds a great deal can be learned from their anatomy.

Like their nearest relatives, the extinct moas and the world's other ratite birds, they do not have a keel to the breast. The pectoral muscles, so prominent in other birds, are small and undeveloped and the bird is quite flightless. For this reason it has no need of a tail and its hidden wings are vestigial. Its feathers lack the unifying barbs and strength of those of flying birds, and the fine, brown plumage closely resembles hair. The kiwis have small eyes and are nocturnal in habits, indicating that the power of sight is not of great significance to them. The nostrils are situated at the tip of the long bill where they are most useful. They have large ear apertures, and well-developed facial bristles indicate that the sense of touch is important to them. The thick, strong legs, with their heavy claws are used to scratch around the forest floor, and also to excavate the nesting burrow.

The kiwis are about the same size as a chicken, and a large female may weigh as much as 7 or 8 pounds. She will lay one huge, white egg, two in some subspecies, that at a pound in weight is the heaviest in proportion to body weight of any bird. Like the other ratites, the smaller male kiwi performs the ten to twelve weeks incubation by himself.

The Common Kiwi *Apteryx australis* is found in three distinct subspecies on North Island, South Island and Stewart Island. It is not uncommon, but has doubtless been much reduced by European settlement and the introduction of various mammals. Only three mammals are native to New Zealand, and two of those are bats. In southern South Island two other kiwis are found, the Great Spotted *A. haasti* and the Little Spotted *A. oweni*.

The well-known, but seldom seen, Kiwi is the national emblem of New Zealand and, like other flightless birds of those islands, has suffered considerably from introduced pests. It is a crepuscular species and lays the largest of all birds' eggs in proportion to its size.

Elephant birds Aepyornithidae

If the legend of Sinbad the Sailor and his encounters with the mythical Roc were not based on the elephant birds of Madagascar and the impression they made on the minds of the earlier mariners to visit that land, then the accuracy of description of this bird would need further explanation. There seems little doubt that several huge birds, some up to 10 feet tall and weighing perhaps a quarter of a ton, survived on Madagascar well into historical times. One species is believed to have survived until 1649. This is prior to the extinction of the Dodo, but it is nevertheless comparatively recent history.

The genus *Aepyornis* consisted of several species, the largest of which *A. titan* was absolutely massive and laid an egg over a foot in length. Such eggs can hold up to two gallons and are the largest single cells known to science. Many complete skeletons have been recovered from the marshes of Madagascar, and a great many bones and egg fragments have been discovered.

Tinamous Tinamidae

Superficially rather dull, grouse-like birds of muted colours, tinamous are, in fact, a surprisingly interesting group of South American birds. They are not related to the partridges or guineafowl which they so strongly resemble. Their nearest relatives are the rheas, and although tinamous show several ratite characteristics, unlike those birds they can fly and are certainly not to be placed in that group. By a process of convergent evolution they have grown to resemble grouse, but that is where the resemblance ends.

Tinamous are primitive birds, indeed it seems likely that the earliest birds to evolve were very similar to them. They are all-purpose birds occupying a range of habitats and niches that elsewhere, in say Africa or Eurasia, would be occupied by more varied, highly specialized species.

Tinamous are a highly successful family that range over a large part of South America. They fly poorly, tire easily and generally rely on their fine camouflage to protect them from predators.

Tinamous are small to medium-large birds found from central Mexico to southernmost Patagonia and Tierra del Fuego. On closer inspection their dull, brown plumage is seen to be beautifully patterned and vermiculated. The larger females are generally more boldly coloured and it is not then surprising that the males perform the domestic tasks of incubation and care of the young. They stand upright often looking almost tailless. The legs are strong and the birds run very effectively, preferring this method of escaping danger to that of flight. Their short, rounded wings propel them through the air quite strongly for a short distance, but their flight is far from accurate and they frequently collide with trees and other obstacles. Even when running they sometimes stumble and fall, and it is not surprising that their most effective method of defence is to stand absolutely still. Equally unsurprising is the difficulty of observing such shy birds.

About fifty species arranged in nine genera are recognized, and they occupy almost every habitat type as well as every region of the continent. Some species are found in the dense, tropical jungles of the Amazon basin, like the far-ranging Variegated Tinamou *Crypturellus variegatus*, although others are confined to the high Andes, like the Ornate Tinamou *Nothoprocta ornata*. Tinamous frequently breed in captivity but they have failed to establish themselves in the wild following attempts at introduction in Britain and North America. Their flesh is said to resemble chicken but with more flavour – doubtless further attempts to introduce such tasty birds elsewhere will be tried.

Tinamous are polygamous. Even within a single species several females will lay one egg in the nests of separate males or several eggs in different nests. Males sometimes incubate different nests one after another, and even cover a fresh egg while still caring for a young chick. Male Bonaparte's Tinamous *Nothocercus bonapartei* gather a harem of three females, and a mutual display ceremony results in some nine eggs in a single nest.

All tinamous' eggs are beautifully glossed and of varied but uniform colours. They are large for the size of the bird, but most females lay comparatively few eggs compared with other similar sized ground-nesting birds. The incubation period is remarkably short, in some cases less than twenty days, and the male often covers the eggs with vegetation when he leaves the nest. The chicks run well soon after hatching, and are able to fly before they are fully grown – a unique achievement for a bird that will seek to avoid such activity for the rest of its life. The breeding season is confined in some species, although others nest throughout the year.

Penguins Spheniscidae

The seventeen or eighteen species of penguins (depending on which authority is followed) are at once among the most familiar and least known birds in the world. They are the comical overdressed little gentlemen that are almost as much an attraction at the zoo as the chimpanzees' tea party, but they are also a group of flightless birds adapted to the harshest environment on earth – the Antarctic and sub-Antarctic Oceans and islands. While most penguins have remained in the extreme south, several species have spread northwards along the line of those cold currents that have their point of origin in Antarctic seas. The Jackass Penguin *Spheniscus demersus* has spread northwards with the Benguela Current to the west coast of southern Africa, while its Pacific equivalent the Peruvian Penguin *S. humboldti* has followed the Humboldt Current northwards as far as the coast of Peru. Cold currents are rich in minerals and life, and the penguins find the rich fishing grounds as much to their liking as productive Antarctic

waters. The Galápagos Penguin *S. mendiculus* has followed the Humboldt Current to the equator. It is clearly related to the Peruvian Penguin, but this small bird is recognized as a separate species found nowhere else.

It is no accident that the world distribution of penguins closely resembles that of the albatrosses. While it may appear strange that a group of birds that has lost the power of flight should share the habitat and range of a group whose members are absolute masters of the air, it must not be forgotten that marine life is concentrated by the food chains of the participants. While albatrosses are surface feeders penguins dive well beneath the surface for their food, but both depend on prey that in turn depends on an ocean rich in life.

Penguins are also closely related to the albatrosses and mollymauks that share their range. Their beaks consist of a series of separate plates that have become fused into a short, stubby bill. In the albatrosses these plates still remain visually distinct.

First used by mariners 200 years ago, the name 'penguin' was originally applied to the Great Auk whose scientific name was *Pinguinus impennis*, and which was slaughtered to extinction by 1844. If they had been discovered earlier no doubt the same fate would have befallen several of the penguins.

Penguins, like the Great Auk, are flightless birds that are perfectly equipped to a life at sea: indeed they are better adapted to an aquatic existence than any other family of birds. The wings are reduced to hard, narrow flippers made up of highly flattened and enlarged bones fused at the elbow. These are used as the sole form of propulsion under water. In effect the birds virtually fly through the water and can swim almost as fast as a seal. They 'porpoise', rising out of the water and remaining clear for considerable 'jumps', before plummeting into the water again.

Of all the world's penguins, the Adelie of the Antarctic is the most numerous and best known. It breeds in dense colonies and survives only by adopting the most rigidly controlled shift system of incubation and feeding. The 'ecstatic' greeting ceremony is thus an important part of maintaining the crucial bond between members of a pair.

Like aquatic mammals penguins often perform like this in groups. They are also able to leap clear of the water to land on ice floes, and Adélies *Pygoscelis adeliae* in particular can leap five or six feet up an ice cliff. It is this explosive speed through the water that makes the birds such excellent fishermen. Their speed has been measured at over twenty-five miles per hour.

Penguins' legs are set well back on their bodies like a seal's flippers. Their feet are webbed and, although they make ideal

The only bird that need never set foot on land, the Emperor Penguin breeds in the harshest conditions found on Earth – on the icecap during the Antarctic winter. Here one has been found in a desolate and featureless snowscape.

rudders while swimming, they are comparatively useless on land. Most penguins waddle along upright like little old sailors freshly ashore, but some are quite fast runners, and others often toboggan along on their tummies over ice and snow.

The largest penguin, the Emperor *Aptenodytes forsteri,* stands nearly 4 feet in height and weighs 75 pounds compared with only 12 inches of the diminutive Little Blue Penguin *Eudyptula minor.* Some fossil penguins stood over 5 feet in height. All species are covered with a thick matting of feathers that grows all over their bodies, rather than in distinct apteria or tracts as in most other birds. These feathers closely resemble the fur of seals rather than the broad feathers of terrestrial birds. They form a thick layer of insulating material that is completely waterproof and of low resistance to drag. Allied with their highly streamlined shape, the penguins are perfectly adapted to the marine world.

Size apart, the major visible differences between the world's penguins is in the region of the head. Most species have a quite distinctive head pattern that distinguishes them from the others. Basically penguins can be divided into five distinct groups, the first of which are the large penguins with an orange-yellow comma extending up the neck to behind the eye. This group consists of the Emperor Penguin and the King Penguin *Aptenodytes patagonica.* The second group comprises medium-sized penguins with yellow or

All of the world's penguins identified, showing clearly the division of these birds into various types: the large, the banded and the tufted. All save the Galápagos Penguin are found in the Southern Hemisphere, mostly around the Antarctic continent.

orange tufts of feathers on the head. Into this group fall the Erect-crested *Eudyptes sclateri*, Macaroni *E. chrysolophus*, Rockhopper *E. crestatus*, Royal *E. schlegeli*, Snares Island *E. robustus*, Fiordland *E. pachyrhynchus* and Yellow-eyed penguins *Megadyptes antipodes*. Only the latter is not placed in the genus *Eudyptes*, and its crests meet at the rear of the head. The third group consists of birds with a single breast band, the Jackass and Peruvian penguins. The fourth group comprises penguins with double breast bands, the Magellanic *Spheniscus magellanicus* and the Galápagos penguins. Penguins that are basically black and white comprise the fifth group, including the Gentoo *Pygoscelis papua*, Chinstrap *P. antarctica*; Adélie, Little Blue and White-flippered Penguins *Eudyptula albosignata*.

As can be seen these groups nearly, but not completely, coincide with generic divisions. In turn each generic division is confined largely to a particular life zone. *Aptenodytes* and *Pygoscelis* are Antarctic; *Eudyptes* is New Zealand based as is the monotypic genus *Megadyptes*; *Eudyptula* is Australian; and *Spheniscus* is temperate South American with a single offshoot to South Africa.

Most penguins breed colonially and are monogamous. A partner that does not reappear at the start of the breeding season will be replaced, although most pairs re-establish themselves at the same nest site year after year. The majority of penguins lay two or occasionally three eggs, but King and Emperor Penguins lay a single egg that is incubated on their feet covered by a special pouch-like fold of skin. In this way these species are freed of territorial problems for their 'nest' is carried around with them.

The Emperor is one of the strangest of birds. It is the only bird species that need never come to land. It breeds on the ice of the frozen Antarctic seas in the middle of the Antarctic winter. Apsley Cherry-Garrard described his expedition to collect Emperor Penguins' eggs at Cape Crozier as '*The Worst Journey in the World*', the title of the book recounting his experiences. No doubt the conditions during the winter on the pack ice are the worst faced by any bird in the world. Perhaps it is not surprising that even something as fundamental to birds as territory is abandoned for the greater need of survival.

The egg is laid in May and June during the period of total darkness. Immediately after laying, the female makes her way over the 50 to 100 miles of pack ice to the sea, leaving the male to incubate the egg for the full sixty-four days that it takes to hatch. During this time males huddle together, taking turns at the edge of the group, backs to the bitter wind. For these sixty-four days, and the preceding journey to the rookery, and the subsequent trek to the sea, the male Emperor Penguin fasts, losing thirty per cent of his total weight in the process. When the chick hatches the male feeds it on a secretion from his crop. Within a day or so the female takes over while the male replenishes his energy reserves at sea. Soon both parents are feeding the chick which joins a creche of fast growing, down-covered youngsters. Each parent picks out its own chick to feed from the creche. Emperor colonies are situated at points where the pack ice breaks up early. In fact the whole breeding biology of Emperor Penguins is designed to ensure that the chicks fledge at the period of greatest food abundance.

That other Antarctic breeder, the Adélie, also manages an extensive fast during the incubation period. Males dispense with food for six weeks and lose up to forty per cent of their body weight. Unlike the Emperors, however, these smaller birds are highly territorial and very aggressive in defence of their patch. Like most other penguins they construct a nest – in this case a pile of stones and pebbles that can be added to only by stealing another Adélie's nest during its absence – and incubate horizontally. The most common cause of friction at an Adélie colony is the arrival of inexperienced, unpaired birds ready to breed at four years of age. They arrive late, take time to pair, and generally intrude into the territory of others. They are, however, less successful breeders. Some Adélie rookeries number up to half a million birds.

While the Adélie and most other penguins nest on open ground, the Little Blue Penguin nests in burrows. The Little Blue has established itself as a true wildlife star in Australia. Such is the tenacity of these birds to their breeding sites that they come ashore at night and pass within yards of crowds of people that have paid to watch their procession up the beach illuminated by floodlights.

For many years the whalers and sealers of the last century and the early part of this also managed to wring a few pints of oil from a penguin. Vast numbers of birds were boiled down for their high oil content, surely as stupid and pointless as any human exploitation of an animal population. Today most penguins are safe, although the Galápagos Penguin probably numbers less than 500 birds. The Antarctic species, however, have recently been exposed to increasing scientific attention and even tourism. Such developments must be monitored for it is often unintentional action that leads to disaster. By disturbing breeding birds, eggs and chicks are left unguarded from the attacks of skuas and sheathbills. Once fledged the penguin's enemies are the Leopard Seal and the Killer Whale.

Divers Gaviidae

Divers are a primitive group of waterbirds whose ancestors can be traced back to the Upper Cretaceous. *Hesperornis regalis* was a huge, North American diver-like bird that fed on fish, boasted a row of gripping teeth, and which was over 6 feet long. Modern divers probably evolved during the Eocene some fifty million years ago, and fossils of several of the living species have been found among deposits laid down in the Ice Age.

There are five species, all found in northern latitudes, several of which enjoy a completely circumpolar distribution. Throughout most of their range they, and particularly their wailing calls, are symbolic of the wild country where naturalists and few others penetrate. Just to see them on the estuaries in winter is to enjoy a vicarious trip to the tundra and wild desolation of the north. There, among the peat bogs, in lakes and lochans, divers make their summer homes.

Divers, called 'loons' in North America probably after 'loonies'

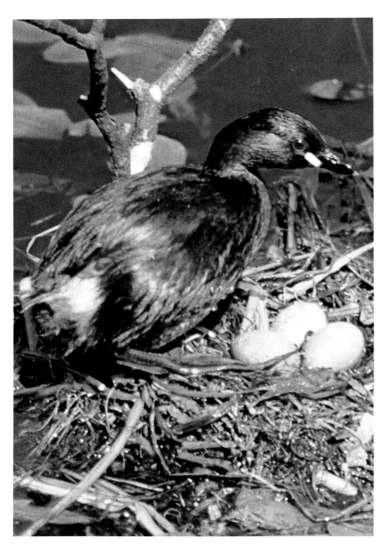

or 'lunatics', are large birds, 2 to 3 feet in length, well adapted to their niche. They are perhaps the most accomplished of all diving birds reaching depths of well over 200 feet, and being capable of spending several minutes below water in an emergency. They normally dive between half a minute to a minute when feeding, but they may swim several hundred yards submerged to avoid danger. Their feet are almost perfect paddles and their streamlined shape, long neck and rapier-like bill are well adapted to an underwater existence.

Like other aquatic species the evolution of divers is a balance between flight and ability in the water. Albatrosses have developed as flying machines, penguins as swimmers. Divers can fly strongly but take anything from twenty to several hundred yards to get into the air. On land they are clumsy in the extreme and as a result make their nest only a few feet from the water's edge, and create a slipway down which they slide at the first sign of danger. They frequently swim with only head and neck above water, but in Japan the local fishermen rely on wild divers to drive shoals of fish into their nets, and as a result the birds have become tame and confiding.

The lakes and other waters on which they breed invariably freeze up during the winter and divers are forced to move to the coast. Several species migrate quite positively southwards several hundreds of miles to gather at milder fishing grounds. The major item of diet is fish but they also take crustaceans and molluscs. They are usually solitary although winter divers sometimes gather in small groups and occasionally in large flocks up to several hundred strong.

The nest is usually no more than a depression near the edge of a lake or on a small island. If available, a fairly substantial mass of

Left Like other members of their family, Little Grebes construct floating nests of aquatic vegetation on which to lay their eggs. The decay of the nesting material produces heat and aids incubation.

Below Divers are expert underwater swimmers, but poorly equipped to come ashore. This Black-throated Diver, like others of its family, nests close to the water's edge and slides to safety at the slightest sign of danger.

aquatic vegetation may be constructed on to which the two large, oval and beautifully marked, brown eggs are laid. Both parents share the month-long incubation and the two months that the young take to fledge. Like young grebes, baby divers are often carried on the backs of their parents. At the end of the breeding season the adults moult and are, for a short time, flightless.

There are five distinct species of diver all belonging to the single genus *Gavia*. The Great Northern *Gavia immer* (the Common Loon of America) and the White-billed Diver *G. adamsii* are the largest of the divers. In summer the Great Northern is a boldly patterned, black and white bird with an iridescent, green sheen over the head and two distinctive, striped collars. It has a strong, thick, tapering bill that is held horizontally as the bird swims. As with the other divers it becomes a nondescript greyish bird in winter. Great Northerns breed right across North America from the Aleutian Islands to Newfoundland, on both coasts of Greenland and in Iceland. After years of speculation and inconclusive evidence, a pair was proved to breed in Britain's Shetland Isles in the early 1970s.

To the north, and almost exclusively in the tundra zone above the Arctic Circle, the Great Northern is replaced by the remarkably similar White-billed Diver. The major distinction between the two species is the size and shape of the bill, which in the latter is both massive and up-tilted. Unlike the Great Northern, the White-billed is essentially Arctic and, although it breeds right across the coastal zone of Siberia to northern Scandinavia, it seldom moves southwards even along the Norwegian coast. Some authors regard these two birds as a single species.

Similarly, many authors regard the Black-throated Diver *G. arctica* and the Pacific Black-throated Diver *G. pacifica* as geographical representatives of a single species. They are certainly very similar although the Pacific diver is slightly smaller and has a greenish gloss over the throat. Both species breed on large lakes which meet all of their summer requirements including food. Red-throated Divers *G. stellata*, in contrast, utilize smaller lakes and flight regularly to fish at larger feeding grounds, often on the sea. They breed further north than the Black-throated species and are generally more numerous. Their thin, almost grebe-like, bill is held at a pronounced tilt as they swim. They have a circumpolar distribution. As their names imply, these species have red and black throats which serve to identify them in summer.

Grebes Podicipitidae

The grebes are an aquatic family that have adapted fully to a waterbound existence. This process has progressed so far that mosts species are weak fliers, and one has lost the power of flight completely. For this reason species have developed in geographic isolation one from another, and several birds have a highly confined range. In contrast others are very widespread birds.

All grebes dive easily and are sleek-plumaged, attractive birds. They can stay submerged for considerable periods hunting and

Once hunted for its plumes, the Great Crested Grebe is a fine example of what rigorous protection can achieve for a wild bird. It is now widespread and numerous in Britain and even nests on city ponds and lakes.

evading predators, as well as human intruders such as birdwatchers. The Little Grebe *Podiceps ruficollis* has the unendearing habit of submerging on sight and rising among aquatic vegetation some yards away, thus effectively disappearing. All grebes have dense body plumage that is waterproof and an effective insulation against temperature change. Most have a distinctive breeding plumage marked with bold areas of colour and often by special nuptial plumes. It was for their thick plumage and elaborate feathers that Great Crested Grebes *P. cristatus* in particular were slaughtered to the point of extinction in many regions at the end of last century.

Grebes have lobed feet like the coots that are highly effective paddles and efficient, if not perfect, rudders in flight. The lack of a proper tail is common to all species. The legs (tarsi) are laterally compressed and thus streamlined to pass easily through water. The bill is either long and pointed to catch fish, or blunt and strong for breaking into crustaceans. The fish-eating species, usually the larger birds, are highly streamlined with long necks designed for underwater pursuit, while those that prey on shellfish are squat, dumpy birds. The difference is the same as that between an air freighter and a jet fighter. The Western Grebe *Aechmophorus occidentalis* is unique in actually spearing its prey.

In the world of animal courtship there are no more strange, elaborate, exciting or moving sights than that of grebes displaying. The sexes are similar and courtship is both highly ritualized and mutual. In mutual courtship each member of the pair reacts to the other and either member may take the initiative. Thus a pair of Great Crested Grebes performs elaborate ceremonies of head shaking, presenting weed to each other while standing up from the water like penguins, a curious head-on approach with necks laid along the surface of the water, and many other ritualized movements. Other species have different rituals, although the dance of the Western Grebe in which the pair come together and literally 'run' side by side over the surface of the water, is probably the most extraordinary. Some of the smaller, less ornate, grebes have a highly vocal courtship, but one which, once again, is mutual. Some

species serenade one another and even 'sing' duets.

Many grebes build floating nests of aquatic vegetation among reeds, or anchored to the trailing branch of a tree or shrub. The bulk of the nest lies beneath the surface, and this floating structure serves to prevent the nest from flooding. Material decaying inside the nest also creates heat which aids the incubation of the clutch.

The eggs are whitish with a blue or green cast but soon become stained a dirty brown-green. On leaving, the parent invariably covers the eggs with material from the nest. Most grebes are solitary breeders, but some like the Horned (Slavonian) Grebe *Podiceps auritus* are distinctly colonial, while others like the Western Grebe are quite definitely so. The two to eight eggs are incubated by both parents and the distinctly striped young are frequently carried on the back of the adults. The young grebes are fed quantities of feathers that the adults pluck from their own backs along with their normal diet. This curious habit, which continues throughout life, is still something of a mystery, although it is claimed that it may aid digestion.

The Pied-billed Grebe is widespread and numerous throughout the United States. The unusually thick bill indicates its preference for seeking slow-moving prey on the bottom of lakes rather than the fast-moving fish preferred by other grebes.

All the grebes nest only on fresh water, usually on lakes, gravel pits, reservoirs, etc. Many species are resident on the same water the year round, others tend to concentrate into flocks on some specially favoured lake, while others frequent the coast. The latter are among the more highly migratory and widespread members of the family. The Horned (Red-necked) *P. grisegena* and the Eared (Black-necked) *P. nigricollis* breed in northern latitudes and migrate to the milder parts of temperate North America and Eurasia. The Great Crested is found across Eurasia into Africa, India and Australasia, and although not such an obvious migrant, does make considerable journeys.

Of the smaller group of grebes, many of which are frequently called dabchicks, the Little Grebe is the most cosmopolitan. It is found through Europe, Africa and Asia as far as New Guinea, but is replaced in Australia by the almost identical Australian Little Grebe *P. novaehollandiae*, which differs by having a black, not red, throat. The Hoary-headed Grebe *P. poliocephalus* found only in Australia and Tasmania, is much the same size as the Little Grebe, but has long, thin, white plumes on the head in breeding garb. The very similar New Zealand Dabchick *P. rufopectus* is also 'hoary-headed'.

In North America the dabchicks are replaced by the Pied-billed Grebe *Podilymbus podiceps* which is a short, stumpy bird with a particularly strong, thick bill marked with a prominent dark, vertical stripe. In 1862 a pied-billed grebe was collected at Lake Atitlan at 5,100 feet in the highlands of south-west Guatemala. When Ludlow Griscom visited the lake in 1929 he realized that the pied-billed grebes there were at least half as large again as the more widespread species, and thus *P. gigas*, the Giant Pied-billed Grebe, was named. Subsequent searches failed to find the bird anywhere but on this fifteen mile lake, and it has more recently been referred to as the Atitlan Pied-billed Grebe. When discovered in 1929 there were about 100 nesting pairs, but in 1966 only eighty-six individuals were counted, sufficient to find the species a place in the Red Data Book.

The 'regular' Pied-billed Grebe earned itself a considerable reputation as a traveller in the late 1960s by making several trans-Atlantic crossings to appear on reservoirs in south-western England. This so delighted the naturalists of Bristol that they promptly adopted the bird as their emblem.

Most of the other grebes are highly localized birds. Two species of the genus *Podiceps* are confined to the island of Madagascar, with Delacour's Little Grebe *P. rufolavatus* being confined to Lake Aloatra. Perhaps geographical rather than personal names should be preferred for birds? Taczanowsky's Silver Grebe *P. taczanowski* is found only at Lake Janin in Peru, the Colombian Eared Grebe *P. andinus* at only a few lakes in the Colombian Andes, and the Short-winged Grebe *Centropelma micropterum* at Lake Titicaca at 12,500 feet in Peru. The latter is totally flightless.

These limited ranges are doubtless the result of the dependence of grebes on water, together with their general lack of a positive migration pattern and weak flying ability. Scientists describe twenty-one distinct forms although these are often reduced to as few as seventeen species.

Albatrosses Diomedeidae

The name 'albatross' alone seems somehow to evoke a spirit of wild adventure, of stormy seas and shipwrecked mariners. Highly pelagic, these birds spend most of their time cruising the greatest of the world's oceans and surviving the worst of storms. There are thirteen species of albatross making up the family Diomedeidae. The name is derived from the Portuguese *alcatraz* meaning 'large seabirds', although they are frequently referred to as 'gooneys' because of their foolishness when faced by man, and as 'mollymauks' from the Dutch *mallemok* meaning 'stupid gull'. The use of mollymauk has become so widespread that ornithologists have adopted it to refer collectively to the smaller species.

Albatrosses are among the longest winged species in the world – the largest, the Wandering Albatross *Diomedea exulans*, measures up to 12 feet across the spread wings. Most are inhabitants of the southern oceans where the winds whip round and round the earth without hindrance from land masses. This is the land of the notorious Cape Horn, perhaps the worst sea passage in the world. Strange as it may seem albatrosses need wind to fly, indeed they fly better in moderate storms and are virtually incapable of rising from the surface in a dead calm. With a good wind they can glide effortlessly for hour after hour with barely a movement of their wings. As the huge southern rollers drive their way round the world, the crests and troughs of the waves create updraughts of air that the albatrosses, as well as their cousins the shearwaters and petrels, take advantage of.

In spite of the fact that fossilized bones have been found in Suffolk in England and in the eastern United States, their method of flying has effectively restricted albatrosses to the Southern Hemisphere. The windless belt of the doldrums forms a virtually impassable barrier to any bird dependent on strong winds for propulsion, in the same way that lengthy sea crossings are an effective barrier to raptors and other birds that depend on the lifting effects of thermals to fly.

Occasionally the highly migratory Black-browed Albatross *D. melanophris* penetrates the doldrum barrier and finds its way into the North Atlantic. These birds have usually been associated with colonies of Gannets. One frequented the gannetry at Mykines, in the Faeroes, from 1860 to 1894, another was seen with these birds on Iceland's Westmann Isles, and one has joined the Gannets on Scotland's Bass Rock every year since 1967. In the same way as the doldrums form a barrier to birds passing northwards, so too do they prevent these vagrants from returning to their proper home. The recent development of intensive sea watching has thrown up a regular number of observations of albatrosses off the coasts of Britain and Ireland, and although these may refer to the movement of the single Bass Rock Black-browed bird, there is a chance that others of this species are wandering the North Atlantic and that they may, therefore, eventually meet up and settle somewhere to breed.

Three species have managed to penetrate the Pacific doldrums and establish themselves in the north of that vast ocean. The Short-tailed Albatross *D. albatrus* was brought to the verge of extinction by the depredations the feather trade made by the end of last century, and survived only on the island of Toroshima in the Izu group, south of Japan. Volcanic eruptions in 1939 and 1941 killed off all the remaining birds, and for a while the species was presumed to be extinct. It was not until 1953 that it was discovered that Short-tailed Albatrosses were once more breeding on the island, and we can only presume that the reservoir of immature birds that remain at sea for the first few years of their lives escaped the effects of the volcano, and had returned to breed and been overlooked during the latter part of the Pacific war. Recent counts on Toroshima show a continuing world population of some twenty pairs.

The Laysan Albatross *D. immutabilis* also breeds on Toroshima but has its main base at Hawaii's Leeward Chain. The total population is of the order of one and a half million birds. Also confined to the Leeward Chain is the Black-footed Albatross *D. nigripes*, with a population of a third of a million birds.

These northern breeding albatrosses are remarkable for the fact that they move southwards towards the equator to breed in the middle of the northern winter. This means that they breed at the same time of the year as the Southern Hemisphere species, but at a totally different season. Nevertheless they manage to avoid the heat of summer and the young fledge at a good time from a food viewpoint.

The Waved Albatross *D. irrorata* actually breeds on the equator itself and is confined to Hood Island in the Galápagos group. With a population of only 6,000 birds it would seem to be in considerable danger, but it is well protected in the Galápagos and the population is stable.

Albatrosses are found on remote, isolated and predominantly inhospitable oceanic islands and come to land only to breed. They find most of their food at or near the surface of the water, and although squid seem to be an important natural item of diet, a large number of species will gather at refuse dumped overboard from ships. Whaling is particularly important as a source of offal in the south, and several species of mollymauks are regular scavengers along with Giant and Pintado Petrels and some other southern seabirds.

At sea albatrosses have virtually no enemies and live to ripe old ages. In fact, like other long-lived birds, they take a long time to reach sexual maturity and pass through a number of immature plumages along the way. This variety of plumages can cause confusion and difficulty for identification because several distinct patterns must be learned for every species. The smaller mollymauks take at least seven years to reach maturity, and the larger species like the Wandering and Royal *D. epomophora* probably take a good deal longer.

Most albatrosses prefer to nest near cliffs where they can get airborne without too much difficulty by simply diving off the cliff top. The Laysan Albatrosses on Midway Island found the runways built by the United States Air Force ideal for both take-offs and landings, much to the consternation of the authorities and at the cost of a strike rate of one in six aircraft movements. Exterminating 60,000 birds made little difference, although levelling the surrounding dune area to eliminate 'lift' created by wind led to a significant reduction in strike frequency.

Above The great Wandering Albatross of the southern seas takes over a year to complete a successful breeding season. Throughout this lengthy period the maintenance of the pair bond is of crucial importance and elaborate greeting ceremonies have been evolved as a result.

Opposite In the Pacific several albatrosses have crossed the equator to establish themselves in the Northern Hemisphere. The Waved Albatross is found only on the equator itself, on the remote islands of the Galápagos.

All albatrosses have elaborate courtship displays that are highly ritualized. That of the Wandering Albatross, for example, consists of much bill snapping and groaning, plus a majestic if somewhat grotesque dance with much wing flapping and prancing. A domed, almost volcano-like nest is built of turf, and the single white egg is laid between Christmas and February. Colonies consist of a scattering of pairs over a fairly large area. Incubation takes seventy days and the first eggs hatch in March. The chick, which is nothing more than a face and a bill stuck on a ball of white fluff, looks extremely comical perched atop its little mound. There it stays for the next eleven months being fed intermittently by its far-ranging parents on a diet of regurgitated fish. Ringing shows that birds that are still feeding chicks may roam over 2,500 miles from their nests. At last the brown-plumaged youngster leaves for the sea at almost the same time that the adults arrive to breed. Although some 'Wanderers' breed every year it is likely that an individual pair will breed only every second season. If to this alternate year breeding routine is added the lengthy maturation period of something in excess of seven years, during most of which young birds are absent from the rookery, it can be seen that keeping an accurate census of populations is difficult, if not impossible. The world population of 'Wanderers' is of the order of 100,000 birds, but they are spread out over a vast range of ocean that extends northwards as far as Tristan da Cunha.

Albatrosses are among the most specialized birds in the world, and there can be no doubt that should economic exploitation of their Southern Hemisphere homes become commercially viable, because of a mineral discovery or some such event, then these magnificent birds would be in very serious danger of extinction.

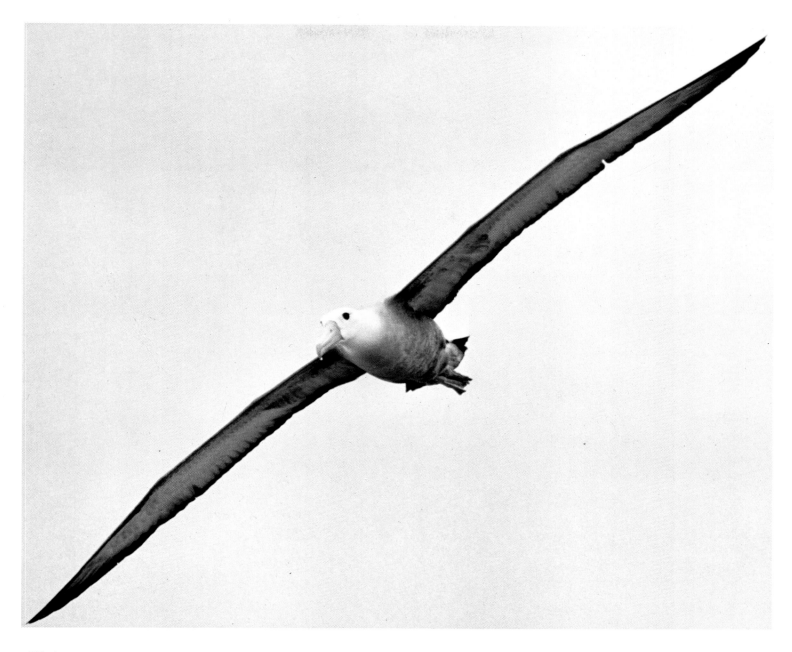

Shearwaters Procellariidae

The Procellariiformes are a relatively small order of about 100 birds that enjoy the distinction, as their previous name of Tubinares implies, of having tubed noses. In all species the nostrils extend on to the bill and are protected by tubes. In some cases these are combined to form a single tube along the top of the bill. All are pelagic birds, spending their non-breeding lives totally at sea roaming the oceans of the world. They have this enormous habitat virtually to themselves and, as a result, the order has adapted to take advantage of every niche and opportunity. No order exhibits such a range of size from the huge 25 pound Wandering Albatross with a 12 foot wingspan, to the tiny, few ounce storm petrels.

The order can be divided into four distinct groups: the Diomedeidae, the albatrosses; the Hydrobatidae, the storm petrels; the Pelecanoididae, the diving petrels; and the group that we are concerned with here, the Procellariidae, the shearwaters. It is a source of some confusion that several shearwaters are in fact as large as albatrosses and yet are called petrels.

All shearwaters and 'true' petrels are oceanic, long-winged fliers in the manner of albatrosses. Many are as economical in flight as

those 'sailplanes', while others are fast-moving birds that fly with considerable wing flapping. While most species hold their wings straight like a glider, others have sharply angled wings reminiscent of a tern or a skua. They are medium- to large-sized birds varying from 1 to 3 feet in body length.

The approximately fifty species are predominantly southern in distribution; roughly two-thirds of the Procellariiformes are found in the southern oceans. They can be divided into four quite distinct groups: the fulmars, the gadfly petrels, the shearwaters and the prions. All are without exception colonial breeders and communal feeders, often gathering at feeding grounds in huge numbers. The larger species, as well as some of the smaller tropical species, are diurnal, but the majority are nocturnal and nest in holes, burrows or crevices.

The extent of their feeding grounds and the restricted nature of suitable nesting areas results in many colonies of shearwaters and petrels becoming extremely large. They are active only at night and nest deep underground, however, and so accurate censuses are very difficult to conduct. This restricted nature of their breeding sites

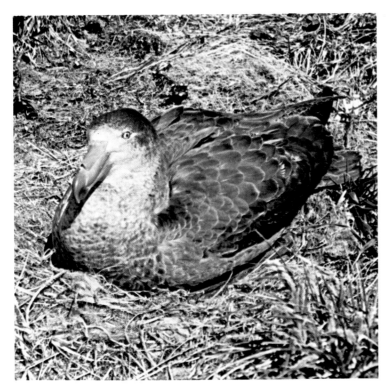

has created a shift breeding system in some cases. At Laysan Island in the North Pacific a group of burrowing petrels arrive in August to be followed by albatrosses in October and Sooty Terns later. At other places some shearwaters nest on the surface while others disappear beneath them in burrows. The use of burrows is primarily a defence against predators, but it also helps to separate the species and enable them to breed, if not side by side, at least in the same tenement.

A shearwater colony at night is a strange and often frightening place. In the late afternoon birds gather offshore, sometimes in enormous rafts. There they will remain until it is totally dark before coming to land. They fly around unseen in the dark, occasionally thumping into the ground on their chests – every shearwater landing is a crash landing. But it is the sound, the shrill, demented cries of the birds, thousand upon thousand of them, that has given rise to so much superstition on the isolated offshore islands where they breed.

All shearwaters take several years to reach maturity and adults

Left The Giant Petrel, sometimes known as the Stinker or Nelly, is a sub-Antarctic species frequently seen scavenging around the whaling operations of the southern oceans. This one was photographed on the remote Crozet Islands.

Below The northern Fulmar was once confined to a few remote stacks and islands in the Atlantic and Arctic Oceans, but has spread in the last 200 years as a result of human fishing activities to almost every cliff in the British Isles.

visit the nest site for a period of several weeks before laying the single egg. The male, at least in some cases, takes the first shift of incubation and the off-duty bird goes to sea often for periods of several days at a time. Manx Shearwaters *Puffinus puffinus* breeding on Skokholm Island off the coast of Wales have been recovered during the breeding season 600 miles away in the Bay of Biscay: and birds from this same colony homed across the Atlantic from New York to their Welsh burrows in a few days.

Incubation lasts from six to eight weeks and the blind, down-covered chick is brooded for a few days and then visited only to be fed. Fledging takes twelve to twenty weeks during which the chick becomes a very fat ball of fluff and is considerably heavier than the adults. Eventually feeding visits become very irregular and the chick finds its own way to sea. It is during this period that most mortality occurs. Young shearwaters are easy prey to gulls and other predators, and once at sea they must quickly learn to feed themselves or starve. Rough seas that prevent them feeding at this critical time can have a disastrous effect on fledging success.

After the breeding season most birds disperse at sea within a particular and established sea belt. Some fly round the world with the great albatrosses, while others simply gather at the best feeding

Right The dainty Fairy Prion is one of the broad-billed petrels often known as whale birds because of their adaptation to feeding on plankton in the manner of whales. They frequent the sub-Antarctic oceans where their food is so abundant.

Below The all-black Sooty Shearwater is one of the most remarkable of travellers. At the end of the breeding season birds move northwards along the western side of the Atlantic as far north as the Grand Banks of Newfoundland. They cross the ocean to Britain and western Europe in autumn, before moving south once more to their breeding colonies.

47

stations within a few hundred miles of their breeding sites. In the Pacific the Short-tailed Shearwater *P. tenuirostris* follows a figure-of-eight migration pattern that takes it in a great loop across the equator into the northern Pacific, in a sweep past Japan and California, before returning to its breeding sites off south-eastern Australia. Similarly the Great Shearwater *P. gravis*, which breeds only on the remote Tristan da Cunha group in the South Atlantic, follows the South American coast northwards after its breeding season to reach the eastern United States in summer, and then moves on with the Gulf Stream to the western coasts of Europe in autumn. Only the recent enthusiasm for sea watching among birdwatchers has revealed the true extent of this migration off the south-western coast of Eire and in the Bay of Biscay.

The fulmars are characteristically shaped, heavily bodied birds of some six species, of which the genus *Fulmarus* has a species in each hemisphere. Formerly confined to a handful of colonies in the North Atlantic, the Northern Fulmar *F. glacialis* has spread over the past hundred years to almost every cliff around the British Isles as well as to France, Norway and elsewhere. The extension of whaling and deep-sea fishing with the consequent abundance of fish waste is the usually quoted reason for this sudden and dramatic increase. Another prominent member of this group is the piebald Pintado Petrel *Daption capensis* which is widespread and numerous in southern oceans, and frequently gathers in great numbers at whaling operations. Also found at whaling sites are the giant petrels, the largest members of the shearwater tribe. Two distinct species, *Macronectes giganteus* the green-billed and *M. halli* the brown-billed bird, have been described recently. Giant petrels are often called 'stinkers' by sailors because of their incredible smell, an odour that can persist in museum skins for years.

The gadfly petrels number about twenty-four species in the genera *Pterodroma* and *Bulweria*; now only Bulwer's Petrel *B. bulwerii* is usually placed in the latter genus. All are similar, fast-flying birds, the larger species having rounded tails and the smaller birds wedged-shaped ones. Most are dark above with white faces.

The most famous of the gadfly petrels, although not the most numerous, is the Cahow *Pterodroma cahow*. Following a famine early in the seventeenth century, caused mainly by the accidentally introduced black rat, the population of Bermuda turned to the Cahow as a source of food. Within a few years protection orders were passed to save the last few birds from extinction. Soon they were forgotten and only in the early part of this century did a couple of specimens come into the hands of scientists who were able to ascribe them to this species. It was not until 1951 that positive evidence of the nesting of the Cahow was obtained on Cooper's Island, Bermuda. Careful and active conservation work had increased the colony to twenty-four pairs by 1966, with an increase rate of one bird per annum.

Another Caribbean Species, the Diablotin or Black-capped Petrel *P. hasitata*, has a similarly checkered history. Its largest colonies were destroyed soon after western colonization, and only occasional records scatter the history of ornithology during the last 200 years. In 1963 a breeding colony was rediscovered at Morne la Salle in Haiti, but it did number some 2,000 pairs. Perhaps other colonies survive elsewhere.

These Atlantic gadfly petrels are difficult enough to track down but the Pacific is littered with mystery. The Réunion Petrel *P. aterrima* is known from only four specimens and a few sightings. Barall's Petrel *P. baralli* nests on Réunion but was discovered only in 1964. A single Magenta Petrel *P. magentae* was collected in 1867 and nothing has been seen or heard of it since. A young Fiji Petrel *P. macgillivrayi* was taken 100 years ago in Fiji but there is no further news. Other species are in a similar state.

The prions are a group of small, blue-grey birds that feed on the plankton of the southern oceans. They were formerly called whale birds because of the habit of straining minute floating crustaceans with the specially adapted lamellae of their bills. The Broad-billed Prion *Pachyptila vittata* has an exceedingly wide bill that gives it an almost frog-mouthed appearance. All are marked with dark markings on the back, nape and tail feathers. Prions often form large feeding flocks where rich upwelling produces plankton-rich seas.

The shearwaters number some fifteen species of strong-flying, typically 'shearwatering' birds. In flight they glide on stiff wings along the troughs of the waves with only a few flaps before turning and setting off on the other tack. They are generally dark above and light below, and the typical shearwaters dive into the sea for their food which consists mainly of fish and squid. Several species gather around fishing boats at areas like the Grand Banks off Newfoundland. Associations here typically consist of Manx Shearwaters, named after the Isle of Man in the Irish Sea whence they have returned to breed after some years' absence, with Sooty *P. griseus* and Great Shearwaters. All are long-distance migrants – a British-ringed Manx Shearwater was recovered on the coasts of Western Australia.

The concentration of breeding shearwaters plus their fidelity to particular colonies has led to considerable human exploitation. Perhaps nowhere has this reached such industrial proportions as on the islands of the Bass Straits and Tasman Sea, where Short-tailed Shearwaters are also called Muttonbirds. Here the birds are still collected as in days gone by, but are now sold in cans under such labels as 'Tasmanian Squab'.

Storm petrels Hydrobatidae

'Mother Carey's chickens' is the name given to the storm petrels by seamen, no doubt following 'Mater Cara', the Virgin Mother and patron saint of all seafarers. Of course, most sailors fail to tell the difference between the approximately twenty species that make up the subfamily, and which appear so similar as they flit over the surface of the ocean.

Storm petrels are tiny seabirds (the largest is only 10 inches in length), predominantly black in colour and with prominent, white rumps. Many are great ship followers and like large House Martins they dip down to the water in the wake of a ship. They feed on the small animals that drift among the plankton and that form the basis of so much of the sea's richness. Where food is plentiful, large numbers of petrels will gather to feed, pattering with their feet on the surface of the sea and bending to pick morsels almost continuously. Some seem to almost walk upon the waters.

On land the legs and webbed feet of storm petrels are almost useless and the birds scramble about low on their tarsi. All dig deep holes in which they lay their single white egg, although some make do with a rock crevice or even a crevice in a sheep pen or abandoned cottage wall. Storm petrels usually nest on offshore islands typically uninhabited and highly remote, and to which they come only in the safety of darkness. Like shearwaters they are highly vocal but their calls are twittering compared with the eerie wails of shearwaters. The breeding grounds of Leach's Petrel *Oceanodroma leucorhoa* around Britain are typical. They are remote, isolated, seldom-visited rocks and total five or six colonies. Leach's Petrel is also found in Greenland, south to Maine and in the North Pacific.

Leach's Petrel is a widespread bird, but it is neither as obvious as its North Atlantic relative the British Storm Petrel *Hydrobates pelagicus*, which is a great ship follower, nor as numerous as Wilson's Storm Petrel *Oceanites oceanicus*, which may be the most

Breeding only on a few isolated islands in the Antarctic, Wilson's Petrels are widespread visitors to the north and contenders for the title of the world's most numerous bird. Their dainty pattering over the surface of the water while feeding is characteristic.

numerous wild bird in the world. The latter regularly visits the east coast of North America and many cross to the Mediterranean, but it nests only on a ring of islands off the coast of Antarctica, making it one of the longest distance migrants of all.

By far the richest concentration of species occurs in the Pacific Ocean off the fishing grounds of Japan, and in the east along the

coasts of Peru. Here they are known as 'bailarines' (ballet dancers), a reference to their peculiar methods of fishing.

Identifying storm petrels at sea (they are nocturnal when they come to land to breed and are seldom seen) is no easy task. Their small size (a storm petrel is about as big as a blackbird), their erratic flight low over the sea and the difficulty of viewing them from the height and speed of a modern liner would pose problems enough, but they also all look basically the same. Most have forked tails, but the degree of the fork plus the exact shape and extent of the white rump, are important features. Several species are light below marked with neck, breast or body bands.

Diving petrels Pelecanoididae

Diving petrels are a distinctive family of the great order of Procellariiformes – the albatrosses, shearwaters and petrels. Like all other members of that order, diving petrels are tube-nosed, but that is about the end of their similarity. In fact they closely resemble the puffins, guillemots and other auks of the Northern Hemisphere, and one or two of the four species are almost identical to the northern Little Auk, a prime example of convergent

evolution – the process by which unrelated species adapt to similar life styles resulting in a similar appearance.

The four species vary in size from $6\frac{1}{2}$ inches to 10 inches in length. All are stockily built birds with elongated and strong heads, short, stubby bills and notably tiny wings. In complete contrast to the easy gliding flight of their relatives the shearwaters and albatrosses, diving petrels fly with rapid, whirring flaps of their wings, just like the northern auks. In the air this seems laboured and tiring, but under water their 'flying' on short, strong wings is efficient and speedy.

Just like auks, diving petrels fly low over the sea before diving headlong into the waves to catch their prey, which consists mainly of crustaceans and small fish. Sometimes these dives barely interrupt their progress as they emerge on the other side of a wave and fly directly onwards through the air. Their dumpy, utility shape is perfectly adapted to their mode of living – it has been derived from the requirements of aerial flight and subaquatic mobility and speed. The balance is so fine that even a partial moult of the wing feathers would render the petrels flightless. They therefore moult the whole lot after breeding, and then find

Diving petrels have adapted to a similar life style as that of the auks of the Northern Hemisphere. As a result, they show a remarkable resemblance to the Little Auk, or Dovkie, of the Arctic seas.

themselves in the same state as their neighbours the penguins.

Like the auks, diving petrels are inshore birds finding their food around the coasts, usually near their breeding colonies. Their breeding biology, however, picks out their close relationship with the rest of the Procellariiformes. They nest in deep burrows excavated in soft soil and lay only a single egg. There is a long incubation period of about eight weeks, and the chick does not leave until fourty-seven to fifty-nine days old. Unlike the other petrels, diving chicks are brooded for about the first ten days of their lives and then visited regularly every day. Doubtless this is in part due to the inshore, and therefore nearby, habitat of the adults. Also unlike other petrels, divers mature early, after about two years, compared with the seven years of the fulmar, and even longer period of the larger mollymauks. On their breeding grounds diving petrels are nocturnal to avoid predation by skuas and gulls, and more recently and seriously, by introduced animals like cats.

The Common Diving Petrel *Pelecanoides urinatrix* is the most widespread of the four species. It breeds at a chain of islands around the Antarctic continent. The Georgian Diving Petrel *P. georgicus* also breeds around the South Pole, but is confined to islands at higher latitudes than the Common species, although the two breed at South Georgia and Heard Island where they occupy different niches. They are so similar as to need an expert view in the hand to distinguish one from another.

The Peruvian Diving Petrel *P. garnotii*, called the 'Potoyunco' by Peruvian fishermen, is confined to the famous guano islands of that country where it burrows a hole in the accumulated guano. Doubtless the removal of this valuable resource has limited the number of petrels that can find a home there. Magellan Diving Petrels *P. magellani* are found only among the maze of islands along both coasts of southernmost Patagonia. They are the most boldly patterned, black and white birds and their appearance led Charles Darwin to draw the parallel between them and the Little Auk of the north.

Tropicbirds Phaethontidae

Tropicbirds are large, gull-like seabirds of the tropical seas that are often called 'bosun birds' because of the similarity between their calls and a boatswain's whistle. The three species are very similar, about the same as a medium-sized gull. The white plumage is sometimes tinged with pink, and in some parts of their range very brightly so. They have varying amounts of black on the wings and a prominent, black eye stripe. All have orange-red bills which in the juveniles are often yellow, so that the colour of the bill alone is no sure criterion of identification. All three species have long, central tail feathers that stream behind them in flight.

Tropicbirds usually appear solo at sea. They fly high above the waves at about 100 feet with strong purposeful beats of their wings. They are highly pelagic and appear briefly around a ship in the middle of the emptiest seas, but do not follow. Food consists of squid and small fish which are obtained by shallow dives from the air.

Tropicbirds nest in rock crevices preferably on cliffs where they can immediately get airborne. Like most other pelagic species they are poorly equipped for life ashore. Their feet are set well back on their bodies on short legs which cannot support their weight. The need for a crevice or nesting cavity which can be defended brings tropicbirds in to conflict one with another, and with other species. Fights are frequent and birds use their sharp, dagger-like bills with effect on one another's heads. It is not unusual to find two tropicbirds with their bills locked together, each unwilling to let the other go. In some areas like Ascension Island in the South Atlantic where the smaller Yellow-billed Tropicbird *Phaethon lepturus* breeds first, the larger tropicbirds cause great damage by evicting the occupants from their nesting holes in the middle of their breeding cycle. On Bermuda, where Red-billed Tropicbirds *P. aethereus* have an isolated outpost, they are a major problem facing the Cahow. By fitting each Cahow nest with a special tropicbird-proof wooden baffle, conservationists managed to save the last couple of dozen of these petrels from extinction.

Courtship among tropicbirds is communal and they breed in loose colonies. Fighting apart, they spend much of the early part of the season chasing endlessly up and down the cliffs in groups of a dozen or so. So obvious are their tail streamers, about 2 feet in length, that they must play a significant role in this part of courtship.

Of the three species of tropicbird, the Red-billed Tropicbird is the most widespread and numerous. Like a large gull, but with a streamer tail, it is encountered right out in the middle of oceans where it feeds on crustaceans and squid.

A single egg is incubated by both parents for six weeks, and the chick takes some three months to fledge. Birds that breed on the equator do so in a continuous stream, rather than during a particular breeding season. Here individuals have abandoned a yearly cycle altogether and on Ascension Island Yellow-billed Tropicbirds breed about every nine months, while on the Galápagos Islands the Red-billed breeds every ten months.

Tropicbirds have similar ranges in the tropical zones of the Indian and Pacific Oceans, while two of the three species also occur in the Atlantic. The Red-tailed Tropicbird *P. rubricauda*, as its name implies, has red tail streamers in the adult. It is the largest of the three and almost completely white in plumage. The Red-billed has a blood-red bill in the adult, but is better identified by the barred and blotched appearance of the wings and back. The smallest tropicbird, the Yellow-billed, is only 12 inches long and shows a distinctive black area on the inner part of the wing extending from the carpal joint.

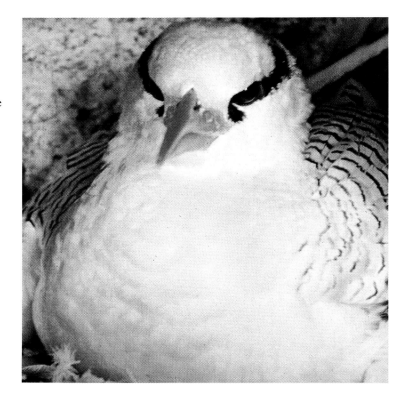

Pelicans Pelecanidae

Primarily famous as a bird whose beak can hold more than its belly can, pelicans are better remembered by those who have seen them for their similarity to a bomber squadron. Out of the rising sun they come, in long, straggling lines and 'V' formations across the sky. One wave follows another, huge birds on huge wings. The leader takes a few wing beats and continues gliding, but the wing beating is taken up by each bird in turn down the line. Clumsy and awkward-looking on land, pelicans are magnificent in the air. Like birds of prey and storks they rely on rising air to keep them aloft, often circling high in the sky on thermals that have risen like bubbles from the land below. They are also adept at utilizing the cushion of air that is created between their wings and the water surface of lakes, and on which they glide equally as effortlessly,

skimming along only a few inches above the surface.

There are seven species of pelicans; some authors recognize six and others eight. They are large birds from 4 to 6 feet in length, all marked by a huge bill and capacious, gular pouch. This latter is used not for holding fish but for scooping them from the water. In use the flexible lower mandibles bend sideways, stretching a net between them. Pelicans are highly gregarious and breed, fly and feed together, often in very large groups. While one species feeds by diving dramatically into the sea like a gannet, others have a

Widespread across Europe, Africa and Asia, White Pelicans breed only at a few isolated and safe areas of marsh. Safety apart, their breeding sites share one common factor – an abundance of fish.

Dalmation Pelican

White Pelican

Pink-backed Pelican

Dalmation

White

American White

juvenile

Robert Gillmor

Brown Pelican

Australian Pelican

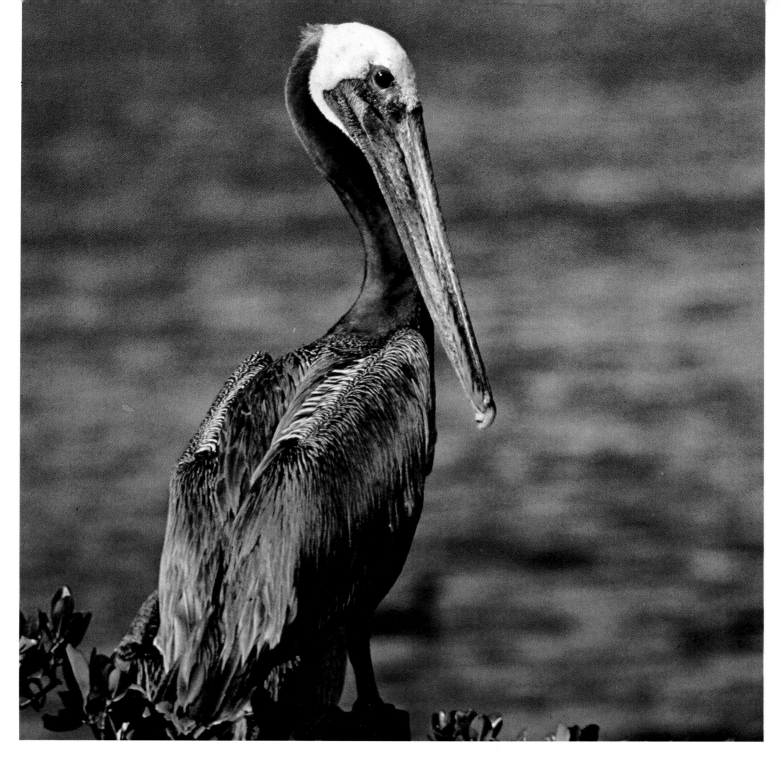

Above The only pelican that dives from the air to catch its food, the Brown Pelican of the New World is also the only purely maritime member of its family. It is particularly abundant among the rich seas of the Humboldt Current of western South America.

Opposite The world's pelicans.

curious co-operative feeding technique. The White Pelican *Pelecanus onocrotalus* gathers in groups of six to eight which swim together in horseshoe formation. Every few yards the birds dip their wide open mouths in unison, creating an almost solid underwater saucer of gular pouch which effectively engulfs any fish in range.

As with most aquatic birds the legs are short and strong, but all four toes are webbed resulting in a huge area of paddle. Set well back on the body they act not only as propellers, but are also used drawn together in great jumping beats to aid take-off over the surface of water. No doubt the pelicans are among the noisiest 'takers-off' in the bird world. Like a submarine the body of pelicans is a maze of air sacs designed for strength and to control their buoyancy in water.

Pelicans breed colonially in marshes and on islands, in trees and on hillsides, constructing a considerable nest of sticks. The one to four eggs are white with a bluish cast that quickly becomes stained. The young hatch completely naked, but soon grow a protective covering of down. A dark brown, woolly covering provides adequate insulation, and the young pelicans soon move about the colony if it is located on flat, dry ground. The young are cared for by both parents and feed directly from the adult's gullet in a primitive and painful-looking performance. They fly after about two months.

Pelicans, although widespread, are by no means numerous. They are found only where fish abound and where man has left them sufficient living space. In Europe such conditions are found only in the Danube delta and in a few spots in Greece and Yugoslavia. The largest colonies are those of the White Pelican at the mouth of the Danube where they breed in the protection of Românian State nature reserves. The Dalmatian Pelican *P. crispus*, which has a short tufted crest and is greyish (not black and white) beneath the wings, is found in the delta in small numbers but also occurs in Dalmatia. This species also breeds to the east extending into central Asia, while the White Pelican breeds eastwards to India and southwards to East and South Africa. White Pelicans are often very numerous on the lakes of the East African Rift Valley. At Lake Shala in Ethiopia, a large colony breeds on one of the lake's islands, but all the birds have to make a flight of several miles and over a range of hills to feed at fish-rich Lake Abiata. A similar situation exists with the American White Pelicans *P. erythrorhynchos* which breed on the Great Salt Lake in Utah. Here the birds have to fly some forty miles to catch their daily ration of some four pounds of fish per bird.

Also found in Africa, as well as southern Arabia and Madagascar, are the small Pink-backed Pelicans *P. rufescens*. In spite of being common, for instance on the Rift Valley lakes, they are never quite as gregarious as their larger congeners. The Grey Pelican *P. philippensis* is found from the Middle East, where it breeds on islands in the Persian Gulf, through Asia to China and the Philippine Islands. It is the Asiatic equivalent of the Pink-backed

Pelican. The Australian Pelican *P. conspicillatus* is the equivalent of the White Pelican in that continent, and the American White Pelican similarly replaces it in North America. The migration of the American Pelican is one of the great animal phenomena. Huge thermals of birds cross mountains and deserts on their way to Central America from their far-flung breeding territories.

The odd bird out of the pelican family is the New World Brown Pelican *P. occidentalis*. It is not only the smallest pelican and a different colour, a deep chocolate brown, but it also has the distinguishing habit of diving for its food directly from the air. Flying overhead twenty feet or so above the surface, it suddenly closes its wings into an arrow and drops headfirst toward the sea. Slow-motion cinematography has shown that at the split second before entering the water, the birds throw back their wings to increase their streamlining and enter the water like a dart. Brown Pelicans are as gregarious as any member of the tribe, and are characteristic members of the guano island avifauna of the rich coastal current of Peru. Here they are regarded as the second or third most important producers of guano. They are also found northwards, however, to Baja California, and through the West Indies to the southern States of the United States.

Gannets and boobies Sulidae

The world's nine species of gannets and boobies are large, strong-flying seabirds with long wings and torpedo-shaped bodies. They have comparatively long, thick necks and, on the ground at least, bear a resemblance to geese that once earned the Northern Gannet *Sula bassana* the name of 'Solan Goose'. They have powerful, dagger-like bills and strong, short legs with large feet that are webbed between all four toes. These are helpful in aiding the take-off of such a heavy bird, but are also utilized as air-brakes when coming in to land.

Gannets and boobies are well adapted to diving and their strong build puts them among the very few birds that can withstand the impact of a 100-foot dive into the sea. Where the fishing is rich large numbers of gannets gather, circling overhead before diving one after another headlong into the water. Fish are grabbed, not speared, and brought to the surface before being swallowed whole. Gannets are exclusively marine and gather at huge colonies on offshore islands, where the fishing within flying range is rich enough

Right and below Of all the birds of the world, many species of colonial seabirds offer the ornithologist the best chances of accurately censussing total populations. Best of all are the gannets found on isolated islands with huge populations concentrated in only a few well-established sites. Most numerous of these is the Cape Gannet found only on a scattering of islands off the coast of South Africa. Here half a million birds may nest on a few rocky stacks.

Opposite Gannets and boobies of the world.

immature

North Atlantic
Gannet

head showing
shorter gular stripe
than Cape Gannet

Australian Gannet
in flight, more
black in wings
than North Atlantic Gannet

Cape Gannet
adults and chick
long gular stripe

Australian Gannet

Brown Booby in flight

White Booby
Atlantic race (Ascension)
has orange feet – on Galápagos
they are slatey to green

male

Blue-footed Booby

female

female

male

Brown Booby

male

white phase

Abbott's Booby

brown phase

Red-footed Booby

Peruvian Booby

Robert
Gillmor

to support their large numbers. While some species breed on isolated islands, others prefer to use large cliff ledges. Even within the species, colonies of the Northern Gannet vary from the flat-topped island of Grassholm off the Pembrokeshire coast of Wales, to the sheer drops of Bonaventure Island in the Gulf of St Lawrence.

The three species of gannets occupy the temperate areas of the world and are the only members of the Sulidae to migrate. It is, however, only the younger birds that fulfil a proper migration. Adult gannets indulge in feeding movements within reasonable range of their breeding sites the year round.

The Northern Gannet is one of the best-studied birds in the world. The late James Fisher made it, along with the Fulmar, very much his own and was responsible, with Gwyn Vevers in 1939, for the first accurate, worldwide census of any species of bird. There is no doubt that the population of the Northern Gannet has doubled (about 160,000 nests) since then. The largest of the colonies, which are confined to the North Atlantic, is at St Kilda where 52,000 birds cling to some of the most fearsome cliffs in the world.

The courtship of the Northern Gannet, along with the other members of the family, has been studied by Bryan Nelson. Pairs occupy a breeding territory about a yard square – the distance they

The Blue-faced or Masked Booby is one of the more widespread members of its family. Of essentially tropical distribution, it plunge-dives for food like the other boobies and has an elaborate battery of courtship rituals which maintain the pair bond in densely packed breeding colonies.

can defend with their sharp bills. Much bowing and scraping, croaking and grunting forms part of various recognition and conditioning displays, to ensure that the pair-bond is maintained through the season. The single egg is incubated by both sexes and there is much squabbling and fighting as birds coming in and leaving inevitably invade neighbouring territories. Many chicks are pecked to death if they leave the nest prematurely due to disturbance. Before it leaves the nest the youngster is starved, and it continues to live on its fat reserves while it learns to fish at sea. Young Northern Gannets pass through a succession of dark brown, speckled plumages before they mature at four years of age.

The Cape Gannet *S. capensis* differs from the Northern Gannet only in having a black tail. It has the largest gannet population in the world with some half a million nesting annually on the guano islands of South Africa. The Australian Gannet *S. serrator* breeds in the Bass Straits and at many islands off the coasts of Tasmania. It also breeds at Cape Kidnappers on the coast of North Island,

Confined to the tropical Pacific coast of America, the Blue-footed Booby often seems foolish in the face of danger. On the Galápagos Islands, where it is numerous, the species will continue with its courtship and nesting routines in spite of a close approach by photographers.

New Zealand. The Australian Gannet has a white tail with a black centre, but is otherwise the same as the other species. Several authors regard the three as races of a single species.

Boobies are stupid, or at least they are thought to be. They continue to show no fear in the face of man in spite of the persecution that they have endured. They survive only because they nest in inaccessible places, or on islands that are seldom visited by man. Six species replace the gannets in tropical waters. Over the years they have accumulated a variety of vernacular names, although the birds themselves are easily separated.

Three species enjoy names that aid their identification and all three are widespread. The Masked Booby *S. dactylatra* has also been called the Blue-faced and White Booby, but Masked is a far better name. It is found in all three oceans – the Atlantic, Indian and Pacific. The Brown Booby *S. leucogaster*, as its name implies, is brown in colouring, but not wholly so. It is completely white below and is found in many areas along with the Masked Booby. The Red-faced Booby *S. sula* enjoys two distinct colour phases – one white in which it resembles a Masked but has red feet, and another which is dull brown.

Three other boobies are more restricted in range and all share a basic plumage pattern of brown wings and white body. The Peruvian Booby *S. variegata* breeds on the seabird islands of Peru and is one of the famous guano birds. The Blue-footed Booby *S. nebouxii* is marked by blue feet and a heavily streaked head and neck. It breeds along the western coasts of Central and South America south to Peru, and is numerous and tame in the Galápagos Islands. Abbott's Booby *S. abbotti* is the rarest of all and confined to Christmas Island in the Indian Ocean. Like the Red-footed Booby it builds its nest in trees where, safe from predators, it survives by laying only a single egg.

Cormorants Phalacrocoracidae

Cormorants are large waterbirds related to the gannets and pelicans with which they share several features. They are generally black with a metallic sheen, but various species have white on the chin, neck or breast, and a brightly coloured area of skin around the eye. As a family they are found along almost every coastline in the world, but are not confined to the sea and some species spend their entire lives on fresh water. Others, like the familiar Common Cormorant *Phalacrocorax carbo*, are equally at home on both fresh and salt water.

All cormorants are fishermen and their structure is adapted to an aquatic existence. The legs are short and powerful and set well back on the body. The feet are totipalmate (all toes fully webbed) and are the major means of propulsion on and below the water's surface. Unlike many other swimming birds they do not have air sacs to aid

Above As the young Shags grow they pass from the reptile-like creatures they resembled when they hatched, through a dark brown stage to fully feathered birds. During this period the adults gradually lose the crest that is such a feature of the species in spring.

Top and above A Flightless Cormorant, photographed on Ferdandina in the Galápagos, tends its young. Like other birds that nest on the equator, these birds breed throughout the year, although they have a quite definite tendency towards a peak breeding season. The Flightless Cormorant is another of those birds endemic to the Galápagos Islands that break so many of the rules of their families. Finding all that it required within a short distance of its island home, this Cormorant had no need of flight.

Opposite Essentially marine in habitat, the Shag breeds in colonies among rocks at the edge of the sea. Its nest of decomposing seaweed together with the remains of partly consumed fish soon create a stench that deters all but the most strong-willed.

their buoyancy, and thus sit lower in the water than, say, the gannets and boobies. They also have the ability to accurately control the depth at which they swim, and frequently proceed with body awash, with only neck and head breaking the surface. Their feathers are not as well insulated as those of most other waterbirds, and they usually spend only a minimum time afloat in order to feed. The habit of standing with wings spread to dry is characteristic of all members of the family.

Cormorants are great fish eaters and, although they generally feed in shallow water, they are quite capable of diving to great depths in search of food. Fish is the prime quarry and as a result the birds are much persecuted by fishermen who see them as direct competitors. They are frequently caught in fishing nets, even at depths of 100 feet or more. In Asia captive cormorants are used commercially by fishermen. The Japanese Cormorant *P. capillatus*, as well as the Common Cormorant, are used in this way, with leather thongs placed around their necks to prevent them from swallowing the fish that they catch, and which they then return to their masters.

Cormorants are of use to man in other ways too. The Guanay Cormorant *P. bougainvillii* is the most numerous of the birds of the Peruvian guano islands, and the largest supplier of the nitrate deposits that are of such commercial importance. These birds swarm by the million over the islands, although in the late 1960s and early 1970s their numbers were reduced by starvation from an estimated twenty million to a fraction of that figure. While the fishing industry of Peru has become a very serious competitor in recent years, there seems no doubt that sometimes the fish themselves do not appear in their normal numbers, so perhaps such fluctuations are part of a natural population cycle. Other cormorants are of equal importance off the coasts of South Africa.

Cormorants are generally colonial birds building their bulky nests on islands, cliffs and in trees. They invariably smell rather strongly of decaying fish remains and droppings, and many visitors are overcome by the stench and are violently sick. The two to four eggs are pale blue or cream when laid, but quickly become stained. The reptilian young hatch naked, but soon grow a covering of protective down. They are fed directly from the parents' bill and soon learn to probe deep into the parents' gullet in a most painful-looking manner. Where colonies are established in trees their foul habits soon kill the trees, and eventually the birds have to seek out another site.

While most cormorants are black, some are marked with a metallic sheen like the familiar Shag *P. aristotelis*, and others have white breasts or are even predominantly white in colour. Some have crests and a considerable number boast areas of colourful, bare skin around the eye and face. Thus the Blue-eyed Shag *P. atriceps* of the Falkland Islands has a bare, yellow face and a bright blue eye ring, while the Red-faced Cormorant *P. urile* of the northern Pacific boasts a large area of bare, red skin on the face.

The Galápagos, invariably the home of the unusual, holds the Flightless Cormorant *Nannopterum harrisi* whose wings have been reduced to mere useless remnants. While most cormorants have to fly strongly to reach their feeding grounds, the Flightless Cormorant is well served by the rich waters that surround its island home. With no predators to fear, the species has no need of flight. Nevertheless it breeds only on two of the most westerly of the islands and numbers no more than 1,000 birds.

A group of small cormorants is often placed in the separate genus *Halietor*. These are essentially fresh water, marsh-dwelling species with long tails and a preference for small fish and crustaceans. Typical of this group is the Pygmy Cormorant *Phalacrocorax pygmaeus* found in south-eastern Europe and throughout the Middle East. In the breeding season it adopts a rusty coloured head and neck, but this becomes black during the rest of the year.

The large Spectacled Cormorant *P. perspicillatus* was discovered in the North Pacific in 1741. Within 100 years it was extinct. It was a poor flier and doubtless succumbed to the sailors of the time, ever on the look out for fresh meat.

Darters Anhingidae

Darters, or snakebirds as they are often called, are freshwater, tropic-based relatives of the cormorants. Several writers consider that all four generally recognized species are simply races of the same bird. While their external appearance, especially their dark coloration, long neck, submerged swimming technique, and particularly the habit of hanging their wings out to dry, marks them as close relatives of the cormorants; they, nevertheless, have a peculiar hair-lined stomach, a pointed not hooked bill, and a unique structure of vertebrae of the neck.

Darters are strictly freshwater birds only occasionally resorting to even the fresh parts of tidal waters. Like the cormorants they dive for fish and, like those birds, the totipalmate feet are used for underwater propulsion, the wings being kept near the flanks. The neck is extra long and kept folded under water ready to dart out (hence the name) and spear a fish. Very few bird fishermen actually 'spear' fish. Most grab them between the mandibles which may be serrated to cope with such slippery prey. Having speared a fish, darters face the problem of transferring it from the bill to the gape, a process which, with great skill, they perform by throwing the fish into the air and catching it.

Darters are almost 3 feet in length, but most of that is bill, neck and tail. In the air they look just like a cross, a likeness that is heightened by their habit of soaring on motionless wings like a raptor. They take to the water rather reluctantly only at the approach of danger and to feed for, like cormorants, their wings are not waterproofed and must be hung out to dry. Like those birds

they have the ability to submerge effortlessly, and frequently swim with only the neck and head protruding from the water like a snorkel.

Darters breed in colonies, often in association with other large aquatic species such as storks and ibises. The nest consists of an untidy structure of sticks or reeds in which are deposited the three to six chalky-blue eggs. Both parents take part in incubation and the chicks are born quite naked. A coat of down is acquired after a few days. If disturbed, the adults will dive from their nests directly into the water even from a considerable height. At first the young are delicately fed on regurgitated fish by the parents, but soon they are poking their bills deep into the adult's gullet in their eagerness to feed. They take five to eight weeks to fledge.

The name 'darter' is applied to all the Old World species, although the scientific and American names stem from the Brazilian Indian name *Anhinga*. The Anhinga *Anhinga anhinga* is found from the middle of the east coast and central Midwest of the United States southwards through Central America to Argentina. It differs from the other darters, but because they are so much alike and with no geographical overlap, identification marks are superfluous.

To the east the Anhinga is replaced by the African Darter *A. rufa*, which is found throughout Africa south of the Sahara wherever suitably rich waters can be found. It is numerous at Lake Naivasha in the Kenyan Rift where birds breed in small colonies low over the

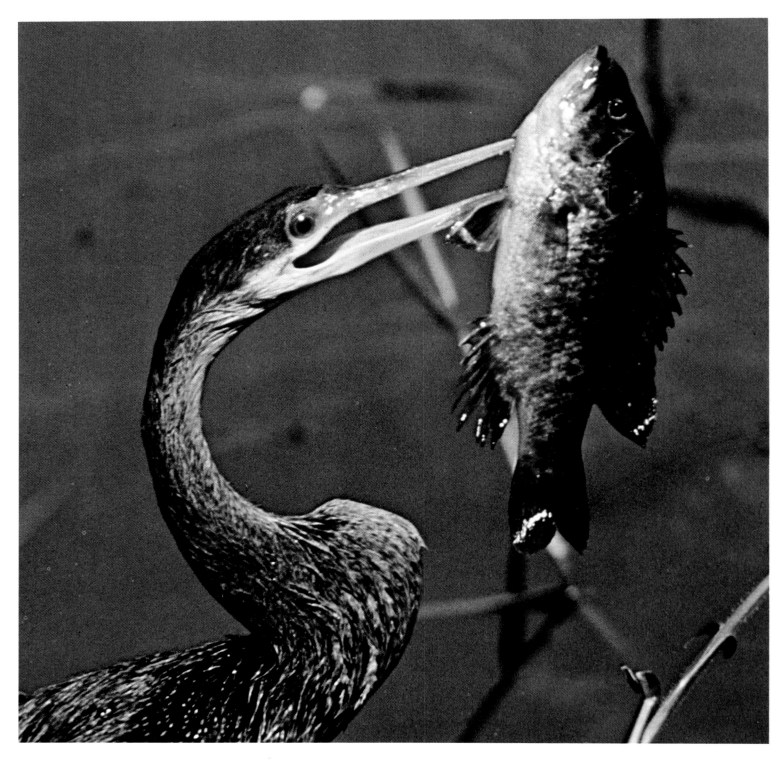

Darters, although closely related to the cormorants, are one of the few birds in the world that actually spear, rather than grab, their prey with their bill. This creates a considerable problem – how to transfer the fish to the mouth.

water among sunken and dying bushes. Such colonies are easily approached but, with an increasing number of nature-tourists visiting the area, they are liable to disturbance. The African Darter is also found in Madagascar where it has formed a separate subspecies, and in the Middle East.

Further east still the African Darter is in turn replaced by the Indian Darter *A. melanogaster* which has a tendency to be lighter on the breast than the other species. It is frequently encountered among the wetlands of India and is particularly numerous at the great marsh of Bharatpur where the wealth of fish supports a large

population of aquatic birds. Its range extends eastwards over most of India through Burma to Indo-China, Malaysia and the Celebes. In some places its nests are built so close together that they interlock in the tree tops. Naturally such dense populations attract predators and at Bharatpur a few pairs of Pallas's Eagle are always on hand to take the young. Indeed these birds seem to specialize on half-grown Indian Darters.

Yet another darter is found in Australasia. The Australian Darter *A. novaehollandiae* is confined to that continent and New Guinea, though it has been recorded in New Zealand.

All darters are found among wooded swamps and are thus most numerous wherever mangroves are found. They find drowned forests to their liking, or areas where dead trees have fallen into the water.

Frigatebirds Fregatidae

Called 'man-o'-war' birds by generations of sailors because of their piratical and menacing habits, frigatebirds are the most aerial of all seabirds. Clumsy and awkward on land, liable to become waterlogged when swimming, frigatebirds are absolute masters of the air and a sure sign of land nearby. They are tropical birds that can hang on the wind for hours on end with barely a movement of their great, long wings; but they can also outfly any seabird they come across, and are adept at picking their food from the surface of the sea without wetting a single feather.

For most of the year frigatebirds earn their living from the sea in the immediate vicinity of their breeding grounds. They follow the tuna shoals and pick off flying fish in mid-air as they attempt to escape their pursuers. They grab jellyfish from the water surface, and spend much of their time chasing boobies, terns and pelicans in

The display of the male frigatebird makes much use of the remarkable gular sac which can be inflated to enormous proportions. This in turn proclaims his ownership of a nest site and attracts a mate.

male Lesser Frigatebird
chasing White Booby

Great Frigatebird
female

Lesser Frigatebird

female

male

Pair of Ascension Frigatebirds

male displaying with gular
sac inflated

female

juvenile

Robert Gillmor

Magnificent Frigatebird

the manner of skuas, forcing them to regurgitate their catch. Like skuas, those marauders of the high seas, frigatebirds are experts at grabbing their bounty before it hits the water.

During the breeding season frigatebirds are found among most large breeding colonies of tropical terns, boobies and other seabirds. The eggs and chicks of these species offer a living to the 'frigates', but they will even take the offspring of their own kind if left unguarded. Hanging effortlessly overhead, a hungry frigate simply waits until an egg or chick is left unguarded before swooping down and picking it up as easily as it would a fish from the sea.

'Frigates' nest on isolated islands and prefer to construct their untidy bundle of sticks in the top of a tree or on a rock from which they can easily get airborne. Their feet are only partially webbed and better adapted to perching than swimming. The male selects the nest site and advertises his ownership to passing females by inflating his huge, red gular sac – one of the most extraordinary sights in the world of birds. Even after pairing the male continues to defend the nest by inflating his sac for hours at a time. But once the egg is laid, the sac has served its purpose and it fades to an orange colour. The six-week incubation period is shared and the naked and blind chick is carefully brooded until it is covered with a strong growth of white down. The young white-headed, frigatebirds

fledge after sixteen to twenty weeks, but they are still dependent on their parents for many weeks to come. During this time they learn the easier tasks of piracy before turning to the more skilful techniques of fishing. The white head is lost after three years when the birds mature.

Two of the five species of frigatebirds are found only in restricted areas. The Ascension Island Frigatebird *Fregata aquila*, for instance, is found only on the isolated Atlantic island of that name. Its population of 2,000 to 3,000 birds makes it one of the rarest of all seabirds, although it does not appear to be in any danger. The Christmas Island Frigatebird *F. andrewsi* is found only at that island and at other places in the Indian Ocean. Both sexes are marked with white on the breast and belly. The other species are more widespread in distribution.

The Magnificent Frigatebird *F. magnificens* is about $3\frac{1}{2}$ feet long and frequents the Atlantic and eastern Pacific. It is replaced in other tropical seas by the Great Frigatebird *F. minor*, which breeds in the Indian Ocean and the western Pacific as well as in the South Atlantic. The Lesser Frigatebird *F. ariel* is the smallest of them all and marked by distinctive white 'armpits'. It breeds in three isolated areas: off the coast of Brazil, off Madagascar and off Australia's east coast. In a few places such as South Trinidad, off Brazil and the Galápagos Islands, two species of 'frigates' are found breeding together.

Herons Ardeidae

These long-legged, cosmopolitan wading birds are among the most obvious and attractive species in the world. They are found in a variety of habitats but they are most concentrated in areas of fresh water where they sometimes gather in great numbers. Many species are gregarious and nest colonially among the tree tops. They are most numerous in the tropics but several species extend north and south into temperate latitudes. Herons enjoy a variety of names that do little to sort them into coherent groups; thus they are variously called 'egrets', 'bitterns', and some plain 'herons'.

Herons are the largest and most varied family of the order Ciconiiformes. They are medium- to large-sized birds, the tallest standing almost 5 feet in height. Much of their time is spent wading on extremely long legs although their feet are not webbed. Instead the fourth toe is well developed and lies in apposition to the other three. Doubtless this helps to spread their weight while wading, but it is perhaps more important as an aid to perching. The middle toe is marked by a serrated claw that is used as a comb to help clean plumage soiled during their often dirty mode of fishing.

All herons have two or more patches of powder-down feathers. These are located on the breast and rump and consist of feathers that grow continuously throughout the year. By rubbing its bill or neck through these feathers, the bird breaks up the ends into a fine powder with which it covers all offending slime and dirt patches. The powder is then removed, together with the slime, with the comb of the middle toe. Like other birds, the herons finish their toilet with oil taken from their preen gland.

Herons are also unusual in having the vertebrae of the neck of unequal length. For this reason many species have a strange serpentine look and carry their necks tucked back on themselves in flight. As anyone who has watched them hunting will know, the neck can be straightened in a flash to catch prey.

In a heron-rich area like the Florida Everglades or Lake Naivasha in Kenya, a huge variety of species can be found. Sometimes there are so many that one wonders how they manage to exist side by side. In fact most species are separated by having quite distinctive methods of feeding, different prey, or both. The Cattle Egret *Ardeola ibis*, for instance, feeds on pasture, often in association with cattle or other animals. The birds depend on their larger associates

to disturb small prey as they move, and often hitch a ride on the backs of their amiable hosts.

In contrast, the Grey Heron *Ardea cinerea* is a stealthy fisherman that wades the shallows and stands stock-still along the banks of streams awaiting his opportunity to grab a fish. One of the most unique feeding methods of any bird is that of the Black Heron *Melanophoyx ardesiaca* which creates a shady canopy, like an old-fashioned photographer's black cloth, over its head with its wings, and hunts below.

Nothing brings out the differences between the species more than watching a line of birds fishing side by side in the same water. While the Squacco Heron *Ardeola ralloides* is busily gulping down fish that seem far too large for its capacity, nearby Night Herons *Nycticorax nycticorax* make do with a number of quite small fry. Bitterns *Botaurus stellaris* are noted for their predilection for eels, and the Green Heron *Butorides virescens* has short legs and frequently dives into the water after prey. Thus while most of us have an image of a heron as a tall arrogant-looking bird that wades in water in search of fish, the reality is by no means as simple. Suffice it that the family is one of the most attractive of all birds.

The majority of herons nest in colonies often in trees, although some species like the Purple Heron *Ardea purpurea* congregate in reed beds and form less tightly packed groups. In the tree tops herons build large, untidy nests of sticks in to which the three to seven unmarked eggs are laid. Very often these colonies are mixed, with egrets and herons together with storks, ibises, spoonbills and other aquatic species. In most cases it is the herons that are the dominant partners. In the Spanish Coto Donaña, for instance, huge, mixed heronries are characteristically composed of Cattle Egrets, with Little Egrets *Egretta garzetta*, Night Herons, Spoonbills and White Storks. In Central America, Cattle Egrets now dominate several of the larger heronries of that continent, but are mixed with Snowy Egrets *E. thula* and Scarlet Ibises. These heronries are very prone to disturbance and are easily destroyed.

Most herons have a distinctive breeding plumage often consisting of a different colour bill or eye rings. This usually lasts only for the courtship period, but is often re-adopted if for some reason the first clutch of eggs is lost, and the birds continue with a replacement clutch. Other species are blessed with fine and beautiful plumes on the chest and back that they raise with great effect like the Peacock's train in display. The Little Egret has particularly fine plumes and its larger congener the Great White Egret *E. alba* was hunted virtually to the point of extinction for its finery. During the fashionable, plume-wearing days of the Edwardian period thousands of egrets were slaughtered for their feathers, and it was perhaps less due to the efforts of conservationists than a simple swing in fashion that the Great White Egret and others managed to survive.

The least typical of the herons are the bitterns, a group that has been placed in a separate family by several authors. Like the true

A young Squacco Heron feeds greedily from its parent's gullet. These herons hunt among shallow, overgrown waters where their prey is as likely to consist of insects and amphibians as small fish. Grasshoppers, crickets and dragonflies and their larvae are all eaten.

herons they rely on camouflage rather than flight for safety. Bitterns are not social like the other species, and they are found together only because of the shortage of their habitat. In fact, bitterns are highly territorial and the only members of the Ardeidae to boast a 'song'. The male bittern develops a specially large esophagus in the spring that enables him to utter a dull booming sound, repeated three or four times. This sound, which is frequently likened to a

The relationship between the well-named Cattle Egret and the various species of large herbivores with which it associates is of benefit to both sides. The Egret feeds on amphibians and insects disturbed by (in this case) the Buffalos while the larger animal is given warning of approaching danger.

foghorn, never appears to be very loud but has extraordinary carrying power. Thus one of the strangest of all bird sounds comes from one of the best camouflaged and least showy species – exactly what one would expect.

Bitterns are brown, streaked birds that have a peculiar habit of pointing their bills skywards when disturbed. In these circumstances they look exactly like the brown reeds that invariably form their background, and they will even sway with the wind in the reeds to perpetuate the illusion. They will perform the same concealment ploy in the middle of a snowscape, a green field or a busy street, which shows the extremely limited framework within which bitterns and many other animals function.

Having attracted a mate by booming, the display of the Bittern consists (as far as we know, for little can be seen of wild birds among the reeds before they build their nest) of an unexciting, slow flap up and down the marsh. Nevertheless, Bittern hunting, exciting or not, was a favourite sport of medieval falconers and the roast bird a special delicacy of kings. Not surprisingly, Bitterns were soon scarce and with the draining of marshes that so fascinated the landowners of the early nineteenth century, the birds disappeared from Britain completely. Their return, earlier than a lot of other similarly dispossessed marsh birds, was a result of a more tolerant attitude towards rare birds and the passing from fashion of the mounted skin collection.

There are twelve species of bittern widely distributed around the world. Many are so similar that several authors have suggested that they should be lumped together. The Least Bittern *Ixobrychus*

exilis of North America, for instance, is very closely related to the European Little Bittern *I. minutus*. Both perch freely on reeds and fly away more like Hoopoes than herons. The males are boldly patterned black, pink and brown birds, but the females are cryptically coloured buffs and browns. Unlike most sexually dimorphic species, male Little and Least Bitterns share the incubation and care of the young among the reeds where their simple basket of vegetation holds the four to six eggs. Despite rumours, there is no evidence to show that Little Bitterns have nested in Britain, although they are being seen with an interesting degree of regularity in the south-eastern corner of Kent.

The tiger bitterns are a separate and quite distinct group that, because of their physical structure, are best called tiger herons. Although they resemble the bitterns in their cryptic coloration, booming calls and solitary habits, they have powder-down patches like the herons. Four species are found in South and Central America with a single species in West Africa and another in New Guinea. This obviously relict distribution has lead several authors to believe that tiger herons are an old-established group that are nearest the ancestral stock from which all of the Ardeidae evolved. Tiger herons build their nests in trees, but little else is known of their lives.

As their name implies, night herons are crepuscular creatures that perform the bulk of their hunting under cover of darkness. They are invariably hunched whether flying or standing immobile on some waterside log. Indeed the only time that night herons show their true length of neck is when they strike head-downwards at some small fish. They are short-legged compared with the typical herons, and most show a pattern of grey or black on the back with bold, dark crown or head markings. The five species that compose the genus *Nycticorax* include the nominate Black-crowned Night Heron *N. nycticorax*, which is one of the most widespread of all birds. In the New World it ranges from Canada to the southernmost tip of the continent. It is found through Mediterranean Europe, almost throughout the whole of Africa to southern Asia and also in Hawaii. The Black-crowned Night Heron breeds colonially in bushes, but even among reeds if tree sites are not available. The three to five blue-green eggs are laid at two-day intervals and incubation begins with the first egg. The young thus vary considerably in size. Night herons flight to and from their daytime roosts to rich feeding grounds, often while the diurnal herons flight along the same course in an exactly opposite direction. The species is migratory throughout its range, and sometimes European birds overshoot to northern temperate countries in spring.

A separate tribe of night herons belongs to the genus *Gorsachius* and is Oriental in origin. Three or four species are confined to the area extending from Japan southwards to Malaysia, but one is found only in Africa. They are solitary birds and, like the bitterns and tiger herons, boom to advertise their presence. One species, the Magnificent Night Heron *G. magnificus*, breeds only in the mountains of Japan's Hainan and Fukien islands. The Japanese Night Heron *G. goisagi* is a solitary nester breeding high in trees. Like bitterns, these birds sometimes indulge in skyward pointing in their efforts to resemble a branch and avoid detection.

The most typical group of herons are daytime feeders. They include the longest-legged and longest-necked species of all, and many have the most pronounced development of nuptial plumes. Many of them nest in large, mixed tree-top colonies.

The eight species of egrets are slim, attractive birds with pure white plumage, or at least a white phase or plumage stage. Widespread and numerous is the Little Egret which, together with the Snowy Egret that replaces it in the New World, is cosmopolitan in distribution. It is one of the most elegant of herons and only yellow feet on black legs jar the sense of beauty. In spring the nuptial plumes fall from chest and back in beautiful, fine filligree patterns – these are the aigrettes of the fashion trade. There are blue and grey colour phases in Africa that form a sharp contrast to the white birds, although they are the same species.

The Great White Egret is also a widespread bird, but one that has been seriously depleted over much of its range. Unlike the Little Egret it needs large reed beds for a home and over much of the world, and Europe in particular, this habitat has been ruthlessly destroyed. In that continent the Great White Egret is confined to a few isolated areas such as the Hungarian lakes and the Danube delta.

The Cattle Egret is one of the most ubiquitous members of the family. Apart from its association with large animals and the advantage it takes, it also managed to spread across the Atlantic during this century and is now well established in Central America, the West Indies and eastern parts of the United States. It has spread to Australia and is quite able to exist away from water provided food is freely available. Cattle Egrets are mainly white, but become buff on the back, breast and crown in the breeding season. At this time the legs also become reddish. Their colonies are often very large and they are frequently the dominant member of mixed heronries.

Among the best known of all herons is the Grey Heron, which is widespread in the Old World and replaced in the New by the Great Blue Heron *Ardea herodias*. In Britain the Grey Heron is the subject of an annual census that shows just how much the bird

Top Normally all white, this dark phase Little Egret is found only on Madagascar and Aldabra in the Indian Ocean. The species itself is widespread and numerous throughout both the Old World and Australasia.

Right The cryptic coloration of the Eurasian Bittern fits well with its crepuscular habits. Confined to large reed beds, the species suffered a considerable decline during the nineteenth century mania for draining marshes, but has made a significant recovery during the present century.

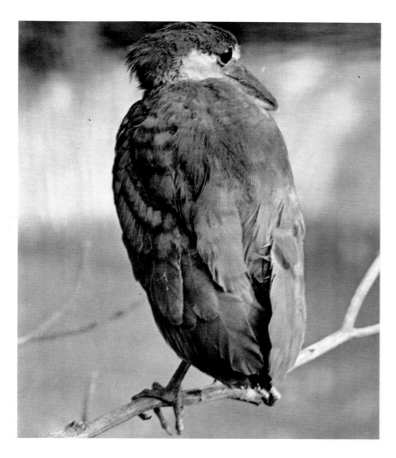

The Boat-billed Heron of the tropical New World is a surprisingly little-known species. It is largely nocturnal, solitary, and feeds mainly on reptiles and small mammals which it grabs with its wide, powerful bill.

suffers during a hard winter, how quickly it recovers, and how the explosion of numbers then slows down and evens out. Many British heronries have been used year after year for hundreds of years.

The Great Blue Heron is widespread in North America extending southwards through Mexico to Central America, as well as to Cuba and Jamaica in the West Indies. Though only a partial migrant many birds move southwards as far as Colombia and Venezuela and it is doubtless as a result of these movements that the bird has become established on the remote islands of the Galápagos. Here they have become as tame as the other inhabitants of these remarkable islands.

A bird that fits into no group at all is the Agami *Agamia agami*, often called the Chestnut-backed Heron, but perhaps better called the Chestnut-bellied Heron after Rudolphe Meyer De Schauensee. It is a beautifully marked bird with fine crown plumes. Its legs are short, but the neck and bill are long and thin. It is found southwards from Mexico to Brazil and Peru.

Herons are easy to keep in captivity and the Japanese royal household has always held these birds in high esteem. One species, the Black-crowned Night Heron, has been elevated to the Japanese aristocracy and other birds are protected as divine messengers. Japan boasts no less than thirteen species of herons and egrets and they breed in vast colonies at the Imperial duck decoys at Shinhama and Koshigaya, as well as at many other traditional sites throughout the country.

Shoebill Balaenicipitidae

The Shoebill *Balaeniceps rex*, often called the Whale-headed Stork, is an inhabitant of the vast papyrus marshes of the Upper Nile water systems. Ornithologists continue to argue about its systematic position and it seems best, at this time, to place it in a family of its own. Standing about $3\frac{1}{2}$ feet high, the most obvious feature of the Shoebill is its quite monstrous and grotesque bill. The bill is used for probing vigorously in the muddy margins of lagoons for its staple diet of lungfish that hide away there. The bird has also been reported to feed on carrion and garfish.

The Shoebill is a slaty grey crowned and backed bird, that invariably holds its head deep in its shoulders. It is wary of human intruders and its habitat and restricted range make it a surprisingly little-known bird. It is solitary in habits, pairs coming together to nest on the ground hidden away in a papyrus swamp. One or two white eggs quickly become stained by decaying vegetation. The Shoebill soars well with neck drawn back on itself like a heron, although the ability to clapper its bill like a stork confuses the systematists. The clapping noise is said to resemble an old fashioned motor cycle or a machine gun, and is performed with the bill pointing skywards.

Surprisingly little else is known about the habits of this remarkable bird, even though it is kept in captivity. It is best looked for along the marshy margins of the Ugandan lakes where it is comparatively common, though it can also be found on the lakes in the Lualaba region of the Congo. Recent exploration has shown it to be present on the Zambian Lualaba, and perhaps other less frequented regions will also prove to hold this secretive bird. Certainly it was once well known to the Ancient Egyptians.

The grotesque Shoebilled Stork is aptly named. It is only found in three remote areas of central Africa where it haunts dense thickets of papyrus. Its staple diet consists of lungfish and the enormous bill is adapted to catching and controlling these slippery creatures.

Hammerhead Scopidae

The Hammerhead *Scopus umbretta*, or Hammerkop as it is generally known, is a medium-sized, 20 inch long bird that shows close affinities to the herons and storks, but which defies any but a cursory attempt at classification. In flight it resembles a goose with a kinked neck, rather than a heron with folded neck, or the fully extended neck of the storks. The name stems from the peculiar shape of the head which is due to the heavy but narrow bill, and the crest of feathers extending from the crown and back of the neck. Its plumage is a sombre shade of brown with a darker crown, and the bill and legs are black. It has the comb-like structure of the middle toe of the herons, but it lacks powder-down patches.

In Africa, south of the Sahara, where it is found, the Hammerkop is the subject of superstition. In particular it is regarded as bad luck to interfere with a nest, which is just as well in view of the obviousness of the structure that the bird builds to rear its family. A huge mass of material is assembled in the major fork of a tree, usually supported by three or more branches. In some areas the birds nest on cliff faces, but the structure remains the same. It consists mainly of twigs welded together with mud. The inner chamber is comparatively small and is entered via an insignificant hole in the side. A nest can be built remarkably quickly and the three to six white eggs hatch out down-covered young, which are looked after by both members of the pair.

Most nests are situated deep in woodland, invariably within a short distance of water, but one pair chose a tree near the centre of Nairobi within the grounds of the National Museum where, of course, it was well protected. Hammerkops are almost crepuscular and are most active early in the morning soon after the sun rises. The food consists of aquatic insects, frogs, fish and worms, which it hunts among mangroves, papyrus beds or even along the banks of quite small streams.

The strangely primitive Hammerkop or Hammerhead is a retiring African bird, most active at dawn and dusk. Its huge nest is built in a tree and is one of the largest structures built by birds, measuring up to four feet across and six feet high.

Storks Ciconiidae

The seventeen species of storks are among the largest and most obvious birds in the world. They are long-legged, omnivorous birds frequently associated with wetland habitats, and form a veritable army of scavengers. Most storks are attractive and graceful birds, but several species are so ugly as to evoke the same sort of revulsion as do vultures. These 'ugly' species most frequently associate with those other carrion eaters.

In Europe, legend has it that storks bring babies and for this reason they are protected and tolerated as are few other large birds. This legendary stork is the nominate White Stork *Ciconia ciconia*. Like the other storks it is a great snapper-up of carrion, frogs, grasshoppers and fish, indeed almost anything that comes its way. It stands nearly 4 feet in height and is predominantly white with, like most other storks, black flight feathers. The long legs and strong bill are red, and the long neck is held straight out in flight and not tucked back like a heron.

White Storks build a huge nest of sticks atop a tree, telegraph pole, chimney, or specially prepared raised platform. The birds are remarkably faithful to their nest sites and will return to the same chimney year after year. They are not highly vocal, although most storks have a characteristic greeting ceremony which involves throwing back the head and clappering with the bill. The sound produced is both loud and far carrying. Once the pair is established every arrival at the nest provokes this elaborate ritual. Intruders, mainly younger unestablished birds, are fought off but sometimes only following the most vicious in-fighting.

White Storks are great migrants and, like the hawks and other raptors, are dependent on thermals of rising air for lift. They are thus quite incapable of flying for long distances across the sea, a fact which helps to explain their extreme rarity in Britain and their concentration at narrow sea crossings. Thus the entire White Stork population of Europe leaves the continent for tropical Africa via the Straits of Gibraltar and the Bosporus. Over 200,000 birds pass over Istanbul every autumn – a spectacular and impressive sight.

This century has seen a startling decline in the fortunes of White Storks in Europe. They have not nested in France, except Alsace, for many years, but they have recently all but disappeared from Holland and Denmark, and are exceedingly scarce in parts of Germany. Whether this decline is due to deaths caused by the proliferation of overhead wires, or perhaps to poisoning via the insecticides used to control African locust plagues, is unknown.

If the White Stork is the best known and studied member of its family, several other members are equally familiar. The three members of the genus *Leptoptilos*, the African Marabou Stork *L. crumeniferus*, the Adjutant *L. dubius* and the Lesser Adjutant *L. javanicus* (both Asiatic species), are all scavengers. All have bare heads and necks like vultures, and the Marabou and Adjutant have long, bare, gular pouches that dangle from their necks. The Marabou is 4 feet tall with a wing span in excess of 8 feet. The bill is thick and heavy but comes to a delicate point which it can use with a certain finesse. On the plains of East Africa the Marabou is one of the most familiar of birds standing atop some bare tree, often holding one knee with the opposite foot.

Another tall African stork is the Saddle-billed *Ephippiorhynchus senegalensis*, which is both colourful and graceful. While the Marabou is often hunched, the Saddle-billed stands upright and alert. It is predominantly black and white, but with a strongly up-tilted red, black and yellow bill.

The African Open-billed Stork *Anastomus lamelligerus* is a small stork less than 2 feet tall replaced in Asia by *A. oscitans*, the Asiatic Open-bill. Both show the strange adaptation of having a gap between the mandibles which meet only at the tip. Doubtless this aids control over their prey which consists predominantly of snails. It is not designed to crush the shells, but to extricate the soft bodies in the manner of the Snail Kite of the New World.

In the United States the Wood Stork *Mycteria americana* is frequently referred to misleadingly as the Wood Ibis, while in Africa the Yellow-billed Stork *Ibis ibis* is similarly misnamed.

Left Like many other long-legged wading birds the Wood Ibis nests in trees in mixed 'heronries' alongside species like the Great White Egret. The black skin of the head and neck is responsible for its American nickname 'flinthead'.

Below The elaborate head-back, bill-clappering greeting ceremony of the White Stork and the bringing of nest material continues throughout the breeding season, even when the young are almost fully grown and ready to fly.

Opposite Grotesque and ugly with their bald, scabby heads and obscene gular sacs, Marabou Storks are familiar scavengers throughout Africa. Often seen alongside vultures, they are similarly masters of the air.

Neither has anything to do with the true ibises, the Threskiornithidae. The Wood Stork is found in the south-eastern United States and is particularly abundant among the swamps of the Florida Everglades. It ranges, however, through Central America south to Argentina. The black bill is long and decurved, and the face is black and bare of feathers. Doubtless the bill shape of this and the Yellow-billed Stork is responsible for their being misnamed 'ibis'.

In Central and South America the Wood Stork can often be found alongside the Jabiru *Jabiru mycteria*, one of the largest of Neotropical flying birds. It superficially resembles the Marabou, but it is a fish eater rather than a scavenger. The American Jabiru should not be confused with the Australian bird of the same name, *Xenorhynchus asiaticus*, which is found from India to Australia, and which is better known as the Black-necked Stork in Asia. It is one of the few solo storks and is seldom found in large groups.

Ibises and spoonbills Threskiornithidae

The ibises and spoonbills form distinct subfamilies of the Threskiornithidae. Both are groups of medium to large, long-legged and long-necked wading birds. While the ibises have long down-curved bills in the manner of the curlews, the spoonbills, as their name implies, have flat, broad ones with a wide sifting plate at the end. Both groups fly with neck extended and legs trailing behind like the cranes, and unlike the herons which tuck their necks back on themselves.

The spoonbills fly with strong, level and purposeful flight, but the ibises are more erratic often gliding and soaring, and landing with a whiffling action like wildfowl. Both groups are gregarious and generally found in association with fresh water. Most are tropical or subtropical in distribution, but should a bird get caught by hard weather it will readily take to feeding on the shore. Many species are white although some are very dark with a metallic sheen, while others are scarlet, red or pink. All have a face bare of feathers that may be black or brightly coloured. They nest colonially in tall trees, sometimes on ledges on cliffs and even among reeds, usually in association with other ibises or with the herons, egrets and storks.

Below Revered by the Ancient Egyptians who mummified them as offerings to their Gods, Sacred Ibises are somewhat unsavoury in their habits. They frequent wetlands where they consume carrion, and flamingo colonies where they are inveterate egg robbers.

They are widespread throughout the tropics with representatives on every continent.

The Sacred Ibis *Threskiornis aethiopica* is the emblem of the British Ornithologists' Union, but is not sacred on that account. It was deified by the Egyptians as the reincarnation of the god Thoth, and was usually represented as an ibis-headed man. The ibis was used in hieroglyphics and can be found on many of the paintings that decorate the tombs of the pharoahs and lesser Egyptian officials. As an act of tribute many ibises were mummified and placed in pots next to burial chambers, and ibises were evidently reared in captivity for the purpose. Even in Egyptian times, however, it is clear that the unscrupulous businessman was at work. While most pots contain the remains of ibises, a great many have only part of the bird, and some a mixture of bones from all manner of birds and other animals.

The Sacred Ibis is now extinct in Egypt and found only in Africa south of the Sahara and in the Persian Gulf area. It is a fine black and white bird with a bald, black head and neck, black tips to all of the wing feathers, and a growth of fine, black plumes on the inner secondaries. The legs are thick and strong but long enough to trail behind the bird in flight. There is a vivid patch of maroon at the base of the underwing during the breeding season. It nests atop thorn trees in company with egrets and herons.

Another species that has declined in the north is the Bald Ibis or

Right One of the rarest birds in the world, the Japanese Crested Ibis, numbers less than a dozen individuals in those islands. Occasional sightings elsewhere suggest that a colony may exist in remote Manchuria.

Below The beautiful Scarlet Ibis of tropical South America is notoriously difficult to approach. Pursued by the plume hunters of the last century it has made a significant comeback among the mangrove swamps from Colombia to Brazil.

Waldrapp *Geronticus eremita*. Once common in central Europe, this species is now found in precarious numbers only in Turkey on cliffs above the village of Biricek where twenty-six pairs bred in 1973, and at a few spots in Morocco and Algeria. It is a short-legged, dark bird with iridescent plumage and a reddish bill. Its face is bald of feathers although a ragged crest hangs from the rear of the crown. It should not be confused with the African Bald Ibis *G. calvus*, which is found among the mountains of South Africa. The World Wildlife Fund is financing protection of the Waldrapp in Turkey but its chances of survival must be considered slim.

Certainly the most beautiful of all the ibises is the Scarlet Ibis *Guara ruber*, which is found from Trinidad and Venezuela southwards, mainly along the coast, to Brazil. This is a gorgeous bird, the adult plumage being a vivid scarlet to which photographer after photographer has failed to do justice. Much persecuted for its feathers, the Scarlet Ibis is still much sought after by natives for its flesh. As a result, it has seriously declined in numbers and has been ever more concentrated into fewer and fewer large colonies.

It nests high in the tree tops overlooking some wild swamp, often in association with the White Ibis *Guara albus*, a similar-sized white bird with a crimson bill, bare face and legs and black tips to the outer primary feathers. This bird breeds as far north as the southern United States in areas where the Scarlet Ibis is only a hurricane-blown vagrant.

The Glossy Ibis *Plegadis falcinellus* is the most cosmopolitan of all the ibises. It enjoys a range that extends eastwards to Australia and westwards through America although it is declining in Europe, where it is now found in the Danube delta and only on passage elsewhere. It is a dark bird with the purplish, glossy plumage that gives it its name. In some areas it gathers in extremely large numbers.

In sharp contrast, the Japanese Crested Ibis *Nipponia nippon* is on the verge of extinction. Once nesting from Ussuriland to Chekiang in China, and from western China to Japan, the species is now down to a few birds breeding on Honshu's western coast on the Noto peninsula, and the offshore Sado Island. It is rigorously protected but this last known colony was nevertheless down to about a dozen birds by the end of the 1960s. Occasional records from Korea, where this ibis formerly wintered in numbers, indicates that another small colony may still survive, perhaps in Ussuriland or in China. The Japanese Crested Ibis is an all-white bird with a shaggy white crest. The face is bare, red skin, and the tail shades from pink to almost crimson. It nests in pine trees.

Another species in danger is the Giant Ibis *Thaumatibis gigantea* which is found only along the Mekong River and its tributaries in strife-torn South-East Asia. There is no evidence of decline but this shy bird has only a limited range along the Laotion and Cambodian borders, and may number only a few hundred individuals.

The six species of spoonbill are, with a single exception, birds of the Old World. Only the Roseate Spoonbill *Ajaia ajaja* is found in the Americas where it is suffering a considerable decline. Persecution in the south-eastern parts of the United States reduced what were once teeming colonies to a few remnants in Florida. Here a last-ditch conservation effort has enabled this fine and colourful bird to survive. It enjoys a large range southwards through the northern part of South America, although the birds are still destroyed, as are migrants reared under the protection of the United States. Thus the latter have not increased as could be expected. Roseate Spoonbills nest among Wood Storks and egrets

One of the most widespread of Old World birds, the Spoonbill is nowhere numerous, however. It nests in trees but seldom among the mixed heronries frequented by its close relatives.

in large, mixed colonies. The Roseate Spoonbill has a bare face and crown with a white neck and back that gradually shades to pink, and finally a deep crimson on the wings and lower body. In the manner of all spoonbills it feeds by sifting food from the water with a curious side to side motion of its large bill.

The Eurasian Spoonbill *Platalea leucorodia* is found through Europe and North Africa into southern Asia. Like the other Old World spoonbills it is an all-white bird with only a tinge of yellow during the breeding season. It is colonial but prefers the company of its own species, and does not join mixed heron colonies as a rule. It breeds as far north as Holland where the birds are migrants, and where a few colonies survive under rigorous protection. In medieval times Spoonbills bred in England, even at Fulham which is now a part of London, and were served at banquets. The Eurasian Spoonbill is replaced by a separate species in other parts of the world: by the African Spoonbill *P. alba* south of the Sahara, by the Lesser Spoonbill *P. minor* in the Far East, and by the Royal *P. regia* and the Yellow-billed *P. flavipes* both in Australia. Several authorities consider that all five would be best grouped into a single species.

Flamingoes Phoenicopteridae

The four living species of flamingo are among the most beautiful, exciting and exotic birds in the world. They are large birds standing 3 to 6 feet in height and flying with neck and legs extended. In proportion to their size they have longer necks and legs than any other bird. They have a peculiar droopy bill that is held upside down to feed, and they are gregarious and occur regularly in very few places.

The largest and most widespread of the four is the Greater Flamingo *Phoenicopterus ruber*, which is found from the Mediterranean, in the African Rift, through the Middle East to India, in the Caribbean, the Galápagos and the lakes of the South American Andes. It varies considerably throughout this range, with the birds of southern Europe being quite white compared with the rosy-red birds of the West Indies, but the Greater Flamingo is most

people's idea of what a flamingo is like. In the Andes the Chilean Flamingo is considerably smaller and has green legs with red knee joints, but is nevertheless considered only a fairly distinctive race of the Greater. Likewise, the pale European birds are a separate race *P.r.roseus*. This species now breeds in Europe only in the Camargue of southern France and sporadically at one site in southern Spain. In India, however, in the great wastes of the Rann of Kutch, over a half a million birds breed with as much regularity as any group of flamingoes – that is five-sixths of the world population of the subspecies.

Flamingoes are highly gregarious and spend all of their lives in tightly packed flocks. The concentration of Lesser Flamingoes *Phoeniconaias minor*, which is confined to the East African Rift at Lake Nakuru, has on several occasions been estimated at over two

A Greater Flamingo preens at an African breeding site. Highly gregarious, these birds are fickle in their nesting habits and are apparently able to maintain their numbers by breeding only every second year or so.

million birds, but they do not breed there. In fact most of the birds disappeared completely until Leslie Brown discovered their breeding grounds on the soda flats of Lake Natron in 1954. In the midst of this barren wilderness, and at a few similar areas in East Africa, the entire world population of the Lesser Flamingo breeds. There are, however, still considerable unexplored areas of the continent that may yet be proved to hold other breeding colonies of this and the Greater Flamingo. The lakes where Ethiopia's Awash River disappears may well hold further breeding colonies, as the 'shotts' in Saharan Morocco are known to do.

Flamingoes are filter feeders sieving minute particles from the water itself. The Lesser Flamingo feeds near the surface and has a large area of laminae with which it sorts its food from the water. In contrast, the Greater Flamingo feeds deeper and takes larger particles with a less elaborate laminae system. The trapped particles are then transferred to the tongue and swallowed. All flamingoes feed in this way but they nevertheless occupy significantly different ecological niches by virtue of their size and the size of their food. Each bird consumes about one-tenth of its own body weight per day, which means a virtually constant routine of filtering throughout the daylight hours. The Lesser Flamingo takes food particles that are less than one-hundredth of an inch long, and it seems extraordinary that such a large bird can live on such tiny items of food. The world's largest known animals, the marine whales, live by much the same method of filter-feeding on small particles.

Flamingoes are unusual birds in more ways than one. They are, for instance, highly irregular breeders, seemingly needing to breed successfully only every two or three years to maintain their numbers. Colonies often become established, pass through the courtship and egg-laying stages, only to be suddenly abandoned. No doubt the birds need the social stimulation of a large colony to bring them in to breeding condition, but in East Africa it is difficult to keep track of which birds are doing what as the various colonies are established and abandoned up and down the Rift. By and large, smaller colonies are less successful, but very often two colonies will breed within a few months of one another at different lakes, and then it is impossible to know if the birds are repeating or completely different individuals. In the Camargue, up to 4,000 pairs nest on average every second year, and these have been studied most thoroughly because there are no other sites within hundreds of miles. Most of the Camargue birds are migratory moving, as ringing has shown, to East Africa.

Flamingo cities are quickly established. Birds are continually courting and displaying one to another and, when they settle on a breeding site, their nests are quickly built. They consist of circular, upright mounds of mud baked hard by the sun with a shallow depression into which the one or two white eggs are laid. Often the site is a low-lying island, but this is frequently awash with water and sometimes birds nest on soda itself. The chicks hatch as tiny, duckling-like balls of fluff, and are fed on regurgitated material from the great height of the adults. At about three days old they leave the nests and join large creches of youngsters, although still being fed by their own parents. It is a further two and a half months before they fly and gain full independence.

Least known of the flamingoes are the three species that nest in the remote lakes of the high Andes. In the region where the frontiers of Peru, Bolivia and Chile meet lies the famous Lake Titicaca, but to the west and south are lakes and huge salt pans where few men penetrate save Indians, and where the climate is so harsh that only flamingoes and their food can survive. On a single day the temperature can range over 100°F. Here the commonest bird is the Chilean Flamingo *Phoenicopterus ruber chilensis*, a race of the Greater Flamingo. The species maintains its migratory habits here and moves from its high-level breeding zones to winter along the Pacific coast. Two other species have never been seen below 7,500 feet and spend most of their lives considerably higher. The Andean Flamingo *Phoenicoparrus andinus* numbers about 100,000 birds, while the James's Flamingo *P. jamesi* has a world population of about 15,000 birds. This bird was rediscovered only in 1956 and its breeding was first proved at Laguna Colorada that year. Now other sites have been found and doubtless others remain undiscovered. In this harsh environment in a corner of the world that holds nothing for man, the birds were safe, but recently commercial taking of eggs for sale and the mass killing of birds for their feathers, has proved a threat to this unique area. Now mining towns are being established and the local indians are not slow to take a commercial opportunity. A severe threat hangs over even this inhospitable place.

A flight of Greater Flamingoes leaves a shallow lagoon – one of the most spectacular of bird sights. These large birds breed in both the Old and New Worlds, but are extremely local and confined to a few huge colonies on each continent.

Screamers Anhimidae

The three species of screamers, strange relatives of the duck and geese, are found among the marshes of South America. They have the strong legs of geese, but not the webbed feet, indeed they show only the slightest sign of webbing on the front three toes. The bill is short and stubby, and there are two spurs at the bend of the wing. They lack the strengthening of the rib cage found in all other known birds save *Archaeopteryx*, and have a network of small air-sacs that covers the body in the manner of a pelican. The hollowness of bones, found in all birds, reaches its peak in the screamers; even their toes are hollow, and few other birds have a uniform covering of feathers rather than distinct feather tracts.

Screamers get their name from their raucous calls which they utter throughout the year to the great annoyance of hunters. Invariably they are first to give the alarm from the marshes where they live. Their long toes support them over floating vegetation, although they are far from being lily-trotters. They frequent damp grazing and can often be seen walking about among domestic animals in the manner of Cattle Egrets, although they are predominantly vegetarians. The Horned Screamer *Anhima cornuta*

also eats insects. It is found through tropical South America and is the most widespread and numerous of the three species. A horn of cartilage, up to 5 inches long, extends in a curve from the crown. Like the other species its call is said to be quite pleasant, but annoyingly repetitive. Outside the breeding season whole flocks of screamers may call in unison and produce a cacophony of sound.

The Black-necked Screamer *Chauna chaviaria* is found in the north in Colombia. Its red face is set against a grey crown and broad black and white neck bands. The Crested Screamer *C. torquata* is greyer and lacks neck bands. It is the bird most frequently found in captivity and the most persecuted of the three.

In addition to their strident calls, screamers are also capable of another sound, audible only when they are near by. This sounds like a dull rumbling and is apparently produced through the air-sacs that cover so much of the body.

The nest is little more than an untidy pile of aquatic vegetation, and the four to six white eggs are incubated by both sexes for forty-two to forty-four days. The down-covered chicks quickly leave the nest and behave just like young ducklings.

Ducks Anatidae (part)

Numerous, gregarious, large and wild – these are the characteristics of ducks that make them one of the prime quarries of the sportsman. For many, the images conjured up are of slippery saltmarshes, thigh waders, a fearful nor'easter and cold trigger fingers, although ducks are not confined to the temperate zone. They are a successful group that have colonized the tropics and adapted to some of the toughest areas of the world.

Closely related to the swans and geese, ducks have webbed feet and water-repellent plumage that enable them to swim buoyantly. Many species dive for their food, although others are surface feeders venturing below water only by the familiar habit of 'up-ending'. They have large, rather rounded bills that reach their ultimate development in the Shoveler *Anas clypeata* in Eurasia, and other species elsewhere.

Nests are usually made on the ground near water, but some species use holes between rocks, and others holes in trees from which the chicks have to leap without benefit of the power of flight. Most eggs are unmarked white with varying castes of blue and yellow. Almost all ducks line their nests with down plucked from the breast by the female herself. The finest and warmest down is said to be that of the Eider *Somateria mollissima*, but it may be that because of their colonial habits Eider down is easier to come by than that of other species. In Iceland huge colonies are protected and farmed for their down. Each time the female lines a nest, the lining is harvested, although never to the point where her tolerance is pushed beyond the limit so that she deserts. The young, which are active soon after hatching, are covered in a protective, camouflaged down.

At the end of the breeding season, ducks shed their flight feathers simultaneously and are, for a period of two or three weeks, completely flightless. The males of some species adopt a special 'eclipse' plumage at this time that closely resembles the muted colours of the female.

Most ducks belong to the distinct subfamily Anatinae, the exception being the whistling or tree ducks of the tribe Dendrocygnini which are closely related to the swans and geese. The eight species are predominantly tropical and, because of their nocturnal habits, are little known. They perch freely on trees, but it is a misnomer to call them tree ducks and the name whistling ducks is to be preferred. In spite of being definitely duck-shaped, whistling ducks stand upright, quite unlike any other group of

wildfowl. They are generally brown birds and the sexes are similar.

Most widespread is the Fulvous Whistling Duck *Dendrocygna bicolor* which has populations in North and South America, Africa and Asia. These populations are quite distinct but they have not evolved into different species. The Red-billed Whistling Duck *D. autumnalis* is found throughout the Americas. It is, perhaps, the most boldly coloured of the whistling ducks with black underparts, rufous back and chest and grey head. The White-faced Whistling Duck *D. viduata* is found in both South America and in Africa south of the Sahara. It is generally darker and more chestnut-

Below The Fulvous Tree Duck is one of the more widespread members of the strange genus *Dendrocygna*, and as likely to be seen among the lakes of Africa as on some Indian jheel.

Opposite Throughout the Northern Hemisphere a brood of Mallard ducklings is one of the common sights of early summer. Up to a dozen eggs may be laid, but predators take their toll during the vulnerable days after hatching.

coloured than the Fulvous, and has a characteristically darker head and pure white face. In Australasia, Oceania and the East Indies, the Fulvous Whistling Duck is replaced by various races of the Wandering Whistling Duck *D. arcuata*, while the Plumed or Eyton's Whistling Duck *D. eytoni*, found in Australia and Tasmania, has developed distinctive plumes along the flanks.

All other ducks comprise the subfamily Anatinae, although the tribe Tadornini, the shelducks and their allies, are another link with the geese. Some authors divide them into *Tadorna* (shelducks) and *Chloëphaga* (sheldgeese). The shelducks are a widespread genus of rather large, goose-like ducks. They are strong-legged, walk well and in some species the female is more boldly coloured than the male. This is not, however, a case of total role reversal as, for instance, in the phalaropes or Eurasian Dotterel. This was perhaps best exhibited in the Crested Shelduck *Tadorna cristata* of Korea, the last example of which was collected in 1916. The Ruddy Shelduck *T. ferruginea* is typical of all shelduck with rufous plumage broken only by a white area at the bend of the folded wing. It is one of the most widespread birds in the world, extending from Morocco to China. In India it is known as the Brahminy Duck.

The Eurasian Shelduck *T. tadorna* is a boldly patterned, black and white bird marked with a broad, chestnut breast band and a red bill. The male has a swan-like knob at the base of the upper mandible. It is essentially a coastal species feeding on saltmarsh and along the tide-line where it sifts molluscs and crustaceans from the mud. At the end of the breeding season the chicks congregate into creches that are cared for by an 'aunt' or two, while the majority of adults fly to traditional and long-established localities to moult. In north-western Europe this moult-migration area lies on the German Knechtsand at the mouth of the Elbe, but other birds gather at Bridgewater Bay in England.

The *Chloëphaga* sheldgeese are a similar group of duck of southern South America. They are found in the Falkland Islands, and in Argentina and Chile south to Tierra del Fuego. Males are usually pure white and the females a mixture of browns, greys and rufous, although in some species the sexes are similar. They are grazers and do not migrate to any extent. The Ruddy-headed Goose *C. rubidiceps* moults its flight feathers gradually over a period and is thus never flightless; the other species may do likewise.

Most numerous, widespread and varied of all the ducks are the dabbling or surface-feeding ducks. In this group the female usually incubates the eggs and cares for the young and is, therefore, a mottled, camouflaged bird. In sharp contrast, the males are boldly patterned, even sometimes gaudy. Most widespread and familiar of all ducks is the Mallard *Anas platyrhynchos*. This is the ancestor of most domestic ducks, the males of which may be all manner of colours, but still boast the ancestral curling feathers of the upper tail. Like other northern temperate species, the Mallard is highly migratory and gatherings of several thousand are not unusual. Wigeon *A. penelope* breed further north and are highly gregarious, often forming flocks in excess of five figures. These surface feeders are predominantly vegetarian and, in winter at least, frequently flight from feeding grounds to a safe roost twice each day. If they are feeding among saltings they will move with the tide rather than the clock.

The torrent ducks of the high Andes are usually included with the dabbling ducks, although they are quite different. They swim like expert canoeists among the high-level rapids of mountain streams, and nest in holes along the river banks. There are six quite distinctive forms, but they are all grouped together into a single species *Merganetta armata*.

Other aberrant members of this group include the extinct Pink-headed Duck *Rhodonessa caryophyllacea*, which was formerly found in north-east India, and the Shovel-billed Pink-eared Duck *Malacorhynchus membranaceus*, which is found in the arid interior of central Australia and is nomadic in its search for wetland. The steamer ducks are flightless birds of southern South America that

Opposite top The finely marked drake Teal, here seen moulting into eclipse plumage in late summer, is one of the most attractive of all duck. In the air it forms dense flocks that fly with many of the characteristics of waders.

Opposite bottom Unlike most ducks, the sexes of the Bahama Pintail are very similar and do not have a special eclipse plumage during the moult. Found throughout the Neotropical region they are largely sedentary.

Above The migratory Garganey leave Britain and Europe completely in autumn to fly across Africa to winter south of the Sahara. This group of drakes have made their winter home at Kenya's lily-strewn lake Naivasha.

Left Adapted to a life among the fast-flowing streams of the Andes, these Torrent Ducks are able to survive the white waters of the most fearful cataracts. Although divided into several subspecies only one full species covers the area from Colombia to Tierra del Fuego.

Below Totally Arctic birds, Steller's Eiders breed only on the most remote and inhospitable coasts around the North Pole. Even in winter they seldom move further than necessary from the edge of the frozen polar seas.

Left The equivalent of the Old World Tufted Duck, Ring-necked Ducks have a boldly patterned bill and a sharp white area at the front of the grey flanks, but they are named after the insignificant ring of bronzed feathers at the base of the neck.

Below The bold black and white plumage, together with the vividly golden eye and elongated tuft of feathers on the crown, easily pick out the Tufted Duck from the all-black Coots that accompany them.

Bottom Confined naturally to the Far East, the handsome Mandarin Duck has proved a popular member of wildfowl collections throughout the World. In many areas these birds have escaped and formed self-supporting feral populations.

Opposite The dainty African Pygmy Geese are, in fact, not geese at all but the smallest members of the duck tribe. They belong to a group of three species, all similar in size, of which the best known is the Indian Cotton Teal.

'steam' across the water surface to escape from danger. Their relationships are obscure.

Next to the dabbling ducks, the diving ducks of the tribe Aythyini are the best known group. They include the familiar Tufted Duck *Aythya fuligula* of Europe, and the Canvasback *A. vallisneria* and Ring-necked Duck *A. collaris* of North America. All dive in various depths of water and for various food. They sometimes gather in immense numbers over rich feeding grounds. Scaup *A. marila*, in particular, are gregarious and huge flocks form over mussel beds.

Often referred to under the general banner of 'seaducks' several of the species are nevertheless as familiar inland as they are along the coast. Thus while the scoters and eiders are essentially marine, the goldeneyes are just as common on fresh water, and Goosanders *Mergus merganser* often gather in larger flocks inland. Scoters are black ducks with a Holarctic distribution. While the females are confusingly brown, the male plumage is broken by different coloured bills and white patches on wing and head. They are essentially marine ducks and are found inland only when driven

Top Scoter are duck of marine habits. They feed over mussel beds close inshore, and come inland only to breed or following storms. The all-black plumage of the males, together with their gregarious habits, make them look like coot at sea.

Left In summer, Harlequin Duck resort to swift-flowing streams like the Torrent Duck of South America, where the dull-coloured females nest along riverside banks. In winter, they take to the sea and some populations perform considerable migrations.

Above The distinctly shaped head and small, round spot in front of the eye characterize the Goldeneye. Its less widespread close relative Barrow's Goldeneye carries a crescent-shaped facial patch.

there by storms. They dive well and feed on the invertebrate fauna of the continental shelf, often in company with Goldeneye *Bucephala clangula* and Long-tailed Duck *Clangula hyemalis*.

In contrast, the sawbills of the genus *Mergus* are fish feeders, the serrated edges of their narrow bills being adapted to grasping slippery fish under water. They are never common, although Mergansers *M. serrator* sometimes gather in flocks of a hundred or

Above A drake Pochard. These attractive little diving duck breed throughout Eurasia, migrating southwards to winter on inland waters in large rafts, often in association with Tufted Duck.

Left The White-headed Duck, the only Old World 'stiff-tail', frequents shallow waters with a strong growth of emergent vegetation among which it searches for food by diving.

more to feed on trapped fish. Drake Smew *M. abellus* are among the most handsome of duck. They come out of the Arctic to winter at a few highly selected localities. Strangely, they find the drinking water storage reservoirs around London particularly to their liking and return year after year.

The stiff-tails are a strange group of freshwater ducks that dive well and invariably feed by night. They boast strong tail feathers that are frequently held vertical, and which perform a rudder function under water. The various species lay large eggs for their size and one species, the Black-headed Duck *Heteronetta àtricapilla*, lays its eggs in other birds' nests like a cuckoo.

Geese Anatidae (part)

Most authors now consider that the swans, geese and ducks belong to a single family, the Anatidae. While they are best treated as one from a taxonomic viewpoint, there is no doubt that at least three quite distinct groups can be separated: swans, ducks and the true geese of the genera *Anser* and *Branta*. Other genera are frequently called geese, but only the strangely aberrant Magpie Goose *Anseranas semipalmata* is dealt with here.

There are fourteen species of true geese, divisible on a generic basis into grey geese (*Anser*) and black geese (*Branta*). They are medium to large waterbirds with long necks, strong and powerful webbed feet and long, powerful wings. They fly strongly and are essentially gregarious, usually occurring in large to exceptionally large flocks. Geese are truly 'wild fowl'. They fly out of the north on prodigious migrations from one end of a continent to another. As they fly their wild echoing calls keep them in contact one with another, the evocation of wild places to those who watch from below. They fly across the sky in skeins (groups in 'V' formation) made up of family parties that have joined together on the tundra and fly together for the winter. These wild creatures are extremely conservative and although the birdwatcher may see a skein once in

a while, to be certain of geese he must travel to one of their known haunts. At a number of traditional sites birds will return year after year at the same time. It may be a late winter site like Slimbridge in England where White-fronted Geese *Anser albifrons* only really begin to arrive after Christmas, or just an autumn stop-over place like Sand Lake in the Midwest of the United States. Here up to two hundred thousand Snow Geese *A. caerulescens* descend on the refuge at the end of their first stage migration from breeding grounds on Hudson Bay. They will stay for the corn thoughtfully provided for them until the hard weather moves them on towards the balmy Gulf Coast of Texas.

Geese are good to eat, but they are even better to hunt. They are so wild that a concealed approach is almost impossible. Their conservativeness is their ultimate downfall, however. Not only do they head for the same places season after season, but when they arrive on location they follow a predictable daily routine. Pink-footed Geese *A. brachyrhynchus*, for instance, feed on fields and flight back and forwards morning and evening to a regular roosting site on sandbanks or shoalings. As they do so a chance of a shot is offered and there, lying in wait, are the wildfowlers. It sounds

Above Ancestor of most domestic geese, the Greylag is the most widespread and numerous goose throughout temperate Europe. Goslings follow their mother across a lake, but would follow any other large object that they encountered and became accustomed to during their first few days after hatching.

Right Wild and dramatic as are the movements of Canada Geese in their native America, in the introduced circumstances of Britain they are resident and tame. A Great Crested Grebe rests alongside this Anglicized pair.

simple but it is not. A strong following wind and the geese will fly too high; a wind from one quarter and they will fly across it to compensate and pass a mile away from the hide. If they all come together there may be the chance of one shot, but most likely the 'wild-goose chaser' will spend the best part of the night in the cold and damp for nothing. No doubt being shot at is one of the factors that makes the geese as wild as they are – and therefore so enjoyable to pursue.

The goose calendar dominates the birds' structure and behaviour in a very obvious way. Their strong flight and long migrations are necessary to escape the harsh conditions of their tundra breeding grounds, where they find comparative safety from predators and a plentiful supply of food during the summer. Courtship is usually performed at some stop-over place en route, so that when the birds arrive at their breeding sites they can get straight on with the business of nesting. There, among the melting ice and newly formed torrents, they must lay eggs which take twenty-four to thirty-two days to incubate. The chicks must change from downy balls to fully fledged, strong flying birds before the snows start to cover the tundra early in the autumn. Time is short for such large birds to rear young, but another factor is important.

All birds change their feathers every year. Most do so gradually over a lengthy period so that they never completely lose their powers of flight. Geese cannot afford to migrate or winter on nine-tenths power and so the adults moult while the youngsters are still growing their first flight feathers. Thus the entire population of geese are flightless for a period of a couple of weeks or so at the end of the breeding season. To escape predators they keep to lakes, rivers and tundra pools, but scientists have taken advantage of their flightlessness to trap them for ringing.

One of the earliest of these scientific round ups involved Peter Scott and the late James Fisher in a memorable trip to a central Iceland glacier where they were to ring 1,000 flightless Pink-feet. For years, thereafter, ringed 'Pinks' were regularly observed and retrapped in the normal wintering areas of northern Britain. Since then literally thousands of geese have been rounded up annually right across the world. Large coloured rings or bands are now used – rings that can be read at long distances and which save the necessity of the geese being recaptured.

The Greylag Goose *A. anser* is the typical goose of temperate Eurasia. Though a migrant, it is found breeding further to the south than the other species and, because of this, it has been tamed and selectively bred by man, and is the ancestor of all our farmyard geese save the Chinese Goose which was domesticated from the Swan Goose *A. cygnoides*. The domestication of the Greylag reached its highest form in eastern Europe, where pâté de foie gras is made by force-feeding geese to flavour their livers – a particularly obnoxious practice.

Greylags are easy to tell in flight because of the bold, grey patches on their forewings, while White-fronts have a bold pattern of barring and blotching on the belly. The other grey geese, the Pink-footed and the Bean *A. fabalis* are often regarded as conspecific (belonging to the same species) even though the Bean Goose is considerably larger than the Pink-footed and has a distinct call note. While British Bean Geese come from the east, the Pinkfeet come from Iceland and Greenland to the north west.

In Asia the Bar-headed Goose *A. indicus* is a migrant southwards from Tibet. It makes one of the most extraordinary migrations of all in regularly flying over the high Himalayan passes at heights of well over 20,000 feet, and has a larger wing area in proportion to size than the other geese. It is gregarious but it is never found in such great numbers as the North American snow geese.

The taxonomics of the snow geese are complex and best left to

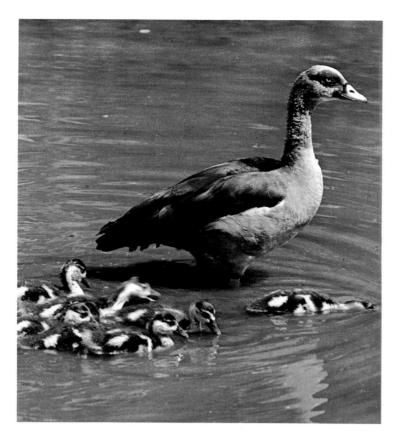

Egyptian Geese are found throughout Africa save the arid region of the Sahara. They swim and dive well, but feed mainly by grazing. They frequently associate at waterholes with the large herbivores of the African plains.

the experts. For our purposes there seem to be only two species: the Snow Goose, which includes the Lesser Snow Goose and the Blue Goose which is simply a colour phase; and the diminutive Ross's Goose *A. rossii.*

The black geese are a more 'contrasty' group of birds, with darker plumage usually including at least some black. Typical is the Brent Goose *Branta bernicla,* called the Brant in North America. Three distinct subspecies are generally recognized. All breed in the high Arctic and migrate to temperate coasts to winter along the shoreline. Due to overshooting and a disastrous decline in their principle food, the eel-grass *Zostera,* the western European population plummeted to an all-time low in the 1940s. International agreement to ban shooting saved the Brent Goose, but the threats to the intertidal area posed by the 1970s yet again threaten this attractive little goose.

According to legend, Barnacle Geese *B. leucopsis* hatch out at the tide-line from barnacles. Actually they breed in the high Arctic and migrate to our shores, but because of their shellfish ancestry they were 'permitted' eating for Catholics on Friday! Barnacles wintering in western Europe are of two quite distinct populations. Some are Siberian birds while others come from Greenland to the west. The two groups never mix, although both find a home in the west of Scotland.

The Red-breasted Goose *B. ruficollis* is another Siberian bird that migrates to winter to the south west in Turkey and around the shores of the Black Sea. It is a fine, attractively coloured bird that occasionally appears singly with flocks of other geese in areas beyond its normal range.

One of the wildest geese of North America, and one much sought after by sportsmen, is the Canada Goose *B. canadensis.* Down the flyways they come along with the more numerous Snow Geese. With every good intention they were introduced into Britain where they have lost their migratory habit, become tame and lack all that makes them appealing. Hardly a sportsman bothers with them, but every so often genuine wild 'Canadas' are wind-drifted across the Atlantic to Europe. In Hawaii, descendants of such disorientated individuals have evolved as a quite distinct species, the Nene *B. sandvicensis.* Here too they lost their migratory habit and even developed shorter wings as a result. Merciless hunting, plus destruction caused by introduced predators, brought the population of this goose down to danger level (about fifty) by the middle of the twentieth century, and only intensive care and breeding in captivity at Slimbridge, England, has enabled the Nene to survive. Birds have now been returned to the wild where, under strict protection, they are beginning to thrive.

The Magpie Goose is placed in a subfamily all of its own. It is a large, boldly patterned black and white bird with long toes that are only partially webbed. It enjoys a progressive moult, rather than a complete one, and in this alone shows that it does not descend from true geese stock like the Nene. The hind toe is strong and the bird perches freely in trees. It was once abundant in Australia but is now confined only to north Australian swamp and grasslands.

Swans Anatidae (part)

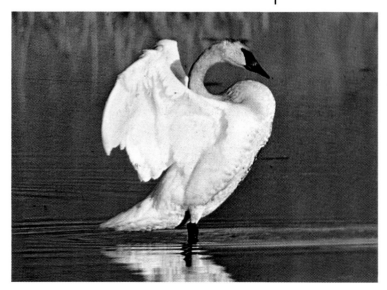

The six species of swans of the tribe Anserini are among the most familiar, decorative and elegant birds in the world, and it is not surprising that man has established a special relationship with them. They play a significant part in mythology (Leda and the Swan), have appeared on coats of arms, have been claimed as the property of kings, given as 'special' presents to dignitaries, and domesticated and used as decoration for thousands of estates. Nowhere, perhaps, has this swan-human relationship reached a higher peak than in Britain where 18,000 Mute Swans *Cygnus olor* belong to the Crown.

Originally domesticated as a source of food and served at important banquets, the Mute Swan was given by 'royalties' to various livery companies that then enjoyed the right to own them. As proof of ownership the companies had to mark the birds they owned with special marks. All unmarked birds belonged automatically to the Crown. The colourful ceremony of swan-

Largest of the swans, the Trumpeter of the North American Rocky Mountain system has been saved from imminent extinction and now prospers in many parts of the United States and Canada.

upping persists to the present day, although only the Dyers and Vintners Companies remain. The famous swannery at Abbotsbury in Dorset is the only other extant 'royalty'. The approximately 700 swans here belong to the Earl of Ilchester.

Our general impression of swans is of large white birds, but young swans, called cygnets, are a dirty brown colour, while two Southern Hemisphere swans are at least partly black. The Black Swan *C. atratus* is completely black, save for a white area on the wings which shows in flight, and was a cause of great wonderment when first brought to Europe from its native Australia. With a wingspan of 6 feet, it is a large unmistakable bird that is easy to domesticate and which now exists in a semi-wild state in New Zealand and Sweden. In New Zealand it thrived so well that control was soon necessary as the birds were interfering with native species. In other parts of the world their lack of success in establishing themselves in the wild is in part due to competition with Mute Swans, but also to the superstition of countryfolk to whom something black is something bad.

In Australia Black Swans are found mainly in the south where huge concentrations can occur. Up to 50,000 have been counted at a single locality. Like the Mute Swan the Black Swan has a beautiful courtship and is seldom vocal. Flocks keep together in flight by the whistle of their wings.

The beautiful Black-necked Swan *C. melanocoryphus* is a slightly smaller bird found in southern South America through the pampas area to Patagonia and the Falkland Islands.

Pride of place among swans goes to the three northern species: the Mute Swan; the Trumpeter Swan (called the Whooper Swan in Europe where it is a separate subspecies) *C. cygnus*; and the Whistling Swan (the Bewick's Swan subspecies in Europe) *C. columbianus*. Of these the 'wild' swans have a special appeal. They have not been domesticated like the Mute, and their calls evoke the wildness of the north whence they come.

The Trumpeter Swan breeds among the muskeg country of Alaska and the Rockies, further south than the Whistling Swan, and at one time it seemed in danger of imminent extinction. Rigorous protection by Federal authorities saved the day. The European subspecies, the Whooper Swan, has never reached such danger levels and breeds in a great belt from Iceland through Scandinavia and Siberia to the Pacific and Japan. In contrast, Bewick's Swan has a far more restricted range on the Siberian Arctic coast, while the Whistling Swan breeds from Alaska across the Canadian Arctic to Hudson Bay.

All four forms are highly vocal and fly south on migration in small 'V' formations. The Bewick's Swan is the longest distance traveller of all, and large numbers leave the Kanin Peninsula area to winter in Holland and Britain. The British Bewick's Swans have been encouraged by Sir Peter Scott's Wildfowl Trust to concentrate and feed on free grain at Slimbridge in Gloucestershire and Welney in Norfolk, and there the wild birds can be approached to within a few feet.

The wild swans are best identified by the extent of yellow on their bills. The smaller Bewick's Swan has a round patch and the Whooper a triangular one. The Whistling Swan has only a tiny comma of yellow at the base of the bill, and the largest swan of all, the Trumpeter, has a completely black bill.

The Coscoroba Swan *Coscoroba coscoroba* is an all-white bird with a startlingly red bill. Its similarity to a farmyard duck shows its affinities to the whistling ducks with which it may properly belong. It breeds in South America over much the same range as the Black-necked Swan.

New World vultures Cathartidae

Vultures, as everyone understands, serve a useful purpose in disposing of dead and decaying animal remains, as well as in cleaning up in areas of poor or non-existent sanitation. This does not make them popular, however. Most people find them quite repulsive, although the ancient Egyptians evidently held them in sufficient esteem to decorate their temples with their stylized likenesses.

The Cathartidae are similar to the vultures of the Old World, but they are, in fact, a quite distinct family. Their similarities are due to a pattern of convergent evolution on continents separated by large areas of inhospitable territory, mainly sea. Fossil evidence shows that the New World species are the more primitive, however, and once occurred in the Old World. Remains of *Gymnogyps amplus*, a close relative of the California Condor *G. californianus*, have been found in the famous Rancho La Brea tar pits, and dated as being from the Pleistocene period.

Like the Old World vultures, the Cathartidae soar on huge, broad wings. The bare head and neck enables them to become fouled up in their efforts to obtain food without endangering their plumage. Their feet are designed for perching not grasping, however, and their bills are quite tiny, like the Old World Hooded and Egyptian Vultures. As a result they are quite unable to penetrate the carcasses of large animals and their clearing up operations, being delayed while the corpse decays, are even more foul-smelling than their Old World congeners. Most species are scavengers, although some are not averse to the chicks and eggs of other birds, and the Turkey Vulture *Cathartes aura* is a serious predator on the guano islands of the Humboldt Current.

The Carthartidae are found throughout the Americas outside the Arctic and Antarctic regions, although like the Old World vultures they reach their greatest numbers in the tropics. They normally nest on cliffs, but take readily to other sites when these are not available. The two or three eggs take five weeks to incubate, and the nestlings a further two and a half to three months to fledge.

The California Condor, with a wingspan of almost 10 feet and a lift-off weight of up to 25 pounds, is one of the largest birds in the world and one of the heaviest of flying birds. First discovered at the end of the eighteenth century, the California Condor was already confined to the area west of the Rockies. Gradually during the nineteenth century it declined and withdrew from its former range, and by the beginning of the twentieth century it was breeding only in California. By 1947 only sixty birds remained in the coastal ranges of the southern and central parts of that State. By 1964 the population had fallen to forty-two birds, with the major concentration in the Santa Barbara and Ventura counties between the Sierra Nevada and the coastal ranges. Here, in the richest State in the World, the last of these great birds are fighting a losing battle against economic development and the increasing pressure of leisure activities and penetration of the countryside. Shooting has been the major cause of decline, at least in this century, and only efficient protection and conservation measures will prevent the California Condor from being shot out of existence. Surely the rich state of California can afford to save the California Condor!

The bird is a huge, black sailplane with prominent white flashes on the wing, and a bare, orange-red head and neck. It is quite unmistakable. Like the Andean Condor *Vultur gryphus*, its breeding cycle is so lengthy that it rears young only every alternate year. The Andean Condor enjoys a far wider range, however, and seems, for the moment, to be in no danger. It is found throughout the Andes range, and is particularly numerous along the cliffs of Peru

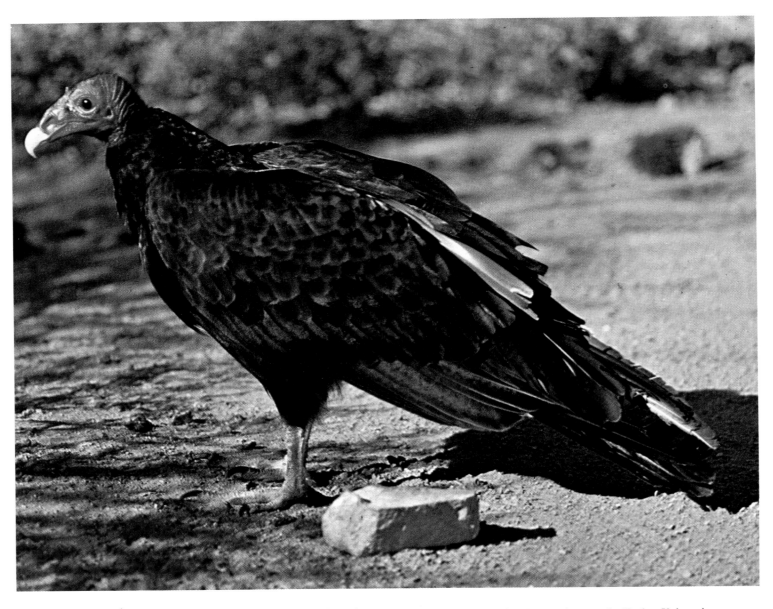

where the cold current is so rich in life. It can be seen feeding along the tide-line along with Turkey Vultures, but is also found in the highest parts of the Andes at over 12,000 feet.

Turkey Vultures are the most widespread of all the New World vultures. They are coloquially called 'Turkey Buzzards' and 'Johnny Crows' in the United States, and are often to be seen clearing up after road accidents involving animals. Their all-black plumage and bare, red head are quite distinctive, although in flight their shape and size are very similar to the Yellow-headed Vulture *Cathartes burrovianus*. Both should not be confused with the stockier Black Vulture *Coragyps atratus* which has a bare, black head and prominent, silver wing patches.

All of these species are liable to poisoning, for in spite of man's continual onslaught the Coyote survives over large areas of North America, and poisoned carcasses are widely used to reduce its numbers. As a by-product this also has the effect of reducing all scavengers. Turkey Vultures are erroneously regarded as carriers of anthrax and other diseases, and predators of young domestic animals in parts of the United States, and this is a source of active persecution and destruction.

The King Vulture *Sarcorhamphus papa* has one of the most extraordinary of animal faces. Its neck is orange as is its bill. Between them are huge, orange wattles, a blackish-purple crown, a purple lappet, a series of buff wattle ridges, and a white eye ringed with crimson. The whole effect is grotesque and dramatic. As for

Above A snapper-up of garbage and waste, the Turkey Vulture is numerous throughout most of temperate and tropical America. In some places it gathers in immense flocks.

Opposite The American King Vulture, so called because of its precedence in the New World vulturine peck order, has one of the most colourful and bizarre faces in the world of birds.

Overleaf One of the world's great rare birds, the Californian Condor, peers from a rocky crag. Inhabiting the sierras that lie behind one of the most affluent regions of the world, the chances of this condor surviving into the next century are remote.

the rest of its plumage, the King Vulture is quite beautiful. Delicate, light buffs marked with black flight feathers make it quite unlike any other New World vulture.

King Vultures are birds of the tropical lowland forests from Central America south to Argentina. They frequently perch and are then inconspicuous, but at other times groups may gather to feed on a carcass and soar together over the trees. The difficulty of obtaining a good viewpoint in the midst of jungle, has perhaps resulted in King Vultures being most frequently seen from mountain ridges. In some areas it is the only vulture present but its dominance at a carcass, as evident by its larger and more powerful bill, is responsible for the vernacular name. Like so many other birds of South America, the breeding biology of the King Vulture has not been studied apart from in captivity.

Old World vultures Accipitridae (part)

Vultures are huge sailplanes, with large, broad wings and tiny tails. They are masters in the air and can stay aloft for hours with only the tiniest expenditure of energy. Round and round they soar in a thermal, higher and higher until they are only dots in the sky. Then they glide off to another area of rising air. If a carcass is discovered, or a predator has killed, they will appear from all directions as if by magic. Despite their size they are not bold birds, and will sit over a carcass for hours if they are at all suspicious.

That so many species can exist side by side is at first confusing, but there is a definite peck order among vultures that is evident by the size and power of their bills. In Africa, for instance, the huge, powerfull bill of the Lappet-faced Vulture *Torgos tracheliotus* is capable of piercing the skin of dead animals. The less massive bills of the griffons *Gyps* species and White-backed Vultures *Pseudogyps africanus* tear at the flesh, while the delicate bills and long necks of the Hooded *Necrosyrtes monachus* and Egyptian Vultures *Neophron percnopterus* are able to enter the carcass and pick the bones clean. The total tidying up operation is completed by the Lämmergeier *Gypaetus barbatus*, often placed in a subfamily of its own, which consumes the bones.

The Egyptian Vulture is also fond of 'tidying up' the eggs of

Ostriches and other large birds. It lifts medium-sized eggs and smashes them to the ground, but larger ones are dealt with by cracking with stones – a primitive use of a hammer as a tool. The Lämmergeier also uses rocks, but drops large bones on to them to break them and reveal the marrow. It has a specially shaped tongue

By a remarkable piece of adaptation Egyptian Vultures have discovered how to break Ostrich eggs with stones. They are not very good at it, and do not quite seem to see the actual connection between rock throwing and egg eating, but it works!

to deal with the extraction problem. The most aberrant of all the vultures is the Palm-nut Vulture *Gypohierax angolensis* which feeds on the fruit of the oil-palm, although it will also take dead fish. Like the Lämmergeier it has a fully feathered neck, the other species having no more than an easy-to-clean covering of down.

Vultures inhabit those parts of the world where carrion is most abundant. They are thus most numerous in Africa and Asia, and fewer in numbers in Europe and the Middle East. The growth of

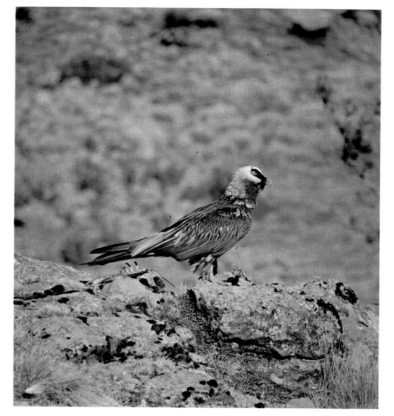

affluence through southern Europe in the last thirty years has led to a serious decline in the number of vultures, but they have also suffered, as have other birds that take carrion, from the habit of putting down poisoned carcasses to kill Wolves and other large and dangerous mammals. No doubt they will become progressively confined to the hills and more remote regions where fatalities among domestic stock are more likely to be overlooked. Even in East Africa there is a marked contrast in the populations of vultures between those parts where cattle are allowed to graze and those where they are banned. There is probably no higher population of vultures anywhere as in the Masai country of southern Kenya.

Vultures are generally rather similar in the air and can be difficult to identify, although an experienced observer should have no difficulty in picking them out as such. There are only fourteen species and these can be divided into quite distinct groups. The Lämmergeier has pointed wings and a long, wedge-shaped tail, while only the Egyptian and Palm-nut Vultures have predominantly white plumage. Each continent has one large, black vulture: in Europe the Black Vulture *Aegypius monachus*; in Africa the Lappet-faced; and in Asia the King or Pondicherry Vulture *Sarcogyps calvus*. Thus only eight species of the fourteen remain and two of those have a prominent, white back-patch in the adult, the African and Indian White-backed Vultures *Pseudogyps africanus* and *P. bengalensis*. Only the six species of griffons and their allies should therefore cause confusion, and here again geographical separation eliminates more of the problems. Underwing and upperwing patterns are the most important field marks and should be carefully noted.

Vultures breed either on cliffs or trees, colonially or singly, but most species have quite definite preferences for one or the other and are either colonial or not. They build huge nests of sticks and

Left An adult Lammergeier, or Bearded Vulture, pauses to pick at the remains of a carcass among broken hill country. This great and rare bird is the final stage in the vulture clean-up operation – it eats the bones.

Below An African White-backed Vulture spreads its huge wings and broad tail as it comes in to land. Its incredibly sharp eyes enable it to see other vultures descending to feed at vast distances.

usually lay one, or sometimes two, eggs that require a lengthy incubation period. This varies up to fifty-three days for the larger species. Fledging takes a further four months.

As the world becomes more tidy as a result of improved hygiene and medical knowledge, vultures will inevitably decline in numbers. While a decline in the need for their cleaning up operations must be a good thing, there seems no danger at present of their imminent demise.

Eagles and hawks Accipitridae (part) and Pandionidae

The kings of the birds, the great and majestic eagles, belong to the family Accipitridae, along with the buzzards, kites, harriers and the true accipiters, the hawks and goshawks. The Old World vultures also belong to this large and diverse family, but are sufficiently distinct to merit separate treatment. Not that many of the groups dealt with here are not distinct enough. The birdwatcher who cannot tell a buzzard from a harrier has not really started, and it is no great accomplishment to separate a kite from a smaller eagle. Thus while the family breaks down quite nicely into separate groups of genera or subfamilies, there are a number of species that provide quite definite links or that are difficult to assign to one group or another. Harrier-eagles and harrier-hawks are cases in point. Authorities usually regard the Osprey *Pandion haliaetus* as

a distinct family, the Pandionidae, but for convenience it is included here.

Together with the Falconidae, these families of birds are often referred to as the birds of prey or raptors. They are generally large birds with sharp talons and powerful, grasping feet with which they are able to kill quite large animals, and sharp, hooked bills that are ideal for tearing flesh. Most species are expert gliders, capable of soaring effortlessly for hours with barely a movement of the wings. With the larger species flapping flight is generally used

An adult Golden Eagle crouches over a mountain hare. These great birds are opportunist hunters and fly low over the hillsides in an effort to take their prey unawares.

only to get airborne, but the true accipiters are strong and agile fliers capable of following and catching a small bird as it darts among the trees of a forest.

Hunting methods vary with species. The larger eagles tend to cruise in the hope of surprising prey or coming across carrion, the kites are great scavengers, and the buzzards customarily hunt from a low perch. All have large eyes set well forward on the head giving

a good area of binocular vision. In some species the sexes have a distinct plumage and in most the female is considerably larger than the male. In the accipiters this size difference may even lead to the male and female taking different-sized prey. The fact that these birds are slow to mature, and pass through a succession of immature plumages, is confusing enough to the would-be raptor watcher. Even when fully adult, however, they are by no means easy to identify. To pick out a bird in flight as belonging to a group is not that difficult. Eagles have large, broad wings, medium-length tails and prominent heads. Buzzards too have broad wings but their tails are short and spread and the head is very small. Hawks have long tails, broad, rounded wings and are generally smaller. Harriers have long, narrow wings and tails and a flapping, lazy flight low over the ground, but when they soar they can be confused with the kites. Fortunately the latter all have a characteristic notch or deep fork in the tail.

Largest and most regal of all the birds of prey are the eagles of the genus *Aquila*, but even these vary from the magnificent Golden Eagle *A. chrysaetos*, which hunts over mountainous areas and is quite capable of killing small sheep, to hangers-on at rubbish tips like the Lesser Spotted Eagle *A. pomarina*.

The Golden Eagle was once found across Eurasia and North America, but persecution waged over centuries has driven it into the hills. Golden Eagles are highly territorial birds and have the

Left A pair of Spanish Imperial Eagles, resplendent with white crowns and shoulders, feed their two eaglets. The subspecies is now one of the world's rarest birds and in imminent danger of extinction. Six or seven pairs attempt to breed each year on the Coto Donaña reserve.

Below Two Bald Eagles, national symbol of the United States of America, dispute a carcass on a frozen lake. Once to be seen throughout North America, the Bald Eagle has been seriously reduced in numbers over the last fifty years.

Below A Crowned Eagle at its tree eyrie with a single young. Although not the largest African bird of prey, the species is probably the most powerful and quite capable of dealing with small mammals.

Bottom A Martial Eagle at its nest with prey caught from the air in a stupendous stoop. This fine African raptor has a slight crest, a bright yellow eye and long, pointed talons ideally adapted to killing birds and smaller mammals.

Opposite Accipiter-shaped for gliding through monkey-haunted forests, the Monkey-eating Eagle is now a rare inhabitant of only the two largest of the Philippine Islands. Its predilection for flying lemurs belies its name.

unfortunate habit of nesting at only one or two traditional sites for generation after generation. They are thus easy prey to gamekeepers and 'sportsmen'. Mostly they nest on crags, although in some parts of the range trees are more frequently used. Golden Eagles lay two eggs, but rear only one youngster. Even when food is plentiful the elder sibling will invariably kill the younger. This habit is quite common among birds of prey. The Lesser Spotted Eagle does the same, although experiments in eastern Europe have shown that Common Buzzards *Buteo buteo* make excellent foster parents, and

can help increase a declining eagle population.

The huge Verreaux's or Black Eagle *A. verreauxi* is not uncommon in southern and eastern Africa. Its staple diet is Rock Hyrax but it will take large birds up to guineafowl size. In flight its all-black plumage is broken only by patches of white on the wings, rump and back, but this bold pattern plus the 'waisted' look of its wings where they join the body, gives it a distinctive flight silhouette.

The Tawny Eagle *A. rapax* is the most abundant of the large eagles. It is found throughout the Old World and is successful partly because of its adaptability. It takes carrion quite freely, is a pirate of other predators, and I have seen it at about 20,000 feet along the flanks of Mount Everest where food is distinctly scarce. It is quite capable of hunting for itself, and will kill rodents on the ground and strike birds in the air. While it is not unusual to see single birds perched on roadside trees and telegraph wires, Tawny Eagles will also gather in flocks at carrion.

In Australia, the Wedge-tailed Eagle *A. audax* has been ruthlessly persecuted because of its alleged depredations on sheep. No doubt these birds, like the Golden Eagle, do take lambs occasionally, but they are quite incapable of killing sheep or even well-grown lambs. No doubt the myth derives from their scavenging operations in which sheep afterbirths and dead lambs provide a plentiful, if seasonal, abundance of food. They are fond of carrion and are thus easy for ranchers to poison. This has seriously reduced the numbers of Wedge-tailed Eagles in many parts of Australia, but they are still common in non-farming areas. Rabbits are a staple item of diet, but wallabies are the natural food.

While the eastern race of the Imperial Eagle *A. heliaca* seems to be holding its own, the Iberian race, the Spanish Imperial Eagle *A.h. adalberti*, is in the gravest of danger and merits a place in the

Left Found virtually throughout the world, the Osprey is entirely dependent on its ability to catch fish by plunge-diving. The impact is so great that the bird often fully submerges. This Osprey is returning to its nest with firmly held prey.

Below Common Buzzards are the typical broad-winged hawks of the Old World. They hunt by pouncing on prey from a low perch and take many small mammals as well as the grass snake seen here.

Red Data Book. The population numbers probably less than 100 individuals, and only those few found on the Coto Donaña Reserve receive any active protection. They are large, handsome birds that feed on carrion and small mammals.

Similar to some of the *Aquila* eagles, and almost as large, the genus *Haliaeetus* comprises a worldwide group of eagles with a liking for fish. Many species are called fish eagles, although the most famous is the Bald Eagle *H. leucocephalus*, national symbol of the United States. Formerly common throughout North America, this eagle has been reduced to a few widely scattered pockets where it survives only under rigorous protection. The largest numbers are found in Alaska where bounties are still paid for their heads. When large numbers of eagles can be seen feeding on an important human food like fresh-run salmon, perhaps the fisherman can be forgiven for seeing them as direct competitors. Large numbers also gather along Alaskan rivers to feed on the dead and dying shoals of Sockeye Salmon which have just spawned.

While some fish eagles are expert fishermen, a great many are scavengers with a penchant for dead or dying fish. They will gather at any carrion or pursue other birds like Ospreys until they disgorge, but their fishing efforts are quite facile. In contrast, the African Fish Eagle *H. vocifer* is, as its scientific name implies, a very vocal species with a shrill, far-carrying cry, and is a particularly good

A Rough-legged Buzzard comes into land at its eyrie. Found further north than the Common Buzzard it is largely dependent on the population of Lemmings for subsistence, although it also takes Ptarmigan and other Arctic grouse.

fisherman. In a gentle curve the eagle will swoop down from its lookout post to snatch a fish from near the surface. At Lake Naivasha in Kenya's Rift Valley, the whole lake is divided up into Fish Eagle territories, and a bird stands sentinel every couple of hundred yards along the shore. Immature birds either trespass or feed from the centre of the lake.

Largest of all is the immense Steller's Sea Eagle *H. pelagicus* which feeds on fish, large birds, and mammals up to Arctic Fox in size, which it takes with comparative ease. Its brown plumage is broken only by the white tail and under-tail coverts, and a white patch at the bend of the wing. Its outstanding feature, however, is the huge, orange bill which is a prominent field mark. It is confined to the most northern part of Japan and adjacent parts of the Siberian coast.

These are the largest and most dramatic of the eagles but they are not the only ones of interest. The Harpy Eagle *Harpia harpyja* is a huge, powerful bird with a white facial disc and two erectile, black tufts to its crown. It feeds in tropical jungles on monkeys, lemurs and other tree-dwelling mammals, which it grabs as it glides among the trees below the canopy. The Monkey-eating Eagle *Pithecophaga jefferyi* of the Philippines is a closely related, though less powerful species, that is in imminent danger of extinction. These species bear some similarity to the various hawk eagles of Africa.

The Osprey is the only bird of prey that is a pure fisherman. It is cosmopolitan in distribution and catches fish by diving feet first into water. It is particularly fond of trout, but will take whatever is available. On returning to Scotland, where it was totally

Opposite Well hidden among the dwarf scrub of the sub-Arctic a female Hen Harrier calls to her mate while incubating her eggs. Compared with the male, the female bird is more sombrely coloured. These circumpolar breeders migrate southwards in winter.

Above The Red Kite is found throughout Europe, predominantly in wooded country. Once widespread in Britain, persecution has eliminated the species from all but a small area in central Wales, where the birds are rigorously protected.

Left A dark phase Honey Buzzard at its nest with two well-feathered youngsters. The Honey Buzzard's feathers are thickly matted to protect it against the attacks of wasps and bees from whose nests it obtains its basic food of grubs.

exterminated by shooting in the nineteenth century, it has re-established itself on a diet of pike, and has now spread to many of its former haunts.

Buzzards are similar to eagles, but are built on a smaller scale. They too are scavengers, but most feed on small mammals as well. The typical buzzards of the genus *Buteo*, known as 'hawks' in North America, are widespread except in Australia and Malaysia. They soar well and frequently perch on posts to hunt for small prey. They are mainly confusing shades of browns and, therefore, sometimes difficult to identify in the field, although some species, like the Augur Buzzard *B. rufofuscus*, are well marked. This African bird occurs in two distinct forms, a dark and a light one. Both have dark, slate grey backs and a distinguishing rusty red tail. They are common birds of telegraph posts in East Africa and often hover like some other *Buteos*. The Red-tailed Hawk *B. jamaicensis* also has a rusty tail as do some of the eastern populations of the Common Buzzard.

The Rough-legged Buzzard *B. lagopus* has a circumpolar

distribution, and frequently **hovers** like a Kestrel in its search for small mammals. Like other Arctic predators it is dependent on the population of Lemmings, and erupts southwards with them over a four or five year cycle. During an eruption Rough-legged Buzzards seem to make quite lengthy sea crossings, which is unusual for a raptor.

Being soaring birds most migratory raptors keep clear of the sea where thermals are not available to give them the lift that they require. Thus European raptors avoid crossing the Mediterranean by flying the narrow straits at each end at the Bosporus and Gibraltar. In North America raptors follow the Appalachian mountain chain where lift is freely available on the updraughts of air that mountains create. Hawk Mountain in Pennsylvania regularly attracts large numbers of 'birders' who gather at

Left A Black-shouldered Kite on its nest in Portugal, perhaps one of only a handful of European nests of one of the world's most widespread birds. Its grey colouring and frequent habit of hovering make this one of the most attractive of raptors.

Below A bird of the African savannahs, the Bateleur is an attractive black and russet bird that spends most of its time gliding on the wing, covering a prodigious mileage.

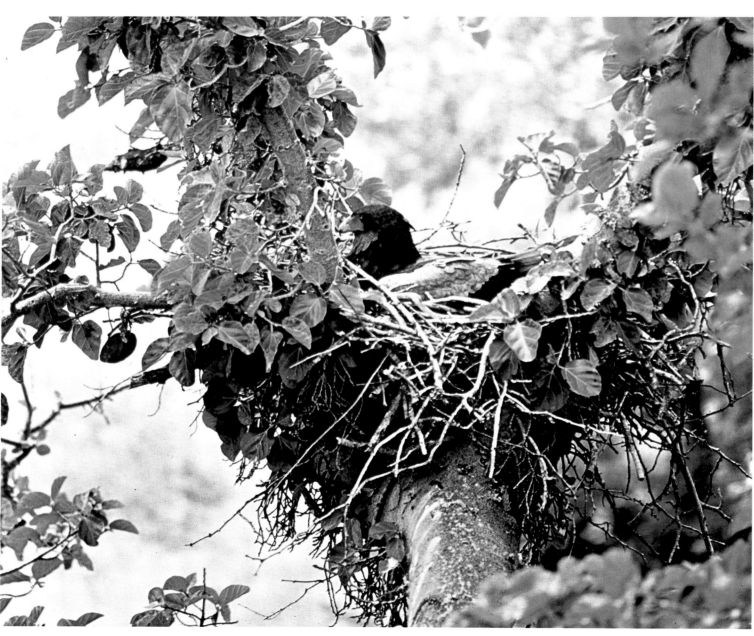

migration time to see these dramatic movements.

Harriers are another cosmopolitan group. They quarter the ground, flying with bouts of flapping interspersed with glides on long, 'V' shaped wings. They are graceful birds, never seeming in a hurry, and they feed mainly on dead or injured birds that are unfortunate enough to come their way. In several species the male is a pale grey and the female a dull, mottled brown – a fact that caused considerable confusion to a previous generation of ornithologists. Several species are associated with marshes and the Hen Harrier *Circus cyaneus* is known as the Marsh Hawk in North America, a cause of considerable confusion with the Marsh Harrier *C. aeruginosus* of Eurasia. Several species are migratory, making long journeys even across the Sahara to winter in East and West Africa.

Although they bear a superficial resemblance to the harriers, kites are more closely related to the fish eagles than the harrier subfamily *Circinae*. The Brahminy Kite *Haliastur indus* is a reddish bird with the white head and shoulders of the African Fish Eagle, but bearing a stronger resemblance in habits to some of the other fish eagles. Kites are essentially scavengers that spend most of their time in the air searching for food. They are expert fliers and can hang stationery on the wind for minutes at a time. Their position is maintained by

The Short-toed Eagle is a true serpent specialist. Recognized by its boldly white underparts it frequently hovers and hangs on the air. Increasing utilization of marginal land with consequent elimination of snakes has reduced its numbers throughout its Old World range.

moving the tail, and by only the minimum use of the wings. This ability to hang in the air gave rise to the name 'kite' for children's paper playthings.

The various black kites are the commonest scavengers in cities throughout the world, although it seems that it was the Red Kite *Milvus milvus* that was the scavenger of the streets of medieval London. Nevertheless, from Cairo to Kathmandu and Nairobi, black kites hang in the air and drop to the streets for scraps. As these cities are cleaned up the kites will doubtless disappear, but that seems a long way off at present. Red Kites are more solitary, woodland birds with deeply forked, translucent, red tails. In Britain they were shot out of existence in all but a few valleys of central Wales during the nineteenth century. Even today they are persecuted by egg collectors, and only gradually are they beginning to spread from their retreat.

The New World has kites of its own, the most remarkable of which, the Snail or Everglade Kite *Rostrhamus sociabilis*, feeds entirely on a diet of *Pomacea* snails. It was formerly quite common in the southern parts of the United States, but has now almost disappeared. Very soon the name Everglade Kite will be completely inappropriate. It is a long-legged bird that hovers low over marshy pools where these snails abound. When one is caught it is taken in the feet to a post or other perch, where the perfectly adapted bill extracts the animal from its shell with a simple twist. The Hook-billed Kite *Chondrohierax uncinatus* performs a similar job on land snails.

The birds of the subfamily Elaninae are also called kites, but they are quite distinct from the other species. Typical and widespread is the Black-shouldered Kite *Elanus caeruleus* (often misleadingly called the Black-winged Kite in Europe) of Africa, Asia and Australia. It is a beautiful grey, white and black bird, with a propensity to perch on telegraph poles and hover when searching for prey. In the western Palaearctic it is confined to a few pairs in Portugal and northern Morocco, where it is exceedingly shy. Over the rest of its range it is an obvious, and easy to see bird. It is replaced by the very similar White-tailed Kite *E. leucurus* in America.

The related Swallow-tailed Kite *Chelictinia riocourii* of Africa is one of the most graceful birds in the world. With grey and white plumage and deeply forked tail it soars catching insects as it flies. It is colonial, migratory and difficult to find in the arid sub-

Saharan zone where it lives. It should not be confused with the American Swallow-tailed Kite *Elanoides forficatus*, which feeds entirely in the air catching insects with its feet.

The Bat-hawk *Machaerhamphus alcinus* is generally placed in a subfamily of its own. It is crepuscular and emerges from its daytime hideaway only when its prey, small to medium-sized bats, are on the wing. It is a silent flier and comes out of the gloom to grab a bat in flight. It is nowhere common over its range in East Africa and Asia, and is solitary and difficult to see. It also takes late flying swallows to vary its diet.

The honey buzzards of the subfamily Perninae are a loosely related group of birds that are difficult to fit in elsewhere in systematic order. The Honey Buzzard *Pernis apivorus* is a buzzard-like bird with broad, barred wings, but with a larger tail and small head set on a pigeon-like neck. It is a migrant to Europe and

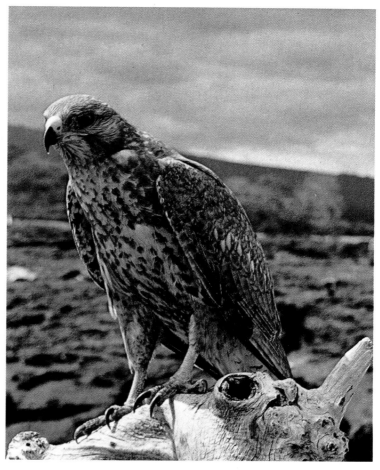

Opposite Short wings and a long tail ideally suit the Sparrowhawk for fast flight and sudden turns in the confined space of woodlands and forests. Its staple diet consists of small birds grabbed in flight.

Above left The large, but remarkably shrike-like Pale Chanting Goshawk perches sentinel on the lookout for small reptiles and mammals. It seldom flies far and gathers its prey in a short but fast glide.

Above right Like other inhabitants of those islands, the Galápagos Hawk is a remarkably tame bird. It is found on most of the major islands of the group and takes reptiles, birds and insects as well as carrion from the edge of the sea.

northern Asia, where it feeds on the grubs of colonial wasps, and has a special covering of armour-like feathers to protect it from these insects' stings. It has a remarkable display flight in which the bird raises its wings and flies fluttering like a butterfly.

Snake eagles live predominantly on snakes and other reptiles that they grasp in their well-equipped talons. They spend much of their time soaring like other eagles, and will kill a snake by biting the head and then swallowing the reptile whole. Best known is the

curiously shaped Bateleur *Terathopius ecandatus*, which seems to be flying backwards across the African sky. In Europe the Short-toed Eagle *Circaetus gallicus* is an all-white bird with an owl-like head and neck, much given to hovering in its search for prey.

The accipiters have been left to the end, although they are in many ways the most raptorial birds of all. They glide effortlessly among the trees of forests patrolling their domain in search of prey. A sudden jink and another small bird is caught in their talons. There are large numbers of accipiters spread throughout the world, but all have the rounded wings and long tails that facilitate changes of direction in confined spaces. The Goshawk *Accipiter gentilis* is the largest and quite capable of downing a Pheasant, while the tiny African Little Sparrowhawk *A. minullus* lives mainly on small birds, but has been known to kill birds of its own size.

Closely related to the accipiters are the chanting goshawks of the African savannahs. Large, handsome, pale grey birds, they sit atop a bush like gigantic shrikes ready to glide down on any unsuspecting lizard, insect or bird. Their long legs enable them to get about on the ground remarkably fast in pursuit of prey.

Falcons Falconidae

We tend to think of falcons as being long-winged, powerful, aerial fighters in the manner of the Peregrine *Falco peregrinus*, but the family is, in fact, a diverse one. It breaks down conveniently into three or four groups: the forest falcons, which live like accipiters and have the long tails and legs of those birds; the caracaras, which are scavengers with vulturine associations; the pygmy falcons or falconets, which more closely resemble shrikes; and the true falcons that are the 'jet fighters' of the bird world.

The forest falcons are sometimes known as harrier-hawks, a term

which adequately describes their appearance and life style, but not their true relationships. They are, in fact, primitive falcons that have adapted to a forest mode of life in South America. They have the long tails and rounded wings of the accipiters, but are generally more shrike-like in their hunting. Whereas a hawk will glide through a forest turning this way and that in its search for likely prey, the forest falcons sit concealed before dashing at nearby prey. This dive and dash mode of hunting is reflected in their prey which consists more of ground mammals and reptiles than the other falcons. The Laughing Falcon *Herpetotheres cachinnans* is a snake-eater quite capable of dealing even with large snakes. Sometimes it bites off the head, but it swallows small snakes whole. Forest falcons of the genus *Micrastur* are similar, but have particularly well-developed ears which they use in hunting. The Barred Forest Falcon *M. ruficollis* makes a speciality of following soldier ants, and preying on the ants' predators. Birds, mice and lizards feature in its diet.

Caracaras are almost exactly the opposite of our usual view of falcons. They are ugly, slow and lugubrious, with none of the fire and dash that we associate with falcons. Above all they are scavengers. In Central and South America they have adapted to a large variety of scavenging niches, niches that in the Old World might well be occupied by the kites. They range northwards to the United States where one species, the Common Caracara *Polyborus plancus*, breeds in central Florida.

Caracaras are long-legged birds that walk well in their search for carrion. Several species are adapted to feeding along the tide-line, walking almost like the Secretary-bird, or alighting at estuary mouths where freshwater fish are killed by the salinity. Worms, rodents, lizards, beetles, and almost anything else that is edible (even vegetable matter), is taken. They are adaptive birds and haunt roads with the sure knowledge that carrion is plentiful, but they have also been known to follow cars and even trains for titbits.

The Johnny Rook *Phalcoboenus australis* (what a superb name for a bird, and so much better than the alternative 'Forster's Caracara') is a native of the Falkland Islands and the cleaner-up of penguin colonies and seal rookeries. It is atypical of caracaras in being dark below, with a yellow cere, and having rusty feathers to the legs. The Common Caracara (the name comes from the call of this species) is a brown bird with close barring below, a bare, red face that extends to the eye and a dark brown cap. Its bill looks longer and more powerful than it actually is.

The Philippine Falconet *Microhierax erythrogonys* is, at 6 inches, the smallest bird of prey in the world, though the better known African Pygmy Falcon *Poliohierax semitorquatus* is only a little larger. Like a small grey shrike, the Pygmy Falcon sits atop some acacia tree watching for a movement from one of the large insects that form the bulk of its food. The male is a fine, powder-grey bird with a black, spotted tail, and white underparts extending to the face. The legs are red and the tiny cere and fine eye ring are similarly coloured, although barely visible in the field. The female is similar, but with an extraordinarily large, chestnut patch on the back. Pygmy Falcons, like most other falcons, do not build their own nest. Instead they adopt one of the social buffalo weavers' nests, a fact which does not seem to bother the weavers, even though the Pygmy Falcon is quite capable of taking small birds.

The true falcons are long-winged, powerful birds that typically hunt in the air. The king of the falcons, the Peregrine, dives on its prey and kills it instantly with a 100 miles per hour strike at the base of the neck. Other falcons hunt in other ways, but they generally kill aloft. Were they to kill on the ground the impact of their dives would be more than sufficient to destroy them.

Falcons have been tamed to hunt for their masters for thousands of years, indeed the sport of falconry is said to have originated in China over 4,000 years ago. It enjoyed its heyday in medieval times when, with elaborate ritual and protocol, it was practised by kings and noblemen. The introduction of the shotgun saw its demise, and it is indulged today by only a few dedicated souls who have the money and time.

A king could expect no greater gift than a pair of Gyrfalcons *Falco rusticolus*, the largest and most powerful member of its family. Only a monarch could fly these kings of the air, which are quite able to knock even a heron from the skies. Gyrfalcons come from the north, from Arctic Canada, Greenland, Iceland, Norway and Siberia. They are huge, grey and white birds with varying amounts of dark speckling in their plumage. The whitest birds of

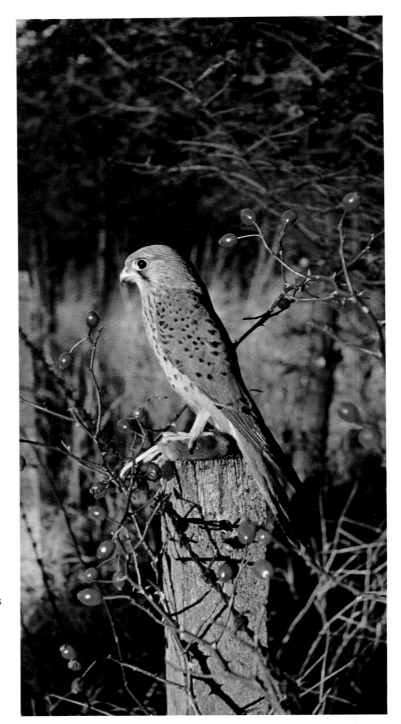

A male Kestrel with a brown rat perches on a fence post. These hovering falcons are widespread in Africa and Asia and depend on small mammals. In cities Kestrels have successfully changed over to a diet of House Sparrows.

all are often referred to in Europe as 'Greenland Falcons'. In the sky they soar on huge, pointed wings that make Peregrines look almost puny. Like other large raptors, Gyrfalcons have fought a running battle first with falconers, then with collectors of skins and eggs, and now with birdwatchers and photographers. In Iceland it is a serious offence to even approach a Gyrfalcon's nest, and photography is absolutely banned.

Peregrines are among the most widespread birds in the world, or at least they were until quite recently. Their favourite prey is pigeons and the falcons have endured a battle waged first with governments, foolish enough to use carrier pigeons for urgent

The beautiful Hobby is a summer visitor to most of the Palaearctic region and feeds on insects and small birds caught in the air. Its speed of flight enables it to catch even the fast-flying Swifts.

messages, and then with the pigeon-racing fraternity. Much reduced, they have nevertheless managed to survive, but the indiscriminate use of toxic and persistent pesticides in the late 1950s was the end for many pairs of Peregrines in Europe, and for virtually the entire population of North America. It is gratifying that in Britain at least, the current restrictions on the use of most toxic pesticides have resulted in a gradual increase in the Peregrine population in the north.

The Peregrine is a superb bird, the master of the air, incapable of being outflown. It can dive, turn, break and jink in a way that no other species can equal. Other falcons are larger and more powerful, but none are so masterful. Peregrines breed on cliffs for preference,

but have also taken to cities for much the same reason as their prey, the feral Rock Dove, has done. Some individuals are particularly faithful to a wintering area and return to the same place or building year after year. Like other falcons they like to bathe every day and will fly for miles to do so.

The most familiar falcons over large areas of the world are the various species of kestrel. The misleadingly called American Sparrowhawk *F. sparverius* is an equivalent to the European Kestrel *F. tinnunculus*. Both hunt by hovering over open country, although the Kestrel has been able to move into the hearts of cities where its diet of small mammals changes to one of House Sparrows. It has also found motorway verges a happy hunting ground. The Lesser Kestrel *F. naumanni*, superficially similar to the Kestrel, is a gregarious bird that finds cathedrals in city centres ideally suited to its needs. It is an insectivorous species that migrates northwards to breed in Europe, before returning to the insect-rich savannahs of

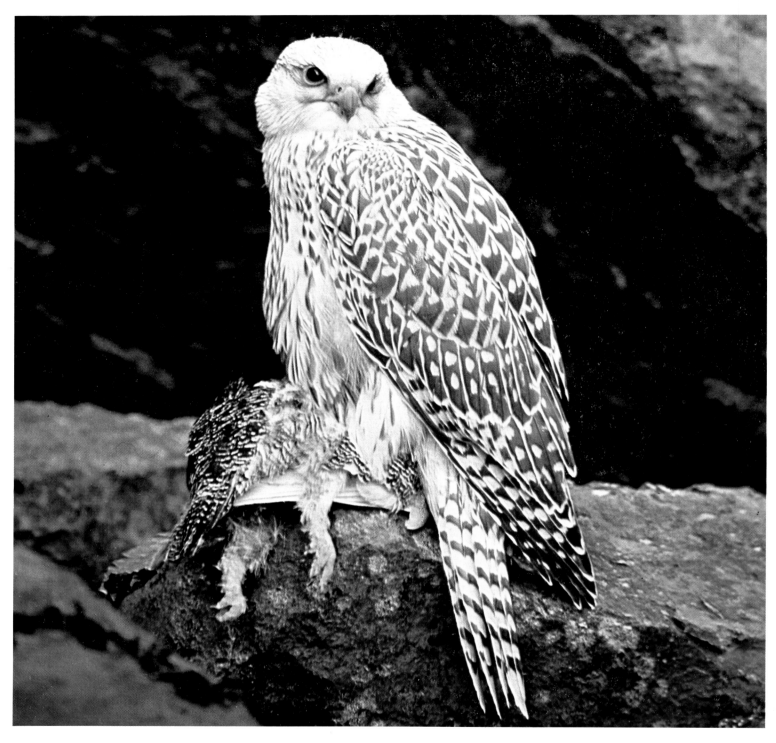

Gyrfalcon with Ptarmigan. This magnificent falcon is the most powerful and lethal of all the aerial killers. Much in demand by those who practise falconry, it is a rare inhabitant of the Arctic lands of Eurasia and North America.

Africa for the duration of the winter months.

The Red-footed Falcon *F. vespertinus* is a similarly gregarious summer visitor to Eurasia. It breeds from the Balkans eastwards across Siberia and in northern China and Korea, but even these eastern birds migrate south-westwards to winter in southern Africa. Occasional parties appear in western Europe in spring. Red-footed Falcons feed on insects which they take on the ground after hovering above them like a Kestrel.

The European Hobby *F. subbuteo* breeds right across the Palaearctic region and feeds on insects and small birds taken in the air. Its ability to catch fast-flying swallows and even swifts is a remarkable achievement, but a highly necessary one if it is to feed a brood.

Strangest of all the falcons is Eleanora's Falcon *F. eleanorae* which has a relict distribution on a few scattered islands in the Mediterranean and adjacent parts of North Africa. It breeds colonially, most nests being built a short distance from the sea. The most usual sites are cliff ledges although crevices and caves are also sometimes used. The eggs are laid at the end of July. Thus when the young falcons hatch, they can be fed on the huge numbers of migrant birds that are then leaving Europe for Africa. Eleanora's Falcons take to the air every evening and collect these night migrants as they fly overhead. They are also quite unique in that they build up larders of corpses to maintain themselves and their chicks during the variable flow of migrants.

Secretary-bird Sagittariidae

The Secretary-bird *Sagittarius serpentarius* stands 3 feet high, resembles the bustards and coursers, and is generally regarded as a bird of prey. It obtains its name from the quills that seem to sprout from behind its 'ears' in the manner of a Dickensian scribe, which seems a shame for it is a fine, graceful bird in its own right.

Unlike most raptors the Secretary-bird walks well on extremely long legs, and a bird may plod up to twenty miles in a day. It finds most of its food on the ground and is quite able to deal with snakes. It grabs them with its strong toes and beats them to death on the ground, while protecting itself from bites with its large wings. To see a Secretary-bird in action is an extraordinary experience. It jumps into the air, stamps and struggles, and virtually turns somersaults in its efforts to confuse and outwit its prey. The Secretary-bird is generally protected wherever it is found, due mainly to its ability with snakes, which has probably been overrated, and perhaps also to its consumption of locusts. It also consumes other reptiles, amphibians, tortoises, rats, and other small mammals as well as young game birds – its only vice. In some areas farmers keep Secretary-birds to keep snakes away.

The bird is basically dove grey in colour, with black on the wings and thighs and elongated central tail feathers. The short, down-curved bill is backed by an area of bare, red and yellow skin.

The Secretary-bird is widespread throughout Africa south of the Sahara, except in the forests of the Congo and adjacent areas, although it is not numerous. Usually only single birds are found, with members of a pair some distance apart. There is evidence to show that Secretary-birds are territorial throughout the year. The nest is constructed atop some tree, often an acacia, in open areas of plains and savannah country. The birds pair for life and are remarkably faithful to their nest site. Thus the huge bundle of sticks grows year by year in the manner of an eagle's eyrie. The two, occasionally three, rough-textured, white eggs take about fifty days to hatch, and the downy young are fed on a diet of small mammals. They fly after about eight weeks.

Secretary-birds often congregate at areas that have been burnt-off, where mammals are deprived of cover and often injured. They take small dead mammals, but not carrion.

The great walkers of the African savannahs, Secretary-birds are long-legged raptors that have taken to a terrestrial life where they feed on insects, small mammals and snakes. They are seldom photographed at the nest.

Megapodes Megapodiidae

'Megapode' literally means 'big foot' in Greek, and that just about sums up the life of the average member of this interesting and unusual group of birds. They are unique in neither incubating their eggs nor feeding nor caring for their young. Each bird digs a large hole in the ground which it fills with rotting leaves and other vegetable debris, often from fifty or more yards around. This is then covered with earth into a mound that in some species may measure up to fifteen feet high and thirty-five feet across. That such a heap can be constructed with nothing more than the feet of a couple of birds is a fair tribute to 'big foot'.

Megapodes are chicken- or turkey-like birds of wooded and open country that walk well and are generally reluctant to fly. Ten distinct species are found from Malaya to Australia, although it is the brush turkey and malleefowl of the latter area that are the best known. Yet the Malleefowl *Leipoa ocellata* is atypical in inhabiting the open, semi-arid brush areas of Australia known as 'mallee'. Most species are dull-coloured birds that prefer to skulk in thick cover and are easy to overlook. Indeed it is only their voices that draw attention to some of the species as they become more vocal at sunset. Food is variable and most megapodes are omnivorous. Insects, reptiles and seeds figure in the diet of almost all species.

The brightest-coloured megapodes, the Maleofowl *Megacephalon maleo* and Moluccas Scrubfowl *Eulipoa wallacei*, boast the simplest nesting technique. This consists simply of digging a hole in the ground, laying the egg, covering with soil, and leaving the sun to hatch it out. On some islands these birds even utilize volcanic activity to help warm the eggs. The Common Scrubfowl *Megapodius freycinet* of Australia also uses the sun directly in this way, although in forested sites it builds the largest of all mounds. One thing is quite clear – these birds are truly experts at artificial incubation, for

while the Scrubfowl will regulate its behaviour according to circumstances, other megapodes are great regulators of the temperature that they create inside their mounds.

The heat of the sun and heat generated by the decay of buried vegetation are the two aids that the megapodes utilize. Malleefowl go to immense length and trouble to ensure that everything is just right. As a basis they excavate a huge hole that may measure twelve feet across and three or four feet deep. Into this every available scrap of vegetation is dumped and then covered with a layer of soil.

The hen excavates a hole in the mound into which the eggs are laid over a lengthy period. Thus the clutch may consist of five or thirty-five eggs. The 'incubation' begins its work at once, and the eggs hatch over a period parallel to their laying. Throughout the incubation period the male Malleefowl is constantly on duty controlling the temperature of the eggs in the mound. He uses his bill as a thermometer and will remove soil or add it as necessary to maintain an appropriate equilibrium. Sometimes the heat created by the decaying vegetation is so great that the eggs have to be virtually uncovered to cool. Incubation may last as long as eight or nine weeks, almost as long as any other bird, during which the male continues to labour with his 'big feet'.

Young megapodes are quite extraordinary. They hatch deep beneath the soil and immediately dig their way to the surface. On emerging they run away on strong legs, and are quite capable of flying within a few hours. They never see their parents and are able

The Malleefowl inhabits the bush country of southern Australia and is responsible for the remarkably large mounds that are such a feature of the landscape. These are artificial hatcheries that the bird constructs to incubate its eggs.

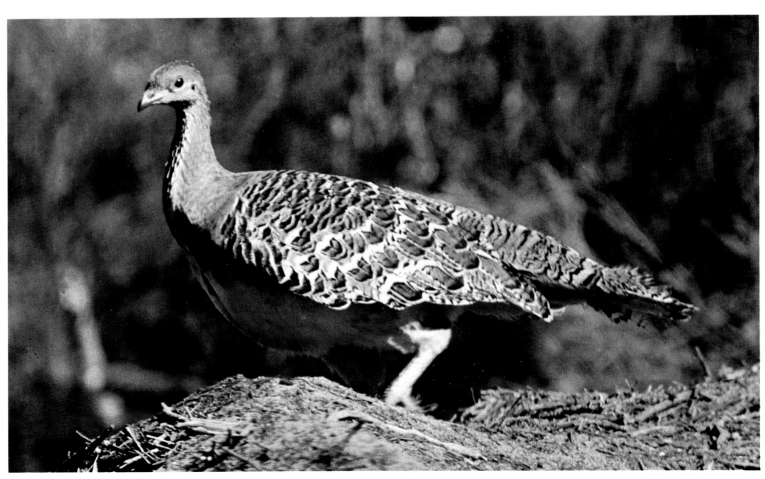

to fend for themselves from birth. The male Malleefowl is very much in charge, he will not let the female lay until the temperature of his mound is just right; other species have different routines.

The Common Scrubfowl is, as we have seen, an adaptable bird. Some of its largest mounds are the products of several pairs of birds, and thus may hatch out quite huge numbers of chicks.

Curassows, guans and chachalacas Cracidae

The Cracidae are large birds varying in length from $1\frac{1}{2}$ to $3\frac{1}{2}$ feet. They bear a strong resemblance to the other Galliformes, in some ways to the megapodes, in others to the pheasants, but their remarkable tree-dwelling habits pick them out from the rest. Not only do they nest and roost in trees, but they are also remarkably agile among the branches and on the ground and run around the

The Common Chachalaca is a member of the Cracidae and a ground-dwelling inhabitant of the forests of Central America. Usually gregarious, it can be found in the extreme south of Texas in the United States.

tropical jungles that form their home with consummate ease.

Their shape is similar to the most primitive of all birds *Archaeopteryx*, with the long fan-shaped tail, broad, rounded wings supporting a plump body, and a long neck and powerful head. As they leap into a gentle glide from one tree to another they behave much as that bird ancestor must have done. They run along branches, jump and land with ease, flutter and glide and are, in a word, at home among the trees.

The various groups share several anatomical features. They have, for instance, the long toes with a particularly long hind toe of the

megapodes, but do not feed by scratching on the ground. Neither do they build mounds. The two or three white eggs are incubated for twenty-two to thirty-four days. Like the other members of the order Galliformes they produce active young, but nesting high in trees poses problems that ground-nesting species do not have to cope with. As a result the chicks hatch with partly grown flight feathers, and can fly after only a few days running around the tree tops. Family parties join together and flocks remain intact until the next breeding season.

The birds feed predominantly on buds and fruit, but are not averse to insects and amphibians and, like the grouse, grit is used to aid digestion. They are quite vocal and a looped trachea helps to produce the far-carrying cries that are typical jungle sounds in South and Central America. The family ranges from the southern United States southwards as far as northern Argentina, and the thirty-nine species are grouped into eleven genera.

The largest birds are the twelve species of curassows. They are predominantly black in plumage and the largest of them all, the Great Curassow *Crax rubra*, is nearly 40 inches long and weighs over 10 pounds. Like other members of the tribe it boasts a curly crest and a pronounced knob, in this case yellow, at the base of the upper mandible. This is swollen during the period of courtship. The Razorbilled Curassow *Mitu mitu* is extraordinary in respect of the strange shape of its bill – the huge, red upper mandible has almost the casque of a hornbill.

Guans are considerably smaller and generally of rather more sombre plumage. Twelve species live in the tops of forest trees where they form large flocks that roam in search of fruit. They have an area of bare skin on the chin or face which is boldly coloured, red, blue or white. In some species the skin extends to form a wattle. Some species boast a prominent crest, and the Horned Guan *Oreophasis derbianus* has a bare, reddish horn jutting from its crown.

The chachalacas are still smaller and more dull. They are predominantly ground feeders, although they are as much at home in the trees as their relatives. They are gregarious and the call from which they get their name often echoes through the forest as each bird takes it up while maintaining the rhythm. Like the other members of the family, the chachalacas are much sought after by hunters and destroyed by 'civilization' as their habitat is converted to different land use.

Grouse Tetraonidae

On 12th August the British aristocracy and rich head for the northern and Scottish moorlands for the opening of the grouse season. There, fortified by the world's best whisky, supported by shooting sticks, and bedecked with tweed plus-fours and deerstalkers, they crouch in trenches while a team of 'gillies' beat the Red Grouse *Lagopus lagopus scoticus* from the heather. The 'glorious twelfth' is as much a social as a sporting occasion, but it has a magic that is shared only with salmon fishing and tiger hunting. Unlike tigers, Red Grouse seem quite able to maintain

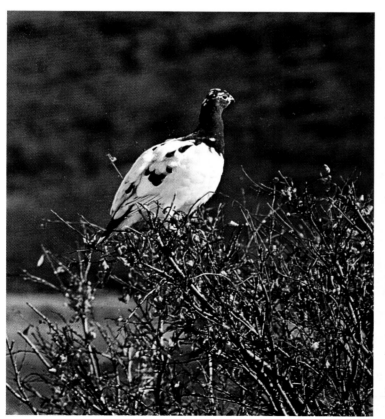

themselves with a little help from gamekeepers.

The seventeen species of grouse are medium to large birds with short, powerful wings that are perfectly adapted to a sprint, but quite incapable of prolonged flight. They fly low over the ground when flushed, and frequently glide for long distances on bowed wings. From a standing start they can accelerate faster than a hawk, but they use this burst of speed only in emergencies. They usually try to avoid their enemies by walking quickly away among cover. All grouse have feathered tarsi that in some species extend to the feet themselves. This may act as a snowshoe, but also serves as insulation against the cold. For similar reasons other species grow a row of comb-like protrusions along the sides of the toes during the winter.

Grouse are dumpy, round-bodied birds with short, stubby bills. The neck usually boasts a patch of erectile feathers, and there is a colourful patch of bare skin around the eye. They vary in size from 1 to 3 feet and in weight from 1 to 14 pounds. Males are often larger than the females and in many species more boldly patterned. Females tend to be cryptically camouflaged and enjoy the facility to disappear completely against a background of rocks and lichens while sitting on the nest. This is particularly true of the tundra species that cannot conceal themselves among vegetation. So dependent is the Ptarmigan *Lagopus mutus* on camouflage for survival, that it moults into an all-white plumage enabling it to hide in the snow that covers its home during the winter months.

Most grouse are resident in the more northern parts of the Holarctic region. Here they manage to eke out a living no matter how severe the conditions. Their shape offers the smallest body surface area in relation to mass, and they have evolved various metabolic and behavioural characters that aid their survival. Like other animals, it is the quantity of food available, rather than the severity of the winter, that determines their survival rate. While the open ground species are the hardiest, life is not much less severe for woodland birds like the Capercaillie *Tetrao urogallus*, and the Spruce Grouse *Canachites canadensis*. Here too the key is the

A Willow Grouse in transitional plumage rests in an Alaskan tree. Its circumpolar distribution is complete if the native Red Grouse of Britain is regarded as conspecific.

quantity of food available throughout the winter. Even before the days of scientific population studies, gamekeepers had recognized the importance of fresh, young heather shoots to their Red Grouse coveys, and instituted a system of rotation burning to provide optimum conditions.

Grouse are among the few groups of birds that exhibit a communal courtship routine. This is most highly developed in the Black Grouse *Lyrurus tetrix* and Capercaillie in the Old World, and in the New World by the Sage Grouse *Centrocerus urophasianus*, the Prairie Chicken *Tympanuchus cupido* and others. In these species, cock birds gather at a lek, a traditional jousting site, where each defends a tiny territory against all comers. Display consists of much bowing and threatening, using the long tail feathers to advantage and puffing up the body to increase its size and threat value. Black Grouse have been particularly tenacious in holding on to their

lekking grounds, even when a formerly remote forest clearing has been converted to the front lawn of a house. Capercaillie, in contrast, form leks deep in the forest itself and, though often consisting of raised ground, the lek is usually dotted with trees. Many Capercaillie also perform solo displays among the trees. The North American species pepper their displays with booming to

Below The strutting postures of the male Capercaillie are adopted during its display among the pines of its forest lek.

Opposite top The Red Grouse, native to the British Isles, is generally regarded as nothing more than a subspecies of the Continental Willow Grouse.

Opposite bottom Most male grouse have special displays that they perform to defend a territory at a lek or attract a mate. Here we see Spruce Grouse (left) and Blue Grouse, two closely related Nearctic species.

which resonance is added by the inflatable air sacs on the sides of the neck. Prairie Chickens are particularly noisy, with booming being accompanied by loud foot stamping as they strut and posture.

In these species, as in the Ruff, the hen visits the lek to be mated and is solely responsible for rearing the young. Only the forest-dwelling Black Cock and Capercaillie are sexually dimorphic among the grouse. The cocks have no need of cryptic camouflage for incubation periods, or for hiding among open grasslands like the North American lek species. Most of the cocks are polygamous or promiscuous, whereas the territorial species, like the Red Grouse, are monogamous.

All grouse nest on the ground. The five to twelve eggs are cryptically coloured and laid on a minimum of nest lining. Incubation takes three to four weeks and the chicks are active and leave the nest soon after hatching. The hen frequently broods the chicks, which are particularly susceptible to cold and wet, and the family usually stays together through the autumn.

Several woodland species are notoriously tame or stupid. When disturbed they fly into a low branch of a nearby tree, where they can be approached almost to within arm's length. The Spruce Grouse is a case in point and its Eurasian equivalent, the Hazel Hen *Tetrastes bonasia*, is another strange bird in this respect.

Their fine eating qualities have put grouse under considerable hunting pressure for centuries, but the vast changes that man has wrought on the landscape have had far more significant effects. The destruction of forests is particularly serious, reducing populations at a single stroke. The Prairie Chicken is now far less widespread than formerly, and the east coast form, known as the Heath Hen, is extinct. The Capercaillie was extinct in Britain by 1760, but has since been successfully reintroduced and now maintains itself well – some foresters think too well for it does considerable damage to young trees. There is no doubt that with a little thought and management most grouse numbers can be maintained or even increased.

A Prairie Chicken in full display with distended orange patches on the neck much in evidence. Like many other grouse the species enjoys a communal joust at a special lekking ground.

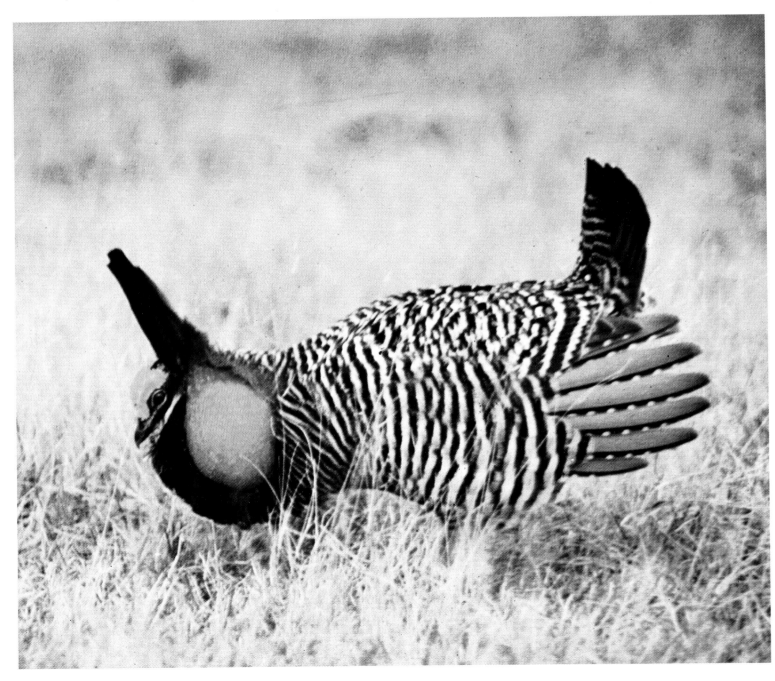

Pheasants, quails and partridges Phasianidae

Closely related to the grouse, guineafowl and turkeys, the Phasianidae are a large group of predominantly ground-dwelling birds comprising no less than forty-eight distinct genera and 165 species. All are round-bodied, plump birds. Most are very good to eat and the family has become one of the prime quarries of man for the sporting characteristics of its members. One species, the Junglefowl *Gallus gallus*, has been widely domesticated and is now the most numerous bird on Earth – it is called the Chicken!

In such a large and diverse group of birds there is inevitably great variation among the individual species. Some, like the smaller buttonquails, are tiny while others, like the peafowl, are large anyway and quite huge when their 'trains' are included. Birds like the Himalayan pheasants are brightly coloured, while many others are dull and sombre. In many species the male is a gaudy dandy, while the female is cryptically coloured for her family rearing functions. All species share characteristics that make them a reasonably well-delineated family, however.

The Phasianidae are ground-feeding birds with moderately long, strong legs. Three strong toes face forwards and one backwards, but many species have a prominent, sharp spur growing from the rear of the tarsus. While they nest on the ground, most species prefer to roost in trees. Their wing surface to bodyweight ratio is not large and most species are incapable of long flights, the Eurasian Quail *Coturnix coturnix* being one of the notable exceptions. Nevertheless, most members of the family have strong, rounded wings that are well adapted to the sudden bursts of acceleration that enable them to avoid approaching danger. Their bills are short and stubby, designed to pick up seeds and scratch around for covered and buried food.

The American quails are very similar to the Old World quails, although separated on various anatomical features such as the stronger and serrated bill. They are small, brownish birds lacking a prominent tail, but boasting a bold pattern of chocolate or black markings on the head of many of the males, which also frequently

A group of California Quail search for food among the snow. The crest on the crown of the males is typical of a small group of closely related birds found in western North America.

carry a crest. They are found throughout the continent in North and South America almost as far as the tree-line, but are absent from most of Canada and from the extreme south. The thirty-six species have adapted to a variety of ecological niches from woodland to desert and mountains, but they are most numerous in the bush country of Mexico and the southern United States.

In the western United States, Gambell's Quail *Lophortyx gambelli* is typical of a group of attractive grey, brown and chocolate, crested quails. Its face is black, the breast dove grey, and a fine 'comma-like' crest graces the crown. Gambell's Quail is a desert-loving species being replaced at higher altitudes by the similar Mountain Quail *Oreortyx picta*, and in the Californian Valley by the California Quail *Lophortyx californica*.

Better known over large areas of the United States is the

Left Yellow-necked Spurfowl are numerous and widespread over much of the dry country of Africa and are invariably tame and approachable. The yellow neck consists of loose, bare skin.

Below Common Quail are found right across the Palaearctic region as summer visitors. Self-effacing and shy, their presence is best indicated by their strange 'quip-quip' calls. In flight, they reveal long, narrow wings which differentiate them from other game birds.

Bobwhite Quail *Colinus virginianus*, which is found in open country and much sought after by sportsmen. It is a brown bird with a distinctive face pattern and, although lacking a crest, the feathers of the crown can be erected. The sporting characteristics of Bobwhite Quails have resulted in them being introduced intentionally as well as accidentally into various other parts of the world. In New Zealand they were unsuccessful in establishing themselves, in strange contrast to the California Quail which was introduced and prospered. In Britain, Bobwhites have certainly bred in the wild, but have not become fully self sufficient. While most quails have short tails, the wood partridges of the genus *Dendrortyx* have them quite well developed. They live in the mountain forests in Central America.

Just as the Bobwhite Quail has been introduced to Europe, so has the Eurasian Quail become established in Texas. In its normal range it is a widespread and numerous migrant, leaving Europe completely to winter south of the Sahara. Its decline is due mostly to the sportsmen of southern Europe, who often slaughter Quail in vast numbers. It is to be hoped that the spread of farming of this species will eventually produce sufficient birds to enable the shooting of wild birds to become uneconomic. Throughout the rest of the Old World there exists a variety of other small quails, some of which are more boldly patterned than the common Eurasian Quail. In Africa and Australia the representative of the genus *Coturnix* are sporadic in appearance and breeding, their numbers and distribution being apparently closely linked to the rains in those parts of the world.

Partridges, and their allies the francolins, have proved among the most satisfactory of all game birds. The Grey Partridge *Perdix perdix* is the classic quarry of hunters throughout Europe. It is an attractive grey, buff and brown bird, with a prominent inverted horseshoe of chestnut on the belly, that lives in small groups (called coveys) on open ground, and that has thrived on agricultural land. It is essentially a ground-loving species that produces a large clutch of eggs, and rears large numbers of young in areas where predators are controlled. The recent decline of the species in England has been blamed on the demise of insects due to spraying, which effectively eliminates the food supply of the newly hatched chicks, so that they starve to death.

One of the most beautiful of the pheasants, the Silver Pheasant is confined to the mountain forests of South-East Asia between 2,000 and 7,000 feet. It is widely kept in captivity where it has prospered, although due to its aggressive nature not more than one male can be kept in the same aviary.

Unlike the Grey Partridge, the Red-legged Partridge *Alectoris rufa* and its allies perch quite freely, and will utter their peculiar and far-carrying cries from perches in trees. In England they are often referred to as 'Frenchmen' or 'French Partridges' doubtless because of their introduction from that country, but they are widespread throughout the continent. Their ecological replacements, in mountains the Chukar *A. graeca*, and in North Africa the Barbary Partridge *A. barbara*, are very similar and require close examination to distinguish in the field.

Francolins, although found in Asia, are typically African birds where over thirty species are found. They are rather larger than the partridges, often with bare patches of skin on the head or neck. Some species are called spurfowl, and some have more than one spur on the tarsi. They are birds of open bush country where their plumage hides them from enemies.

The pheasants are a group of large, brightly coloured birds that are often kept in captivity, and are almost as decorative as the similarly easy-to-keep wild-fowl. Their centre of origin is Asia, and they reach their peak of development in areas bordering the Himalayas. Nearly fifty distinct species are recognized, but the most beautiful live in the remote areas of northern China. Here is found Reeves' Pheasant *Syrmaticus reevesii*, for example.

Like other hen pheasants, the female Reeves' is a dull, cryptically coloured bird in contrast to her mate, which is covered with black-bordered, golden feathers, has a black and white marked head, and a tail that may be four times its body length. Here too is the

The Grey Jungle Fowl replaces the more widespread Red Jungle Fowl in southern India. Similarly, it inhabits forests and has been kept in captivity with considerable success. All three species of jungle fowl are confined to India and South-East Asia.

Golden Pheasant *Chrysolophus pictus* with the male displaying the most vivid rusts and golds, with a canopy of gold and black feathers that trail along the neck and which are erected in display. Lady Amherst's Pheasant *C. amherstiae* of south-central China boasts a similar ability, but its plumage is boldly black and white with iridescent green and blue on the back, and a dash of red in the tail.

All of these pheasants are ground-dwelling birds that find most of their food by scratching and probing the earth. They are not migratory, although some species of high altitude will descend to lower levels in winter. Most species live in areas with severe winters, and are then confined to forests where they find shelter from the extreme conditions that prevail on the hills. The Common, or Ring-necked, Pheasant *Phasianus colchicus* is a native of the southern areas of the Palaearctic region, from the Caucasus to the China Sea. It is primarily a marshland bird but it has taken freely to woodland and coverts where introduced in most of Europe and North America. It is one of the most shot birds in the world and has given rise to a huge industry, the sole aim of which is to provide the maximum of birds for sport.

High in the Himalayas lives one of the most elusive of all birds,

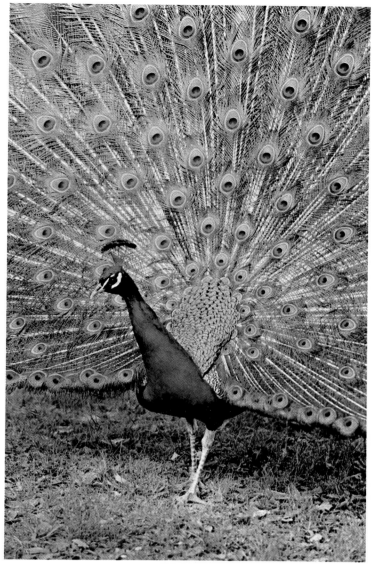

Above The Common Pheasant is found from the Caspian region across Asia to China, but has been successfully introduced in Europe, North America, New Zealand and Australia for its sporting characteristics.

Right The magnificent train of the Peacock, more accurately known as the Blue Peafowl, is an adornment to many formal gardens. It is a native of India where its shrill cries may be heard over long distances. In the wild it is found in open country with some scrub, near cultivated areas.

the Blood Pheasant *Ithaginus cruentus*. Even in winter this bird is found along the mountain passes of Nepal, eking out a living among the snow drifts. It is a rare bird and seldom kept in captivity. The various species of monals and tragopans too find their homes among these mountain fastnesses.

Lower down, in the jungles that border the great river systems that originate in the Himalayas, are two of the best-known birds in the world. The Blue Peafowl *Pavo cristatus*, better known chauvinistically as the Peacock, is widespread throughout the Indian subcontinent. It needs little description save to point out that the magnificent train that it displays during courtship is not a tail, but

the elongated feathers of the upper-tail coverts. In spite of its dimensions, the train does not hinder the bird either when perching or in flight.

The Red Junglefowl, replaced in south and south-west India by the Grey Junglefowl *Gallus sonneratti*, is the ancestor of the domestic Chicken. It is a somewhat secretive forest species and bears a strong resemblance to the domestic Bantam.

Guineafowl Numididae

Guineafowl are large gallinaceous birds similar to the turkeys of the New World. Apart from an outpost in Arabia they are restricted to Africa and its satellite islands, although one species, the Helmeted Guineafowl *Numida meleagris* has been widely domesticated, and is found throughout the world. Despite breeding in captivity since Greco-Roman times, no distinctive forms have evolved, and the descendant stock is exactly the same as that found in the wild.

All guineafowl conform to the same basic and unmistakeable shape. The head and neck are bare and scraggy and set on a rotund, pear-shaped body that is effectively tailless. The legs are strong and the hind toe is at a higher level than the front ones. Wings are rounded giving the bird quick acceleration although, like grouse, they prefer to glide and cannot fly for long distances. Like other members of the order, Guineafowl spend a lot of time walking and

scratching about in the ground for food.

The typical guineafowl are found in the dry bush country of Africa. They do not penetrate the Sahara proper, but are found northwards through East Africa to the Red Sea. They avoid the tropical rainforest areas of West Africa.

Most common and widespread of this group is the Helmeted Guineafowl. Several authors have described the subspecies of this bird as a distinct species, on the basis of different shaped helmets and patterns of spotting. In East Africa Helmeted Guineafowl are frequently encountered feeding along the roadside. Flocks are usually small, but in particularly arid areas they gather in huge numbers at waterholes. These nomadic flocks sometimes walk huge distances in a day, but many groups are faithful to a particular location. In the heat of the day they shelter from the sun beneath a

Helmeted Guineafowl frequent open bush country throughout Africa and are usually encountered in small flocks. Their diet is varied but the need to drink regularly takes them to waterholes in vast numbers. They nest low among vegetation.

thick bush, which they become understandably loath to leave.

Vulturine Guineafowl *Acryllium vulturinum* owe their name to the vulture-like look of their bare head and neck, surrounded at its base with a ruff of attractively striped feathers. They are found only in the Somali corner of East Africa in the most arid subdesert zone. They are, for instance, quite common in the Samburu area of the North-western Frontier Province of Kenya, where they share a

habitat with Dik–dik and Gerenuk. Here they gather to drink at the river, but elsewhere they live miles from the nearest water and survive.

These open-area guineafowl lay up to twenty buff-white, spotted eggs in a simple scrape in the ground. The nesting habits of the remainder of the family are unknown, indeed few Europeans have ever seen the rare White-breasted Guineafowl *Agelastes meleagrides*, which is found in the forests of Ghana. The Black Guineafowl *A. niger* is similarly shy, with its black plumage offset only by a bald, red head. These forest guineafowl are usually seen singly or in small family parties, but the truth is that we know little of their habits at all.

Turkeys Meleagrididae

Our Christmas dinner may scale more, but the wild turkey of North America rarely exceeds 20 pounds in weight. Females weigh only half as much. In spite of such a payload turkeys fly strongly, although the longest recorded flight is barely a mile. The Common Turkey *Meleagris gallopavo* is the most numerous and widespread of the two species – the Ocellated Turkey *Agriocharis ocellata* is a

diminishing bird of Central America confined to Honduras, Guatemala and Yucatan. The male Common Turkey is slightly thinner than its domestic counterpart, but has similar iridescent, black plumage with brownish wings, and a white-tipped tail that is fanned and cocked in display. The head and neck are bare and large wattles of red skin dangle from a vividly blue head. The effect when

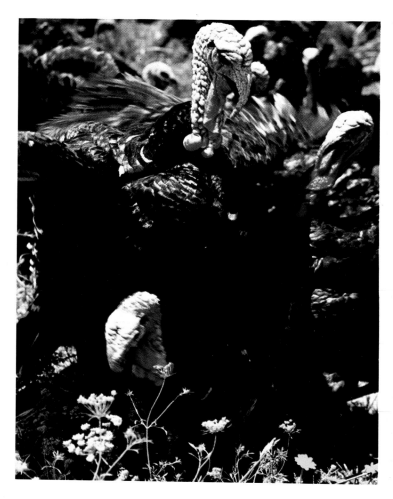

Native of North America the Turkey is a favoured domesticated fowl in many parts of the world. Fights between males are frequent both in the wild and in the confines of captivity.

the bird calls its 'gobbling' cackle is grotesque – all wattles and noise – but apparently effective, for the male turkey is invariably surrounded by a harem of hens.

Turkeys are birds of the woodland glades, not a habitat that has been extensively preserved in the United States. Here they feed on seeds from the forest floor, although they will also take large quantities of insects. Outside the breeding season the sexes segregate into separate flocks. The display of the male turkey in spring consists of much gobbling and prancing with wings dragging on the ground and tail well spread. This attracts a harem of hens that crave his attentions.

The nest is tucked away on the ground beneath dense vegetation and the eight to fifteen eggs take the hen twenty-eight days to incubate. The chicks stay with the hen until the following winter.

In spite of being kept in captivity for several hundred years, the turkey stock remained very similar to the wild bird until quite recently. Huge, white turkeys are now much favoured by the poultrymen who rear them, though perhaps less so by the customer.

The Ocellated Turkey is considerably smaller and a male will grow to only half the weight of the common species. Its body plumage is tipped with green and the tail feathers are greyish, tipped with blue and buff. The bare head is blue with only a modicum of red wattles on the crown and around the eye. The display and breeding routine are very similar to the common species, although the sexes do not divide into separate flocks. The Ocellated Turkey is a forest-dwelling species that prefers to fly rather than run to safety. It frequently raids fields of cereals and corn in late summer.

Hoatzin Opisthocomidae

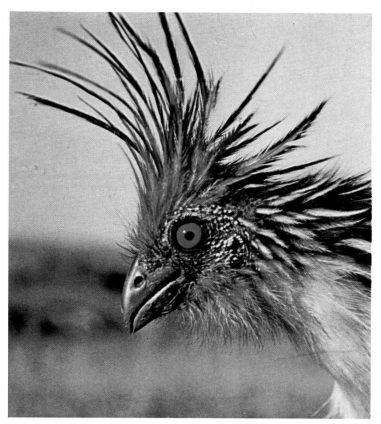

The Hoatzin *Opisthocomus hoazin* bears a superficial resemblance to the currasows and guans found alongside it, but it is a problem bird. For years systematists debated its position in the avian scheme of things, and at one time it was almost placed in an order of its own. It is a strange bird, a bird with confusing features that serve to make it quite unique.

Two feet in length but still a lightweight: the Hoatzin is mostly tail and neck with only a small body between. It is a vividly coloured bird, brightly golden on the chest with a scalloped, brown back, golden-tipped tail, and a long but ragged crest of gold on the crown. The eye is a vivid red, and the surrounding bare skin cobalt blue. It inhabits the Amazon basin extending northwards into Venezuela, but is found only among riverside jungles. Its legs and feet look more powerful than they are, and the bird often helps support itself on its breast, which is covered with thick skin. Its flesh is unpleasant, although indians sometimes take eggs.

So far, so good: but the Hoatzin has a number of strange features that together picks it out from all other birds. The bill is short and decurved, but unlike most other species, the upper mandible is not fused with the skull. Instead, it is independently articulated like that of the parrots. The red eye is protected by eye lashes like those of mammals. Its crop, instead of being a food store like that of other birds, is used as a gizzard, and is thus greatly enlarged and muscled to grind down food.

The Hoatzin is a strange bird reminiscent of the ancestors of all birds. It flies poorly and uses its wings as it clambers about riverside trees. The chicks have claws at the bend of the wing to help them climb, and they can swim as soon as they leave the nest.

Hoatzins breed in trees and males may take more than one mate. The two or three yellow eggs are spotted with pink, and are incubated for twenty-eight days. The first down is very thin and the newly hatched chicks soon develop a second coat of dark brown.

If the adult Hoatzin is unusual, the chick Hoatzin is extraordinary. Soon after hatching it leaves the nest and begins clambering about the tree tops, using its well-developed feet and the special claws that are present at the bend of each wing. In this respect it resembles the bird ancestor *Archaeopteryx*. These claws are shed soon after fledging and are not present in the adult. Of the several birds that boast wing claws, only the Hoatzin chick uses them for climbing. The young chick also swims well at a few days old, and uses its wings to dive beneath the surface. The adult Hoatzin spends most of its time climbing, and uses its wings to aid its grip. It seldom flies more than a few yards, and the muscles of the breast are very poorly developed. Its most common form of aerial activity is a shallow glide over open water.

Whether the Hoatzin is a primitive link with *Archaeopteryx* or a highly specialized 'modern' bird, is unsettled. The fact remains, however, that it is a great puzzle and a species that needs more study. Unfortunately it is becoming progressively more difficult to find the Hoatzin as man penetrates further into its habitat.

Mesites Mesitornithidae

Mesites are one of the least-known families of birds in the world and, like other groups of little-studied birds, they are difficult to classify. The three species are confined to Madagascar where they inhabit forests that offer protection not found in mainland Africa. All three are less than a foot long, and are dull, brown birds with few distinguishing features. They are usually likened to that highly confusing group, the babblers.

The mesites do not fly well and are reluctant to take to the air at all. One species, Bensch's Monia *Monias benschii*, apparently has the wings to support itself, but has yet to be seen in the air, even when provoked. It is a ground-dwelling species that hunts the forest floor where it feeds on insects and fruit. It resembles a passerine, but its gait is characteristic of the members of the order Gruiformes, with a bobbing motion of the head like a chicken. Surprisingly, the nest is built a few feet up in a tree, and the bird climbs up to it. A single, white egg is laid on a platform of twigs lined with grass, and the male incubates and cares for the chick by himself. Females are brighter and have a circle of mates in whose nests they lay.

The other mesites have not lost the power of flight, but they otherwise resemble the Monia in habits. The Brown Mesite *Mesoenas unicolor* is a dull, rusty brown bird with slate grey wings and a creamy nape stripe. Bensch's Monia is similarly brown above with a nape stripe, but with a white breast speckled with black like a thrush. The bill is long and down-curved for probing in the ground. The possession of five patches of powder-down, which is used for cleaning the plumage, is unique among the Gruiformes.

Buttonquail Turnicidae

Buttonquail, hemipodes or bustard quails, are found throughout the warmer parts of the Old World, and are most numerous in Australasia. They closely resemble quails, so much so that even experienced ornithologists sometimes confuse them. Their secretive habits make them one of the least-observed groups of birds in the world. Indeed most of our knowledge of their lives has been obtained from the study of captive birds.

Varying in size from 4 to 7½ inches, buttonquails are dumpy, rotund birds with short tails, hunched shoulders and a short, thin bill. They are generally dull coloured, but with bold patterns of barring on the chest and usually some chestnut below. Like many other ground-dwelling birds, they have only three toes. The wings are rounded and not long and pointed like the migratory Eurasian Quail, and they normally fly only short distances when flushed before dropping into cover. Food consists of seeds and shoots, together with insects. They are predominantly solitary although some species do form flocks of twenty to thirty birds.

Like other secretive birds the buttonquails have well-developed voices, or at least the females do, for it is they that are dominant in breeding matters. They are more boldly coloured than their mates, and probably lay several clutches of eggs to be tended by different males. The nest is a scrape lined with grasses, and the four eggs are cryptically coloured. The very short incubation period, only twelve to thirteen days, is followed by an incredibly fast development by the chicks, which are active at birth, can fly in a fortnight, are independent in six or seven weeks, and have bred (in captivity at least) within three months.

Only one buttonquail is found in Europe where it is misleadingly called the Andalusian Hemipode *Turnix sylvatica*. In fact this bird is found in Africa south of the Sahara, and through India and the Far East as far as the Philippines. It is more widespread in North Africa than in Andalusia in southern Spain. The alternative names of Striped **or Little** Buttonquail are far to be preferred.

The Lark-quail *Ortyxelos meiffrenii* of the southern Sahara is the odd one out of this family. While the other buttonquails are so very similar, the Lark-quail looks more like a lark than a quail, and lays only two eggs. In flight a black and white wing pattern forms a diagnostic feature.

Plains-wanderer Pedionomidae

Formerly regarded as a member of the family of buttonquails, the characteristics of this strange bird are sufficiently distinct to make most authorities place it in a monotypic family of its own. The Plains-wanderer *Pedionomus torquatus* is very like the buttonquails although it has the distinctive habit of standing upright rather than crouching. It has a hind toe, lacking in the buttonquails, and lays pointed not ovate eggs. It lives in the open grasslands of Australia where it is confined to the populous south-east of the continent. No doubt disturbance has reduced its numbers, but although most records come from Victoria, the chances of seeing this bird in the wild are virtually nil. It is extremely reluctant to fly and will crouch for concealment, both factors which mean it is only very rarely seen. The majority of Australian ornithologists have never seen the Plains-wanderer.

Knowledge of the life of the Plains-wanderer is very limited but it seems that it may be, if not nocturnal, at least crepuscular. It is probably nomadic and dependent on climatic factors for its appearances. The female is the more boldly coloured of the pair and takes the larger role in courtship. Her plumage has strong similarities with the buttonquails, with a striped neck and chestnut breast patch. The male is more subdued in colour and performs all of the incubation and tending of the chicks. The four greenish eggs are spotted. They are laid in a simple scrape, usually beneath a tuft of grass.

Cranes Gruidae

No more beautiful or appealing group of birds exists on earth than the fourteen species of crane. Cranes are long-legged, long-necked birds, whose trumpet calls evoke the spirit of the wilderness where they live. They are birds that are becoming progressively more rare as civilization comes to more and more wild places. They are birds that are in danger, but birds to which few people can fail to respond.

The largest cranes stand 5 feet in height. They are delicately coloured, grey and white birds with distinctive heads and crowns usually with a dash of crimson. Like storks they fly with head and neck extended and long legs trailing out behind. In all species the innermost secondaries are greatly extended to form a drooping train over the tail. Cranes are highly gregarious and vocal; in fact most have a peculiarly shaped trachea that enables them to produce their loud, trumpeting calls. The smaller females do not always share this vocal ability to such a refined degree.

Cranes live on the ground and breed in marshy wildernesses. They are catholic about food and exist on a mixed diet of vegetable matter and animals such as worms, mice and insects. Most birds apparently pair for life.

Cranes are highly migratory and regularly follow the same route year in, year out. They are as conservative about their wintering places as they are of their breeding stations, and even appear at the same stopover places along their route. European Cranes *Grus grus*,

Common Cranes migrate in flocks and frequently feed and display at regular stopover points along the way, as here in southern Sweden at the famous Hornborgasjön.

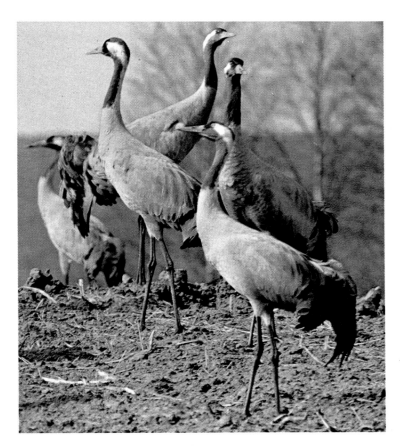

for example, migrate right across north-western Europe in flocks totalling several thousand. In autumn they rest among the heathlands of southern Belgium before moving across France along a narrow path from which they seldom deviate. Thousands of Cranes visit France annually although they are exceedingly rare apart from along this corridor. Most birds move on to winter in southern Spain in long lines or 'Vs', just like skeins of geese stretched out across the skies. Occasionally a freak weather situation may blow these strong-flying birds right off course, but the flocks that ended up along the south coast of Britain one year are unlikely to be repeated. In Britain Cranes are distinctly rare.

In spring Cranes arrive early in Sweden and mass at the lake of Hornborgasjön awaiting the northern thaw. Here in April they are one of Europe's greatest wildlife spectacles. The birds resort to the surrounding fields by the thousand, and perform their elaborate and fascinating nuptial dances. With shrill cries, individuals, pairs or whole groups jump into the air, wings raised or stretched sideways. They bow, freeze, throw their heads back and cry. In a modified form such dances are continued throughout the year by all species of cranes.

Cranes usually gather a nest together, although some simply lay their two eggs, sometimes one or three, in a bare hollow. The eggs are usually a dull buff colour spotted with brown, but at least one species lays an almost pure light blue egg. Incubation, which is shared, takes four to five weeks and the young, which closely resemble overlarge sandpipers, are sandy balls of fluff that can run about more or less immediately. They fly some two and a half months after hatching.

Most cranes belong to the typical genus *Grus* which consists of ten species, no less than three of which are sufficiently rare to merit a place in the Red Book. Rarest of all are the great Whooping Cranes *G. americana* of North America, which maintain a population of about fifty birds that commute the length of the continent from their wintering grounds on the Gulf Coast at Aransas, Texas, to the muskeg country of Wood Buffalo National Park. All the way along this 2,300 mile flight the Whooping Cranes are watched for by eager-eyed conservationists. Year after year the excited count at Aransas raises and lowers the hopes for this magnificent white crane with its black wings and bare, red skin on the face. It is interesting and encouraging that Whooping and other cranes breed in zoos, although there must be serious fears of their ever being able to survive in the wild.

Almost as rare is the Manchurian or Japanese Crane *G. japonensis*. Its scientific name and the fact that it has its strongest population on the island of Hokkaido in Japan, justify this bird being known coloquially as the Japanese Crane. The Japanese Crane breeds in the Amur River valley in eastern Siberia where some 200 to 300 birds spend the summer, and has a stronghold of approximately thirty pairs at Lake Khanka. Outside this area reports are all very much past history over the Manchurian part of its range, and it is quite possible that the populations no longer exist. Evidence comes from Korea, formerly a major home of wintering cranes and where reports are now very few. In Japan the bird survived in tiny numbers in the Kuccharo Marsh in eastern Hokkaido, but the population has recently built up to about 150 individuals. These birds are resident.

The situation is very critical with these two birds but most of the other species survive in the face of serious dangers. The Sandhill Crane *G. canadensis* of North America is stable at about 200,000 birds, but several distinct subspecies are in danger. The Siberian White Crane *G. leucogeranus* formerly bred right across Siberia but is now confined to a few isolated pockets, the major one of which boasts about 700 pairs and lies between the Rivers Yana and Alazeya. The world population of this bird, which is similar in appearance to the Whooping Crane, is now less than 2,000 birds. Most winter in China but a considerable population is found in northern India, particularly at Bharatpur, near Agra. The direct line north-eastwards from there leads to one of the breeding areas, but across the Himalayas. As Siberian White Cranes have been observed at over 14,000 feet there, perhaps this is a normal part of their migration.

Three other genera of cranes exist, all with a distinctly African centre of distribution. The Wattled Crane *Bugeranus carunculatus* is a dark bird marked by two long wattles that dangle from the face. During ritualized dances the wattles flap wildly adding considerably to the effect. It is confined to southern and eastern Africa. The Stanley Crane *Anthropoides paradisea* is confined to South Africa. It

Below Cranes migrate like geese in great V-formations across the sky. These Common Cranes were photographed en route between their Scandinavian breeding grounds and their winter quarters in Iberia and North Africa. Like geese they follow narrowly defined routes.

Opposite Crowned Cranes frequent open areas of Africa south of the Sahara where their courtship displays have inspired the local natives to create ritualized dances based on the strange antics of these attractive birds.

is a graceful grey-blue bird with dark plumes. A third African species, the Crowned Crane *Balearica pavonina* is more widespread and numerous over Africa south of the Sahara. A dark bird, its most prominent feature is the fine, golden crest that it erects on its crown, but the bold pattern of white and gold with brown plumes is particularly noticeable in flight. Crowned Cranes are essentially gregarious and gather in flocks with the hordes of other waterbirds at favourite East African rivers and marshes.

The Demoiselle Crane *Anthropoides virgo* is one of the smallest of the cranes. It breeds in a broad sweep across central Asia to the Black Sea, and again across North Africa from Tunisia to the Atlas Mountains of Morocco. It winters in Africa, and from the Middle East to India, but is nowhere very obvious or common. Its grey and black plumage is plumed at the tail and breast.

Limpkin Aramidae

The Limpkin *Aramus guarauna* looks like a curlew, is related to the cranes, lives like a rail and feeds almost exclusively on snails like the Everglade Kite. It is not then surprising that it is placed in a monotypic family. The name stems from its peculiar gait which is almost a limp.

Just over 2 feet in length, the Limpkin is a brown, mottled bird, with white flecking on the neck. It has long legs with a long hind toe like the rails, but a long, powerful, down-curved bill like a wader. Its food and method of operation are the same as the waders. Unlike most of those birds it is not a migrant, and is resident from the southern United States through Central America, the West Indies southwards to Argentina. Its wings are small and rounded, and it has the reluctance to fly that characterizes the members of the rail family.

The Limpkin lives in swamps with a strong covering of undergrowth where molluscs, particularly snails, are abundant. Like the Everglade Kite, the Limpkin has evolved a method all its own to deal with snails, which it is adept at finding. Taken in the

Limpkins frequent mangrove swamps through Central and South America where they live on an almost exclusive diet of snails which they extract from their shells with their specially adapted bills.

bill the snail is wedged between roots of a tree or bush, and the open mandibles inserted at either side of the snail's operculum, or lid. Then with a twist the animal is drawn from its shell. The almost total overlap in range between the Everglade Kite and the Limpkin is due to the predominance of the snail *Pomacea caliginosa* in the diet of both birds.

In the United States Limpkins are found in the mangrove swamps of Florida and Georgia. Their numbers were once seriously reduced by shooting, for they are excellent eating, but they can normally be seen now at the refuges of Lake Okeechobee in Florida and Lake Okafenokee in Georgia. They have prospered under protection but the more insidious dangers of drainage and leisure development now threaten these and the other waterbird communities of Florida.

Limpkins usually nest on the ground, though some nests have been found at a considerable height among waterside bushes, where they gather an untidy mass of sticks and aquatic vegetation together. The four to eight eggs are buff spotted with brown and both parents share the incubation. The active young hatch after twenty-eight days and are covered with a concealing and protective layer of down. They are fed by the adults even after they are fully grown.

Trumpeters Psophiidae

It is a tribute to the jungles of South America that three birds about the same size as a domestic Chicken, living in flocks of hundreds, renowned for their extremely loud calls, easily tamed, good to eat and enthusiastically hunted, should remain so little known. The three species of trumpeters are attractive relatives of the cranes and rails. They live among jungle clearings often forming flocks of a hundred or more. They are dark in coloration and are weak fliers, spending most of their time foraging on the forest floor for fruit and insects. They escape predation by running rather than flying, although they invariably roost in trees.

The trumpeters are best known for their calls which echo through the jungle. Their extreme sociability makes them an easy prey to be 'called up' by artificial imitations of their trumpeting, and they are easily shot and are absent as a result from the areas around villages.

Courtship, consisting of dance-like posturing, is similar to that of the cranes, and the nest is placed in a hole in a tree. The eggs are said to number from six to ten and incubation may be undertaken by the female alone. The chicks are reported to leave the nest soon after hatching, but the intimate life of the trumpeters is still surprisingly little studied.

All three species are black with different coloured 'ends' created by the feathers of the scapulars and tertials. The Common Trumpeter *Psophia crepitans* has a grey 'end'; the Green-winged *P. viridis* has a glossy green 'end'; and the White-winged *P. leucoptera* a white 'end'. Trumpeters are handsome birds that have been successfully kept in collections but which have yet to breed in captivity.

The White-winged Trumpeter inhabits the lower regions of the Amazon basin where its loud calls are a feature of the cacophony of sound of the tropical jungles. The white 'ends' to the wings of this species are clearly seen.

Rails Rallidae

The rails comprise about 130 varied species that include birds generally referred to as crakes, moorhens, coots and gallinules, as well as rails. In general they are long-legged birds adapted in various ways to an aquatic environment. They are generally sober in coloration and, although they make regular and lengthy migrations, they are not strong fliers. Migrant rails are prone to kill themselves on overhead wires, and some authors have suggested that this danger is in itself sufficient to place whole species in danger of extinction.

Despite this lack of aerial power, rails have proved highly successful colonists. In the Pacific, with its plethora of islands scattered across the ocean, rails have established themselves and, in many cases, developed into quite separate island species. On many islands they have lost the power of flight due to the lack of predators – it is just not necessary to fly if there is nothing to fly from. Unfortunately their island homes have been progressively invaded by man over the past few hundred years, and with him have come pest species such as rats and cats. The rails are quite unable to exist alongside these predators, and no less than fifteen species have become extinct during the last 100 years. Most of these are single island species, but for this very reason they are of immense interest to the ornithologist.

Most rails are secretive and many are seldom seen. They are thus easy to overlook and even after a thorough search it is a bold man that declares a rail species extinct. For similar reasons new species of rails are still being discovered on islands that have never been intensively worked by scientists.

Rails are generally thin birds ('thin as a rail') with narrow bodies that pass through vegetation smoothly and easily. They have long necks and legs and generally walk with a bobbing head motion like a chicken. The tail is flitted as they walk, exposing the often boldly patterned under-tail coverts which serve as a contact signal, as well as a territorial flag. Hidden deep in thick vegetation they maintain communication by producing some of the most extraordinary calls in the animal world. In the evening, in particular, many species utter a prolonged territorial calling. The Spotted Crake *Porzana porzana* is often semi-colonial and utters a continuous 'quip-quip-quip' note that has been likened to the drip of a tap into a large, half-empty tank of water. Other species boast equally remarkable calls.

Typical rails are dull, mottled and camouflaged birds with long legs and long toes that enable them to spread their weight over aquatic vegetation. Their bills are usually long and they feed mainly on animate matter. They are not adverse to raiding other birds' eggs and young, and the Water Rail *Rallus aquaticus* has on several occasions been observed grabbing and drowning House Sparrows. This group of rails, of which the genus *Rallus* is typical, is found throughout the world, although the Water Rail is the only Palaearctic representative. In North America the Virginia *R. limicola* and King Rails *R. elegans* are both found on freshwater marshes, and the Clapper Rail *R. longirostris* is a saltmarsh species. Other members of the genus are widespread in Africa and Australia and its associated islands. One species can still be found on the island of Guam in the Pacific Ocean, although other island species, including one from Tahiti, have become extinct.

Crakes are generally thought of as similar to the rails but with shorter, stubbier bills. They are equally at home in thick vegetation and many species are aquatic. The Corncrake *Crex crex* is a summer visitor to Eurasia which has been seriously affected by the mechanization of farming and the quicker-growing varieties of cereals. Once a common bird over most of the British Isles it is now found in numbers only on the northern offshore islands. It winters in Africa and has, therefore, to run the gauntlet of the 'sportsmen' of the Mediterranean.

The crakes of the genus *Porzana* are a cosmopolitan group that includes several other long-distance migrants. The Little Crake *P. parva* is about 7 inches long yet regularly migrates in and out of Europe, as does its congener Baillon's Crake *P. pusilla*. In Africa these Palaearctic birds can be found alongside the resident and charming Black Crake *Limnocorax flavirostra*. With an all-black, sooty plumage, red legs and yellow bill, it is one of the most boldly coloured of its family. It is usually easy to see, although it takes to cover at the slightest disturbance.

Most crakes and rails build a substantial nest of vegetation low down among dense herbage. The six to twelve white to buff eggs are spotted or boldly blotched with red or black, and are incubated by both sexes. The down-covered young leave the nest soon after hatching and are tended by both parents.

At the other extreme of the family are the coots whose feet have evolved grebe-like lobes for swimming. Coots most closely resemble grebes in foot structure and, although they dive clumsily, they are among the more successful bird groups. They sit buoyantly on the water and surface with the bouncy quality of a cork released under water. Their all-black plumage is relieved only by a bold shield on

Opposite Hidden away in a dense bed of reeds and sedges a Water Rail incubates its eggs. Although difficult to observe, the species is probably more widespread and numerous than is generally imagined. It is more often heard than seen and its typical call is a mixture of grunts and screams.

Below The American Purple Gallinule is a skulking species found in swamps throughout much of Central and South America. Birds that nest in the southern United States are migrants and, being poor fliers, often end up way off course.

the forehead. In the Common Coot *Fulica atra* this is pure white, but in the Crested Coot *F. cristata* the white shield is surmounted by two red knobs that swell during the breeding season. Doubtless this is an aid to specific identification and prevents hybridization. Where they are found together the Crested Coot is a more skulking bird, finding most of its food among dense vegetation and the shallow edges of the water. Common Coots, in contrast, often pack together over deeper water.

The majority of the world's coots are found in South America where there are seven distinct species. All are slaty grey in plumage with varying coloured legs and bills and particularly varying frontal shields. The Red-gartered Coot *F. armillata*, for instance, has a yellow bill backed by a red frontal shield bordered with yellow. Two of these South American species, the Giant Coot *F. gigantea*, which is over 2 feet in length, and the Horned Coot *F. cornuta*, are both found only on some of the highest of the Andean lakes.

Coots build a floating platform of vegetation on which to lay their eggs, although the Horned Coot is unique in using stones for its nest. All of the species are good swimmers and they avoid danger by running away over the surface of water rather than by taking flight. If sufficiently provoked they will take to the air, but their flight is very laboured and does not usually last long.

Gallinules, of which the best known example is the Moorhen *Gallinula chloropus*, called the Common Gallinule in America, share some of the features of both rails and coots. They are frequently shy and skulking, but are also boldly coloured and boast the forehead shield of the coots. The Moorhen swims well, but most gallinules prefer to walk and aquatic species have long toes like lily-trotters. The American Purple Gallinule *Porphyrula*

martinica is a boldly coloured, purple-breasted bird with yellow legs, red and yellow bill and a white frontal shield. It is frequently caught up in the hurricane stream that sweeps the West Indies in autumn, and occurs at out of range stations as a result. Throughout the rest of the world, from Africa to Australasia, it is replaced by the similar but conical-billed Purple Gallinule *Porphyrio porphyrio*, which is associated with dense aquatic vegetation and particularly with shallow, lily-covered waters. In some areas this larger bird is quite common.

One of the most fascinating of all the gallinules is the Takahe *Notornis mantelli* discovered in 1849, although described earlier from fossil remains. Reports (mainly skins) of the Takahe were few

and far between and eventually ceased altogether in 1898. It was not until Dr G.B.Orbell made a purposeful search in 1948 that anyone saw a live Takahe. The rediscovery of this 'extinct' species, and its subsequent protection at Lake Te Anau, is one of the success stories of conservation. There may be 200 to 300 birds in this general area of the Murchison Mountains of New Zealand's South Island. What is so remarkable is that *Notornis* was, in fact, named from fossils, indicating its lengthy sojourn in an area where it must have once wandered alongside moas. If a brilliantly coloured bird the size of a small turkey can escape observation for nearly half a century, what other rails are still tucked away among the forests of other less-accessible islands?

Finfoots Heliornithidae

The finfoots are one of those strange families that link the rails to the bustards. They are related to the coots, but most closely resemble grebes to which they are not related at all. Some look like darters, although they do not spear fish like those birds. There are three species of finfoot, one to each of the world's major land masses, each placed in a distinct genus, but each sharing a similar ecological niche and life style.

Finfoots are shy birds of narrow streams. They are seldom seen and little studied, so that only the barest details of their lives are known. Most ornithologists that have seen these birds have seen the

pair that inhabit Mzima Springs, deep in the heart of the Tsavo National Park, Kenya. Here in the early mornings, long before the tourists arrive, the African or Peter's Finfoot *Podica senegalensis* can be seen swimming from one side of the pools to the other, for finfoots spend most of their time among the thick, floating vegetation of the edges of streams. At Mzima their neighbours are

The strange Peter's or African Finfoot is an inhabitant of deep, clear, flowing waters, but invariably spends much of its time hidden among emergent vegetation.

the Hippopotamuses that likewise enjoy the crystal clear water which so swarms with fish. The African Finfoot, however, like its congeners, feeds mainly on insects, crustaceans, frogs and other amphibians, and only the tiniest of fish.

The African Finfoot is almost 2 feet in length. The male has a dark head and neck with a greenish caste, and a large, bright red bill. The body, although seldom held awash like the darters, floats low in the water and the resemblance to a grebe is quite uncanny.

The two creamy and brown, spotted eggs are laid in a substantial structure of twigs and rushes lined with grasses and leaves, and invariably placed in a riverside tree, or among flood debris where it is well hidden. The exact roles in breeding remain unknown.

When feeding the finfoots keep well hidden, examining the underside of leaves for the larvae of insects which are their major food. Finfoots regularly perch out of the water where their immobility successfully hides them against predators and prying eyes. The African Finfoot is found in suitable areas throughout Africa south of the Sahara. The American Finfoot *Heliornis fulica*, often called the Sungrebe, is an inhabitant of the area from southern Mexico to northern Argentina, while the Asiatic species, known as the Masked Finfoot *Heliopais personata*, ranges from Malaya through Sumatra.

Kagu Rhynochetidae

The Kagu *Rhynochetos jubatus* is the sole member of the Rhynochetidae and has caused so much confusion among systematists that it is placed in a suborder of the crane-rails all by itself. It is about the same size as a chicken but with longer legs and a more upright posture. It is a dove grey bird with long, erectile plumes that hang down from the crown. Its beautiful nuptial display, which has been studied in captivity, reveals to the full the startling black, white and red pattern of the wings. This display has led some authors to see a close relationship with the Sunbittern. The legs and bill are both red.

New Caledonia, the only place where the Kagu is found, lies 750 miles east of Australia. It is a ridge some 200 miles in length by 30 miles wide, and was discovered by Captain Cook in 1774. Its virgin forests were settled and exploited soon after and the French discovered the Kagu in 1860. Since then human influence on the environment has brought what is virtually a nocturnal and almost flightless bird to the extreme danger point. Dogs, pigs and hunting took their toll but forest clearance had a more wholesale and permanent effect. A few Kagus have been kept in zoos but they are seldom bred in captivity. The only chance of survival for this most interesting and aberrant species lies in the creation of reserves by the government and local ornithological society of New Caledonia.

Kagus are vocal at night in their forest home and although they are difficult to study, several writers mention peculiar antics which involve much twisting and turning and even chasing their own tails. The nest is built on the ground and is similar to that of the crakes and rails. Both parents incubate the single egg which is buff streaked with darker brown. The chick, which is abundantly covered with down, hatches after thirty-six days.

Sole member of its family, the Kagu is found only on the island of New Caledonia in the South Pacific. It is virtually flightless and in considerable danger from introduced pests.

Sunbittern Eurypygidae

The Sunbittern *Eurypyga helias* is the only member of its family. As it walks the river banks of its South American home it looks like a combination of goose and anhinga, although it is generally placed between the rails and bustards, along with the finfoots, seriemas and Kagu – all birds whose taxonomic position is uncertain.

The Sunbittern is 18 inches long and walks with a horizontal carriage on long legs and unwebbed feet. Its head is carried on a longish, slim neck and the plumage is beautifully mottled with blacks, browns and whites that effectively camouflage the bird beneath the trees that line the river banks. Here it is hidden by the mottled sunlight. The long, thin bill is adapted for catching fish and crustaceans in shallow water. A fierce, red eye stands out from a black head marked by two white stripes, while the only other colour of note is the bright, light maroon patch on the spread wing. These patches of colour are obvious in display where the bird indulges in the most extraordinary contortions. With tail spread and cocked,

The Sunbittern is another of those species which virtually defy classification. It haunts the rivers of Central America and the Amazon basin and is particularly fond of shrimps and crabs.

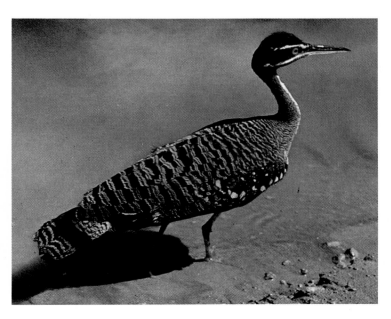

and wings spread like some heraldic emblem, the Sunbittern stands stock-still for minutes on end. It also adopts a more simple head-down posture that is similarly held for long periods. But it is when the bird emerges into an open patch of sunlight that a strange, dancing frenzy comes over it.

The nest consists of a bundle of twigs and leaves constructed ten to fifteen feet high in a tree in which two or three reddish eggs are laid. The down-covered chicks hatch after about four weeks and are tended by both parents. The Sunbittern takes well to captivity and has bred quite frequently. It is found in the wild from Central America southwards and throughout the Amazon basin. In this wilderness it seems secure.

Seriemas Cariamidae

The two species of seriemas are tall, walking birds of southern and central South America, which spend most of their time pacing gracefully across the pampas and bush country of Argentina and adjacent states. The body, generally brownish in colour, terminates in a long tail. The legs are long and powerful with three toes pointing forwards and a vestigial one raised and pointing to the rear. Like the Secretary-bird of Africa, their powers of dealing with snakes have often been exaggerated, and they do not have the immunity to snake bites with which they have been credited. Large ants and other insects form the bulk of the diet, but, like the Secretary-bird, they do kill snakes. They are not averse to lizards and take quite large amounts of fruit and other vegetable matter.

The best-known seriema is the Crested Seriema *Cariama cristata* which stands 30 inches high and is widely distributed over rolling grasslands. It is brownish grey in colour with long, red legs and a down-curved, crimson bill. A tuft of feathers sprouts from the forehead over the upper mandible. The long tail is boldly tipped with dark and light bands. The Crested Seriema is exceedingly reluctant to fly and escapes from predators by running to cover. The nest, which is usually placed near the ground, is composed of sticks, and the two eggs are white with a pink flush that soon fades. The down-covered young are cared for by both parents.

Burmeister's Seriema *Chunga burmeisteri* is found only in north-western Argentina and the adjacent Chaco region of Paraguay. It is a larger and heavier bird with a more prominent crest and frequents more bushy country than the Crested Seriema. It is much hunted and is difficult to observe. Both species take well to captivity and have bred.

The Crested or Red-legged Seriema frequents open thorn country where its long legs carry it many miles a day in search of prey. Its reputation as a snake killer is, like that of the Secretary-bird, probably exaggerated.

Bustards Otididae

The Great Bustard *Otis tarda* and the Kori Bustard *Ardeotis kori* share the distinction of being frequently referred to as the world's heaviest flying birds. In fact that distinction probably belongs to the Mute Swan, but it does indicate the size of these birds.

Bustards are a family of medium to large, ground-dwelling birds of open, rolling savannah country. They are confined to the Old World, and all but a handful of the twenty-two species are found in Africa. They are strongly built with thick necks and long, strong legs. The three toes form a running foot and most species utilize their speed on the ground to escape predators. The plumage is usually dull browns and mottled greys, but in many species the male is more brightly marked than the highly cryptic female. These brighter colours are usually confined to the neck which is the centrepiece of the elaborate courtship displays of the bustards.

Bustards are often gregarious and form considerable flocks in favourable areas. Being large as well as good to eat, they were formerly served at royal banquets in medieval England; even today they are much persecuted and hunted. They prefer open country and are most numerous on the plains of East Africa where several species occur side by side.

Huge numbers of Great Bustards formerly roamed the steppes of Russia where mile after mile of uncultivated grassland provided them with an ideal habitat. Today, those grasslands are devoted to cereal production and Great Bustards are disturbed and their eggs and young destroyed by mechanical farming. The Great Bustard also formerly bred throughout temperate Europe, but is now confined to a few isolated pairs in Rumania, Hungary, Austria, Spain and particularly Portugal. These birds occasionally manage to rear a brood in a cereal crop and thus stave off what must in the end be local extinction. Attempts were made in the early 1970s to reintroduce the Great Bustard to Britain where it was exterminated by 1845.

The Great Bustard is a brown, white and black bird that flies with powerful and purposeful beats of its huge wings. In display it raises its tail and produces the most extraordinary fans of feathers to turn itself into a moving ball of feathers and plumes. A red gular sac is inflated and stands out from the muted background colour of the neck. No doubt it also plays a part in the remarkable calls produced by the males in courtship.

The other European species, the Little Bustard *Otis tetrax*, is far smaller and in flight shows more resemblance to a duck than to the

Opposite A rare photograph of the Great Bustard on its nest in Portugal. This huge bird has suffered greatly due to persecution and to the ploughing of the open plains that it favours. Many birds now nest among crops and their eggs and young are frequently destroyed by agricultural machinery.

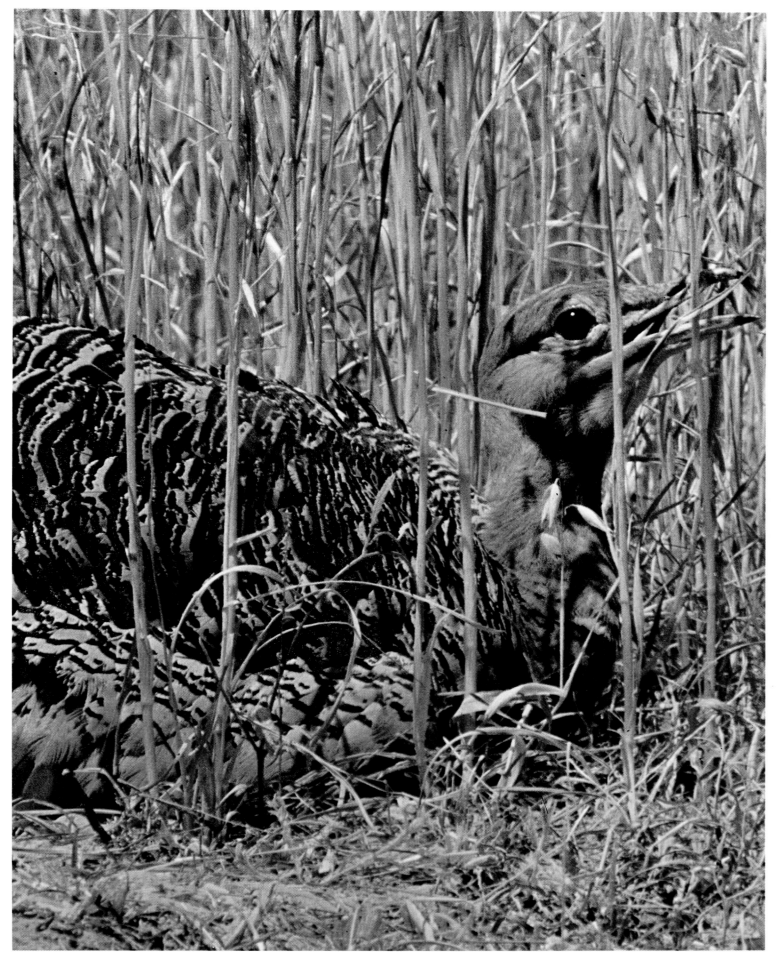

goose-like Great Bustard. It is more widespread and numerous in Europe and can be found in large flocks, even in intensively cultivated areas. The male is distinguished by a black and white neck collar.

The Kori is related to a group of large bustards found across the whole range of the family as far as Australia. It is common enough in East Africa and may weigh up to 40 pounds. It attracts considerable attention from tourists by virtue of its special relationship with Carmine Bee-eaters, for which it provides a mobile perch and flusher of prey as it walks among the tall grasses of the plains. Like the other bustards and plains' game it likes to shelter in the shade of a tree, even though open grassland with good visibility is its proper home.

The Kori is replaced in India by the Great Indian Bustard *Choriotis nigriceps*, the rarest of all the world's bustards and also one of the heaviest. Once found throughout the subcontinent it survives only in a few isolated pockets: in the remote areas of Rajasthan, Kutch and in the Deccan. The agricultural revolution is the major factor in this decline, although such a large and obvious bird of open country could not fail to be hunted. Fortunately, several

bustards (including the Great Indian Bustard), are now being bred in captivity.

The Australian Bustard *Eupodotis australis* is similar to the Indian Bustard and it too is hunted particularly during its winter wanderings.

The Arabian Bustard *Andeotis arabs* is found throughout North Africa and southern Arabia over much the same sort of country as the Houbara Bustard *Chlamydotis undulata*. Both prefer arid areas, and the Houbara in particular is noted for its lengthy migratory flights. Some seventy years ago these flights quite regularly brought the eastern race of the Houbara, MacQueen's Bustard, to western Europe and Britain. Today, with a greatly reduced population, it is an exceptional vagrant. These desert bustards may have suffered little change of habitat but they have been persecuted by the new machine-gun carrying 'sportsmen' of the Middle East.

The vast majority of other bustards are found in Africa and many of them bear personalized names – Denham's Bustard *Neotis denhami*, Heuglin's Bustard *N. heuglinii* and so on. In India there are two bustards that are called floricans: the beautiful Bengal Florican *Houbaropsis bengalensis* which roams northern India and the Lesser Florican *Sypheotides indica*.

Jacanas Jacanidae

The seven species of jacanas are placed in no less than six distinct genera. They are medium-sized water birds with the distinction of having quite extraordinary feet. The toes are exceptionally long with straight claws that accentuate their length. The claw of the hind toe is even longer than the toe itself. The legs are long with an unusually prominent shin that gives the birds a peculiarly stilt-like character. These physiological quirks are adaptations to the jacanas' unique habitat. They live and feed walking over floating aquatic vegetation – a fact that gives rise to their alternative name, lily-trotters. In fact, the name jacana is derived from the South American and is Portuguese in origin. Several authors prefer lily-trotter for the Old World species. The long toes enable the birds to spread their weight over a large surface area and they are adept at running over the surface of water-lilies.

Jacanas are colourful birds with the sexes similar. The female is a shade larger than her mate and has the same frontal shield. These shields are boldly coloured and, in the case of the Australian Jacana or Lotus-bird *Irediparra gallinacea*, extended almost into a cock's comb.

Jacanas pick insects and other aquatic life from the surface of the water and vegetation. Like coots and rails they prefer to run over the water rather than take to flight to avoid danger. Also like those species, they have a curiously Chicken-like gait that involves jerking the tail and head. When they eventually become airborne the dangling legs trail behind, just like those of a Moorhen. They are not strong fliers and two species, the African Jacana *Actophilornis africana* and the Madagascan Jacana *A. albinucha*, lose the power of flight altogether by moulting their flight feathers simultaneously like geese and ducks. Jacanas swim well and will dive to feed as well as to hide themselves from danger.

The nest is a mass of rotting vegetation anchored to floating vegetation in the manner of a grebe's nest. The four eggs are beautifully marked with veins of black or dark brown running over a lighter background of buffs and olives. The incubation period is from twenty-two to twenty-four days and the African Jacana has been noted holding the eggs against its flanks, perhaps to prevent them becoming covered with water when the birds' weight sets the nest awash. Certainly this species regularly carries its chicks beneath

its wings as it walks about the lily pads. The chicks are precocial and covered with a striped down – a condition only found elsewhere in their close relative, the Painted Snipe.

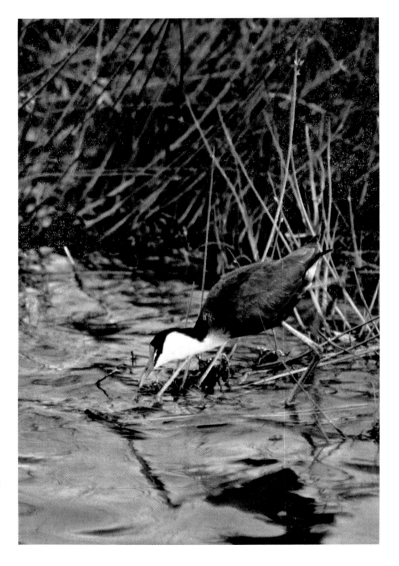

The huge toes of the African Jacana spread its weight and enable it to walk daintily over floating aquatic vegetation. As with all jacanas, it has been given the colloquial name of lily-trotter as a result.

The Pheasant-tailed Jacana *Hydrophasianus chirurgus* of Asia has long, black plumes extending from the tail, with a white head and breast and a conspicuous patch of yellow on the nape. Sometimes the tail feathers are broken off and lost and the bird can then be confused with the Bronze-winged Jacana *Metopidius indicus* which is often found alongside. The Pheasant-tailed Jacana is unique in that the female produces up to ten eggs in the nests of different males. The males are then given the task of incubating the eggs and looking after their particular broods.

The best-known and most familiar of all these tropical species is the African Jacana. It is a strong, chocolate brown coloured bird with a white breast and neck and a blue frontal shield that extends over the crown. A black eye stripe extends down the nape to the back. It is familiar on lakes throughout Africa south of the Sahara, reaching perhaps its greatest density on lily-covered lakes like Kenya's Lake Naivasha.

Painted snipe Rostratulidae

Painted snipe are not really snipe at all, although they do bear a strong resemblance to those birds. In particular the longitudinal striping of the head, the long, straight bill, the largish eyes and general proportions give these birds a resemblance to snipe that is yet another case of convergent evolution. Their life styles have much in common, although painted snipe also have strong affinities with the crakes, rails and jacanas.

There are two species of painted snipe: the Painted Snipe *Rostratula benghalensis* found throughout non-Saharan Africa, the Middle East including Turkey but not Europe, India, China, most of South-East Asia and Australia; and the South American Painted Snipe *Nycticryphes semicollaris* which has clearly spread from southern Africa to the marshes of the Argentine and adjacent pampas. They are very similar in appearance but in each case the female is larger and more gaily coloured.

The head, neck and breast are a dark, chocolate colour broken by a prominent, white eye ring that extends to a comma behind the eye, and a white crown stripe. The mantle is separated by a white area extending from the breast almost as an outline to the folded wing, which is prominently barred with vermiculations of black and white. The bill is a pale flesh colour with a noticeable droop near the tip, and the legs are similarly flesh coloured with very long toes. The South American species differs in having a web between the toes, as well as a more down-curved bill and a wedge-shaped tail.

Like true snipe, painted snipe are secretive hideaway birds of swamplands overgrown with dense vegetation. They are adept at wading through thick mud where the sensitive, soft tip to the bill searches out worms, molluscs and insects. They are seldom seen, since in many parts of the world they prefer the cover of rice paddies. They are extremely difficult to flush, and fly, like rails, with their feet dangling behind them.

Female Painted Snipe have an elaborate courtship ritual in which the rows of spots on the wings are displayed by bringing the spread wings forward, twisted towards the tip of the bill. The bold spotting of the spread tail is similarly displayed. Females hold territories and it is the males that are attracted and dominated. The males alone incubate the eggs for nineteen days and care for the young. Their mates are never faithful, however, searching out another male once they have completed a clutch. Four eggs are laid in a cup of grass constructed by the male on damp ground. They are pale yellow, blotched with black and purple. The young are covered with down and are active from birth. The South American Painted Snipe (of which the female is larger and brighter), shows no role reversal, however. The two eggs are white mottled with black.

The female Painted Snipe has a well-developed trachea, but the species is not highly vocal. The female is said to hiss and growl. A whistle is the call used to keep flocks together, for outside the breeding season painted snipe occur in small flocks and roam from one feeding ground to another. Nothing is known of their migrations.

Oystercatchers Haematopodidae

Varying in size and coloration, the four to six species of oystercatchers form one of the most distinctive of bird families. Each species has an 'oystercatcher' quality that is unique and precludes confusion with any other group of birds. All are members of the same genus.

Oystercatchers are boldly patterned black, or black and white birds with brightly coloured reddish or orange legs and bills. They live by the shoreline, their long, heavy, orange-red bills being adapted to dealing with the abundant intertidal bivalves. Prey found above the high water mark is smashed, but that found below water is neatly prised open and clipped from its protective shell.

Oystercatchers are essentially marine and are found on almost every type of coastal habitat from estuaries to sandy and rocky shores. The Common or Pied Oystercatcher *Haematopus ostralegus*, however, breeds well inland along the rivers of South Island, New Zealand, and some authors regard these birds as a separate species *H. finschi*. Oystercatchers have recently spread inland along the shingle-banked rivers of northern England, although they have bred in similar sites in Scotland for years. Even these inland birds resort to the coast outside the breeding season where they form large, extremely noisy, piping flocks several thousand strong. Like watchdogs, oystercatchers are seldom quiet and still. As several thousand take to flight their calls are, at once, an evocative sound of the mudflats and saltings. To the birdwatcher walking the dykes they are considered a nuisance, however. They are also looked upon as a pest by shell fishermen who see their depredations of the cockle beds as direct competition. For this reason oystercatchers are seldom protected species.

The Common Oystercatcher breeds throughout temperate Europe eastwards to the Caspian Sea and the Siberian steppes, in southern Africa and in Australasia. Over parts of this vast range various subspecies have been described including the melanistic mutants of New Zealand and the British subspecies *H.o. occidentalis*. The American Oystercatcher *H. palliatus* is generally regarded as a separate species, as is the Black Oystercatcher *H. bachmani* of western North America. The Sooty Oystercatcher *H. fuliginosus* is found around the coasts of Australia alongside the common bird, known locally as the Pied Oystercatcher. The Sooty Oystercatcher is an all-black oystercatcher, as is *H. ater* of Argentina, Chile and the Falkland Islands. Yet another distinct species, *H. leucopodus*, is also found in this area.

Clearly, the exact systematics of this group have yet to be fully worked out, and it seems very likely that eventually the situation will be resolved to perhaps four species covering all the different

Overleaf The Painted Snipe, together with its close relative the South American Painted Snipe, is placed in a family on its own. It resembles a snipe but it is, in fact, more closely related to the jacanas.

137

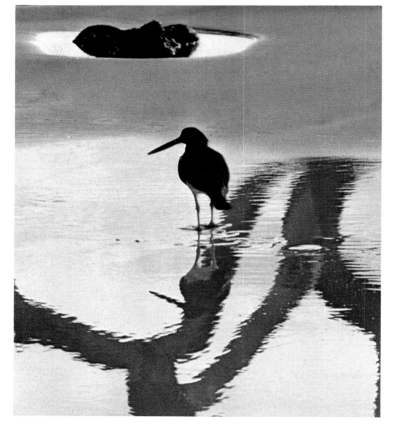

Opposite top The Oystercatcher is a typical member of the shorebird community and frequently forms large, vociferous flocks over favoured feeding grounds. Though predominantly coastal, it breeds inland over vast areas of central Asia, and has recently spread to breed along many rivers in northern England.

Opposite bottom The boldly pied Oystercatcher is one of the most obvious members of the shoreline community. Its predilection for cockles has brought it into sharp conflict with shell fishermen and control campaigns have been undertaken in several parts of the world.

plumage patterns. In the meantime it is perhaps best to regard the genus *Haematopus* as consisting of a superspecies.

All species have an elaborate piping ceremony in which small groups of birds walk together in hunched attitudes with bills pointing obliquely towards the ground. This serves not only to isolate the pair from the flock, but also to space out the pairs within the loose colonial arrangements within which oystercatchers breed. Colonies are often mixed with other species including terns *Sterna* species and gulls *Larus* species. Conflict between the species is commonplace.

Oystercatchers lay three eggs, (but sometimes two or four) in a bare scrape on the ground often among shingle where their cryptic colouring effectively hides them. The chicks hatch after twenty-seven days and 'freeze' at the alarm call of the parents that frequently indulge in an elaborate injury-feigning routine to distract intruders.

Plovers Charadriidae

Along with the sandpipers (the Scolopacidae) plovers make up the great majority of what in America are called 'shorebirds' and in Europe are generally known as 'waders'. Both families are large, although both are also quite distinct, with only a very few uncertain species that could equally be placed in both families. Most notable

Below A Little Ringed Plover settles on its well-camouflaged eggs. The species has spread northwards during the present century.

of these are the turnstones, which are treated as sandpipers in this book.

There are then fifty-six species of plovers that possess various vernacular names around the world. The family is dominated by two genera *Vanellus* and *Charadrius*, the lapwings and true plovers, which between them account for fifty species. For this reason, if for no other, it would seem sensible to use names linked with genera rather than misuse other names like dotterel, which has been widely applied to various Australasian species.

The typical plover is from 6 to 16 inches in length with medium to long legs, but with only a moderate length bill. Indeed, compared with many sandpipers' the bill is short and stubby. The body shape is somewhat rotund but the plovers as a whole are fast runners. The long wings are typical of all waders and the flight is both strong and direct. Several species have a short, talon-like spur at the bend of the wing, as in the Spur-winged Plover *Vanellus spinosus*. Unlike the sandpipers they are not cryptically coloured, but rely on their disruptive plumage to escape detection. Seen on their own, away

Right One of the very few asymmetrical birds in the world, the Wrybill is found in New Zealand and its bill always turns to the right. It breeds on South Island and migrates to the bays of North Island to winter.

Below A Lapwing settles on its nest in open meadow country in Holland. Even today its eggs are considered a delicacy and are taken in great numbers during the early part of the breeding season in that country.

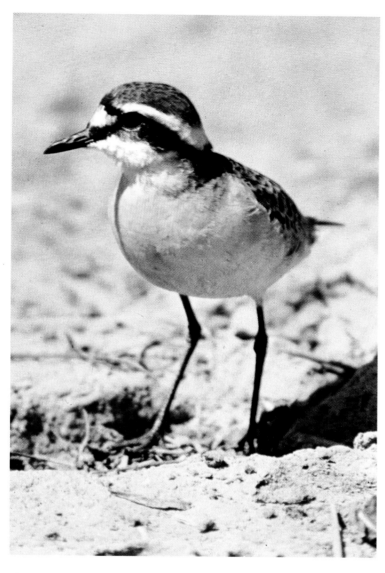

Many plovers have adapted to arid environments, including Kittlitz's Plover of Africa, which is found around freshwater margins as well as in open sandy areas some distance from water.

Lapwing *Vanellus vanellus* is a particularly fine exponent, drawing an intruder away from the danger zone with a convincing 'broken-wing' and much flapping erratically into the air.

The true plovers, sometimes called the 'sand plovers', are small to medium birds, darker above than below. The Ringed Plover *Charadrius hiaticula* of Eurasia and the Semipalmated Plover *C. semipalmatus* of America are typical, and incidentally considered to be conspecific by many authors. They are $7\frac{1}{2}$ inches long, brown above and white below with a black band across the tail and a disruptive pattern of black rings and bars across the crown, head and breast. This pattern is common to many members of the genus. They most commonly nest near the coast but enjoy an immense breeding range that stretches from temperate western Europe to the high Arctic. They can be found on any bare open area, even including crops. Like thrushes, they spend much time standing still before pattering off over the ground and stopping again. They feed mainly on crustaceans that are picked from the surface of mud, and on insects hunted among shingle or lichen-covered tundra. Outside the breeding season they migrate to temperate estuaries and shores, but seldom form large flocks.

The Ringed Plover's close relative the Little Ringed Plover *C. dubius* is a highly migratory species that leaves its breeding range completely. Similar in shape and coloration to the Ringed Plover, it is slightly smaller and breeds at freshwater sites inland in the temperate boreal zone. Over much of Europe it finds the shingle banks of rivers a suitable habitat, but in Britain it has spread since its first colonization in the 1930s via freshly created gravel pits.

In the Middle East the true sandplovers are the ecological counterparts of the 'ringed' plovers of the north. In keeping with their habitat they are buffer, more washed-out in coloration with less pronounced ringed patterns. The Greater Sandplover *C. leschenaultii* breeds from Turkey eastwards across the Middle East into Asia. It is similar in outline to the other species but has a chestnut, not black breast band, and chestnut above the eye. Like many other species of ground-nesting tropical birds it often has to protect its egg against overheating rather than chilling. Thus it frequently stands over its eggs and even buries them beneath the sand.

Although a true member of the genus, the Killdeer *C. vociferus* of North America occupies a similar niche to the Old World Lapwing. It has two black breast bands and a strangely elongated rust red wedge-shaped tail. Its loud ringing 'kill-dee' call is as familiar to the American birder as the Lapwing's 'pee-wee' is to the European birdwatcher. It is a bird of grassy fields and breeds throughout North and Central America south to Peru.

The plovers of the genus *Pluvialis* are larger and more bulky birds than the true plovers. All have distinct breeding plumages which typically consist of black underparts, but which in the New Zealand Dotterel *P. obscurus* are a rusty brown. No doubt this species, which is confined to New Zealand, evolved from migrant stock that remained behind as the others returned northwards to breed. The three other *Pluvialis* species are all long-distance migrants.

The Golden Plover breeds in northern Europe eastwards into adjacent parts of Asia, and is replaced in eastern Siberia and North America by the closely related and very similar Lesser Golden Plover *P. dominica*. The latter truly spans the globe, moving from the Arctic southwards across the Pacific to Australia, over the Atlantic to Argentina, and across 6,000 miles of ocean from Alaska to the islands of Hawaii. Both birds are golden on the back and wings.

The Grey Plover *P. squatarola* is larger than the Golden Plover and easily identified in winter plumage by the black 'armpit' effect

from their normal backgrounds, many plovers appear boldly patterned with large areas of black, brown and white. Against a bare area of shingle, sand or even earth, however, they disappear effectively as soon as they stand still. Many ornithologists have seen their first Dotterel *Eudromias morinellus* high on some Arctic *fjell*, and then discovered that they are in the middle of a considerable flock of birds that they simply had not seen.

Like the sandpipers, plovers are gregarious for most of the year. They are waders that usually feed at the water's edge rather than actually in it, but this nevertheless has a considerable concentrating effect. Flocks of two or three thousand are quite commonplace, but they never form the dense masses of species like Knot and Dunlin.

Some species adopt a special breeding plumage. The Golden Plover *Pluvialis apricaria* and the other members of that genus sport a boldly black face, breast and belly during the summer, that is moulted completely in winter. The nest is placed on the ground and is usually unlined, although several species use a few bents and others gather odd items around them as they sit. Four cryptically coloured eggs are usual, although some, like the highly aberrant Wrybill *Anarhynchus frontalis* of New Zealand, lay only two, while yet others produce a clutch of five. In general both parents participate in incubation and the care of the chicks, which are nidifugous (leave the nest soon after hatching). An exception to this rule is the Dotterel which follows a phalarope-like role reversal routine in which the duller coloured male incubates the eggs and looks after the young. Many species defend their camouflaged eggs and young with an elaborate injury-feigning distraction display. The

The Wattled Plover is a noisy inhabitant of marshlands throughout southern Africa. The yellow wattle extending from the base of the upper mandible is a good field mark but, being shared with other African plovers, is not diagnostic.

of its axillaries. Whereas Golden Plovers are fresh marsh and grassland birds the Grey Plover is essentially a shorebird, and sometimes gathers in dense flocks on favoured estuaries, where it feeds on the open mud flats. It is a high Arctic breeder nesting on the tundra of the extreme north of Siberia and North America where it is called the Black-bellied Plover. It migrates as far as Chile and Australia, although many birds remain in northern, temperate lands.

Lapwings are medium-sized plovers with diverse plumage patterns. They have rounded rather than pointed wings, and one or

more of the following features: a crest, facial wattles and wing spurs. Most lapwings are found in Africa, there are none in North America and only a couple have penetrated northwards into Europe. One of these, the Common or Eurasian Lapwing, is both widespread and numerous. A foot in length, its name is derived from its peculiar 'lapping' flight and rounded wings. In spite of this it is a long-distance migrant and boasts a complex system of movements at all seasons. It is predominantly a bird of moist grassland and as soon as frost threatens it is off in search of milder climes, only to return as soon as there is a thaw. In many parts of western Europe Lapwing's (usually called 'plover's') eggs are a delicacy and even in conservation-minded countries like Holland the first clutches are regularly collected for the gourmet.

The other European lapwing is the Spur-winged Plover, a recent colonist of the Balkans from Asiatic Turkey. It breeds throughout the Middle East to North Africa and can be found in winter southwards to Africa and eastwards into India. It is a boldly patterned, brown, black and white bird that stands on long legs, making it appear larger than it is. Southwards in Africa it is replaced by the similar, but differently coloured, Blacksmith Plover *V. armatus*. This bird is a common sight in East Africa where it mixes easily with the large herbivores of the game parks. The name comes from the similarity between its call and the sound of a hammer on an anvil.

A few species do not belong to any of these dominant genera. The Dotterel breeds in the tundra zone of Eurasia and migrates southwards to the Mediterranean region in winter. The only other member of its genus is the Tawny-throated Dotterel *Eudromias ruficollis*, which breeds only in southernmost South America. The Wrybill of New Zealand is quite unique in having a bill that turns sideways to the right, but no doubt the bill would be equally effective if it turned to the left. In all other appearances it is similar to a ringed plover. It feeds under stones on the beaches where it gathers in flocks of up to 1,000 birds in winter.

Sandpipers Scolopacidae

The name sandpiper evokes images of wild desolate shores, although it is sometimes applied to all waders quite indiscriminately. In fact there is no vernacular equivalent of the Scolopacidae with which we are concerned here.

Waders belong to the Charadriiformes, an order which includes the gulls, terns, skuas, thick-knees, and so on. In North America they are collectively described as shorebirds – a misleading term, since many species do not frequent the shore at any time of the year and most do not breed within miles of the tideline. The group or tribe of waders can be divided into plovers, phalaropes, stilts, shanks and sandpipers, but both of the latter belong to the Scolopacidae.

The sandpipers then are a large group consisting of some seventy-five species divided into twenty-one distinct genera. They are as diverse as any group of birds, and although the most widespread family in the world, occurring on every continent and almost every small island, they remain unfamiliar to those who have no interest in birds. Waders are birdwatchers' birds.

Despite the fact that they vary in size from 5 to 25 inches, all share some characteristics. By and large they are aquatic species that find much of their food by wading in shallow water. They have long legs with four toes, although the Sanderling *Calidris alba* has only three toes and spends more of its time running than any other

sandpiper. Some species have exceedingly long legs that trail behind them in flight. They also have long necks and a bill that is at least as long as the head and sometimes considerably longer. While many species have straight bills used for picking food from the surface of mud and along the water's edge, others have extremely long bills that may be straight, heavily decurved or recurved. Many sandpipers have very characteristic methods of feeding and depend on length of leg and structure of bill to separate out their distinct ecological niches.

Most sandpipers are cryptically coloured above and white below. Mottled greys and browns are seldom very distinctive and many people find the members of this family extremely difficult to identify. In summer some species adopt a special nuptial plumage which consists of a black or russet breast and belly. No doubt this destroys their otherwise highly effective countershading and serves to pick them out from their background.

All the sandpipers are strong fliers and each shows a distinctive combination of wing bars and tail pattern that serve very well as field marks. Thus of two very similar species, the Dunlin *C. alpina* and Curlew Sandpiper *C. ferruginea*, the Dunlin has a wing bar and a central tail stripe whereas the Curlew Sandpiper has a wing bar and a white rump. These patterns help to maintain contact between members of a flock, a process that is aided by their similar, but

A flock of Dunlin, the most common wader of the Northern Hemisphere, pauses at a safe rocky refuge at high tide. These birds form huge flocks in estuaries and along open shores.

equally distinctive, calls.

Strong flight is a necessity for highly migratory species like the sandpipers, most of which breed in the Northern Hemisphere and make long flights southwards to winter. Several of the high Arctic breeders migrate to the Southern Hemisphere. During these flights many are highly gregarious and gather together into quite immense flocks. Dunlin and Knot *C. canutus* in particular often form flocks thousands strong, such is the wealth of life to be found between the tides. These flocks often rise in the air forming a dense cloud that is sometimes dark and sometimes light as the birds turn this way and that as one against the sky. How they manage to synchronize their turns with these complex aerial manoeuvres remains unexplained. On favoured estuaries counts of the open shore sandpipers, that is, the true shorebirds, may reach six figures.

During low water they will spread out over the mud or sand flats busily feeding in their non-stop manner. Little groups will fly and some species will tend to gather together. Slowly, as the tide rises, they will be forced on to ever smaller feeding grounds. At high tide all the birds of the estuary will gather at an established and often traditional roosting site. Here, perhaps 100,000 birds will be forced together into an acre or so. The lives of these shorebirds are governed by the tides, not by night and day and the normal clock that we use.

Sandpipers are great travellers; in fact some have been referred to as 'globe-spanners'. They breed in the Arctic and winter as far south as land goes, but they also make some of the strangest journeys. The Ruff *Philomachus pugnax*, for example, breeds right across Eurasia to the Bering Straits. These far-eastern birds do not, however, migrate along the Pacific coast but fly westwards right

across Siberia to western Europe. That they could find the same conditions in Japan, only a fraction of the distance away, just adds to the curiosity. Ruff are also known to make direct migrations across the Mediterranean and Sahara, a severe test of any flying machine. Many other waders, however, perform equally amazing feats of endurance. The Wood Sandpiper *Tringa glareola* stops off in the Camargue of southern France to 'take on fuel' (put on reserves of fat) for its Sahara crossing. Several Nearctic species like the famed Eskimo Curlew *Numenius borealis* breed in northern Canada and then fly eastwards out over the Atlantic before making a landfall in South America. This looks a strange and inexplicable route on a normal map projection, but on a globe it is apparent that the route is a great circle, the shortest distance between two points on the earth's surface. That the same birds often return by the longer overland route is just another of the strange facets of the lives of these birds.

Essentially terrestrial, several waders take to the trees during the summer, however. Most do so simply to proclaim their ownership of a territory, but a very few, such as the Green Sandpiper *Tringa ochropus*, actually nest among the trees in the disused nests of other birds. Most waders declare their territories with a song flight and loud calls. These calls have an evocative and curiously wild, ringing quality, although they are far from melodious. The display flight itself is performed on stiff, jerky wing beats often mixed, like a dove, with glides and hovering. In the case of snipe, the song flight consists of a series of climbs and dives during which the stiff outer-tail feathers beat through the wind creating a whiffling noise referred to as 'drumming'. This places the snipe among the very few ornithological 'instrumentalists'.

Ruff, on the other hand, behave much more like grouse. The males gather at a communal lek where they direct elaborate displays of aggression against each other in defence of a territory that is often

Above Two Ruff, resplendent in their full nuptial plumage, take time off for a quick preen of their finery. The traditional lekking grounds of this species attract many birds, although it is only the dominant males that are regularly visited by the reeves.

Right The delicately marked and widespread Whimbrel is a diminutive version of the Curlew. It breeds further north than the Curlew and has a more pronounced migration pattern as a result.

less than a yard across. Making much of the 'ruff' of feathers around the neck together with their head plumes, the birds gather morning and evening to joust like medieval knights for the favour of their ladies, the reeves. The ruffs are of different colours: blacks, whites and rust coloured, yet colour seems of little significance in battle. The reeves visit the lek to choose a mate and invariably select a Ruff at the centre of the lek that seems to perform little display. This is a dominant male, his position is secure and he can mate with the reeves, his only contribution to the rearing of the young, without fear of interruption. The less well-established Ruffs are continually fighting for their territories.

Most sandpipers construct a simple cup of grasses on the ground to hold their four cryptically coloured eggs. Some species lay only two or three eggs, but the usual clutch of four are highly pyriform (pear-shaped) and fit together like the segments of an orange. This shape enables the incubating bird to cover the large mass of its eggs. The young are active from birth and are covered with cryptically coloured down. They further avoid danger by 'freezing' at the parental alarm call.

The largest of the Scolopacidae are the curlews. The Eurasian Curlew *Numenius arquata* is 23 inches long with an extremely long, down-curved bill for probing deep into estuarine mud in its search for worms. Its near relative the Whimbrel *N. phaeopus*, the

Hudsonian Curlew of North America, is smaller with distinctive stripes on the crown, but most of the other members of the genus are very similar to the Eurasian Curlew. The Eskimo Curlew was once abundant in North America, but was hunted to the point of extinction by the professional shooters of Labrador where the bird

Above A Woodcock stealthily approaches its woodland nest among the dead leaves that it so much resembles. Nests of this species are notoriously difficult to locate and usually found only by accident.

Left A Great Snipe in its strutting display photographed in a Swedish bog. Like Ruff, these birds gather at an established lek each morning and evening to establish their right to mate.

gathered in immense numbers in autumn. Now there is just an occasional record from the Gulf Coast in spring.

Woodcock *Scolopax rusticola* are waders that have abandoned the shores and marshes and turned to a forest existence. Their delicate browns and fawns are mottled into the most effective cryptic camouflage, making them quite invisible apart from their large, dark eye. The eyes are set exactly at the sides of the head giving the bird complete 360 degree vision, and binocular vision both in front and behind. The roding flight of the Woodcock consists of a circle around its territory on slow beating wings, during which the bird utters a deep 'tissuping' call. The regularity with which the birds follow the same flight path for lap after lap made them a simple target, but breeding season shooting is now banned in most countries. Woodcock are also unusual in carrying their young, one at a time, tucked between their legs.

The highly cryptic snipe are one of the most widespread groups of birds. The Common Snipe *Gallinago gallinago* breeds right around the Northern Hemisphere with outpost populations in South America and Africa. Like the other snipe it has an unusual tail that is not only used as a 'musical instrument', but also has an unusual number of feathers. The Pintail Snipe *G. stenura* of Siberia has no less than twenty-six feathers in its tail.

The New Zealand Snipe *Coenocorypha aucklandica* has developed a number of island subspecies. It has the habit of nesting in burrows created by other birds – an unusual practice for a wader.

The 'shanks' and their allies belong to the *Tringa* and other closely related genera. All are long-legged waders often with names that refer to their leg colour. By and large they prefer fresh marshes, although several species gather in large numbers on estuaries. The largest is the Greater Yellowlegs *Tringa melanoleuca* of North America. Like the other 'shanks' it is more often found in small flocks than in the huge packs of some of the *Calidris* sandpipers. The Greenshank *Tringa nebularia* is more or less a Palaearctic equivalent. Like the Yellowlegs, its feet trail behind the tail in flight. It is a long-distance migrant moving from northern Europe and Siberia, where it nests among the marshes of the northern forests, to Africa south of the Sahara.

Redshank *T. totanus* are the odd ones out in the genus. They are frequently found on the open shore and sometimes gather in large flocks. Their strident alarm calls are the earliest signal of danger to the birds of the estuary and a great annoyance to the approaching birdwatcher. They nest in a variety of situations and frequently perch on fence posts during the breeding season. The high-flying display flight, performed by as many as forty birds together, clearly

Right Essentially terrestrial birds, many waders, however, have the habit of perching on posts and even the tops of trees during the breeding season. They invariably call alarms or utter their piping territorial songs like this Redshank.

Below The boldly broken plumage pattern of the Ruddy Turnstone is an effective camouflage against the rocks and lichens of the North American tundra where it nests. Outside the breeding season it haunts rocky shores in small flocks.

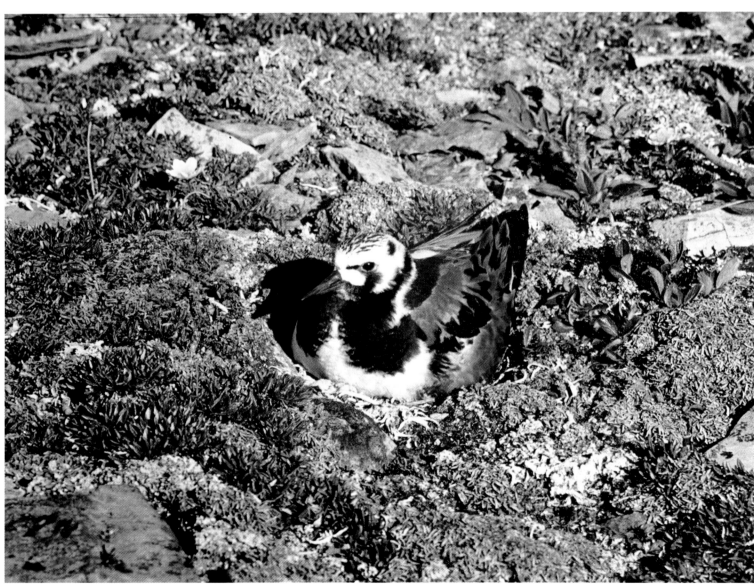

shows the large, white trailing edges of the wings.

The Eurasian Common Sandpiper *T. hypoleucos* and the Spotted Sandpiper *T. macularia* of North America are often thought to be conspecific, although in breeding dress they are quite distinctive. Both frequent rivers and both have a pronounced bobbing motion of the body.

The Wandering Tattler *Heteroscelus brevipes*, often called the Grey-rumped Sandpiper, is the best-known of a group of Polynesian sandpipers. It breeds in Siberia and winters in Australia. The Polynesian Tattler, *H. incanus* migrates to Hawaii and the islands of Polynesia, but two species have become extinct on these islands while Peale's Sandpiper *Aechmorhynchus parvirostris* is found only on the tiny islands of the Paumotos.

The sandpipers of the *Calidris* group are shorebirds. They are small, highly active birds found in huge flocks along the shore and on estuaries. Most of them are confusing and a group of Nearctic species is collectively known as 'peeps'. Most of these birds breed in the north and perform long migrations. They are widespread on migration and the Knot and Dunlin form the largest flocks of all waders. The Least Sandpiper *C. minutilla* of the Nearctic and the Palaearctic Temminck's Stint *C. temminckii* are the smallest of all sandpipers, being little more than 5 inches in length. Like other Arctic breeding species they are often exceptionally tame and allow a close approach. Sanderling are almost pure grey and white in

Numerous and widespread though it is, the Bar-tailed Godwit breeds so high in the Arctic that nests are seldom found outside the Soviet Union and Alaska. This bird was photographed in northern Scandinavia.

winter and are the most active of all the sandpipers. They feed on sandy shores at the very edge of the water which they follow up and down the beach with the waves. Their consumption of energy must be enormous. The Spoon-billed Sandpiper *Eurynorhynchus pygmeus* of far-eastern Siberia shows a unique feeding adaptation in its large, spatulate bill. The turnstones, in contrast, have a highly adapted feeding behaviour and a rugged frame to enable them to turn over stones along the shore. The Common Turnstone *Arenaria interpres*, the Ruddy Turnstone of North America, is one of the most widespread birds being found from Australia to Britain in both directions round the world.

The dowitchers breed in Arctic North America extending westwards into Siberia. They bear a strong resemblance to snipe in shape, but lack the cryptic striping of those birds. This Long-billed Dowitcher was photographed off range in Britain.

Godwits, and their Nearctic equivalents the dowitchers, are among the largest of the sandpipers. They are tall, elegant birds with long legs and long, straight, sometimes upturned, bills. In summer they adopt a red plumage, while winter sees them grey, brown and rather drab. In general they prefer the open shore where they form closely knit flocks, usually quite separate from other species. The Black-tailed Godwit *Limosa limosa* breeds in the boreal zone of Eurasia and has recently recolonized England. It is a bird of supreme elegance and great beauty. Its North American equivalent is the Hudsonian Godwit *L. haemastica*.

The two species of dowitcher, the Short-billed *Limnodromus griseus* and the Long-billed *L. scolopaceus*, were distinguished only in the 1950s and present as difficult a field identification problem as any. They are quite unique in having a remarkable division of labour in which the female incubates the eggs and the male cares for the young.

Avocets and stilts Recurvirostridae

Seven species comprise the Recurvirostridae, a group of large, long-legged, boldly patterned waders that form part of the great order of Charadriiformes which includes the waders, gulls, terns and auks. There are few bird families that are as cosmopolitan as the avocets and stilts, and there is hardly a significant area of the world where one or more of these birds is not found.

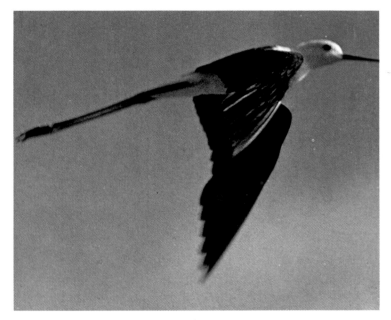

Dominant among the group are the avocets of the genus *Recurvirostra*, large, black and white birds with delicate upturned, awl-like bills. Like the rest of the family, there is little or no difference in plumage between the sexes. The Avocet *R. avosetta* is a pure piebald with long, grey legs and a dark bill. It is found in Europe and across the rest of the Palaearctic region as far east as China. In the north it extends as far as the Baltic but is rather more common in the Mediterranean. Like the other avocets it is a saline-loving bird and feeds on saltmarshes and estuaries in the north, and in similar areas as well as saltpans in the southern part of its range, which extends into Iraq and Baluchistan.

Extinct as breeding birds in Britain for nearly 100 years, Avocets returned to breed in Suffolk in eastern England in 1947, and are now well established at two sites where they can be watched from the comfort of hides provided by the Royal Society for the Protection of Birds. Avocets are exceptionally common in Holland and almost the total population of western Europe gathers on the great mudflats of the Dutch and German Waddensee in autumn. The 10,000 birds then move southwards to winter on the great estuary of the Tagus in Portugal, although a few spend the winter in south-western England and in western France.

Left The long, pink legs of the Black-winged Stilt trail out behind it in flight, but enable it to feed in deeper water than most other waders. The species is found on every significant land mass in the world.

Below The delicate, black and white Avocet has long legs that enable it to wade among the shallow lagoons that it favours. The fine, upturned bill is used to sift food from the muddy bottom with a side to side scything motion.

The American Avocet *R. americana* resembles the European bird but sports a cinnamon wash over the head and neck during the breeding season. It is similar in habitat to the European bird and is found west of the Mississippi north to southern Canada, migrating to central America in winter. The two other avocets are similar in plumage to the American species, having reddish suffusions of varying densities over the head and neck. *R. andina*, as its name implies, is found in the Andes and has been graced with the vernacular name of Chilean Avocet. It is most at home on the high altitude lakes that are such a feature of those mountains, and which also provide a home for several species of flamingo. The Chilean Avocet is generally darker than the other species. The Red-necked Avocet *R. novaehollandiae* has an almost rust red head and neck. It is confined to Australia but has managed to appear occasionally in New Zealand.

Avocets wade easily and gracefully and will swim quite readily. They are typically found in shallow water where they sift small organisms from the surface of the mud with a distinctive scything action of their heads and bills. Avocets invariably nest in colonies laying their four eggs (sometimes as few as two or as many as eight) in a simple, bare, sandy scrape or a perfunctorily lined hollow. This is usually only a few inches above water level and a sudden rise can lead to disaster. Nests may be as close as a couple of feet but are usually further apart. Both sexes share in the incubation of the typically wader-shaped and coloured eggs which hatch after twenty-two to twenty-five days. The chicks immediately fend for themselves although the adults tend and protect them from marauding gulls for some ten weeks. Avocets are particularly vociferous in defence of their colonies, 'yelping' loudly at intruders.

The other members of the family all belong to monotypic genera, although the Stilt *Himantopus himantopus* has a number of distinct subspecies and geographical forms. It is also the most widespread member of the family and has the distinction of having the longest legs of any bird in proportion to its body length, apart from the various species of flamingo.

Like the Avocet, the Stilt is a black and white bird with, in this case, a less piebald effect. Its bill is short and fine and ideally adapted to picking food from the surface of water as it wades on its long, pink legs. These trail behind distinctively in flight. Again, like the Avocet, it usually breeds colonially: on the only occasion in ornithological history that the Stilt bred in Britain, two pairs turned up on an obscure sewage farm. When sitting on its eggs the Stilt has a considerable legroom problem that it solves by folding them back on themselves behind it. In Europe the subspecies is called the Black-winged Stilt, in North America the Black-necked Stilt. In New Zealand there is an all-black form (the tendency for all-black birds in those islands is curious) that consists of melanistic mutants. Intermediate forms are also found and these birds are generally considered to be the same as those found in Australia where they are called Pied Stilts.

Also confined to Australia is the Banded Stilt *Cladorhynchus leucocephala* which is found in various parts of southern Australia and sports a rust red breast band in the adult. Otherwise it is similar to the *Himantopus* stilts except perhaps that it is even more colonial. It nests on temporary floods in the interior, sometimes in huge numbers, and feeds on the freshwater shrimps that abound in the ponds.

The odd one out in this family is the Ibisbill *Ibidorhyncha struthersii*. It breeds only in the mountains of the Himalayas and their subsidiaries. It is a grey-brown bird with a black breast band and black face, and with a prominently down-curved bill. Like an ibis, in flight it looks longer in front than behind, and its rounded wings with their white patches are prominent. The Ibisbill is found in small groups along fast-flowing, glacier-fed streams. It frequently ducks beneath the water as it feeds by probing its bill round and beneath boulders. A few birds migrate to lower levels in winter.

Phalaropes Phalaropodidae

The three species of phalaropes form one of the most interesting and attractive of bird families. They are miniature sandpipers that have adapted to an aquatic life style and spend much of their time swimming. This adaptation is longstanding and the family is now quite separate from the other members of the Charadriiformes.

Indeed, each of the species is itself quite distinct from the others and placed in a separate genus by all leading systematists.

Wilson's Phalarope *Steganopus tricolor* is the largest of the three and found only in the Americas. The Grey Phalarope (called the Red Phalarope in North America) *Phalaropus fulicarius* is intermediate in size between Wilson's and the Red-necked Phalarope (called the Northern Phalarope in America) *Lobipes lobatus*. This apparent absurdity in vernacular names is due, in part at least, to *Phalaropus* being red on its North American breeding grounds, but grey in autumn when it reaches Europe. Nevertheless there is a good case, as elsewhere, for standardizing names.

Phalaropes, looking for all the world like peeps or stints, swim buoyantly on the duck-like plumage of their bellies. In effect, they virtually sit atop the water rather than in it and, like corks, they bob up and down over the waves. Their feet have become semi-webbed and their legs laterally flattened to speed them through the water. Like moorhens they have the engaging habit of bobbing their heads backwards and forwards as they swim. The Red-necked Phalaropes and Grey Phalaropes have so adapted themselves to an aquatic existence that only seldom do they set foot ashore outside the breeding season. At other times they resort to the sea and live a mariner's life out on the open oceans.

All phalaropes are highly migratory, Wilson's moving southwards to South America where it feeds like a wader at marshy pools and lagoons, while the two pelagic phalaropes winter at several richly

The misleadingly named Grey Phalarope is, in fact, rust red in summer and grey only in autumn when it visits Europe. In North America it is called the Red Phalarope with more justification.

The male Red-necked Phalarope (Northern Phalarope in North America) takes full charge of incubation and care of the young while his mate cavorts with other males and produces more clutches of eggs. As in the other phalaropes, the female is the more brightly coloured of the pair.

endowed areas of cold upwelling, as off the western coasts of South America and South-west Africa. They arrive by an oceanic route that keeps them well clear of the coasts, and share their winter quarters with other great concentrations of seabirds. The Red-necked Phalarope also winters in the northern Indian Ocean and apparently reaches this area by an extended overland migration from Siberia via the Caspian Sea.

For most birdwatchers phalaropes are to be seen only on their breeding grounds or occasionally in autumn when bad weather, and particularly Atlantic gales, cast them ashore in large numbers. At such times they may appear anywhere. Like storm petrels they are too small to sit out a gale and have to run before the weather in their search for a lee shore. Grey Phalaropes breed in Iceland but are so frequently seen off the west coasts of Europe that many Greenland and Canadian birds must pass offshore en route to West Africa. Wilson's Phalaropes are confined to the New World but have occurred with increasing regularity in autumn in the British Isles. No doubt they were previously overlooked.

Phalaropes have an unusual love life. The females are gaudier than the males, in fact they are the most brightly coloured of all the plovers and sandpipers – generally a dull group of birds. They arrive first on the Arctic breeding grounds in June, and stake out their territories. They take the initiative in courtship but little or no part in incubation and care of the young. They are often apparently promiscuous and in many areas leave the vicinity of the nesting grounds once they have laid their eggs.

The nest and four eggs closely resemble those of the sandpipers and the chicks are active at birth. Phalaropes are territorial but also loosely colonial and at the end of the breeding season vast numbers of these little birds gather at suitable bays and inlets in the tundra. All three species feed by picking food from the surface of water, although on occasion they up-end like ducks. Wilson's Phalarope is the only species that also regularly feeds by wading. Phalaropes pirouette, spinning round and round, in their efforts to disturb food and, judged by their persistence, this method is apparently highly successful. On their breeding grounds all are highly confiding little birds and show no fear of man. There are instances of males returning to incubate eggs nestled in a human hand and of them swimming between a photographer's legs. The species are easily identified in summer but are separated at sea in winter only with great care.

Crab-plover Dromadidae

The Crab-plover *Dromas ardeola* is the sole member of its family. Current opinion tends towards thinking that this medium-sized, black and white wader is most closely related to the stone curlews and thick-knees, but for the moment at least it is placed in a family of its own. Its overall shape and structure certainly bear a similarity to several members of the Burhinidae, most notably the Indian Stone-plover, but it also has several other features that make it unique.

It is a fine-looking bird some 15 inches in length and boldly patterned black and white like an Avocet. In flight this pattern is quite distinctive and, indeed, there should be no difficulty in identifying a Crab-plover. Quite characteristic is the large, black bill which bears a strong resemblance to that of a gull with a pronounced gonys, and sharp, dagger-like point. The long, strong legs are similar to those of the thick-knees and are slate grey.

The Crab-plover is a coastal species restricted to the northern and western shores of the Indian Ocean. It is found as far south as Madagascar, but it does not breed beyond Mombasa. It feeds on molluscs and crabs which it breaks into with hammer-like stabs of its powerful bill. Outside the breeding season it forms noisy flocks and, although generally said to be far from shy, it is difficult enough to approach within photographic range – so much so that really good photographic portraits do not exist. In suitable habitats it forms quite large flocks.

The nesting habits of the Crab-plover are also aberrant for a member of the Charadriiformes. Like few other species these birds nest underground, but unlike the others they have adopted the white egg that is usual in other hole-nesting species. The single egg is laid in a chamber at the end of a four foot-long tunnel.

The Crab-plover is colonial and although the young chick is able to run about like other members of the order, it nevertheless remains inside the burrow and is fed by both parents.

Found only along the shores of the Indian Ocean, these Crab Plovers were photographed at Kenya's Mida Creek, one of their regular non-breeding haunts.

Thick-knees Burhinidae

Thick-knees, stone-runners, stone curlews, plus a hundred other colloquial names, have been lavished upon the nine species that comprise the Burhinidae. They are large birds from 14 to 20 inches long and are found throughout the world except in North America and New Zealand. They remain a comparatively little-known family, however, for they are crepuscular and retiring by nature. The countryman usually knows them well enough, thus the wealth of nicknames, but over most of their range there is little guarantee of being able to find them in a particular area.

The thick-knees are closely related to the plovers and sandpipers, but bear a strong resemblance to the bustards, and share a number of habits and features with these birds. They have long, strong legs with well-developed toes for running. The joint of the tarsus and the shin (which is really the ankle since birds stand on their toes) is thickened and prominent and gives rise to the vernacular name, although perhaps 'thick-ankle' would be more accurate. The plumage is buff streaked with blacks and browns and the head is

Opposite A Stone Curlew sits on its nest with its mate and a newly hatched chick behind. Dependent on open, sandy or grassland areas with plenty of bare soil, the species is suffering a considerable decline as marginal land is put under the plough.

invariably marked with bold stripes. The bill is about the same length as the head in most species, but in some is thickened and longer. The wings are long and angled in flight and there is often a wing bar. The yellow eye is large in proportion to the bird and is an adaptation to a nocturnal mode of life.

Thick-knees are well-camouflaged birds, most active at dawn and dusk and spend much of the day hidden on the ground. They will allow a very close approach and fly only when they are almost stepped upon. Their far-carrying, wailing cries at dusk are responsible for a great many ghost stories – almost as many as those attributed to Barn Owls and nightjars.

Two, occasionally three, eggs are laid on the bare ground where their cryptic coloration enables them to merge effectively with the background of bare, sandy soil often broken by stones. Both members of the pair share the incubation which takes twenty-five to twenty-eight days. The chicks are covered with greyish buff, streaked down and crouch prone, necks stretched along the ground, when the parents give the alarm. They leave the nest almost immediately and fend for themselves straight away. The Water Dikkop *Burhinus vermiculatus* of Africa nests along the shoreline

and wherever possible among crocodiles. No-one knows why it should choose such unsavoury neighbours, but the species also has a penchant for laying its eggs on the droppings of Elephant and Hippopotamus.

Most other thick-knees prefer dry, sandy wastes where they feed on insects, beetles, lizards and vegetable matter. They run in the manner of plovers with short bursts broken by statue-like stillnesses. They will flatten themselves to avoid detection, but often incubate in an upright position and rest on their tarsi like Marabou Storks.

Of all the thick-knees, only the Stone Curlew *B. oedicnemus* is migratory. It is found across Europe and North Africa through the Middle East to India, and is a summer visitor to the more northern parts of its range. In Britain its decline has been blamed on the ploughing of much marginal land, particularly downland, and on the afforestation of other areas formerly regarded as wasteland. As a result, it has taken to arable land and there it loses successive clutches to agricultural activities. It is now rare. Its migratory habits result in it being the only species that forms flocks; up to 100 birds are found together in autumn parties prior to migration.

Coursers and pratincoles Glareolidae

This small group of wader-type birds can be conveniently divided into two quite distinct groups: the nine coursers including the Egyptian Plover *Pluvianus aegyptius*, and the seven pratincoles. Both groups are long-winged, fast-flying birds that clearly belong to the Charadriiformes.

The coursers are long-legged, running birds of the arid, semidesert zone. They are confined to the Old World, with a centre of origin clearly in Africa where seven species are found. A single courser, misleadingly called the Australian Dotterel *Peltohyas australis*, is found in that continent, and another, the Indian Courser *Cursorius coromandelicus*, in India. A further Indian species, Jerdon's or Double-banded Courser *Rhinoptilus bitorquatus*, has not been seen in India since 1900 despite searches by ornithologists, and

Below The strange Egyptian Plover is a close relative of the pratincoles and coursers and, like them, shows a preference for the dry, arid areas of Africa. It frequents the sandbanks of rivers and runs about actively in pursuit of insects.

Right A Temminck's Courser settles on its two eggs laid on open ground with not so much as a pretence of a nest. It is an inhabitant of Africa's arid savannahs.

is now regarded as extinct. It should not be confused with the Double-banded Courser of Africa *R. africanus*.

Coursers are creamy, sandy coloured birds that merge well with the wastes where they live, and avoid danger by running rather than by flight. Their rounded, plover-like heads are marked with eye-stripes and the bill is thin, tapering and slightly down-curved. As with other running birds the hind toe has been lost. Most species lay two or three well-camouflaged eggs, although the African

A Collared Pratincole pauses from migration beside a drying out waterhole. Although related to the waders, pratincoles fly like terns and feed by pouncing like a thrush.

Double-banded Courser lays only one. Desert country experiences some of the most dramatic changes of diurnal temperature, and while it can be scalding hot during the day, the nights can be exceptionally cold. Thus the problem of incubation is one of maintaining a reasonable temperature and avoiding extremes. The coursers thus sit tight at night, but often stand above their eggs to shield them from the heat of the sun during the day. When they are disturbed coursers will tiptoe away with shoulders hunched.

The Cream-coloured Courser *Cursorius cursor* is a familiar bird of the Sahara edge that has extended its range into the Middle East. Nowhere a regular migrant, its nomadic flights have nevertheless taken it all over Europe, although it breeds no nearer than North Africa. It is distinguished by the pale blue area bordering the crown. Temminck's Courser *C. temminckii* is a bird of Africa south of the Sahara. It is considerably smaller than the Cream-coloured Courser and has a chestnut crown and a dark breast patch.

Pratincoles are tern-like: they have the long wings and buoyant flight of those birds, but look less uncomfortable on the ground.

They are buff brown in colour, 7 to 9 inches long (although their long wings make them seem larger in the air), and they merge well with the bare ground that they favour. The seven species range from Africa and Europe to Australia and most are migratory.

Pratincoles are gregarious, migrating in noisy flocks and forming scattered colonies on low lying sandbanks or islands. They usually manage to breed at the end of the rainy season when freshly emerged sandbanks are their favourite sites. They sometimes make mistakes with their timing and colonies are washed out. The two or three eggs are cryptically coloured and incubation is shared by the pair. Like terns, disturbed pratincoles will fly overhead noisily. The down-covered chicks are active on hatching.

The species migrate through Europe. The Collared Pratincole *Glareola pratincola* comes to Europe to breed while the Black-winged Pratincole *G. nordmanni* passes through eastern Europe on its way to breeding grounds further east. It has black, not chestnut, underwing patches, but may well be a simple subspecies of *pratincola*.

The Little Indian Pratincole is a pale, sandy, undistinguished bird that nests along the rivers that run down from the Himalayas. A strangely aberrant species, the Australian Pratincole *Stiltia isabella*, has long legs like a courser, but the long wings of a pratincole. Nevertheless, it lives in the manner of a pratincole.

Seed-snipe Thinocoridae

Seed-snipe look like finches and are closely related to the waders and other members of the Charadriiformes—facts which fit in very well with their name, for they live on seeds and fly like snipe. They are purely South American, being found throughout the region of the Andes, through southern Patagonia, Tierra del Fuego and the Falkland Islands. Four distinct species are divided into two genera varying in size from that of a lapwing to a small plover. They are plump, ground-dwelling birds, with short legs and a rather long

A White-bellied Seedsnipe among the grasslands of Patagonia. Despite their superficial resemblance to small game birds and their finch-like bills, these birds are most closely related to the waders.

neck and dove-like head. The short bill is typically conical as in other seed-eaters. They are well-camouflaged and prefer to run from danger and crouch on the ground rather than fly. They spend much of their time in flocks, like the Snow Buntings of the north, but unlike Snow Buntings, fly fast and direct.

Seed-snipe are bare-ground birds being found from the high tundra-like edges of the snowline to the desolate shores of the sub-Antarctic seas. The four plover-like eggs are laid on the ground. In the White-bellied Seed-snipe *Attagis malouinus* these are green with darker markings to match the background of its moss-covered habitat, but the three other species have buff coloured eggs with dark markings to merge with the dry ground that they prefer. So well do the White-bellied Seed-snipes' eggs match their background and so remote is their range that the first nest was discovered only in 1959. The better known Pygmy Seed-snipe *Thinocorus rumicivorus* has the habit of burying its eggs when it leaves its nest.

Sheathbills Chionididae

Sheathbills are medium-sized, all-white, grouse-like birds that inhabit the Antarctic continent and various sub-Antarctic islands. They are squat, dumpy birds with thick, powerful bills and a comb-like sheath covering the upper base that shields the nostrils and gives them their name. The wings are short, but marked with carpel spurs like several members of the plover family.

Sheathbills are members of the Charadriiformes and are regarded as a link between the gulls and the waders, the dominant members of that order. They probably most closely resemble the ancestral form of both groups.

Sheathbills are terrestrial birds and the only Antarctic birds with unwebbed feet. Their plumage is entirely white and the strong legs are blue-grey. The cheeks are wattled and yellowish in colour. Sheathbills are the most voracious scavengers of the Antarctic. They are in constant attendance at all penguin colonies and seal rookeries, not only looking for the afterbirths and dead youngsters but also for the off-chance of a poorly chick, misplaced feed, or any other source of food they can snap up. To increase their chances at penguin colonies they are a constant nuisance to adults trying to feed their chicks. Apart from scavenging and piracy they feed on the animals that live or are cast up along the Antarctic shores and for which they hunt with their short but powerful bills. Sheathbills prefer to escape danger by running rather than flying, although they have been seen hundreds of miles from land. They frequent Antarctic bases and regularly raid the rubbish dumps along with Antarctic Skuas. Whaling stations naturally attract large numbers.

Sheathbills are solitary breeders creating a nesting crevice among

The sheathbills are the natural scavengers of the Antarctic. These Yellow-billed Sheathbills breed on the coastal islands of the South Shetlands, Orkneys and Sandwich Islands and migrate northwards to the Falklands and adjacent coasts of South America to winter.

a tangle of boulders where the two, sometimes three, large, pale brown eggs are laid. Incubation, which is shared, lasts twenty-eight days. Usually only a single chick is reared.

Two species of sheathbill are recognized. The Yellow-billed Sheathbill *Chionis alba* is found in the southern Atlantic, whereas the Black-billed Sheathbill *C. minor* breeds on Kerguelen and Prince Edward Islands, and the Crozets.

Skuas Stercorariidae

Skuas are the pirates of the high seas and open oceans. The name itself probably comes from the birds' distinctive cry, although in America three of the four species are referred to as jaegers which ultimately derives from the Norse word *jaga* meaning to hunt. All

four species are pelagic and all find a considerable proportion of their food by pursuing other seabirds and robbing them in flight.

Skuas are gull-like birds varying in size from the small Long-tailed Skua *Stercorarius longicaudus*, which measures some 14 inches without the tail, to the 23 inch long Great Skua *Catharacta skua*. They are long-winged, brown birds that bear a superficial resemblance to medium-sized immature gulls. All have wedge-shaped tails with central tail feathers that extend to a greater or lesser extent behind them, but which are frequently broken or missing. They show a variable white flash in the wing and a dark hood in the pale phase.

Great Skuas are always dark, but the other three are either light or dark phased. Dark phased birds are an almost uniform greyish brown in colour with the white wing flash, while pale phase birds have greyish brown wings, are white below with a dark cap and a variable amount of yellow on the lores. Above all it is their flight that most readily identifies skuas. The wings are long and sharply angled, and cut scythe-like through the air when chasing some poor tern, itself no mean flier. Skuas are expert chasers, but even when migrating along the coast their flight has a characteristic purposeful

quality that is not seen in the flight of gulls.

The Great Skua, called the Bonxie in its Shetland base, has an unusual range. It breeds in the North Atlantic where it very nearly became extinct and was saved only by rigorous protection on the island of Unst in Shetland. It has now spread to several other eastern Atlantic islands. Another population is found thousands of miles away in the Southern Hemisphere on a circle of islands surrounding the Antarctic continent. Several distinct subspecies have been recognized there.

Great Skuas frequently follow ships and their diet varies from waste thrown overboard to the offal of the whaling fleets. They pursue other seabirds until they drop or disgorge their catch, and are adept at diving to catch their bounty in mid-air before it has

These Antarctic Great (sometimes called Brown) Skuas are displaying on their breeding grounds. One has been colour-ringed on both legs to ensure its recognition at a distance without recourse to trapping.

time to fall into the sea. In the north, Great Skuas breed on open marshlands and rob nearby seabirds of their eggs and young. They also take petrels when they can find them.

In the south, they are particularly numerous around penguin colonies, a large rookery of which will support a fair-sized population of skuas. Skuas are not in the strict sense colonial, but they tend to nest together over a favoured hillside where each defends its nest site and small territory. An advertising display consists of a raucous call with the wings thrown back.

The two eggs are laid in a hollow on top of a small knoll from which the sitting bird can see for a considerable distance. The non-incubating bird frequently stands on guard alongside its mate. Usually only a single chick is reared from the two eggs. The pair will remain faithful to the same nest site year after year. Some northern birds cross the equator in winter, but there is no evidence of the two populations mixing.

Pirates of the high seas, Arctic Skuas nest on open ground north of the tree line where they continue their predations on birds while adding small mammals like Lemmings to their diet.

The largest of the three other skuas is the Pomarine Skua *Stercorarius pomarinus*. Like the other skuas, it is marked by elongated central tail feathers, which in this case are thick and twisted giving the bird a curiously attenuated shape, rather like a frigatebird. Its heavy body is a good identification feature when the central feathers are absent. Again, like the other skuas, it has a circumpolar breeding distribution and nests on the open tundra of Siberia and North America. It is absent from Scandinavia. As with the Long-tailed Skua, it is dependent on the population of Lemmings during the summer. In a good Lemming year it will raise more young, and in a poor Lemming year will not bother to breed at all. The birds from western Siberia, at least, migrate directly out to sea between Iceland and the Faeroe Islands to winter off the coast of West Africa.

Up to a third of the length of the Long-tailed Skua consists of the two central tail feathers. The birds are light, airy fliers and breed further north than their relatives. Dark phase birds are now exceptionally rare, a fact which simplifies identification. On its breeding grounds the Long-tailed Skua is fearless in defence of its nest and will dive-bomb and sometimes even perch defiantly on

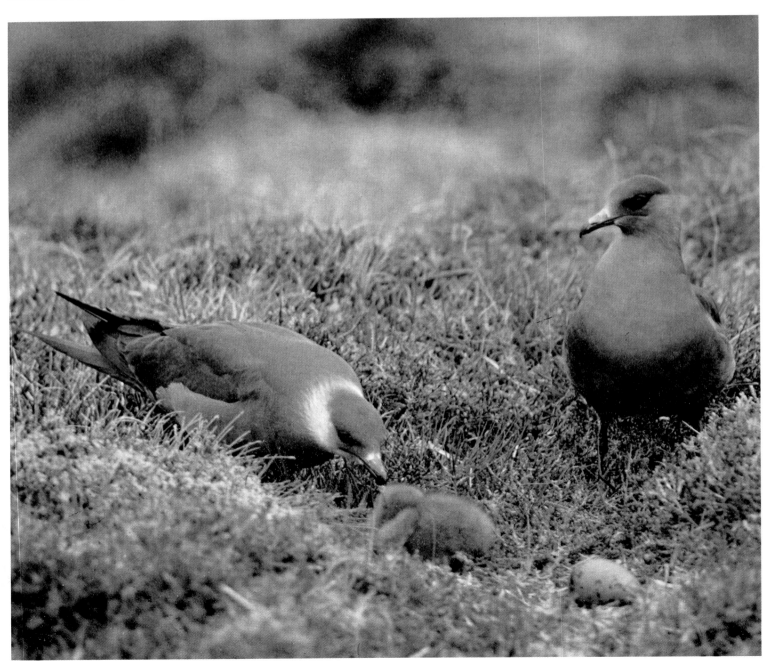

intruders who have approached too close to its nest.

The Arctic Skua *S. parasiticus* is the most common skua in European waters and also the best known. It breeds around the world in the tundra zone, extending southwards to Britain in the Atlantic. It is a vigorous tern chaser and marked by two extended central feathers projecting three to four inches beyond the tail. In the south of its range most individuals are dark phase, while in the extreme north almost all are pale. The two interbreed quite freely. Arctic Skuas, like the terns they pursue, are long-distance migrants and a large population winters off the coast of southern Brazil.

Gulls and terns Laridae

The Laridae are divided into two quite distinct groups of predominantly white or light grey seabirds. The terns are buoyant fliers with long, pointed wings and forked tails. Many are long-distance migrants and most have long, pointed bills which are used for fishing or picking food from the surface of the water. Despite their webbed feet they are not good swimmers.

The gulls, in contrast, are generally larger birds with a heavy bill and body and long, but more rounded, wings. They are the best known of all seabirds, although most of the forty or so species seldom venture far from the coast. They are common and noisy around harbours, and because of their outstanding ability to adapt to new food sources, have prospered and spread inland in many areas.

No doubt gulls started as beachcombers. They are adept at hawking along the coasts and picking up whatever scraps of food the sea casts up. With the advent of organized fishing, however, fish scraps and refuse soon became a major source of food. Sewage outfalls provided another new food supply and rubbish tips drew birds inland. The provision of large areas of water for drinking supplies adjacent to every large city offered the gulls a safe roost from which to explore the full potential of city life and its food supplies. No gull has taken advantage of this new mode of life as fully as the Black-headed Gull *Larus ridibundus*. Well accustomed to life inland, it breeds among other places in the very heart of eastern Europe (as far as one can get from the sea). Black-headed Gulls formerly wintered around the coasts of the North Sea. A hundred

Gregarious at all times, Black-headed Gulls nest colonially in marshes and bogs. There is little harmony in the colony and bickering continues throughout the season.

years ago they arrived in London and have been there ever since. Now they are almost as cheeky as House Sparrows in coming to the hand to feed in city parks and open spaces. Other gulls have followed their lead.

Most gulls, irrespective of where they breed, have remained coastal, but they are also opportunists and their increasing populations have brought them into conflict with people as varied as airport controllers, waterboard officials and conservationists. Even bird protectionists have found the increase of these species a great danger to other less successful birds, on the eggs and young of which they prey during the summer months. Fireworks and falcons have been used to clear them from runways and reservoirs, but conservationists have found that only nest destruction will actually reduce their numbers and the damage they do to other wild birds.

Gulls are medium to large birds that fly effortlessly, often soaring in the manner of raptors or following ships on bowed, gliding wings. Their feet are webbed and they swim buoyantly on the top of the water. Their bills are large and powerful, and in some species almost hooked like a raptor's. They are gregarious throughout the year, breeding in colonies on cliffs, isolated moorlands and, most recently, on the roofs of factories. In winter large numbers gather at rich feeding grounds and truly staggering concentrations will flight up to twenty miles to a safe communal roost. Some coastal roosts hold over 100,000 birds.

The nest is usually a tangle of grasses and the two or three eggs are cryptically blotched browns and olives. In some areas they are sold as 'plover's' eggs. The young are nidifugous but they usually remain at the nest until they fledge.

Two gulls, the Kittiwake *Rissa tridactylus* and Sabine's Gull *Xema sabini*, are the only species regularly seen in the middle of oceans, although only the former is truly a pelagic species and finds the majority of its food from the ocean. Even the Kittiwake, however, seems to have increased, and has now taken to breeding on man-made structures like warehouses and the ends of piers.

Gulls can be divided roughly into two general groups: the hooded gulls and the non-hooded gulls. The Black-headed Gull is an example of the hooded type. In summer it adopts a chocolate coloured cap that covers its face and of which only a vestigial spot behind the eye remains in winter. Other hooded species have black and grey hoods of varying extent. The unhooded species include the wide-ranging Herring Gull *Larus argentatus* and its allies. These are generally larger birds with more powerful bills and stronger heads and necks. They are more marine than hooded birds.

The Herring Gull and the Lesser Black-backed Gull *L. fuscus* of Europe form a ring species. They are quite distinct in Europe where they overlap, but between them they encircle the globe. As one progresses eastwards, the various subspecies intergrade, gradually becoming lighter, until arriving back in Europe the Lesser Black-backed Gull has become the Herring Gull. No doubt in Europe they are separate species for although they nest alongside each other they seldom interbreed. At other points around the world, however, they are simply subspecies of one and the same bird. While the Herring Gull remains largely resident, the Lesser Black-backed Gull is a considerable migrant moving southwards out of Europe to the coasts of tropical Africa.

Several other unhooded gulls enjoy a circumpolar distribution. The large, virtually white, Glaucous Gull *L. hyperboreus* is the terror of the Arctic seabird colonies in summer with a particular predilection for Little Auks. Its all-white primaries – most other large *Larus* gulls have black wing tips marked with white mirrors – give it a distinctive appearance that is shared only by the similar

Top One of the few species of gulls of truly oceanic distribution, Kittiwakes build substantial nests on the smallest of cliff crevices.

Right A colony of Mediterranean Black-headed Gulls. These birds show to advantage the pure black hood, the white marks above and below the eye, and the lack of wing tip pattern.

but smaller Iceland Gull *L. glaucoides*. The latter does not in fact breed in Iceland but constructs its nest further north than most other birds along the coasts of Greenland and other Arctic islands. Two other extreme northern birds, the Ivory Gull *Pagophila eburneus* and Ross's Gull *Rhodostethia roseus*, are but rare vagrants out of their Arctic homes. The Ivory Gull breeds as far north as land extends and winters at the edge of the pack-ice itself. Its all-white plumage is an obvious adaptation to this environment, but it has a curious pigeon-like shape. Ross's Gull has a very strange breeding pattern. It breeds only along a few remote Siberian rivers and then migrates northwards to winter in the Arctic Ocean.

One of the largest of the gulls is the Great Black-backed Gull *Larus marinus*. It effectively replaces the Glaucous Gull to the south and is dependent for its summer survival on colonies of seabirds. Outside the breeding season it is more marine than most gulls. Its huge, heavy bill is a symbol of its murderous capabilities.

Like the Great Black-backed Gull, many gulls have distinctively coloured bills. The dominant pattern is yellow with a red spot and experiments have shown that this combination provokes most pecks from chicks of the species concerned and which, as a result, evokes food from the parents. The courtship and breeding behaviour of several of the colonial gulls has been well studied and has added significantly to our understanding of all animal behaviour.

The hooded gulls are generally smaller and more frequently breed inland. Franklin's Gull *L. pipixcan* breeds throughout the prairies of North America and migrates to winter along the Pacific coasts of Peru and the rich Humboldt Current. The graceful Grey-headed

Above Widely distributed on both sides of the Atlantic, the Herring Gull is a colonial breeder that prefers to nest on the flat tops of islands, although it also favours broken cliffs and even the roofs of factories.

Below Bearing a superficial resemblance to the widespread Great Black-backed Gull, the Pacific Gull boasts an even more massive and deeper bill. It is found along the shores of southern Australia and feeds on carrion, birds and eggs.

Gull *L. cirrocephalus* of the Rift Valley Lakes of East Africa is another essentially inland species. All of these gulls lose their hoods in winter. The Little Gull *L. minutus* at 10 inches is one of the smallest gulls. It is quite numerous in parts of eastern Europe and often associated with marsh terns whose feeding methods its own most resemble.

Several of these hooded gulls have shown a tendency to wander, and while Bonaparte's Gull *L. philadelphiae* and the Laughing Gull *L. atricilla* have appeared in Europe, there are many records of Black-headed Gulls along the eastern seaboard of the United States.

While the juveniles of many gulls, particularly the larger species,

Left The Grey Gull is one of the very few uniformly dark gulls. It is abundant along the Pacific coast of South America, but flies inland to breed in the seclusion of rock-strewn deserts where no single plant can manage to survive.

Below The attractive Swallow-tailed Gull is found only on the Galápagos Islands where its fine, grey plumage and confiding habits win the heart of scientists and tourists alike.

are various shades of brown and quite different from the adult plumage which they take four years to acquire, other species are brown as adults. The Lava Gull *L. fuliginosus* of the Galápagos is well-camouflaged against the background of volcanic debris. Another Galápagos gull, the Swallow-tailed Gull *L. furcatus*, is a quite beautifully marked bird with sooty coloured plumage and distinctive bill and eye markings. Like many other birds of those islands it is exceptionally tame.

Terns too are predominantly white in colour, although many have dark caps and a few have black or brown plumage. They are lighter fliers than gulls and although generally smaller, some species, notably the Caspian Tern *Hydroprogne caspia*, are as large as a Herring Gull. Terns have short legs and usually a prominently forked tail.

Most species nest on the ground where a simple scrape suffices

to hold the two or three eggs. Unlike the birds themselves, the eggs are cryptically coloured like those of many waders and other ground-nesting species. They are highly gregarious birds and, although they usually nest in quite sizeable colonies, a few species like the Sooty Tern *Sterna fuscata* of tropical seas gather at some colonies by the million. Such gatherings are among the most spectacular wildlife sights on earth. On the Dry Tortugas, the southernmost of the Florida Keys, Sooty Terns were virtually exterminated in the nineteenth century by the wholesale collection of eggs. Only under the most strict conservation measures has the colony returned to something like its former abundance. Sooty Terns lay a single egg, but on Ascension Island in the South Atlantic the birds breed every ten months. Despite being greatly decimated by persecution and particularly by cats and rats that have been introduced to the island, Sooty Terns manage to swamp predators by their very numbers. Few colonial birds show such a high degree of synchronized laying. One of the largest Sooty Tern colonies is on the island of Des Noefs, the southernmost of the Amirantes Islands which lie in the Indian Ocean south of the

Sooty Terns breed in dense colonies on isolated islands. In several parts of the world these colonies reach staggering proportions and are frequently harvested by regular visits from commercial egg collectors.

Above Long-distance migrants on their way along the coasts of southern England. Most are Common Terns, but the lower bird is a Roseate Tern distinguished by its finer, all-black bill.

Right The delightful and delicate Fairy Tern breeds on isolated islands throughout the tropics. The impression of a large eye is created by a patch of black feathers surrounding the true eye. The birds lay their eggs in forks of trees without recourse to nests.

Seychelles. Here, literally the whole island is covered with nesting birds. Over a quarter of a million eggs are taken every year apparently without effect on the colony.

Around many colonies of Sooty Terns a few hundred or even thousand noddies are sometimes difficult to spot. The Common Noddy *Anous stolidus* nests in bushes or low trees, but frequently has no choice but to lay on the bare earth. It is a chocolate brown bird with a white cap – almost the reverse of the usual tern pattern. The closely related Fairy Tern *Gygis alba* – not to be confused with the Australian species of the same name which is like a Little Tern *Sterna albifrons* – is one of the world's most beautiful birds. It is pure white with a black spot that includes the eye, making it look overlarge. It breeds only on islands among the tropical seas and lays its single egg on the branch of a tree. Of the typical terns, none are more widespread than the Arctic Tern *S. paradisaea* and Common Tern *S. hirundo*. The Arctic Tern replaces the Common Tern to the north, but the two are so similar that they are often referred to as 'commic' terns. The Arctic Tern is one of the greatest of all migrants. Birds from Greenland cross the Atlantic on a great circle route and pass along the coasts of Africa to winter among the pack-ice of the Antarctic. They thus enjoy more hours of daylight than any other creature on earth, and regularly cover 22,000 miles per annum on migration alone. Certainly they cover twice or perhaps three times as many miles as the average family car in a year. The fact that their life span is also twice as long adds to the sense of wonder.

Arctic Terns nest near the tide line on sandbanks and low islands, and along Arctic rivers. They are gregarious and given to fierce displays of anger at intruders. Their sharp, red bills are quite excellent daggers and can cause painful wounds to the scalps of the would-be tern watcher.

Above Scattered on islands throughout the tropics, the Brown Noddy is one of the most widespread of birds. Where trees are available the birds prefer to nest among the branches, but they also nest freely on the ground, as here.

Opposite Most graceful and elegant of all the terns, a Black Tern stands over its eggs and newly hatched chick. Found on both sides of the Atlantic these birds delicately pick their food from the surface of the water in flight.

Marsh terns build quite elaborate nests of floating debris anchored to aquatic vegetation. They are small, dark terns with almost square tails and a delicate, graceful flight that enables them to pick their food from the surface of water. In winter and during immaturity they are similar to the other terns – whitish with a dark cap.

Most widespread and numerous of the marsh terns is the Black Tern *Chlidonias niger* which breeds right across the United States

Above Royal Terns nest in dense colonies along the coast of Africa and on both sides of tropical North America. The family bond is unusually strong for a seabird and parents continue to feed their young for several months after fledging.

Right Sandwich Terns are temperamental birds. They nest closely packed together, but are erratic in their choice of nest sites and will abandon a traditional site overnight. The sudden 'dreads', in which the whole colony takes to the air, are a little-understood feature of their lives.

and throughout Europe and adjacent areas of Asia. Over the whole of this range it is a summer visitor and has recently returned to breed in Britain after an absence of 100 years. It usually builds a floating nest among swamps though sometimes it nests on solid ground. Ideal conditions are provided by a good deal of open water with plenty of aquatic vegetation. Black Terns can then find an abundant supply of aquatic insects and their larvae, as well as leeches, snails, tadpoles and frogs, all picked from the surface.

An aberrant member of the subfamily is the delicately marked Inca Tern *Larosterna inca* of the Pacific coast of South America. This graceful bird of slate grey plumage has a vivid red bill and legs, and a plume of white feathers growing over the eye. Unlike any other tern it breeds in burrows.

Skimmers Rynchopidae

Skimmers are the only birds that have the lower mandible longer than the upper, and have a quite unique method of fishing. Authorities have disagreed about the exact mechanics of their fishing technique, but basically it consists of a controlled flight over still water, trailing the extended lower mandible through the surface thus creating a line of light. Formerly it was thought that the birds simply closed their mandibles on a fish that happened in the way, but more careful observation has shown that the birds, having created the line of light, then return along the same path to pick up fish attracted to it.

An African Skimmer slices through the water with its extended lower mandible. This strange performance attracts fish to the line of light and the Skimmer then picks them from the water.

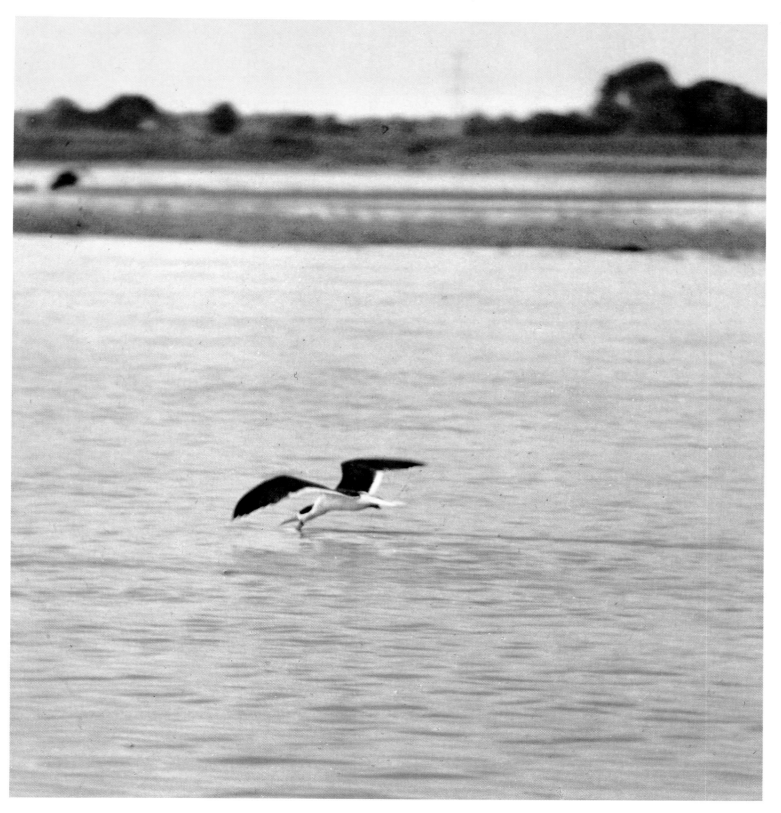

169

Built like a large tern, two of the species of skimmer are freshwater birds of tropical areas. The third American bird is essentially coastal. They replace each other geographically: the Black Skimmer *Rynchops nigra* of America being replaced by the African Skimmer *R. flavirostris* in that continent, and by the Indian Skimmer *R. albicollis*. The distinctions between the species are quite minor and irrelevant.

Skimmers are black above and white below, with red legs and a red base to an otherwise black bill. They are quite unmistakeable. They fly tern-like with purposeful beats of the wings and, as they plough their furrow along the surface of the water, the head is held still while the body moves to compensate. Like that of a cat, the pupil of the eye consists of a vertical slit that is quite unique among birds.

Skimmers gather on sandbanks along slow-moving rivers, sometimes in small flocks, sometimes by the thousand. Their hunting is so dependent on still water that floods will lead to a rapid disappearance of a resident flock. They tend to hunt at dawn and dusk and also during the night, when presumably the trail of light that they create across the surface is more obvious, and when their unique eye structure can be put to best use. Like terns, flocks of skimmers sometimes indulge in aerial manoeuvres when their cries, a shrill 'kek-kek-kek', form a loud accompaniment.

Skimmers nest in small colonies on the open sand of a river bank or confluence. A colony in Virginia, in the United States, consists of over 4,000 pairs and is far larger than any other known colonies. Colonies are generally exclusive, although some colonies include a mixture of other species that share the same habitat. Thus in India, colonies of *R. albicollis* frequently have a mixture of River Terns and Little Pratincoles.

The clutch consists of two to four eggs which are cryptically coloured and are incubated by both sexes, although the female takes the larger share. The chicks leave the nest immediately and can swim well. The mandibles are equal at birth but soon develop the adult pattern. They are then black with a narrow, pink base. Skimmers are generally confiding at their colonies, but are sometimes difficult to approach.

The Black Skimmer is found on the Atlantic coast of North America southwards along both coasts of South America. It is the largest of the three species. The African Skimmer is found throughout Africa, and the Indian Skimmer from India eastwards to Vietnam.

Auks Alcidae

The auks are the northern counterpart of the penguins of the Southern Hemisphere. They are medium-sized, black and white seabirds that adopt an upright posture on land, swim well, and propel themselves under water with their wings. They are colonial breeders and come to land only to nest. They are not related to the penguins; their nearest relatives are the gulls and waders of the great order Charadriiformes, whereas the penguins are closest to the albatrosses and petrels. All the living auks can fly and even the extinct and flightless Great Auk *Pinguinus impennis*, although it gave its name to the penguins, still retained vestigial flight feathers. This is a fine case of convergent evolution – two groups of birds occupying a similar niche although geographically isolated.

Auks have a circumpolar distribution, although nineteen of the extant species are found in the Bering Sea region between the Soviet Union and Alaska. Compared with this, the North Atlantic boasts a meagre total of six species.

Auks are birds of the temperate and northern seas and are seldom found further south. They feed over the continental shelf and are infrequently seen on the open oceans. Most dive for fish which they pursue by 'flying' under water. In this dense medium their strong, short wings carry them along at a good speed, whereas in the air the

Opposite left Seldom seen far from their chain of high Arctic breeding colonies, Little Auks may nevertheless be one of the most numerous of birds. Their single egg is laid in a rock crevice or burrow.

Opposite right Razorbills occupy the deeper crevices among rocks neglected by other cliff-dwelling auks. Like the Guillemot they are frequent victims of marine oil pollution and apparently in serious decline throughout their North Atlantic range.

Below Wings whirring vigorously, a Puffin comes in to land at its cliff top nesting site. The catastrophic decline of this formerly abundant little bird has been attributed to marine pollution of a variety of sources.

same wings seem to work overtime to keep the birds airborne at all.

Auks nest colonially, sometimes in huge numbers. The Little Auk *Plautus alle*, which nests only on the highest Arctic islands, breeds in colonies millions strong and is a contender for the title of the world's most numerous wild bird. Many species favour cliff ledges, yet others are happy with the flat tops of isolated stacks, with crevices in cliffs and among the boulders at the foot of cliffs. Others nest in burrows which they excavate for themselves in the soft soil of islands. The chicks of cliff-nesting species leave their ledges within two weeks of hatching, whereas burrow-nesting birds remain in the safety of their bunkers for up to two months. Cliff-nesting auks huddle together on their tiny ledges where the single, large egg is adapted to spin rather than roll off into the sea below. Most birds sit upright, their weight supported on their tarsi. Incubation resembles that of some of the penguins with the egg straddled between the legs.

Most birds are black, or dark brown, and white and are usually called guillemots in Europe and murres in North America. The Common Guillemot *Uria aalge* and Brünnich's Guillemot *U. lomvia* have circumpolar distributions. The Brünnich's Guillemot is

perhaps the more numerous although the Common Guillemot
breeds further south and is thus more familiar. While these birds
nest on the most precipitous cliffs, the Black Guillemot *Cepphus
grylle* finds a home among the rock debris along the water line. It is
basically a black and white bird but has the most vivid red feet and
a similarly coloured inside to the mouth. All other auks show a
similar arrangement of coloration: black and white plumage with
colour, if any, confined to the feet and head and particularly the bill.
The Black Guillemot too is found both in the Pacific and Atlantic.

The Razorbill *Alca torda* nests in crevices tucked away behind
the ledges of the guillemots, and is marked with a series of vertical
lines across the bill. Its close relative the Great Auk was confined to
only a few remote North Atlantic islands within historical times.
Standing 30 inches in height it provided fresh meat during the
great age of sailing, and was finally exterminated on 4th June 1844
on the island of Eldey off northern Iceland, when two adults were
killed and their single egg smashed. By a strange twist of fate Eldey
is now carefully protected as the last Icelandic home of the Little
Auk, only a few pairs of which now breed. The last British Great
Auk was killed on Stac-an-Armin of the St Kilda group in 1840,
because it was 'thought to be a witch'. Skins of Great Auks still
exist in several museums and collections, and fetch small fortunes
when they come up for auction.

It is, however, in the Pacific that the greatest numbers of auks,
or alcids as they are frequently called in America, are found. The
Atlantic Puffin *Fratercula arctica* is replaced in the Pacific by the
very similar Horned Puffin *F. corniculata*. Both have brightly
coloured, horned plates that develop on their bills during the
breeding season. This almost parrot-like structure is used in a
mutual fencing display in which the bills of the two birds are
smacked together. Many other puffins and auklets boast brightly
coloured bills and sometimes head plumes as well. The Tufted
Puffin *Lunda cirrhata* has long, golden plumes hanging from above
and behind its eyes to the base of the neck. The Crested Auklet
Aethia cristatella boasts a thin, white plume behind the eye, but also
a forward-curving 'quiff' from the forehead.

Puffins are not only the 'dinner-suited gentlemen' of the clan,
but they are the best walkers. Like sailors freshly ashore they
waddle along, and virtually run as they patter over the ground to

The centre of auk distribution is the Bering Sea where a large variety of
species, including these Crested Auklets, can be found. Their range extends
from the Aleutians to the islands of Japan.

take flight. Like that of other hole-nesters, their single egg is round
and white. After six weeks the young puffin is heavier than its
parents and is deserted, and finds its own way to sea under cover of
darkness.

Several of the Pacific murrelets have little or no ornamentation
and are unusual in other ways too. Craveri's *Endomychura craveri*
and Xantus's Murrelets *E. hypoleucus* breed in the south in Lower
California and then migrate northwards to winter. The chicks are
almost ready to leave as soon as they hatch, and regularly take to
the water when two days old.

Kittlitz's Murrelet *Brachyramphus brevirostris* posed a problem
for many years and its breeding grounds were discovered only
recently among the tundra slopes above the tree-line in Alaska. The
breeding grounds of the Marbled Murrelet *B. marmoratus* have still
to be discovered.

For centuries auks have been taken for food by island peoples.
In the Soviet Union, on the islands of Novaya Zemlya, the
guillemots are virtually farmed, and most communities that have
come to depend on these seabirds as a source of food have always
been careful to control their 'take' within the limits that the
population can stand. One such community was that of St Kilda in
the Outer Hebrides in Scotland. Here the islanders took thousands
of Puffins and other seabirds annually. When the islands were
evacuated in 1930 the Puffin was numbered in millions; today
counts show a fast declining population to be measured only in
thousands. The use of the sea as a dump for our industrial waste,
the run-off of agricultural chemicals, the general pollution level of
the planet – all must be at work in what certainly is a most
catastrophic decline.

Other auks are more frequent victims of oil pollution and as it is
now difficult to find a patch of sea that does not contain droplets of
oil, it is no surprise that these species, particularly the guillemots,
are declining rapidly as well. Provided we stop using the sea as a
dump, and that we run out of oil within the next twenty years as
predicted, it is just possible that some of these birds will survive.

Sandgrouse Pteroclididae

Despite the fact that they are ground-dwelling birds with a squat carriage and a strong, swift flight, sandgrouse are completely unrelated to grouse. Their nearest relatives are the pigeons and doves and they have the small head and stumpy bill of that family, although lacking the colourful cere at the base of the bill. They are a desert and semidesert group of birds and their colourful plumage, which boasts patches of yellow, orange and chestnut, is an effective camouflage in these arid surroundings. Birds of the most arid conditions are paler than those that are able to find some shelter from the sun beneath vegetation.

The sixteen species are found through southern Europe, over the whole of Africa and the Middle East into southern Asia. Most are sedentary but one species, Pallas's Sandgrouse *Syrrhaptes tibetanus*, breeds in central Asia and formerly erupted in vast numbers into areas where it was otherwise unknown. Noted eruptions took place in 1863, 1872, 1876, 1888 and 1908. These migrations took the birds as far west and east as they could go, to the British Isles and Peking respectively. In Britain at least, birds stayed on and managed to breed thousands of miles off range.

Pallas's Sandgrouse are birds of the vast grassland steppes of

Most northerly of the sandgrouse, the Pin-tailed is typically an inhabitant of arid stony wastes from southern France and Spain through North Africa to the Middle East. Throughout most of its range it is the commonest sandgrouse and flocks of several thousand birds occur.

southern Russia and other provinces of the Soviet Union. Doubtless when a mild winter enabled plenty of birds to survive and was followed by a good breeding season, the population of sandgrouse became too much for the area and vast numbers took off. While this is typical of northern birds and mammals it is unusual in non-Arctic species, but then the range of temperature in central Asia is as extreme as anywhere. Eruptions were comparatively regular until the early twentieth century, and the only major change at that time seems to be the opening up of southern Siberia and the changing of steppe into cereal-producing prairie. Perhaps the destruction of habitat has since prevented the build-up of numbers that is required for such eruptions to occur.

Sandgrouse fly on long, pointed wings and are as powerful and swift as the fastest pigeons. They are usually found in small parties, often families, but sometimes band together into larger flocks that roam in search of food. They are adapted to a semidesert existence in a variety of ways. They have a thick skin covered with a heavy layer of protective down, which serves to insulate them against the extremes of temperature experienced in desert areas. Considering the amount of time spent walking, the legs are extremely short and stubby, and the birds waddle along like freshly ashore sailors.

Sandgrouse drink regularly every day, some species soon after dawn, others before dusk. As so much of their habitat is arid, barren and waterless, they regularly fly for miles to obtain their daily ration of water. Some have been proved to fly round journeys of over seventy-five miles to water, a flight of some two hours' duration. Birds are tenacious of their drinking spots at which they gather day in, day out, often in vast numbers. Literally tens of thousands of birds will gather at a rough water hole but their behaviour there is even more remarkable. Most species drink in the early morning. Parties circle overhead to see that all is clear before plummeting down from the sky to alight a few yards from the water's edge. They quickly run to drink and are off again into the air after only a three or four seconds' drinking. The whole process takes less than ten seconds per bird. Some small parties arrive and leave together, but sometimes the milling mass becomes a continuous stream that lasts for minutes.

Sandgrouse drink without raising their heads, in the same manner as pigeons, but they have a unique system of carrying water to their chicks among the dense feathers of their breasts. On arrival back at the nesting area chicks come to the parent's breast and take the water directly from the feathers. This method of carrying water is unique in the animal world. As soon as they can fly they accompany the parents on regular visits to the water hole.

With such gatherings it is not surprising that predators are frequently attracted to lie in wait for the birds. Raptors are often numerous and crocodiles have been known to take them, but man is a more destructive predator and there are many areas where huge daily kills are obtained. Pallas's Sandgrouse often live so far from water that a daily flight is impossible, and the birds must take what little they can from dew and temporary pools.

Sandgrouse vary in size from 9 to 16 inches, yet they all look very much the same in flight. They are bulky, long-winged birds with pointed, often attenuated tails. The males have distinctive face patterns, but they are not always easy to see. Flying sandgrouse present a considerable identification problem. Two features are particularly important: most species have breast and belly bands and the exact extent and position of these should be noted. Note should also be taken of the length of the tail feathers. Even when good views of males on the ground are obtained, careful note of all plumage details must be made.

Pigeons and doves Columbidae

The name pigeon is generally used to describe the larger members of the Columbidae, and dove is reserved for the smaller and more dainty species, yet there is no hard and fast rule of usage. Thus the Bleeding Heart Pigeon *Gallicolumba luzonica* might well be called a dove, and the Stock Dove *Columba oenas* is typical of what we generally call pigeons. This lack of specificity is not surprising in view of the number of species in the family.

Some 255 species of pigeons and doves are recognized and divided among forty-three genera, yet all share pigeon-like characteristics that make them one of the most clear-cut of avian families. Even the extinct Dodo *Raphus cucullatus* and Solitaire *R. solitaire* exhibited the same qualities, for they were nothing more than overlarge, flightless pigeons. Some authors prefer to divide the pigeons up into several distinct families, the Otipiphapidae (Pheasant Pigeon), the Gouridae (crowned pigeons) and so on, but this is not generally regarded as valid.

Many authors regard the pigeons and doves as closely related to the sandgrouse. They both drink by a head-down sucking method and share various other anatomical characteristics, but the sandgrouse are more properly regarded as relatives of the plovers.

Pigeons and doves then share, to a considerable degree, common characteristics. They are large-bodied, densely plumaged birds that characteristically perch. They exhibit a variety of attractive and colourful plumages yet most birdwatchers regard them as boring birds, since they sit and appear to do nothing for much of their time. Some species, however, are intensely interesting and easy to study. Some again are renowned only for their nuisance value and others for their powers of migration. One could suggest other candidates for the title of the world's most boring birds.

Pigeons have long, pointed wings and well-developed flight muscles. They are extremely powerful fliers and very fast over long distances. The Rock Dove *Columba livia* has been tamed for thousands of years, partly as a source of fresh meat, but also because of its remarkable homing ability, speed and stamina. News of battles was frequently sent by carrier pigeons in Greek times, while more recently pigeons were used by the combatants during the First World War. Only during the current century have electrical devices supplanted the pigeon as a messenger. Yet millions of birds are still kept by pigeon racers to participate in long-distance events across Europe. No doubt racing pigeons navigate by the same methods that guide migratory birds, but their flights are evidently completed by their knowledge of their local areas. Rock Doves and racing pigeons have only the Peregrine Falcon to fear in the air.

Other pigeons and doves also fly well. They flight to and from their roosts and are generally gregarious by nature. Huge numbers will gather at good food supplies and their essentially vegetarian diet has brought them into sharp conflict with farming interests. In Britain in particular, an all-out war has been waged against the Wood Pigeon *C. palumbus* for its depredations on crops. That this has been only moderately successful is a remarkable compliment to a bird that, like most other pigeons, lays only two eggs.

The tail of pigeons is moderate in length and generally broad, although the pretty Namaqua Dove *Oena capensis* of Africa has a remarkably long tail. The species is also unusual for its marked sexual dimorphism, the male having a mask of black that extends down the breast. Most pigeons and doves are sexually similar. Pigeons have short, down-curved bills with a bare cere where the bill meets the head and through which the nostrils protrude. The legs are short, which is surprising in view of the amount of time spent walking.

Most species breed in trees, but some nest on the ground and others, like the Rock Dove and its feral descendants, on cliffs and buildings. All species construct a flimsy platform of twigs on to which the two, sometimes one or three, oval, white eggs are laid. Incubation is shared and the chicks hatch naked and helpless. A sparse down covering quickly gives way to full feathering, and the youngsters often fly within the remarkably short time of two weeks from hatching.

Young pigeons are fed on 'pigeon-milk' when they hatch. This is similar in nutritional terms to the milk produced by mammals, but actually consists of the broken-down lining of the crop. It is produced by both parents during the first few days after hatching. Thereafter the young are fed on the masticated remains of adult food which they take from the gullet of their parents in the manner of cormorants.

Display, as anyone who has sat and watched pigeons in a park will know, is quite fascinating. Males puff up their breasts and strut about like turkey cocks, tails spread and with much bowing. Such bowing and scraping is often accompanied by quiet 'cooing'. Indeed most pigeons 'coo' in a characteristic manner throughout the year. Despite being initially pleasant, such repeated calling eventually becomes a nuisance. Hotel keepers in Ramsgate, England, have complained that immigrant Collared Doves *Streptropelia decaocto* are preventing their guests from sleeping and have suggested a control campaign.

Several species, notably the Wood Pigeon, have well-developed aerial displays. These consist of a steep climb, often accompanied by wing-clapping, followed by a glide on 'V' shaped wings before another steep climb. The process may be repeated several times.

Among birds, few species can parallel the success story of the Collared Dove. Even as recently as 1930 it was confined, in Europe, to the Balkans. Within forty years it had spread to the Atlantic coast of France, to the Scottish Isles, to southern Scandinavia, and looks all set for colonizing Iceland, Greenland and perhaps North America. No satisfactory explanation for this success has yet been postulated. It is tame and confiding and feeds mainly on spilt grain and poultry food.

In sharp contrast, the Passenger Pigeon *Ectopistes migratorius*, once found by the million in the prairie lands of North America and thought by some to be the most numerous bird in the world, was hunted out of existence last century in the space of a couple of decades. Wilson, the distinguished American ornithologist, estimated these birds to be present in single flocks containing thousands of millions, and the fact that all these pigeons could be hunted to extinction gave a tremendous boost to the worldwide

Left The White-bellied Plumed Pigeon, boldly marked with a red face pattern and spike-like golden crest, is found in the arid interior of northern Australia. Its localized distribution indicates its need for plentiful supplies of water.

Below The Turtle Dove is a summer visitor to the western Palaearctic region and migrates southwards to winter in Africa. It also breeds among the oases in the central Sahara and along the Nile Valley. Turtle Doves prefer open country provided some corner is available for nesting.

Found throughout most of Africa south of the Sahara, the African Green Pigeon is nevertheless seldom very numerous. It builds a flimsy nest of twigs and feeds predominantly on fruit, particularly figs. Its plumage serves as good camouflage amongst the foliage of fig trees.

conservation movement. The last Passenger Pigeon, Martha, died in Cincinatti Zoo in 1914.

The pigeon centre of radiation lies in the Asian–Australasian area where a greater wealth of species is found than anywhere else. Among these are the magnificent crested pigeons. Larger than a domestic Chicken, these beautifully blue birds wander the forest clearings of New Guinea like Asiatic turkeys. They have fine, filigree crests that can be erected to form a beautiful fan, and which have been an attraction to the endemic New Guinea dandies. They are also good to eat and this has led to their disappearance around most villages.

Many tropical pigeons are boldly coloured birds that live predominantly on a diet of fruit. They are forest birds and often vie for attention with the noisier parrots and parakeets that share their habitat. Many of these pigeons have large gapes to enable them to swallow fruit whole, but others have a specially constructed jaw that can expand like that of some snakes.

Parrots Psittacidae

The Psittacidae are a large family, comprising over 300 distinct species, but are nevertheless remarkably 'self-contained' and clearly demarcated from their closest relatives, the pigeons and turacos. Varying in size from $3\frac{1}{2}$ inches to $3\frac{1}{2}$ feet, every species retains an essential parrot quality, however, that makes it almost impossible to mistake an individual for anything other than a parrot.

A wealth of vernacular names has been lavished on the family of which parakeet, lorikeet, cockatoo and macaw are the most common. Taxonomists have tried to divide this huge group into several distinct families, but current opinion relegates these to no more than tenuous subfamilies.

Parrots are gaily and boldly coloured birds. Their plumage, which is evenly but thinly distributed over their bodies, consists of patches of solid colour, often sharply contrasting one with another. Only in a minority of birds do colours merge. Thus red patches abut blue patches, and yellows interrupt greens. A large number of species boast considerable areas of green and it needs no great powers of deduction to work out that these multi coloured birds are found in the canopy of tropical jungles.

The most obvious clue to familial identity is the beak, which in all species is sharply hooked and down-curved. This is essentially a fruit-eating bill, although in a very few species it has been adapted to other purposes. Many Australian parrots, for instance, are ground dwelling and feed predominantly on seeds. With the Kea *Nestor notabilis* of New Zealand, the hawk-like bill of a parrot has been converted for flesh-tearing scavenging.

Many parrots have long tails, sometimes extremely so. They are invariably pointed and give the bird a highly characteristic silhouette as it flies over the tree tops. Parrots have long, pointed wings and fly fast overhead, normally in small groups. They are often gregarious, although the very large gatherings of Budgerigars *Melopsittacus undulatus* at Australian waterholes are unique.

Like the woodpeckers, parrots have two toes pointing forwards and two pointing backwards – a design ideally suited to clambering about in trees. The feet are also used for grasping food, and parrots are unique in bringing held food up to the bill to eat, a habit that endears them to visitors to zoos and is one of their attractions as pets. Their ability to mimic, however, along with their splendid colours, is probably a more important factor in this respect.

Parrots are generally easy to keep and maintain and Budgerigars in particular are kept as pets in enormous numbers. Selective breeding has produced a variety of colour strains far divorced from the natural green and yellow birds of the Australian savannahs.

The African Grey Parrot *Psittacus erithacus* is generally considered to be the best of the mimics yet it in no way compares with the greatest of all talkers, the Indian Mynah. Some parrots seem to burst into an appropriate 'Hello – how d'you do?' but since they will also produce an inappropriate pneumatic drill, it seems unlikely that they understand what they are saying! While parrots in captivity may live to the ripe old age of eighty, birds in the wild can seldom survive as long.

Parrots nest in holes, usually in trees but sometimes among rocks or in termite mounds. The virtually flightless Australian Ground Parrot *Pezoporus wallicus* nests on the ground among grass, but the New Zealand Kakapo *Strigops habroptilus*, while also unable to fly, manages to clamber to natural holes in rocks and trees. The two to five white eggs hatch after about three weeks. The helpless young are fed by both parents on predigested food that is regurgitated.

Parrots are found throughout the tropics extending into temperate regions in South America and in Tasmania and New Zealand. The only parrot to be found in temperate North America, the Carolina Parakeet *Conuropsis carolinensis*, was hunted to extinction in the nineteenth century. Parrots reach their greatest abundance in the jungles of Amazonia and the wastes of Australia. Most species are resident, although Australian species are noted nomads.

The Kea is found in New Zealand and is a high-altitude scavenger that has recently adapted from a vegetarian diet to one of carrion. Keas are often accused of killing sheep, but there is no evidence that they have yet learned to do this. Their dull, green, scaly plumage is broken by a vivid red and yellow underwing that

Opposite top The broad-winged flight silhouette of the Kea of New Zealand picks out its high-level life style. Capable of eating almost anything, this aberrant parrot has recently acquired a taste for carrion.

Opposite bottom The Kakapo is a largely nocturnal parrot with poorly developed muscles that preclude true flight. It is found among the native forests of New Zealand and, like so many endemic birds of those islands, is in grave danger of extinction.

shows in flight. They are tame birds and will readily approach, investigate and start to dismantle a parked car!

Also found in New Zealand is the Kakapo, formerly called the Owl-parrot because of its nocturnal habits and similarity to those nocturnal predators. Kakapos have evolved similar flat, well-feathered faces and the soft plumage of owls, but have also become flightless and feed almost entirely on vegetable matter. They live in remote valleys in South Island and are only very rarely found by expeditions.

Among the lories and lorikeets of Asia and Australasia, Rainbow Lorikeets *Trichoglossus haematodus* are remarkable for their sound commercial sense. Basically flower feeders (but also partial to fruit) and playing a significant part in pollination, these highly gregarious birds descend by the thousand to feed from the hand like pigeons in a town square. At one site on the coast of eastern Australia they perch on visitors and pose for their photographs like the good 'public relations officers' they are.

The largest group of parrots is the Psittacinae that includes the macaws, lovebirds, Budgerigars and many parakeets. They are a widespread subfamily found predominantly in the warmest parts of the tropics. The largest and most colourful are the fifteen species of macaws found in South America. The Blue and Yellow Macaw *Ara ararauna* is the most familiar of all. It inhabits the periphery of the Amazon basin and is a large, startlingly coloured bird. It is gregarious and extremely noisy, uttering a variety of loud and piercing shrieks and yelps. It was one of the first South American birds to be brought to Europe from the New World and has been widely kept in captivity ever since.

Also included in this family, and in contrast to the huge macaws, are the lovebirds, all less than 7 inches in length. They are usually found in small groups, and the affection showed one to another is responsible for their common name. The ten species of hanging parrots of the genus *Loriculus* are remarkable for their habit of hanging upside down to feed. They were formerly called 'bat-

Left One of the most gaily coloured members of a colourful family, wild Rainbow Lorikeets regularly flock in vast numbers to bird gardens in eastern Australia.

Above Like many other Australian parrots, the Cockatiel is a strong-flying, gregarious bird. This female at her nest hole has her crest raised in curiosity. Perhaps she can see her own reflection in the camera lens.

Opposite Lovebirds. From top to bottom. Madagascar, Nyassa, Abyssinian, Black-cheeked, Black-collared, Fischer's, Red-faced, Peach-faced, Masked.

Overleaf This fine Roseate Cockatoo inhabits the non-forested areas of Australia and, like so many other parrots, forms dense flocks at favoured feeding grounds and around water holes.

parrots' for this reason. They are widespread in Asia and include the smallest of all parrots the Orange-fronted Hanging Parrot *L. aurantiifrons* of New Guinea, little more than $3\frac{1}{2}$ inches in length. This hanging parrot is rivalled in size only by another group of New Guinea based parrots, the pygmy parrots of the genus *Micropsitta*, none of which measures more than 4 inches in length.

Widely kept in captivity are the cockatoos of the subfamily Cakatocinae found in Australasia. These large birds boast erectile crests that makes them another favoured group for captivity. Their deep, powerful bills are capable of cracking palm nuts, one of their favourite foods.

Best known and most widely kept of this group is the Greater Sulphur-crested Cockatoo *Cacatua galerita*, an all-white bird marked with a large, yellowish erectile crest. Widespread in Australia, apart from the arid interior, and New Guinea, it inhabits woodlands usually within a short distance of water. It is a gregarious bird outside the breeding season and often forms substantial flocks.

The Roseate Cockatoo *C. roseicapilla* is similarly a gregarious bird and will even flock into city squares. It is a fine deeply pink bird marked with a white crest and is generally called the Galah in its native Australia.

179

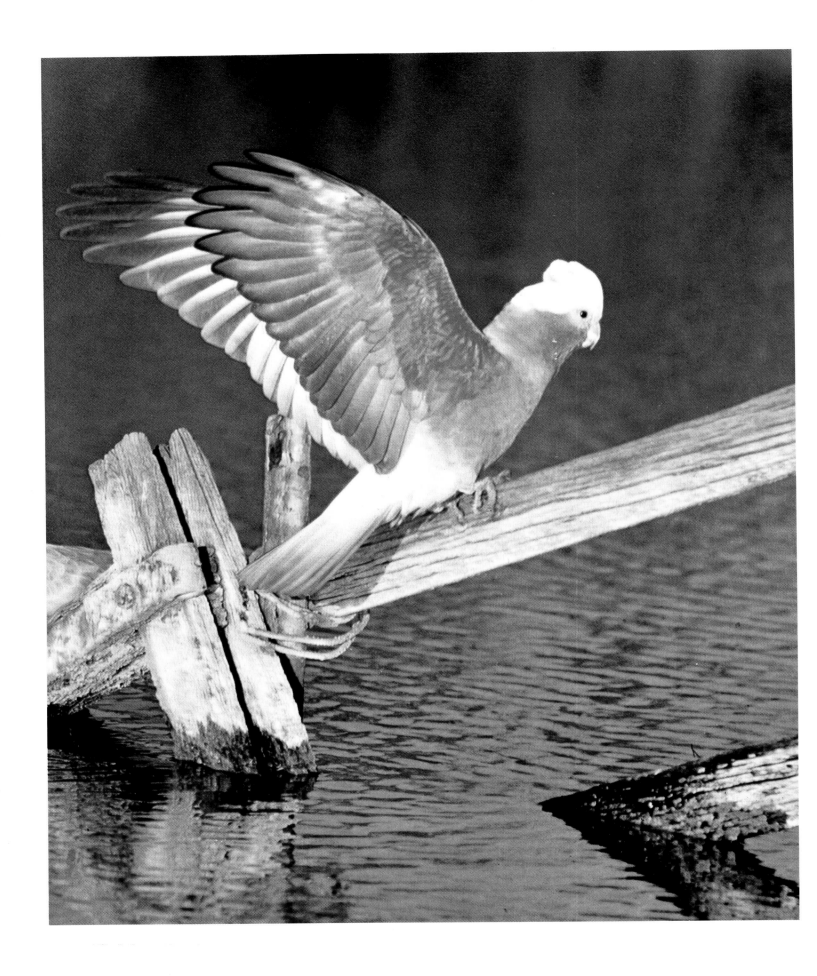

Turacos Musophagidae

The eighteen species of turacos are arboreal birds of central and southern Africa that are well enough known to have accumulated several distinctive vernacular names. Southern species are often called go-away birds after the 'go-awaa' call of the genus *Corythaixoides*. Others are called louries and yet others plantain-eaters because of their assumed predilection for plantains, or bananas. In fact, while all turacos live predominantly on a diet of fruit, there is no evidence for such preferred food items. Most turacos are 15 to 18 inches long, although the Great Blue Turaco *Corythaeola cristata* is over 2 feet in length.

Turacos are colourful, long-tailed birds, green and blue in colour with crimson primary feathers that show well in flight. While the bright colours of most birds are due to refraction of light by their feather structures, those of the turacos are true pigments. Thus a red primary will, when mixed with water, dye the liquid red, a fact which has led some writers to believe that rain in tropical jungles will wash the colour from the living birds. In fact, the birds manage to maintain their colours throughout the year. Indeed, those that live in the dense jungles created by heavy rainfall are more densely coloured than those that prefer the dry thorn scrub of the African savannahs, and which are 'washed-out' in comparison.

Turacos, in spite of their obvious colouring, are extremely difficult to see among foliage. In trees, they clamber about with considerable agility and are easily overlooked as they perch stationary along a branch. They live in small bands and are most obvious as they fly, one after another, from tree to tree. They have broad, rounded wings and their flight invariably seems laboured. Like commandoes, they seem to wait for the bird ahead to land safely before the next in line sets off across open ground.

Below Although colourful and large, the Great Blue Turaco, like other members of its family, is by no means obvious among the African woodlands from which it obtains its diet of fruit and berries.

Right The Bare-faced Go-away-bird inhabits the dry acacia country of the African savannahs. Despite its size and obvious voice it has the remarkable ability to enter a tree and disappear from view completely.

Among the trees their search for fruit is thorough and systematic. They climb and run along branches easily, using their wings and feet. The fourth toe, like that of the Osprey, is set at right angles to the foot and may be used forwards or backwards. No doubt this aids their tree-climbing abilities.

All species have a crest or mop on the crown and this, together with the face pattern, most easily identifies the individual species. Hartlaub's Turaco *Tauraco hartlaubi* has a prominent, white comma before the eye, whereas Livingstone's Turaco *T. livingstonii* has a simple, white line around the red eye patch. This species has a bold, green crest in contrast to the reddish, white-tipped crest of Fischer's Turaco *T. fischeri*, which otherwise has a similar face pattern. Ross's Turaco *Musophaga rossae* is an all-blue bird with a reddish wing and crest and bold, yellow face pattern.

The White-bellied Go-away bird *Corythaixoides leucogaster* is one of the all grey and white savannah turacos well known to all visitors to East Africa. In loose parties these birds fly noisily from one bush to another, seeming huge in the air, but disappearing completely as they land in the centre of the next acacia. Their extremely long and rounded tails give them a quite unique aerial outline.

Turacos nest in trees where they build a pigeon-like platform of twigs. The two eggs are white, or masked with a slight cast of plain colour. Incubation takes about eighteen days, and fledging about four weeks. Like the great climbers they are, young turacos will leave the nest long before they can fly to clamber about the tree tops. A strong wing claw helps them on their way like the young of that other arboreal species, the Hoatzin of South America. Chicks are fed on predigested fruit, but surprisingly little is known of the lives of these large but retiring birds.

Cuckoos, anis, roadrunners and coucals Cuculidae

Everyone knows the Cuckoo's secret, but few know just how widespread the habit of brood parasitism is. While the European Cuckoo *Cuculus canorus* is infamous for its habit of laying eggs in the nests of other birds, few realize that all the forty-five other species in the Cuckoo's subfamily do so as well, and that some members of another related subfamily within the Cuculidae are also parasites. This form of roguery is not confined even to the family, however. American cowbirds of the Icteridae are as varied as the cuckoos themselves in this respect. The honeyguides, well known as indicators of the presence of bees' and wasps' nests, lay their eggs in the nest holes of other birds. While it is well known that the Cuckoo evicts its nest companions, the honeyguide chick has two sharp hooks at the tip of its bill which are shed after performing their infanticidal function. Other families too are brood parasitic, some of the weavers lay their eggs in other bird's nests and so do most of the widow birds. In South America, even a duck, the Black-headed Duck, regularly utilizes the nests and services of other aquatic birds.

The cuckoos then are not unique, but they are the most fully adapted to a parasitic mode of reproduction. The family gets its name from the call of the common European species which utters a distinctive call of 'cuck-oo, cuck-oo, cuck-oo' during spring in the woods. It is also the derivation of the old English word 'cuckhold'. Very few birds have such a distinctive voice that their name is the same in almost every language. For while 'cuckoo' is spelt differently in different countries, the derivation and pronunciation are the same.

The Cuculidae are generally slim birds with long tails, ranging in size from 6 to 26 inches in length. The legs are short except in the quite distinctive ground-dwelling species. The outer toe is reversible and the stout bill slightly down-curved. A great variety of plumage patterns exists, although many species are of muted browns and greys in coloration.

Most of the 125 species are tree-dwelling, but a few are terrestrial. The majority fly strongly and some species of high latitudes perform lengthy migrations. The European Cuckoo regularly flies across the Sahara to winter in tropical Africa.

As indicated by the wealth of vernacular names, the Cuculidae is a highly diverse family. Not only are there cuckoos, anis, roadrunners and coucals, but also guiras, ground-cuckoos, couas, koels and a yellowbill. Faced with such diversity, generalizations tend to be meaningless and discussion of the various subfamilies is of far greater value.

The Cuckoo is the best known of the subfamily Cuculinae. It

Below The Cape Robin of South Africa is host to a young Red-chested Cuckoo. Like the Eurasian Cuckoo the chick will not tolerate any other occupants of its foster home and soon ejects the eggs of the true owner. Feeding on a diet intended for a larger brood it soon grows larger than its foster parent.

Opposite Eurasian Cuckoos soon grow too large for their nests and then form perches for their foster-parents. In this case the foster-parent is a hard-worked Dunnock.

breeds right across Eurasia and over large parts of Africa. Throughout this vast range it encounters a variety of possible foster-parents and both its behaviour and type of eggs are adaptations to this diversity. The female Cuckoo lays four or five eggs, each in a separate host nest over a period of nine to ten days. Each female produces a particular type and colour of egg and specializes in a particular species as host. Thus those Cuckoos that lay bluish eggs seek out the nests of Dunnocks, those that produce spotted eggs find Reed Warblers' nests, and so on. Having arrived on her territory and mated, the female Cuckoo spends much of her time spying on suitable foster-parents and noting their state of progress in nesting. Success depends on placing her egg in the nest before incubation commences, but during the egg-laying period. By carefully controlling the nesting activities of his local population of Meadow Pipits, the late Edgar T. Chance was able to make exact predictions about their state of readiness for the Cuckoos that he studied.

It is clear that the Cuckoo must be a champion nest finder, and while it probably uses the favourite 'wait and see' method of the old oologists, it also has a special flight that aids its search. In this it so resembles a raptor that small birds leave their nests to mob it thereby giving an approximate, if not exact, nest location to the Cuckoo.

The female Cuckoo removes one of the host's eggs and lays her own in the tiny (in comparison to her) nest. As this may be domed, as in the case of the Common Wren, the manoeuvre may be quite complex. The Cuckoo's egg is remarkably small for the size of the adult and has a very short incubation period – just twelve days. It thus hatches before or at the same time as those of the host and the young cuckoo is soon busy, instinctively pushing the eggs or other young from the nest. Despite such losses the foster-parents continue to feed the voracious youngster, which soon grows larger than themselves. The ejection of rivals for food is essential to the survival of the young Cuckoo, for to make up its bulk it needs all the food that the combined efforts of its foster-parents can supply.

The Cuckoo is the best-known member of the subfamily, but the other members are not without interest. The Great Spotted Cuckoo *Clamator glandarius* favours the nests of crows and magpies. The Koel *Eudynamys scolopacea*, which breeds from India to Australasia, is parasitic on the House Crow and frequently lays several eggs in the same nest. The resulting chicks closely resemble crows even after fledging. The Drongo Cuckoo *Surniculus lugubris* of South-East Asia is unique among cuckoos in having a forked tail. In fact it closely resembles the drongos which it parasitizes. Young Drongo Cuckoos even have the dark feathers tipped with white of the immature drongo. The Drongo Cuckoo also utilizes a variety of other hosts including shrikes and warblers.

The cuckoos of the subfamily Phaenicophaeinae are non-parasitic. They build shallow nests of twigs in trees and lay two to six blue eggs, which they incubate and care for themselves. While most are tropical, some species have extended into temperate climes. The familiar Yellow-billed Cuckoo *Coccyzus erythrophthalmus* of the United States extends northwards as far as Canada. A totally tropical member of the subfamily is the strange Squirrel Cuckoo *Piaya cayana* which is confined to the dense jungles of Central and South America. Here it glides between trees on small, rounded wings that are quite unable to support sustained flight. It spends most of its life, as its name implies, running along forest branches with the sure-footedness of a squirrel. It nests in dense undergrowth and the chicks feather early and leave the nest for the safety of the canopy when barely half the size of the adults.

The members of the subfamily Crotophaginae are sociable, and the anis and their curious relative the Guira Cuckoo *Guira guira,* of South America, adopt an extreme form of social nesting. The three species of anis are black birds, with long, square tails and stubby, thick bills. They feed in the manner of tick-birds, but are not such excellent fliers as the oxpeckers of Africa. They are found in small

184

flocks during the day, but may gather in larger numbers to roost.

The nest is built in a tree, either by a single female or by a whole flock. Once one hen has commenced incubation, another will lay her eggs in the same nest. Up to 100 eggs have been recorded from a single nest. Sometimes the eggs of the Guira Cuckoo may also be found in an ani's nest. When the chicks hatch, the entire flock will join in the feeding. Anis are cautious birds and spend much time spying over their surroundings. They fly weakly and usually in a line like jays.

The best-known members of the subfamily Neomorphinae are the roadrunners of Central America. The Greater Roadrunner *Geococcyx californianus* is well known to every visitor to the American west. It frequents the semidesert country of Arizona and California, and while most visitors do not see its nest among the cactus they do see the bird itself crossing roads. It is a great runner capable of speeds of over twenty miles an hour, but a decidedly weak flier. It escapes predators by dodging between cacti and manages to avoid cars with the same display of agility.

It feeds by making sudden pounces on insects, lizards and snakes, although its predilection for snakes has been grossly exaggerated. As an obvious and attractive member of the desert fauna a considerable amount of folklore has accumulated about the Greater Roadrunner. In particular, stories associated with its snake-eating habits abound. A favourite one is that when bitten, the bird rushes off and swallows a particular herb as an antidote.

The Greater Roadrunner's nest is an untidy bundle of twigs lined with bones, snake skins and paper. The three to seven white eggs are incubated by the hen for nineteen days, and the nestlings hatch over a period of several days.

The couas of the subfamily Couinae are found only on Madagascar, and the nine or ten species are little known. They are generally gregarious and are not parasitic. Most species are terrestrial in habits, but the Crested Coua *Coua cristata* is a forest-dwelling bird.

Couas are slim birds with long tails and of generally dull plumage. The wings are round and short and although they have not lost the power of flight, most species will take to the air only in the direst emergency. They feed on insects taken on the ground, but also on fruit. Nests are constructed of twigs in low trees.

The twenty-eight species of coucals are found from Africa across Asia and Australia to the Solomon Islands. They are dark coloured, medium-sized, ground-dwelling birds. When they take to the trees their every action seems clumsy and they frequently appear to be clowning. They have long, rounded tails, short, rounded wings and stubby, hooked bills. They feed predominantly on insects as well as lizards and even young birds. The roughly constructed, domed nest is placed on the ground and the three to five white eggs are incubated as they are laid. The resulting brood is thus diverse in age and size.

Opposite top The Smooth-billed Ani is found from the West Indies through Central America to Ecuador and Argentina. Throughout this vast range it is an inveterate hunter of ticks from the backs of cattle.

Opposite bottom The Greater Roadrunner, so called because of its habit of streaking across desert roads, is found in arid country from the southern United States through Mexico. The tail is frequently cocked when the bird is stationary.

Below The Pheasant Coucal is a large bird of well-watered countryside that is surprisingly easy to overlook. It is found throughout northern Australia and New Guinea and feeds on insects and other animate prey.

Owls Strigidae and Tytonidae

The amalgamation of the two families of owls for convenience needs little justification. The barn owls (Tytonidae) are quite clearly distinct from the typical owls (Strigidae), but they have so much in common, that separate accounts would be repetitive and pointless. As an order (Strigiformes), owls have a quite definite character that might best be summed up as their 'owlness'. Anyone can identify an owl and they have accumulated as much folklore as any other group of birds. Paradoxically, they are thus familiar and yet, because of their mainly nocturnal activities, unfamiliar. We know their sounds, but seldom see them. They are responsible for many of the 'ghosts' of the churchyards and the 'murderous' cries from the woods.

Owls are nocturnal raptors and exhibit well the adaptations to predation and a night-time existence. They have the large eyes and binocular vision of the diurnal raptors, the hawks and falcons, but also the ability to turn the head through 180 degrees or more to see directly behind them. Like other nocturnal birds their plumage is cryptically camouflaged, and they have soft tips to the wing feathers that make for silent flight.

Their habits mean that they rely on calls to locate one another and they are extremely vocal at certain times of the year, when territories are being staked out and pairs established. As with other groups of animals, some owls have readapted to a diurnal existence while still maintaining much of their 'owlish' way of life.

Owls have sharply hooked bills like the diurnal raptors, although in most species much of the bill is hidden by the feathers of the face. Humans like owls because they have flat faces like ours, evolved to accommodate their huge eyes and give them the binocular vision that all predators require, and which enable distances to be judged. Owls have a facial disc that almost seems to funnel the light into their eyes. They have good ears, but the two tufts of feathers at the top of the head of many species are not related to hearing at all. Like diurnal birds of prey, owls have a soft cere around the nostrils, but this is seldom visible below the facial feathering. Thus the face of an owl is strangely appealing. They seem more intelligent than they are, and we invest them with human qualities: hence phrases such as 'wise old owls'.

Most owls are various shades of browns, mottled for camouflage, the basic purpose of which is to render them inconspicuous during the day. Thus a woodland owl is typically brown and buff like a woodcock or nightjar, but owls that live in northern forests are often grey rather than brown, and the Snowy Owl *Nyctea scandiaca* is white, or barred white, to blend with its background of snow-covered tundra.

Owls vary in size from the Elf Owl *Micrathene whitneyi* of North America, which is a bare 5½ inches in length and nests in holes in cacti, to the great eagle owls which stand over 2 feet high. All have sharp talons, with two toes pointing forwards and two pointing backwards, ideal for grasping prey. Like the raptors, it is the feet that are the hunting weapons and of which one should beware. Naturally such variation in size indicates a similar variation of prey. While small mammals are the mainstay of the medium-sized owls, the larger birds take animals the size of rabbits, and are not averse to taking another owl if they come across one. In contrast, the smaller species are often insectivorous, feeding on the abundant insect life to be found in the tropics.

Our knowledge of the food of owls is gleaned, not from direct observation, but from the careful examination and analysis of their pellets. Most birds have the ability to cast up the remains of food that they cannot digest in the form of pellets. These are seldom

found because of their size, but all large predators bring up quite large pellets consisting of fur, bones and other indigestibles. A scattering of grey, sausage-like pellets beneath a tree is a sure indication of a predator roost, usually an owl. The size and shape will indicate the species and a careful dissection of the pellet will

Confined to the northern tundra zone, the ghostly Snowy Owl nests on the ground. The size of its clutch and the number of fledged young is almost entirely dependent on the number of Lemmings.

reveal bones of mammals and perhaps birds that have been eaten. This is a particularly useful source of information on the food of owls, and tells us that most owls are the friends of farmers rather than their enemies. It tells us, for instance, that Tawny Owls *Strix aluco* may live on small mammals in the countryside, but that in city centres they have adapted to a diet of House Sparrows. Mammalogists are particularly keen on studying owl pellets, for with small, secretive nocturnal mammals often the only evidence of their presence is the appearance of their remains, particularly their skulls, in the pellets of owls.

In the great conifer belt of the Northern Hemisphere, the owls are not only dramatic and appealing, but are also dependent on the population of Lemmings. These small mammals vary in abundance over a five to six year cycle and so too do the various predators that depend on them. The Long-tailed Skua and Rough-legged Buzzard are two examples that come to mind. Snowy Owls in

particular vary enormously in number from year to year and when the Lemmings erupt the Snowy Owls tag along behind following their food supply. In such seasons they are found far outside their range and regularly penetrate well into the United States. A great many of these Snowy Owls are shot at such times, although from a population viewpoint, it is probably not important.

Other species, like the Hawk Owl *Surnia ulula* and Great Grey Owl *Strix nebulosa*, are less eruptive, but do breed further south during years of high Lemming population. It is almost as if the birds know that it will be a bumper year, and that they will be able to breed in areas to the south that are not usually able to support them. Even the Snowy Owl lays a larger clutch at such times than it does in years when prey is scarce. In this way it is able to rear the maximum number of young. Even if the food supply suddenly disappears, owls are able to ensure that they rear at least some youngsters by commencing incubation with the first egg. Almost any picture of an owl family will show the extreme variation of age and size in a brood of owlets. Indeed, the youngest member of a brood is often killed and eaten by its stronger siblings.

Young owls hatch blind and deaf and are covered in white down. They are fed on small titbits of food by their parents, but are soon

Opposite The Great Grey Owl enjoys a circumpolar distribution among the great coniferous forests of the north. Nowhere numerous, this elusive species extends its range southwards in times when the small mammals on which it depends abound.

Below 'Air brakes' spread, eyes down, and 'landing gear' at the ready a Screech Owl prepares to land. This species is found from Mexico northwards to the tree line and will eat virtually any living creature.

able to manage quite outlandish prey that often seems beyond their capacity. Owls have lived to ripe old ages in captivity (an Eagle Owl died at the age of sixty-eight years), but life in the wild is probably not much longer than two or three years after fledging.

There are ten distinct species of barn owls, although the Barn Owl *Tyto alba* is one of the most widespread birds in the world. Over thirty distinct subspecies have been described. It is, without doubt, one of the most beautiful of birds. The facial disc is white and heart-shaped and the eyes are small and dark. The breast is white, but a golden cinnamon in some colour phases. The upperparts are the same golden cinnamon with jewel-like speckles of black and silver that seem almost decorative rather than purposeful. On silent wings Barn Owls fly like 'ghosts' low over fields and along the edges of woods. They usually nest in large holes in dead and dying trees, but have successfully switched to man-made structures and barns in particular. It is perhaps short-sighted of farmers to remove hollow trees and, at the same time, pull down old barns and replace them with modern storage covers that offer no home to these owls.

Only the bay owls of Asia and Africa are linked to the eight species of barn owls. Like those species they have long, well-feathered tarsi, but the facial disc is not as geometrically satisfying and they have a less appealing appearance. As with many other tropical owls, little is known of their life histories.

Their liking for buildings, and for church towers in particular, has resulted in the white Barn Owl being responsible for a great many ghost stories. No doubt their wailing, mournful cries do nothing to ease the imaginations of those that find dark nights and graveyards unconducive to relaxation.

Of the typical owls the most impressive are the twelve species of eagle owls of the genus *Bubo*. Well over 2 feet in length, these powerful birds are able to deal with quite large prey. The Eurasian Eagle Owl *B. bubo* is among the largest of all owls. It is a brown, barred bird with prominent 'ear' tufts, huge yellow eyes, and a set of quite fearsome talons. Despite the fact that stories of Eagle Owls attacking any intruder of their nests have probably been exaggerated, they could no doubt inflict really nasty injuries should they feel so inclined. With the persecution that these birds have suffered throughout their range, such stories may well help to protect a progressively rare bird.

Eagle Owls nest on the ground and lay their two to four eggs in unlined depressions. The male supplies the food which varies according to locality and altitude, for these birds have been found at over 15,000 feet in the Himalayas. Young have been brought hares, duck, rats and mice, but the owls will deal quite happily with hedgehogs and even large crows and hawks. In Africa the Eagle Owl is replaced by the grey-coloured Milky Eagle Owl *B. lacteus*,

Carrying a large, winged insect, a Boobook Owl lands at its nest site. This small owl is found throughout the wooded areas of Australasia and is named, after the aboriginal, by its call note.

by the Mountain Eagle Owl *B. capensis* and, in savannah country, by the Spotted Eagle Owl *B. africanus*. All three are large, strong birds, although the Milky Eagle Owl is the most powerful. It will take birds as large as guineafowl and medium-sized bustards. In North America the genus is represented by the Great Horned Owl *B. virginianus*.

Some of the strangest and least known of owls are the species of

fishing owls of which one is Pel's Fishing Owl *Scottopelia peli*. Found throughout most of Africa south of the Sahara, ornithologists resident within the range curiously enough neither see nor hear of this bird from one year to the next. As a result little is known of its life except its distinctive 'whoomm-hutt' call. Its plumage is mottled brown with quite distinctive, creamy eyebrows, almost like the Spectacled Owl *Pulsatrix perspicillata*. It has long legs, featherless tarsi, and serrated toes as adaptations to catching fish as they come into the shallows to feed at night. Unfortunately, very little is known of the fishing techniques of Pel's Fishing Owl, but it is also said to feed on rats and other small mammals. It is

Despite its localized name, the Ural Owl is found from Scandinavia across Asia to the Pacific in the coniferous forest zone. It also breeds in southern Europe and in an isolated area of southern Asia.

seldom found away from riverine forests.

Also unusual is the Burrowing Owl *Speotyto cunicularia* of the American prairies. While owls are well protected in woodland and forest areas, there is plenty of food to be found on the prairies where hideaways are non-existent. The Burrowing Owl has adapted to this environment by taking to the ground, and developing long legs with which to excavate a roost of its own as well as to run to cover when disturbed. Its prey consists mainly of large insects, but it also takes reptiles and amphibians as well as the young of Prairie Dogs and other species whose burrows it commandeers.

The Short-eared Owl *Asio flammeus* is one of the diurnal owls. Its range is circumpolar in the north, but it is also found in southern South America, in the West Indies and high in the Andes on the equator. It would be very difficult to find a more unusual range

A Long-eared Owl photographed with wings spread as it comes in to land. This widespread woodland species is seldom very vocal and because of its soft call is easily overlooked.

than that of this bird. It is also unusual for an owl to be a regular migrant, abandoning the more northerly parts of its breeding range for the temperate zone in winter. The numbers of small mammals determine the number of owls, and in suitable areas where numbers of prey are high, large concentrations of owls may come together to roost in such places as old barns. Short-eared owls are largely nomadic and their mobile existence enables them to take advantage of any food supply that presents itself. This is in contrast to the vast majority of owl species which are territorial, and probably develop the expertise that comes with familiarity of a particular hunting area.

It is surprisingly easy to overlook an owl. Elf Owls have been present in gardens in Arizona for years without being discovered, and for a long time these little birds were thought to be confined to desert areas with cacti. In fact they also frequent pine woods and have probably been attracted to habitation by the concentrations of insects that gather beneath street lights. Elf Owls nest in holes in cacti excavated by woodpeckers.

Oilbird Steatornithidae

The Oilbird or Guacharo *Steatornis caripensis* is one of the strangest birds in the world. Despite being related to the nightjars and bearing some resemblance to the owls, it is, in fact, quite isolated and distinct. The name stems from the old Indian practice of obtaining oil for cooking from the extraordinarily fat, young Oilbirds in the same manner as island communities have utilized young Fulmars.

Oilbirds are mottled brown with black and white spots. They have strongly hooked bills surrounded by bristles, long, pointed wings spanning almost 3 feet, and long tails. The legs, like those of the nightjars, are short and weak. The eyes are large, as befits a nocturnal species, and the birds live deep in caves leaving only after dark to feed on the abundant local fruits. They are found over most of northern South America from Peru to Venezuela and in

Trinidad. Oilbirds are nowhere common and are totally dependent on the presence of suitable caves. They are thus confined to mountainous districts, although some can be found in sea-caves in Trinidad.

Oilbirds live so deep in caves that they are unable to see to fly. Instead, they navigate by an echolocation system similar to that used by bats. As they fly the birds produce a high-pitched, clicking sound that is bounced back to them by the walls of the caves. They also produce harsh, screaming cries that probably serve to maintain the colonial aspect of their lives.

Colonies may vary in size, but most consist of thirty to fifty pairs. The birds leave their caves under shelter of darkness and fly up to fifty miles in their search for food. With their bills they grab fruit directly from trees as they fly past and carry it back to their roosts in their stomachs.

Nests are placed on cave ledges and consist of regurgitated fruit together with the birds' droppings. The two to four white eggs are incubated by both parents for thirty-three days, and the chick remains in the nest for a further four months before flying.

The nocturnal, fruit-eating Oilbird lives deep in caves where it finds its way about in complete darkness by an echolocation system similar to that used by bats. Because of disturbance several of its better-known haunts are strictly protected.

Frogmouths Podargidae

Frogmouths are nightjars that have taken to the trees. Like the other Caprimulgiformes they are cryptically coloured with vermiculations of greys and browns streaked with blacks and whites. Instead of resembling the ground, however, they merge perfectly with lichen-covered trees where they nest and spend most of their time. Frogmouths retain the large gape of the nightjars, but are not aerial feeders and do not have their long wings and tails. Indeed, the wings are short and rounded and the tails quite stubby. They hunt in the manner of shrikes, descending from invisibility within a tree to snatch insects, snails, frogs and even small mammals, from the ground. They also take small birds and some fruit.

Frogmouths build a nest of twigs in the fork of a tree and camouflage it with lichens. One or two eggs are laid and incubated by the female alone. Both parents share in feeding the young which take about a month to fledge. Like the nightjars, frogmouths are active at dawn and dusk and rely on their colouring for daytime concealment. Several species 'freeze' when disturbed in such a way as to bear an uncanny resemblance to a broken branch. Like the nightjars they have peculiar and characteristic calls that are repeated seemingly endlessly.

The twelve species are found from Australasia through to Malaysia and vary in size from 9 to 20 inches. Nowhere are they common and comparatively little is known of their lives.

The cryptic coloration and strange posture enable the Tawny Frogmouth to pass unnoticed as an old stump as it sits on its tree fork nest. It feeds shrike-like by pouncing on ground-dwelling insects.

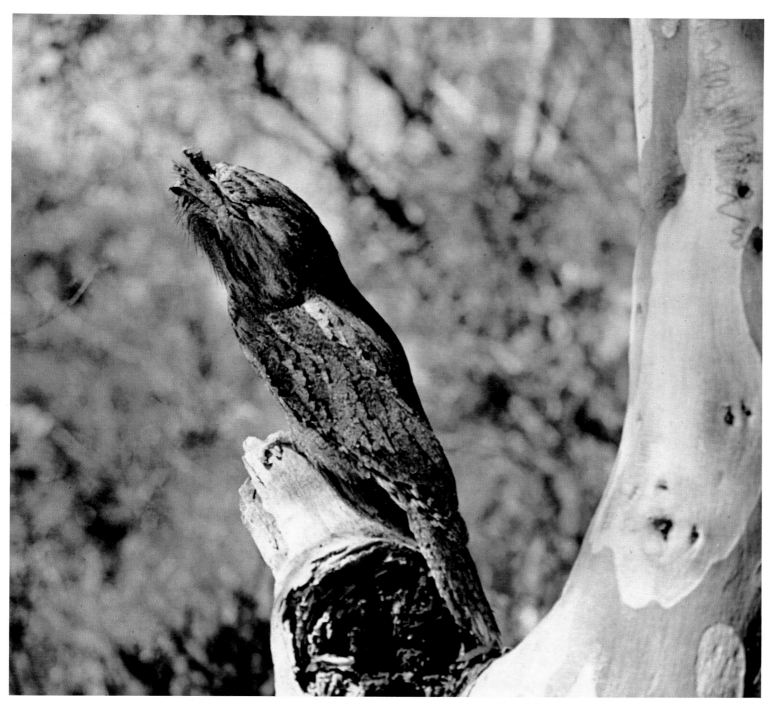

Potoos Nyctibiidae

Potoos are nightjars turned nocturnal flycatchers. While most of the Caprimulgiformes hawk for nocturnal insects on long wings and tails, the potoos sit atop a stump or fence post before darting out after some nocturnal insect. Like a flycatcher they return to the same hunting post. As typical nightjar-type birds they are beautifully camouflaged with greys and browns, and when sitting on an old stump look like nothing more than an extension of the wood. During the day they often sit along a branch but during the nesting season they choose an old, broken stump upon which to lay their single, spotted egg. For most of the time they relax with eyes open and head forward, but if disturbed they will stretch upright and close their eyes to the merest slits. They then blend perfectly with the branch and in such attitudes they are quite approachable, content in the belief that they are unseen. When provoked, however, the disturbed bird will open its eyes and gape and snap with its bill in the most startling manner.

Potoos are found through the West Indies and adjacent areas of Central and South America. There are five distinct species, but only the Common Potoo *Nyctibius griseus* and Giant Potoo *N. grandis* are at all well known. In these species incubation is shared by both members of the pair, but incubation and fledging periods are unknown. The chick is covered with white down and brooded almost continuously by the adults.

The Common Potoo is found in Central and South America in open wooded country where, resembling an extension of a post or stump, it is easily overlooked. It feeds in the manner of a flycatcher.

Owlet-frogmouths Aegothelidae

The eight species of owlet-frogmouths are confined to New Guinea and Australia. Like other members of the Caprimulgiformes they are cryptically coloured and active at dawn and dusk. They are similar to the frogmouths, nightjars and potoos, but the facial feathers of the owlet-frogmouths give them the flat-faced appearance of an owl – an impression heightened by their habit of sitting as upright as a potoo. Unlike most other members of the order they sit across, rather than along, branches. Owlet-frogmouths are almost as vocal as the other families uttering a faint 'churr' like that of the nightjars.

Owlet-frogmouths are found in bush and forest country and, while they hawk for insects like the nightjars, they take most of their food on the ground like the frogmouths. They will rise from the ground to take flying insects, but the vast majority of their prey consists of flightless insects caught on the ground. Their legs are long and strong, at least compared with nightjars, indicating an ability to move about easily on the ground.

Thus within the Caprimulgiformes there are individual families that catch their prey by hawking in the air (nightjars), by pouncing shrike-like (frogmouths), flycatcher-like (potoos), and on the ground (owlet-frogmouths).

Two clutches are usually laid between September and December and the three or four rounded white eggs are laid in a hollow tree which is lined with leaves or animal fur. It is reported that the leaves are replaced by fresh ones as they become soiled and wither. This is an unusual but charming habit for a hole-nesting species. The white, down-covered nestlings soon grow a brown, immature plumage.

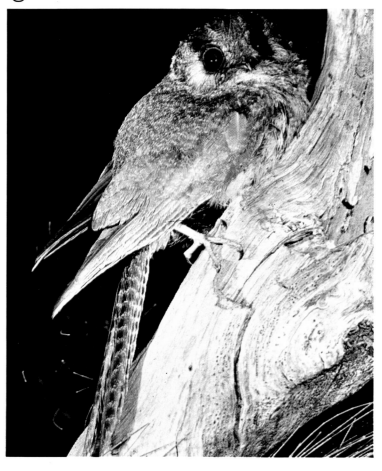

The Australian Owlet-nightjar is a large-eyed, nocturnal species found in the wooded parts of Australia and Tasmania. It feeds by hawking like a nightjar, but also pounces on insects on the ground.

Nightjars Caprimulgidae

Goatsucker, night hawk, poor-will and chuck-will's-widow: these and a host of other strange names have been heaped upon the nightjars. Almost every countryman in every part of the world, apart from New Zealand and the Pacific islands, knows their calls which are invariably prolonged and monotonous. Few have ever seen them, however.

Nightjars are birds of dawn and dusk. During the day they lie up, concealed by their superbly cryptic plumage. Then, as the last rays of the sun disappear, they begin to call. The common European Nightjar *Caprimulgus europaeus* utters a continuous 'churring' call that varies in volume as the bird turns its head this way and that. The Gaboon Nightjar *C. fossii* utters a continuous 'tok-tok-tok-tok' call that never varies in pitch.

After a period of calling the birds normally go on the hunt. Like all nocturnal species they are soberly dressed in mottled browns and buffs, although when they fly some of the males show white or cream patches on the wings or tail that serve to identify them to females. Silently they glide and hover like giant-sized moths, flitting almost lazily over the ground around trees and bushes. They are complete masters of the air, indeed their short, weak legs are barely sufficient to support the body let alone to walk on. If a nightjar wishes to move only a yard or so it will fly rather than walk.

Flying on soft wings, the nightjars hawk for moths and other large, nocturnal flying insects which they take in the air with their huge mouths. Like some other aerial feeders they have a strongly developed set of rictal bristles that aid the funnelling effect of a large mouth.

The camouflage of the nightjars is so perfect that they can often be approached to within a few feet before flying. It is perhaps no accident that they keep their eyes closed during the day, for they are large eyes adapted to nocturnal use and ruin the effect of camouflage if open. Cryptic plumage tends to be so similar between species that the birds have to rely on calls and other signals to identify one another, and this is also the key to the would-be nightjar-watcher. While a few species have elongated feathers that they wave like flags, most nightjars have a very distinctive voice which can be learned and then provides instant recognition.

As it flits among vegetation, the European Nightjar sometimes utters a sharp 'kwik-kwik' call that seems to serve as a contact note. It also indulges in aerial displays involving the male twisting his tail to the vertical, and then clapping his wings together with a loud smack. Other nightjars have a more involved aerial display.

The Pennant-winged Nightjar *Semeiophorus vexillarius*, for instance, has the innermost primaries extraordinarily extended to twice its own length. As it flies, the brown and white feathers flash in the air. This bird is silent and it seems that fluttering pennants are a satisfactory substitute for a far-carrying cry. No doubt the handicap of such appendages to the wing does hinder the flight of the bird, and it is not surprising that they are broken off as soon as they have served their purpose in courtship. The similarly endowed Standard-winged Nightjar *Macrodipteryx longipennis* is hampered by having a single long shaft extending from each wing with the usual feather structure apparent only at the tip.

All nightjars nest on the bare ground where one or two blotched

Found throughout most of North America, the Common Nighthawk nests naturally on the ground among scant vegetation. It has, however, found that the flat roofs of office blocks offer a satisfactory substitute and has penetrated quite large cities as a result.

The Red-necked Nightjar is found only in Iberia and adjacent parts of North Africa. Typical of the other nightjars in habits, it is most frequently seen rising from little-used tracks in the headlights of cars.

or mottled eggs are laid. Both sexes share the parental duties of incubation and care of the young. The Common Nighthawk *Chordeiles minor* of North America has responded to a disappearing habitat, a factor that progressively more of the nightjars are having to face worldwide, by taking to the lonely flat roofs of skyscrapers and office blocks to nest. Indeed this species now seems more common in towns than in the countryside.

Nightjars find their proper home in the tropics where insect life is abundant. Here, several species may live side by side, for there are some sixty-nine species to be found in the world. Those nightjars that exist in temperate latitudes, including the European Nightjar, are summer visitors migrating towards the equator for the winter. Some of these migrants manage to rear a couple of broods during their brief summer sojourn.

The American Poor-will *Phalaenoptilus nuttallii*, so named because of its call, has in recent years been responsible for raising the controversial question of hibernation once more. This time it has been shown that these birds do hibernate to pass the winter in crevices of canyons in Arizona. Temperature and metabolism are reduced to tick over levels until the birds emerge the following spring. Birds even return to the same spot to hibernate in successive winters.

To most people nightjars are things that make noises in the night and it is perhaps not surprising that they should be the subject of so many strange country tales. Sucking the milk of goats is as strange as any, and although it doubtless stems from the habit of taking insects disturbed by animals, it shows how imaginative and gullible folk can be.

Swifts Apodidae and Hemiprocnidae

Swifts are the most aerial birds in the world. It may be that other groups cover a larger annual mileage, but there can be no doubt that no birds fly longer hours or even faster than the various swift species, nor is any group of birds so perfectly adapted to an aerial existence. Swifts catch and eat their prey on the wing, they gather nesting materials on the wing, they mate on the wing and there is sufficient evidence to show that at least some species spend some nights actually sleeping on the wing. This does not mean that they sleep for a regular eight hour stint, but that the catnaps that they take during the night are sufficient to sustain their metabolism.

The swifts, which are related to the hummingbirds and which some authors regard as very close relatives, are usually regarded as a suborder containing two families. The Hemiprocnidae is composed of three species of crested swifts found only in South-East Asia and the western Pacific. The Apodidae consists of some sixty-three species of typical swifts found almost throughout the world except in southern South America. Asia supports the greatest populations of swifts, but most of the better-known species are cosmopolitan.

The Apodidae consists of two distinct subfamilies based on the presence or absence of spines at the end of the tail feathers. The spines of the Chaeturinae aid the bird when clinging to its nest site or roost, while the Apodinae have a different clinging adaptation, the fourth toe is capable of facing forwards. Within the spine-tailed swift group the genus *Collocalia* consists of some twenty species of very similar, highly confusing cave swiftlets that breed colonially, are famous as the producers of birds' nest soup (said to taste like a superior consommé), and are so much in need of systematic work as to leave a large element of doubt about how many distinct species there are.

Also members of this subfamily are the large spine-tailed swifts of

One of the most remarkable of all birds' nests, the Palm Swift glues a few feathers to the underside of a palm frond, and then sticks its two eggs to the nest. On hatching the chicks must immediately grasp the nest with their claws and cling there until ready to fly.

the Far East among which are included the fastest birds on earth. All the true spine-tailed swifts (not the swiftlets) build similar nests in similar situations in hollow trees where the structure is glued to the inside wall of the hollow. The Brown-throated Needletail Swift *Hirundopus giganteus* of India, Java, the Celebes and Philippines is so large that it lays its eggs in the base of a hollow tree. This species may well be the fastest animal in the world, being capable of speeds of up to 200 miles an hour.

Best known of the spine-tailed swifts is the Chimney Swift *Chaetura pelagica* of North America which, like some others, has taken to nesting in man-made equivalents of hollow trees. Large factory chimneys will hold several nests of the Chimney Swift glued to the smoky inside, and on migration huge spirals of birds develop above a favoured roosting site before they dive by the thousand down into the chimney. Ringers, or in America banders, have been able to mark thousands of birds at these roosts. Chimney Swifts gather windblown material and break off dead twigs to form their nest cup glued to the chimney side.

The cave swiftlets stick their nests to the walls and ceilings of caves often by the thousand in suitable areas. Like bats and oilbirds, several of these birds find their way about in the total darkness of the deeper caves by echolocation. Some species construct their nests out of pure saliva without a mixture of bark, feathers or other material. These nests, primarily those of the Edible-nest Swiftlet *Collocalia fuciphaga*, are the most sought after and prized for soup manufacture. When the birds have constructed their nests they are immediately knocked down by 'specialized trapeze artists' with long bamboo poles. Subsequent repeat nests have a significant increase in impurities – the birds simply run out of spit – but are collected and refined nevertheless.

One of the strangest nests of all is built by the Palm Swift *Cypsiurus parvus*. This 4-inch long bird sticks a pad of feathers to the underside of a palm frond and then sticks its egg to the feathers. Incubation consists of the bird clinging to the frond and covering the egg. Despite the fact that the nest and egg get blown about in the wind the real problem arises when the chick hatches for, although naked like other swifts, it must immediately cling to its nest until completely fledged and ready to fly. This instant flight ability is, of course, one of the characteristics of all swifts, for most of them rise from the ground only with the greatest of difficulty. Thus young swifts spend a long time in the nest between hatching and fledging. They must fly and feed themselves perfectly first time – there are no second chances.

The fork-tailed swifts of Central America build long, tubular structures hanging from rocks, branches and under the eaves of houses. The tube, which may be up to two feet long, is entered from the bottom and the eggs are laid on a shelf in the globular top chamber.

Of the other typical swifts, the Eurasian Swift *Apus apus* is by far the best known. It breeds over large areas of the Palaearctic and has, in most areas, adapted to man-made habitats. Like the other swifts, it is totally dependent on flying insects but, being a migrant to northern latitudes, it has evolved a series of fail-safe mechanisms to protect itself and its offspring. If the Eurasian Swift arrives during inclement weather it will quickly make a reverse migration to milder climes. It can leave its eggs in a state of suspended development without harming them, and the chicks are able to subsist on their own body fat when the adults are unable to find sufficient food to feed them. There is even some evidence suggesting that these birds can induce a state of torpidity, and exist without temperature control for short periods.

The three species of the family Hemiprocnidae, the crested swifts,

While most Common Swifts nest in holes in buildings this bird has retained the original habit of nesting in a hole in a tree despite the presence of a small wasps' nest above its head.

are found in South-East Asia and are streamer-tailed birds of brighter colours than the almost uniformly slate brown and white typical swifts. Like the parakeets with which they frequently share their forest home, they fly on long wings with much flapping and,

with their tail feathers pressed together, produce a strongly attenuated shape. With a close approach their crests can often be seen in flight. They are less aerial than the other swifts and parties frequently become inconspicuous as they roost together on the branch of a tree for anything from a few minutes to an hour or more. The nest is nothing more than a few feathers and pieces of bark stuck to a branch with hardened saliva on which the single egg is glued.

Hummingbirds Trochilidae

The Cuban Bee Hummingbird *Mellisuga helenae* has a body just a shade over $\frac{1}{2}$ inch in length. The bill is a similar length and, together with its long tail, the bird measures $2\frac{1}{4}$ inches overall. It weighs less than 2 grams and its wings beat fifty to eighty times a second producing a high pitched hum. It feeds entirely on and around flowers and supports its high metabolism mainly on nectar. It is the world's smallest bird and almost an 'honorary insect'. It is also just one of the 320 species of hummingbirds that comprise the Trochilidae, one of the most extraordinary families of birds in the world.

Hummingbirds have a characteristic mode of flight that produces the hum that gives them their name. They are confined to the New World and have no exact ecological counterpart in the Old World. The nearest group is the sunbirds. The sunbird 'jewels' of Africa and Asia have iridescent plumage and a similar diet of nectar and insects, but they are nowhere near as aerial as the 'hummers'. Furthermore, they do not show the variety of forms exhibited by

the hummers and as a group are not as individually distinguished.

Hummingbirds vary in size from the minute Bee Hummingbird to the Giant Hummingbird *Patagona gigas* of the High Andes, which is the same length as a thrush, about $8\frac{1}{2}$ inches. The majority of species are about $3\frac{1}{2}$ inches in length. They are most numerous among the subtropical cordilleras of the Andes–Amazon area in Ecuador, Colombia and neighbouring parts of Peru. Here, the lushness and altitudinal range combine to produce a wide variety of ecological niches that hummingbirds have evolved to fill. Away from this region, to the north and south, the number of species declines rapidly. Nevertheless, hummingbirds are found from Alaska south to Tierra del Fuego. These hummingbirds of higher latitudes are of necessity migratory and the Ruby-throated Hummingbird *Archilochus colubris* makes a quite remarkable flight across the Gulf of Mexico and the West Indies to South America. This extraordinary journey for a bird that is only $3\frac{1}{2}$ inches long has become one of the bases in the study of avian metabolism and of

Like most hummingbirds, this Sparkling Violet-ear enjoys bathing. It is extremely vocal for a hummingbird and is also unusual in that the male takes his turn with incubation. The plumage of this species is one of the most brilliant of the violet-ears.

the consumption of fat during migratory flight.

Some hummingbirds are of sombre plumage, but the vast majority are brightly coloured with patches of high iridescence. Like the sunbirds of Africa, it is often difficult to pick out the exact colour as the hue changes with the reflection of light. This makes for considerable difficulty in identification, a skill not aided by the extreme mobility of the birds. Hither and thither they fly at quite extraordinary speeds, still for a moment, but then off once more to another flower. A perched bird gives an opportunity for study, but normally only a brief one. From their vivid colours come many of their names – ruby, topaz, amethyst, and so on. Others are named after their bills or tails which in many species are highly developed.

Each hummingbird has evolved a bill to enable it to collect nectar from a particular flower or group of flowers. In one case a scientist was able to predict the existence of an unknown flower by an examination of a hummer's bill. He was proved correct when the flower was later discovered. Most hummingbirds have long bills that enable them to reach deep inside flowers without soiling their plumage, but flowers are themselves extraordinarily beautiful and strangely shaped organisms. The Sword-billed Hummingbird *Ensifera ensifera* has the proportionately longest bill of all birds. It is quite as long as the bird itself and forms what is a highly effective nectar 'pipeline'. In contrast, the Buff-tailed Sicklebill *Eutoxeres aquila* boasts a strongly decurved bill for probing its favourite flower.

Tails too are highly variable, although not for the same reasons as bills. In general, hummingbirds have long tails composed of broad feathers that act as an effective rudder and brake. While many have rounded tails, other shapes include square-ended, forked, streamered and scissor-shaped. Some tail feathers show quite extraordinary development. The Spatuletail *Loddigesia mirabilis* from Peru has only four tail feathers, but the outer pair are greatly extended, cross over and end in large racquet-like tufts. The Black-throated Trainbearer *Lesbia victoriae* has long streamers that are several times longer than the head and body, and yet, like a peacock, it manages to fly efficiently. All of these tails as well as the iridescence of the body plumage are used in display, for hummingbirds are highly territorial birds.

Hummingbirds live solitary lives coming together only to mate. The males are extraordinarily aggressive in defence of their territories. They will chase out their own kind and even attack a large raptor or owl should it be foolish enough to venture within their boundaries. Many species apparently assemble at display grounds where the males perform the most elaborate aerial displays to attract a mate. When a female approaches, the male may display in the air above her perch. Mating often takes place in flight, a habit shared with the hummingbirds' nearest relatives the swifts, but by few other birds.

The duties of rearing the young invariably fall entirely upon the female which lacks the bright display colouring of the males. Anyone who has seen gaily coloured male hummingbirds darting through the mottled sunlight of a forest clearing will appreciate their lack of suitability for nesting duties. The tiny cupped nest, often smaller than a matchbox, is placed on a horizontal branch and covered with camouflaging lichens and mosses. The two eggs are white and rely on the muted colours and insignificance of the female for their safety. Incubation is a lengthy process lasting from fourteen to nineteen days. The young hatch naked and blind and take a further twenty-two to twenty-four days to fledge. Such lengthy pre-fledging periods are commonly found among birds that are completely dependent on flight and which must be first-flight experts in order to survive. The youngsters do not grow down, but pass directly into an immature plumage stage which, apart from

being duller, is similar to that of the adult female.

While many things about hummingbirds are unusual and fascinating, it is their aerial mastery that picks them out from the rest of the birds of the world. Only the Giant Hummingbird seems capable of anything like normal flight, the rest buzz about just like insects. Photography of hummers in flight calls for an elaborate array of sophisticated electronic equipment, flash guns and automatic trip devices. The results reveal the quite incredible powers of these tiny little birds. They have all the manoeuvrability of a helicopter and more besides. They can hover head motionless before a flower. They can fly upwards, downwards, sideways, on their sides, on their backs, they can even do battle in the air. Unlike any other bird they can fly backwards. They have the largest sternal keel in proportion to their size of any bird and this supports the largest proportionate flying muscles. High speed cinematography has shown how the wings of a hummingbird move backwards and forwards creating lift in both directions. It shows how the wings can move independently, and how many times per second they beat.

A Glittering-bellied Emerald, caught in flight by the speed of the flash, feeds predominantly along forest edges often at considerable heights from the ground.

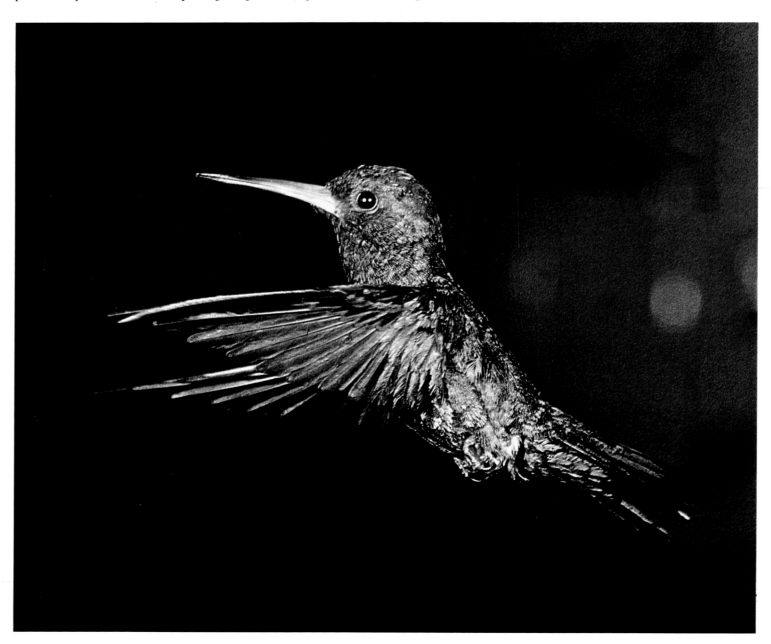

During the display of the male the audible 'buzz' of his wings indicates a wing-beat rate in excess of 100 beats per second.

As with helicopters, this manner of flight is highly expensive on fuel. To cope, the hummingbird must take on fuel in the form of nectar or insect food at frequent intervals. During the hours of darkness this is not possible and hummingbirds are able to lower their body temperatures by over a third and regularly enter a state of semitorpidity, to tide them over during the night. This is similar to the torpid state in which the American Poor-will passes the winter in some parts of the western United States, but the hummingbird may do so *every* night.

Nectar, then, is the 'high-octane fuel' that keeps hummingbirds airborne, but, as already mentioned, they also take insects. The birds are not capable of manipulating the mandibles to catch and consume insects, nor do they use the tongue as do the woodpeckers. Instead the prey is taken in flight when the insect is forced into the open gape by the speed of the moving bird. Nectar is also taken in flight, but while a moth may suck it up through its proboscis, a hummingbird moves its tongue in and out between nectar and bill. The feet are small and weak and used only for perching. Thus hummers cannot cling to flowers in the manner of sunbirds. Indeed, even when they take to the air they do not push off with their legs, but simply rise on their wings.

Despite its size the Ruby-throated Hummingbird regularly migrates across the Gulf of Mexico, covering a distance of some 500 miles in a single non-stop flight. It is one of the better-known and more distinctive members of the family.

Opposite A female Black-chinned Hummingbird sits on her neat nest of fibres lashed to a horizontal branch by cobwebs. This bird breeds in the western United States and migrates southwards to Mexico to winter.

Above A young Broad-tailed Hummingbird, lacking the red on the throat of the adult, is photographed on a conifer in the Rocky Mountains in North America. Like other northern hummingbirds it is a migrant.

Over the greater part of the eastern United States the only hummingbird is the Ruby-throated Hummingbird. Its prodigious migrations across the Gulf of Mexico – 500 miles without a stopover – make particularly critical demands upon the bird's metabolism. Ruby-throated Hummingbirds have been clocked at speeds of up to 60 miles per hour flying alongside cars, although wind-tunnel experiments indicate a maximum of only half of this speed. Like other hummers the Ruby-throated Hummingbird produces its own 'hum' in flight, and experiments have shown that this is because whatever the airspeed, the bird continues to beat its wings at fifty-three beats per second. To cope with increased wind speed the bird simply changes the angle of its wings. As with other birds, the muscle responsible for the downward beat of the wings is considerably heavier than that powering the upbeat. While the upstroke muscle in most birds is about two per cent of the weight of the downstroke muscle, in the Ruby-throated Hummingbird the figure is nine per cent.

Before setting out on migration the Ruby-throated Hummingbird, like other long distance migrants, puts on a store of fuel in the form of fat. During its migratory flights this is used up. Calculations have shown that on migration this hummingbird crosses the Gulf of Mexico at a steady 25 miles per hour in twenty-five hours.

These calculations are made more complex by the extremely small size of the subject. All living things use energy to maintain their body temperature and hummingbirds, by virtue of their small size and comparatively large surface area, should use proportionately more energy to maintain their body heat. In fact they have a copious covering of feathers (940 on a Ruby-throated Hummingbird) that acts as highly efficient insulation and allows maximum energy to be utilized for flying.

The Ruby-throated Hummingbird penetrates into southern Canada yet it is not the most northern of hummingbirds. That distinction goes to the Rufous Hummingbird *Selasphorus rufus* which breeds as far north as southern Alaska. Here it frequents mountains up to 11,000 feet high, and evidently migrates vertically as the lowlands become drier during the course of the summer. They will feed on whatever flowers happen to be available, although their predilection for red objects was demonstrated to the members of an expedition to Admiralty Island, who found Rufous Hummingbirds buzzing about tomato cans and a red handkerchief. The male Rufous Hummingbirds are polygamous and the nests of a single male are often closely grouped, although tended by different females.

To their downfall, but to the relief of taxidermists, hummingbirds have a tough skin, and their exceptionally fine colours made them much in demand at the time when no lady's hat was complete without a bird in it. A London dealer imported almost half a million hummingbird skins in a single year during the nineteenth century, and tens of millions of birds must have perished for the sake of the millinery trade while the fashion lasted. Most skins ended up on hats, but some were made into brooches while others were mounted under glass domes to be placed between the aspidistra and the portrait of the Queen.

Most birds were collected by natives and among the mass of

material, ornithologists were able to identify a wealth of new species. Unfortunately the exact place and date of collection was often missing, and to this day some species of hummingbirds are known only from one or two specimens rescued from the fate of female adornment.

Some of the tropical species of hummingbirds are highly localized but there is no reason to suppose that they are in any danger. Doubtless the opening up of the Amazon will take its toll, but it will also provide opportunities for study that have been hitherto impossible. In their approach to man, hummingbirds are fearless. They will come to special sugar feeders even when supported from a human hand.

Mousebirds Coliidae

The mousebirds, or colies as they are often known, are so peculiar that they have been placed in an order of their own – the Coliiformes. The six species all belong to the same genus, however. Mousebirds exhibit a variety of structural peculiarities. The species are very similar and the sexes alike. The plump, rounded body carries a tail that is almost three times its length and markedly tapered. The head is crested and the stubby bill down-curved. All four toes can be pointed forwards, although two may point backwards in the manner of a woodpecker. The claws are long and sharp, and this enables the birds to climb about among the dense vegetation of thorn bushes where they are effectively hidden. The

The long tail of this White-backed Mousebird projects well beyond its nest. A South African representative of this largely Ethiopian family, it is a highly gregarious bird and a common fruit-eater.

name mousebird stems from their climbing habits and shyness.

Mousebirds are usually seen appearing from the centre of a dense bush one after another before disappearing into the next. They are highly gregarious at all times of the year and even 'off duty' nesting birds will form flocks. They fly fast on rounded, whirring wings and often manage a glide before landing. Their similarity to overlarge Long-tailed Tits has been noticed by many visitors from Europe. Unlike most other birds, the feathers of mousebirds grow all over their bodies and not in tracts.

Mousebirds are great fruit eaters and will excavate the flesh of a fruit through a small aperture while leaving the skin intact and the fruit on the tree. They are often regarded as pests by farmers particularly for their depredations on buds and shoots. They are found only in Africa south of the Sahara but are widespread and common in many areas.

Trogons Trogonidae

The thirty-five species of trogons are among the world's most colourful birds. They are found in all tropical areas from South and Central America, to Africa south of the Sahara, and in Asia. That such a distribution should be exhibited by such a sedentary family has led ornithologists to believe that this is merely a relict distribution of a group that was once far more widespread. Fossil remains from France support this conclusion.

Trogons vary between 9 and 14 inches in length and are exceptionally brilliantly coloured. The breast is often red, but also yellow, green and blue. Upper parts are green or brown, but also sometime blue. Bold patches of colour are obvious when the birds are seen closely, but in the dappled light of their jungle homes these same patches tend to break up the bird's outline in an effective camouflage.

All trogons have short, rounded wings and long tails, but they are not weak fliers like the turacos. They do not fly long distances, but they feed in the air in the manner of flycatchers. Far Eastern species feed entirely on insects caught in this way, but Neotropical birds also eat considerable amounts of fruit that they pluck in flight before consuming on a favoured perch. Like several other groups of perching birds, trogons have two toes pointing forwards and two pointing backwards. In their case, however, it is the first and second, not the first and fourth, that point backwards, a feature unique among birds. Like other aerial feeders the legs and feet are weak, being merely used for perching, and the birds appear to sit upright on their bellies.

Trogons nest in holes which they excavate themselves in soft and decaying wood. Their weak bills, although ideal for catching flies, are ill suited to drilling living timber. Some species find termite mounds make ideal nesting sites and the Gartered Trogon *Chrysotrogon caligatus*, which lives along the forest edges of Central America up to 5,000 feet, frequently excavates its nest chamber in the paper nests of social wasps. While digging, the Gartered Trogon feeds on the wasps and their grubs, and seems to be immune from stings.

Trogons lay their two, three or four oval eggs directly on the hole floor with no attempt at lining the chamber. These are white, sometimes with a bluish or buff tinge. Both sexes – the female is invariably duller than her mate – share the incubation which lasts seventeen to nineteen days. The young are born naked and fly after sixteen to twenty-three days.

Most resplendent of all the trogons is the Quetzal *Pharomachrus mocino*, often called the Resplendent Quetzal. In this vividly green, blue and crimson bird the upper-tail coverts are extended to form a train as long as the bird itself. This is the national bird of Guatemala and long sacred to the Aztecs and other ancient civilizations. Its hole-nesting habits are not conducive to keeping the elongated feathers in the best of condition, and they are often broken and worn by the end of the season.

The members of the genus *Harpactes* are the only Oriental trogons and widespread in Malaysia where eight of the eleven species are found. Though they are remarkably similar to trogons found elsewhere in the world, these Asiatic birds are not great fruit eaters. Insects form the bulk of the diet though small reptiles and amphibians are also taken. Leaf buds are important on a seasonal basis.

Museums are remarkably careful with their collections of trogon specimens, for the birds have the thinnest of skins, and feathers fall from them at the slightest handling. Indeed, most collectors find them almost impossible to skin intact.

The Resplendent Quetzal boasts one of the longest tails of all birds. Its vivid green plumage made its feathers much prized by the Aztecs who inhabited Central America prior to the Spanish conquest.

Kingfishers Alcedinidae

Kingfishers, one could be forgiven for assuming, are the 'kings of fishermen'. However, while some species are quite definitely experts at dealing with the small fishes on which they feed, a great many members of the Alcedinidae do not only never fish, but do not even live near water. Like shrikes, they are great watchers and waiters, and while the familiar kingfisher of Europe or North America sits patiently overlooking some stream, many of his tropical cousins sit equally still, overlooking nothing more than insect-ridden scrub. Even known fishermen sometimes take insects if they are presented.

Kingfishers are a boldly coloured group of birds closely related to those other 'jewels' the bee-eaters and rollers, and to the hornbills. The eighty-six species vary from 4 inches to over 18 inches in length and they are found throughout the world, save its northern and southern extremities. Most species are not migrants, a fact that makes the temperate species particularly prone to hard weather. The short legs are weak and merely serve to perch, two toes being joined together almost throughout their length. The bill is often brightly coloured and is large and well adapted to fishing. However, it is generally accepted that the kingfisher's bill was adapted to their original dry land habitat, and that it just happens to be suited to an aquatic existence – scientists refer to this as 'preadaption'. The Shovel-billed Kingfisher *Clytoceyx rex* of New Guinea has developed a powerful, blunt scoop of a bill that is ideally adapted to digging. It is hardly surprising that its favourite food is earthworms.

All kingfishers nest in holes. The fish-eating species use holes in the banks of streams that they excavate themselves, and the dry land species nest in ready-made holes in trees or in termite mounds. Like other hole-nesting species the two to seven eggs are white and are laid on the bare floor of the hole. Reports of kingfishers laying their eggs on a nest of fish bones refer to the accidental accumulation of food remains in the nesting chamber. Both members of the pair share in the incubation and care of the young.

The kingfishers are divided into three subfamilies: the Cerylinae which are 'fishermen', the Daceloninae which are forest or woodland species; and the Alcedininae some of which are fishers and others not.

Typical of the Cerylinae 'fishermen' is the Pied Kingfisher *Ceryle rudis*, which is found throughout Africa and parts of Asia. Its bold, black and white plumage and general noisiness make it difficult to overlook as small groups chase one another low over the water. It invariably fishes from the air by hovering and is then solitary and silent. It is a confiding little bird and can often be approached very closely. In contrast the Giant Kingfisher *Megaceryle maxima* is a huge 18-inch bird that fishes from a perch. It too is found in Africa but is by no means as common as the Pied Kingfisher. Its North American relative, the Belted Kingfisher *M. alcyon*, is a familiar bird along the banks of streams and rivers. It is a fisherman with the same predilection for minnows as the Common European Kingfisher *Alcedo atthis*. Like that species it will emerge from the water with its catch; twist it and bang it against the perch to stun it, before turning the unfortunate fish

Opposite The Little Kingfisher of northern Australia and New Guinea is one of the smallest members of its family. It frequents rivers, creeks and lakes that are overgrown with emergent vegetation.

Below The White-breasted or Smyrna Kingfisher breeds from Turkey to China and feeds on a variety of small reptiles, amphibians and small birds as well as fish. The choice of habitat is equally catholic.

Right Kookaburras, the Laughing Jackasses of Australia, are kingfishers that need little water. They inhabit woodland areas of eastern Australia and live on a diet of insects, snakes and other reptiles.

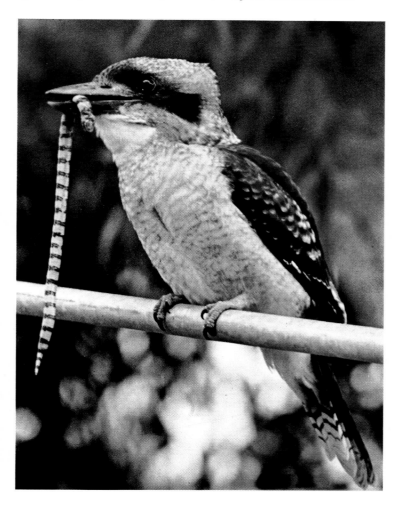

The Brown-hooded Kingfisher is an African species that inhabits open bush country in South and East Africa. Like other 'dry' kingfishers it feeds rather in the manner of a shrike.

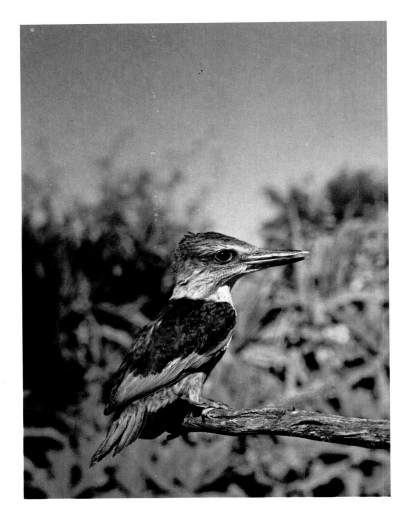

headfirst to swallow it. Both species will visit the shoreline in hard weather, for when the streams and ponds freeze over there is no food for the kingfishers.

The Dacelonidae contain many kingfishers of arboreal habits. In general they are less brightly coloured than the 'fishers' and their browns and greys merge easily with their background. Most notable of this group is the Laughing Kookaburra *Dacelo novaeguinae* of Australia. In fact there are two kookaburras, the Laughing and the Blue-winged *D. leachii*. While the Blue-winged Kookaburra is found around the warmer northern half of Australia, the Laughing Jackass, as it is often known, is a bird of the eastern half of the continent that has been successfully introduced into Western Australia and Tasmania. Its rolling, laughing call is one of the best-known sounds in the animal world. It is well known to be partial to the young of other birds and snakes, as well as insects and small reptiles. The fact that kookaburras often call together in chorus only serves to heighten their notoriety.

Northern New Guinea is one of the centres of world kingfisher distribution. No less than twenty-four species are found on the island. The Little Kingfisher *Alcyone pusilla* at 4 inches is the smallest kingfisher in the world while others are among the largest. The Hook-billed Kingfisher *Melidora macrorrhina* excavates its home in the nests of tree-dwelling termites, and finds its food on the ground among the leaves of the forest floor. Most of New Guinea's kingfishers feed on the great wealth of insects to be found there. Some specialize in winged insects, others in beetles, while some, like the Blue-black Kingfisher *Halcyon nigrocyanea*, feed on almost anything that comes their way on land or in the water. Mangrove Kingfishers *H. chloris* from south-east Africa apparently feed almost entirely on crabs.

Todies Todidae

The five species of todies are confined to the West Indies. They are 4 to 4½ inches long and all share the same basic plumage pattern. Indeed, some authorities have suggested that the five forms are merely geographical races of a single species, so difficult are they to tell apart. Fortunately both the Narrow-billed Tody *Todus angustirostris* and the Broad-billed Tody *T. subulatus* are found on the single island of Hispaniola, and live together in close proximity without apparently interbreeding. Thus these two at least seem quite distinct species, and there is no reason why the other three should not be treated similarly. While the Narrow-billed Tody is a mountain bird of tropical jungles, the Broad-billed Tody favours dry lowland areas. The other species are more catholic in their choice of habitat, for each is confined to a single island. The Cuban Tody *T. multicolor*, the Jamaican Tody *T. todus*, and the Puerto Rican Tody *T. mexicanus*, are all basically similar in plumage.

Todies are close relatives of the kingfishers and motmots and like them have partially united toes pointing forwards. They are rotund little birds with bright green backs, crimson patches of beard, yellow under-tail coverts and a vinous wash along the flanks. The bills are sharp and dagger-like and held at an angle of 45 degrees to the horizontal.

Todies are insectivorous, feeding mainly on flying insects that are captured flycatcher-like in the air. They favour hunting low over the ground and are often easy to overlook. They are territorial birds

The dainty todies are a family of similar West Indian birds closely related to the kingfishers that, like kingfishers, excavate holes in banks in which to nest. This bird is the Puerto Rican Tody.

and usually found either singly or in pairs. The male is extremely vociferous in defence of his patch and utters a variety of rattling calls.

Todies nest in burrows which they excavate in soft banks, and the entrance hole is no larger than that used by a tit or chickadee in an artificial box. The tunnel may be up to a foot in length. Both sexes share in the incubation of the three or four spherical, white eggs and in caring for the young.

Motmots Momotidae

Motmots are beautifully coloured, green or rufous birds with a strong physical resemblance to the bee-eaters of the Old World. They have the same bold colours, particularly about the head, the strong, down-curved bills and the elongated tail feathers. Nevertheless, these New World birds are more closely related to the kingfishers and the diminutive todies.

There are eight distinct species of motmots, ranging from Mexico to Argentina. Their distribution coincides with that of the Central and South American forests, because unlike the majority of bee-eaters, motmots are solitary, tree-loving birds. Their wings are short and rounded and not swallow-like as in the bee-eaters, their bills are serrated, and their foot structure is very similar to that of the kingfishers with three forward-pointing toes and one backward.

The most prominent feature is the tail, the central feathers of which are extended. When these are freshly grown they are covered with vanes as are normal feathers, but as the bird preens and brushes the tail against vegetation the innermost vanes become broken-off leaving a naked shaft with a broad tip of vanes at the end. The bird often twitches its tail as it sits along a branch, and it has the curious habit of holding its tail sideways.

Like the other members of its small family, the Turquoise-browed Motmot is a bright green and blue bird marked by an extended tail. It is found only in Central America.

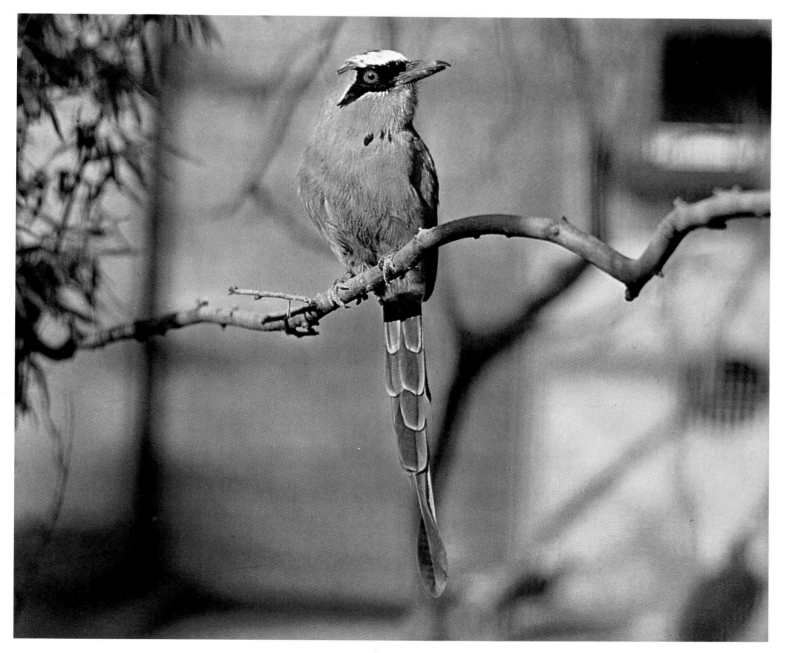

Motmots feed on insects which they grab from vegetation, the ground and occasionally in flight. Like the bee-eaters they beat their prey before swallowing it, although, in general, they are not dealing with harmful stinging insects. They take all manner of food including fruit.

Like kingfishers and bee-eaters, motmots excavate a nesting tunnel in a bank of soft earth. This may be up to six feet in length and the three or four eggs are white. Incubation, which is shared, lasts about three weeks and the young take a month or more to fledge. They are fed on a mixture of insects and other animals, but fruit becomes important as they grow to maturity.

The Blue-crowned Motmot *Momotus momota*, by virtue of its preference for the edges of forests, is one of the more familiar members of the family. It has taken to living in agricultural plantations with success. Its bright colours make it an attractive aviary bird and it is widely kept in captivity.

Bee-eaters Meropidae

Bee-eaters are an Old World family consisting of twenty-five of the most colourful birds. Varying from 6 to 14 inches, the length of the larger species includes the elongated central tail feathers that are such a feature of these birds.

Most bee-eaters are a vivid green, but some are red and others brown. Without exception their colours are bright and various, giving rise to the nickname 'rainbow bird' in many parts of the world. They are expert fliers, and in the air, because of their long wings and agility, they are reminiscent of the swallows. Their habit of perching on trees before diving off after insect prey is similar to that of the flycatchers, although their coloration and occasional habit of taking prey from the ground is more akin to the shrikes.

As their name implies, bee-eaters are the great enemy of bee-keepers. They feed mainly on bees and wasps that they catch in flight in their long, tapering, decurved bills. The unfortunate insect is treated to a bout of beating and wiping on the ground or branch before it is swallowed. No doubt this is an adaptation to dealing with stings. In most parts of the world bee-eaters are well liked and in the tropics they consume vast numbers of locusts.

The brightly coloured Red-throated Bee-eater inhabits the arid Sahel zone immediately south of the Sahara. It is resident, comes regularly to feed in gardens and breeds in colonies that may reach considerable proportions.

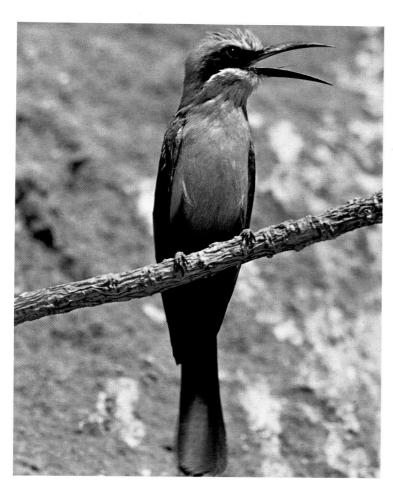

Some of the migratory species, especially the European Bee-eater *Merops apiaster*, present a serious menace to apiarists. When the species bred in Britain in 1955, far north of its normal range, the birds took to a Sussex sandpit surrounded by the orchard land that is the centre of British bee-keeping.

Bee-eaters spend most of their time perching on their weak, kingfisher-like legs in trees and more recently along telegraph wires. They also hunt from the air. Parties, especially migrants, are more often heard than seen as they circle high overhead, hawking like swallows. Their characteristic flutey, whistling calls are far-carrying and essential to keeping flocks together. Bee-eaters are gregarious birds hunting and migrating in parties, often more than a hundred strong, and nesting in colonies consisting of ten to many hundreds of pairs.

Most bee-eaters excavate a chamber in a sandy cliff in the manner of a kingfisher or the Sand Martin, but the Australian Rainbow Bee-eater *M. ornatus* prefers to dig into level ground and even European Bee-eaters do so in 'cliffless' areas like the Coto Donaña of southern Spain.

The tunnel is normally several feet long, and the unlined nest chamber at the end holds two to eight white eggs. Incubation takes twenty to twenty-two days, and fledging a further month. Both sexes participate in excavating the chamber and rearing the young.

Left The White-fronted Bee-eater is an ecological replacement of the Red-throated Bee-eater in the savannah lands of East and Central Africa. It is slightly longer and heavier than that bird, but lives a remarkably similar life.

Below The curious relationship between the Carmine Bee-eater and the Kori Bustard seems to be rather one sided. The Bee-eater uses the huge bird as a mobile perch, swooping off from time to time to catch insects that the Bustard disturbs.

The largest colonies are those of the Carmine Bee-eater *M. nubicus*, which is found throughout tropical Africa, although their breeding colonies are few and far between. In some cases, several thousand pairs of these birds gather at traditional nesting sites. Their vivid, carmine plumage with the elongated central tail feathers, is broken only by the iridescent, bottle green colour of the head and a few pale blue feathers on the wings. When large numbers are together the spectacle is one of the most colourful wildlife shows on earth. Like other bee-eaters, the Carmine Bee-eater is a partial migrant with some populations moving slightly southwards.

From their tropical origins bee-eaters have spread to areas from where they must, of necessity, migrate. The European Bee-eater breeds throughout the Mediterranean, northwards around the Black Sea, and eastwards to Pakistan. Some winter in India and in the Aden area, but the vast majority of birds migrate to Africa where they are numerous and widespread. Some colonies have become established in South Africa and these birds migrate northwards to winter.

The Rainbow Bee-eater migrates northwards out of Australia to winter in New Guinea and the adjacent islands. Here it may come across the Red-bearded Bee-eater *Nyctyornis amicta* which is essentially a forest-dwelling species. It is a vivid, green bird with pink forehead and a bright crimson beard. Unlike other bee-eaters it is catholic in its tastes and has been frequently observed clambering about among the branches of trees in its search for insects. Sometimes, it probes for grubs like a woodpecker, while at other times it hovers to take caterpillars. It is found in forest clearings and excavates its nest along the banks of a stream. Its close relative, the Blue-bearded Bee-eater *N. athertoni* is similar but it has a blue rather than a crimson chin, and is said to attract insects because of this colour.

The Little Green Bee-eater *M. orientalis* is a widespread, common bird from The Gambia across Africa and Asia to Malaya. But a population has broken away to occupy the Nile Valley where it has become a migrant. In summer it is found in the great delta of that river, while in winter it moves southwards and can then be found among the great temples of upper Egypt.

One of the most curious habits of any bird is that of the Carmine Bee-eater. A great many birds feed on or in association with large mammals or reptiles, but there are few others that use another species of bird as a perch. The Carmine Bee-eater is particularly fond of perching on the backs of Kori Bustards although it will also use the large game animals of Africa. While the Bustard snaps up any immobile creatures it comes across, the Bee-eater swoops off to catch insects that fly as they are disturbed. Presumably this one-sided relationship is simply tolerated by the Bustard.

Cuckoo-roller Leptosomatidae

The Cuckoo-roller *Leptosomus discolor* of Madagascar is an aberrant relative of the true rollers and the ground-rollers. It is 17 inches long and, unlike the other rollers, the sexes are dissimilar. The male is an iridescent, green-grey which may, in some lights, reflect a copper colour. Below, it is a paler grey which extends in a band across the nape. The feathers of the face extend forwards to cover the base of the upper mandible. The female is a browner bird with black barring.

Cuckoo-rollers are noisy, gregarious birds of the forest canopy. They feed on insects and arboreal reptiles and are particularly fond of hairy caterpillars. Parties of the birds fly gracefully overhead on their large, slow-beating wings, skimming the tree-tops. When calling from a perch the crest is raised and the throat extended to produce a loud whistle. Like the true rollers they have weak legs and feet and are capable of turning the fourth toe to face backwards. Breeding data are scant but the eggs are white and laid in a tree hole.

Rollers Coraciidae

Members of the family of rollers are among the most colourful of Old World birds. The eleven species of true rollers are found from Europe to Australia centred on tropical Africa where seven species are found. Ground-rollers are usually accorded subfamily rank, because they are confined to Madagascar where, together with so many other bird groups, they have evolved separately.

True rollers are predominantly blue in colour and acquire their name from the tumbling aerobatics that they perform during nuptial displays. They are compact birds about 9 inches to 13 inches in length, although several species additionally boast long tail streamers. While the Abyssinian Roller *Coracias abyssinica* has simple streamers, those of the Racquet-tailed Roller *C. spatulata* are tipped with vane-like racquets. Most beautiful of all, the Lilac-breasted Roller *C. caudata*, has a simple, but deeply forked tail.

Rollers have strong, powerful heads like the larger gulls and the shrikes, with medium-sized down-curved bills. Their feet are weak with the two forward toes partly joined and the fourth toe reversible – ideal for perching, but of little use when walking. On the ground, rollers seem almost legless and shuffle about in the most ungainly manner. They feed like shrikes by pouncing on insect prey from a prominent perch.

Rollers like to perch and it would be forgivable to think that telephone engineers have lined the roads of Eurasia and Africa specifically for their benefit. Throughout their range rollers are more often seen on wires and poles than anywhere else. In Rumania one spring I remember counting European Rollers *C.*

garrulus on every alternate pole for mile after mile across the Dobrudja plains. When put to flight the birds would simply move down the line a couple of poles, perhaps bursting into a bout of 'rolling' along the way. During these performances the birds twist this way and that, seemingly tumbling through the air in a blaze of blue.

Rollers eat mainly insects but they will also take small birds. They are most numerous around locust swarms which they follow as a mobile feast. The summer fires of the African savannahs also attract large numbers to feed on crippled prey brought out into the open.

Rollers nest in holes, often in trees, but also in banks. The three to six white eggs are laid in an unlined nest, and both parents tend the chicks which hatch naked and helpless.

The European Roller is 12 inches long. It is coloured pale cobalt

Top left The Lilac-breasted Roller is one of the most beautiful members of its family. Its finery is shown to advantage during the rolling courtship flight that gives these birds their name.

Top right A Eurasian Roller at its nest hole in a pine in southern Europe. This colourful summer visitor feeds on insects, reptiles, small mammals and birds which it hunts from a perch.

Right Dollarbirds are rollers found from Australia northwards to India and Korea. They are predominantly insectivorous and catch their prey mainly on the wing. Like other rollers they nest in natural holes.

blue below, and the back is a rusty brown, with black primaries and centre tail feathers. It is widespread throughout Europe, although it is confined further south in the west than in the east. It reaches southern Sweden and as far north as Leningrad in Russia, but it is absent from all but southernmost France and is not found in Britain. Like other rollers that have moved into temperate lands, it is a migrant moving southwards into Africa to winter.

Broad-billed rollers are generally rather duller than the true rollers and do not tumble in the air in display. The Broad-billed Roller *Eurystomus glaucurus* of Africa is a reddish brown bird with deep blue wings and a prominent, yellow bill. Better known is the widespread Dollarbird *E. orientalis*, named after a round, silver patch in the wing which is translucent and about the same size as an American silver dollar. It breeds from India to Australia with the outer range populations migrating back to their tropical centre of origin which extends from Malaysia to New Guinea.

They are jungle-fringe birds, perhaps more fond of hawking for insects in flight than the other species. They are most active at

dawn and dusk, flying on slow, steady wingbeats like nightjars in their search for food.

Ground-rollers are long-tailed, squat-bodied, short-winged birds with long, powerful legs and sharp, down-curved bills. This group of five Madagascan endemics is recognized as a subfamily, although several authorities have treated it as a separate family with some justification. Certainly, their resemblance to the true rollers is slight and their terrestial habits are totally different.

Four of the five species live on the forest floor flighting to a perch on short, rounded wings only when disturbed. A fifth species lives in the semidesert of the south-western part of the island. This bird, the Long-tailed Ground-roller *Uratelornis chimaera*, looks very like the Roadrunner of America.

Almost everything known of this strange and interesting group has been gleaned from natives and remains to be verified by ornithologists. The eggs are apparently spotted or white and laid in a hole in a bank excavated by the bird itself. Natives also report that they hibernate!

Hoopoe Upupidae

Like a sewing machine, the Hoopoe *Upupa epops* prods the lawns of gardens throughout the Old World. Thoroughly, and in the most business-like manner, it searches and probes head-down, seemingly oblivious of all around it. In many parts of the world it allows the closest of approaches, but get too close and its light cinnamon plumage bursts into bars of black and white as it flies to cover.

The Hoopoe is the sole member of the Upupidae and is represented by nine distinct subspecies scattered over most of the Old World continents. There is little difference between them, and all are quite unmistakable. The body is pale cinnamon verging on orange, with the back and wings prominently barred with black and white. An erectile crest is usually carried flat on the head extending behind the crown.

Several authorities have suggested that the Hoopoes be divided into several quite distinct species. Their case is based on small, but

arguably significant differences of plumage. Certainly other genera are divided on just as slight differences.

Hoopoes are ground-feeders with strong walking legs and well-developed feet. In the northern parts of their range they are migratory, and in Europe northward-bound migrants often overshoot to northern latitudes such as Britain, where they occasionally stay to breed in the southern counties.

The female is slightly duller and smaller than the male and takes full responsibility for incubation. The nest is placed in a hole, a tree, a bank or among rocks, and the four to six pale blue eggs are usually laid in an unlined nest. The Hoopoe has an unenviable reputation for foul personal habits, because nothing is removed from the nest chamber and the eggs are soon stained by the female's droppings. The male feeds the female on the nest for the eighteen days of incubation. The naked young take three to four weeks to fledge.

The Hoopoe gets its name from its gentle repeated 'poo-poo' call which is surprisingly far-carrying. The reactions that it provokes over its wide distribution are varied, but it is generally tolerated. In some parts of Asia it is considered a delicacy, whereas in other areas it is strictly taboo as food.

The boldly coloured Hoopoe is a widespread inhabitant of open woodland and gardens throughout the Old World. Numerous populations have been recognized but they are all generally regarded as belonging to a single species.

Wood-hoopoes Phoeniculidae

Often classified with the Hoopoe in the Upupidae, the wood-hoopoes are a distinctive group of six species found only in Africa. They lack the bold pattern and terrestrial habits of the Hoopoe. Their slim shape is accentuated by a long, stiff tail and they are inconspicuous in their aboreal habits. Like tree-creepers, wood-hoopoes have long, sharp-clawed toes, ideally suited to climbing trees where, in the manner of those birds, they pick insects from the bark. Their long, decurved bills are also similar to the tree-creepers'.

They are medium-sized birds, 9 inches to almost 18 inches long. In colour they are generally dark with a strong metallic gloss that gives them a brightly coloured appearance in some lights. The long tails are spotted with white and the bills are brightly coloured red or orange. Though generally difficult to see over most of their range, in some places, wood-hoopoes can be quite confiding. The Green Wood-hoopoe *Phoeniculus purpureus*, for instance, visits bird-tables among the large gardens that surround Lake Naivasha in Kenya.

All wood-hoopoes prefer open acacia to dense forest, and their distribution reflects this predilection. Several species occur around the edges of tropical rainforests, but seldom venture far inside. The Forest Wood-hoopoe *Scoptelus brunneiceps* is a case in point, and even though it feeds mainly in the canopy it is confined to open woodland and forest clearings.

Like Hoopoes, wood-hoopoes nest in holes and have little use for nest lining. The three pale grey-blue eggs are incubated by the female alone and she is a particularly tenacious sitter. The nests are quickly fouled by the bird's droppings and a notably unpleasant smell issues from the hole. Outside the breeding season wood-hoopoes are both noisy and gregarious.

Like an overlarge tree-creeper, the Green Wood-hoopoe spends most of its time climbing trees where it picks insects from the bark with its long, decurved bill. It will, however, come to food put out for birds in gardens.

Hornbills Bucerotidae

The forty-five species of hornbill are among the strangest of the world's birds. All are larger than 15 inches in length, and some grow to almost 5 feet. The huge ground hornbills walk the plains of Africa at gazelle height and look immense when they take to the air.

All hornbills are marked by a huge bill, which is often topped by an almost equally huge, red, yellow, or horn-coloured casque. In some species the casque is considerably larger than the bill because, despite its proportions, the hornbill's bill is of no significant use to it for feeding. While most of these casques are hollow, one species has a solid lump of ivory that natives carve in the manner of mammalian ivory.

This grotesque, over-weighted front-end is only partially balanced by the long, usually rounded tail, and in flight hornbills look like huge crosses in the sky. Their characteristic flappy flight is interspersed with glides and seems both light and uncertain.

Apart from the ground hornbills, the legs are short, and the front three toes are partially joined. Hornbills live predominantly in forests, but several species are common across the savannahs of East Africa. Hornbills tame easily and are frequently kept as pets and even totems by natives – their peculiar nesting habits making them a symbol of marriage fidelity. Around most of the modern safari lodges hornbills have become as much a part of the landscape as the Marabou Storks, and a considerably greater attraction. Large flocks of Red-billed Hornbills *Tockus camurus* congregate at the sounding of the lunch gong at Tsavo National Park's Kilaguni

Lodge. Here, birds and tourists eat together.

More normal hornbills live on a diet of fruits, berries, insects, small mammals, lizards, and so on. While some species do tend to specialize, others are virtually omnivorous. Whatever they feed on, the birds swallow their food whole, usually by throwing the fruit or animal into the air and allowing it to fall into their gullet. Indigestible remains are regurgitated. The habit of tossing food into the air is easily transferred to other objects and tame hornbills will amuse endlessly by throwing sticks and other things.

The nesting habits of the hornbills are extraordinary. Having found a suitable hole and laid her one to five, commonly two, eggs the female is sealed in by the male which brings mud to mix into a rock-hard, cemented structure across the hole entrance. Only a narrow slit remains open and for the period of incubation and at least part of the fledging period the hen remains in her cramped hole totally dependent on the male for food. In some species it is the hen herself that barricades the entrance with mud and saliva brought by her mate. While incubating, the female uses the period of activity to pass through a moult. Males may visit the sitting female up to once every half-hour.

Incubation may last from thirty to fifty days and fledging may take as long. Female Silvery-cheeked Hornbills *Bycanistes brevis* have spent as long as 112 days incarcerated in their holes, and doubtless some of the larger species spend even longer periods. When the young are well grown the hen hacks her way out of the

Left With its huge bill and well-developed casque, the Great Hornbill seems curiously top heavy in appearance. It inhabits lowland forest in western India and is also found from the Himalayan foothills into Malaysia.

Above Two closely related species photographed together. The difference in bill size as well as colour is clear between the Red-billed Hornbill (above) and the Yellow-billed Hornbill (below).

Opposite The Ground Hornbill of Africa is a hunter of the plains of southern Africa. Although easily overlooked as it walks among tall grass, in the air its enormous size is impressive.

chamber, a process that may take almost a day. At first, for lack of exercise, she is unsteady on her feet and incapable of flying. Once she leaves, the youngsters patch up the entrance which is once more reduced to a slit. Now, both parents are free to bring food, and before long the youngsters are able to hack away the mud and leave themselves. They too are often unsteady and incapable of flight.

There are, of course, modifications of this technique. Species that lay only two eggs are often maintained by the male alone, the female remaining inside the nest hole until the youngsters are ready to fledge and then leaving with them. The ground hornbills *Bucorvus* species apparently do not bother with mud at all – perhaps the female's bill is a sufficient deterrent to would-be intruders. Hornbills are, of necessity, clean nesters. Food debris is carefully passed outside and both female and chicks void through the slit.

The ground hornbills are all black with red wattles on the head. They consume huge quantities of grasshoppers and other terrestrial insects as well as lizards, amphibians, and small mammals. Like the Secretary-bird, with which they are often found, they seem quite

able to deal with snakes. On some occasions the male of these species may actually relieve his mate on the nest. Ground hornbills are used as disguises in the Sudan where natives tie a stuffed head to their own while they crawl towards their prey on all fours through the tall grass that the hornbills inhabit.

Hornbills are found throughout Africa into Asia, Malaysia, the Far East as far as the Philippines, to New Guinea and the Pacific Islands. Of all the tree-dwelling species the largest is the 5 feet-long Great Hornbill *Buceros bicornis* of western India and South-East Asia. This huge bird looks very strange perched in a tree, although the trees among which it lives are constructed on the same lavish scale. The birds roost communally, and it is probable that this is associated with their diet of fruit. Where abundance of fruit occurs, gregarious hornbills will be more likely to find it. Despite their size, Great Hornbills also adopt the practice of sealing the female into her nest hole. The large tail feathers are much in demand for head-dresses by the primitive tribesmen of the hill country in which they live.

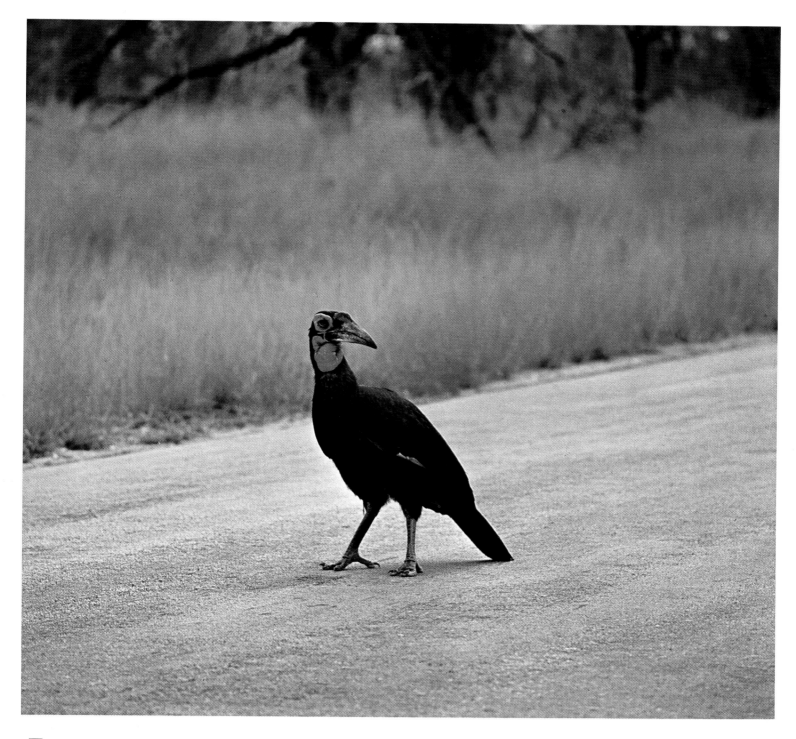

Jacamars Galbulidae

Superficially, the jacamars resemble the bee-eaters of the Old World but they are members of the order Piciformes, and are most closely related to the puffbirds and woodpeckers. Like bee-eaters they are slim, brilliantly coloured birds with extended tails and long, pointed wings. They catch their prey in flight with great aerial mastery, and they excavate their own nest holes in river or roadside banks. There the similarity with the bee-eaters ends, because jacamars are solitary, forest-dwelling birds.

Like the flycatchers, jacamars sit on the exposed branches of some tree or bush alert for passing prey. They prefer to live at the edge of forests, in clearings, or over streams. Their favourite prey is the large, colourful butterflies and dragonflies that most other birds ignore. They suddenly dart from their perch and grab the

insect with their long, thin bills, often with a loud snap of the mandibles. Returning to their perch the insect is beaten roughly on a bough to remove the wings, before the soft body is swallowed.

Like other aerial species, jacamars have weak feet and legs. Most have two toes pointing forwards and two back, although in the genus *Jacamaralcyon* the second hind toe has been lost. Males, like hummingbirds, are brightly coloured in iridescent, metallic hues. Green and bronze predominate, their shades changing as they catch the light. The birds vary in size from 5 to 11 inches, the largest being the Great Jacamar *Jacamerops aurea* of Central and South America. Females are generally more dull. Their calls carry a long distance, and, at least in some species, are not unpleasant to the ear. The little trills of the Rufous-tailed Jacamar *Galbula ruficauda* are,

Opposite Jacamars are birds of forest clearings, perching on exposed branches and darting after insects. **1**. White-throated Jacamar **2**. Brown Jacamar **3**. Dusky-backed Jacamar **4**. Pale-headed Jacamar.

in fact, quite melodious.

Jacamars excavate their own tunnels in the manner of bee-eaters. These are about twelve to eighteen inches deep, and the female usually does most of the work. It is she also that incubates during the long hours of the night, although she is relieved by her mate during the day. The unlined chamber contains two to four unmarked, white eggs, and the down-covered chicks hatch after twenty to twenty-three days.

Both parents bring food and scraps, and the droppings of the young soon foul the nest. Strangely enough the same hole may be used in following years despite the risks of parasitic infection. Fledging takes twenty to twenty-five days.

Puffbirds Bucconidae

Puffbirds like to perch. They sit on some exposed branch or tree along the forest edge in upright postures awaiting the first sign of movement by a passing insect, caterpillar, or lizard. In such attitudes their feathers are puffed out giving them a bulky appearance, as well as their common name. Most are dully coloured birds, but those of the genus *Monasa* are boldly patterned black and white, and are often called 'nunbirds' as a result. Most species are oblivious of fear and are called 'stupid johns' by the natives of Brazil where the majority of species are found.

Puffbirds have two toes pointing forwards and two back. Their bills are broad and chunky and ideally suited to catching small insects in flight. They also take prey from the vegetation and sometimes from the ground in the manner of shrikes. The thirty species are found predominantly in the Amazon Basin, although some have spread northwards into Mexico and some south to Paraguay. Most puffbirds are solitary, but nunbirds often gather in flocks. They are generally silent and at most utter high-pitched squeaks and whistles.

The White-whiskered Softwing *Malacoptila panamensis*, with its northern and western distribution, is the only species that is at all well known. The male is a rich brown in colour with lighter underparts; the female is more dully coloured. Along with other puffbirds they have a strong growth of rictal bristles which help to funnel aerial prey into the large mouth.

They nest in a burrow which they excavate themselves in sloping ground. The entrance is camouflaged with twigs and leaves. The

Puffbirds are stolid inhabitants of the tropical jungles of South America. They live on insects, excavate nest holes in banks or termite hills and sing pleasing duets. This species is the Sooty-capped Puffbird.

tunnel descends gently for about eighteen inches, and the nesting chamber at the end is lined with dead leaves. The two or three glossy, white eggs are incubated by both sexes, the male taking the night shift and the female the day. Other species have a more normal, alternate short shift incubation schedule. The naked and blind young are brooded by the male alone while the female performs all of the foraging and feeding. After a few days the chicks move to the tunnel entrance in their eagerness to be fed, although they return to the chamber to spend the night behind a screen of leaves that they erect themselves. Fledging takes about three weeks.

Barbets Capitonidae

The seventy-six species of barbets are closely related to the Old World honeyguides and the New World puffbirds, giving a clue to their extraordinary pan-tropical distribution. Doubtless, these three groups have evolved from a common ancestor that was once widespread throughout the tropical regions of the world. Today they are found in tropical America, in Africa south of the Sahara, and in the Far East. They are best represented in Africa, where more than half of the species are found, and in Asia. Only two genera occur in America, but they are among the most colourful members of the family.

Barbets vary from 3½ to more than 12 inches long, but the majority are sparrow-sized, chunky birds. They have a strong growth of rictal bristles, or in some species actual tufts of feathers, and from this stems the common name. Their bills are generally strong – in the case of the Toucan Barbet *Semnornis ramphastinus* of Colombia and Ecuador massively so – though they are not as powerful as those of the woodpeckers. As a result their nesting chambers, which otherwise resemble the woodpeckers', are generally excavated in dead or dying trees where the wood is softer and more accommodating. Some species habitually excavate their holes in termite mounds.

Barbets are resident throughout their range and are generally weak fliers with short, rounded wings. They have strong heads and dumpy bodies of green or similar colouring. Most species boast bold flashes of colour on the head. These may be reds or blues, yellows or even black, and are crucial for identification. In most species the sexes are similar. The barbets' feet are strong with two toes pointing forwards and two back although they are not as powerful as those of the woodpeckers.

The attractively spotted D'Arnaud's Barbets live in open bush country in East Africa, in contrast to most other members of their family which are woodland birds. They are also unusual in excavating nest holes in the ground rather than in rotten trees.

The Yellow-fronted Tinker Barbet is an African species with a predominantly western distribution. The thick woodpecker-like bill and arboreal habits are typical of the family.

Barbets are birds of the forest spreading into more open areas only where trees are plentiful. In Assam they are found in the shade of the tea plantations, as well as in the surrounding forests. Some African species are found in the savannahs, but only where acacias provide them with perches. Several of the long-tailed species, such as D'Arnaud's Barbet *Trachyphonus darnaudii*, have the habit of sitting very still among the foliage of a tree and effectively disappearing like a wryneck. Yet this barbet is exceedingly confiding and will come to feed at table at the game lodges of Kenya. Barbets are predominantly vegetarian, feeding on fruit and seeds. The young, however, are often fed on insects and some species are purely insectivorous.

Several of the Asian and African species are renowned for their calls and are often referred to as 'brain fever birds' by white settlers enduring the heat and humidity of the tropics. Their calls, at first pleasing, are continued with a monotony that eventually becomes infuriating. The Coppersmith, or Crimson-breasted Barbet *Megalaima haemacephala*, derives its name from its endlessly repeated metallic note. It is a medium-sized, green bird, short-tailed and dumpy in appearance, with a crimson breast and forehead and a yellow throat. Like other barbets it hunts among the outer branches of the canopy, although it is quite capable of clinging to the trunks of trees in the manner of a woodpecker. It is found throughout India, Sri Lanka, and Burma and its voice, at least, is a characteristic sound of that part of the world. Some pairs of barbets produce quite appealing duets.

The large Red and Yellow Barbet *Trachyphonus erythrocephalus* of Africa is a boldly patterned bird with the deeply undulating flight of a woodpecker. It is found in the bush country that stretches from Somaliland to northern Tanzania, and nests almost exclusively in termite hills. Its unmistakeable 'toogle-doogle' call is repeated endlessly, sometimes in a chorus of several birds at the same time.

Barbets are hole-nesters, for preference in rotten trees, but also in banks. Like those of the woodpeckers, the entrance hole expands into a downward cavity in which the two to five white eggs are laid. Both parents participate in the incubation and feeding routines. African species often play host to the honeyguides' chicks which have formidable hooked bills at birth.

While most barbets are solitary, the small tinker-barbets of the genus *Pogoniulus*, no more than $3\frac{1}{2}$ inches long, are gregarious and even nest in colonies. They spend much of their time fighting noisily as they move through the forest. Typical of these smaller birds is the Prong-billed Barbet *Semnoris frantzii* of the New World. It is strictly vegetarian, and gregarious, so much so that the birds will roost together in disused woodpecker holes like wrens. Up to sixteen have been counted in a single chamber at night.

Honeyguides Indicatoridae

Honeyguides are nondescript little birds closely related to the barbets. They are generally dull green, olive, brown, or grey with little to distinguish them other than white markings on the tail. One species has splashes of orange on the rump and forehead which, in comparison with the other thirteen species, makes it boldly coloured. Yet behind this dull exterior, honeyguides are among the most interesting birds in the world.

Their names, both scientific and common, stem from their habit of leading man to the nests of bees and wasps. But this is no simple 'follow and see' routine. Two honeyguides, including the Greater Honeyguide *Indicator indicator*, actively lead men and animals to the nests of these insects. Having located a nest the bird will approach a native and call loudly to attract attention. It fans its tail, displaying the white patches to advantage, and then flies conspicuously a short distance into the bush. Gradually it leads the person towards the nest, which may be as much as a quarter of a mile away, all the time displaying vigorously. At the end of this performance it waits while the nest is robbed and the honey taken, before feeding on the wax cones that remain. Invariably some of the honey is left, because it is a native superstition that a reward for the bird should be left to encourage it to come again. Indeed, this superstition takes a stronger

A Lesser Honeyguide attacks a piece of honeycomb which it has taken from a wasps' nest. Its unique ability to extract food value from the indigestible wax is aided by special stomach bacteria.

form in which the unrewarded bird will next time lead the unsuspecting to a lion, snake, or some other danger.

Basically, honeyguides feed on insects, particularly bees and wasps, and have a particularly thick skin perhaps as a protection against stings. Many insects are taken in the air.

The honeyguide is unique in feeding on wax, which is highly indigestible and of low nutritional value. But the honeyguide's intestine contains a peculiar bacterium that aids digestion. There is some evidence that honeyguides are gradually abandoning their guidance of natives in many areas, perhaps due to a lack of success as Africans become less dependent on gathering and hunting, but there is no doubt that this strange symbiotic behaviour is inherited. The honeyguides are also brood parasites in the manner of a cuckoo leaving the upbringing of their young to other birds. No doubt the habit originated in conjunction with the Ratel or Honey Badger which inhabited this region long before man appeared on the scene. Even today the Ratel often benefits from the unusual association.

Honeyguides lay their eggs in the nests of barbets and woodpeckers, although the Greater Honeyguide boasts a list of over forty species which it has been known to parasitize. Other honeyguides make use of the open nests of whiteyes and flycatchers. When the young honeyguide hatches it is armed with a hook at the tip of its bill with which it quickly dispatches the other occupants of the nest. The growth drops off after a week or so when its function is fulfilled. The youngster is then cared for by its foster parents so that it has no chance of learning its peculiar honey-indicating habits from the adults of its own species.

Toucans Ramphastidae

Toucans are a New World family consisting of five genera divided into thirty-seven distinct species. They are confined to the dense tropical jungles of the Amazon Basin and adjacent areas, and their name stems from the 'tucano' given them by the Tupi indians of Brazil. They vary from 12 inches to 24 inches in length, but in some species over half of this is made up by the bill, which is such a feature of the family.

All toucans have huge, boldly coloured bills which give them a distinctly out-of-balance appearance. In fact, the bills are masterpieces of engineering, being both exceptionally strong and exceedingly light in weight. Beneath the hard sheath they consist of a honeycomb of bone, pound for pound one of the strongest forms of construction. The plumage of toucans is frequently black, although many of the smaller species are sombre greens. All have bold patches of colour particularly on the head and neck. Some are

Closely related to the toucans, the araçaris boast similar outlandish bills that may serve several distinct functions. The Black-necked Araçari is found in forests and plantations from the Amazon basin northwards to Colombia.

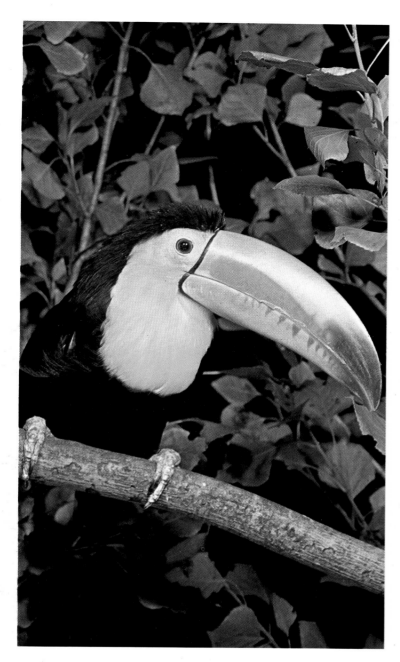

The Keel-billed Toucan has one of the brightest coloured bills in a well-endowed family. It is found from Mexico to Venezuela and is widely kept in captivity. It feeds freely on fruit and insects.

The toucan's bill and its function have been a cause of considerable debate among ornithologists. Some suggest that it may play a significant part in courtship. But although birds have been noted clappering their bills together, passing food to one another, and even mutually preening, its role in courtship has yet to be proven. Others suggest that it is ideally adapted to reaching out for fruit, but other birds manage quite well without such a bill. Yet again it has been suggested that the bill is an intimidation to would-be predators and that toucans defend their nest holes against intruders with a flash of their bill, or that it effectively scares other birds from the nest so that the toucan can feed on their young. Whatever the truth, toucans do sometimes find their bills an encumbrance. Food, taken delicately in the tip, has to be thrown into the throat with an upwards jerk of the head. And both long bill and long tail are embarrassments in the narrow confines of a nest hole.

Toucans are strong-legged birds with two toes pointing forwards and two back. They are essentially arboreal and find most of their food among the canopies of trees where they are easily overlooked. Fruit is the dominant food though insects and other items are also taken, particularly when feeding young. The wings are rounded and the larger species fly with a series of flaps followed by a lengthy glide. The smaller araçaris and toucanets have a more direct flight.

They are generally gregarious and noisy birds with a well-developed sense of curiosity. They roam the forests in search of food, although the toucanets of the genus *Aulacorhynchus* make vertical migrations in the Andes synchronized with the different ripening times of fruit and berries.

Toucans nest in natural holes or in those of woodpeckers, sometimes evicting the owner to do so. While they may enlarge the entrance and clear away the debris from the nesting chamber they do not excavate themselves. Nest height depends entirely on the height of the chosen hole and may vary from a few feet to near the top of a forest giant. The two to four white eggs are incubated by both parents and hatch very quickly, perhaps in as little as sixteen days. During this period the sitting bird often leaves the nest after short stints of incubation, but one bird always maintains an all-night vigil. The young toucans hatch naked and are slow to develop. They remain blind for up to three weeks and do not fledge, even in the smaller species, for over six weeks.

In the Collared Araçari *Pteroglossus torquatus* the nest may be invaded by several adults (or subadults) soon after the eggs have hatched. The extra birds may be the young of a previous brood, but nevertheless a hole must be a very cramped place in such circumstances. All the birds roost together in the hole, and all bring food for the developing young. It is perhaps just as well that toucans have a tail structure that enables them to tuck it up out of the way over their backs. When roosting outside the safety of the nesting hole they tuck their bills beneath the feathers of their backs and throw the tail upwards to cover it.

white with orange eye patches, others white with blue, and yet others yellow, red, or green. The colours of the face tend to accentuate the bill itself making it appear even longer and more massive than it actually is. It also varies considerably in colour, sometimes within the single species as with the Keel-billed Toucan *Ramphastos sulfuratus*. The bill of this bird may consist of patches of almost any colour at all. Within the bill the tongue is itself a peculiar structure reaching to the tip of the bill and being serrated and notched near its tip. The end is covered with bristle-like structures.

Woodpeckers Picidae

The woodpeckers are a well-defined family of thirty-six genera divided into 209 species. Two distinct subfamilies, the Jynginae (wrynecks) and Picumninae (piculets) are separated from the true woodpeckers, the Picinae. Woodpeckers are widespread and well distributed in forest country throughout the world save in Australasia and Madagascar where they are not found. Almost all species are dependent on forests for their livelihood and the true

woodpeckers are the most highly adapted for a life in and among the trees.

The legs and feet are strong with well-developed claws. The second and third toes point forwards with the first and fourth pointing backwards. In the three-toed woodpeckers the normal vestigial first toe has been lost completely. The feet are ideally suited to clinging to the trunks of trees, and most members of the family spend much of their time climbing tree trunks and major branches in search of food. The bill is strong and pointed, and used for chiselling for insects and their larvae in and below the bark. When an insect hole is found the woodpecker inserts its extremely long tongue to extract its prey. This tongue, which is barbed at the tip and covered with a glue-like secretion, sticks to the insect or larva which is then extracted and swallowed. Many woodpeckers have tongues almost as long as their bodies and a unique retraction system in which the root of the tongue curls around the rear of the skull, over the eye, sometimes being anchored behind the eye and in some other species at the base, or even tip, of the upper mandible.

The woodpecker's tail is pointed, or occasionally rounded, and the shafts are extremely strong. It is used during climbing, and when the bird is hacking into a tree the tail forms the third leg of a tripod providing a firm support. The strength of this comparatively small bird is remarkable as it chips wood from the trunk of a living tree. Firmly supported by its 'tripod' the whole force of the body is used, as the chisel bill is thrown at the wood. The neck seems to arch back like a spring between each well-directed chisel movement. In fact, the neck is long, but exceedingly strong and well muscled, while the head is strong, powerful, and well insulated with bone to withstand the continued shock of impact.

Woodpeckers feed by searching the bark of trees for insects. Starting at, or near, the base they will work their way systematically upwards around the bole prodding all the time with the bill. When found, a short burst of chiselling is usually sufficient to open a

Above Change-over at a Wryneck nest sited in a tree hole. This widespread, but easily overlooked, species is a summer visitor across the Palaearctic region from Britain to Japan.

Opposite A female Green Woodpecker brings a mouthful of ants to its eager young. The species' predilection for this food means that it is frequently seen feeding on the ground, unlike most other members of the woodpecker family.

cavity for their tongue to do its work. Nearing the top of the trunk the bird then flies down to the base of one nearby to repeat the process. Feeding on such small prey, woodpeckers spend the bulk of their day searching for food. In doing so they are often oblivious of the approach of humans, although some of the larger species often keep the trunk of the tree between themselves and an observer while they continue with their work.

In many parts of the world several species of woodpeckers live side by side, sometimes even feeding in the same tree. That two such similar birds can co-exist in this way indicates either different food or different feeding methods. It is, of course, very difficult to ascertain what food a given species is taking, but in the case of the familiar Greater Spotted Woodpecker *Dendrocopus major* and Lesser Spotted Woodpecker *D. minor* of Europe, the larger bird feeds on the trunk while the smaller feeds on the outer branches. Similar habitat differences between 'pairs' of species can be found in other parts of the world.

Several woodpeckers have adapted to more open conditions and are less dependent on forests that the typical birds. The Green

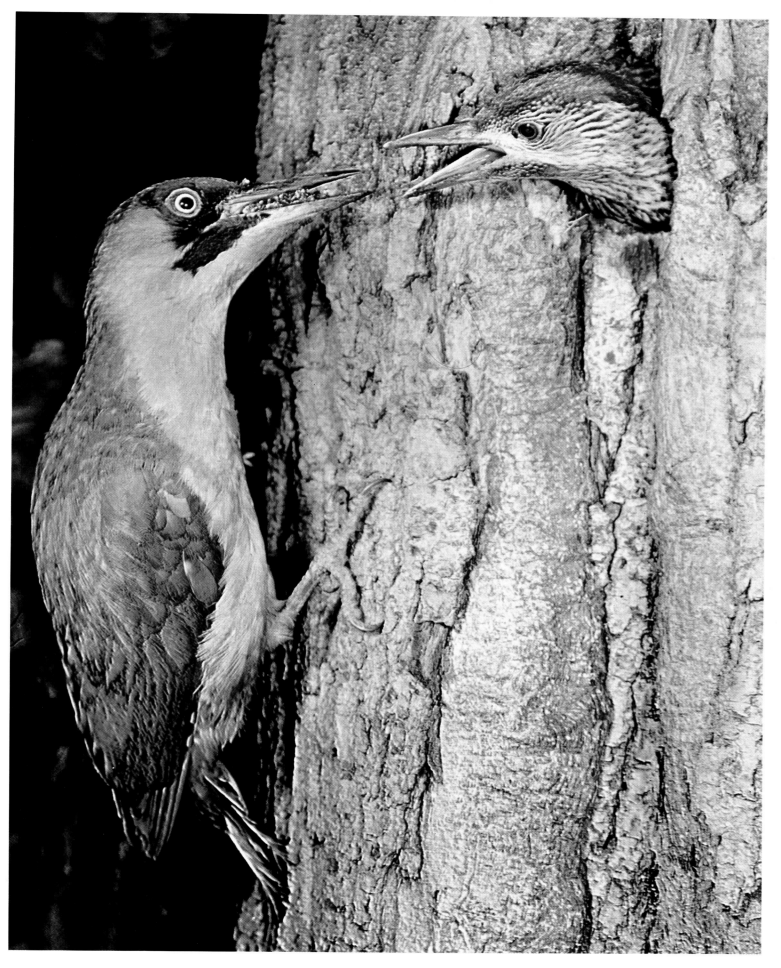

A Yellow-bellied Sapsucker at its nest hole in the western United States. As the name implies, these birds drill holes into the living tree and return later to consume the sap that has accumulated.

Woodpecker *Picus viridis*, for example, frequently feeds on ants on the ground, using its bill to excavate their nests and its long tongue to extricate the insects and their pupae. The American flickers are even more emancipated from the forests and habitually feed on ants. Even the coating of their tongues is alkaline to deal with the formic acid of ants. While the North American Red-shafted Flicker *Colaptes cafer* and Yellow-shafted Flicker *C. auratus* still retain the arboreal nesting habits of woodpeckers, some South American flickers have abandoned the trees altogether and excavate their holes in banks or termite mounds. One species, the Andean Flicker *C. rupicola*, has even become a colonial nester, in sharp contrast to the solitary lives lived by the majority of woodpeckers.

Most woodpeckers are medium-sized birds between 5 and 12 inches in length, but some are considerably larger. The Black Woodpecker *Dryocopus martius* of Eurasia is 18 inches long, while the Ivory-billed Woodpecker *Campephilus principalis* of the southern United States is 20 inches long. Such birds need very large trees in which to nest, and while there is no evidence of a serious decline of the European bird the Ivory-bill has for long been on the verge of extinction. Indeed, many ornithologists regarded it as extinct by the 1950s, although the early 1970s saw a few reports based on intensive searches for the bird. The trouble is that the old stands of primeval timber required by the Ivory-bill are few and far between and strictly limited in size. It is surely only a matter of time before it succumbs.

The typical woodpeckers are highly territorial but seldom very vocal. The Green Woodpecker has a high-pitched 'yaffling' call that echoes through the forests, but many other species are instrumental in defence of their domains. Using a dead branch as a sounding board, they peck out a loud, far-carrying, rhythmic beat with their bills. This 'drumming', as it is called, serves the same purpose as song in other species.

Having established a territory and found a mate, woodpeckers excavate a nest hole in a living or dead tree. A hole is bored inwards and then an oval chamber is excavated downwards. Chippings are simply dropped in a tell-tale pile beneath the hole with no attempt at hiding or dispersal. Most woodpeckers are secure in their nests, although several species are spied on by usurpers such as Starlings and Jackdaws and dispossessed before they have time to breed. Their habit of excavating a new hole every season makes old holes available to many other birds that are quite incapable of boring their own. Nevertheless, there is frequently a shortage of suitable holes in many managed woodlands.

The two to eight white eggs are laid on a bed of wood chippings and incubation is shared by both sexes. The naked and blind young hatch after eleven to eighteen days and both parents participate in the feeding and brooding routines. Fledging takes as long as thirty-five days, but the young often clamber about the nest tree before they are able to fly.

Considerable opinion has claimed that woodpeckers cause great damage to forests and that many species are incompatible with modern forestry practices. Certainly they do cause damage and can easily kill a tree in which they excavate a nest. Nevertheless, all damage has to be set against the beneficial effects that the birds have in keeping control of the harmful wood-boring insects on which they feed. Few foresters today look upon the woodpeckers with anything but a friendly eye. Even that curious North American genus, the sapsuckers, with their liking for feeding on the sap that runs from the scars that they create on trunks, do no permanent harm to the trees. They quickly heal and, in any case, even sapsuckers take vast quantities of harmful insects.

Woodpeckers can be a nuisance, but not to foresters. In several parts of the world, notably in the United States, wooden telegraph

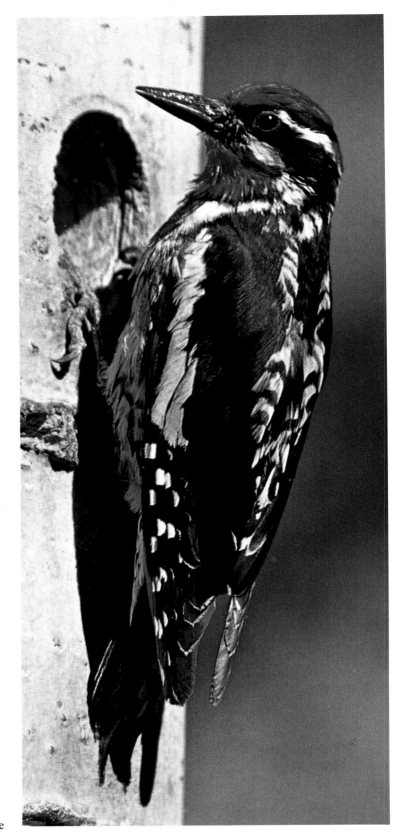

poles offer ideal nesting sites in otherwise unsuitable areas. The resulting weakening of the poles often makes them susceptible to winds and the inevitable cuts in communications are annoying and expensive to repair. The only answer has been to use the more costly metal poles which are woodpecker-proof.

Wooden telegraph poles are also used by the Acorn Woodpecker *Melanerpes formicivorus* as storehouses for its favourite food – acorns. Drilling an exact sized hole in a pole the woodpecker inserts

A female Great Spotted Woodpecker feeds horizontally in much the same way as it does on the vertical trunk of a tree. Feet set well apart, it creates a tripod by pushing down with its strong tail.

and wedges an acorn there for future use during less bountiful seasons. Some poles are pock-marked all-over in this way.

Most widespread and numerous of all the world's woodpeckers are the 'pied' woodpeckers of the genus *Dendrocopus*. Their Holarctic distribution makes them as familiar in North America as they are in Europe. All are black and white or greyish birds marked with various patterns on the back that are crucial for their accurate identification. Some have bold white oval patches on the back, whereas others have a ladder-like pattern of horizontal bars. In all species the male is marked with an area of red on the crown or nape, although in some cases, as with the Red-cockaded Woodpecker *D. borealis* of the southern United States, the red area is minimal. Like all other woodpeckers they fly in a deeply undulating manner. A few, strong flaps are followed by a brief dive before rising once more on their wings. Also like other woodpeckers they are largely sedentary, although some of the northern woodpeckers that feed frequently on ants make considerable journeys during the autumn

and winter months on forays for food.

The subfamily Jynginae consists of two closely allied species of wrynecks. They are primitive birds of cryptic coloration, and obtain their name from their ability to turn their necks in all manner of unlikely ways. Many ringers have been aghast to find that a trapped wryneck was dead in their hands with the head hanging limply from the body only to have the 'dead' wryneck flay away from them. The Palaearctic Wryneck *Jynx torquilla* is a summer visitor to Eurasia and one that is fast declining in certain parts of its range including Britain. There it is confined to the extreme south-east and probably numbers less than twenty pairs. This comparatively sudden decline has been blamed on a number of factors, but is in strange contrast with the bird's recent colonization of Scotland. No doubt the latter indicates an extension of the range of Scandinavian birds.

Wrynecks are not chisel-billed and rely for food on insects, particularly ants, picked from the surface. They do not climb like the woodpeckers and use natural or old woodpecker holes in which to nest. The six to nine white eggs hatch in about two weeks and the young fledge three weeks later after being fed on ants and their eggs. Their repeated 'ku-ku-ku-ku' cries cease after nesting has

229

started, but start again about five weeks later indicating a second brood.

Piculets are tiny birds all less than 5 inches in length. Three species are found in Asia, one in West Africa and the rest in tropical South America. Such a distribution indicates a very ancient group of birds. They are greenish grey above with white, heavily spotted underparts. The crown is usually black with scarlet or orange areas, duller in the female. They hunt for prey on the bark of trees and excavate their nest holes in dead and rotten trees where they also break away the crumbling wood to find insects and their larvae.

Broadbills Eurylaimidae

The broadbills are a widespread, Old World family of squat, gaily coloured, perching birds that, because of a number of structural peculiarities, are placed in their own suborder, the Eurylaimi. They vary in size from 5 to 11 inches, and have short, rounded wings and rounded tails. Several species have very short tails which accentuate their 'dumpy' appearance. They have fifteen (not fourteen) vertebrae in the neck, but still seem almost neckless and their heads are large compared to the rest of their bodies. Some species are bright green in colour and others predominantly green, but blue, black, and red are also found.

Broadbills have their centre of distribution in the islands of South-East Asia particularly in Sumatra and Borneo. Their range extends eastwards to the Philippines and westwards into India, and there is a secondary area in the forested regions of West Africa. They are forest birds, but some species visit cultivated land and gardens. They are generally insectivorous and pass through forests in noisy parties in their search for prey among the upper branches of large trees. Some species are expert flycatchers; the larger species take the occasional frog or lizard, and the green broadbills of the genus *Calyptomena* feed predominantly on fruit.

The bill is, as their name explains, broad and blunt, and in the case of the green broadbills, partially covered with feathers that extend forwards over the bill in the manner of a Cock-of-the-Rock. They are generally unafraid of humans and stand completely still when alarmed, relying on their camouflage.

The nest of a broadbill is suspended, invariably over water, in the midst of dense jungle. In this the birds resemble some of the weavers and the Penduline Tit, except that a broadbill nest may be as much as five feet long. It is constructed of twigs, bamboo leaves, grasses, and creepers, and is entered through a small opening in the side which is decorated with a porch and a handy perch. In a chamber in the middle the two to six creamy, pinkish spotted eggs are laid. Little more is known of the breeding biology of these fascinating birds other than in some species the nest may be the result of the co-operative efforts of several birds. Both sexes apparently feed the chicks.

Woodcreepers Dendrocolaptidae

The forty-six species of woodcreeper are birds of the South American forests extending from the Argentine to southern Mexico. All but five are called 'woodcreepers', and the remainder 'scythebills' for obvious reasons. Their habits and appearance are similar to the northern treecreepers but there is no direct relationship. They are tree-climbers boasting the strong tail shafts of the woodpeckers, but without the chisel-like bills. Like the treecreepers they pick most of their food from the crevices of bark and have evolved a large range of bill shapes to suit particular types of food. Indeed, because most species are dull browns of various shades with little else to distinguish them, it is the shape of the bill that is of primary importance in identification.

Many woodcreepers have straight bills, but some are delicately up-curved and others extremely long and decurved. The Red-billed Scythebill *Campylorhamphus trochilirostris*, for example, is 12 inches long, but this includes a bill chord (the shortest distance between the base and the tip) of 3 inches, whereas the Wedge-billed Woodcreeper *Glyphorynchus spirurus* has a stout $\frac{1}{2}$ inch-long bill in which the lower mandible is upturned. The legs are short, and the feet strong and long-clawed for gripping bark.

Most woodcreepers have an arboreal mode of life, flying from the top of one tree to the base of the next before working their way upwards once more, but the Great Rufous Woodcreeper *Xiphocolaptes major* quite frequently feeds on the ground in northern Argentina, while the Scimitar-billed Woodcreeper *Drymornis bridgesii* does so in woodland. As with other Neotropical

Right Of Central and South American distribution, the numerous woodcreepers are well adapted to their life of picking insects from among the crevices of bark. This is the Plain Brown Woodcreeper.

Opposite The Lesser Green Broadbill inhabits the tropical forests of Malaysia where it lives on a diet of fruit. Despite its bold colouring it is a shy bird and easily overlooked in the green of the jungle. The plumage of the female is less intense.

families, several species have highly restricted ranges. Snethlage's Woodcreeper *Xiphocolaptes franciscanus*, for example, is found only on the western bank of the Rio São Francisco at Minas Gerais in Brazil, and doubtless the opening up of the Amazon Basin will produce other, similarly localized, species.

Woodcreepers are solitary birds, but their calls are commonly heard. Shrill whistles, melodic trills, and harsh nasal calls are produced by different species, and some even produce a woodpecker-like drumming on a dead branch.

They nest in holes, but lacking the ability to excavate their own holes thay are dependent upon those abandoned by woodpeckers and on natural holes in decaying wood. Often the adults have to squeeze themselves into the nesting chamber. Comparatively few nests have been described and even fewer well studied, so that our knowledge of the family's breeding biology is limited. Some species at least line their selected hole with dead leaves which are replaced throughout the nesting period. The Streak-headed Woodcreeper *Lepidocolaptes souleyetti*, which is a medium-sized bird of northern South America, lays two or three white eggs which take fifteen days to hatch. The young of this species fledge in nineteen days.

Ovenbirds Furnariidae

The ovenbirds form one of the most diverse of all the families of birds. The 221 or so species vary in almost everything except their Neotropical distribution and general drabness. All are smallish birds, less than 11 inches long, and virtually without exception are coloured dull browns above and lighter fawns below. Many species tend to russet on the tail and rump, although the White-cheeked

Spinetail *Schoeniophylax phryganophila* has a yellow chin which renders it a more distinctive member of the family. Thus, the

A skulking species of dense South American forests, the Rufous Spinetail is easily overlooked as it haunts the thick undergrowth, feeding on insects. It often duets with its mate.

ovenbirds are particularly difficult to differentiate.

Yet this uniformity of aspect is relieved by the variety of forms and habits of the individual genera and species. In particular, their vernacular names are remarkably accurate indications of the ways in which the birds live. The vast majority are forest birds, with a strong centre of distribution in the Amazon Basin and adjacent areas of tropical rainforest, but ovenbirds are found from the seashore to the treeless zone of the high Andes. From the marshes of the great rivers to the dry savannahs of bush and scrub.

The true ovenbirds of the genus *Furnarius*, called honneros in South America, are responsible for the family name. They build large mud nests that are baked hard and secure by the heat of the sun. The widespread Rufous Ovenbird *F. rufus* of southern Brazil and northern Argentina is perhaps the best known of all the species. It builds a large mud nest in open places like the tops of posts or under the eaves of houses. The simple sphere of mud is entered via a hole in the side which in turn leads down a spiral corridor before a second hole guards the nest chamber itself. These nests are often taken over by swallows in subsequent seasons which suggests that, despite their complexity, they offer no real defence against determined small predators.

The miners of the genus *Geobates* get their name from the tunnel that they excavate up to ten feet long leading to their leaf-lined nesting chamber. They are ground-dwelling birds, like the majority of other ovenbird groups. The foliage-gleaners, too, excavate nest holes in the ground, but are characterized by their warbler-like habit of searching the leafy canopy in search of insect food. Several distinct genera numbering nearly thirty species fall into this group. Another group is the treehunters of the genus *Thripadectes*. These birds frequent forests and live in the manner of woodcreepers picking insect prey from the bark of trees. As a result, their tails are quick to wear and the shafts protrude from the rest of their feathers. Unlike the true woodcreepers they have not developed stiff tail feathers to give them the full support that such a life would demand.

The spinetails, too, have the shafts protruding beyond the rest of their tail feathers, but they are predominantly marsh-loving birds with highly elongated tails in the manner of the Asiatic wren-warblers. Some spinetails have tails up to three times as long as their bodies.

The leaf-scrapers of the genus *Sclerurus* spend much of their time on the forest floor turning over leaves in the manner of a thrush. Indeed, they closely resemble a short-tailed thrush.

The shaketails shake their tails in the manner of wagtails, and it comes as no surprise to learn that they frequent mountain streams, although they also like sewage works. It needs little imagination to guess at the life style of the earthcreepers of the genus *Upucerthia*.

The thistletails *Schizocaca* species have long, attenuated tails with ragged tips, and the thornbirds *Phacellodomus* species are birds of predominantly dry, open areas. Prickletail, brushrunner, barbtail, recurvebill – all are indicative of the nature or habits of the birds concerned.

Ovenbirds, then, live in a variety of ways and in a variety of places. They are predominantly insectivorous and are notable for using almost every conceivable type of nest and nest site except the simple cup of so many other birds. Some construct 'ovens' and some mine tunnels: still others build domed structures near the ground or in the tops of trees. The firewood-gatherers build huge structures consisting of quite large twigs, while the Rufous-fronted Thornbird *Phacellodomus rufifrons* constructs a huge communal nest high in a tree within which five or more pairs may breed. Largest of all the 'single' nests is that of the White-throated Cachalote *Pseudoseissura gutturalis*.

Despite their huge range and variety of species the breeding biology of ovenbirds remains much of a mystery. Incubation may last from fifteen to twenty days and the fledging period from thirteen to eighteen days. Nearly all species lay white eggs, although some have a clear blue caste. The eggs number three to five, but clutches of up to nine are known.

Antbirds Formicariidae

Antbirds are a large family comprising over 220 species of predominantly forest-dwelling birds. Their distribution is centred upon the vast forests of the Amazon Basin, although they extend northwards through Central America as far as southern Mexico, and southwards to the scrublands of northern Argentina. Like that other large Neotropical family, the ovenbirds, the antbirds are rather dull and drab. Their plumage is predominantly brown, but some species are grey, black and white, or rusty in colour. They vary in size from 4 to 15 inches and, for the most part, have medium-length, stubby, down-curved bills. They are most at home on the forest floor, but many species frequent the secondary growth of jungle below the canopy.

Many species bear the common name of antbird, but others, because of an apparent resemblance to other groups of birds, bear the prefix 'ant-' followed by the name of another species. Thus, there are antshrikes, antvireos, antpittas, antwrens and so on. In many cases this similarity is totally misleading, while in others it seems well founded. Antvireos, for example, do resemble the vireos of North America in the structure of their nests and in their habits, but antwrens resemble wrens only in size. Antpittas are perhaps the best named of all. Antpittas are not a colourful group, like the Old World pittas, but they are short-tailed birds of the forest floor that make themselves very inconspicuous.

Several species habitually prey on ants and others feed in association with columns of marching ants preying on the insects that the ants disturb. But a great many antbirds have nothing to do with ants at all and are totally misnamed. Most species are insectivorous and a great many find their food on the ground. The wings are generally short and flight is used to avoid danger, to reach a secure nest site, and for very little else. The legs and feet are understandably well developed and strong. Despite a poorly developed syrinx, antbirds are remarkably vocal. Their calls are said to vary from the harsh to the musical, and several species have well-developed calls which are frequently repeated. Not surprisingly, in view of their habitat, many species are easier to identify by voice.

Many antbirds build a simple cup nest either on the ground or in a low fork in a tree. Some species sling their nest between branches in low bushes. The clutch consists of two or three white eggs marked with brown, cinnamon, or mauve. Incubation takes between fourteen and seventeen days and fledging a further nine to thirteen days. These bare bones of the antbirds' breeding biology have been gleaned from only a handful of species and the vast majority of these birds remain totally unknown.

The Rufous-necked Antthrush *Formicarius analis* breeds in holes in rotten trees, as may other species. In the Black-crested Antshrike *Sakesphorus canadensis* both members of the pair share the incubation and care of the young, but it would be wrong to assume that this applied to all members of the family. As with many other Neotropical families generalizations are full of dangers, but it does seem that antbirds mature very quickly once hatched and are able to leave the nest after a very short fledging period.

Some species of antbirds are highly localized, occurring within a single valley, or along a single mountain range within the great Amazon forests. The Argus Bare-eye *Phlegopsis barringeri*, for example, is known from only one specimen taken at Nariño in Colombia. The Rufous-fronted Antthrush *Formicarius rufifrons*

owes its identity to two females collected at Madre de Dios in south-eastern Peru, and to date no-one knows what the male may look like at all. Other antbirds are equally local in their occurrence, but doubtless with the progressive opening up of their habitats and the increasing attention being paid by ornithologists to the Neotropical zone we may soon know much more about these birds.

Antpipits Conopophagidae

Antpipits are closely related to the antbirds and ovenbirds with which they share a home in the forests of South America. All eleven species are less than 6 inches long and all are denizens of the forest floor. They are insectivorous, but differ from the antbirds in the structure of their bill which is broad like a flycatcher's rather than narrow like a shrike's. An alternative name for the whole family is 'gnateaters' and most of the species bear this common name.

Food is taken from the ground, and the antpipits' wings are short and rounded and quite unsuited to sustained flight. Antpipits are seldom seen because of the very nature of their lives although they are not shy. Most of their time is spent among vegetation and they are, in any case, generally dull in coloration. Only two genera are recognized, but the differences between them are so significant that some recent workers have abandoned the family Conopophagidae altogether, placing the genus *Conopophaga* with the Formicariidae (the antbirds) and the genus *Corythopis* with the Tyrannidae (the tyrants). Whatever the merits of such an arrangement, there are significant differences between the two genera.

The genus *Conopophaga*, claims nine of the eleven species, and these are pitta-like birds with a strong resemblance to the antpittas. They are long-legged, short-tailed birds mainly rich brown in colour, but with patches of rust, black and white in their plumage. Several species boast a white eye stripe. Their general dumpiness is accentuated by their loose feathering. Their vocal equipment is poorly developed, confirming their alliance with the antbirds, and their most remarkable sound is the 'spitting' of the Black-cheeked Gnateater *C. melanops* which has given rise to their local name 'cuspidor'.

These birds nest on or near the ground constructing a deep cup of dry leaves. The two yellow eggs are spotted with brown. Both members of the pair share in incubation.

The two *Corythopis* species are slimmer, more elegant, long-tailed birds bearing a much closer similarity to the Old World pipits. The Ringed Antpipit *C. torquata* inhabits the forest floor and even has the wagtail-like habit of bobbing its tail. Between them the two species cover the continent from Colombia and Guyana to Paraguay and northern Argentina.

Tapaculos Thinocryptidae

The twenty-nine species of tapaculos are ground-dwelling birds of the more open areas of South America. They reach their greatest density in the Andes of Chile, and many species are confined to mountains and their adjacent high-level forests. In the southern parts of their range, tapaculos can be found down to sea-level in open bushy country.

All tapaculos are essentially terrestrial species and among the poorest fliers of all birds. The wings are short and rounded, and the flight muscles of the breast soft and poorly developed. The feathers of the tail, which are quite long in some species, are soft and of little use for in-flight steering. Instead they are often carried cocked high above the back like a wren. The legs are long and powerful and, in contrast to the breast muscles, those of the thighs are well developed. Tapaculos spend almost all their lives on the ground and habitually run into cover to escape danger.

They are plump birds varying in size from 4½ to 10 inches. Most are brown or buff in colour, though several species are boldly

marked with chestnut or black. The darker birds spend much of their time out of the light in the deepest thickets, but the buffer, more sandy coloured birds frequent the savannahs and dry, open grasslands. No matter where they live, tapaculos are shy and inconspicuous. At the slightest sign of danger they will run with huge strides into cover and even when feeding make only the briefest of dashes across open ground.

Nests are usually placed on the ground, but some species excavate their own burrows and others construct a domed nest a few feet up in a dense thicket. The two to four large, white eggs are incubated by both sexes and the chicks hatch with a thin covering of down.

Perhaps the tapaculos' saving grace from a birdwatcher's point of view is their voices. Their calls are generally monotonous, boring, and difficult to locate, although they are identifiable. The Black-throated Huet-huet *Pteroptochos tarnii* of Chile and Argentina frequents thick forests and bamboo thickets, but its repeated 'huet-huet-huet' call is a well-known and characteristic sound.

Pittas Pittidae

Pittas are among the most colourful birds in the world, but also among the most secretive. Bold patches of colour – blues, reds, violets, greens, indeed almost every colour of the rainbow – mark them all. But all are lost in the deep gloom of the tropical forests in which they live.

Pittas are ground-dwelling birds with long legs and strong feet. They can hop remarkably quickly over the ground and avoid the gaze of intruders by this means rather than by flight. Their wings are short and rounded, but they fly strongly, and several species regularly migrate long distances. Their tails are short, in some cases

merely a tufted remnant rather than a true tail, giving them a curiously rounded shape reminiscent of a courser. They vary in size from 5 to 11 inches and have short, down-curved bills.

Pittas are most numerous in South-East Asia where more than half of the twenty-three species are found. Two species are found in the tropical forests of Central Africa, three species reach Australia, and the Fairy Pitta *Pitta brachyura* penetrates the Palaearctic in China and southern Japan. These temperate-breeding pittas regularly migrate to tropical climes to winter, the northern populations of the Fairy Pitta moving southwards to winter in Borneo. En route some birds are attracted to lights like other migratory birds.

This strangely disrupted distribution, and particularly the isolated species in Africa, led to the conclusion that pittas are an ancient group of birds that were once far more widespread through the tropics than at present.

They live on insects gleaned from the forest floor, although the Noisy Pitta *P. versicolor* has the thrush-like habit of breaking open the shells of snails on a favoured anvil. This bird is also fond of slugs. Like other members of the family the Noisy Pitta is a highly vocal bird. Most pittas have characteristic calls, but they also have a common quality of trilling or whistling. But for their calls pittas

Like the other members of its family, the Noisy Pitta is a brightly coloured bird that feeds on insects and other small creatures found on the forest floor or among dense undergrowth.

would be even less well known than they are at present.

Pittas build a large, domed nest, frequently on the ground, and invariably low down among forest vegetation. The roots of trees are a favoured site as are fallen trees. Nests up to thirty feet from the ground are known, however. The two to five white eggs are boldly marked with maroon or purple and are incubated by both parents. The young hatch helpless and are cared for by both sexes. Nothing appears to be known about the length of the fledging period.

Asitys and false sunbirds Philepittidae

This family consists of two genera, each having two species that live in the forests of Madagascar. The two asitys are pitta-like birds that are essentially arboreal, inhabiting secondary growth. The false sunbirds, as their name implies, bear a close resemblance to sunbirds and feed on the flowers of the forest in a similar manner. Indeed, for some time they were classified as sunbirds, but recent work has shown that they are quite distinct and that they share a primitive ancestry with the asitys. Asitys and false sunbirds show few affinities with any other family of birds.

Asitys are stocky birds about 6 inches long with short, rounded tails. The wings, too, are short and rounded, and the legs strong, though not as long as the pittas'. The bill is broadbased and of moderate length. The Velvet Asity *Philepitta castanea* is an all-black bird with the merest trace of yellow on the wings. It is marked by a large, blue wattle around the eye that extends to the base of the bill. The Velvet Asity frequents the forests of eastern Madagascar where it is generally unobtrusive and inactive. It feeds on fruit and builds a penduline nest with a side entrance protected by an awning. The three eggs are pure white. These stark facts are all that

is known about the bird's breeding biology, but that is more than is known about any of the other members of the family. Schlegel's Asity *P. schlegeli* is a similar, but yellower bird with black only on the head. It is found in the western forests of Madagascar.

The Wattled False Sunbird *Neodrepanis coruscans* is found in the eastern forests of Madagascar, and is a small 3½ inch-long bird with a long, down-curved bill. It is cobalt blue above and yellow, spotted with black below. It, too, has a prominent, light blue wattle around the eye. It is basically solitary and feeds on insects and on nectar in the manner of a sunbird. The remaining species, the Small-billed False Sunbird *N. hypoxantha* is olive green about the head and nape and less spotted below. It inhabits the central forests of the island, but is known from only a few specimens and may now be in danger of extinction.

Opposite The Small-billed False Sunbird (above), may be extinct. Its bill allows it to probe tree-blossoms for nectar and insects. The quiet and rather inactive Velvet Asity favours the middle storeys of moist forests, where it seeks small fruits.

237

New Zealand wrens Xenicidae

The New Zealand wrens are a family of small, greenish yellow birds endemic to those islands. They are plump, round-bodied birds with small remnant tails and are reminiscent of tiny pittas. Like other New Zealand birds they have suffered considerably from introduced predators, and one species, the Stephen Island Rock Wren *Xenicus lyalli*, was discovered by a cat in 1894 on a small island in the Cook Strait and was promptly exterminated by the same beast. The lighthouse keeper who owned the cat was the only person ever to see this species alive.

Similarly, the New Zealand Bush Wren *X. longipes* was once widespread in forests, but it is now no longer found on the main islands. Little is known of its life history.

Fortunately, the two remaining species have fared better and have been well studied and photographed. The South Island Rock Wren *X. gilviventris* is an alpine bird confined to the mountains of that island. It is less than 4 inches long, and it never retreats lower than the scrub zone and ekes out a living among the fallen rocks of

The New Zealand Rock Wren is a seldom-observed inhabitant of rock-strewn mountain slopes on South Island. Similar to the other members of this small, endemic family, it has probably suffered less as a result of colonization than its congeners.

the mountain screes. Most of its life is spent hidden in rock crevices searching for beetles and other insects. Its nest is hidden deep among the rocks or among the branches of scrub and is entered through a tunnel. The two to five white eggs are incubated by both parents. Finding Rock Wrens is difficult because they are most often out of sight. Their calls are thin and high-pitched and easily overlooked. The birds seldom fly, and when they do it is only for a few yards. Their most characteristic habit is a bobbing motion of the body in the way of a wheatear.

The Rifleman *Acanthisitta chloris* is the most widespread of the New Zealand wrens. It is little more than 3 inches long, and is found throughout the forested regions of both main islands as well as on the smaller ones. It is the New Zealand equivalent of the treecreepers, and feeds by climbing the trunks and branches of trees probing for insects in the bark. Riflemen nest in tree holes or in nest boxes where these are made available. The two or three white eggs take twenty to twenty-one days to hatch and are incubated by both parents. There is some evidence of polygamy which reduces the part played in breeding by the male. The chicks take twenty-four days to fledge, but may then participate in feeding a second brood.

Tyrant flycatchers Tyrannidae

Tyrant flycatchers form one of the largest of bird families. More than 360 species have been described, and although some authorities recognize as many as 380 species, there seems little doubt that an overdue revision of the family would considerably reduce both of these totals.

Tyrants are a family of primitive passerines of considerably more

The Eastern Phoebe, widespread in the eastern United States, is popular with farmers because of its depredations on harmful insects. It frequently nests among boulders alongside streams.

ancient ancestry than their Old World equivalents, the Muscicapidae, which they resemble superficially. Like the Muscicapidae, the tyrants are predominantly aerial feeders, pouncing on passing insects and catching them with an audible snap of the bill. But like the flycatchers, they return to their favoured perch to consume their prey at leisure, often beating larger insects to kill them and break them up. Typically, they sit upright on a prominent perch with feet withdrawn into the plumage of the belly. The feet are weak with two of the toes partially joined. The bill is broad and there is a strong growth of rictal bristles.

Tyrants vary in size from 3 to 9 inches, although some species have particularly long tails that may double their length. They are generally dull in colour and the sexes are similar. Sexual dimorphism occurs only in the few species where the male is brightly coloured and where the dull colours of the female have survival value. Most birds are capable of raising the feathers of the crown into a crest which may then show a patch of bold colouring. Thus, a totally drab brown bird like the Royal Flycatcher *Onychorhynchus mexicanus* may, when roused, produce a fine semicircular crest of crimson feathers spotted and tipped with black and mauve.

Tyrants are American birds and have their centre of distribution in the tropical forests of South America. They have, however, spread to every part of the continent that provides insect food, but only seven species have reached Alaska and no more than ten are found in Tierra del Fuego. As is to be expected, these southern and northern birds are migratory, most moving back to their area of origin to winter, although the Eastern Phoebe *Sayornis phoebe* moves no further south than Mexico. Tyrants inhabiting the high Andes perform a vertical migration to winter in milder climes.

Tyrants have elementary vocal equipment, but many boast memorable, if simple, calls that have given them their names. The Wood Pewee *Contopus virens* is a case in point. It breeds in large areas of North America where its incessant 'pee-e-wee' can become quite nerve-racking.

These are the main characteristics of the 360 or so species of tyrant flycatchers, but there is great variation in structure and behaviour. Indeed, almost every departure from the generalization can be found.

Thus, while *most* tyrants *are* flycatchers, some behave more like warblers scouring the forest canopy in their search for insect food. Many species eat berries and fruit, while others, such as the Kittlitz Ground Tyrant *Agricornis livida*, behave more like shrikes, swooping down on lizards, amphibians, and even small mammals. The Derby Flycatcher or Great Kiskadee *Pitangus sulphuratus* has even learned to fish. With its bold yellow breast, well-marked, black-and-white head pattern, and strongly hooked bill, this bird bears a strong resemblance to several of the shrikes of African bush country.

Birds of open country have developed special song flights with which to defend their territories. Airborne, they utter their harsh, chattering calls, but some species are capable of producing quite sweet melodies. Few are as demonstrative as the familiar Kingbird *Tyrannus tyrannus* of North America. The Kingbird not only attacks its own kind, as most birds do, but also any other interloper. It is particularly aggressive towards birds of prey, chasing them until they are well away from its domain. Such fearlessness makes the Kingbird a particular favourite and the native indians of North America nicknamed it affectionately 'Little Chief'. The Kingbird is a dull grey above and white below. Its crest is seldom erected, but when it is it shows a deep crimson flare of colour. It is particularly fond of bees and regularly attacks hives with complete disregard for stings. Needless to say, the Kingbird is unpopular with bee-keepers.

Many of the tyrants are dull and similar. Indeed, some North American birds are exceedingly difficult to identify and are often lumped together in the same way as European birdwatchers lump *Phylloscopus* warblers, but others are highly individual. The beautiful male Vermilion Flycatcher *Pyrocephalus rubinus* is a vividly crimson-headed and crimson-breasted bird with black upperparts. In contrast, his mate is a dull grey with a streaked breast and the merest touch of rufous on the flanks. Vermilion Flycatchers are found from the southernmost United States through Central and South America to Argentina.

The Scissor-tailed Flycatcher *Muscivora forficata* similarly breeds in the southern States extending northwards into Kansas and Missouri. It is an average-sized tyrant, but the extended streamers of the tail make it, at 16 inches, the longest member of the family. It is a fine, pearl grey bird with a touch of crimson on the crown and

Resplendent in his black and red plumage, a male Vermilion Flycatcher perches near his nest. The species breeds from the southern United States southwards to Patagonia. Many birds migrate into the tropical forests of the Amazon to winter.

bend of the wing. The tail feathers, which are at least twice as long as the body, are boldly patterned black-and-white. While most tyrants that migrate do so during the hours of darkness, the Scissor-tailed is a diurnal migrant forming loose flocks.

With such a large and varied family it is only to be expected that there would be considerable variation in breeding habits. The majority of species build cup-shaped nests, but these vary from the large and untidy to the neat and frail. Many are placed in the crotch of a tree, but others favour the outer branches. Some species produce domed nests with side entrances, while others suspend substantial structures within which the nesting chamber is concealed. Yet others nest in holes and the Great Crested Flycatcher *Myiarchus crinitus* uses old woodpecker holes as well as nest boxes where these are provided. This species also has the curious habit of decorating its nest with the shed skins of snakes.

For some time it was considered that this might be a defensive technique, but as it has recently shown itself to be equally fond of old polythene doubtless it is mere decoration. Other birds frequently take over the old nests of ovenbirds while others, notably the Phoebe, construct their own mud nests under bridges or some stream-side ledge of rock.

A clutch of two or three eggs is usual, but four is quite common among migratory species. Egg colour varies considerably, although a base of white, sometimes with a green caste, is the general rule. They may be spotted, blotched, or veined with a variety of different colours. Incubation, which is invariably performed by the female alone, varies from fourteen to twenty-three days and similarly, fledging may take from thirteen to twenty-three days. Tropical species may breed several times within a year and several temperate species breed twice.

Manakins Pipridae

Manakins are active, colourful birds of tropical American forests from Mexico to northern Argentina. Few species are larger than 5 inches in length and yet they are among the most obvious of birds. They may be divided into two rough groupings: those that are dull coloured with plumages dominated by greens and yellow; those with predominantly black plumage broken by bold patches of colour, and in which the females are dull and greenish. Thus, the Grey-headed Manakin *Piprites griseiceps* is an example of the dull green birds being marked with only a white eye ring, while the Long-tailed Manakin *Chiroxiphia linearis* is a boldly black bird with a scarlet crown and vividly blue back. The central tail feathers are extended to double this bird's length. The female, too, has extended tail feathers, but is green in colour. The dominance of brightly coloured patches in these birds' plumage is tied in with their highly elaborate and ritualized displays which are quite unique.

Manakins are dumpy, short-tailed, stubby-billed birds of the forest. They feed mainly on small fruits which they pick in flight but supplement their diet with insects. They are among the most conspicuous of the birds that wander through the forest in nomadic bands, and are generally confiding and tame enough to allow a close approach.

Nests are slung in a fork of a bush usually low down over water. The female lays two brown-spotted eggs in the nest that she builds alone, and is totally responsible for the incubation and care of the young.

The most interesting aspect of the lives of manakins is their intricate courtship behaviour. This has been particularly well studied by Dr David Snow, the well-known British ornithologist. The manakins of the genus *Manacus*, which includes the Black-and-

The Blue-backed Manakin is one of the more colourful members of this fascinating South American family. At its communal display grounds much use is made of the vivid patches on the crown and back.

white Manakin *M. manacus*, were studied by Snow at the New York Zoological Society's field station in the Arima Valley of Trinidad. He found that these birds occupy a lek or jousting ground almost throughout the year save only when undergoing their annual moult. Each bird clears its own 'arena' carrying away twigs and leaves so that only bare ground surrounds its perch. Usually the perch is a single sapling only a few feet high, but sometimes subsidiary saplings exist within the cleared area. The male, surrounded by other manakins, each on its own territory, displays in the most extraordinary manner with much jumping and posturing, all the while accompanied by a variety of noises made by the wings, and particularly the specially strengthened secondary wing feathers. Females visit these courts and are mated on the perch after briefly joining in the display.

Other genera of manakins perform their dances at selected sites high in trees, while some prefer to wiggle their bodies from side to side in a head-down attitude. Yet others perform the most extraordinary crawling display on the ground. In the Blue-backed Manakin *Chiroxiphia pareola* two males join together to dance before a female. Jumping up and down alternately when faced with a potential mate, the two perform a sort of leap-frog display in which they take each other's place in turn. In the Swallow-tailed Manakin *C. caudata* several birds have been recorded collaborating in a similar display.

In the Black-and-white Manakin less than half of the nests produce young, predation, mainly by snakes, accounting for the rest. Faced with such a low rate of reproduction, manakins live fairly long lives for their size, and an average adult can expect to live for upwards of three years. First year males are unable to obtain a place at a lek and do not breed.

Cotingas Cotingidae

Cotingas are among the most diverse, colourful and bizarre birds in the world. They are related to the manakins and tyrants, and range from 3½ to 18 inches in length. They are found in tropical Central and South America extending northwards to the southern United States in the case of the Rose-throated Becard *Platypsaris aglaiae*, and to the West Indies in the Jamaican Becard *P. niger*.

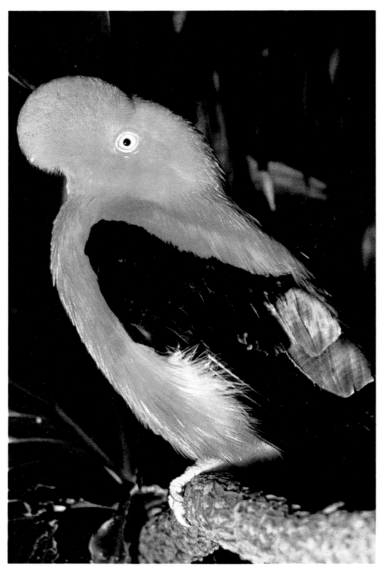

Cotingas really are an extraordinary family. They vary from the brilliant to the dull, from the terrestrial to birds of the forest canopy. Many are decorated with the most outlandish appendages to their plumage, which are without exception used in courtship displays.

In such a diverse family it is extremely difficult to generalize, but cotingas have broad, hooked bills, rounded wings and strong legs and feet. Almost all species are arboreal and feed on fruit and insects. They are generally solitary birds but they may be seen in pairs or occasionally in family parties. Many of the species are boldly marked and obvious birds, but they are little known, performing both their courtship and breeding cycle high in the tree tops. Most commonly found in tropical forests, they extend into the montane area in the Andean foothills where they occupy pine and oak forests. The name 'cotinga' stems from the indian name for the White Bellbird *Procnias alba* meaning 'whitewashed'. This species is one of the very few white tropical forest birds.

The bellbirds are good examples of the more bizarre members of the group. The three South American species are pure white or silver in colour, a plumage otherwise found among birds only in alpine-Arctic species. They are distinguished by wattles on the head and, in the case of the Bearded Bellbird *P. averano*, by a cinnamon head and black wings. The Bare-throated Bellbird *P. nudicollis* is pure white broken only by a greenish blue area of bare skin around the eye and throat. Like other bellbirds it utters an extraordinary ringing, far-carrying call that gives it its English name. The Three-wattled Bellbird *P. tricarunculata* of Central America is a rusty brown bird with a white frontal half. Three, long, pointed, almost snake-like wattles hang from the base of the bill and the neck. The Bearded Bellbird has a mass of such wattles hanging from its neck in the manner of a beard.

Perhaps the most extraordinary of all cotingas are the umbrella birds of the genus *Cephalopterus*. The Ornate Umbrella-bird *C. ornatus* is a black, crow-sized bird marked with the most elaborate crest of curled feathers which it can raise to cover its head and bill like an umbrella. From its chin extends a huge wattle which may be over a foot in length and is covered with short, square-ended, scale-like feathers. The wattle of the Long-wattled Umbrella-bird *C. penduliger* is even longer and may reach as much

Left An Andean Cock-of-the-rock with expanded crest held forward over the bill. It constructs a swallow-like nest against the wall of a cave and exists on a diet of fruit.

Opposite The shrill cries of the Bare-throated Bellbird echo through the forests of its South American home. The bare, green skin of the face contrasts with the all-white body, a plumage pattern seldom found among passerines.

as 18 inches in length. In the Bare-necked Umbrella-bird *C. glabricollis* the wattle is unfeathered and bright red in colour.

The magnificent cocks-of-the-rock are sometimes placed in a separate family, the Rupicolidae, by some authors. But, in truth, the systematics of the whole of the Cotingidae are in need of critical examination, and these birds are best kept within the family until such a re-examination has been made. The two species are very similar birds and basically separated by the different colour of their plumage. They are found only in northern South America and the Cock-of-the-rock *Rupicola rupicola* is confined to the Guianas and northern Brazil, being replaced westwards by the Andean Cock-of-the-rock *R. peruviana*. The plumage of the Cock-of-the-rock is bright orange, while its Andean counterpart is bright red with black wings and tail.

Both species are marked, in the male at least, with a fine erectile crest that forms a continuous and smooth fan on the head. In the nominate bird this crest has a black band near the tip. The secondary feathers are square cut and held above the folded primaries. Like the manakins, cocks-of-the-rock form a communal display at a lek. Males gather on the ground in a forest clearing, in the same manner as many of the temperate grouse, and display one to another. Grotesque postures are adopted to show their finery to its best and they have the curious habit of remaining motionless for minutes at a time in a favoured pose. The more dull, greenish females are attracted and mated on the lek and are then solely responsible for the duties of nesting.

A mud cup glued to the entrance of a cave serves as a nest for the two eggs. It is sometimes reinforced with twigs. Often, several nests are placed together at the same site forming a small colony of females.

In general, the nests of cotingas are as variable as the birds themselves. Some build domed nests with a side entrance, others construct platforms of twigs, while still others nest in holes in trees. The three species of tityras (genus *Tityra*) are hole nesters with a curious parasitic method of evicting the rightful owners from holes that they fancy. The tityras fill a woodpecker's hole with sticks and twigs faster than the owner can remove them. Eventually the woodpecker gives up in disgust and the tityra lines its hole with leaves to form a nest.

Tityras are shrike-like birds with silvery plumage and black facial masks that shine in the dappled light of the forest. Like other cotingas they have bare face patches.

Plantcutters Phytotomidae

The three species of plantcutters are similar birds grouped into a single genus. They inhabit the more open areas of western South America, and although they are related to the cotingas they bear a strong physical resemblance to the grosbeaks and buntings of the Holarctic region. They are about 7 inches long, and frequently sit at the top of a bush or shrub in agricultural areas where they give vent to a discordant, whistling song. Males show a certain amount of rufous on the breast according to the species and vary from the Reddish Plantcutter *Phytotoma rutila* which is brightly orange, through the Peruvian Plantcutter *P. raimondii*, to the Chilean Plantcutter *P. rara* which is all grey.

Plantcutters are marked by a strong finch-like bill which is finely serrated and ideally designed to cut through the softer parts of vegetation. Leaves, buds and fruit fall easily to this bill and their wasteful eating habits bring plantcutters into sharp conflict with farmers, particularly fruit growers. In some areas extensive control measures have been undertaken, but they make no significant difference to the species' population. They are not gregarious birds and seldom form flocks of more than a dozen individuals. They are nomadic outside the breeding season and roam the countryside in their search for food. This seldom amounts to a regular migration.

The Reddish Plantcutter is common on the pampas of Patagonia extending northwards through Argentina and Paraguay to Bolivia. The nest consists of a platform of twigs placed in the middle of a bush and lined with a neat cup of bents. The two to four eggs are greenish, spotted with dark brown and, although the female alone incubates, both members of the pair share in caring for the young. The nesting habits of the other two species are very similar.

The Chilean Plantcutter is found in south and central Chile and an adjoining area of Argentina. It is predominantly a bird of orchards and open country, but it is found at heights as much as 6,500 feet in the foothills of the Andes. The Peruvian Plantcutter is isolated in the coastal areas of north-western Peru.

Lyrebirds Menuridae

The lyrebird was discovered in 1798 near Sydney, Australia, and the first one arrived in Europe the following year where it was described by Major General T. Davies and named *Menura superba* in 1802. At first, its remarkable similarity to gallinaceous birds led to its classification as a pheasant, but later study, particularly of its nesting habits and extraordinary vocal ability, convinced ornithologists that it should be placed with the passerines. Lyrebirds show few characteristics shared by other birds, but together with the scrub-birds it is placed in a subfamily of its own. The only other lyrebird, Prince Albert's Lyrebird *M. alberti*, was not discovered until 1849, and even today little is known of the life style of this highly localized bird.

The Superb Lyrebird is now a national emblem of Australia and appears as a symbol in a variety of forms, most notably on postage stamps. Unfortunately, the pose depicted is but a momentary one as the bird brings its tail over its back at the start of its display when it forms the 'lyre' shape.

Both sexes are dull brown birds with longish necks, short stubby pheasant-like bills and the long, strong legs and feet characteristic of fowl. They live on the floor of dense, dark forests by scratching in a chicken-like manner among fallen leaves for worms, beetles and insects. The female has a longish brown tail, but that of the male is quite breathtaking. The outer feathers, which form the frame of the lyre, are about 30 inches long, broad and boldly marked with crescents of brown on a buff to white background. The two central tail feathers are narrow wire-like structures, while the rest of the retrices are inordinately long, barbless plumes of white. In display the male raises his tail overhead and bows it down to touch the ground in front of him. It then covers him completely and the whole is shimmered conspicuously while the bird utters a loud and varied repertoire of calls.

Lyrebirds breed during the Australian winter when their food is most plentiful and easiest to obtain. Males make several clearings within their strictly defended territory and construct small mounds on which they display. A single bird may boast upward of a dozen such arenas on which he will perform several times a day. The female alone carries out the duties of nest building, incubation and feeding and tending the young, but there is no evidence of

Native to eastern Australia, the Superb Lyrebird inhabits dense forest where it feeds on the ground in the manner of a pheasant. Its magnificent tail is shimmered during display to attract a mate.

polygamy on the part of the Superb Lyrebird.

The nest is a large structure of twigs with a side entrance, constructed on the ground or occasionally in a tree. The female may take up to a month to build her nest and then lays a single brown egg spotted with grey. Incubation is frequently delayed a few days and the egg is protected by a covering of down that the hen plucks from her own flanks. When eventually incubation begins the egg takes more than five weeks to hatch and the chick is born virtually naked. Unlike the gallinaceous birds it remains in the nest for about six weeks until it is well grown. By this time it is invariably too large for the nest and frequently it has to break it open to poke its head through to be fed.

Both sexes are extremely vocal, but the male is generally thought to be the most brilliant mimic in the animal world. He has a 'shoo-shoo' call of his own, but he increases his repertoire with the calls of parrots and many other birds as well as of forest mammals. All are reproduced with extraordinary accuracy as are the unnatural sounds that are picked up from the activities of man. Cars and horns are simple, but the Lyrebird will also manage power-saws and even the shouts of forestry workers. As with other mimics we have no understanding of the value to the species of repeating other sounds.

While the Superb Lyrebird is found over much of south-eastern Australia, Albert's Lyrebird is confined to forests in the south-east of Queensland and the adjacent north-east of New South Wales. Its displays are less dramatic than those of the Superb Lyrebird and made from a shallow depression cleared in the rainforest. Little else is known of its life.

During the heyday of fashion at the end of the nineteenth century, thousands of Superb Lyrebirds were shot for their plumes. Fortunately, they survived and are now strictly protected, although forest clearance is a continuing threat.

Scrub-birds Atrichornithidae

The two species of scrub-bird were discovered in the middle of the last century – the Rufous Scrub-bird *Atrichornis rufescens* in south-eastern Australia, and the Noisy Scrub-bird *A. clamosus* 2,500 miles away near Perth in south-western Australia. Their discovery was widely reported in scientific circles and was the cause of considerable debate among contemporary ornithologists. The scrub-birds proved to be the nearest living relatives of the famous lyrebirds, even though only 6½ to 8 inches in length. Following its discovery in 1842 about twenty specimens of the Noisy Scrub-bird were collected before 1889 – thereafter none. Before long the bird was recognized as being extinct, because several expeditions failed to find it in the Albany area south of Perth. Then, in 1961, Harley Webster rediscovered the bird at Two People Bay some twenty miles east of Albany.

Almost instantly, the area was declared a reserve by the State Government and its 13,000 acres proved to hold about 100 birds. Despite further searching it has not been relocated outside this area. A proposed development at Two People Bay was cancelled and the birds have subsequently been rigorously protected. Perhaps the greatest danger now stems from fire, because this part of Australia

The Rufous Scrub-bird is found only in south-eastern Australia where its dull coloration and secretive behaviour make it difficult to observe. It hunts the forest floor for insects, worms and other small animals.

is noted for the ferocity of its bush fires, one of which could wipe out the Noisy Scrub-bird for ever.

Its cousin, the slightly smaller Rufous Scrub-bird, faces no such danger. It has a wider, if still restricted, range in the forests of north-eastern New South Wales to southern Queensland, and breeds within several national parks in this area.

Scrub-birds are dull brown birds finely barred with black. The wings are short and comparatively useless, while the tail is long and rounded. The legs are long and powerful and the feet are large with strong toes. They feed on small animals gleaned from the ground – predominantly insects with worms, snails and terrestrial crustaceans. The birds run well and fly little.

Scrub-birds are remarkable in lacking a wishbone and in having only poorly developed clavicles. Both species have shrill whistling calls, particularly the Noisy Scrub-bird which also boasts a sweet and melodious song. Both build large, domed nests on the ground with side entrances. A lining of pulped vegetation is added which has the consistency of papier-mâché, and which resembles nothing more than grey cardboard. Two eggs are laid and incubation takes about fourteen days.

Doubtless the two scrub-birds once occupied the whole of southern Australia but, following the Pleistocene Ice Age, a period of marked aridity separated the two populations into their present toe-holds at the very corners of the continent.

Larks Alaudidae

To rise early in Europe is to be 'up with the lark', an acknowledgement of the goodwill shown towards one of nature's finest songsters – the Skylark *Alauda arvensis*. Like the other seventy-four species of lark, the Skylark is a dull brown bird with a voice that belies its unassuming plumage. Rising upwards from some meadow it is one of the first birds to sing in the mornings of spring and summer. It breeds across the Palaearctic region from Britain to Japan and from the Arctic to North Africa.

Some larks are boldly patterned like the Shore Lark *Eremophila alpestris*, called the Horned Lark in America, or the finch-larks of Africa, but most are sombrely coloured in shades of brown that merge well with their preferred backgrounds. They vary in size from 5 inches to 9 inches and are a remarkably homogeneous group. Birds of open country, from Arctic wastes to semidesert, they walk rather than hop and have the claw of the hind toe more or less extended like the pipits and wagtails. Some species prefer to run rather than fly to avoid danger and are exceedingly difficult to flush. My first views of Dupont's Lark *Chersophilus duponti* in Morocco were only obtained, after two days spent quietly watching likely spots, by running through suitable territory to make these long-legged birds show themselves. Even then the birds flew only a few yards before alighting and out-distancing me on foot. Larks, then, are great walkers.

Most species prefer open country although some, like the Woodlark *Lullula arborea*, habitually alight on small bushes and fence posts and prefer more broken bushy country. The Skylark is often seen on agricultural land and has benefited and spread following man's clearance of the natural forests that once covered large areas of temperate Europe. No doubt other larks have similarly benefited and increased their range in other parts of the world.

Larks have short, pointed bills ideally suited to their mixed diet. Most species have a slight down-curve to the bill, although only Dupont's Lark rivals the lengthy curve of the Bifasciated Lark *Alaemon alaudipes*. This large, desert-loving lark is often called the Hoopoe-lark because of the bold pattern of black and white on the wings. It, too, can be difficult to flush, although when it flies in its undulating way it is quite unmistakeable. The long, decurved bill is used to probe the earth in its search for food. Yet other larks have strong, finch-like bills, such as the Bimaculated Lark *Melanocorypha bimaculata* of the Middle East and its cousin, the more widespread Calandra Lark *M. calandra*. But none equals the Hawfinch-like bill of the Thick-billed Lark *Rhamphocoris clot-bey* which can crack the toughest skins of desert seeds and insects.

Most larks have a crest or, at least, can raise the feathers of the crown to give a crested appearance. The Skylark is well marked in this way, but in southern Europe two larks that live side by side in Iberia and North Africa have very pronounced crests. The Crested Lark *Galerida cristata* is exceedingly difficult to distinguish from the Thekla Lark *G. theklae*, but is more widespread and occurs in many areas where Thekla Larks are absent.

The Shore Lark, too, has a crest of sorts, but this is condensed into two prominent horns that extend from the black area of the crown. This is the only lark to occur in the New World, save for the Skylark which has been introduced successfully to Vancouver Island in British Columbia. The Shore Lark has a totally circumpolar distribution extending in the Americas as far south as Mexico. Because of the harshness of its Arctic breeding grounds it is at least a partial migrant and it is doubtless this fact that has led to its establishment in the high Andes of Colombia and status of South America's only lark.

But the centre of lark distribution is Africa where some two-thirds of the world's species can be found. Large numbers of bush-larks and finch-larks are found nowhere else and their similarities can cause considerable confusion to the beginner in African ornithology.

The Desert Lark is found from the Sahara to the arid lands of the Middle East. Over this large area it varies enormously in coloration depending on the background against which it occurs.

The species of finch-larks in particular are an elusive and confusing genus. Reminiscent of nothing more than a group of diminutive sparrows, they are brown above and black below, with variable areas of white about the head, flanks and rump. They are distributed over the open and drier parts of Africa in an intricate patchwork that extends, in the case of the Black-crowned Finch-lark *Eremopterix nigriceps*, from the Canary Islands to India. The latter continent also has its own Ashy-crowned Finch-lark *E. grisea*.

The finch-larks are ground feeding birds much given to flocking and are easily overlooked. Grass seeds form the basis of their diet, but insects are also taken. In spite of the species being so similar several of them will readily associate in composite feeding groups,

Throughout Europe and the Mediterranean, the Wood Lark is found in open country with scattered trees. Its decline in England has been correlated with the demise of the rabbit.

though there is no evidence of inter-breeding.

Many larks form flocks outside the breeding season, and while the African species are essentially nomadic, many of the northern species perform lengthy migrations. The migration of Skylarks is often difficult to detect over countryside where they breed, but every October huge numbers flit over the rooftops of London.

The songs of the larks are particularly melodic in spring. Many are uttered in a hovering display flight like that of the Skylark, but

The attractive Temminck's Horned Lark is the desert equivalent of the widespread and strangely distributed Shore Lark. It frequents broken ground along the northern edge of the Sahara.

others sing from posts, rocks or, in the case of the Woodlark, even the tops of small trees. Several African species of the genus *Mirafra* clap their wings as they descend during their display flight, a fact that has proved a useful identification aid and given rise to names such as Flapper Lark *M. angolensis* and Clapper Lark *M. apiata*.

Without exception, larks nest on the ground constructing a scrape or neat cup lined with grass into which the three to five lightly camouflaged eggs are laid. The nest of some African larks often has a dome of grass over it, while that of the desert larks is sometimes protected from wind-blown sand by a pile of small pebbles. The female takes the dominant role in incubation but both sexes feed the growing chicks.

Several larks have evolved well-marked subspecies, but the desert larks of the genus *Ammomanes* vary enormously in coloration according to the earth colour of the area they inhabit. Thus, the Desert Lark *A. deserti* occurs in six distinct subspecies across North Africa alone. What is more, different coloured birds can be found in differing landscapes within a few miles of each other. While some of these forms can be ascribed to distinct subspecies it is perhaps wiser to say that, within this species, populations have become adjusted to the coloration of their habitat. Thus, while some birds are sandy red in colour others are slate grey.

Larks, especially the European species, have long been considered a delicacy and large numbers have traditionally been slaughtered, particularly in the Landes coast of south-west France. Even today, the slaughter runs into millions of birds. Despite the lack of evidence to the effect of such killing on the populations concerned, it seems that the practice will soon be made illegal by a French government.

Swallows and martins Hirundinidae

Swallows are among the most popular and appealing of the world's birds. They are swift-flying masters of the air with a propensity to nest confidingly close to man, often on his artefacts. The seventy-eight species have an almost world-wide distribution and many are migrants which herald the return of spring according to popular sayings.

The swallows are quite distinct although they are sometimes confused with swifts. Indeed, the similarities are a result of convergent evolution in which two separate families have adapted to a common aerial life style. Swifts are longer winged and usually fly higher than the swallows, a fact that makes them less well known to the casual observer.

An adult Swallow, red throat bulging with insects, arrives at its nest in a disused house. Found in both Old and New Worlds this long distance migrant is seen virtually throughout the globe.

Swallows are smallish birds from 4 to 9 inches in length, with longish forked tails often extended by streamers consisting of elongated outer tail feathers. The wings are long and pointed, but not sickle-shaped like many of the swifts. Flight is masterful and the birds use their large wing areas to perform erratic manoeuvres in the air as they hawk for the insects that form the bulk of their diet. They also drink from the air by sweeping low over ponds and scooping water from the surface. They perch frequently, but the legs and feet are weak and often invisible as they squat on their bellies on wires or bare twigs. On the ground they look almost legless and walk awkwardly. Most species alight only to gather mud for their nests. The bill is tiny, but in the manner of most aerial feeders it is backed by a huge gape into which insects are gathered as the bird flys through their swarms.

Most swallows are dark above and light below. The upperparts are frequently boldly coloured with iridescent blues, purples and greens, while the underparts and rump are often rufous. The sexes are similar, although minor differences can be seen in the field in

Wings spread, a Sand Martin leaves its nesting burrow. Found throughout the Northern Hemisphere, these little birds are gregarious during every aspect of their lives.

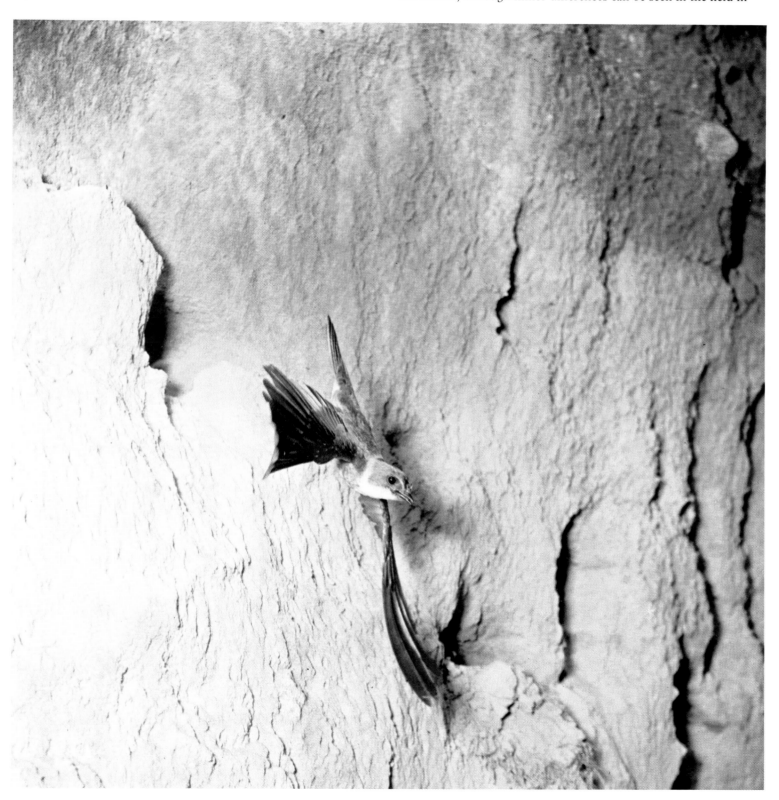

some species. In the Barn Swallow (the Common Swallow of Europe) *Hirundo rustica*, for instance, the length of streamers can be seen as the birds sit on telegraph wires above an observer. The outer tail feathers of the male are considerably longer than those of his mate.

Most swallows are gregarious, nesting, feeding, sleeping and migrating in flocks. Colonies of Sand Martins *Riparia riparia*, for instance, often consist of several hundred pairs, while communal roosts of these birds and Barn Swallows among reeds on migration may reach a quarter of a million individuals. This habit of roosting among reeds is doubtless responsible for the old myth that swallows spend their winter in hibernation at the bottoms of ponds, a theory that must have seemed no more far-fetched than their disappearance in autumn due to a complete migration out of Europe. Certainly, we are in danger of becoming blasé about the incredible journeys made by swallows and other small birds.

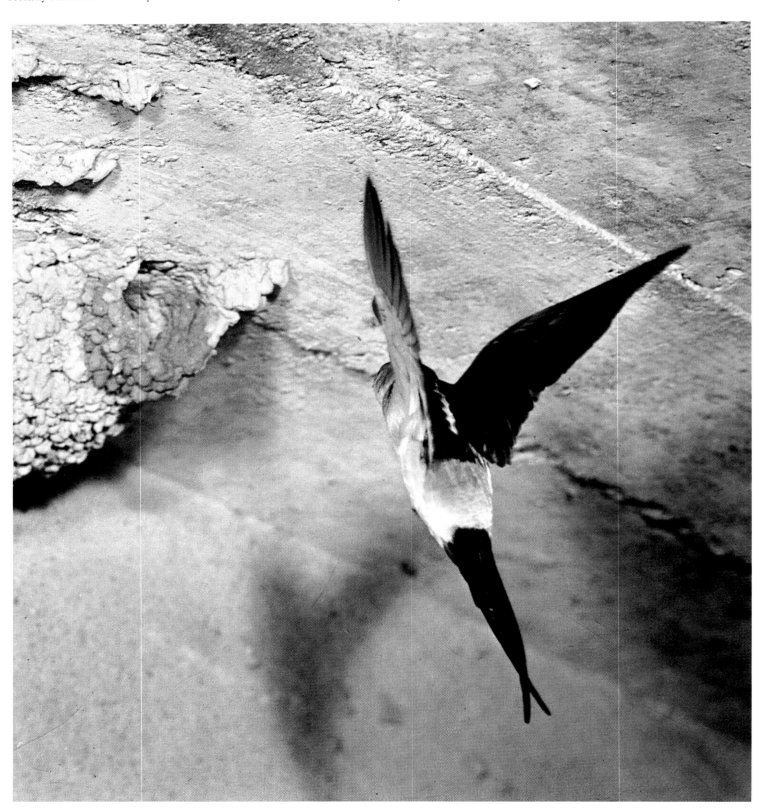

A Red-rumped Swallow arrives at its bottle-shaped nest beneath a concrete bridge. The nearest globules of mud, darker than the rest, have been recently added and have not yet dried.

Vocally swallows are not great performers. Mostly, they utter twittering notes and contact calls, but several manage to string together a quite pleasant jingle of song. The male Barn Swallow, which arrives on territory before his mate, sings pleasantly every morning from a wire or bare branch near his favoured nest site. Courtship, which consists of much aerial chasing, is invariably accompanied by much calling.

The migrations of swallows are extraordinary. British Barn Swallows pass across the Mediterranean and Sahara to winter in a restricted zone in the very southernmost part of South Africa. This journey of over 8,000 miles makes them one of the longest-distance land-based migrants in the world. Dependent on flying insects, their spread northward across Europe in spring has been shown to coincide closely with the 48°F isotherm. Thus, the first arrivals in Britain are in the south-west followed by a northwards movement along the shores of the Irish Sea.

Barn Swallows, as their name implies, nest almost exclusively in association with man. Barns, sheds and outhouses are so frequently used that it is difficult to see how widespread these birds could have been before man began to construct them. They are solitary nesters and an established pair will behave aggressively towards other prospecting birds. House Martins *Delichon urbica*, in contrast, are colonial nesters favouring the eaves of houses where their dome-shaped nests may be clustered so closely together that they overlap to form a large conglomeration of mud. Their distribution over much of their range is dependent on the presence of buildings, although in remote areas they will nest on cliffs and in caves.

Like many other swallows and martins (there is incidentally no real significance in these two names) these birds construct a nest of small, rounded, mud bricks built up layer by layer. Mud droplets are gathered in the bill from the edge of some pond or puddle near the nest site. Having chosen an appropriate site, the first job is to build a firm foundation of mud bricks against the vertical wall. One pair of swallows that nested in my kiln spent several days trying to get this foundation to stick, at the end of which a large area of the wall was covered with incomplete half-circles of mud with droplets all over the floor. As Swallows prefer to build their nests on a ledge I nailed up a simple platform on which the birds immediately built, and successfully raised two broods.

After the first half-circle has been laid, the mud bricks must be allowed to dry before the second layer is added, and so on until the structure is complete. Each course of mud is stuck to the previous one, the whole being reinforced with grasses and straws to form a solid mass. Red-rumped Swallows *Hirundo daurica* build their bottle-shaped nests in the same way, except that their favourite sites are usually beneath horizontal overhangs and under bridges.

The Eurasian Sand Martin is a bank-dweller nesting in holes that it excavates in soft, sandy cliffs. Doubtless the growth in the number of such pits to satisfy the ever-expanding construction industry has helped the Sand Martin spread.

The fine, green-backed Tree Swallow *Iridoprocne bicolor* of North America is a natural cavity nester that prefers to nest in existing holes in trees. Often, it occupies the disused chambers excavated by woodpeckers, but it takes readily to nest boxes and is now widespread wherever such homes are provided. Even more successful is the Purple Martin *Progne subis* which has spread northwards from the southern United States due to the erection of martin boxes. Many of these are dovecote-like structures with 'flats' or 'apartments' to accommodate many pairs, forming a virtual martin tenement block.

While the nesting habits of swallows are so variable, their reproductive cycle is remarkably uniform. They lay three to seven white eggs, which are often more or less speckled with brown. The young take a long time to fledge, often more than three weeks, and are then supported by the adults until they have mastered the art of aerial hunting for themselves. Many species rear more than one brood.

Several of the swallows have extremely large ranges occurring on both sides of the Atlantic and through Asia. The Barn Swallow is a case in point, but the Sand Martin also occurs in the New World where it is known as the Bank Martin.

While rough-winged swallows appear in both Old and New Worlds they are not the same birds. The American Rough-winged Swallow *Stelgidopteryx ruficollis* has the edges of its outer primaries serrated like the Old World birds, and nests solitarily in tunnels excavated in banks. The other rough-wings are of purely African distribution and belong to the genus *Psalidoprocne*. They nest on ledges or in natural holes and bear a superficial resemblance to aerial drongos with their deeply forked, lyre-shaped tails. Also African is the strange Grey-rumped Swallow *Pseudhirundo griseopyga* which nests in rodent holes made in level ground.

The odd bird out of the swallow family is the African River Martin *Pseudochelidon eurystomina* which is sometimes placed in a family, or at least a subfamily, of its own. It is a bulky, black bird with red beak and eyes and is confined to certain areas of the River Congo, where it forms large colonies in holes excavated along the river banks. Three white eggs are laid and the birds winter in coastal marshes.

Pipits and wagtails Motacillidae

Pipits and wagtails are slim, ground-loving birds with a world-wide distribution, absent only from the islands of the Pacific. They walk rather than hop, and many species bear a marked similarity to those other great passerine walkers, the larks. They have the long toes of larks with extended hind claws which, in the case of the Yellow-throated Longclaw *Macronyx croceus*, is double the length of the foot. The longclaws live among the marshes of Africa where they tiptoe over aquatic vegetation in the manner of jacanas.

About forty-eight species are currently recognized, but they are divided among only four or five genera: *Anthus*, the pipits; *Motacilla*, the wagtails; and *Macronyx*, the longclaws, are the dominant groups. All share a variety of common features that include gregarious habits, avoidance of perches, a wagging or rather bobbing of the tail, deeply undulating flight and vociferous calling.

Pipits are found throughout the range of the family. In general, they are dull brown, streaked birds with longish tails marked by white outer tail feathers. Their general similarity makes them difficult to identify and the unenthusiastic tend to dismiss them in bulk as 'sparrows', a fact which makes them particularly attractive to the keen field man. Fortunately, all pipits have distinctive calls that, once learned, are a certain means of easy identification, for they call continuously. Pipits frequent open ground being most common on mountains, tundra and along the shore line, although they are also found on pastures among domestic animals.

Most widespread of all is the large Richard's Pipit *Anthus novaeseelandiae* a rare, but often overlooked, autumn visitor to Britain, that breeds from western Siberia right across Asia to Australia. In India it is a common bird often foraging on lawns in suburban gardens. Not surprisingly it occurs on grassland in Britain. The characteristic sparrow-like 'churrup' is an easy means of identifying this large, darkish pipit. Also widespread are the Rock and Water Pipits *A. spinoletta*, races of the same species with a circumpolar distribution. While both races occur along coasts in winter, the Rock Pipit remains to breed, whereas the Water Pipit takes to the hills and frequents mountain streams.

Many pipits are highly migratory; indeed, the family as a whole

Above Although it nests on the ground in true pipit fashion, the Tree Pipit inhabits open areas with a plentiful supply of trees from which it can launch into its distinctive song flight.

Left A Blue-headed Wagtail, one of the most widespread of the many races of the Yellow Wagtail group, pauses at the rim of its nest. It is this subspecies which occupies the heart of continental Europe.

boasts numerous long-distance migrants, although few make journeys as lengthy as those of the Tree Pipit *A. trivialis*. This species leaves Europe completely in autumn and many birds penetrate deep into Africa. The Tree Pipit is unusual among its family in preferring broken country with trees on which to perch. It feeds on the ground but it sings from the top of a tree and has a delightful song flight performed as it drops to the ground like a parachute. Several other pipits have similar displays including the common and widespread Meadow Pipit *A. pratensis*, which is the most numerous of the pipits in Britain and north-western Europe. It frequents moors and coasts alike and is found almost as high as any other bird among the mountains of Scandinavia. Climbing a mountain you expect the birds to change as zone succeeds zone, but the Meadow Pipit is ever-present.

To the north the Meadow Pipit is replaced by the delightful Red-throated Pipit *A. cervinus*. While this species is like a dark Meadow Pipit through most of the year, in spring it dons a rust red face and chest. It breeds from northern Scandinavia eastwards across Siberia and migrates through the eastern Mediterranean to winter in East Africa. Thus it is only a rare, passing visitor to Britain.

The southern parts of Europe boast the Tawny Pipit *A. campestris* which is a large, light sandy coloured pipit. Typically, it is found in the arid regions of the Mediterranean, but it penetrates as far north as the Baltic in eastern Europe.

Wagtails are generally larger and more attenuated in shape than pipits with longer tails that seem permanently in motion. Save for the Forest Wagtail *Dendronanthus indicus*, all belong to the genus *Motacilla* and bob their tails up and down. The Forest Wagtail moves its tail from side to side.

Typically, the wagtails are water birds, found along streams or among marshes. The White Wagtail *M. alba*, colloquially called the Water Wagtail and officially the Pied Wagtail in Britain, ranges across Europe and Asia and through much of Africa. In several areas it has developed quite marked subspecies, several of which have been accorded full species status by some authors. Certainly, the black and white pattern of the plumage varies considerably from area to area.

Even more diverse are the plumage patterns of the Yellow Wagtail *M. flava*. Ranging across the Palaearctic and into the New World in Alaska, the various populations of Yellow Wagtails seem to be in a state of evolutionary flux, because while certain apparently well-defined subspecies inhabit distinct geographical areas, birds of other subspecies turn up with such remarkable regularity that the consensus of scientific opinion favours mutation rather than migration as their origin. Yellow Wagtails are green and yellow in colour with long tails marked with white outer feathers. It is, however, in the coloration of the head that most variation occurs. The British bird *M.f. flavissima* has a yellow head, whereas European birds *M.f. flava* have a blue head. Thousands of miles away on the Kirghiz Steppes of Siberia another yellow-headed bird *M.f. lutea* occurs.

One quite remarkable member of the family is the Yellow-throated Longclaw. A bird of the marshes and grasslands of Africa, this brown-backed, yellow-breasted bird is marked by a horseshoe of black on the throat. That this plumage pattern so closely resembles the meadowlarks of temperate North America is an extraordinary example of convergent evolution, because the birds are in no way related.

Pipits and wagtails are a remarkably self-contained family. All are insectivorous birds, that nest in a simple cup of bents on the ground carefully covered with grasses or hidden among rocks. Some species nest in trees sometimes making use of the disused nests of other species. While the female pipit is solely responsible for incubation, the male wagtail frequently takes a turn on the nest. The usual clutch is four to seven eggs and second broods are quite common.

Cuckoo-shrikes Campephagidae

The cuckoo-shrikes are neither cuckoos nor shrikes, and are not even related to either of these disparate families. Many species do, however, closely resemble those birds in both plumage and form. The Common Wood Shrike *Tephrodornis gularis* of India, for example, looks just like a shrike with its grey plumage, long, graduated tail, and short, stubby bill. The Barred Cuckoo-shrike *Coracina lineata* of Australasia is a large, grey bird marked with bold black and white barring below, just like a cuckoo. Basically such resemblance is superficial, because the cuckoo-shrikes are essentially arboreal birds of the forest edge.

The Common Wood Shrike is an inhabitant of Asia where it is found in small, easily overlooked parties that scour the branches of trees in their search for insects. It is most unlike a shrike in behaviour.

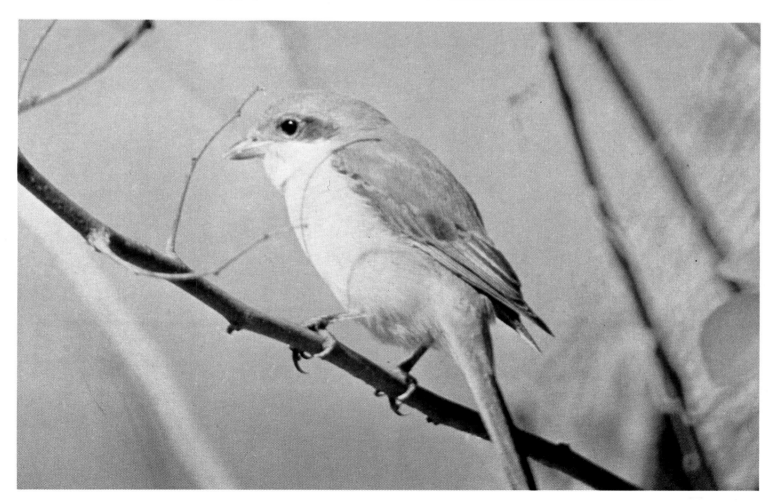

They frequent wooded country and gardens and are typical members of the nomadic parties that roam through tropical woodland. They are found from Africa, through Asia to Australasia, though the minivets are found as far north as Japan. These birds of the genus *Pericrocotus* are the only brightly coloured members of the family and are Asiatic in distribution. They are 8 or 9 inches in length with long tails and boldly patterned in reds, oranges and black. The females are generally more dull and, in some cases, quite differently coloured in greens and browns. They are noisy birds, much given to appearing in small flocks that scour the canopy in search of food. As with the other cuckoo-shrikes they take a great many caterpillars as well as adult insects. Surprisingly enough even the brightly coloured, crimson species are not obvious among the red-flowered forest trees of early spring.

The Ashy Minivet *P. divaricatus* is the most northern member of the family breeding through Japan to Amurland. It migrates southwards and is the only long-distance traveller among the cuckoo-shrikes. Nevertheless, the White-vented Cuckoo-shrike *Coracina novaehollandiae*, migrates considerable distances, moving from south-eastern Australia and Tasmania to New Guinea to winter. It is aptly called Summer-bird in Tasmania.

Minivets build their neat, lichen-camouflaged nests on a high branch of a tree, where the two to five eggs are laid in a neat little cup. Invariably, it is only the female that incubates and tends for the young, although in some of the other cuckoo-shrikes the male helps to build the nest and takes his turn on the eggs.

Dominating the family are about forty species of the genus *Coracina*, mostly referred to as cuckoo-shrikes, but some bear the vernacular 'greybird'. They are wide-ranging birds extending from Australia to Africa. They all share the basic pattern of dull grey plumage and forest habitat. They have long, pointed wings and long, rounded tails and fly well among the trees. The bill is shrike-like, marked with a notch and there is a strong growth of rictal bristles. The feathers of the back have stiff shafts and can be erected. They can also be shed like those of the pigeons and it has been suggested that this acts as a defence when the bird drops feathers to distract a would-be predator.

Quite aberrant is the Ground Cuckoo-shrike *Pteropodocys maxima* of Australia. This 14 inch-long bird spends most of its time foraging on the ground. Like the other cuckoo-shrikes, however, it nests high up in a tree. It is a slim, elegant, grey bird marked with grey barring on the breast and rump, and by black wings and tail. This sharp colour contrast is particularly evident when the birds engage in a courtship ritual which consists of raising and lowering the closed wings alternately. Most other cuckoo-shrikes have similar courtship displays. Ground Cuckoo-shrikes occur in the dry wastes of the Australian bush in small, nomadic flocks. Gregariousness continues into the breeding season, when several birds may combine to tend a brood. There is even evidence of more than one female laying in a nest.

Bulbuls Pycnonotidae

The bulbuls are a homogeneous group of Old World, tropical passerines that reach their greatest development in Africa, where all but one of the genera occur. All species share a characteristic shape and 'jizz' that make them quite unmistakeable – their 'bulbulness'. They are found throughout Africa, except in the driest parts of the central Sahara, through southern Turkey and the Middle East, India, China and South-East Asia, and as far east as the Wallace line that separates Australasia from the Orient. One species, the Brown-eared Bulbul *Hypsipetes amaurotis*, breeds in Japan and migrates southwards to winter in Korea. Another, the Red-whiskered Bulbul *Pycnonotus jocosa*, has been introduced into Australia where it is the bane of the fruit farmer's life.

The members of this large, 120-species family are 6 to 11 inches in length, with broad, rounded wings and long, rounded tails. The legs are strong and the birds spend much time on the ground or perch acrobatically on bushes or reeds. The medium-length bill is fine and clearly down-curved, and many species have erectile crown feathers that sometimes form a quite definite crest.

Most bulbuls are sombrely clad in browns and buffs which, at first sight, are confusing. But many boast bold patches of colour on the under-tail coverts and clear, sometimes colourful, face patterns. Thus, the common bird around the gardens of Kenya is the Common Bulbul *P. barbatus* with deep yellow under-tail coverts, whereas in India it is the Red-vented Bulbul *P. cafer*.

The greenbuls, as expected, are greenish rather than brown in colour, and the bristle bills have the growth of rictal bristles shared by all bulbuls, particularly well developed. But these are elusive forest birds. All bulbuls are basically woodland birds, but a great many have adapted to more open country, particularly farmland, while some find the company of man congenial. Despite their dull coloration they are friendly and confiding and, even away from habitation, allow a close approach before flying away to cover. Their inquisitiveness leads them to perch and watch more often than to flee. When they do fly they do so low and directly like a thrush, but they cannot sustain such flight for long and are generally resident throughout their range.

Outside the breeding season bulbuls are gregarious and vocal,

Widespread in Africa and adjacent parts of the Middle East, this Common Bulbul is perched to drink the nectar from the common aloe flower found widely in South Africa.

roaming forests and gardens in noisy parties. They feed predominantly on fruit and berries, although some species feed in the manner of sunbirds on nectar from flowers, while others glean insects from the leaves of trees in the manner of warblers. There are well-authenticated instances of bulbuls being drunk and disorderly following their consumption of decaying and partly fermented fruit.

Most bulbuls build their nests among low bushes, but some of the more strictly forest species do so high in trees. The two or three, occasionally four or five, boldly marked eggs are laid in a cup of bents and roots set in a considerable structure of twigs. The male feeds his mate on the nest, but seldom participates in incubation. Both parents feed the young with insects and later berries.

Typical of the more open-country species is the Common Bulbul of Africa. It is found throughout most of that continent south of the Sahara, except the extreme south-west. It extends along the Nile Valley even into the heart of Cairo where it can be seen on hotel balconies overlooking the river. It is found throughout the Mahgreb of north-west Africa, but has not crossed the Straits of Gibraltar into Europe. This is also the bird found in southern Turkey, around the eastern end of the Mediterranean, and extending southwards along the eastern shore of the Red Sea.

Throughout this vast area it is found in association with man and is particularly fond of agricultural land where it is a considerable pest. Not only does it eat fruit, but its rape of the new season's buds is as destructive as that of the European Bullfinch. Like several other pest species it apparently enjoys the ability to breed at almost any time throughout the year. There is considerable variation in the plumage of the Common Bulbul, and even the characteristic yellow area around the vent is missing in the population of the Sahel zone immediately south of the Sahara.

The greenbuls are more typically birds of forests, difficult to observe, and just as confusing once seen. They are exclusively African and largely confined to the tropical rainforests of the west. A subgroup is found among the forests of Madagascar where they have been given unlikely names like tetraka and foditany. One or two species are found in the montane forests of East Africa.

Several of these greenbuls have highly restricted ranges. The Mountain Greenbul *Andropadus montanus*, for example, is found only in a few areas of the Cameroon Mountains from 3,000 feet to 6,000 feet and virtually nothing is known of its life. Like the other bulbuls, greenbuls are noisy, but some are far more melodic and tuneful, while others are comparatively good songsters.

Leafbirds Irenidae

Irenidae is the family name of three quite distinct groups of birds – the leafbirds, the fairy bluebirds and the ioras. All are Far Eastern in distribution and of forest habitats, although several species have adapted to clearings and are common in gardens. They are colourful birds, predominantly green in colour except for the fairy bluebirds which, as their name implies, are blue and black. The wings and tail are well proportioned and the birds fly well. The legs and feet are strong and the bill is moderately sized, slim and down-curved. The leafbirds are vocal, producing musical trills as well as mimicking other birds. They feed predominantly on fruit and are of a gregarious nature. The ioras, the smallest members of the family, are solitary, however, and feed predominantly on insects.

The eight leafbirds proper are 7 or 8 inches long and feed in the canopy of the rainforests that stretch from India to the Philippines. They are green in colour marked with splashes of black and yellow. Most widespread is the Golden-fronted Leafbird *Chloropsis aurifrons* which is found from India eastwards to Vietnam. Its black facial mask extends on to the breast and is edged with a bright golden border. It is a popular cage bird in the East though it does not mix well with other species. In contrast, the Blue-masked Leafbird *C. venusta* is found only in Sumatra where it is rare. It is an exceedingly beautiful bird and the smallest member of the genus. Females are generally duller than their mates.

The leafbirds construct a delicate little nest well hidden in the fork of a tree. The three or four light grey or pink eggs are speckled and streaked with reddish brown. They feed predominantly on fruit and berries, but also take insects and nectar from flowers. They are highly gregarious forming flocks that roam the forest canopy.

The two fairy bluebirds are about 9 inches long and, like the leafbirds, are gregarious fruit-eaters. They form small flocks that frequently gather noisily at wild fig trees. One species, the Philippine Fairy Bluebird *Irena cyanogaster*, is confined to those islands, while the Blue-backed Fairy Bluebird *I. puella* is more widespread from India and Malaysia to Vietnam. Both species are blue and black in colouring and some authors regard them as members of the family of Old World orioles.

The ioras are yellow-green birds with black markings. They are solitary and insectivorous, and the Common Iora *Aegithina tiphia* is frequently found in gardens throughout the Far East. Its extraordinary display flight consists of the bird climbing high into the air before fluffing out its feathers into a ball and dropping slowly downwards, all the while producing a thin tin-whistle note. Like the other leafbirds they construct a delicate little cup in a fork of a tree using spiders' webs as binding.

Shrikes Laniidae

Shrikes are passerines turned birds of prey. In many parts of the world their unendearing habit of impaling their prey, which varies from insects to small birds, on thorns or barbed wire has earned them the name 'butcherbirds'. In fact, they are ferocious and, for their size, quite capable of dealing with large prey. Typically, they perch on some prominent bush and, hawk-eyed, watch for some passing insect or small bird. They prefer to live in open country, where they are able to dart down upon their unsuspecting victims. Much of their food consists of large insects taken on the ground. The erection of telegraph wires has been a boon to shrikes, and throughout their range these are now among the most favoured perches.

Shrikes are small to medium-sized birds, with strongly hooked bills marked with a bold notch on the upper mandible. The legs and feet are strong, and although the birds kill with their bills, unlike the hawks and owls which do so with their talons, the feet are used for grasping prey in the dismembering process. The tail is usually, though not always, long and rounded, and the birds sit characteristically upright. While most shrikes of temperate latitudes are sombrely coloured in greys and blacks, those of the tropics, particularly Africa, are often boldly coloured with reds and yellows. Young birds are frequently mottled browns, as are some adult females. Flight is direct and low and invariably ends with a sharp upswing to another perch.

The true shrikes of the subfamily Laniinae best exhibit the familial characters: the Great Grey Shrike *Lanius excubitor* is a case in point. It is a dove grey bird some 9½ inches long, with a long, attenuated, black tail and black wings broken with a bold white wing-bar. The bill is solid and hooked with a well-developed notch, and a black mask extends from the gape through the eye to the lores. It enjoys a circumpolar distribution and, although it is found in France and around the Mediterranean, it does not breed in Britain. Along with the Loggerhead Shrike *L. ludovicianus*, it is the only shrike found in the Americas. Several other shrikes boast a similar plumage pattern including the smaller Lesser Grey Shrike *L. minor* which has a more southerly distribution, and a group of African shrikes often jointly referred to as fiscal shrikes. The fiscals are typical birds of the bush country of East Africa and have adapted well to the growth of new cities, where they penetrate the suburbs and live in close proximity with man. The Grey-backed Fiscal *L. excubitorius*, in particular, shows its ease with man by frequently perching on car doors, wing mirrors and the like. It is also one of the few truly social shrikes, and small groups can frequently be seen 'squabbling' along fences. In fact, these gatherings seem to serve some social function and have been labelled 'dances' by some authors.

The Red-backed Shrike *L. collurio* is the only member of the family to breed in Britain, but it is fast declining and is now

Above Male and female Red-backed Shrikes feed their hungry brood. This widespread Palaearctic species migrates eastwards out of Europe to winter in East and South Africa, Arabia and India. It is declining at the edge of its range in Britain.

Opposite A Great Grey Shrike incubates its eggs in a pine tree. This is the most widespread of the shrikes found in America, across the Palaearctic region and throughout northern Africa and India.

confined to a few southern counties. No doubt this must be, in part at least, due to the destruction of the heathland which it prefers, but perhaps other causes are also at work. Its closest relatives seem to be the Bay-backed Shrike *L, vittatus*, Rufous-backed Shrike *L. schach* and Brown or Red-tailed Shrike *L. cristatus*. As all visitors to India will know there is plenty of room for confusion between these birds.

Many of these typical shrikes are long-distance migrants quite capable of making journeys of several thousands of miles. The vast majority winter in Africa and there, no doubt, lies the centre of origin of the family.

The bush-shrikes are an African subfamily of boldly marked, often quite colourful birds. They are distinctly less obvious than the true shrikes and often very difficult to observe. The bush-shrikes of the genus *Telophorus*, for example, keep very much to the interior

of bushes and dense thickets, while members of the *Tchagra* hunt on the ground under bushes, running about like rodents in the process. Fortunately, almost all are highly vocal and utter some of the most characteristic calls of Africa. Sometimes, members of a pair will duet, but the uninitiated will find it difficult to decide where one bird ends and its mate begins. Many of these songs are quite delightful to the ear, though a beginner in African ornithology will find identifying them a considerable problem.

The boubous of the genus *Lanarius* are another vocal group that often duet during courtship, but which are otherwise shy. Most species boast at least part of their plumage a rich glossy black together with white, crimsons and yellows. Some of the more brightly coloured species are called gonoleks. As would be expected from their common name the most frequent call is a soft, but far-carrying, 'boubou', but the birds also snarl and chatter one with another. Studies have shown that there are various, but established,

combinations of calls and that these are accompanied by various postures which act as visual signals between the pair. Thus, most duetists perch within a few yards of one another although distances of over a hundred yards have been recorded. Each bird has its own singing part and never adopts that of its partner. Fortunately, the boubous are curious birds and can be tempted out into the open by unusual sounds. The puff-backs of the genus *Dryoscopus* boast an erectile patch of white feathers on the rump.

Helmet-shrikes, so called because of the feathers that extend over the base of the bill and the rounded shape of the head, are another group of African shrikes comprising the subfamily Prionopinae. They are notable for their social behaviour which extends to the actual business of nesting. They form quite distinct colonies and several birds will often combine to build a single nest and feed the chicks. The seven species are quite distinct from the rest of the family in behaving non-aggressively, and lacking the sharply hooked shrike bill. They feed mainly on small insects and build beautiful nests camouflaged with lichens, quite unlike those of other shrikes. They are confiding with man and have a strange butterfly-like flight.

A summer visitor to the Mediterranean, a Woodchat Shrike perches sentinel on the look out for insects and reptiles. Throughout its range this bird is easily spotted along telegraph wires.

Vangas Vangidae

Vangas are found only on the island of Madagascar where, from a common shrike-like ancestor, they have evolved to fill a variety of ecological niches. Like the honeycreepers of Hawaii and the finches of the Galápagos, vangas exhibit a considerable variation of bill shape, but, unlike those families, the exact purposes of these sometimes extraordinary beaks remain unknown. That they became established on Madagascar a long time ago is evident from the variety of sizes and plumage patterns, but no doubt they have evolved to occupy otherwise vacant niches from a common colonizing ancestor. Only twelve species are generally recognized, but several authors have recommended that the Kinkimavo *Tylas eduardi* and the Coral-billed Nuthatch *Hypositta corallirostris* should be added to the family, and Stuart Keith tells me that his work on the avifauna of the island is constantly producing more birds that should rightly be regarded as vangas.

In size vangas vary from 5 to 12 inches and are predominantly black and white birds, with bold patches of chestnut and blue. Many species have a strong, heavy bill, but they vary from the long, thin bill of the Sickle-bill *Falculea palliata* to the huge wedge shape of the Helmet-bird *Euryceros prevostii*. Several authors have suggested that the latter should be placed in a family of its own.

Vangas are gregarious birds of the forests that forage among the trees for insects and other prey. The larger species will take lizards and tree frogs. They are generally noisy birds and readily associate with one another and with other species that roam through the canopy. Unfortunately, breeding behaviour has been little studied, but recorded nests consist of a cup placed in a tree holding three or four spotted eggs.

The Sickle-bill was originally called 'bird-baby' by the local natives, a reference to its loud crying call. It is a large bird with white head, neck and underparts, and black wings and tail. Doubtless the long, decurved bill acts as a probe, but the birds are difficult to observe as they hunt in the high canopy of Madagascan forests.

The Hook-billed Vanga *Vanga curvirostris* is also black and white and marked by a strongly hooked bill. The natives called it 'vanga' and this has since become the name for the family. It is generally less gregarious than other vangas and is said to be rather slow and deliberate in its movements.

Smallest of all is the Red-tailed Vanga or Tit Shrike *Calicalicus madagascariensis*, which is less than 6 inches long, and finely marked with rufous, grey and white with a black patch on the throat in the male. It has a short, stubby bill.

The largest bill of all belongs to the Helmet-bird. Laterally compressed, like that of the anis of South America, the huge black bill extends on to the forehead in a ridge. The bird is black in colour with a bold area of chestnut extending from the mantle down the rump to the central tail feathers.

Waxwings, silky flycatchers and Hypocolius Bombycillidae

The waxwings and their allies form a ragbag of a family, but with the members sharing certain characteristics. Further comparative study is necessary before the various groups and their relationships can be determined, but it seems likely that at least two distinct families would be created in the process. Recent work on the Palmchat, formerly included in the Bombycillidae, has resulted in splitting this bird off into a monotypic family, the Dulidae.

The Bombycillidae, as at present constituted, consists of three waxwings, four silky flycatchers and the Hypocolius *Hypocolius ampelinus*. They vary from 6 to 9 inches in length and are attractively plumaged in muted colours. All eat large quantities of berries and fruit, have soft plumage and poorly developed vocal organs. And there the similarities end.

The waxwings are birds of the northern coniferous forests enjoying a circumpolar distribution. The silky flycatchers are found in Central America, and the Hypocolius in the Middle East around the Persian Gulf extending northwards along the Tigris-Euphrates complex, and in an isolated area of Saudi Arabia near Mecca. Such a strangely disjointed distribution is unusual among birds indicating that the family, or at least its ancestors, was formerly more widespread. Certainly, the extant members show closer relationships with each other than they do with any other group of birds.

The three waxwings are placed in a single genus and closely resemble one another. They are chunky birds, softly coloured in dull pinks and greys, with a bold splash of colour on the wings and tip of the tail. The name stems from the red, wax-like protuberances on the tips of the secondaries of the Waxwing *Bombycilla garrulus*, called the Bohemian Waxwing in North America, and the Cedar Waxwing *B. cedrorum*. The Japanese Waxwing *B. japonica* lacks these appendages, but is otherwise similar to the two more widespread species. The Bohemian Waxwing, as it is perhaps best called, is found throughout the northern boreal zone except eastern Canada where it is replaced by the Cedar Waxwing. At 8 inches it is the largest of the three.

Waxwings are highly gregarious birds, best known for their irruptions southwards into the more populous temperate regions of Europe and North America. In normal years waxwings are found in their northern forest homes where they roam nomadically in flocks several hundred strong in search of berries which are their principal food. It is difficult to map their range accurately because of their irregular habits, and in some seasons they breed hundreds of miles further south than in others. About every five or six years the population builds up following a mild winter and good berry crop and birds will breed in areas where they are usually only irregular winter visitors. Should such seasons prove bountiful the population of waxwings will reach an exceedingly high level and flocks will take off in autumn in their search for food. Usually this is triggered off by the comparative failure of the berry crop over the 'normal' range.

In these seasons flocks of Bohemian Waxwings appear in areas where they are never seen in 'normal' years. They cross the North Sea to winter in Britain where they are as likely to appear in suburban gardens as at the more usual 'rare bird', coastal sites. Flocks usually number twenty or thirty birds, but sometimes several hundred will gather along a berry-rich hedge. The largest flocks are found in autumn immediately following the arrivals, but in some years even the earliest birds do not arrive until the New Year. What happens to these out-of-range birds we do not know, and perhaps it does not matter from the point of view of the species. There is, however, some evidence of a return movement in spring on a very reduced scale. What is clear is that the huge population of some Arctic animals is too large for the food supplies available, and that the surplus population then moves out enabling the birds that remain to eke out an existence. Ornithologists are becoming progressively convinced that the occurrence of many so-called rarities is due to similar pressure of population in their breeding areas.

Waxwings usually nest in conifers well out on a branch. The untidy nest is composed of twigs and bents lined with hair and feathers and the clutch varies between three and five eggs. The chicks are fed exclusively on insects, but the adults take buds as well as berries in season.

The silky flycatchers, too, subsist mainly on berries and are prone to wander nomadically in search of them. Mistletoe is particularly favoured. Best known of the four species is the Phainopepla *Phainopepla nitens* of Mexico and the south-western United States. The male is an all-black bird with a soft but prominent crest and a

Named after the red, wax-like protrusions that grow on their wings, Waxwings are irregular migrants from the great forests of the Holarctic region where they breed among the conifers.

vividly red eye. The primaries show broadly white in flight. The nest, like that of the waxwings, is an open cup built exclusively by the male which performs the bulk of the incubation of the two or three grey-white, speckled eggs. Unlike other members of the family the Phainopepla and the other silky flycatchers take large quantities of insects which they catch flycatcher-like in the air. The female Phainopepla is a dull grey and much more difficult to find than the more boldly coloured male.

The Hypocolius is a long-tailed, grey, shrike-like bird slightly smaller than the Bohemian Waxwing. It is found in semidesert country as well as among the lush groves of rivers. In the desert they are shy birds, whereas in the gardens of river towns they are bold and tame. They feed mainly on fruits and berries, particularly the mulberry, and have a habit of leaving the discarded skins below the food tree. They are generally silent and fly directly into the centre of a tree to disappear completely from view.

Palmchat Dulidae

The Palmchat *Dulus dominicus* is found only on the island of Hispaniola and adjacent Gouave Island in the West Indies. Formerly classified with the waxwings and silky flycatchers, the Palmchat is treated as the sole member of a separate family, the Dulidae. It differs from the Bombycillidae in having more coarse, less silky plumage, a stouter bill, and particularly in its communal nesting habits. About 7 inches long, the Palmchat is dirty green above and white below, boldly streaked and blotched with dark green. Its legs and feet are strong and the slightly hooked bill is stout and powerful. It feeds principally on berries and fruit, predominantly on those of palms, as well as on flowers.

This nondescript little bird is numerous and widespread on the islands it inhabits and is, at all times of the year, gregarious. It is particularly numerous among lowland palm groves where it constructs a bulky nest at the junction of the palm trunk and the fronds. Such nests may completely encircle the trunk and provide a home for up to thirty pairs. Though they join together in this way, each pair retains its own entrance hole and tunnel leading to its nest chamber which is lined with grass and pieces of bark. Occasional nests may be found in pines, but these are invariably small and provide a home for only two or three pairs. The four eggs are white spotted with grey.

Sometimes Palmchats will repair and add to an existing nest but, as the nests often fall to the ground when the palm fronds are shed, they frequently have to start from scratch. Doubtless such large nests act as a secure defence against predators.

Dippers Cinclidae

Dippers are a family of passerine birds that have taken to an aquatic existence with only the slightest of physical modifications. They are robust, wren-shaped birds with short tails that are invariably held cocked. The legs and feet are strong and equipped with sharp, gripping claws. The wings are short but powerful. On the basis of external appearance alone it would be a bold ornithologist who deduced an aquatic existence for such a bird.

Dippers are 'water walkers'. They do not walk upon the waters like the jacanas, but under the water along the beds of fast-flowing streams – a habitat shared with no other species of bird. They are

A nestful of young Dippers photographed alongside a hill stream in the Cairngorm region of Scotland. Confined to fast-moving water, Dippers have a patchy distribution throughout the Palaearctic region.

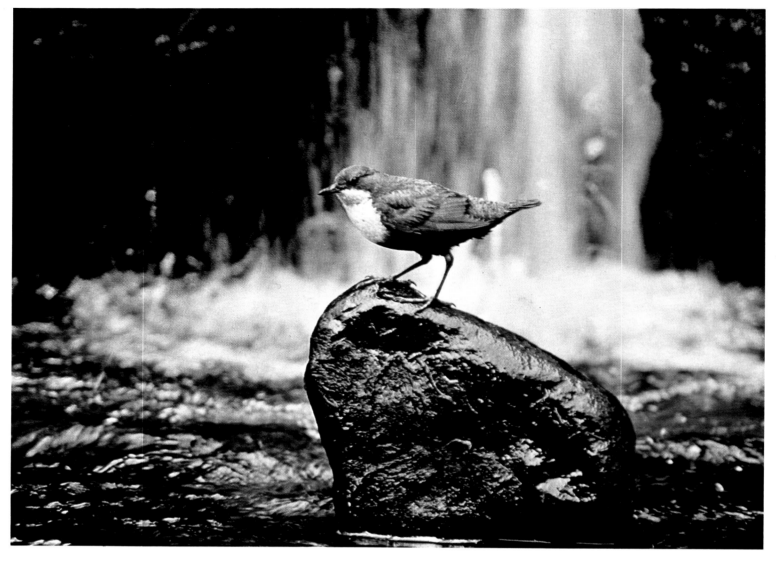

Dippers are most often seen perched on boulders alongside mountain streams. They dive and use their wings in their search for food, although they are also effective underwater walkers.

confined to the Northern Hemisphere, but are widespread in hilly and mountainous districts where water flows quickly. Even in winter, when some populations are migratory, they will search out such habitats. In southern and eastern England where they do not breed, migrant dippers can only be found on streams where weirs have been constructed or the water flows fast for natural reasons.

The Eurasian Dipper *Cinclus cinclus* is 7 inches long and dark chocolate brown in colour. The chin and breast are pure white. It breeds throughout Scandinavia, in northern and western Britain, through Spain, southern France, the Mediterranean countries and the Balkans to the Middle East south of the Caspian. It is found in the Urals and Himalayas extending northwards into Central Asia and in an isolated pocket on the Pacific coast of Manchuria. The American Dipper *C. mexicanus* is similar in build, but lighter and greyer in colour and lacks the white breast of the Eurasian species. It is found throughout the western mountain districts of North America from Panama to Alaska. The White-capped Dipper *C. leucocephalus* inhabits the mountain streams of the Andes. The Brown Dipper *C. pallasii* inhabits northern Asia to Japan and overlaps with the Eurasian Dipper in the Himalayas, where it lives at lower levels on larger streams and rivers.

Like other aquatic species dippers have very dense plumage, with a thick layer of insulating down next to the skin. This covering is

waterproofed by preening, and the dippers have huge oil glands several times as large as any other passerine. The nostrils can be covered with a special cover and a nictitating membrane clears the eyes of water.

Dippers wade happily in water, picking insects and particularly their larvae from the stream bed. They can hold themselves down on the bottom in quite deep water and frequently dive after food using their short, powerful wings for propulsion. They often do swim but the legs and feet are not specifically adapted to do so and have to work very hard. Dippers dive from the surface, from boulders and from flight, but usually they simply wade into deeper water and begin to swim.

The dipper's territory is long and narrow. A single pair will occupy up to two miles of river which they will defend vigorously against intruders. Usually they fly about their domain low over the water, but sometimes an individual will take a short cut across a bend and then often fly between bordering trees. They regularly perch on boulders and their droppings are the best sign of their presence.

The birds construct a wren-like, domed nest in a cleft among stream-side rocks, but man-made structures such as bridges are increasingly preferred. The well-hidden structure is covered with moss and the four or five white eggs are laid in a bed of grasses or leaves. Incubation by the hen takes sixteen days and it is she that takes the dominant role in feeding the youngsters which fledge in two or three weeks. The young dippers take to the water immediately. Second broods are common.

Wrens Troglodytidae

It is strange to think that while the Wren *Troglodytes troglodytes* was regarded as the 'king of the birds', and was referred to affectionately as 'Jenny Wren' in medieval times, it always has been the only wren to occur in Europe and Asia, and there are another fifty-nine quite distinct species to be found in the New World. Yet this tiny bird with the powerful melodic voice is still very much a favourite and subject of much folklore in Europe. Its scientific name stems from its habit of creeping among dense vegetation and of nesting in cavities in rocks. *Troglodytes* literally means 'cave dweller'.

Wrens, then, are a New World family most closely related to the dippers and mockingbirds. Only the single species has crossed the Bering Straits via Alaska to invade the Old World, which is surprising in view of its undoubted success. In America the same bird is called the Winter Wren, because while it breeds right across the northern part of the continent it appears over most of the United States only as a winter visitor south to the Gulf Coast.

Wrens are short-tailed, brown birds varying from under 4 inches to about 9 inches long. Their wings are short and the body plump. The legs are well developed and the bill thin and narrow. All wrens

are unmistakeably wrens, no matter what their size or habitat. They are most numerous in Central America, although they are poorly represented in the West Indies. There, only the widespread House Wren *T. aedon* occurs in any numbers and then only as far as Dominica. This made all the more interesting the discovery in 1926 of the Zapata Wren *Ferminia cerverai* in a small marsh in southern Cuba. Despite searching, this single spot remains the only known locality for the species.

While the Common or Winter Wren is well known for its catholic choice of habitat, and is just as much at home in woodland or in the most inhospitable, rock-strewn islands, in the New World each wren has seemingly adapted to a different niche. Thus, some species are found on bare, rocky mountain slopes while others prefer saltmarshes. There are desert species, and those most at home on the dark forest floors of tropical jungles or in suburban gardens.

One of the largest members of the family is the Cactus Wren *Campylorhynchus brunneicapillus* of the southern and western United States and Mexico. It is generally wren-like in behaviour except that it does not cock its tail. It is a brown, mottled bird marked with a rust-coloured cap, a prominent white stripe above the eye and distinctly speckled underparts. These are birds of semidesert areas where they perch freely on cacti and feed on beetles, grasshoppers and occasionally on lizards. They also occur around buildings where they are generally quite tame. The nest is flask

Found in the arid south-west of the United States and adjacent parts of Mexico, the Cactus Wren lives among the stands of the cholla cactus. It is a huge bird and more like a thrasher than a wren.

Opposite Finding a Wren's nest in a strawstack is only a little easier than finding a needle in a haystack. Despite its small stature the species has spread right across the Northern Hemisphere from its American origins.

shaped and constructed in a thorn bush or cactus, or occasionally on a building. Unlike most birds the Cactus Wren occupies its nest throughout the year and even young birds, that have recently fledged, build themselves a nest home. A pair of birds may construct a small series of nests, but only one is used for breeding. This desire for a home is doubtless due to the need for insulation against the extremes of temperature experienced in deserts, but even the Common Wren roosts regularly in its nest holes. Up to sixty of these birds have been found in a nest box in England.

The most widespread of the New World wrens is the Short-billed Marsh Wren *Cistothorus platensis* which breeds from the forest zone of southern Canada southwards through the United States and Central America to the southernmost tip of the continent at Tierra del Fuego. It is about 4 inches long and is found in dry marshes in the northern part of its range and in grasslands further south. It is highly territorial and has the usual wren-type loud song. The nest, which is domed, is placed low down among vegetation, and the four to eight white eggs are incubated by the female alone.

One of the most striking features of the Troglodytidae is the number of subspecies that have developed, particularly in the Common Wren. The birds seem able to colonize quite remote islands and then become resident. In time they form a quite distinct subspecies and we have the Shetland Wren *T.t. zetlandicus*, the St Kilda Wren *T.t. hirtensis*, as well as the Cretan Wren *T.t. stresemannii*, and so on. In the Aleutians no less than eight distinct subspecies can be found along the chain of islands.

Mockingbirds and their allies Mimidae

The mockingbirds, catbirds and thrashers are a New World family of some thirty-one species of slim, medium-sized birds, with a propensity to mimic the songs of other birds. They most closely resemble the thrushes and wrens, particularly the latter in habits. They live on or near the ground in dense vegetation where they feed on insects and berries. The legs are strong and powerful, the tail long and often flicked upwards, and the bill well developed and

A Galápagos Mockingbird photographed on Santa Cruz Island. An immigrant from America, the different species or subspecies present a fascinating systematic tangle that had considerable influence on the work of Charles Darwin.

down-curved. They vary in colour, but greys and browns predominate and several species are boldly streaked. While they are well known for their songs, their expertise in mimicry has probably been exaggerated. The huge variety of calls produced is bound to coincide with those of some other birds and the extent of true mimicry is less than ten per cent.

Best known and loved is the Mockingbird *Mimus polyglottos* of the United States. A fine, grey and white, $10\frac{1}{2}$ inch-long bird, it sings virtually throughout the year and is vigorous in defence of its territory. Living often in close association with man, Mockingbirds sing from rooftops and telegraph poles as well as from more natural sites. The continuance of song into the small hours aids their adoption as the Nightingale of America. No doubt they do mimic very well and pick up the songs of other birds as well as whistles and other artificial sounds. A population in Florida has even been credited with faithfully reproducing the song of the Nightingale learned from genuine Nightingales in captivity nearby.

Over most of their range Mockingbirds rear two or three broods per season and rush through the breeding cycle in a breathtaking month. Incubation apart, the sexes share the nesting activities.

Isolated on the Galápagos Islands, 600 miles off the coast of Ecuador, the Galápagos Mockingbird *Nesomimus trifasciatus* has developed a variety of island species or subspecies in geographical isolation. They are dull grey, boldly streaked birds with sharply decurved bills and, like all the creatures of those islands, totally unafraid of man. They live predominantly on insects, but will gather crumbs from picnics, and eat the eggs of the Waved Albatross while it stands by and watches.

The Catbird *Dumetella carolinensis* is a familiar bird over large areas of the United States. Like the Mockingbird it lives happily in close association with man, and gets its name from the cat-like 'meeows' it produces. All grey with a black cap and rust-coloured under-tail coverts, it is a handsome bird, although it is no vocal match for the 'Mocker'. It migrates southwards to winter from the Gulf States to Panama.

The thrashers are more shy, preferring the cover of dense vegetation and living on or near the ground. They feed on insects and fruit, and have shorter wings and longer tails than the mockingbirds. The large Brown Thrasher *Toxostoma rufum* is 12 inches long. It is a handsome chestnut brown above, and the underparts are white, boldly streaked with black. It sings usually from the cover of bushes and characteristically repeats each phrase twice. The nest is well hidden among dense vegetation and consists of a bulky cup holding two to five eggs.

Brown Thrashers are found throughout the eastern United States as far west as the foothills of the Rockies, and are migratory in the northern part of their range. A single bird once arrived in Europe.

Accentors Prunellidae

Accentors are small, shuffling, little birds almost exclusively found at high altitudes and equally exclusively confined to the Palaearctic region. Not surprisingly the only species that is at all well known is the odd one out and not a high-altitude bird – the Dunnock *Prunella modularis*.

Accentors are dun coloured with little, if any, bold markings. They hop or run low down over the ground just like small rodents. They have rounded wings with ten primaries, and although they produce a sweet tinkling song, they are not as vocal as most tundra and bare landscape birds. The bill is slender and pointed, and the birds feed extensively on insects in summer, and seeds in winter,

Dunnocks often nest near the ground, frequently in close association with man. In habits they are atypical of the rest of the accentor family, which consists predominantly of montane birds.

taking grit to aid digestion in the crop. The accentors are generally regarded as being relatives of the thrushes.

Several species are found above the tree-line in mountainous areas where they creep among rocks and dwarf vegetation. They are extremely tough birds, and while some accentors do make migrations, at least to lower levels in winter, several manage to survive some of the worst conditions on earth. Like other montane birds they are shy rather than timid, and readily approach mountain walkers to collect the remnants of their meals. The family centre of origin is in central Siberia and the birds are most numerous in the Himalayas. In the Khumbu area near Everest I was able to watch several species hopping around the tiny drystone walls of the Sherpa villages before disappearing into thick vegetation. One bird, the Orange-breasted Accentor *P. strophiata*, sat atop a bush and sang, just like the familiar European Dunnock. Several other species prefer vegetation to open areas, though at high altitude. The Maroon-backed Accentor *P. immaculata*, which is also found in Nepal, prefers damp areas surrounded by conifers, whereas the Robin Accentors *P. rubeculoides* at Khumbu preferred the shelter of rhododendrons.

Dunnocks are woodland birds that have turned to hedgerows and gardens with the felling of forests. They are even resident in central London and hop about the park shrubberies seemingly oblivious of man. In other parts of their range they penetrate high into mountainous areas as, for instance, in the Caucasus and Pontic Alps. While resident in Britain, Dunnocks that live on the continent of Europe perform considerable migrations. Some pass through Britain and have been recovered as far south as Spain, and the species is a regular winter visitor to North Africa.

The nest is built in a low bush by the female and consists of twigs and dried grasses, lined with hair and moss. The three to six pale blue eggs are incubated by the hen for twelve days, and the chicks are fed by both parents for a similar period before fledging. The species is multibrooded over much of its range.

The Alpine Accentor *P. collaris* is a larger bird with flecks of brown along the flanks and a neat enclosed bib of dark spots beneath the chin. Nesting at high altitudes where the season is short, both members of the pair take a full part in the business of breeding. In this way they manage to rear two broods per season and the young of the first brood leave the nest before they are capable of flying. The youngsters are fed on a diet of insects and predigested seeds from the parents' crop. In winter Alpine Accentors descend to lower levels and some individuals manage to wander well away from their nearest breeding area.

Thrushes Muscicapidae subfamily Turdinae

Thrushes are a familiar world-wide subfamily occurring naturally in almost every part of the globe except for a few Pacific Islands, the polar areas and New Zealand. Throughout their range they are regarded kindly by the human population and many species are treated with particular affection. The Blackbird *Turdus merula* and Song Thrush *T. philomelos* have been successfully introduced to New Zealand, leaving no significant land mass on earth where thrushes cannot be seen.

No doubt part of their popular appeal stems from their songs, because the subfamily includes some of the most beautiful of bird singers – the Nightingale *Luscinia megarhynchos* perhaps the best of all, the Song Thrush, the Wood Thrush *Hylocichla mustelina*, and so on. Thrushes are large and obvious birds, and several species have lived successfully in close association with man for many years. Blackbirds can be found in every garden in Britain, while the

American Robin *T. migratorius* occupies a similar niche in America.

Thrushes form a subfamily of the great family of the Muscicapidae. Some authors prefer to treat them as a distinct family but they show such close relationships with the other groups that they all are best placed together in a family that comprises more than 1,000 species, or roughly an eighth of the world's birds. Thrushes are most closely related to the Old World warblers and flycatchers, but also to such diverse groups as the babblers and the curious bald crows, the picathartes.

The thrush subfamily includes not only the true thrushes of the genus *Turdus* and their allies but also the chats, wheatears, robins, redstarts, solitaires and wren-thrushes. Typically, they are ground-dwelling birds of medium size with well-developed wings and tails. They fly strongly and directly and have well-developed legs and feet. Many are highly migratory. They are predominantly

The unthinking way in which British colonists named any red-breasted bird a 'robin' led to the confusing situation whereby the American Robin – really a thrush – was christened.

insectivorous, but many species take worms and crustaceans and resort to berries and fruit in season. Primarily, they are birds of open countryside, but thrushes occupy scrub and forest areas and are common birds of farmland and gardens. Some species are essentially arboreal. Such a range of habitats is, perhaps, not surprising in view of the existence of more than 300 species in the subfamily.

No doubt the thrushes originated in the Old World, but they colonized North America in earliest times and have evolved quite distinctive forms in the New World. Their general robustness and adaptability no doubt account for their enormous success. Thrushes have even colonized some of the most remote land in the world. They are found on Hawaii, the West Indies and even on Tristan da Cunha, that remote speck in the middle of the southern Atlantic. Some of these island species were wiped out with the arrival of man and particularly of rats and cats from his ships. Such extinctions represent the only black mark in an otherwise highly successful subfamily career.

The typical thrushes are best represented by the sixty-strong genus *Turdus*. This includes such familiar Old World birds as the Blackbird, Song Thrush, Mistle Thrush *T. viscivorus*, the Redwing *T. iliacus* and Fieldfare *T. pilaris*. The American Robin represents the genus in the New World. Most *Turdus* thrushes are birds of

open country that resort to bushes and trees in which to breed. They find much of their food on the ground and hunt in the characteristic 'freeze and dart' method that is shared by so many members of the subfamily. A Blackbird on a lawn will stand completely still, head turned to one side, as if listening for the movements of some insect or worm. With a sudden dart it leaps forwards probing into the earth to emerge with a worm or some smaller item of insect prey. Large prey is wiped on the ground before being swallowed. In the autumn, thrushes take to the trees and bushes to consume berries, and for species like the Fieldfare, Arctic berries are an essential part of the yearly diet. In temperate Europe Blackbirds make an excellent job of cleaning up windfall fruit such as apples and pears from the ground, although they also damage fruit on the trees.

Thrushes are highly territorial birds and males have well-developed songs with which to defend their territories. The traditional quality of such territories was remarkably demonstrated in a north London suburb when, during the bitter winter of 1962–63, a large proportion of the resident Blackbirds succumbed. The following spring members of a greatly reduced Blackbird population spent so much of their time fighting over territorial boundaries that, instead of making up the numbers with a successful breeding season, they actually produced fewer birds per pair than normal. What had happened was that so many birds had died and with them the knowledge of traditional territorial boundaries, that the new population was confused.

Blackbirds build a strong cup of bent grasses reinforced with mud to hold their four to six bluish, brown blotched eggs. The female performs most of the incubation, though both members of the pair feed the chicks. When they fledge the brood is divided between the parents which continue to feed them for several days. Nests are usually placed low down in bushes, but Blackbirds in cities often choose tall trees where they are safe from the attentions of small boys. In some city parks nest sites are so scarce that the birds will build another nest on top of an old one for year after year. Other suburban birds will nest on window sills, against drainpipes and in old sheds. There are several examples of Blackbirds nesting in cars that were in daily use. They usually manage to rear three, sometimes as many as five, broods in a season.

Song Thrushes, too, manage to exist in city centres, but they are not as common as Blackbirds. They have the unusual habit of breaking snail shells to extract the animal by beating them on an anvil – a convenient rock or stone. The Song Thrush nest is lined with a layer of mud and is one of the easiest of birds' nests to recognize.

Many of the thrushes are highly migratory. The Fieldfare and Redwing both breed among the dwarf birches and other Arctic vegetation and regularly migrate to Britain and temperate Europe

Below A winter visitor from northern Europe, the Fieldfare frequents fields and orchards in Britain. This bird finds windfall pears a satisfactory source of food.

Opposite Deep among the Palaearctic birch and pine forests a pair of Redwings have built their neatly camouflaged nest. Like other northern thrushes, they migrate to winter in more temperate climes.

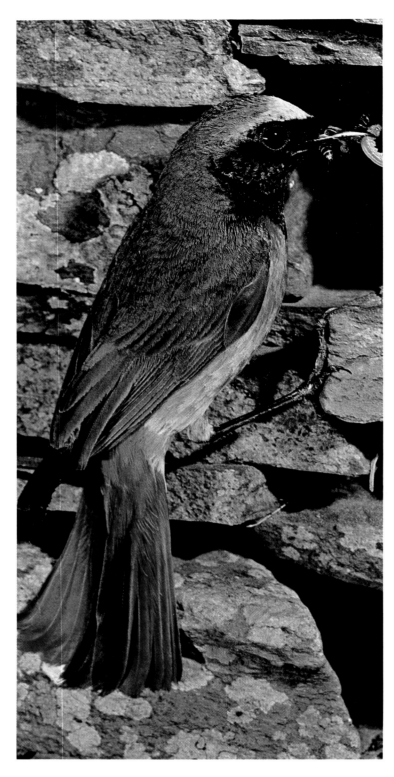

Left One of the most handsome members of the attractive chat family, a male Redstart with a green caterpillar pauses outside his nest hole. Widely distributed through Europe the Redstart migrates across the Sahara to winter.

Opposite A male Stonechat, head concealed behind a magnificent emperor moth, attempts to see that all is clear before approaching his nest.

and winter from the Gulf Coast southwards into South America. They are excellent songsters and build neat, cup-like nests low down in bushes or on the ground.

The rock-thrushes are birds of the Old World that frequent rocky ground from southern Europe across Asia and deep into Africa. Most are marked with some area of cobalt blue and some with areas of red. The Eurasian Rock Thrush *Monticola saxatilis* is a beautifully marked, blue-backed bird with a rusty red area extending from the breast to the tail. It frequents inland crags as well as rocky coasts from Spain across Asia to Japan. The Blue Rock Thrush *M. solitarius* is uniformly dark blue and black, and over much of its range more common than the Rock Thrush. It is confiding and a regular inhabitant of ruins from Portugal to at least India. I have seen them among the Roman ruins at Merida, at Minoan sites in Crete, flitting from wall to wall in the ruined Armenian cities of eastern Anatolia, and perching on the buttresses of the deserted city of Fatepur Sikri in India. They are truly the archaeologist's friend and must be as familiar to him as the Robin *Erithacus rubecula* is to the English gardener.

Of all the chats the Robin is probably the best known in Britain. During the great age of exploration and settlement homesick British immigrants were quick to give the name of their beloved and familiar garden bird to any bird with a red breast. Thus, the American Robin is, as we have seen, a true thrush and not a chat, but its red breast was enough for the early settlers. There are similar examples from Africa to Australia, indeed, anywhere that British families have settled. In India, where red-breasted birds were difficult to find, a familiar, black garden bird was christened the Indian Robin *Saxicoloides fulicata* because it has red under-tail coverts. Over most of its range the Eurasian Robin is a woodland bird that is generally shy, but in Britain it is a tame bird of gardens. It comes readily to food, occupies nest boxes, perches on forks next to gardeners, and can even be tempted to enter houses and perch on the hand for food. It is bold and pugnacious in defence of its territory and was one of the first species to be studied with regard to territory. Robins are territorial throughout the year and in winter non-migrating females have a territory of their own. The red breast is the releasing signal and even a tuft of red feathers placed within a Robin's territory will elicit display and eventual attack and destruction. As male and female are identical it is only by behaviour that the sexes recognize one another during pair formation in spring.

Robins are partial migrants and northern birds that migrate to Britain can often be told by their skulking behaviour. They receive a royal welcome from British resident Robins and in autumn the hedgerows are often alive with dispute. British Robins migrate from the north and are resident in the south. Between, it is usually the females that migrate, while the established males stay on territory.

Their place as garden birds is taken on the continent by the Redstart *Phoenicurus phoenicurus*, which is a bird of open woodland in Britain. It breeds across Eurasia and a considerable number of subspecies has been recognized. Like the other redstarts it flicks its tail frequently and feeds in the manner of the other chats by pouncing from a perch to the ground in pursuit of prey. This group of birds includes some of the most colourful and delightful species to be found in the Palaearctic fauna. The Bluethroat *Luscinia svecica*, a dull brown bird in winter, adopts a colourful breeding plumage of deep blue bordered with red and black on the breast, and marked with a red or white spot in the middle. It is found throughout Europe and migrates to Africa and to India and other

where they do not breed. There they roam the fields in nomadic flocks and feed along the hedgerows. The more northern populations of Blackbirds also migrate and sometimes arrive along the east coast of England in huge numbers in late October and early November. As its scientific name implies, the American Robin too is a long distance migrant. Breeding northwards to the tree-line it migrates the length of North America to winter in the Gulf States southward through Mexico.

Also migratory are the North American forest thrushes of the genus *Hylocichlas*, the Wood, Hermit *H. guttata*, Grey-cheeked *H. minima* and Swainson's Thrushes *H. ustulata*, and the Veery *H. fuscescens*. All are smallish, brown thrushes with speckled breasts. They nest in coniferous or mixed woodland across North America,

parts of southern Asia. The Red-flanked Bluetail *Tasiger cyanurus* is a deep blue above with pale rust along the flanks in the manner of a Redwing. Migrating eastwards from Finland and northern Russia it is a rare bird in western Europe and gave me great pleasure when I first saw it in Nepal.

Another distinct group is the wheatears and chats which extends across the Palaearctic with a single outpost in the New World in Alaska. Wheatears are some 6 inches in length and totally birds of open country reaching their greatest density of species across North Africa and the Middle East. They perch on the top of some small boulder or rock and bob in characteristic fashion when alerted by danger. The basic pattern is a lightish body, dark wings and a white or lightish rump patch. Many of the species are very similar and, where they occur alongside each other, pose interesting problems of identification. They nest in crevices in rocks, or in disused burrows of rodents, sometimes in level ground. The more northern species are highly migratory and the Common Wheatear *Oenanthe oenanthe* is one of the first summer visitors to return from the south.

Closely related are the chats of the genus *Saxicola* that prefer areas of scrub to those of bare ground. The Stonechat *Saxicola torquata* prefers dry heathlands, while the Whinchat *S. rubetra* is a bird of damper areas. The beautiful Pied Stonechat *S. caprata* is common among the reed-strewn marshes of India where it can be found alongside the Stonechat, which occurs in darker, and more confusing forms.

Oddest of all the thrushes is the Wren-thrush *Zeledonia coronata* of the mountains of Central America. It lives on the forest floor and is generally shy and elusive. Its short tail is held cocked and it has the short wings of a wren.

Babblers Muscicapidae subfamily Timaliinae

Babblers, as their name implies, are noisy birds. Throughout Africa and Asia, which are the centres of babbler distribution, groups of these birds produce many of the characteristic sounds of the jungle and bush country where they live. They are, however, a complex group. Many authors treat the babblers as a distinct family, while others regard several of the tribes as distinct subfamilies. Certainly, they are a diverse group of birds about which generalizations are either vague or misleading. The subfamily, as treated here, includes the often recognized subfamilies Orthonychinae, the ground-babblers; the Timaliinae, the true babblers; the Panurinae, the parrotbills; and the Picathartini, the picathartes or bald crows.

All are small to medium-sized birds with short, rounded wings and characteristically laboured flight. The feathers are soft and vary in colour from dull, to bright and colourful. The tail is frequently long and rounded, although in some species it is square and in others quite short. The legs and feet are strong and the bill usually well developed, sometimes with a distinct hook at the tip. Babblers live on or near the ground and are generally gregarious forming noisy flocks. Chattering calls keep the flock together, but many species have pleasant and distinctive songs. They usually inhabit thick vegetation from forests to reed beds, and only a very few species are seen with any frequency in parks and gardens. They build cup-shaped or domed nests near the ground.

Babblers are Old World birds, and only one species, the Californian Wren-tit *Chamaea fasciata*, has invaded the Americas. They are well represented from Africa through Madagascar to India, most of South-East Asia and China, and Australasia. A single representative, the Bearded Tit *Panurus biarmicus*, occurs in Europe.

The ground-babbler or rail-babbler group is Australasian in distribution and includes such apparently dissimilar birds as the logrunners, the whipbirds and quail-thrushes. The logrunners are thrush-like, ground-dwelling birds that have evolved strong spine-like tail feathers (like woodpeckers) to aid their digging activities. They feed among the debris of the forest floor and are confined to the mountainous zones of eastern Australia and Papua. The larger species, Spalding's Logrunner *Orthonyx spaldingii* is restricted to a small area of northern Queensland, whereas the Spine-tailed Logrunner *O. temminckii* is more widespread. It is a dull brown bird marked only by an orange patch on the chin. Both species build domed nests on the ground.

The four quail-thrushes likewise resemble thrushes, but are more cryptically coloured like quails. They inhabit a variety of landforms, from forests to dry, stony areas of semidesert. They walk deliberately picking up insects as they go and nest on the ground where they construct a deep cup of grasses. Both parents participate in nesting duties.

Most elusive of all the ground-babblers are the two species of whipbirds. They are fond of thick cover and their presence is usually indicated only by their calls – a series of low-pitched whistles followed by a quite definite whipcracking call. The Eastern Whipbird *Psophoides olivaceus* is dark brown in colour, with a long, black tail and a black crest that can be raised, but its most distinguishing feature is a white chin patch. It is found throughout eastern Australia. In contrast, the Western Whipbird *P. nigrogularis* is found only in four isolated pockets in southern and western Australia and, as a result, merits a place in the Red Book of endangered species.

The typical babblers comprise more than 140 species widespread through Africa and Asia. Some species are quite colourful but the group also includes many that are so similar and so lacking in distinguishing features as to cause many visiting birdwatchers great problems.

The jungle babblers of the genus *Trichastoma* are small, brown birds with longish, slightly down-curved bills. They skulk in the dense undergrowth of the jungle floor in the forested regions of Africa, and in Malaysia east to the Philippines. They are noisy but extremely difficult to observe, and only very occasionally will they come out into the open at the forest edge. Some species occasionally catch insects in the air in a clumsy fashion like a House Sparrow. They are usually gregarious and roam along what seem to be habitual paths at regular times. Domed nests are constructed on the ground and often hidden away in a bank.

The Wren-tit of the western coastal States of the United States is an undistinguished little bird of uniform, dull grey-green colouring with a long, rounded tail. It is always found in thick cover, but because it is the only babbler in the New World, it poses no identification problems. It sings throughout most of the day during summer from the bush-clad hillsides where it lives. These are highly territorial little birds and seldom move far from their area of birth.

Most typical of all the babblers are the twenty-five species of the *Turdoides*, which include those birds that come nearest to Europe and penetrate the Palaearctic region. They also include the Common Babbler *T. caudatus* and Jungle Babbler *T. striatus* that are so familiar to visitors to India. These are predominantly thrush-sized

276

Opposite Typically babbler in shape, the finely plumaged Arrow-marked Babbler is an inhabitant of African bush country and gardens. Like some other babblers it has a prominently coloured eye.

Left A male Bearded Tit shows the fine black moustaches after which it is named. Confined to dense reed beds the species is a prolific breeder, but suffers heavily during hard weather.

Below The White-necked Bald Crow or Picathartes builds a swallow-like nest deep inside an African cave. The species is very localized, liable to disturbance and has seldom been photographed.

less than ten individuals, but they are gregarious the year round including the breeding season. These babblers feed on insects and spiders, but also take quantities of berries in season. The Common Babbler is more terrestrial than most and frequently adopts a cocked-tail attitude. It runs well with shuffling gait, but flies only short distances on its rounded wings. Birds nest throughout the year and three or four pale blue eggs are laid in a cup lined with hair and small leaves. Both sexes share the nesting duties.

Most westerly of all the Old World babblers is the light brown Fulvous Babbler *T. fulvus* found across northern Africa as far as the Atlantic coast of Morocco. In this region it inhabits palm groves among the oases and river courses of the Saharan edge.

Also included in this tribe are the fourty-four species of laughing thrushes of the genus *Garrulax*. They are more boldly coloured than the *Turdoides* babblers, are larger, and some species are crested. In many respects they live up to their scientific name in bearing a strong resemblance to the jays. The White-cheeked Laughing Thrush *G. leucolophus* is remarkably jay-like in shape and behaviour. Parties of these brown, white-headed birds can frequently be seen in various parts of India and will even come to bait, feeding in the most greedy manner. Some species even hoard acorns like the jays. The nest is an untidy affair and when the two to four eggs hatch, the chicks may be fed by more than two adults.

Best known of the parrotbills is the least typical – the Bearded Tit. It breeds throughout Eurasia, but has a highly broken distribution. The Bearded Tit is comparatively rare in western Europe because it is dependent on large areas of pure reed which have declined as a result of drainage. Like miniaturized babblers, Bearded Tits fly low

birds of dull and confusing grey-brown plumage. They live in thick cover and although the two Indian species often frequent parks and gardens they never venture truly out into the open. They always feed on the ground in the shadows, and leap into the undergrowth at the slightest sign of danger. Most parties are small consisting of over the reed-tops uttering a high-pitched 'pting' call. The males are beautifully marked with chestnuts, greys and two black moustaches. In recent years their numbers have increased as the result of a high rate of reproduction so that every autumn sees an irruption from their breeding marshes in Holland and eastern England. Several new colonies have been established.

The parrotbills proper are birds of Asia from the Himalayas, across China to Korea. Clothed in various shades of chestnut, cinnamon and white, and with long tails and short, stubby bills they are a particularly well-defined group of babblers. Varying in size from 4 inches to a foot in length these are predominantly mountain birds inhabiting low scrub and bamboo thickets. One species, Heude's Parrotbill *Paradoxornis heudei*, is found only in extensive reed beds along the lower reaches of the Yangtze. Parrotbills are predominantly insectivorous, but they do resort to bamboo shoots and seeds in season. The strong finch-like bill is adapted to tearing open bamboo to seek out the insects that live in the pith. The nest is placed in a tree or shrub and consists of a cup made from bamboo leaves lined with grasses and roots. The clutch varies from two to five eggs. Outside the breeding season they roam in parties up to thirty strong.

The two species of *Picathartes* are birds of the West African forests from Sierra Leone to the Cameroons. They are large, long-tailed birds characterized by a lack of feathers on the head exposing areas of brightly coloured skin. They nest only deep in caves where they construct swallow-like cups of mud against the walls. The Grey-necked Picathartes *P. oreas* is the more widespread and better known of the two. It is grey above and white below with blue, black and red about the head. It inhabits caves and feeds among the bat droppings that accumulate below its home. This highly specialized habitat makes the Grey-necked Picathartes a particularly elusive bird, and very few ornithologists have had a chance to study it. When these birds leave their caves they venture no farther than the dense growth of ferns that surrounds the entrance or, at very most, to nearby lush, overgrown streams. Nests are sometimes placed in the light at the cave entrance, but others are well inside in almost complete darkness. The two eggs are incubated by both parents.

Being so primitive and so restricted, the picathartes are in grave danger from disturbance. The possible exploitation of bat guano would lead to instant extinction for both species.

Gnatcatchers Muscicapidae subfamily Polioptilinae

Gnatcatchers are an exclusively New World subfamily found from southern Canada southwards to Central and South America. They are closely related to the Old World warblers, but they must have become established in the Americas a considerable time ago, because they form a quite distinct group.

Gnatcatchers are, in the main, less than 5 inches in length. They are dove grey birds with long, black tails that are kept continually in motion. They inhabit the canopy where they glean insects from the outer branches and leaves of forest trees, sometimes hovering like a *Phylloscopus* warbler or a Goldcrest. A small group of four species known as gnatwrens are of more exclusively tropical distribution and find their living among the secondary growth of the forest.

Most of the species are very similar, the males marked with a black facial mask during the breeding season. They have a sweet, high-pitched, little song and a warbler-like call note. Gnatcatchers favour trees near water, often in swamps, in which to build their deep, little, cup-shaped nest. It is constructed of grasses and plant fibres bound together with spiders' webs and camouflaged with pieces of lichen. The four or five pale blue eggs are spotted with brown, and both sexes share the incubation for the thirteen days that they take to hatch. The chicks, which are fed by both parents, fledge after ten to twelve days. Two broods are regularly reared in the south, but the migratory northern birds are single brooded.

Outside the breeding season gnatcatchers are generally found in small flocks and frequently mix with other species to roam the

The delightful Blue-grey Gnatcatcher builds a fine little cup of a nest, bound together with cobwebs and camouflaged with lichens.

canopy in search of food. Best known and most familiar is the Blue-grey Gnatcatcher *Polioptila caerula* which has an extensive range from southern California eastwards across the United States to the coast of New England and southwards into Guatemala. It is the more northern populations of this species that migrate to the Gulf Coast and beyond.

Old World warblers Muscicapidae subfamily Sylviinae

There are about 320 Old World warblers and they are small, rather dully coloured, confusing birds. American 'birders' sometimes find them totally baffling in much the same way as the European birdwatcher is baffled by the autumn plumages of the unrelated American warblers. Yet both groups of birdwatchers find their own warblers fascinating and are delighted to be confronted with a 'difficult' one. Imagine the joy of sorting out your first Blyth's Reed Warbler *Acrocephalus dumetorum* from a lifetime's contact with the common Reed Warbler *A. scirpaceus*: or of finding and identifying a Dusky Warbler *Phylloscopus fuscatus* way off course on an English east coast marsh. Such joys are clearly for the enthusiast.

Warblers are closely related to the Old World chats and flycatchers and to the Australian wrens, often called warblers, of the subfamily Malurinae. They are most numerous and widespread in the Palaearctic and Oriental regions and particularly in Africa between the Sahara and the Zambesi. Three species – the two

Above Smallest of European birds, the Goldcrest breeds among coniferous woodland and spends the winter roaming in flocks, often in association with tits.

Right A typical inhabitant of the Mediterranean scrub, the Sardinian Warbler is readily identified by its red eye-ring. The black cap of the male is another good field mark. The female is shown here.

Regulus and the Arctic Warbler *Phylloscopus borealis* – have penetrated the New World, and while the 'crests' are well established, the Arctic Warbler, like the Common Wheatear, returns to the Old World to winter in Asia. This species has also extended its range westwards into northern Europe, but still retains its old-established habit of migrating eastwards into Asia instead of southwards into Africa.

Warblers are small birds varying in size from $3\frac{1}{2}$ inches to 8 inches. They have ten functional primaries, as against the nine of the New World warblers, with average to long tails. The legs and feet are not strong and the bill is thin and pointed. Most are active birds feeding predominantly on insects which they glean from trees and bushes, although some species feed on the ground and even the leaf warblers, more properly birds of the canopy, will do so if needs dictate. Birds such as the Chiffchaff *P. collybita* which arrive early at their breeding sites can frequently be seen feeding in this way. Warblers are generally pleasant songsters and some species, in particular, the Blackcap *Sylvia atricapilla,* vie with the Nightingale for the title of world's top songster. The warbling of so many species is responsible for the subfamily name, and a most useful aid to the identification of what can be a difficult group.

Warblers inhabit a variety of habitats from the canopy to the ground including heather, scrub, marshes and reed beds. They are territorial in the summer, but frequently band together with other species to roam appropriate habitats in winter. At such times they associate with birds as diverse as the European tits and Asiatic flycatchers and nuthatches. They are predominantly insectivorous, but several species evidently rely on soft berries such as blackberries to fatten up prior to autumn migration. They also take nectar from flowers in the manner of sunbirds or hummingbirds. I remember handling a number of migrant Chiffchaffs in spring with nodules of pollen attached to the feathers at the base of the upper mandible. Scientists at the Royal Botanic Gardens at Kew identified the pollen grains as coming from flowers in southern Iberia.

Many warblers perform quite extraordinary migrations for such tiny birds. Several are regular trans-Saharan migrants and must be able to fly for up to forty hours non-stop to cross that desert and the Mediterranean without alighting. European birds migrate predominantly south-westwards, but the Lesser Whitethroat *S. curruca* and others move south-eastwards into Asia. Some species exhibit a migrational divide in which western populations move south-west while eastern populations fly south-east. Birds from Scandinavia and eastern Germany may move in either direction. This strange division seems to be more due to the pattern of colonization after the great Ice Age than to the presence of the Saharan barrier to the south.

Several authors have attempted to divide up the warblers into neat groupings such as 'leaf', 'marsh' and 'scrub' warblers which unfortunately do not work. The best divisions are those based on scientific grounds – the generic names.

The warblers of the genus *Phylloscopus* are small, predominantly green and yellow birds that feed mainly in the canopy. In the Himalayas, from where they originate, over twenty species may be found. All are similar and, being continuously active, they are extremely difficult to see and identify correctly. They flit hither and thither, leaning out to peck some morsel from a twig, hovering to explore the underside of a leaf, and catching flies in the manner of a flycatcher. Only occasionally will a bird stop to preen. Many species

Left The orange breast and white moustache are the key features of the Subalpine Warbler, a skulking inhabitant of Mediterranean scrub. The female is drabber but both sexes have an orange-red eye ring.

Below Most widespread and numerous of the genus *Cisticola*, the Fan-tail Warbler builds a fine purse-shaped nest of vegetation bound together with cobwebs.

are almost identical in plumage pattern and are best told apart by song. Others have varied patterns of wing bars, rump patches and crown markings that pick them out from the rest provided all these points can be seen.

The nest is generally placed on or near the ground, is domed and incubation is performed by the female alone. Some males participate in feeding the young, but not all. The first brood is usually five to seven eggs although the second, where it is reared, is usually slightly smaller.

In Britain the Chiffchaff and Willow Warbler *P. trochilus* are both common summer visitors. They are so similar that even experts often lump them together as 'phylloscs'. The colour of the legs, dark in the Chiffchaff, is useful as is the comparative extent of the supercilium, longer and more bold in the Willow Warbler. But these are fine points to pick out from a fast-moving bird. The songs, however, are quite distinct consisting of a sweet descending trill of

The uniformly undistinguished Marsh Warbler is a melodious summer visitor to most of Europe that builds its nest among waterside vegetation.

the Warbler and a monotonous repeated 'chiff-chaff-chiff-chaff' of the Chiffchaff.

Sylvia warblers inhabit more open brush country and are often found in scrub and along hedgerows. Many species are marked with dark heads or caps and the basic plumage is predominantly grey or brown. Several species occur in the Mediterranean in the prickly scrub that is generally referred to as 'macquis'. Here they live a secretive life searching the low vegetation for insects and their larvae. Most common and widespread is the Sardinian Warbler *S. melanocephala*, a grey warbler with a black head and startlingly red eye ring. Like all the *Sylvia* warblers it has a certain irascible quality as it perches head down en route from one twig to the next. The Spectacled Warbler *S. conspicillata* and the Subalpine Warbler *S. cantillans* frequent similar habitats.

Most of these small birds are migrants, but the Dartford Warbler *S. undata* is a resident that suffers severe casualties during hard winters. It breeds in southernmost England and seems permanently in danger of local extinction. It is a shy little bird that frequents dense clumps of gorse and is difficult to see. During spring,

however, it sings from the tops of bushes with its long tail up over its back.

The Desert Warbler *S. nana* lives in the semi-desert areas along the northern edge of the Sahara and in the Middle East. Its light, sandy coloration is in sharp contrast to the rest of the genus.

The 'marsh' warblers, predominantly of the genus *Acrocephalus*, are dull brown birds with either plain or striped backs. They have rounded tails and are among the most difficult birds to identify in what is a very difficult subfamily. Many inhabit dense reed beds and show themselves very little, though others have characteristic song flights that are quite distinctive. The Fan-tailed Warbler *Cisticola juncidis*, which is only 4 inches long, bobs in the air

uttering a deep 'zip-zip-zip' call that is repeated until it becomes almost boring. It is, in this way, quite unique among the *Cisticola* in being easy to identify. This predominantly African genus is so confusing that even ornithologists that live in the region are not always sure of their birds. Surely no other group of seventy-five species of birds in the world poses so many problems. Their nests, globular structures bound with spiders' webs, are superb creations.

Typical *Acrocephalus* warblers are the Reed and Marsh Warblers *A. palustris*. They are almost identical and best separated by habitat and song. Like other members of the genus they produce a basic song consisting of several 'churrs' followed by several 'churrucs', but the Marsh Warbler is a superb songster and includes phrases that are never heard from a Reed Warbler, including imitations of other birds.

Another group, the *Locustella*, are striped birds of reeds and marshes that are highly secretive and spend most of their time low down in dense vegetation. Their songs consist of a reeling like that of an insect, often likened to that produced by a fisherman's reel being wound in. Here the difficulty is to identify the songster from the other 'reelers' by its pitch, an impossible task for anyone without a well-developed sense of tone.

The Grasshopper Warbler *L. naevia* is widespread throughout

Opposite top A summer visitor to western Europe and North Africa, the Melodious Warbler seeks its food in a deliberate manner – quite unlike most other European warblers.

Opposite bottom The stitching along the leaf edges of this Black-necked Tailorbird's nest has come undone. The species is widespread and numerous in southern Asia.

Below Changeover time at a Wood Warbler's nest. As one bird leaves with a faecal sac, its mate arrives with food in the form of a large insect.

Britain and Europe and has recently found that young plantations of conifers offer a suitable alternative to the fast-disappearing reed beds. Its nest is acknowledged as among the most difficult of all to find, because it is entered through a long tunnel and is completely covered with vegetation.

Another group of European warblers, the *Hippolais*, is as difficult to identify as any. Here the problem is to pick out various fine anatomical points from what are basically dull, unmarked birds. They are larger than many other warblers and less inclined to flit about. They often feed by reaching out rather than flying, and have a characteristic disregard for foliage which they brush through rather than slip through like the more graceful species.

The wren-warblers of tropical Africa and Asia are long-tailed, little birds predominantly greenish in colour, but frequently marked with patches of rust colour. In India several species are common

garden birds including the superbly creative Tailorbird *Orthotomus sutorius*. These birds construct their nest inside one or two broad leaves that they sew together with a neat row of stitches of plant fibre. This chamber is lined with grasses, plant down and animal hair.

Showing a close resemblance to several of the *Phylloscopus* warblers are the 'crests' or kinglets sometimes placed in a separate family – the Regulidae. Four species are generally recognized, two in the Old World and two in the New. All are greenish yellow in colour, 4 inches or less in length and boast vivid splashes of red or gold across the top of the crown. They are birds of coniferous forests and build globular nests at the tops of the higher branches of a pine. They are active birds constantly searching for insect food among the pine needles. They often hover, and frequently mix with bands of tits in winter.

Australian wrens Muscicapidae subfamily Malurinae

The Australian wrens are a complex subfamily of the Muscicapidae that consists of several more or less well-defined groups. They carry such names as wren-warbler, bristle-bird, whiteface, thornbill, chat, warbler, songlark, as well as grasswren, scrubwren and simply wren. They have no direct relationship with the true wrens of the Troglodytidae, although many species resemble them in stature and behaviour. Their nearest relatives are probably the Old World warblers – the Sylvinae – and some authors regard several groups

treated here as better placed in that subfamily. Typical Australian wrens build domed nests with a side entrance, and lay two to four eggs, but others construct open cups.

Most clearly defined of all the groups are the birds of the nominate genus *Malurus*. They are small, long-tailed birds,

The brightly plumaged male Variegated Wren is typical of the Australian blue wrens. Its long tail is invariably held cocked.

frequently boldly marked with cobalt blue, and often considered most closely related to the babblers. They are social birds that feed mainly on insects and can be found in a wide variety of habitats throughout Australia, Tasmania and New Guinea.

The males of several species vie one with another for the title of most attractive Australian bird. The Black-backed Wren *M. melanotus* is a deep cobalt blue marked with a black eye stripe that continues around the nape. Like the other species, it frequently cocks its long, blue tail. The Variegated Wren *M. lamberti* also has a blue head, but this is bordered on the back and breast by lines of black and flame orange. The Blue-and-white Wren *M. leucopterus* too is a finely marked and attractive bird.

While these birds are attractive to look at, they also exhibit one of the strangest forms of social behaviour to be found among birds. Each small group maintains and defends a territory from which it drives invaders from neighbouring groups. Members of the group combine to build a single, globular nest in which the female of the dominant pair lays her eggs. All members of the group, which includes other full adults, then take turns in incubating the eggs and brooding and feeding the young. This is doubtless an adaptation to the often harsh conditions that the birds encounter in Australia. Sometimes, single pairs do nest by themselves, but their success rate is generally low.

The habitats of these wrens vary considerably, but they all occupy much the same niche, feeding on or near the ground on small insects. They fly on whirring wings and generally prefer to hop into cover. If the nest is threatened the entire group will perform a distraction run fluttering this way and that over the ground.

The emu-wrens of the genus *Stipiturus* are also found in Australia and closely resemble the blue wrens. They are also short-winged, long-tailed birds with a characteristic stocky shape. But while blue wrens are often open and obvious in habits, the emu-wrens are very inconspicuous. The Common Emu-wren *S. malachurus* is found in south-eastern and south-western Australia with almost 1,000 miles separating the two populations. It is a brownish orange bird with a bold spot of pale blue on the breast, not that anyone but the most fortunate or persistent will ever see it. The tail, which makes up 3 inches of the 5½ inches of the bird's length, is virtually transparent and always looks ragged and worn with only the shafts appearing at all conspicuous. The birds build domed nests low down in dense vegetation, and though little is known of their breeding behaviour they do seem to move about in small groups.

The grass-wrens of the genus *Amytornis* are similar ground-dwelling birds of the drier parts of Australia. They are dependent for breeding on the effect of rain on the spinifex grass.

The Australian chats *Ephthianura* species form a group of largely nomadic species dependent on rainfall for their breeding season which is, therefore, highly erratic. They are boldly marked, chat-like birds that build cup-like nests in low, dense vegetation. They have quite curious distribution ranges. The Yellow Chat *E. crocea*, for example, occurs in four areas of marshy swampland in northern Australia, each separated from the others by several hundred miles of unsuitable territory. The Crimson Chat *E. tricolor* is a vividly crimson bird with the black of the back extending across the face. It is found in eastern and western Australia. White-faced Chats *E. albifrons* are essentially wetland birds with a propensity to form quite large flocks outside the breeding season. Such flocks are nomadic.

The most aberrant members of the subfamily are the songlarks of the genus *Cinclorhamphus*, best known for their aerial song flights and extreme difference in size between the sexes, greater than in any other passerine. They are bulky, strong-flying birds that nest on the ground in the manner of larks. Both species are migratory. In the Rufous Songlark *C. mathewsi*, at least, the males are polygamous, mating with as many as three different females.

Old World flycatchers Muscicapidae subfamily Muscicapinae

The Old World flycatchers are a large group of insectivorous birds that reach their greatest development of species in Africa, Asia and Australasia. They have flat, broad bills with a strong growth of rictal bristles and typically catch their prey in flight, often with an audible snap of the bill. They sit sentinel on some prominent perch watchful for a passing insect after which they dive, catch it and return to their perch to consume. A great many species feed in this characteristic manner, but there are others that behave more like warblers and chats.

Flycatchers vary in length from 4 to 8 inches. Some species are brightly coloured and sexually dimorphic, while others are duller with the sexes usually being similar. They have long wings and are agile fliers – they have to be. Most of the Eurasian species are migrants. The tail is usually short, but the *Rhipidura* have long, fan-shaped tails and several species have elongated and decorated tails. Some birds boast brightly coloured wattles about the eye. In contrast with their close relatives the thrushes and warblers, song is poorly developed, and usually consists of a repetitive trill. As you would expect the legs and feet are weak and simply used to perch. The typical flycatcher posture on a branch is upright with the feathers of the belly almost resting on the perch.

The subfamily can be further subdivided into three quite distinct groups: the typical flycatchers, the monarchs, and the fantails.

The typical flycatchers include the species that are regularly seen in Europe and which breed across Eurasia. These are the expert insect catchers. They are generally subdued in colour. They nest in holes and on ledges. The sexes share the duties of rearing a family, though the female takes the larger part.

The Pied Flycatcher *Ficedula hypoleuca* is a 5 inch-long, black-and-white bird that is a summer visitor to its breeding range. The wings are marked with white flashes and there is a white spot at the base of the upper mandible. It frequents hillside woodlands and is numerous in the northern and western districts of Britain. It takes readily to nest boxes and is generally encouraged in forestry areas. The female is browner and more dull in colour, though still with the lighter flash on the wing. Pied Flycatchers are numerous in Scandinavia and, migrating south-westwards, large numbers frequently make their landfall on the east coast of England together with Willow Warblers and Redstarts. They are the 'bread-and-butter' of the British student of migration.

The similar Spotted Flycatcher *Muscicapa striata* is slightly larger and a dun brown bird boldly streaked on the breast. It lives in gardens and orchards, and frequently nests on buildings and in sheds. Its delicate little nest needs a shelf to support it, and the birds will readily take to an open-fronted nest box. Its general lack of fear has taken it deep into the suburbs of large cities and even into the parks and gardens of the city centre.

Red-breasted Flycatchers *Ficedula parva* are of more easterly distribution and migrate eastwards into Asia and away from the strong flush of birdwatchers found in western Europe. Little more than 4½ inches in length, they are dainty birds marked in the male during the summer by a red chin and upper breast. The female and male in winter are dull brown, undistinguished birds, but with the characteristic habit of cocking the tail upwards to reveal two white

Opposite top A male Pied Flycatcher visits his mate during incubation inside their hollow-tree nest site. This summer visitor to Eurasia frequents open woodland, often near streams.

Opposite bottom The Rufous Fantail is well named. Its finely bound nest is lashed to a horizontal fork with cobwebs and insect silk.

Above left The Red-breasted Flycatcher is a summer visitor to the northern part of the Palaearctic region and only a scarce wanderer to western Europe. This male shows the characteristic red-throat and white tail patches.

Above right The male Flame Robin was named by early English settlers for obvious reasons. In fact it is a member of a widespread group of Australian flycatchers.

areas at the sides. They also boast a narrow, white eye ring. They are winter visitors to India where they are common in open woodland and scrub.

The flycatchers of the genus *Newtonia* are confined to the woodlands and forests of Madagascar. They are dull grey, little birds with long tails, well-developed legs and feet, and behave more like warblers than typical flycatchers. They usually occur in parties, associate with other forest birds, and are invariably tame and approachable. The four species are difficult to separate and their breeding habits are little known.

In contrast, the Australian flycatchers of the genus *Petroica* are generally called robins, and behave more like chats than flycatchers.

They are often boldly coloured birds and the male Flame Robin *P. phoenicea* has a vivid red breast with black-and-white upperparts. They inhabit the forests and bush country of Australia, although they may be found in more open areas in winter. They sing well and are highly territorial, even ensuring that the human trespasser passes safely out of their patch. They feed in the manner of chats dropping from a low perch to take prey from the ground, although they also scour the trees like warblers. The nest is a beautiful construction made of grasses, lined with hair and fur, and placed neatly in a fork. It is often camouflaged with lichens and mosses. Two species occur in New Zealand, one of which is called the New Zealand Tit *P. macrocephala* because of its resemblance to those birds. It is found only in the undisturbed areas of native forests.

The monarchs and paradise flycatchers are brightly coloured birds of the forest. The feet and legs are small and weak, and though they do take insects on the wing their more typical method of feeding is a more warbler-like searching of the canopy and outer branches of trees. They join mixed species parties in winter. Monarchs are found from India to the Philippines southwards into Australia, while the paradise flycatchers of the genus *Terpsiphone* inhabit a wider area extending from Africa to Japan. The latter are

The long tail of the African Paradise Flycatcher is all that can be seen from below. The male takes his part in incubation and care of the young – an unusual event for such gaudy birds.

among the most beautiful birds in the world. The tail feathers, particularly in the males, are greatly extended, in some species amounting to twice the body length. They weave deep, cup-shaped nests into a minor fork of a tree or shrub, and the two to five white eggs are spotted with red.

The Asiatic Paradise Flycatcher *T. paradisi* has a huge range from Iran to Korea through Malaya and Sumatra. About seventeen distinct subspecies have been recognized some of which are confined to islands or island groups. It also occurs in a variety of plumages of which the white phase and brown phase are the extremes. In general, the head is black marked with a blue eye ring and bill, and a pronounced crest. The rest of the plumage is either cinnamon brown, pure white or variations between. The tail varies with age and does not reach its full length until the bird is three years old. Despite its tail the male paradise flycatcher takes his turn at incubation with the feathers hanging out behind the nest.

The fantails are another group of flycatchers that inhabit Asia and Australasia. Their long tails are continually wagged and spread as they move through the low undergrowth which they prefer. Many species are found in close association with water, and one, the Willie Wagtail *Rhipidura fuliginosa* of Australia, is so named because of its resemblance to the British Pied Wagtail. Most fantails are clothed in subdued colours, but often show bold patches of colour in the spread tail. The Rufous Fantail *R. phoenicura*, for example, has a bold patch of rufous orange at the base of the spread tail. It builds a delightful cup of bents held together with cobwebs and placed neatly on a horizontal fork.

Fantails inhabit the forest edge and have benefited from clearing and agricultural activities. They are highly territorial, but band together in winter to form small flocks that often frequent farms with livestock. Several species feed on insects disturbed by animals.

Whistlers Muscicapidae subfamily Pachycephalinae

Whistlers are found from Australasia northwards to Malaya and eastwards across the islands of the Pacific. They are named after their deep, penetrating calls and are generally thick-billed birds bearing a strong resemblance to shrikes. Lacking the flattened bill of the true flycatchers, they do not catch insects in the air, but search tit-like the branches and leaves of trees and shrubs.

The Golden Whistler *Pachycephala pectoralis* is a dull brown bird above with a black head and breast band enclosing a white chin patch. The underparts are yellow. This general description belies the enormous diversity that can be found among these birds which vary both in coloration and structure through their vast range. Some have thick, heavy bills, others thin and narrow ones. Some are large and some are small. The breast band is narrow or wider, and the colour of the underparts varies from primrose to deep

The Shrike-tit bears a remarkable resemblance to a Great Tit but with the head and bill of a shrike. It feeds by tearing and hammering at the bark of trees to reveal insects and grubs.

orange. The species offers one of the best examples of colour variation of any bird. The song of the Golden Whistler is a characteristic series of loud whistles ending in a loud crack. The bird can be stimulated into song by the report from a gun.

The Crested Bellbird *Oreoica gutturalis* inhabits the dry interior of Australia and is a long-tailed, lark-like bird marked with a prominent crest and black breast patch. The song which gives it its name is usually produced from a prominent perch, repeated endlessly throughout the day and is strangely difficult to locate. Food consists predominantly of insects. The nest is usually sited in low bushes and consists of a deep cup of twigs lined with roots and decorated around the rim with torpid or immobilized hairy caterpillars. It has been suggested that these may act as a food reserve, but as they are added to the nest before the eggs have hatched and sometimes even before they are laid, their function is not definitely known. They may equally act as a deterrent to would-be predators. Both sexes share the nesting duties. The plumage of the young birds resembles that of the female during the first year.

Titmice and chickadees Paridae

Bold and aggressive, confiding and tame – these are the apparently conflicting ingredients in the titmice character. No group of birds has established such a close relationship with man, or one that gives so much pleasure. They are friendly garden birds, always the first to the scrap basket and nut bag, and invariably the first occupants of nest boxes. But while such characteristics go to make up our impression of the tits, many species are secretive and elusive and seldom, if ever, meet man if they can avoid it.

The titmice are small, colourful birds patterned in bright blues and yellows, although some are black and grey. They have rotund bodies with short, but powerful bills and strong legs and feet. The wings are generally quite well developed and they fly well, but rather like tiny transports than swift fighters. They are intensely active birds and form flocks that roam woodlands and gardens through the winter. Never still, tits always seem to be searching. They flit among the canopy, picking this way and that for insects and their larvae, frequently turning upside down to examine the underside of leaves and twigs. Indeed, they actually seem to prefer this topsy-turvy life and will feed on ripening fruit in this manner.

Originally forest birds, tits have taken well to gardens. Their ability to deal with hard-skinned fruits and berries has been transferred to peanuts, rich in protein, but totally foreign to their normal diet. They are also fond of coconuts and of fat. How they first discovered the cream of milk we shall never know, but many country milkmen have to ensure that bottles left on doorsteps are covered as a protection against attack from these birds. Tits will happily rip the metal top from a milk bottle to get at the cream inside. By one means or another they are well able to cope with severe winters, but there can be little doubt that these adaptable little birds are to a greater or lesser extent dependent on man for their survival at such times.

The family has often been subdivided by systematists into subfamilies of the long-tailed tits, the Aegithalinae; the penduline tits, the Remizinae; and the typical titmice, the Parinae. Some authors have treated each group as a separate family. Certainly, they have different nesting habits. The typical tits are hole or cavity-nesters, while the long-tailed tits construct a beautiful, lichen-covered dome, and the penduline tits a hanging basket.

Characteristic of the typical tits is the Blue Tit *Parus caeruleus*, well known to every bird gardener in Britain. Little over 4 inches in length, Blue Tits are conspicuous and noisy for their size. The crown and wings are bright blue, with the mantle green and the underparts yellow. The face is marked with black-and-white. In many areas they are the most numerous and widespread member of the family, being equally at home in remote woodlands and city centres. Dependent for nesting on natural holes in timber, they have taken readily to nest boxes. These are prospected throughout the winter and in the early spring the female begins to use the selected box as a roost. Later she lines it with moss forming a cup of grasses in one corner in which to lay her ten to sixteen eggs. The timing of laying is absolutely crucial. The young Blue Tits must hatch at exactly the same time as the flush of green caterpillars on which they are to be fed. And yet this event must be predicted at least a month ahead by the adults. Doubtless there is a connection between the caterpillar flush and another food source on which the female is able to find sufficient nourishment to enable the eggs to be formed inside her, for in a little over a fortnight the female Blue Tit lays her own weight in eggs. The female takes the major, if not exclusive, role in incubation though she is fed on the nest by the male. Both parents bring food to the growing chicks. As there is only one caterpillar flush each year the Blue Tit is single brooded. Other tits have a similar routine.

The Great Tit *P. major* is a more widespread bird throughout the Palaearctic and Oriental regions, from Ireland to Java. It occurs in a variety of forms, for instance as the Grey Tit in India, but is typically blue above and yellow below with a black cap and black stripe down the middle of the chest. This stripe is broader on the belly in the male than the female, and the only sure method of distinguishing the sexes in the field.

Great and Blue Tits are the dominant species in the mixed flocks of tits and other birds that haunt the woods of winter. They are always noisy and utter a variety of calls. The Great Tit alone has been credited with no less than fifty-seven distinct call notes. Other tits that join these nomadic bands include the Marsh *P. palustris* and Willow Tits *P. montanus*. The latter is unusual among tits in excavating its own nest hole. Having only the usual tit-type bill it chooses rotten wood and stumps, but enterprising bird gardeners have persuaded this bird to use nest boxes by filling them with expanding polystyrene in which the birds then peck a cavity.

The genus *Parus* is also found in the New World where tits are generally referred to as chickadees, a name derived from their calls. Most common and widespread is the Black-capped Chickadee *P. atricapillus* which bears a close resemblance to the Old World Willow Tit. Like that bird it prefers to excavate its own nest hole, a habit shared with three other American species. Their habits are

The European Crested Tit builds its nest in a cavity in a rotting conifer stump. It is dependent for its winter survival on ripe pine seeds and hibernating insects.

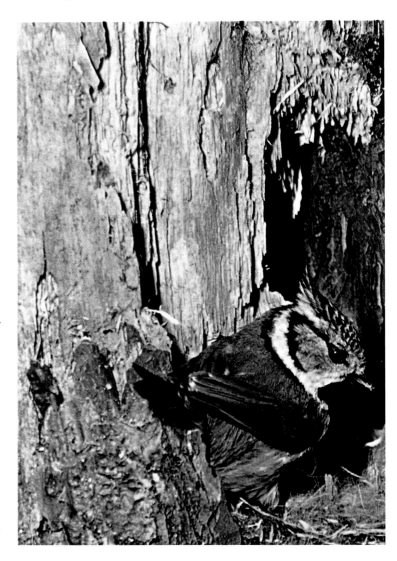

similar to the Old World species.

Crested tits, too, have a Holarctic distribution being represented in Europe by the Crested Tit *P. cristatus* and on the other side of the Atlantic by the Tufted Tit *P. bicolor* and other species. These are birds of pine forests that share a characteristic crest of feathers on the crown. In the Crested Tit this is boldly barred black-and-white, though in the New World species the crest is shades of plain grey or black.

Most tits are resident, although when populations build up irruptions sometimes occur. One such irruption brought huge numbers of European Great and Blue Tits to Britain in the mid-1960s.

The long-tailed tits are a group of small birds marked with tails as long as their bodies. The Long-tailed Tit *Aegithalos caudatus* is a black-and-white bird with a long, black-and-white tail. It is essentially gregarious and parties of birds play follow-my-leader from tree to tree. Their characteristic shape in flight is quite unmistakeable. They breed in a continuous belt across Eurasia from Britain to Japan and Kamchatka, extending southwards to the Persian Gulf in the Middle East. Long-tailed Tits build one of the finest of birds' nests. Placed in dense cover in a bush or in creeper,

the nest is an upright oval with a side entrance. It is constructed of moss bound with spiders' webs and hair and camouflaged with lichens. As the eight to twelve chicks grow the nest stretches to accommodate their increasing bulk. The female performs the major part of the incubation though the male is active in feeding the young. Long-tailed Tits form flocks outside the breeding season, but invariably keep themselves to themselves.

One of the most attractive members of the subfamily is the Asiatic Red-headed Tit *A. concinnus*. Grey above it boasts a rusty crown and rusty flanks that extend in a band across the breast. A black eye stripe extends to the side of the nape and there is a black spot in the centre of the breast. It is found in China extending southwards into Vietnam and westwards to the Himalayas and is exclusively a hill bird. It is usually found between 3,000 and 12,000 feet among forests and more open bush-clad areas.

Best known of the Remizinae is the Penduline Tit *Remiz pendulinus*. Like the other members of this subfamily it constructs a hanging nest with an entrance near the top. It is found across Eurasia, although in western Europe it is confined to the shores of the Mediterranean. There has been some evidence of a spread northwards in recent years and the Penduline Tit has the distinction of having been added to the list of Dutch birds before being seen in that country. Ornithologists discovered a disused nest after the birds had left in autumn.

The Tufted Tit of the United States is a characteristic bird of woodland and gardens. It is vocal and gregarious and destroys harmful insects.

The tail of the Long-tailed Tit can prove something of an embarrassment in the confines of its domed nest. It solves the problem by tucking it up over its back.

They often feed high up in trees, but nests are invariably placed over water. They can be found along the banks of rivers and streams as well as along the fringes of marshes. Some birds breed among reeds and many take to the reed beds outside the breeding season. Like weaver birds, Penduline Tits take a considerable time to build their nest. The male is usually the instigator although both sexes work on the main chamber. The six to eight white eggs are incubated by the female alone.

In the New World the subfamily is represented by the Verdin *Auriparus flaviceps*, a 4 inch-long, grey bird with a golden yellow head and a patch of chestnut at the bend of the wing. It is found only in the desert country of northern Mexico penetrating the United States in Arizona. It lives among the scattered thorn trees of the desert and is seemingly independent of water supplies. The nest is a cunningly designed, globular structure protected by outwards projecting thorns and lined with softer fibres. The nest chamber is reached via a tunnel in the side that affords protection against predators. Unlike most other Paridae it does not form flocks in winter. It will visit bird-tables and is quite common in the suburbs of desert towns.

Nuthatches Sittidae

Nuthatches, so called for the ability of some species to hack open hard-shelled nuts, are small, rather tastefully coloured birds that find a living typically among the trunks and major branches of trees. Some prefer rocks and rock faces, but feed in much the same manner. Predominantly insectivorous, the more northern species feed on seeds during the winter which they often hide away in the manner of jays.

They are strongly built, 'neck-less' birds with powerful legs and feet and sharp claws that enable them to cling to bark or rocks without the support of their tails. They climb equally well

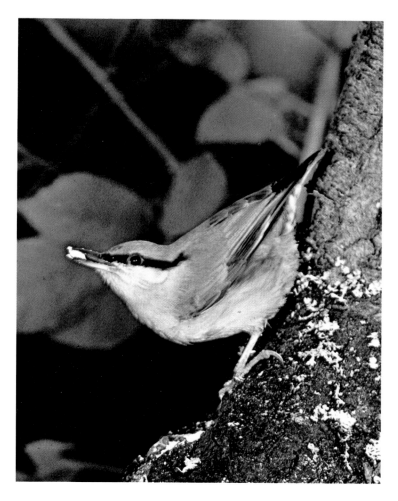

The Nuthatch climbs as well downwards as it does upwards. It is a successful species found from the Atlantic to the Pacific Oceans and from Norway to Vietnam.

against possible shortage during the winter months.

Nuthatches nest in holes, either natural or those of woodpeckers, but always make a point of plastering the inside of the entrance with mud. They also take to nest boxes where similar mud-plastering is performed whether or not it is necessary. Doubtless such plastering reduces the size of the entrance hole to prevent predation.

Nuthatches are usually resident, although individuals will attach themselves to a foraging party of tits in winter. They are frequent visitors to gardens and will feed quite readily at bird-tables.

Remarkably similar in plumage pattern is the Rock Nuthatch *S. neumayer*, a bird of south-eastern Europe and the Middle East. These birds are found throughout their range in limestone areas where bare rocks afford them a home. They are insectivorous and prefer cliff faces, from sea-level to over 6,000 feet, which are cracked and pitted by the weather. Their shrill, whistling calls are characteristic of many of the ruins of ancient civilizations throughout their range. Rock Nuthatches build a large, bottle-shaped nest of mud securely attached to an overhanging rock which provides shelter against rain and sun. It is entered via a tunnel just large enough for the bird to squeeze through. The mud, which is often an inch thick, takes a long time to collect and the finished structure may total nearly a thousand times the weight of the bird.

The forests of the Himalayas and other parts of Asia are a home to a variety of nuthatches including the Chestnut-bellied *S. castanea* and Velvet-fronted *S. frontalis* which are typical members of the bird flocks that wander through these areas of woodland. The Velvet-fronted is one of the most handsome of all the nuthatches. The back and wings are a bright cobalt blue while the bill is bright coral red – a vivid bird even among the colourful inhabitants of tropical forests.

The sitellas of Australia and New Guinea resemble the other nuthatches in structure, but are rather dull in comparison, being clothed in shades of grey and brown. Unlike the other species they are gregarious birds that pass through areas in loose flocks roaming this way and that, up and down trees. They build cup-shaped nests in the fork of a tree, camouflaged with flakes of bark.

The Wallcreeper is large for a nuthatch. Its light grey coloration merges well with the sheer rock faces where it lives. It is an expert climber and can even cling to the ceiling of an overhang or cave. When it flies the vivid maroon wings are eye-catching, but it is an elusive bird and high on the 'wanted' list of many birdwatchers. It is found exclusively in mountain regions from the Pyrenees eastwards to the mountains of eastern Asia. In the Alps it is found up to 9,000 feet and in the Himalayas up to 16,000 feet. In winter many birds descend to the lower slopes and some regularly frequent church spires in the centres of Alpine towns.

The male chooses a nest site and advertises with nuptial flights that show the bold colour of the wings to advantage. Indeed, constant wing flicking is performed throughout the year. The female builds the nest, which is placed in a rock crevice, and incubates the three to five eggs alone. Both sexes feed the young which take almost a month to fledge.

downwards as upwards. Most are various shades of blue above with pinks, oranges and reds below. Many species show a bold, black eye stripe. The bill is strong and tapered and makes both a fine probe and an excellent hatchet.

The vast majority of species belong to the genus *Sitta*, but the two treerunners or sitellas of Australasia are placed in the genus *Neositta*, and the Wonder Treerunner or Pink-faced Nuthatch *Daphoenositta miranda* of New Guinea in a genus of its own. The Wallcreeper *Tichodroma muraria* is also generically isolated.

Typical of the family is the Eurasian Nuthatch *Sitta europaea*, found from Spain to the shores of the Bering Sea, and southwards through the Orient. Dove grey above and buff below with the merest touch of chestnut along the flanks, it is a common bird of both deciduous and coniferous forests. Its shrill, whistling call or the hacking noise of its attacks on a nut often draw the attention of the passer-by to this charming little bird. Like a treecreeper it works its way over the trunks of trees probing here and there for insects and their larvae. It breaks nuts by carrying them to a favoured niche where they are wedged firmly to bring the bill into play. The seasonal abundance of nuts in autumn has led to hoarding by the Nuthatch which hides nuts wedged between bark as a hedge

Treecreepers Certhiidae

Treecreepers are small, tree-climbing birds striped with black and brown above, with light buff or white underparts. They have long, sharp claws that enable them to grip bark, and stiff, usually abraided, tail feathers with strong shafts that support them in the manner of a woodpecker. The bill is long, thin and decurved and used for probing rather than hacking or chiselling like the

woodpeckers and nuthatches. In many respects treecreepers resemble the various groups of woodcreepers (family Dendrocolaptidae) of South America.

Treecreepers feed in a characteristic manner starting at the base of a tree and climbing steadily skywards probing here and there in search of insects and their larvae. Near the top of a tree the bird

A crevice-nester, the Treecreeper uses its long, thin bill to probe for insects hidden among the crevices of bark as it climbs ever upwards. The specially thickened shafts of the tail feathers serve as a prop against the trunk.

will suddenly fly off to the base of the next to repeat the process. Though usually solitary, several birds may join the flocks of tits that roam the woods outside the breeding season.

Most successful of the five species is the Common Treecreeper *Certhia familiaris* which enjoys a Holarctic distribution. In America it is known as the Brown Creeper. It is a bird of both deciduous and coniferous woodland and its range extends southwards into more southern climes in most of the major mountain ranges of the Northern Hemisphere. It is thus found extending southwards into Central America among the high mountain extensions of the Rockies, and in the Old World occurring in isolated populations in the Pyrenees, the Pontic Alps and Caucasus, and in the Himalayas. In this last region it meets up with three of its congeners, the Himalayan Treecreeper *C. himalayana*, the Brown-throated Treecreeper *C. discolor*, and Stoliczka's Treecreeper *C. nipalensis*. Indeed of the five species only one, the Short-toed Treecreeper *C. brachydactyla*, does not occur in this part of Asia. Instead its range overlaps that of the Common Treecreeper over most of the European mainland. Where the two inhabit the same region the Common species generally breeds at higher altitudes.

The Common Treecreeper typically nests in a crevice behind a piece of loose bark, but will also take to nest boxes and frequently utilizes the narrow gaps between planks in coal sheds and outhouses. The chamber is lined with grasses with a neat cup of hair and moss. The five to seven white eggs are finely marked with reddish spots. Incubation is shared, though the female performs the larger part, and lasts for fourteen to fifteen days. Fledging takes a similar period and family parties usually remain together for some time thereafter. Second broods are very unusual.

The Short-toed Treecreeper is, in general, the more common of the two species over much of Europe and inhabits the lowland woods and forests occupied by the Common Treecreeper in Britain. Doubtless the Common Treecreeper arrived in that country first and occupied both niches, for on the continent it is a bird much more characteristic of coniferous forests. The best means of differentiating between the two is by the buff flanks of the Short-toed and by their different call notes. In the early 1970s the Short-toed Treecreeper was discovered in Britain and may well be set for a take-over of its proper niche. Habitat apart, the birds live remarkably similar lives.

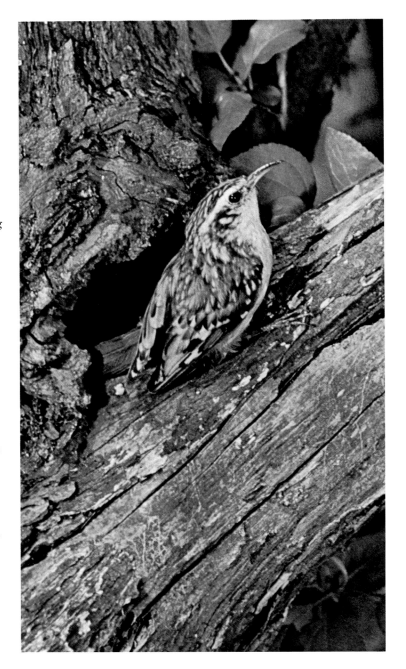

Australian treecreepers Climacteridae

The six species of Australasian treecreepers have variously been placed among the treecreepers, the nuthatches and even the warblers. That they are today invariably accorded full familial rank shows that their true origins have long since disappeared. No doubt they originated from some group of Old World passerines and have since adapted to fill an otherwise vacant niche in Australasia. Other diverse families have filled similar niches in every other forested part of the world.

Australasian treecreepers are dull brown, striped birds with vivid orange wing patches that show only in flight. They vary in size from 5 to 7 inches and are generally longer in the tail than either nuthatches or treecreepers. Like the former, they climb without recourse to tail support and do not have the stiffened retrices of the true treecreepers. The bills are fine and suited to picking rather than chiselling, but they are seldom as long as those of the Certhidae. They feed like these birds by systematically searching the bark of trunks and major branches of trees. Some

species feed on the ground and inhabit the drier and more open areas of Australia.

The nest is built in the hollow of a tree, either in the trunk or in the cavity formed by a broken branch, but sometimes also in a rotting fence post. The cup consists of strips of bark and dried grass lined with feathers or wool. The two or three eggs are white spotted with rust brown and both parents participate in the nesting routine. These birds often rear a second brood.

Outside the breeding season the Australasian treecreepers are sedentary and do not join mixed bird flocks like many other species. Five species are found in Australia, while the White-throated Treecreeper *Climacteris leucophaea* is confined to the forests of the mountain slopes of New Guinea.

Opposite Popularly called Tree-creeper in Australia, this species actually belongs to the family of nuthatches. It builds a well-camouflaged nest covered with scraps of bark.

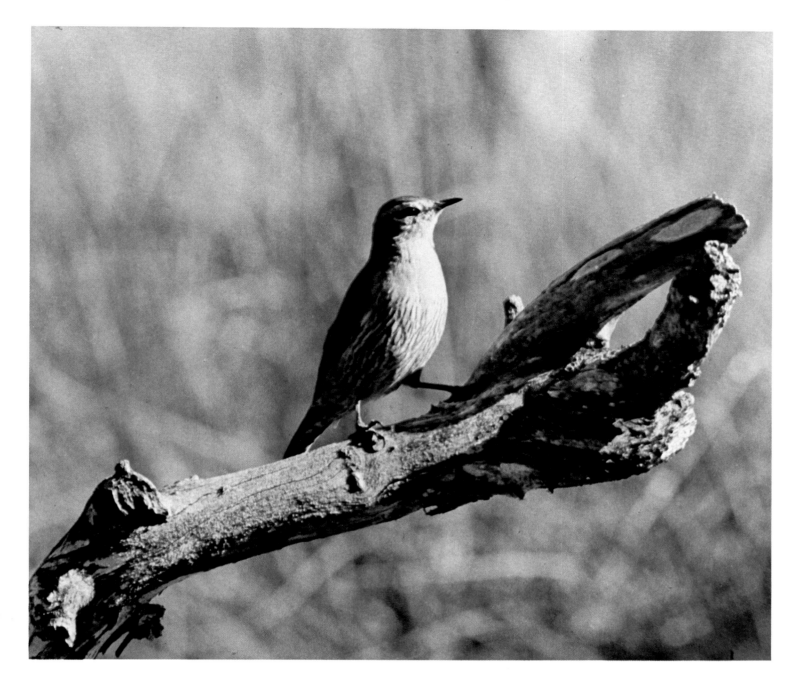

Flowerpeckers Dicaeidae

Flowerpeckers are small birds that can frequently be seen on flowers, feeding on nectar or on the insects attracted to it. They are, however, neither as insectivorous nor as dependent on flowers as the sunbirds which they closely resemble. The major items of diet are fruit and berries, and many species have a close and beneficial relationship with the various species of parasitic mistletoe. They play such a large part in spreading this unwanted plant that several flowerpeckers are regarded as pests in various parts of Asia, while in Australia *Dicaeum hirundinaceum* is called the Mistletoe-bird.

Unlike the sunbirds, flowerpeckers have short, thin or stubby-shaped bills, with the outer third of the mandibles finely serrated. They are generally boldly coloured with large patches of contrasting plumage. In these species the sexes are usually dimorphic, while in those of more sombre hue they are invariably similar. The tongue, which is shorter than that of the sunbirds, is similarly tubed towards the tip, doubtless to facilitate feeding on nectar. The seven Australian pardalotes (genus *Pardalotus*), often called diamond-

birds, are an aberrant group of boldly spotted birds with short, stubby bills lacking serrations. They feed almost exclusively on insects and their larvae which they glean from the outer branches of trees.

Flowerpeckers are widely distributed in Asia from India eastwards across China to the Philippines, and southwards to Australasia and the Pacific islands. They reach their greatest variety of species in the Papuan-New Guinea region and in the Philippines, and in both regions the majority, if not all, of the species are endemic.

In parts of Asia some flowerpeckers are familiar garden birds and only seldom found in forests. All species build a globular nest that is frequently pear-shaped and suspended from a thin branch. Most utilize the fibrous down of the silk-cotton tree lined with rootlets. The usual clutch is two or three white eggs, sometimes with a few spots, and incubation is by the female alone.

The pardalotes excavate a tunnel, often in level ground but also

Known as the Diamondbird in its native Australia, the Spotted Pardalote digs a burrow in which to lay its eggs and rear its young. It is a most attractive and colourful bird.

in banks, leading to their underground nesting chamber. This may be up to two feet in length and a domed structure of strips of bark and grasses is created in which the three to five eggs are laid. Excavation is shared by both members of the pair.

Habitat varies according to the species and its range. Many birds frequent rainforests, but some prefer more open and drier areas while others live among thickets of bamboo. The Mistletoe-bird, for example, is found throughout Australia, save for the arid interior, frequenting habitats as varied as forests and plantations. It is a tiny bird, little more than $3\frac{1}{2}$ inches in length, boldly marked with red, black and white. Despite such splendid plumage it spends so much of its time high in trees that it is not at all well known. It lives mainly in small groups and is of great benefit to mistletoe in spreading its seeds. When a bird eats a mistletoe berry the soft, outer part passes directly to the stomach, while the hard seed is channelled into a by-pass system and voided in a matter of minutes. Larger species of flowerpeckers achieve a similar result by seeding the berry in the bill and wiping it from the mandibles on a branch.

The nest, like that of other flowerpeckers, is suspended and invariably decorated with odds and ends like the dried castings left by wood-boring insects. Nest building and incubation is by the female alone.

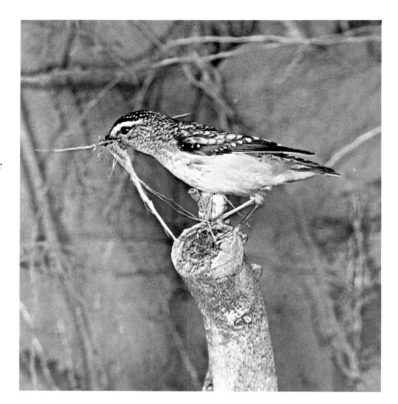

Sunbirds Nectariniidae

Sunbirds are the Old World equivalent of the New World hummingbirds, and are bright, metallic-coloured birds that feed on flowers and the insects they attract. While the hummingbirds are extremely diverse in shape and size and feed predominantly on the wing, the sunbirds exhibit less aerial mastery and are remarkably similar in structure. Typically a hummingbird will hover before a flower and insert its highly specialized bill into the corolla to drink the nectar. Sunbirds sometimes hover in this manner too, but more frequently perch on the flower or an adjacent stem and reach into the flower to drink. Faced with a flower with a long corolla, the sunbirds pierce the flower near the base and take the nectar from the side.

Sunbirds vary from a little under 4 inches to over 8 inches in length, and the males particularly are marked with bright metallic colours that are extremely difficult to reproduce in printed form. As they move, the angle of the light brings out different colours, giving rise in descriptions to such terms as 'bright metallic green-blue' and 'bronzy-green'. Such colour changes can lead to confusion in the field, although the birds form a distinctive family and one that should cause little difficulty to identify as such. Females are generally duller, although in some species they have patches of iridescence like their mates.

Sunbirds are active little birds, feeding in almost warbler-like manner flitting hither and thither in search of insects, pausing now and again to drain a flower. They are not truly gregarious and gather in numbers only where concentrations of blooms provide a more than adequate supply of food. Individuals will, however, sometimes join mixed species flocks and roam nomadically through the forest, their 'chinking' metallic call notes easily picking them out from the rest of the birds. They are, however, far from being purely forest birds and the various species can be found in a variety of habitats from dry scrub to dense, tropical jungle. Many species frequent agricultural land and several are common garden birds, particularly in Asia.

Sunbirds are well adapted to their lives among the flowers. They have rounded wings with ten primaries that propel them through the air with a flitting, warbler-like flight. The legs and feet are strong, unlike those of the hummingbirds, and the bill is invariably down-curved. While hummingbirds exhibit a huge range of bill forms, the sunbirds are remarkably uniform varying only in length, and then never to the extremes of the New World birds.

The family is particularly numerous in Africa and over half of the 105 species live in that continent south of the Sahara. They are also numerous throughout the Far East from India eastwards through Malaysia to Australia. The eastern end of the Mediterranean has its own sunbird, the Palestine or Orange-tufted Sunbird *Nectarinia osea*, a fine iridescent blue and green bird with black wings and a tuft of orange-yellow feathers below the bend of the wing. This species also occurs in south-western Arabia and in central Africa south of the Sahara.

One of the most widespread and familiar of African species is the Scarlet-chested Sunbird *N. senegalensis*. A velvet black in body colour, this bird is marked with a bold patch of scarlet extending from the throat to the breast and by iridescent green areas on the crown and chin. It is common and confiding around the safari lodges of Kenya. In some parts of its range it overlaps with the very similar Hunter's Sunbird *N. hunteri*, although the latter is a replacement species in the more arid areas of eastern Kenya and Somaliland.

Like the other sunbirds these birds build suspended, oval-shaped nests constructed of roots and other fibres bound together with spiders' webs, and with a neat entrance hole in the side. They are often placed among bushes, while most other sunbirds prefer high trees. The usual sunbird clutch of two streaked and spotted eggs is generally laid, but sometimes there may be only one egg. The breeding season coincides with that during which most flowers are in bloom and, therefore, with the onset of the rains. They are generally thought of as resident or at most nomadic, although recent ringing recoveries show that the Scarlet-chested Sunbird, along with some other species, has a distinct migration pattern over

The Scarlet-chested Sunbird is found throughout southern Africa wherever there are flowers to feed on. The striking metallic colours of its plumage change in the sunlight.

at least part of its range.

Equally well known in southern Africa is the Malachite Sunbird *N. famosa*, a vividly green bird with extended central tail feathers. It makes vertical movements coming lower in winter from the heights of nearly 10,000 feet up to which it breeds. This is one of the many longer-billed sunbirds and, like the others, is equipped with a tubular tongue through which to drink nectar. Its bill is serrated, an adaptation to grasping insects, and it even takes small lizards from time to time. The female is duller in colour and marked with the emerald green of the male only along the primaries and upper-tail coverts.

Among the many familiar Asiatic species the Yellow-backed Sunbird *Aethopyga siparaja* is one of the most beautiful. Its crimson head, back and breast are marked with two distinctly mauve moustachial stripes, a feature that shows particularly well when the bird sings from the top of a bush. It is widespread in the hilly districts of northern India, through Burma and Malaysia. Throughout this area it is generally outnumbered by the Purple Sunbird *Cinnyris asiatica*, a metallic purple-blue bird that is common around Indian gardens.

The spiderhunters of the *Arachnothera* are a distinctive group of ten species in which even the males are dull in coloration. Most are dull green or brown birds, more or less streaked with darker hues. Their bills are long and only the occasional bright patch of colour on the rump serves to distinguish them. They are found throughout South-East Asia and vary in size from 6 to $7\frac{1}{2}$ inches in length. In many ways these birds are unfortunately named, for they eat spiders no more than the other sunbirds, and regularly feed on nectar.

Perhaps their most outstanding characteristic is the building of intricate and beautiful nests. These are either cup-shaped and hung from a leaf by a stitching of cobwebs, or flask-shaped where the top of the nest is formed by the leaf to which the rim is neatly fastened.

Throughout their range sunbirds are vivacious and attractive birds in their own right. Comparisons with hummingbirds tend to do them less than justice.

White-eyes Zosteropidae

The most remarkable thing about the eighty odd species of white-eyes is that they all look the same, or at least nearly so. They are small birds with green backs, yellowish underparts and only a ring of white feathers around the eye to distinguish them. Most are between 4 and 5 inches in length and have their centre of distribution in Indonesia. From there they extend northwards to Japan, eastwards through the islands of the Pacific, southwards to New Zealand and westwards through Africa to the coast of Guinea.

The white-eyes are compact, warbler-like birds that show a considerable resemblance to the willow warblers of the genus *Phylloscopus* and, like those birds, live among the canopy of forests and other wooded areas. They have longish wings with nine primaries, the tenth being virtually absent, or at most vestigial. The bill is thin and pointed like the *Phylloscopus*, and adapted to picking insects and their larvae from among the leaves. The tongue is tipped with fine, bristle-like structures leading several authors to regard them as most closely related to the honeyeaters.

Like the willow warblers, white-eyes generally move about in flocks and are restless little birds. They flit this way and that, just like the warblers, and after the breeding season quite large flocks join together to make nomadic movements. Only the most northern populations are truly migratory, but these nomadic flocks are evidently responsible for the colonization of new breeding areas by various populations.

Throughout the Pacific and Indian Oceans there are scattered endemic species of island white-eyes. Indeed the colonization of New Zealand from Australia is said to date only from the 1850s. Their flocking behaviour makes it very likely that off-course

297

The olive green coloration and white ring about the eye are typical of the widespread *Zosterops* family. This bird is a Pale White-eye.

vagrants will be accompanied by some of their fellows, thus increasing the likelihood of quick colonization. As they adapt to their new environments, the white-eyes tend to change with a certain uniformity. They are inclined to become less yellow and more grey or brown, larger in size, and gradually lose their diagnostic eye ring. Whether or not such adaptations are part of becoming more general, less specialized birds as suggested by Lack, remains to be shown. What is certain is that island species that have evolved from different ancestral species, do tend to look alike. This is a case of 'mini' convergent evolution. Sometimes these highly similar island species are separated by thousands of miles of oceans, while in some places two species breed on the same island. In such cases ornithologists have been able to ascertain that they have different ecological niches, and can even determine which was the first colonist.

It seems quite extraordinary that while three distinct species inhabit the tiny Norfolk Island off the coast of Australia, the whole continent of Africa can boast only four species. The latter figure follows extensive museum research by the late Reg Moreau, doyen of African ornithologists, who found such variations in plumage that only this handful of species could satisfactorily be distinguished.

Despite the wealth of species in the Far East, most study has been concentrated on the Grey-breasted White-eye *Zosterops lateralis* in New Zealand. Here the birds form winter flocks that are remarkably stable and also resident. They divide up in spring and males re-establish themselves in their territory of the previous year, possibly even pairing with their last year's mate. The song is a canary-like trill. Other white-eyes sing well and loudly and are commonly kept as cagebirds.

Unlike the willow warblers, most white-eyes nest in trees, slinging a cup between the arms of a fork. The two or three eggs are white or pale blue and are incubated by both sexes.

Though most white-eyes are placed in the single genus *Zosterops*, many of the island species have been placed in monotypic genera, or in genera consisting of closely related birds from island groups. The Olive Black-eye *Chlorocharis emiliae*, however, is found in two areas of Sumatra and is unique in having a black, not white, ring about the eye. It is otherwise green and yellow in colour. The Cinnamon White-eye *Hypocryptadius cinnamomeus* has a cinnamon-coloured eye ring that exactly matches its plumage, giving the impression that it has no eye ring at all. It is found only on the southern islands of the Philippines. Both of these untypical species inhabit the forests of the mountainous interiors of these islands.

Honeyeaters Meliphagidae

The honeyeaters originated in the Australasian region and have spread through New Guinea to the adjacent islands of South-East Asia as far as the Wallace Line. One species, the Brown Honeyeater *Lichmera indistincta*, occurs on Bali and several species have reached Hawaii. There are honeyeaters in New Zealand and on many islands of the Pacific. A single genus *Promerops*, the sugarbirds, occurs in southern Africa, but there is considerable doubt about including these birds in the Meliphagidae. Their geographical isolation from the rest of the family plus certain differences in habits indicates the need for a reappraisal of their taxonomic position.

Honeyeaters, as their name implies, feed on flowers in the manner of sunbirds and while some species bear a close resemblance to those birds, the majority of honeyeaters are larger and more robust in build. Indeed the family is so diverse that some species more closely resemble warblers, flycatchers, thrushes and even jays. This radiation of a family to occupy otherwise vacant niches is remarkably similar to that of the marsupials which, although obviously sharing a common ancestry, have evolved into mouse-like creatures as well as the large kangaroos.

All honeyeaters live an arboreal existence. They are generally gregarious and aggressive, particularly to other species. Most are rather dull in colour, many have areas of bare skin about the head, and some are quite bald. Often these areas of skin are marked with colourful wattles particularly around the eye. The bill is thin and down-curved and several species have elongated sickle-like bills. The tongue is 'bristled' at the tip and, along its basal half, can be curled to form two tubes for sucking in nectar.

Originally birds of forest and woodland, honeyeaters have adapted well to changes in habitat and several species are now common birds in gardens and orchards. Nectar is an important food item, but most species take a great many insects and many eat quantities of fruit. Indeed, in some parts of Australia they do considerable damage to the crops of fruit farmers. No honeyeater can do without trees, but their habitats vary from dense tropical forests to the dry and arid mallee scrub of the interior. Some are coastal and frequent marshes and mangrove swamps, while others prefer bare, open areas of sand.

With such a vast range and such variation in habitat preference, it is not surprising that several species are restricted to particular islands. Here they tend to be less specialized and to have suffered considerably from man's activities. On the islands of Hawaii, for example, the distinct genus *Moho* has been virtually eliminated as a direct result of man's persecution. The native peoples were particularly proud of capes made from the feathers of these birds, and in addition large-scale destruction of the natural habitat has followed in the wake of the white man. Frequently referred to as O-os, these birds have gradually disappeared from island after island in the Hawaiian chain. The Oahu O-o *Moho apicalis* was extinct soon after 1837; the Molokai O-o *M. bishopi* by 1904; and

A Yellow-tufted Honeyeater feeds its well-grown chicks. The species is common in parts of its Australian range and is sometimes responsible for considerable damage to fruit crops.

the Hawaiian O-o *M. nobilis* thirty years later. The fourth and final species, the Kauai O-o *M. braccatus*, disappeared about the same time, but was relocated in the Alakai Swamp in 1960. No more than twelve birds survive. Several other endemic island species are in danger of extinction and the wealth of honeyeaters in New Guinèa must be considered at risk as the island struggles into the twentieth century.

Honeyeaters are tree-nesters that usually construct their delicate cup-shaped nests at some height. Several species show colonial inclinations and a great many prefer to nest alongside streams and lakes. The *Meliphaga*, a large genus of Australian and New Guinea species, has the unusual habit of plucking its nest lining from the backs of cows, while the White-eared Honeyeater *M. leucotis* has even been known to attack man to the same end. Honeyeaters lay from one to four eggs, depending on habitat, and most of the incubation is performed by the female.

One of the most widespread and certainly among the better-known members of the family is the Blue-faced Honeyeater *Entomyzon cyanotis*. It is found in northern and eastern Australia and, being an adaptable bird, has benefited considerably from man's

efforts to change the face of that land. At 12 inches in length it is one of the largest members of the family, brown above and white below with a black head marked with a large and conspicuous area of bright blue skin on the sides of the face. Like other honeyeaters it displays considerable agility as it works its way through the trees in search of insects, berries and, of course, nectar. Blue-faced Honeyeaters are aggressive towards intruders and will flock in noisy profusion around birdwatchers and owls. They will build their own nests in the forks of trees, but they prefer to take over those of other species, particularly babblers (family Muscicapidae), which they will sometimes drive away. An individual invariably adds its own nest cup to these structures and lays two or three well-marked eggs. It is multi-brooded.

Some of the Blue-faced Honeyeater's favourite victims are another group of honeyeaters, the friarbirds, five species of which are found in Australia. The name derives from the bald tonsure-

Opposite The Leatherhead Friarbird, like the rest of its congeners, is rather dully coloured with an area of bare skin on the head.

like head of the Noisy Friarbird *Philemon corniculatus*. All are dull brown in colour with varying degrees of black baldness. They feed predominantly on nectar and the head often becomes covered in hard pollen. Despite their size, from 9 to 13 inches in length, they are frequently observed catching insects in flight.

New Zealand boasts its own honeyeaters among which pride of place must go to the Tui or Parsonbird *Prosthemadera novaeseelandiae*. Its resemblance to a curate is quite remarkable. The plumage is all black broken only by a small bib of white feathers that protrude in two tufts from the centre of the neck, and by a ring of fine filigree plumes that hang to form a collar. The Tui

is a bird of the original New Zealand forests and is still widespread and comparatively common where these remain. It is a noisy bird producing high pitched calls, some of which are outside the range of the human ear.

The two species of sugarbirds share many of the characteristics of the rest of the family including tongue structure and nectar feeding habits. This may, however, be a result of convergent evolution. The Cape Sugarbird *Promerops cafer* is found only in the Cape region of South Africa, and is a brown bird marked with orange on the breast. Its tail feathers are over three times its own body length. Feeding like the other honeyeaters, it is particularly fond of the blooms of protea bushes and its breeding season coincides with the high season of these shrubs. It invariably builds its cup-shaped nest in a protea bush as well.

Buntings Emberizidae subfamily Emberizinae

Though generally referred to as buntings, the Emberizinae are essentially New World in origin and the majority of species that occur in that area are called sparrows. This misleading vernacular usage should not hide the clear relationships between this distinct group of seed-eating, long-tailed, ground-dwelling birds. The taxonomy of the subfamily is reasonably clear, but the

Below The Slate-coloured Junco breeds in the northern woodlands of North America migrating southwards to winter among the farmsteads and suburbs of the United States.

relationship with the finches, Galápagos finches, the sparrows and weavers, and other similar groups, is so complex that several authors have suggested that they should all be placed in a single family, the Fringillidae. In this work we take the Emberizidae to include the cardinals and grosbeaks, the tanagers and Swallow-tanager, and the honeycreepers – a group of well over 500 species.

Buntings and New World sparrows are generally rather dull in coloration with plumages of blacks and browns, and yellows and chestnut. They are mostly about 6 inches in length, with longish tails, and have strong perching feet and legs. The bill is short and

The White-crowned Sparrow breeds in open northern areas of North America where it behaves in typical bunting-like fashion. The conspicuous white crown and eye stripe show well here.

stubby and well able to deal with the seeds that form the bulk of the adult diet. The wings are variable in shape, from long and pointed to short and round, but most species fly well and strongly. Many of the more northern species are migratory.

The Snow Bunting *Plectrophenax nivalis* has the distinction of being the most northerly breeding land bird, but the subfamily is immensely successful and can be found almost throughout the world. Habitat varies too, and buntings are found in almost every habitat type except for dense forests. Open bush country and grassland are especially favoured and the prairies of central North America are the home of a number of species. Others frequent reed beds and the House Bunting *Emberiza striolata* is seldom found far from human habitation. In the heart of Casablanca it actually feeds inside blocks of flats and hotels showing a lack of fear that even the House Sparrow cannot claim. That this bunting is advancing northwards in Morocco could auger well for a new European breeding bird before too long.

Typical of the Old World buntings is the Yellowhammer *E. citrinella*, a markedly yellow bird with a chestnut mantle and rufous rump. It frequents heaths and dry agricultural land throughout Europe, and the more northerly populations are migratory. The male has a jingling, little song much like many other buntings, delivered from the top of a bush. The nest may be on the ground or neatly placed in a low tree, and the three or four eggs are incubated predominantly by the more sombrely coloured hen. Several broods are raised in a season and, in the autumn, quite large roosts are occupied. Even in winter, however, Yellowhammers

are not truly gregarious and although flocks of several hundred may gather in extreme, hard weather, they soon break up when more normal conditions arrive.

Another 'yellow' species is the Black-headed Bunting *E. melanocephala*. This brightly coloured bird is marked with a black cap and is exceedingly numerous in the Balkans to which it is a summer visitor only. In winter the species moves eastwards towards India returning to Europe only in May.

The Reed Bunting *E. schoeniclus* is another black-headed bunting, but is more or less confined to marshy ground. Breeding right across Eurasia from the Atlantic to the Pacific, it has evolved a number of distinctive subspecies marked by varying shapes of bill. In general the bill is thicker and more robust in the southern populations, and some authors regard the Thick-billed Reed Bunting *E.s. pyrrhuloides* as a distinct species. The range of variation, however, seems to indicate that all forms are not yet sufficiently distinct to merit specific status. Most of these larger-billed forms are almost entirely confined to reed beds, while northern birds are more catholic in habitat choice. In Britain Reed Buntings are occurring with increasing regularity in plantations and even in suburban gardens.

Typical of the North American buntings is the White-crowned Sparrow *Zonotrichia leucophrys*. Breeding across the Canadian white coronal stripes are distinctive, but also shared with the White-throated Sparrow *Z. albicollis*. These are birds of open country occurring on tundra and among high mountains, but they are also found in gardens and even along the edges of forests.

Many of these American 'sparrows' are remarkably similar and best separated on the basis of head pattern. In particular it is of crucial importance to note the extent and exact placement of the small, yellow patches that are present in so many species.

One of the least distinguished of these birds is the Ipswich Sparrow *Passerculus princeps* which breeds only on low-lying Sable Island off the coast of Nova Scotia. Unlike so many island endemics, the Ipswich Sparrow regularly migrates to winter along the adjacent coast of the mainland while maintaining its specific integrity on isolated breeding grounds. It bears a marked similarity to the widespread Savannah Sparrow *P. sandwichensis* and there are cases of these birds reaching Sable Island and interbreeding with the Ipswich Sparrows.

A more clearly marked bird is the Slate-coloured Junco *Junco hyemalis* which breeds throughout the boreal zone of North America and winters through the United States. It arrives with the first snows and frequently gathers in flocks around buildings where there are plenty of seeds. It sometimes combines with other sparrows to form mixed flocks, although by and large the Junco remains faithful to a small wintering area.

The sierra finches of the genus *Phrygilus* are found only among the Andes of South America, and are well named after their distinguishing characters. They are birds of the high mountains, found at lower altitudes only when driven there by hard weather. Typically 'bunting' in shape, their plumage patterns are quite distinct from the better-known Northern Hemisphere species. They lack eye or coronal stripes, and many are boldly marked with rufous or gold.

Arctic extending southwards through the Rockies to southern California, the species is highly migratory wintering in the southern States and as far south as Central America. The bold black and

Cardinal-grosbeaks Emberizidae subfamily Pyrrhuloxiinae

The cardinal-grosbeaks, together with their allies the saltators and Dickcissel *Spiza americana*, are a group of New World buntings widely distributed from Canada to Argentina. They are woodland birds with robust, thick-set bodies, longish tails and strong, seed-cracking bills. This last characteristic is particularly well developed in the grosbeaks, which have bills as bulky and powerful as the Eurasian hawfinches. The males are invariably colourful birds of bold reds and blues, while females are generally more dull and less easily distinguished. They are solitary birds and do not usually form flocks, indeed many cardinal-grosbeaks remain in pairs on the same territory throughout the year. Much of their food is gleaned from the forest floor, but their nest sites vary from the ground to tall trees.

Males sing well. They take little part in incubation, but some do help with nest construction, feed their mate on the nest, and bring food to the young. While members of five genera are found in North America, the family centre of distribution lies in tropical America.

Most familiar is the Cardinal *Pyrrhuloxia cardinalis* occurring in the southern United States southward through Mexico to Central America. Within historical times the species has extended its range northwards and is now well established in New York, New England and southern Ontario, while remaining essentially non-migratory. No doubt this spread is, in part at least, due to encouragement by man, for the Cardinal is an attractive and well-loved bird, and a frequent visitor to bird-tables. It is also an adaptable bird with a

catholic choice of habitats. It needs dense thickets, but does not mind whether these are in swamps or city centres. The diet is predominantly vegetarian with seeds of various plants high on the list. Sunflower seeds and maize kernels are neatly shucked with the robust bill.

The male Cardinal has a pleasant song and is highly territorial. In display much use is made of the crimson plumage, especially the contrast with the black areas around the face. The crest is raised and he regularly feeds his mate in courtship. Once paired the sexes often perform duets in which the theme is taken up alternately. The neat cup of roots and twigs is placed in a low bush and the two to five greyish, speckled eggs are incubated by the female. The male tends the chicks once they are fledged for two or three weeks before his strong territorial instinct is reasserted and he drives them away.

The closely related Pyrrhuloxia *P. sinuata* is a similar, but greyer bird marked with crimson only about the face and wings. Its thick bill is distinctly notched, a useful field mark by which to separate immature birds of both species. As with the Cardinal, seeds are the dominant food item, but the Pyrrhuloxia inhabits the desert regions of Mexico and thus enjoys a different diet. It is most common in the Sonoran Zone between 2,000 and 3,000 feet, being absent from true desert as well as the more lush areas around towns. Its song is remarkably similar to that of the Cardinal although the female never sings. The nest is placed in a thorn and the two or three eggs are incubated by the female alone.

The male Cardinal with its all-crimson plumage and short crest is an unmistakable bird through the eastern and southern United States and Mexico.

Outstanding among the grosbeaks is the Blue Grosbeak *Guiraca caerulea*. This finely patterned bird, radiant blue in colour broken only by a few patches of chestnut on the wings, is found right across the United States migrating to Mexico, Central America and Cuba in winter. It is found in rough, overgrown country, along hedgerows and regularly comes to gardens. The bill is adapted to crack hard seeds and the stones of fruit, but large quantities of insect and soft seed food are also taken. This diversity of food is a fine balance of gain and loss to the farmer, for while the birds take cereals in quantity, they also destroy many insect pests.

The only other 'blue' bird is the Indigo Bunting *Passerina cyanea* which lacks the chestnut on the wings, is smaller, and boasts a less massive bill. It is found throughout the eastern United States migrating southwards to Mexico and Central America in winter. The nest is placed among thickets of blackberry or bamboo and also in cotton plantations. The clutch of three or four eggs is frequently added to by parasitic cowbirds, and as many as four of these birds' eggs have been found in a single nest.

Largest and most distinguished of all the Pyrrhuloxiinae are the typical grosbeaks including the Rose-breasted Grosbeak *Pheucticus ludovicianus*. The female resembles nothing more than an over-large, thick-billed sparrow with boldly striped head, but the male is a distinguished black bird marked with a red breast and white underparts. It inhabits the northern deciduous forests and adjacent areas of conifers from Nova Scotia westwards through the Great Lakes region to the Canadian prairies. In the west it is replaced by the Black-headed Grosbeak *P. melanocephalus*, and in the area of overlap hybridization is not uncommon.

The Rose-breasted Grosbeak is not an obvious bird and is best seen in spring when the male sings from a prominent perch and performs a fluttering display flight. Food consists of insects and seeds, and attacks by these birds cause considerable damage to the crops of fruit farmers. The thick bills can cope with the shells of hard seeds and deal neatly, if disastrously, with spring-time buds.

Unlike the other members of the subfamily, the male takes an active part in incubation, sometimes even singing on the nest. Rose-breasted Grosbeaks are migratory, leaving their breeding areas completely to winter in the southern United States southwards through Central America to Colombia.

Tanagers Emberizidae subfamily Thraupinae

The tanagers are a typically colourful group of tropical birds found throughout the warmer parts of the New World. Indeed, hummingbirds apart, they are the most numerous and obvious of Neotropical birds and exactly what the average visitor expects tropical birds to be. Part of the great family of Emberizidae, they resemble the buntings and cardinals in structure, with short, strong, vegetarian bills and characteristic finch-like bodies. The feet and legs are well developed for they are an essentially arboreal group. Most species are brightly coloured in a profusion of hues. Bright greens and yellows, reds and blacks, blues and golds all can be found boldly splashed in large patches of colour. In general the sexes are similar, but in the four species that have penetrated the United States and which migrate southwards to their ancestral home, only the males are bright and even then only during the summer months. These are the most pronounced sexually dimorphic birds among the tanagers and the only ones to show a seasonal plumage change.

Tanagers range in size from 4 inches to the 8 inches of the Thrush Tanager *Rhodinocichla rosea*, an aberrant ground-dwelling

bird with the habits of a thrush. It is found in forests throughout Central America and, despite its bright pink breast, is difficult to observe. It is a fine songster and the sexes frequently sing antiphonally.

The typical tanagers, however, are poor songsters and not as strongly territorial as many birds. They frequent forest canopy, but are more at home in open areas and particularly where agricultural land is mixed with woodland. They are fruit-eating birds, but also take large quantities of insects. The Summer Tanager *Piranga rubra* frequently feeds by taking insects in the air in the manner of a flycatcher. This fine, crimson bird breeds across the southern United States into Mexico, and migrates southwards to Central America and onwards as far as Ecuador. The female, like the male in winter, is a dull orange-brown bird. They frequent mature, open, deciduous woodland and the cup-shaped nest is placed on a horizontal branch. The four or five eggs are incubated by the female alone, for even when the sexes are similar, male tanagers take no part in the process of incubation. The male will, however, bring food to his sitting mate and takes an active part in feeding the chicks. These northern migratory species lay larger clutches than their tropical congeners, but the latter often manage two or three broods to compensate.

The Summer Tanager is particularly fond of bees and wasps and will regularly hunt at the entrance to hives and nests. It will take the larvae if it can gain access, but even away from nests it shows a marked preference for these insects.

Its close relative, the Scarlet Tanager *P. olivacea*, is marked with black wings on a scarlet body and is of more northern distribution. It is a bird of the forest canopy and its nests provide a frequent home for the eggs of the cowbirds.

Euphonias are the only group of tropical tanagers that show a similar sexual dimorphism to the migratory North American species. The males are boldly patterned in blues and yellows, but the females are dull green. They are robust little birds with stubby bills and short tails and are particularly fond of mistletoe berries. More

Left The little-known Plush-capped Finch breeds among the high sierras of the Andes above 7,000 feet.

Below The well-named Seven-coloured Tanager is an inhabitant of South America that feeds predominantly on berries and fruit.

than any other group of birds they are responsible for the spread and distribution of these parasites. Many species are remarkably similar in plumage patterns and can be difficult to identify as they feed in small flocks among trees.

The generic name of the euphonias *Tanagra* must not be confused with the genus *Tangara* which consists of forty-six species of typical tanagers. The latter are boldly coloured and the sexes are similar. They frequent the canopy of tropical forests where they forage in small, mixed flocks. They are generally quiet, none has a well-developed song, and can be exceedingly difficult to identify high up against the light. They are active and fast moving. In coloration they are among the most vivid of tropical birds. The Seven-coloured Tanager *T. fastuosa* is a remarkable motley of colours like a patchwork quilt. Blue, green, black, purple, orange and red can all be found on this remarkable little bird.

Much in demand as cagebirds, tanagers have always been attractive to man. In the heyday of the skin trade hundreds of thousands of birds were shipped dead and alive to Europe and North America to decorate ladies' hats. Among them, inevitably, ornithologists were able to identify species new to science, and in some cases a single skin saved from a hatter is all that we have of a species. Even the area of origin is uncertain in some cases.

The *Tangara* build cup-shaped nests and the two or three eggs are incubated by the female alone. Being forest birds their nesting habits are little known and those of several species have never been described. In contrast the nests of the *Tanagra* are domed and entered via a hole in the side. Both groups are multi-brooded.

An aberrant member of the subfamily is the Plush-capped Finch *Catamblyrhynchos diadema*, often placed by some authors with considerable justification among the cardinals. It is confined to the high altitude forests in the northern parts of the Andes and is chestnut below and brown above with a characteristic 'plush' cap of yellow feathers on the crown. Its short, stubby bill is conical and more like a cardinal than a tanager.

Swallow-tanager Emberizidae subfamily Tersininae

The Swallow-tanager *Tersina viridis* is the sole member of this monotypic subfamily, and despite similarities to the true tanagers it differs in several notable respects. It is the only tanager to nest in a hole, the only species with flycatcher-like long wings and weak legs, and has a completely different palate structure from the other tanagers. The male is a boldly patterned cobalt blue bird with a black facial mask, black primaries edged with blue, and black barring on the flanks. The female is green above and lighter below with bold, green barring on the flanks. The species is found throughout the forested areas of South America, being absent only from the high Andes and the more open country from Uruguay southwards. Its movements are little known, but birds that nest in Trinidad and Venezuela are completely absent outside the breeding season. Throughout its range it is an uncommon bird, despite the male's colouring and propensity to display itself from a perch.

Placed in a family on its own, the Swallow-tanager is found throughout the forested regions of South America, but is generally uncommon.

Swallow-tanagers form flocks exclusively of their own species that wander through the forests in search of fruit and insects, some of which are taken on the wing. The male establishes a territory around the nest site which is defended by a 'churrupy' song. It is he who chooses a site, but this is carefully inspected by his mate who sometimes rejects it and finds her own.

Swallow-tanagers excavate their own tunnel in a bank, and it is the onset of the rainy season that sets both sexes gathering nesting materials. The chamber, which is some two feet underground, is a small cup constructed of roots and grasses. The three orange eggs are incubated by the female alone and it is she who raises the chicks to fledging. The male may feed freshly fledged youngsters. There is some evidence to show that male Swallow-tanagers take two years to reach sexual maturity – unusual for a passerine.

Honeycreepers Emberizidae subfamily Coerebinae

Honeycreepers are colourful relatives of the tanagers that have often been accorded full familial rank by ornithologists. They can be divided neatly into two convenient groups on a basis of plumage and feeding methods. While the typical honeycreepers are brightly coloured and feed by inserting their long bills into the corollas of flowers to drink the nectar, the flowerpiercers are more sombrely clad and feed by piercing holes in the sides of flowers.

Both groups are well adapted to their mode of life having bristle-like protrusions on the outer edges of the tongue with curling and, in some cases, tubing of the inner (basal) half. The typical honeycreepers are boldly patterned in blues and blacks and the bill is generally decurved, though not always very long. The females are duller and more like both sexes of the flowerpiercers. They range throughout Central America, through South America and the West Indies. They feed in the forest canopy, although several species are found in more open areas and around agricultural land. The Bananaquit *Coereba flaveola* is, perhaps, the most successful member of the subfamily, being one of the most numerous and widespread birds in the West Indies. It is black above broken by a contrasting yellow rump and has yellow underparts. The head is black with a bold white supercilium and

Widespread through Central and South America, the Bananaquit is often found in gardens. It feeds on insects and nectar.

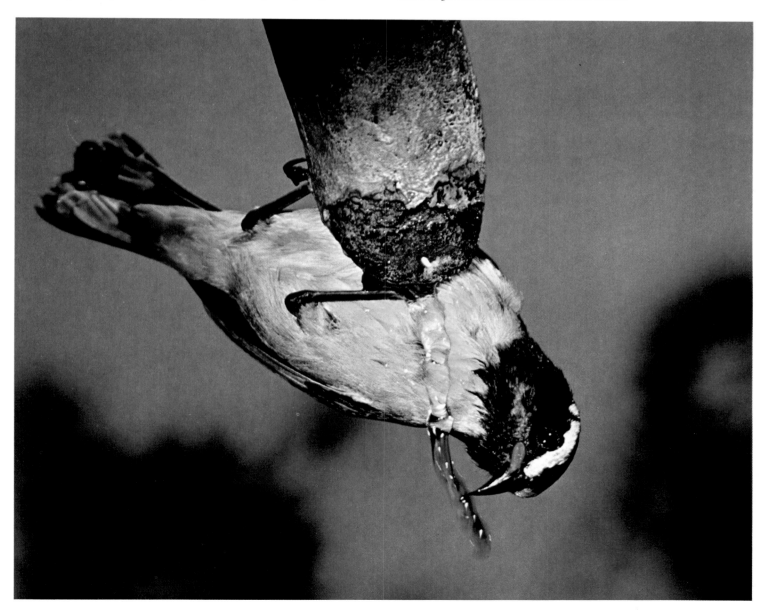

307

the gape retains a wide, crimson edge like that of a recently fledged bird. Outside the West Indies it is found in Central America and throughout the vast forested regions of South America. In the West Indies, however, it is a common garden bird and frequently enters occupied houses to raid the table in its search for food.

The nest is a suspended, globular structure hung from an outer branch of a tree and is usually easy to find. The two or three eggs are incubated by the female alone, but both parents feed the nestlings, apparently on nectar. The profusion of empty Bananaquit nests is explained by the species' habit of roosting each separately in a nest. While nectar is the main food the birds also take large quantities of insects and their larvae.

The flowerpiercers, of which ten species are recognized, have a beautifully adapted bill. The upper mandible is up-tilted and sharply hooked, while the lower is shorter and sharply pointed. The birds feed by hooking the upper mandible over the base of a flower and then piercing it with the lower, thus allowing the tongue access to the nectar.

Flowerpiercers vary in length from 4 to 7 inches, and are birds of

mountain forests with a centre of distribution among the eastern foothills of the northern Andes. They breed during the season of most abundant flowering, in Central America from November to January, but further south at virtually any time of the year. The nest is a cup constructed by the female alone and two eggs form the usual clutch. Both parents tend the growing youngsters and feed them on regurgitated insects, doubtless laced with nectar.

The honeycreepers build cup-shaped nests similar to the flowerpiercers and lay two eggs. The young, however, are not fed on regurgitated food, but on insects brought in the bill by both parents. Unique among honeycreepers in having a dull winter plumage, the Red-legged Honeycreeper *Cyanerpes cyaneus* is nevertheless one of the best known. The male in summer is a radiant little blue and black bird, found from southern Mexico to Brazil. It feeds on nectar and insects as well as on bananas and oranges, and is particularly fond of feeding in association with the Golden-naped Woodpecker. When the latter has broken the hard outer casing of fruit the Red-legged Honeycreeper moves in to help dispose of the inside. Its nesting habits are similar to the other honeycreepers.

Wood warblers Parulidae

The wood warblers, or New World warblers as they are sometimes called, are unfortunately named. They neither warble nor are they related to the typical Old World warblers of the Muscicapidae. While some species resemble warblers in habits, scouring the trees in search of insects and their larvae, others show a marked resemblance to treecreepers, mockingbirds or flycatchers. Many species are named 'warbler', but some are called 'redstart' and still others 'chat'.

There are approximately 113 species, divided among twenty-six genera. They are found throughout the Americas from Alaska to southern South America. The northern species, including representatives of over half the genera, are highly migratory and the

spring passage of these birds across the continent is one of the highlights of the North American birder's year. Empty woods are suddenly alive with birds of a dozen or more species, and while the watcher in a London park may pick up five or six species of migrant on a spring morning, his equivalent in Central Park, New York, will be unhappy with anything less than twenty species. He will, however, face considerably more danger and most New York park watchers now hide their binoculars inside their jackets.

A male Yellow Warbler, boldly streaked with light chestnut on the breast, pauses at his nest. The female's plumage is duller and lacks the streaking. The species breeds from Alaska to Peru.

The various waves of north-bound migrant wood warblers are then a great joy to birders. All are resplendent in their full and distinctive breeding dress and easy to identify. But, as with so many New World migrants, in fall they moult into dull greens and look remarkably similar. This is when the field expert really comes into his own searching out fine points like wing bars, rump patches and leg colour to identify his birds. 'See the warblers in the spring' is the continuing advice of American birders. In contrast most of the tropical species boast the same plumage throughout the year.

Wood warblers are small birds, the largest, the Yellow-breasted Chat *Icteria virens*, measuring 7½ inches in length. They are active birds feeding among trees and bushes, although the range of habitats occupied covers almost every type available in the

continent. A majority are woodland birds, but they also occur in marshes, agricultural land and gardens, and among desert scrub. While many birds are yellow, others are black and white, red and black, orange and so on. They feed predominantly on insects gleaned from vegetation, but a great many berries are taken in autumn and winter. Some species feed on the ground and the first Myrtle Warbler *Dendroica coronata* to be recorded in Britain was found feeding on a bird-table.

Nest sites are equally variable and while most of the resident species nest on the ground, the migratory birds will construct their nests in bushes, in trees, against banks and even, like the Prothonotary Warbler *Protonotaria citrea*, in holes. Eggs are white and variously spotted, and clutches vary from two to five eggs. Northern species produce larger clutches than tropical birds.

Despite their distinctive calls, the wood warblers are no great songsters. Most songs are repetitive and thin, but they are nevertheless an invaluable guide in the field.

The Yellowthroat breeds throughout the United States and southern Canada among marshy vegetation, where it is generally tame and confiding. The male retains his striking plumage throughout the winter.

One of the more remarkable characteristics of the family is the propensity to produce hybrids. Brewster's and Lawrence's Warblers are distinctive forms of hybrid between the Blue-winged Warbler *Vermivora pinus* and the Golden-winged Warbler *V. chrysoptera* produced where their ranges overlap in the eastern United States. These hybrids are capable of breeding and thus give rise to a variety of second generation birds. Hybrids are produced by other wood warblers, sometimes even by birds of different genera.

Undoubtedly the rarest member of the family is Kirtland's Warbler *Dendroica kirtlandii* which numbers no more than 1,000 birds at the start of the breeding season. First discovered in the middle of the last century the breeding grounds in lower peninsula Michigan were not located until 1903. Thorough investigation revealed a breeding range of about eighty by a hundred miles and a habitat preference for regenerated thickets of jack pine. This exclusive habitat – the birds move in from six to thirteen years after destruction by fire when the pines are between six and eighteen feet high – is exceedingly limited, but recent conservation efforts have organized burning on a rotation basis to ensure the continued existence of the right habitat for this unique little bird. It is protected in reserves in Michigan, but still has to make the long journey each spring and fall to and from its winter quarters in the Bahamas.

In contrast the Yellow Warbler *D. petechia* is widespread from northern Alaska southwards to Colombia and Peru, and winters in Central and South America. Thus over part of its range, at least, it is a resident. Its bold yellow plumage, marked with orange streaks on the breast, makes it one of the most distinctive of the wood warbler family but in the fall the more dull-coloured birds can be confused with other species.

With such a vast range it is not surprising that there should be considerable variation in plumage, and at one time three distinct species were recognized. Yellow Warblers inhabit damp thickets and swamps, often associated with mangroves in the southern part of their range. In the United States they frequently appear in gardens and are as much a warmly welcomed sign of the approach of spring as the arrival of the first Swallow.

The Black and White Warbler *Mniotilta varia* is a boldly black and white, streaked bird of deciduous woodland, found throughout the eastern and central parts of the United States and southern Canada. Like a nuthatch it gleans a living by picking insects and their larvae from the bark of tree trunks, which it climbs with consummate ease both upwards and downwards. Like those birds it has strong legs and feet with sharp, rounded claws. It is an early spring migrant from South America and in the fall is among the last of the summer visitors to leave the forests.

The Prothonotary Warbler is a hole-nesting wood warbler and, as a breeding bird, confined to the eastern half of the United States. Though not generally widespread, it is common among willow- and cypress-bordered swamps and is easy to observe in the appropriate habitat. It is confiding and will readily take to nest boxes and all manner of other artificial holes, though it breeds naturally in holes in trees. With its orange-yellow head and breast, grey wings and green back the male Prothonotary Warbler is a beautiful bird.

The American Redstart *Setophaga ruticilla* is a wood warbler turned flycatcher, and not a redstart at all. Like the Old World flycatchers it has a thin, but broad bill and a strong growth of rictal bristles. The wings are long and the broad tail is often fanned and cocked. The male is a black and red bird with a bold red wing bar and red patches on the outer tail feathers. Females and immature males are uniformly grey with white patches in the tail.

Like a flycatcher the Redstart feeds by snapping up insects in the air, but also frequently works the canopy like a warbler and with a characteristic fluttering action. As with other members of the Parulidae it is the female that builds the nest and incubates the eggs. In suitable deciduous habitats densities of up to seven pairs per acre may be found. They nest through the boreal zone of North America and winter from Mexico southwards to Colombia and Venezuela and throughout the Caribbean.

Several wood warblers are endemic to the West Indies. The almost black Whistling Warbler *Catharopeza bishopi* is confined to the small island of St Vincent, while the rare Semper's Warbler *Leucopeza semperi* is found only on St Lucia.

Hawaiian honeycreepers Drepanididae

No group of birds exhibits the phenomenon of adaptive radiation more dramatically than the honeycreepers of the Hawaiian chain. From a single ancestor, probably a member of the Parulidae of America, a variety of species has evolved to fill a range of previously vacant niches. Even Darwin's finches of the Galápagos do not exhibit such an extreme range of adaptations. There are twelve or thirteen living species, plus a number of comparatively well-known birds that are now extinct. No doubt the process of evolution, especially in the speeded-up 'hot-houses' of remote islands, is extremely wasteful and it is to be expected that some forms will disappear as others move into their places; but the human colonization of Hawaii and the introduction of foreign pests no doubt accelerated the demise of some species.

Honeycreepers are 4 to 8 inches in length, and may be divided into a black and red group consisting predominantly of nectar-eaters, and a yellow-green group of which many are seed-eaters. A more conveninent division, however, is to examine the structure of the bills of these birds, for as with the Galápagos finches it is in this respect, indicating adaptations to different foods, that the honeycreepers differ most dramatically.

The nectar-eaters of the subfamily Drepanidinae are reddish in colour with longish, decurved bills. The Iiwi *Vestiaria coccinea* (almost all Hawaiian honeycreepers have local names) has the longest bill of all and feeds on the flowers of the lobelia family and in particular those of the mamani tree. The shorter-billed species are both dependent on the ohia lehua tree, and while the Apapane *Himatione sanguinea* is still quite numerous, the Crested Honeyeater *Palmeria dolei* is distinctly rare. These birds also eat insects.

More specifically an insect-eater is the Kauai Akialoa *Hemignathus procerus* which feeds in the manner of a treecreeper, probing with its long bill among the bark of trees. It also feeds on nectar. One of its congeners, now unfortunately extinct, the Akiapolaau *H. wilsoni* had the most extraordinary bill. While the upper mandible was long and decurved, the lower was short and wedge-shaped. This lower mandible was used woodpecker-fashion to chip away the bark of trees to reveal insects, which were then extracted with the probe-like upper mandible.

Another insect-eater, the Akepa *Loxops coccinea*, has the mandibles slightly crossed to facilitate the extraction of insects from buds and leaved cocoons. The closely related Amakihi *L. virens* is the most widespread and numerous of all the Hawaiian honeycreepers, perhaps because it is more catholic in its taste of food. These birds take nectar and insects, but also berries and fruit.

Another insect-eater with strange habits is the Pseudonestor *Pseudonestor xanthophrys*, an extremely rare if not extinct inhabitant of the island of Maui. Its massive bill is used to break dead twigs from branches and expose various species of leghorn beetles and their grubs.

Of the finch-type honeycreepers, the Finchbill or Laysan Finch

Feeding methods of two extinct Hawaiian honeycreepers. The Akiapolaau (above) used its short, stout, lower mandible to chip away bark and the long, decurved, upper mandible to extract insects. The Akialoa probed bark crevices with its long, sickle-shaped bill.

Psittirostra cantans is the most successful. It is more generalized than the other species and takes insects, seeds and carrion. It is adept at breaking open the shells of seabirds' eggs and can be found among the islands' terneries in some numbers.

Other honeycreepers are exceptionally well adapted to particular foods. The Ou *P. psittacea*, for example, feeds predominantly on the flowers of the Screw Pine, while the Palila *P. bailleni* feeds on seeds of the mamani tree.

Honeycreepers show remarkable similarity in breeding behaviour. They build untidy nests of twigs and grasses usually in trees or bushes. The clutch of white, spotted eggs usually numbers two or three. Honeycreepers are not aggressively territorial and, though other birds may be driven from the vicinity of the nest, some species, at least, form flocks even during the breeding season.

Of the twelve or thirteen species, six or seven are considered sufficiently rare to merit a place in the Red Book. Even some of the remaining six species have subspecies in danger of local extinction.

Vireos, shrike-vireos and pepper-shrikes Vireonidae

Closely related to the New World warblers, the vireos nevertheless have a character all of their own. They feed among foliage in the manner of the warblers, but prefer secondary growth to the canopy, and exhibit a deliberateness about their searching that is quite unlike the flitting gracefulness of the warblers. Where a warbler will hover before a leaf to get at its underside, a vireo will reach or even hang upside down to glean a hidden insect. Like the warblers they are green above and light below, but they do not exhibit a seasonal change of plumage, and the sexes are similar. They vary in size from 4 to 6 inches, and many species are remarkably similar so that their vernacular names frequently pick out the finer points of difference. Thus we have the Red-eyed, White-eyed, Grey-headed, Yellow-throated, and so on.

In general the legs are stronger and the bill thicker and more powerful than the warblers. Many species have a slight hook at the tip of the mandibles together with a small notch. The two distinctive tropical subfamilies, the pepper-shrikes and shrike-vireos, have these features highly developed, and live on large insects which they frequently tear apart in shrike fashion, while holding them in their feet.

Vireos live in thickets where they hunt among the outer branches of bushes at no great height from the ground. Some species prefer the canopy, but they never feed on the ground. Almost without exception they are highly vocal, but even their most ardent admirers would hardly call them melodious. The northern species,

in particular, sing throughout the long days of summer, and the Red-eyed Vireo *Vireo olivaceus* churns out a thousand songs an hour throughout the Canadian spring, summer and autumn. Males will even sing while incubating. Each member of the family has a distinctive song and these are invaluable to birdwatchers in

The well-named Red-eyed Vireo incubates on its nest nearly slung between the branches of a fork. Widespread in North America it leaves the continent completely in winter.

identifying what can be a very confusing group.

Vireos are New World birds, probably the equivalent of the Old World white-eyes, although they bear some similarity to the flowerpeckers. They are widespread throughout North America, but most of these species migrate southwards to Central or South America to join species that are resident in those areas. Doubtless their origins lie in these southern regions. The large genus *Hylophilus*, consisting of some fifteen species, is resident in South America. These birds, generally known as 'greenlets' (an old name for all the vireos), inhabit the undergrowth of tropical forests and frequently join mixed flocks of birds that roam those areas. They are remarkably similar in appearance, lacking the distinguishing marks that characterize the northern vireos. They have longer bills, but feed in much the same manner as the others.

All vireos build a cup-shaped nest suspended between the branches of a horizontal fork. The eggs are white and invariably spotted, often quite heavily. Incubation is generally shared as one would expect with species in which the sexes are similar.

Of the twelve vireos found in North America, the Red-eyed is by far the best known. It breeds in the eastern half of the United States and across southern Canada from the Atlantic to the Pacific, extending northwards through the prairie states. Despite its retiring qualities it is, perhaps, the commonest bird of the deciduous woodlands. It is rather dull in appearance, olive green above and white below, with a grey crown and strong, white supercilium. The vividly red eye is diagnostic at close quarters, but lacking in immature birds, that is, those most likely to occur as off-course vagrants. The whole population migrates southwards

overflying the Gulf of Mexico to Yucatan, before moving southwards to the forests of Venezuela and Colombia. It prefers deciduous woodland but can also be found in mixed woods, for the essential requirement is a strong growth of secondary bushes and saplings. The hammock nest is neatly bound with cobwebs, and the four eggs are incubated probably by the female alone. Incubation and fledging periods are both about twelve days. The birds are occasionally double-brooded. Throughout the summer insects are the dominant item of food, but as autumn develops the birds progressively turn to berries. No doubt this plentiful food supply helps them to put on fat prior to their long migrations.

The three species of shrike-vireos have heavy, shrike-like bills and are more brightly coloured than the typical vireos. They are found through Central America and northern South America, but because of their habit of feeding high in the canopy little is known of their lives. Their nests and eggs have not so far been described. The Chestnut-sided Shrike-vireo *Vireolanius melitophrys* is a bright green-backed bird some 7 inches in length. The head is boldly striped with black, yellow and grey, and the chestnut on the flanks extends to form a breast band. It inhabits oak woods from 4,000 to 10,000 feet from southern Mexico to Guatemala, and is usually found in pairs.

The two pepper-shrikes are similarly resident, non-gregarious birds that frequent secondary forest vegetation. They fly weakly and catch large insects in the middle and upper storeys of the forest. The nest resembles that of the typical vireos, and the two or three cream eggs are blotched with brown. The thick, hooked bill is ideally adapted to tearing large insects to pieces.

Icterids Icteridae

The icterids, frequently referred to as the New World orioles, are a large family closely related to the tanagers and cardinals. Indeed, the family is so diverse in almost every aspect of its natural history that several species pose real systematic problems. It includes the orioles, blackbirds, cowbirds, grackles, meadowlarks, oropendolas, caciques and other equally distinctive groups. This diversity of form and behaviour makes a general summary difficult.

The family is found throughout the New World, save the extremes of the continent in the north and south. Most species are woodland birds, but the meadowlarks feed in open country while others are marsh dwellers and one species is found in dry, desert

The Yellow-rumped Cacique is a gregarious and noisy bird that breeds in colonies in the manner of weavers. It is found from Panama to Bolivia.

country. Sexual dimorphism is the rule and this applies to size as well as to colour. The more northern species are highly migratory and in most species the male takes little or no part in nesting duties. As a result, promiscuity and polygamy are widespread. The cowbirds are parasitic breeders like the cuckoos. Most icterids are gregarious, living and migrating often in large flocks, and the tropical oropendolas and caciques are colonial breeders.

The family diversity is best shown by the variety of feeding habits. Almost all species take both vegetable and animal food depending on the time, place and availability. Grackles, for instance, are virtually omnivorous and feed on small birds and their eggs as well as on insects, fruit and seeds. Cowbirds too eat a range of foods, including ticks taken from the backs of animals on which they sometimes gather in numbers. Tropical species are mainly fruit-eaters, but may also drink nectar and catch insects. Many birds feed on the ground and the Bobolink *Dolichonyx oryzivorus* has become something of an inland 'turnstone'.

Icterids vary from 6 to 20 inches in length and many are predominantly black in colour, although 'icter' is the Latin word for yellow. Streaking is rare and most birds are boldly marked with patches of red or yellow. They have strong bills which, in the oropendolas and caciques, have developed a shield at the base of the upper mandible like a coot. Like other New World passerine families, the icterids have nine primaries and rictal bristles are generally absent.

Nests are as diverse as the birds themselves for while the orioles construct beautiful, hanging structures, the meadowlarks build a simple dome of grasses on the ground. The colonial caciques and oropendolas build slim, hanging nests that may measure several feet in length with up to 100 nests suspended from the same tree – a fabulous sight in the tropics where these birds are found. Eggs, which number two or three in the tropics and from four to six in temperate latitudes, are generally white sometimes with a blue or green cast. They are spotted or blotched with various shades of brown, and incubation by the female lasts from eleven to fourteen days. It is she who cares for the young, although in some species the male helps with feeding.

While most icterids are highly vocal, the thirty or so orioles of the genus *Icterus* are outstanding. Their flute-like whistles echo through the woods of North America as well as the tropical forests where the majority of species occur. In many birds the females sing as well as the males, and there seems to be little difference in the quality of song between the more brightly coloured and more sombrely hued species.

The male Baltimore Oriole *Icterus galbula* is a fine orange and black bird and a migrant to the eastern part of North America. His mate is generally more sombrely coloured in yellows and greens, although she may be quite orange and resemble the male. In western North America the species is replaced by Bullock's Oriole *I. bullockii*, and the two frequently hybridize in Midwestern areas of overlap. The resulting brood can pose considerable identification problems.

The longest-distance migrant of all is the Bobolink which shows not only sexual dimorphism, but a seasonal change of plumage as well. The breeding male is black below and on the face, with a broad, white bar on the folded wing and a white rump. The back is broadly striped black and buff and the nape is also buff. The female closely resembles several of the New World sparrows with the boldly striped crown of the bunting family. The bill is short and stubby like those birds. The Bobolink migrates from eastern North America via the West Indies to South America as far south as Buenos Aires in Argentina. In winter plumage the male resembles the female.

The cowbirds, with the exception of the Bay-winged Cowbird *Molothrus badius* which rears its own young albeit often in an appropriated nest, are brood parasites. Most of them are not particularly choosy about foster parents, simply watching a victim prepare its own nest and then laying a single egg. Surplus eggs are removed in the manner of some of the cuckoos. The Screaming Cowbird *M. rufoaxillaris*, however, victimizes only its congener the Bay-winged Cowbird. Cowbird eggs have a short incubation period and generally hatch in advance of those of the host. Nevertheless the host's own brood are usually reared as well.

The two species of meadowlark, Eastern *Sturnella magna* and Western *S. neglecta*, are so similar that, where they occur together, call is the best means of identification. They are birds of open country with a remarkable resemblance to the Yellow-breasted Longclaw of Africa. Despite similar habits and plumage, and notwithstanding a considerable overlap in range, the two do not hybridize.

Finches Fringillidae subfamilies Fringillinae and Carduelinae

The finches are a widespread group of small, seed-eating birds that had their origins in the Old World. Their exact systematic place is obscure and several authors have grouped them together with the buntings, cardinals, and Darwin's finches, to form one great family of seed-eating birds. Here we include the Darwin's finches, together with the two subfamilies that are the subject of this entry, to make up the family Fringillidae.

Finches are found throughout Eurasia, have penetrated and spread throughout the western Americas, and are widespread in Africa. They are dainty, attractive birds perhaps originally found in clearings and along the woodland edge, but now abundant in a variety of habitats from deep forest and mountain tops, to the arid wastes of deserts. Along with this spread into differing habitats has gone an adaptation to differing ways of life. The species have adapted in a variety of ways, but they vary most in the structure and size of their bills. While the Eurasian Goldfinch *Carduelis carduelis* has a delicate, fine-pointed, little bill, the Hawfinch *Coccothraustes coccothraustes* has a huge stone-breaker, and the grosbeaks have massive bills that are as large as their heads. The crossbills, as their name implies, have crossed mandibles specifically adapted to extract the seeds from pine cones. Yet young crossbills are born with quite normal uncrossed bills. All finches are adapted

to seed-eating, but while the Goldfinch delicately picks seeds from thistle heads, the Hawfinch can crack even cherry stones.

Several species have adapted well to the seed-rich areas provided by agriculture, but few can be considered pests on this account. One quite serious pest, however, is the Bullfinch *Pyrrhula pyrrhula*. This species breeds across Eurasia from Britain to Japan and the male, with his fine, pink breast and black cap, is a particularly attractive bird, and much in demand as a cagebird in many areas. Bullfinches eke out their diet of seeds, as do the other finches, through the winter, but are prone to eat buds in spring. In particular they turn their attention to the early buds of fruit trees and thus come into conflict with owners of orchards. Even the small gardener, with his two or three apple trees, can find no place in his heart for the Bullfinch. Ian Newton has shown, however, that it is only in following seasons in which the crop of ash seeds is poor, that the birds do really extensive damage to trees. Thus fruit farmers can predict severe attacks by the birds and concentrate their control measures accordingly. Instead of trapping in spring, when the damage occurs, it has been found much more effective to trap in autumn, thus reducing the whole of the winter population and conserving the crop of ash seeds by spreading it throughout the winter among a smaller population of birds.

Bullfinches are usually found in pairs, but Chaffinches *Fringilla coelebs* and Bramblings *F. montifringilla* are invariably gregarious birds. Unlike Bullfinches they feed predominantly on the ground and can often be found in huge flocks feeding on waste and weed seeds in autumn and winter. The Chaffinch breeds across Europe into Russia, in parts of the Middle East and in North Africa. In Scandinavia its range overlaps that of the Brambling, but in general that species is a more northern bird breeding among the birch forests of the taiga edge. Its range extends across Eurasia to Kamchatka on the Pacific, and it moves southwards to cover the range of the Chaffinch in winter. Among the birch woods it is one of the commonest birds, but in winter it is invariably outnumbered by the Chaffinch, once thought to be the most numerous bird in Britain.

The delicately marked Chaffinch builds a finely camouflaged nest in the fork of a tree, frequently a birch, as here. This is the male bird, the plumage of the female lacking most of his colours.

315

The males of both Chaffinch and Brambling are attractive birds, but while the Chaffinch has a grey head, that of the Brambling is black in summer and mottled with orange in winter. The females are duller versions of the males, but in all plumages the Brambling has a bright white rump that is particularly noticeable in flight.

Both species are largely dependent for their winter survival on the crop of beech-mast, and are numerous among beech woods at this time. If the crop fails they resort to open fields, farmyards and, in the case of Chaffinches at least, suburban gardens. The nests of both species are neat cups placed in the fork of a tree, often a birch, and beautifully camouflaged with lichens.

Both species migrate from the northern parts of their range to winter in more temperate climes. Chaffinches, at this time, frequently form into flocks and migrate by day. Like most finches they call continuously in flight.

One of the best known of all finches is the Canary *Serinus canaria*. Found only on the Canary Islands off the Atlantic coast of Africa, the Canary is one of the most numerous and widespread captive birds in the world. Selective breeding has produced a variety of different forms, many of which are grotesque, but the native bird is green above streaked with dark and greenish yellow below. That such a nondescript bird should have proved such a popular cagebird is due almost entirely to its fine song. In its native islands the Canary builds a neat, cup-shaped nest placed among bushes. The three to five eggs are incubated by the female alone, although

Above Enjoying a Holarctic distribution, the Redpoll is a bird of birch and coniferous forests. Its 'zitting', nasal call is a characteristic sound in areas where it breeds.

Opposite The Scarlet Grosbeak breeds right across Eurasia in coniferous forest and montane uplands. In some areas it is a common village bird.

the cock feeds her on the nest and also helps to feed the chicks. Like many other finches, the Canary clears away the droppings of its youngsters only for the first few days after hatching. Thereafter these are left on the rim of the nest.

Similar to the Canary is the more widespread Serin *S. serinus*. Once confined to the northern and western Mediterranean, this bird has enjoyed a most remarkable extension of range over the last hundred years and can now be found as far east as eastern Anatolia and as far north as southern Sweden. It has colonized parts of southern England in the last fifteen years, and is worth watching for throughout northern Europe.

Serins are gregarious little birds that feed on the ground on a variety of seeds. They are marked with a bold yellow rump and are favourite cagebirds in parts of Iberia where they are so numerous. No doubt the spread of agriculture has aided the spread of the Serin.

Similar in size to the Serin are the Redpoll *Acanthis flammea* and Twite *A. flavirostris*. While the Redpoll is essentially a woodland

bird with a propensity to haunt coniferous forests, the Twite is a bird of open moorlands. The Redpoll has a circumpolar distribution in the northern boreal zone. It is particularly associated with birch and is more common when these trees produce a good crop of seeds. Though basically a streaked, brown bird with a black bib and red on the crown, the plumage varies considerably and several distinct subspecies have been described based on size and the amount of white in the plumage. Usually the Arctic Redpoll *A. hornemanni* is regarded as a distinct species breeding north of the forest zone among the dwarf bushes of the tundra, but there is so much variation that it is not at all clear what the exact systematic position should be.

The Twite is even duller in colour than the Redpoll, and also lacks the high-pitched nasal call note that so easily picks out that bird as it flies. It breeds in northern Britain and through Norway and adjacent parts of Sweden. There is then a huge gap in distribution until it is found once more in the Caucasus extending southwards through the Middle East. It is also found among the Himalayas and northwards across the central Asian plateau to the Aral Sea. In Tibet it breeds up to 15,000 feet, but in Britain it is found from sea-level to 4,000 feet. In parts of Scotland it is a familiar bird around houses and replaces the House Sparrow in more isolated areas.

Among the 'red' finches the several genera tend to occupy distinct ecological niches. The *Leucosticte* are found only among high mountains in eastern Asia and western North America. The *Rhodopechys* are desert birds, and the largest genus, the *Carpodacus*, are birds of more moderate climes. One of the most widespread species is the Common Rosefinch or Scarlet Grosbeak *C. erythrinus*, which breeds in a northern belt right across Eurasia from the Baltic to the Pacific. It also breeds among that vast stretch of mountains from Turkey, where I found it a common village bird in the Pontic Alps, through the Himalayas to central China. The male is bright scarlet on the foreparts, while the female is simply sparrow-like, and best distinguished from females of that bird by the bold speckling on the breast.

Best known of the desert-loving species is the Trumpeter Bullfinch *Rhodopechys githaginea* whose rasping call is familiar to all visitors to the Valley of the Kings at Luxor in Upper Egypt. Although it blends well with the sandy rocks among which it lives, it is a surprisingly pinkish bird, the male being marked with a bright pink bill. It breeds throughout the Sahara region through the Middle East to northern Iran, where it feeds on the seeds and buds of desert plants. Similar, but less widespread, is the Crimson-winged Finch *R. sanguinea* which inhabits dry sub-desert areas at higher levels. It can be found among the Moroccan Atlas, the high plateaux of eastern Turkey, extending eastwards to Mongolia. It is a chunky looking bird that stands upright like a wheatear and is marked with vinous pink areas in the wing. Like the other members of the genus, Crimson-winged Finches do not migrate and local birds simply form flocks and move lower as the weather dictates.

Crossbills are among the few asymmetrical animals in the world, and also among the most specifically adapted. Their expertise at extracting the seeds from pine cones is well known, but they will eat a variety of other seeds when forced to land in unsuitable treeless areas.

Like several other species of the northern boreal and tundra zones, crossbills have an irruptive migration pattern. When a bumper breeding season is followed by a poor crop of pine cones, large numbers will take off in late summer for areas well beyond their normal range. The Common Crossbill *Loxia curvirostra*, perhaps more than any other irruptive species, is prone to establish itself in these new areas and settle down to breed in subsequent seasons. Thus while Scottish Crossbills have been present for years in the old Scots pine areas of the Spey Valley, there are now several areas of England and Wales that have breeding colonies of

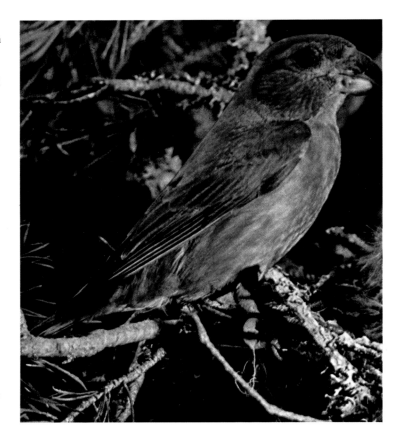

Above The male Parrot Crossbill pauses at its nest to regurgitate to its hungry youngsters a milky liquid made from pine seeds.

Opposite The massive bill of the Hawfinch gives the bird a curiously cross-patch look, but also imparts to it the remarkable ability to break into cherry stones.

these birds established over the last 200 years. No doubt the new coniferous plantations offer them a home in areas that were formerly outside their range, a fact that was taken advantage of, particularly in the 1960s.

Pine cones open very early in the spring and as a result Crossbills are remarkably early breeders. Nesting may commence in December, but is in full swing by January and February. The most usual nest site is a spruce or pine and the nest itself is placed at the end of a high branch. The three or four eggs are incubated by the female who is fed by her mate at regular intervals. No doubt her reputation as a close sitter is an adaptation to the harsh conditions under which she breeds, for the eggs would chill very quickly at this time. After the hatch the blind and naked chicks are brooded by the female and fed by the male. Later both parents participate in feeding the young on predigested pine seeds. They take about twenty-five days to fledge – a very long period among passerines.

Among the finches the genus *Carduelis* has been the most successful in invading the New World and some thirteen species are found in North and South America. Best known is the American Goldfinch *C. tristis* which breeds right across the United States, in parts of eastern and western Canada, and into northern and eastern Mexico. The male is a boldly patterned yellow and black bird that moults in autumn into a dull greenish plumage similar to that of the female. Like the European Goldfinches they are fond of the seeds of thistles and teazles and are most commonly found on waste ground where they join flocks of other birds.

Like most of the finches, the American Goldfinch is one of the most attractive of birds. It has a pleasant song and is confiding enough to visit bird-tables on an increasing scale.

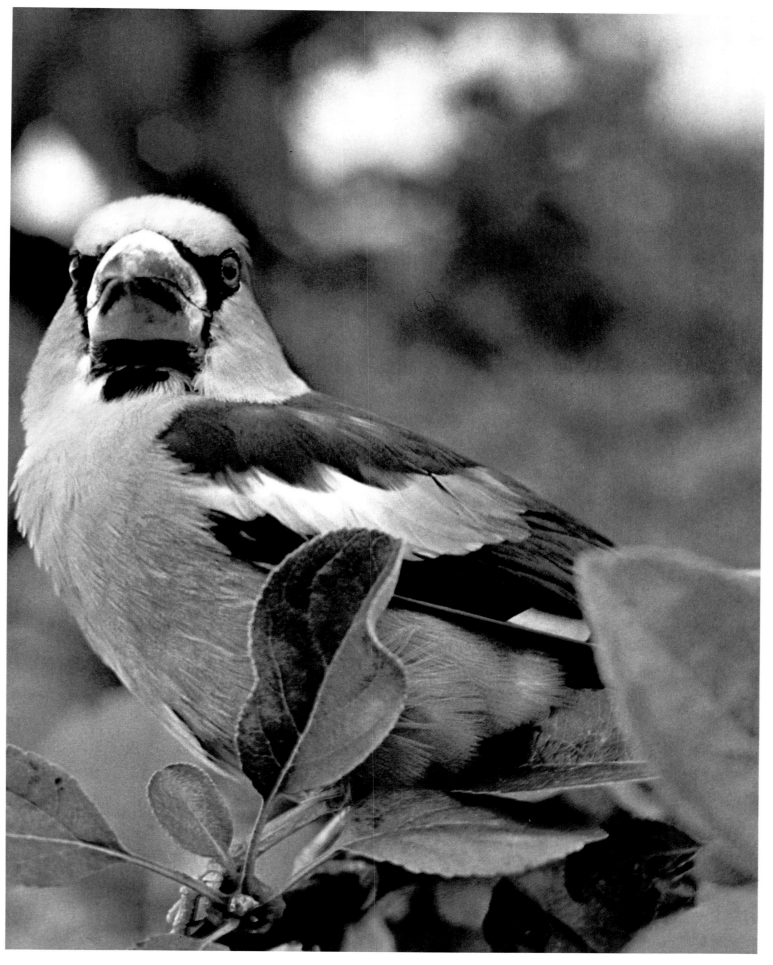

Darwin's finches Fringillidae subfamily Geospizinae

It is fitting that the small subfamily of endemic Galápagos finches should continue to bear the name of Darwin. On these islands, more than anywhere else, the theory of natural selection, which culminated in the publication of the *Origin of Species* in 1859, was crystallized in his mind. At first, as we know, he was more taken with the diversity of tortoises that he found there, but later the importance of the nondescript, little birds became obvious.

From an original colonizer thirteen distinct species have evolved in less than a million years, perhaps considerably less. The only other passerine birds found on these islands are four distinct but closely related mockingbirds, two tyrant flycatchers and the Yellow Warbler, a recent arrival that is still virtually indistinguishable from its mainland ancestor. This poverty of species does much to explain how the original finch-like colonizers were able to move into and occupy a variety of vacant ecological niches. The Galápagos Islands are of volcanic origin and have risen from the sea some 600 miles from the coast of Ecuador. All of their fauna and flora have flown or drifted over the sea and while no doubt other animals may

continue to colonize them, the difficulties are immense. Though generally thought of as confined to the Galápagos, another member of the Geospizinae was discovered on the Cocos Islands 600 miles north of the Galápagos in 1891.

As with the honeycreepers of Hawaii, Darwin's finches differ most markedly in the structure of the bill. Some retain a moderately sized finch-like bill, while others have evolved a mammoth nut-cracking bill like the grosbeaks of America and the hawfinches of Eurasia. Others have parrot-like bills and one has virtually become a warbler with a thin insect-eating bill. The most curious of all is the Woodpecker-finch *Camarhynchus pallidus* which boasts a strong, chiselling bill and lives like a woodpecker. It has not, however, adapted the long tongue of those birds, but has compensated by developing the habit of picking cactus thorns and

The strong, conical bill of the Medium Ground Finch of the Galápagos Islands is adapted to seed cracking. It is a member of the unique subfamily found only on those islands.

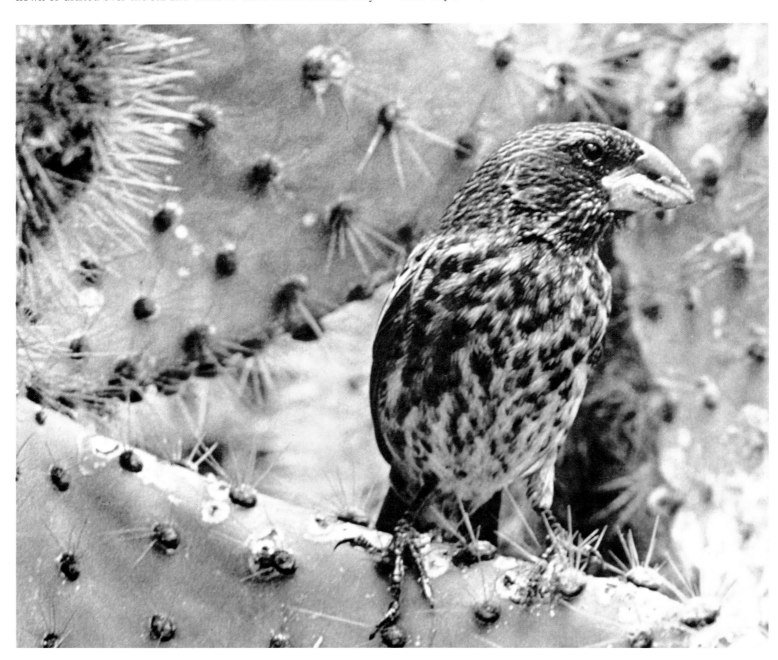

using these to probe for insect grubs as a tongue substitute. The use of tools is an accomplishment restricted to only a handful of wild animals.

Like the other members of the subfamily, the Woodpecker-finch has a streaked, dull grey-brown coloration. Other finches are similarly streaked, entirely black, or something between the two. Males are in general black and females grey, but this also varies according to age, and young males closely resemble the females.

Within a single genus the species may be remarkably similar in plumage pattern but can usually be told apart by bill shape and size. The larger bills are powerful enough to crack hard seeds, whereas the smaller and more delicate bills are better suited to picking small seeds from the ground. Thus the Large Ground-finch *Geospiza magnirostris* is of the grosbeak type, whereas the Small Ground-finch *G. fuliginosa* is the more dainty bird. Within the same genus are two species which are largely dependent on the prickly pear for their food – the cactus ground-finches.

The tree-finches are similarly differentiated by bill size and diet. Some are seed-eaters, others insect-eaters, and some take both. This group includes the Woodpecker-finch.

The Warbler-finch *Certhidea olivacea* is distinctly orange in colour and flits through bushes searching for insects just like a warbler. The similar Cocos Finch *Pinaroloxias inornata* takes insects as well, but also feeds on nectar from flowers.

Most species of Darwin's finches are sufficiently distinct to be able to live alongside one another, and several species are found on most of the islands. The cactus ground-finches, however, occupy different islands, indicating that competition between them may still persist.

Nests, which are built during the rainy season about Christmas time, are untidy, domed structures with a side entrance. The male is the constructor and the female chooses between the several that he offers her. Incubation is by the female alone although both sexes bring food to the chicks.

Weaver-finches Estrildidae

The exact relationship between the various groups of Old World seed-eaters is confused and authorities have adopted various schemes to show their relationship. Others, perhaps in despair, have lumped them all together. There are, however, several well-defined groups such as the weavers, sparrows, whydahs and waxbills, within which it may be difficult to assign certain 'difficult' species, but which have a typical structure and life style of their own. The difficulty is to decide whether such groupings deserve familial

rank. In this book we treat the weavers, sparrows and whydahs as a single family, the Ploceidae, while the weaver-finches are placed separately in the Estrildidae. That both families contain birds with common names such as 'weaver', 'sparrow', 'finch', and so on, does

A pair of Red-cheeked Cordon-bleus. Only the male has the diagnostic cheek patches that give the species its name. This species is widespread in tropical Africa and popular as a cagebird.

Right A Zebra Waxbill pauses at its domed nest. The species is found through most of Africa south of the Sahara.

Opposite Found in the more arid parts of Africa the Cut-throat Weaver is named after the obvious crimson mark across the neck of the male bird. The Cut-throat Weaver is another popular cagebird.

not help to make the division any clearer.

The 108 species of weaver-finch are small birds, widespread in the Old World tropics from Africa across Asia to Australia and the Pacific. They are generally colourful and even the more dully coloured species are boldly marked. Reds, greens, mauves, blues and yellows predominate in many species, although some are striped like zebras and others are almost uniform in coloration. They have short, stubby, seed-eating bills, often brightly coloured, and prefer open areas of grassland or bush country. Their food, which consists of the small seeds of grasses, is taken on the ground and they invariably form flocks throughout the year. Sometimes these groups may reach enormous proportions. Though the pair bond is particularly strong, various species show a tendency to colonial nesting and their domed or globular nests decorate a chosen tree in profusion. The clutch is often large, up to ten white eggs, and incubation and care of the young is shared to a greater or lesser extent.

The chicks are remarkable for the colourful pattern of the inside of their mouths. A white or yellow gape is boldly decorated with spots or lines of black, and when begging for food the chicks sway their open mouths in a peculiar fashion. No doubt this stimulates the parents to feed them and makes the mouths more obvious in the darkened interior of the nest, but this cannot be the full explanation, for other hole-nesting species survive without such elaborate behaviour patterns. The various species of whydahs that parasitize the weaver-finches have evolved similar gape patterns to their hosts, although some authors regard the gape patterns as a sign that the whydahs and weaver-finches are closely related.

Young weaver-finches breed at the age of a few months and invariably well within their first year. This high breeding rate together with their brightly coloured plumage and general restlessness make them popular cage birds, and there is a thriving trade in exporting birds from Africa and Asia to Europe. Only their lack of song prevents them from becoming perfect cagebirds – a factor for which conservationists should be grateful, for untold numbers of these attractive little birds die in transit.

The waxbills of the subfamily Estrildini are found in Africa, with two species in Asia and one in Australia. They vary in size, in power of bill, and thus in the types of seeds that they eat. Different species have attracted a variety of common names such as 'firefinch', 'twin-spot' and 'cordon-bleu'. The last are among the most beautifully marked of birds, with fine areas of pale blue in the plumage. The Red-cheeked Cordon-bleu *Uraeginthus bengalus* is one of the most commonly imported cagebirds. It is light brown above and pale blue below, the male being marked with crimson patches on the cheeks. This species is widespread in the non-forested areas of Africa and feeds on the ground on seeds that it gleans by scratching in the earth. It will also raid termite mounds and feeds the newly hatched young on these and other insects.

The grassfinches of the Erythurini are of predominantly Australasian distribution and are also favourite cagebirds. They include the Zebra Finch *Poephila castanotis*, the parrotfinches of the genus *Erythura*, and the quite exquisite Gouldian Finch *Poephila gouldiae*. The last, found in northern Australia, is beautifully marked in green, pale and cobalt blue, crimson and deep yellow. It occurs in three distinct phases in which the colour of the head varies from crimson to black and yellow. The black-headed form is the most common, while the yellow-headed variety is distinctly rare.

Unlike most other estrildine finches, Gouldian Finches feed

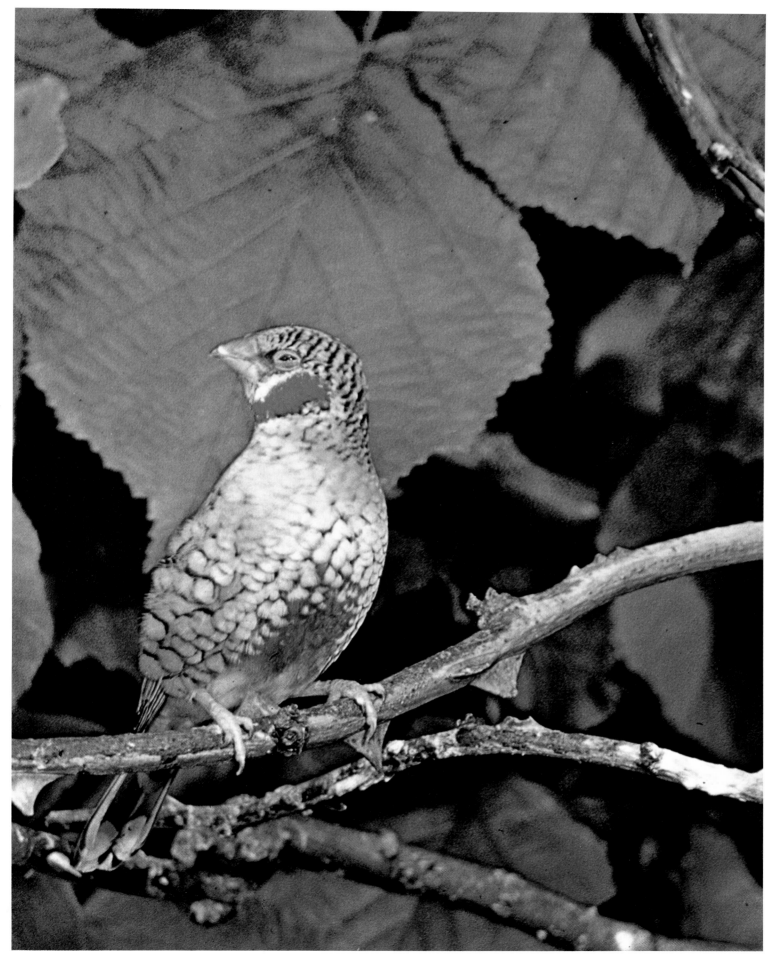

largely on unfallen seeds which they take directly from ripening grass. They are found in open bush country, but seldom far from water. Their breeding coincides with the latter part of the rainy season when grass seeds are plentiful and when the sun provides plenty of heat. Indeed they seem unhappy at anything less than 100°F. They build no nest, but occupy a hollow in a tree or termite mound. They are gregarious and frequently gather hundreds strong at water. In a drought the birds become nomadic in their search for water.

The mannikins, not to be confused with the manakins of tropical America, are a rather subdued group of weaver-finches found from Africa to Australia, but with a very definite centre of origin in Malaysia and adjacent parts of the Far East. Best known is the Java Sparrow *Padda oryzivora* which, though native to Java, Sumatra and Bali, has escaped from captivity and established itself over large areas of Asia. It is an attractive bird with dull plumage broken by a bold, black and white head pattern and a strong, deeply pink bill. Despite its importance as an agricultural pest it is surprisingly little studied outside captivity. In Java it lives in villages, while in China its relationship with man extends to picking out fortune-telling cards in markets. Of course, these birds are specifically trained for the purpose, but they doubtless show an impartiality in keeping with their status.

They build domed nests under the eaves of houses and the four or five white eggs hatch after thirteen or fourteen days. The young are fed on insects, but soon change to the more usual diet of grass seeds.

One of the African mannikins is the well-known Cut-throat Weaver *Amadina fasciata*. This brown, mottled bird marked by a broad, crimson patch across the throat is found in the more arid regions of Africa where, despite its comparatively large size (5 inches) it is easily overlooked. 'Cut-throats' are somewhat sporadic in their appearances being either quite common or completely absent. They breed during the height of the dry season. The domed nest is built in a hole in a tree or building, though the birds regularly take over the nests of other weavers.

Weavers, sparrows and whydahs Ploceidae

The Ploceidae are a large family of Old World seed-eating species that includes many widespread and well-known birds. Yet it is a difficult family to summarize. It has close relationships with the weaver-finches and the true finches, and is easily divisible into three quite distinct groups which are usually accorded subfamilial rank. Birds vary in length from 4 to 10 inches and are generally gregarious. They are seed-eaters with thickish bills and are particularly abundant in open country. Several species have multiplied rapidly with increased forest clearance so that they are among the most serious pests in the world. The House Sparrow *Passer domesticus* has been introduced to many parts of the world and has invariably thrived, often to the annoyance of the human population. The Red-billed Quelea *Quelea quelea* forms such truly gigantic flocks in several parts of Africa that its depredations have been likened to those of locusts, and similar elaborate control measures have proved necessary.

The largest members of the Ploceidae are the buffalo weavers (subfamily Bubatornithinae), familiar to visitors to the game parks of East Africa. The Buffalo Weaver *Bubalornis albirostris* is boldly black in the male marked with a large, pink bill, and mottled brown in the female. The White-headed Buffalo Weaver *Dinemellia dinemelli* is cream on the head, nape and underparts, and brownish grey above with a particularly bright crimson rump. Both inhabit the more arid areas of Africa, feed on seeds and insects, come to safari lodges for bread, and build thorny nests in bushes.

The true weavers (subfamily Ploceinae), which account for some ninety species, are predominantly African birds with a handful of representatives in Asia. They are highly gregarious and nest in colonies often close together, in some cases combining to build a single great structure within which each pair has its own nest chamber and entrance hole. The more usual nests are globular structures suspended from trees in groups. Many species have bold areas of yellow or red in their plumage, and some are remarkably similar in appearance. In Kenya, for example, I was able to sort out a half dozen species in all of which the body was yellow and the face black. Others had rust or even orange faces and heads. They feed in flocks and, like the buffalo weavers, are bold and tame around safari lodges.

The nest, which is invariably constructed of green stems which turn brown as they die, starts as a single loop suspended from an outer branch of a bush or tree by the male. This is then used as a display perch as the bird flutters its wings while hanging upside down. The male continues its construction, but as soon as it is finished he starts another to attract another mate. Polygamy is widely prevalent among these true weavers.

Globular nests are common, although several species construct long entrance tunnels to protect their eggs and young. Such a form of construction, together with the location of the nest at the very tips of branches, would seem to offer satisfactory

Below The ubiquitous House Sparrow is found wherever man has established permanent settlements and takes advantage of his fondness for feeding birds.

Opposite The scourge of African agriculture, the Red-billed Quelea is one of the few great avian pests. It is also a finely marked bird.

security against predators, but the weavers also bolt and bar the door by frequently building over water or close to the nest of bees or wasps. Such elaborate nest protection devices are probably necessary for these gregarious birds building such obvious nests.

Most magnificent of all these constructions is that of the Sociable Weaver *Philetairus socius* of South and South-west Africa (subfamily Passerinae) which produces the largest of all birds' nests. Placed in a thorn, usually an acacia, these may measure twenty feet by fifteen feet by ten feet and form a home for up to a hundred pairs. Totally communal behaviour of this sort is unusual among birds, for though each pair has its own entrance and nesting chamber, more effort is put into the total structure than to the individual parts. Thus partition walls tend to be flimsy. The top is thatched with straw and is completely waterproof like that of an English country cottage. In spite of this communal nesting, the Sociable Weaver is strictly monogamous.

Sociable Weavers bear a strong resemblance to sparrows. Their crowns are chocolate and their cheeks white with black bibs. The back is brown with creamy edges to the feathers giving a 'scalloped' effect. They feed in flocks on dry, open ground and are apparently less dependent on water than many other weavers.

The Red-billed Quelea inhabits the more arid areas of Africa and is widespread from Senegal to the Red Sea and southwards to South Africa. It is brown above, the feathers of the back and wings being broadly edged with cream, has a golden crown, a dark brown face patch and red bill and legs. For such a pest it is a remarkably attractive bird. When I found them in Samburu National Park in the northern frontier district of Kenya, I came across a flock of about 100 individuals feeding among dry, open scrub, but in many areas they gather in millions to feed on crops of rice and cereals. Around Lake Chad in northern Nigeria a single tree may hold 6,000 nests, while a single colony covering some 500 acres may boast as many as ten million nests. The destruction caused by these flocks is incalculable, and in areas where poverty is so prevalent it is not surprising that man has tried everything to rid himself of the Quelea plague. Dynamite and fire are frequently used to destroy nesting colonies and roosts. Villagers take to the fields with rattles and drums, flame throwers are used to set fire to colonies and in South Africa over 400 million birds were destroyed in four years by aerial spraying. Yet the Quelea still exists in enormous numbers. All the control measures seem to do is to kill off the surplus population that would die anyway during the dry season. The problem of control is aggravated by the fact that Queleas are remarkably quick nesters. They descend on an area and take only two weeks to incubate their eggs and another two weeks for the young to fledge. They are immensely successful breeders and nearly ninety per cent of eggs result in fledged young. As soon as their highly synchronized breeding is completed Queleas start to roam. They breed only once a year but never do so in the same place in successive years. In fact they breed in many inaccessible areas and thus build up a reservoir population that is able to move into any area where extermination measures have reduced their numbers.

Traditionally small boys were used to guard the fields against bird flocks and this is still the most effective, if time-consuming, method of protecting crops. Control measures clearly do not work and agriculturalists are progressively coming round to the idea of crop protection. One by-product of the Quelea problem is the increased supply of valuable protein in the poorer areas of Africa, for while one bird is insignificant, a dishful makes a substantial and nourishing meal.

As successful in its way as the Quelea is the House Sparrow, now established on every major land mass in the world save Greenland and Antarctica. Familiar, cocky and aggressive, the Sparrow is *the* household bird in many parts of the world. It nests in our houses, feeds on our garbage, and raids our fields. It was well established in North America on the coast near Baltimore by 1868, but within twenty years it had occupied every one of the

Above The generally tame and approachable White-headed Buffalo Weaver is marked by a vivid red rump pattern in flight.

Below A Black-headed Weaver clings to the underside of its suspended nest in display. The male flutters his wings in this position to attract a mate.

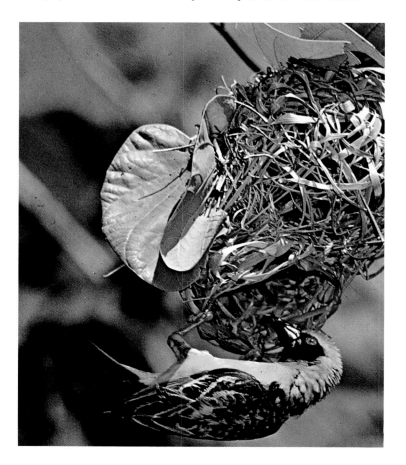

United States. In South Africa it presses steadily northwards. It is becoming more common in eastern Australia, has overrun New Zealand, and is widespread in South America. Doubtless it will eventually cover the earth.

Unlike Queleas, Sparrows breed almost throughout the year in temperate zones. This is, in part, accounted for by their catholic taste in food, for they eat what they can get, from bread to buds and grass seeds. In London numbers declined with the demise of the horse-drawn carriage and cart and the consequent decline of grain spillage, but they are still common and plentiful throughout the city.

European Sparrows sometimes make considerable journeys in their first year, but are thereafter resident. They will nest in the same site year after year, and even a nest site movement of 100 yards is unusual. The three to six grey, blotched eggs are incubated mainly by the female and hatch after twelve to fourteen days. The young, which are fed on a variable diet, fledge some eleven to eighteen days later. A further clutch is started within ten days, and a breeding pair will produce an average of five fully fledged young that survive at least to the autumn. Most nests are placed under eaves, but tree nests are quite common in country districts and Sparrows also take over House Martin nests with some regularity.

The Snow Finch *Montifringilla nivalis* is a chirpy, sparrow-like bird that lives at high altitudes in a scattered belt from the mountains of Spain to the Himalayas. It breeds above 4,500 feet and up to 16,000 feet, but is not found lower than 9,000 feet in the mountains of eastern Anatolia. Despite their barren habitat, Snow Finches are not shy and in the Alps regularly haunt picnic spots on the high-level passes between Switzerland and Italy. A handful of grain regularly attracts a flock of these birds on the Grossglockner Pass.

Two peculiarly African genera are the *Vidua* and *Euplectes*, both often called whydahs or widow-birds with varying degrees of accuracy and considerable and permanent confusion. As their common names also include 'indigo bird', 'weaver' and 'bishop', it is simplest to use the generic name.

The *Vidua* whydahs are brood parasites in the manner of cuckoos. The largest males are boldly patterned in black, white and orange-yellow with long, broadly vaned tails. The Pin-tailed Whydah *V. macroura* is a black and white bird with elongated, but narrow, tail feathers and marked by a conical, red bill. Several species parasitize the weaver-finches of the genus *Pytila*, the grenadiers and their allies – indeed the distribution of these whydahs coincides more or less exactly with that of their preferred hosts.

The indigo birds, often placed in the genus *Hypochera*, but now usually considered *Vidua*, present remarkable problems. There may be a single, highly variable species, or perhaps up to a dozen or more. They parasitize the various African firefinch species.

The *Vidua* whydahs do not have the means or behaviour patterns necessary to kill or evict the chicks of foster parents, but they do have the brightly coloured and patterned gapes of their siblings.

In contrast the *Euplectes* bishops and whydahs rear their own young. The males of several species have elongated tail feathers during the breeding season and are predominantly red, marked with bold patches of black. All are gregarious, but at the commencement of the breeding season males leave the flocks to establish their territories. These are defended by elaborate postures, and patrolled on noisy wings to attract a female. Jackson's Whydah *E. jacksoni* has a communal courtship dance in which the males establish a tiny, circular territory from which they leap into the air.

Males construct the framework of the nest while the females finish the structure and are solely responsible for incubation and care of the young. As soon as one nest is established the male constructs another and attracts another mate. A single male may have a harem of three to six mates.

Starlings Sturnidae

Starlings are the wide boys of the bird world. Cocky and aggressive, and often flashily dressed, they waddle with a swaggering gait over the ground sometimes bursting into a hopping run in their efforts to be first at food. Throughout their range they are among the most familiar of birds having built up a specially intimate relationship with man. As a result, several species have been introduced to new continents where they have inevitably thrived and, in some cases, reached pest proportions. Indeed it was the very success of the introduction of the Common Starling *Sturnus vulgaris* to North America that led the United States government to establish laws controlling the importation of alien birds.

Starlings vary from 7 inches to 1½ feet in length, although the larger species are invariably long-tailed. The bill is longish, often slightly decurved, and the legs are strong and well adapted to walking. Although starlings were probably forest birds by origin, they prefer open areas and feed predominantly on the ground. A great many species are omnivorous, which accounts for their success, and agriculturalists are continually balancing the beneficial effects of their depredations on populations of harmful insects against their destructive raids on crops. Cereals and fruits are particularly prone to attack.

Basically dark in colour, many starlings have a bright, iridescent quality about their plumage, particularly during the breeding season. The Common Starling, for example, moults only once a year at the end of the breeding season into a boldly speckled plumage. Gradually, however, the buff tips to the feathers are abraided and by spring a glossy, metallic sheen covers the body, producing purples and blues as the sun catches the feathers. Several African starlings are exceedingly brightly coloured with purples or blues, oranges or yellows boldly spread over the body. The genus *Spreo*, winch includes the Superb Starling *S. superbus*, is particularly notable for its brilliance. As with many other starlings, these birds are tame and confiding and regularly haunt villages and safari lodges. The Superb Starling is a bright metallic green above, with the dark blue of the head extending to the breast where a white ring separates it from orange underparts. While this species is often dominant, aggressively chasing other birds from food, the secondary starling varies according to the locality. At Kenya's Amboseli National Park, for instance, the Superb Starling is the dominant bird, while Hildebrandt's Starling *S. hildebrandti* is also found. Eastwards, in the adjacent Tsavo National Park, its place as second bird to the Superb is taken by the magnificent Golden-breasted Starling *Cosmopsarus regius*. The latter is slightly larger-bodied than the Superb, but an extremely long tail extends its overall length to nearly 15 inches. It is purple above, green on the head, and bright yellow below. It feeds naturally on termites, but readily comes to bird-tables at lodges.

Also found in the same areas, but never as confiding as the others, is the dull grey Wattled Starling *Creatophora cinerea*. At times this bird feeds on ticks from wild animals and domestic stock, but it is best known as a major predator of locusts. When locusts lay their eggs Wattled Starlings commence breeding as well. The chicks fledge just in time to catch the young locusts at the flightless hopper stage. Being so dependent on these nomadic insects, Wattled Starlings have little choice but to abandon the usual starling habit of nesting in holes in trees or buildings. Instead they construct large domes of twigs and grasses on a colonial basis. Often two or three nests are woven together, and as many as a dozen may be found in the same tree. These birds are also unusual in going completely bald and growing long wattles during their irregular breeding season.

Another irregular breeder is the Rosy Starling *Sturnus roseus* of the Middle East. Similarly dependent on insect swarms, this bird nests colonially among rocky hillsides and at the end of a successful breeding season irrupts into areas where it does not otherwise occur. At such times it appears regularly in eastern Europe, and may sometimes stay on to breed for a year or so. I remember seeing flock after flock of these fast-flying birds passing over Lake Van in eastern Anatolia in June. Their movements had a certain purposeful quality and only a few came to land.

In Asia the various species of mynahs are common and widespread. They have the usual cockiness of the family and can be

Left The Common Mynah is an inhabitant of Asia from India to Malaya that has been successfully introduced to many other parts of the world where it has become a pest.

Below The Violet Starling is found throughout Africa south of the Sahara, but is generally less common than many of its congeners.

Opposite One of the world's most successful birds, the Common Starling has benefited from man's actions and has established itself in parts of the world where it is not naturally found.

found from Delhi airport to the more remote Himalayan villages. In India several species occur side by side including the Common Mynah *Acridotheres tristis*, which inhabits almost every part of that continent and is ubiquitous in towns and cities. *Gracula religiosa*, the Hill or Talking Mynah as it is often called, is less common and best known for its ability to mimic. In the wild it picks up a variety of calls of other birds, but in captivity it is regarded as one of the very best talking birds. The Common Mynah, like the Common Starling, has been introduced to many parts of the world including Australia, South Africa and New Zealand, and in some areas is now considered a pest.

Best known of all introduced species is the Common Starling. Released in 1890 in New York's Central Park it has spread throughout the United States and is now as numerous as the human population. In American cities, as in London and other parts of their native range, Starlings regularly flight to roost in the warmth of the city centre. In vast numbers they occupy the ledges in Trafalgar Square seemingly oblivious of the noise below, and the flashing on and off of neon signs. The noise they create is deafening and their droppings do considerable damage to buildings as well as unfortunate passers-by. Various deterrents including shooting, broadcasting warning cries, and a sticky glue on the ledges, seemingly have little effect on the birds, which may fly for up to twenty miles morning and evening to the city centre.

When radar was first used scientists were confused by rings of 'angels' passing every morning over their screens. Concentric rings of light spread out over a short period of time like the rings caused by dropping a stone into still water. Investigation showed that the rings on the screen were composed of Starlings leaving their roosts and flying out to feeding grounds.

The two species of oxpeckers are starlings that have adapted to a life on the move. As their name implies, they live on oxen and the various species of large African game. Zebras and giraffes may be virtually covered with birds, while buffalo allow intimacies that show that they must value the company of these birds. Woodpecker-like they clamber over their hosts prying into ears and nostrils in their search for ticks. They are difficult birds to approach and regularly sound the alarm by flying off with noisy calls long before the animal itself shows any fear. In this way they perform a further service to the plains game of Africa.

The two species can be distinguished by the colour of the bill, and while the Red-billed *Buphagus erythrorhynchus* nests among rocks and the thatch of native huts, the Yellow-billed *B. africanus*

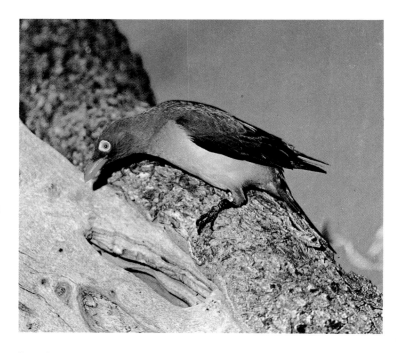

Oxpeckers invariably nest in holes in the dead boughs of trees up to eighty feet from the ground. This makes them quite inaccessible and they are consequently little studied. This is the Red-billed Oxpecker.

breeds in holes in trees.

The rarest member of the family is Rothschild's Starling *Leucopsar rothschildi* which was described as recently as 1912. It is found only on the island of Bali, and was quite common in the Bubunan area of the north coast until bird dealers discovered its potential. Capture has since reduced its numbers and some hundreds are now in the hands of zoos and aviculturists. Fortunately the species breeds well in captivity, but it still remains unprotected in its native land.

Starlings generally nest in holes in trees and many species are aggressive enough to usurp the homes of woodpeckers. Several nest in buildings, while a few build domed nests in trees or excavate their own holes along the banks of streams. The four or five eggs are in general incubated by the female, but both sexes share in caring for the young. Fledglings lack the iridescence of the adults.

Old World orioles Oriolidae

Orioles are colourful birds of the tree tops best known for their flute-like calls. They are found exclusively in the Old World from Africa eastwards through Asia to Australia, and reach their maximum density of species in the region of Malaysia where several species have evolved in the geographical isolation of islands. The Oriolidae are not to be confused with the orioles of the New World (family Icteridae) for, despite various physical similarities, the latter are most closely related to the tanagers, another exclusively New World group.

Old World orioles are predominantly yellow and black in coloration, but the females are generally duller and often streaked. Island orioles also tend to be less brightly coloured. In some species black is dominant, while in the Maroon Oriole *Oriolus traillii* the body is a deep reddish maroon. The bill is strong, of medium length and often slightly decurved. Orioles vary in size from 8 to 12 inches and are birds of woodland, feeding predominantly among the canopy. In spite of their bright plumage, they are more frequently heard than seen, although a glimpse of a vividly coloured, yellow bird, flying in a lilting almost woodpecker-like

fashion, is sufficient for identification. They take a great many insects, but most orioles turn to fruit and berries in autumn, to the annoyance of fruit farmers. Four Australian species are, in fact, called 'figbirds' because of their predilection for these fruits, while the Golden Oriole *O. oriolus* regularly turns to figs as it passes through the Mediterranean region on migration.

All but a handful of orioles belong to the genus *Oriolus* and only the Golden Oriole, which penetrates Europe, is at all well known. This bright yellow and black bird breeds throughout continental Europe, eastwards as far as central Asia. In Britain it is of irregular spring occurrence and occasionally remains to breed in the woodlands of southern England. It is a late arrival and departs early on its journey to Africa south of the Sahara. Like the other orioles, it feeds almost entirely in trees, and builds a hammock-shaped nest attached to a horizontal fork. Both sexes share the nesting duties, while it is the female that performs the bulk of the building. The two to four eggs, occasionally six, hatch after fourteen or fifteen days and produce naked and helpless young. Orioles are unusual in preying on the hairy caterpillars that most

A summer visitor to Europe, the Golden Oriole slings its nest between the branches of a tree fork. Its loud, flute-like call is a characteristic sound of European and Asiatic woodlands.

birds leave alone. These are vigorously brushed against a perch to remove the fluff before being eaten.

Many of the tropical species are more or less resident, and most of those that have been studied resemble the Golden Oriole in details of breeding behaviour. In several species, however, the female performs the bulk of the incubation, although she is frequently fed on the nest by her mate. Best known is the Indian

Black-headed Oriole *O. xanthornus*, which is widespread throughout that continent eastwards through Burma to Malaysia. It is a brilliant, yellow-bodied bird, marked with black wings, head and bib and by a red bill. The sexes are similar, the female being only a little duller than her mate. Like other orioles they are solitary birds fond of tall jungle trees, as well as agricultural areas.

The Australian figbirds, in contrast, are gregarious and given to travelling in noisy flocks. They are basically green in colour with areas of black on the wings, tail and head. The males have an area of bare, red skin around the eye, and the bill is shorter and more hooked than that of the typical orioles. Their coloration makes them difficult to observe among the foliage of the tree tops, and their constant calls bear a strong resemblance to those of parakeets. Their nests are more flimsy structures than those of the orioles, being constructed of twigs and placed among the outer branches at the top of a tree. They have a tendency to gregariousness even during the breeding season.

The four species, which obviously evolved from a single ancestor, are found along the coasts of eastern and northern Australia, with one species confined to Java, and another to a maze of islands immediately to the north. As their name implies figs are an important item of food, but they also consume quantities of other fruits and berries.

Drongos Dicruridae

The first bird I saw in India was a Black Drongo *Dicrurus macrocerceus* flitting about the customs building in the middle of the night at Delhi airport. The species was to prove a constant companion for the remainder of my stay in that country.

From Africa and throughout Asia it is difficult to travel far without seeing at least one member of this twenty strong family. They are easy to identify. Most species are black with deeply forked tails and long, pointed wings. The bill is wide, slightly hooked and backed by a strong growth of rictal bristles. The feet and legs are weak, and the birds spend much of their time perched prominently on the look-out for passing insects.

In many areas several species of drongos live apparently side by side and, sharing such features as shape and coloration, can be difficult to identify specifically. In this connection the amount and distribution of iridescence in the plumage is critical. Fortunately this varies considerably, but further helpful points in the field are the exact extent of forking in the tail and the length, or lack, of a crest. While the normal drongo tail is forked with the feathers splaying outwards at the tips, some species have extended outer tail feathers which sometimes have the barbs of the feathers worn off except at the tips. The Great Raquet-tailed Drongo *D. paradiseus* is an example, where the tail more than doubles the bird's overall length. This species, which enjoys a patchy distribution throughout India extending eastwards into Burma, also boasts a prominent crest extending from the forehead. Other species have crests that may be up to 5 inches in length.

Some drongos are more or less grey below, as with the White-bellied Drongo *D. caerulescens*, which I found quite scarce in India. Like other drongos the White-bellied is a good mimic.

Although numerous and obvious, drongos have been little studied outside museums. The roles of the sexes in the breeding cycle have not been ascertained for many species, and few nests have been described. The Black Drongo weaves a fine cup of bent grasses on to a horizontal fork, and lays three or four white or pink eggs which are spotted with brown. Incubation, which is apparently shared, takes some two weeks and both parents feed the young. Breeding drongos are highly aggressive and will attack other species that come too close to their nest. Hawks are pursued unmercifully and even human intruders are beaten off. As a result several other birds have adopted the habit of breeding near a drongo's nest to enjoy the protection that these birds afford.

Whereas most drongos are solitary and can be seen evenly spaced out along roadside telegraph wires, those species which occur in forests tend to be more gregarious. Bronzed Drongos *D. aeneus* are invariably in the van of mixed parties of birds found in the jungles of the Himalayan foothills.

The only drongo not placed in the *Dicrurus* is the small Mountain Drongo *Chaetorhynchus papuensis* which is found in New Guinea and has twelve, not ten, feathers in the tail.

A common bird of the Indian scene, the Black Drongo is most frequently seen perched along roadside posts and fences.

Wattlebirds Callaeidae

The story of the wattlebirds of New Zealand encapsulates that of so many of the birds native to these and other islands when faced by human colonization, and the inevitable introduction of a foreign fauna that follows. Three species, generally thought of as being most closely related to the starlings, Apostlebird and bowerbirds, were once widespread on the main as well as the outlying islands. They were not great fliers, finding their living on the ground or by jumping from branch to branch, and tree to tree among the forests. Within a short period of mass settlement, and particularly of the introduction of foxes and rats, the Huia *Heteralocha acutirostris* was extinct. The species was remarkable for the sexual dimorphism of

The seldom-photographed Saddleback is a member of the New Zealand wattlebird family, a group that has suffered considerably following European colonization.

the bill, being starling-like in the male and extremely long and decurved in the female. Such a difference of structure would seem to indicate a difference in ecology, but reports show that the members of a pair sometimes cooperated in obtaining beetles from dead or dying timber. The male evidently chiselled away the bark enabling the female to insert her flexible bill to obtain the food. It is to be regretted that this fascinating species was exterminated before modern field workers had had a chance to investigate fully such an unusual adaptation.

The Kokako *Callaeas cinerea*, like the other wattlebirds, is marked by two, fleshy wattles extending from the sides of the gape. These are orange in the North Island subspecies and blue in the South Island bird. The latter has been seen only three times in the last twenty-five years, but the North Island bird is more widespread and may be adapting to live with the threats that led to the extinction of the Huia.

The Saddleback *Creadion carunculatus* situation is grave. Once widespread, the bird is now confined to a few offshore, rat-free islands. Even these, however, are not proof against such pests and when rats got ashore on the 'muttonbird' islands off the coast of South Island, the population was decimated in a matter of months. Only the action of the Wildlife Service saved the subspecies from extinction. Birds were caught and transferred to other islands where the rats had not yet landed, and where they are now safe. But the near disaster could be repeated, and it will need an ever-watchful eye to ensure that the two remaining wattlebirds survive.

Magpie-larks Grallinidae

The magpie-larks, or mudnest-builders as they are sometimes called, inhabit the Australasian region and consist of two distinct subfamilies that apparently resemble one another only in the construction of their nests.

The Magpie-lark *Grallina cyanoleuca* is a thrush-like bird, boldly marked in black and white, that is common and widespread in Australia. Its predilection for feeding along the margins of water, as well as its dependence on mud for nest building, ensure its absence from the more arid areas of the interior, but it is common enough in the suburbs of even large cities to have acquired a special place in Australian hearts. That the birds also eat the snails that carry the noxious liver fluke, as well as taking ticks from animals, is a further cause of endearment to farmers.

The nest, which is constructed of mud reinforced with grasses, is placed on a horizontal bough and may weigh over 2 pounds. Adult birds remain in pairs on territory throughout the year and large flocks of Magpie-larks invariably consist of immature birds. Both sexes share in building the nest and in the incubation and care of the young.

The Torrent-lark *G. bruinji* is similar to the Magpie-lark but is found only along the mountainous streams of New Guinea. Little is known of its life.

The Apostlebird *Struthidea cinerea* is over a foot in length and a dull, grey, striated bird with a thick, stout bill. It inhabits the dry areas of eastern interior Australia and feeds on the ground in open country. Its mud nest is placed on a horizontal branch and is unusual in being constructed communally. Groups, invariably consisting of twelve (sometimes more) individuals – hence the common name – live together with females laying eggs in each

The Magpie-lark is a boldly pied bird of Australia that builds a substantial cup of mud as a nest. It is generally found near water.

other's nests and all the members sharing incubation and the care of the young.

White-winged Choughs *Corcorax melanorhamphus* are also communal nesters, but inhabit the damper areas of eastern Australia. Remarkable as it may seem, individual Choughs remain faithful to the group for life. Young birds join the group and simply replace older birds that die. They feed with long, decurved bills picking among leaves of the forest floor, but they also occur in more open areas and overlap the range of the Apostlebird.

Wood-swallows Artamidae

The wood-swallows, or wood-shrikes as they are often called, are aptly named, for while they are relatives of neither swallows nor shrikes, they show similarities to both of these families. Typically they sit in small, huddled groups atop some dead tree in open areas, and swoop out shrike-like on long, swallow-type wings in search of insects. Despite their somewhat stocky appearance, they are exceedingly graceful birds in the air. The long wings, which extend almost to the tip of the tail when folded, have the triangular shape of the hirundines. They flutter and swoop after insects and soar on spread wings over their favoured perch.

Wood-swallows are of Australasian origin, but they have spread

The White-breasted Wood-swallow is a gregarious bird that feeds in the manner of a hirundine. It breeds throughout Australia and migrates northwards in winter.

throughout the islands that separate that continent from the Asian mainland and one species, the Ashy Wood-swallow *Artamus fuscus*, is widespread from India to southern China. All are varying shades of grey and white, with dark face patches and lighter bills. They vary in size from 5 to 8 inches, have wide gapes and short legs in the manner of swallows and flycatchers. They are unique among passerines in having powder-down patches like the herons with which they dress their plumage.

Wood-swallows nest in stumps or in the crotch of a tree, invariably at a considerable height from the ground. The Little Wood-swallow *A. minor* of the arid Australian interior is aberrant in preferring crevices in cliffs or caves. The two to four, spotted white eggs are laid in a neat, unlined cup and incubated by both parents for twelve to sixteen days. Both birds participate in feeding the chicks and are joined by immature and unsuccessful adults in this chore. Young birds take two years to reach maturity, although they may be stimulated by rainfall to breed at the age of six months.

Of the ten species, six occur in Australia and between them cover the continent. Several are migratory both there and in Burma, but some are probably better described as nomadic in their movements. They often form mixed flocks, and most species are at least loosely colonial during the breeding season. The birds also roost communally and groups of ten to fifteen birds may commonly be found huddled together. There are even reports of up to 200 birds being found roosting in a tightly packed mass.

Butcherbirds Cracticidae

The family Cracticidae consists of some nine or ten species of medium- to large-sized birds of Australasia that lack a satisfactory English family name being variously called bell-magpies, crow-shrikes and song-shrikes. Fortunately the family divides easily into three distinct groups: the butcherbirds, the bell-magpies and the currawongs.

The Cracticidae are strongly built birds, varying from little under a foot to just under 2 feet in length. They have large, powerfully hooked bills, fly strongly and several species are of black, or black and white plumage. They tend to be gregarious and are invariably noisy, uttering some of the most characteristic of Australian natural sounds.

The butcherbirds of the genus *Cracticus* are the most numerous species. They are shrike-like, with the habit of impaling their prey on thorns in the manner of those birds. They are essentially tree-dwelling birds, although they are by no means confined to forests and frequently swoop to the ground in true shrike manner in search of prey. They are thick-set birds, with large heads and strongly hooked bills. They feed on large insects, as well as on small birds and mammals, and are predominantly black, white and grey in colour. They are noted for their beautiful songs, and some writers consider the Pied Butcherbird *C. nigrogularis* to be a contender for the title of the world's greatest songster. Butcherbirds are strongly territorial and will drive off other species and attack human intruders.

The Bell-magpie *Gymnorhina tibicen* is a bird of more open areas, and one of the most obvious of birds in the agricultural regions of Australia. It occurs in various forms, white-backed and black-backed, which were formerly regarded as distinct species. These birds feed largely on the ground on a diet of insects and small reptiles, eked out with occasional carrion. They have a strongly developed sense of territory and are aggressive to their own kind as well as to humans. Their bell-like songs, often produced in chorus, are familiar throughout much of Australia.

Currawongs are large, black birds reminiscent of crows, with areas of white in the rather long tail. Two species of currawongs are now generally recognized, but there is considerable variation in

The Grey Butcherbird is a shrike-like inhabitant of Australia that impales its prey on thorns to form a larder in the way of those birds.

plumage characters and the two are best distinguished by song. That of the Black Currawong *Strepera graculina* is responsible for the vernacular 'currawong', whereas the Grey Currawong *S. versicolor* utters a bell-like note.

Both are forest birds of eastern Australia that take a variety of foods from insects and mammals to birds and their eggs. They form flocks during the winter, but are typically territorial during the breeding season. The nest is placed in a fork of a tree.

Bowerbirds Ptilinorhynchidae

The bowerbirds and birds of paradise perform some of the most elaborate courtship displays of all birds. The families are closely related and share the same range in New Guinea and northern Australia but, while the male birds of paradise attract mates by the most remarkable dancing and show of finery, male bowerbirds construct special courting grounds to secure themselves a female. Indeed, though the behaviour and biology of this family is remarkably little known, the structures that they build are a constant source of fascination to everyone with an interest in birds.

Two bowerbirds, commonly called catbirds, of the genus *Ailuroedus* do not build bowers at all. A close relative, the Tooth-billed Catbird or Stagemaker *Scenopoeetes dentirostris*, clears an arena which it then covers with freshly plucked leaves. Other, and more typical, bowerbirds build a variety of bowers which fall

Attracted by the decorated bower of a male, this female Satin Bowerbird pauses before the entrance to the male's playground. As can be seen, this bowerbird has a particular preference for blue objects.

into roughly two types: a maypole type and an avenue type. The former consists of a central pole around which the bird places a pile of twigs which may grow to a height of nearly ten feet and resemble nothing less than a small native hut. The latter type is an avenue of twigs with brightly coloured objects gathered and placed at either end. All of these birds, save only the Golden Bowerbird *Priondura newtoniana*, are confined to the forests of New Guinea and are little known.

The male Golden Bowerbird is some $9\frac{1}{2}$ inches in length and vividly coloured in golden yellow and brown. His mate, like other female bowerbirds, is much duller, being brown above and grey below. Immatures are similar to the female in colour. It takes some three or four years for the birds to reach sexual maturity – an unusual length of time for passerines.

Golden Bowerbirds are found only on a few scattered mountains above 2,500 feet in northern Queensland and then only in the heart of thick, forested country. The male chooses two

saplings and constructs his major maypole around one. This normally grows to a height of four or five feet, but frequently higher. The secondary pole is similarly covered, but to a lesser height. The whole is decorated with lichen, and the display perch between the two poles with pale flowers.

On this elaborate perch the male sings and displays in a fluttering manner to the female whenever she appears. After mating the female goes off on her own to build the nest, lay the eggs and hatch and care for the young, the male taking no further interest in the proceedings. Like the other bowerbirds, the Golden is a very accomplished mimic, and accurately repeats most of the songs of other birds found in the adjacent forest.

Best known of the bowerbirds, however, are the various species of avenue-builders of the genera *Ptilonorhynchus*, *Chlamydera* and *Sericulus*. These birds cover the cleared ground with a shallow platform of twigs, and then construct an avenue of vertical interwoven twigs which may sweep upwards to meet at the top and reach a considerable height. At each end the birds gather together a collection of objects that are gaily coloured, often blue and sometimes shiny. My friends Hans and Judy Beste discovered a Spotted Bowerbird *Chlamydera maculata* that had stolen five pounds of roofing nails to lay out at the entrances to its bower. Each nail, and there were hundreds of them, had been carried from a farmer's barn over a quarter of a mile away. Their partiality towards shiny objects has led this species to gather glass and coins as well as natural objects. Spotted Bowerbirds often construct several bowers within a few yards of one another.

The Satin Bowerbird *Ptilonorhynchus violaceus*, in contrast, has a preference for blue objects with which to decorate its playground. At one end of the avenue it will gather blue flowers and berries, snail shells and bones, but given a chance it will add blue bottle-tops – a particular favourite – and pieces of plastic.

The Bestes, who were busily filming one male Satin Bowerbird, moved some of the objects that it had so carefully placed on its playground. Within minutes the bird returned and, with much

The brightly coloured Regent Bowerbird is found only in the dense forests of eastern Australia. It is one of the less well known of the avenue builders.

clucking, put each back in its original place. A similar experiment with a Tooth-billed Catbird consisted of turning over all the leaves, that the bird had carefully placed upside down, to show their shiny surface. Within minutes the bird returned and quickly rectified the situation. The process was repeated several times, but always with the same reaction from the bird.

The avenue-builders are apparently never satisfied with their handiwork. They will bring new sticks for their bowers and will, on occasion, tear down a wall and completely rebuild it. They also have the curious habit of painting their avenues with the juices of berries. Having squashed the berries in the bill they draw the twigs of the bower between the open mandibles so that they are covered and stained. Some authors report that Satin Bowerbirds will, at times, use a wad of bark as a brush, one of the very few examples of tool using among animals.

The point of this elaborate building is to attract a mate, and when a female approaches, the male bowerbird immediately begins to display. He dances round and round the bower, which is the centre of his attention, and does not approach the female. Such displays may continue for weeks before the female reaches breeding condition, enters the bower and shows her willingness to mate. Only this invitation triggers the male bowerbird to transfer his devotions from his playthings to the female.

Various explanations have been offered for this strange, indeed unique, behaviour pattern. Perhaps most likely it is a displacement activity stemming from the fact that most male passerines build nests. In this case the male takes no part in nesting, but builds a bower instead. Certainly for much of the courtship period, which may be very extended, the male bowerbird pays more attention to his bower than he does to his potential mate.

Bowerbirds vary in size from 9 to 14 inches. They have short wings and tails, but strong legs, and bills which are often slightly hooked. They spend most of their time among trees and feed predominantly on fruit, with an admixture of insects. They are mainly bright in colour with many species boasting patches of orange or red in the plumage. Several species have colourful crests or ruffs that are raised in display.

Birds of paradise Paradisaeidae

The first birds of paradise reached Europe with the explorer Magellan and so astonished the Spaniards that they thought that they must have come from paradise. Indeed, though the trade in their skins increased, it was not until 1824 that it was discovered that the birds came from the forests of New Guinea and its adjacent islands. Within a few years vast numbers of skins were being imported to the excitement of contemporary ornithologists and the delight of fashionable ladies, whose hats they were to adorn. Fortunately changes in fashion and restrictions in New Guinea stopped the trade before it was too late, but one can understand the fascination created by the immensely beautiful plumes of these birds.

There are about forty birds of paradise and they are the most colourful and beautiful birds in the world. While some are simply black decorated only with iridescence and wattles, others are fabulously colourful with elongated plumes and streamers that take on the most bizarre shapes. Whereas the more sombrely coloured birds are monogamous forming a permanent and exclusive pair bond, others are polygamous, the male taking no part in the reproductive cycle save mating. The gaudy plumes are used as signals to attract the females, but the displaying and posturing are so elaborate that the usual description of 'dance' is totally inadequate to describe them.

Some birds display in the tree tops, whereas others clear a space on the forest floor on which to perform. Some display communally, like manakins and grouse, while yet others hang upside down from a branch to show their finery to effect. The females of these species are invariably dull in plumage and totally different in appearance, a factor, no doubt, which helps to explain the high percentage of wild hybrids that occurs among this family, and which the highly developed plumes and ritualized display seek to overcome.

Birds of paradise are medium to large birds and essentially arboreal, feeding on fruit, insects and amphibians. Their nearest relatives are the bowerbirds from which they differ little in structure, but considerably in behaviour. It is no accident that the two families share a remarkably similar distribution.

Most familiar of these birds are the larger species of the genus *Paradisaea* found among the coastal forests of New Guinea. The Raggiana Bird of Paradise *P. raggiana* is a fine, maroon bird with a golden crown and emerald green face and about 18 inches in length. Its red plumes extend in bushes from its flanks and form a gentle curve when the wings are raised in display. A near relative, the Emperor of Germany's Bird of Paradise *P. gulieimi*, sways to and fro on its perch until it gradually topples forward and hangs upside down while continuing the performance.

The 13-inch Twelve-wired Bird of Paradise *Seleucidis melanoleuca*

has yellow plumes extending from the flanks. In display the wings are raised to allow these soft plumes to shimmer, while a green chin patch spreads into a heart-shaped fan. Most remarkable of all, however, are the six wire-like feather shafts that extend from the

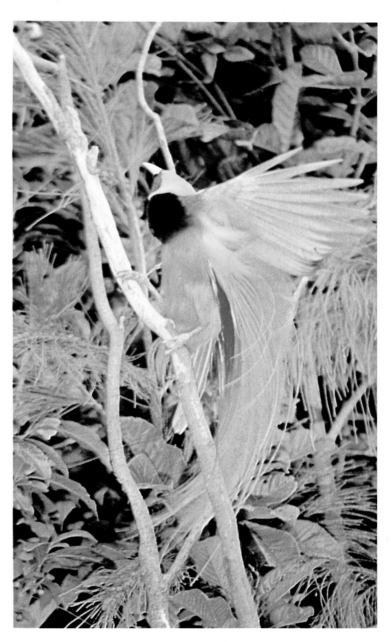

The Greater Bird of Paradise displays its finery to advantage. This is one of the better known and easier to see members of this New Guinea family.

flank plumes and bend forwards towards the head.

Several species have 'wire-tails' including the fine, red Little King Bird of Paradise *Cicinnurus regius* whose long wires end in twisted discs of feathers; and the Magnificent Bird of Paradise *Diphyllodes magnificus* whose gold and green plumage terminates in two purple 'wires' extending lyre-shaped from the centre of its tail. The Blue Bird of Paradise *Paradisaea rudolphi*, whose plumes and wings are differing shades of blue, shows its 'tail-wires' to advantage by displaying upside down.

The gold and black King of Saxony Bird of Paradise *Pteridophora alberti* is only 8 inches in length but from its nape extend two wide plumes fully 18 inches long. These birds live high among trees in the interior, and are greatly prized for their feathers by native tribesmen who favour the plumes as nose decorations. This species displays communally and the gathering grounds are kept strictly secret by the tribesmen. Longest of all is the Ribbon-tailed Bird of Paradise *Astrapia mayeri* whose tail feathers stream some 3 feet behind it. This bird was not discovered until 1938, and even then was described from a few tail feathers that were adorning the head of a native tribesman.

Even apparently dull birds can suddenly become quite startling during display. The Superb Bird of Paradise *Lophorina superba* is an all-black bird with a touch of iridescence on the breast as it feeds among the trees. During courtship, however, the breast feathers spread into a wide fan, as wide as the bird is long, while those of the back are raised to form an even larger cape.

Only two species of birds of paradise occur both in New Guinea and Australia. One of these, the Magnificent Riflebird *Ptiloris magnificus*, so called because of its 'rifle-crack' call, is a large, blue bird that spreads its rounded wings in display to form a huge shield. The head is then slowly bent backwards and moved from side to side at gathering speed.

Not surprisingly most of our knowledge of the behaviour of birds of paradise has been gleaned from the study of birds in captivity. Some species are so rare that the little information we have is based on a few museum skins. Doubtless the situation will improve as central New Guinea is opened up and developed for minerals and agriculture. But herein lies the danger. The more accessible these birds become, the stronger the likelihood of their being destroyed as the twentieth century fells the forests in which they live.

Crows Corvidae

Placed at the end of the list by most modern systematists, crows are the most advanced and intelligent of birds. They are also among the most successful and familiar to the countryman virtually throughout the world. Crows are as common in nursery rhymes as they are in history, and as much a subject of folklore and legend as any other avian family. Magpies are noted for their thieving, Jackdaws for their intelligence, crows for their fearlessness, while Britain is said to be doomed if the Raven *Corvus corvus* ceases to live in the Tower of London. The reasons for assigning such powers to the crows are not difficult to deduce. Despite endless persecution they have proved an enormously successful family; they are absent only from New Zealand and Polynesia. The more obvious species are black, and country people have always surrounded black cats and birds with a certain magic. Several species exhibit a high level of social behaviour that is otherwise unknown in the bird world. Above all it is perhaps the craftiness of the crows that country people so admire. Many species live in close contact with man, but they seldom if ever lose their lack of trust.

The 103 species can be subdivided into typical crows, jays, magpies and smaller, more specialized groups such as choughs and nutcrackers. They are highly adaptable birds taking a wide variety of foods and changing from one to another according to time, place and season. They will eat fruit, berries and seeds, small mammals and young birds, and are not averse to carrion. The predilection shown by many species for rubbish tips is indicative of their opportunism, and I have seen House Crows *C. splendens* behaving like oxpeckers on the backs of domestic buffalo in India.

Crows are large birds, and indeed the Raven is the largest of all passerines. The bill is powerful, often slightly hooked, and quite long. The legs and feet are strong and most crows walk well and run with an ungraceful cantering action. They also fly well, although wing shape varies from long and pointed to short and rounded, depending on life style. Many species feed on the ground and successfully drive larger birds away from food. It is perhaps this aggressiveness, rather than their shape, that makes small birds mob them in the manner of hawks. The sexes are similar and, although the male takes no part in incubation, he does feed his mate on the nest and takes a full share in feeding the young.

Nests, which are bulky structures of twigs often bound together with mud, are placed in trees and bushes, or on cliffs and buildings. Eggs vary in number from two to nine and incubation may take up to three weeks. The chicks hatch blind and helpless

and fledging takes some three to six weeks.

Crows are often highly social, nesting in colonies like the Rook *C. frugilegus* which has given its name (rookeries) to all colonies of birds, and even some mammals. These birds inevitably nest high in the tree tops, usually near the centre of a village. Jackdaws *C. monedula*, in contrast, are hole-nesters, and while their natural habitat is sea and inland cliffs, they have been able to spread into new areas by the adoption of buildings, and in particular churches, as cliff substitutes. Within a colony a remarkable level of peace is achieved. Occasionally a bird will challenge the peck order, but if a serious fight develops between two members the rest will move in to keep the peace. Nevertheless the colony will not tolerate intruding Jackdaws and unite to drive them away.

Some northern crows do perform quite lengthy migrations. Hooded Crows *C. corone cornix*, a race of the Carrion Crow *C.c. corone*, regularly winter in southern England hundreds of miles from their nearest breeding grounds. I have seen parties of Jays *Garrulus glandarius* flying over the office blocks of central London in autumn, while nutcrackers *Nucifraga* species irrupt irregularly into areas at least 1,000 miles from their normal range. However, most crows are sedentary and subject, at the very most, to short, hard-weather movements.

The typical crows of the genus *Corvus* are the largest and most advanced of all. They are generally black in colour with some species having a more or less glossy sheen, while others have an admixture of grey or white. They are found throughout the range of the family, save South America. The Carrion Crow is typically pugnacious and partly rapacious. It feeds mainly on the ground and nests high in trees or on cliff ledges. While it has penetrated central London it nevertheless remains wary of man and will seldom allow a close approach. Though they occupy distinct ranges, the two subspecies interbreed quite freely in areas of overlap.

While Carrion Crows are invariably solitary, their close relative the Rook is essentially gregarious. Not only do Rooks nest colonially, but they feed in flocks and are particularly dependent on arable land where they frequently gather in large numbers. The two species often confuse the layman, but the Rook is a smaller bird with a bare area of grey skin surrounding the base of the bill.

Opposite Steller's Jay inhabits the Rocky Mountain system from the Aleutians to Panama where it frequents coniferous forests. It is larger than most other North American jays.

Opposite An Alpine Chough soars over its mountainous home against a dramatic backdrop of the Swiss Alps.

Above Two House Crows. Tame and bold throughout the Oriental region, they frequent streets, gardens, rubbish tips and even the backs of buffalo. House Crows are never found away from human habitation.

The large Raven is a bird of wild places enjoying a Holarctic distribution. Its size, heavy head and bill, and wedge-shaped tail easily distinguish it from the other all-black species. It nests on cliffs and is quite common in some coastal areas where seabirds and their eggs and young ensure an adequate supply of food. Although hated by sheep farmers, the Raven is probably guilty only of consuming the afterbirths and still-born lambs. Certainly its depredations on healthy, young lambs have been overstated.

Several other ravens occur in the drier and more rugged parts of Africa. The White-necked Raven *C. albicollis* has a particularly heavy bill and is marked by a white crescent on the nape. Further north the Thick-billed Raven *C. crassirostris* is found only in Ethiopia where it is a familiar sight among the high plateaux and gorges of that mountainous kingdom.

The jays are more colourful, woodland birds with rounded wings and longer tails. They are widely distributed, and were the first of the crows to invade the New World. A variety of species has evolved, particularly in the west, and jays are the only members of the family to have spread as far as South America. The widespread Common Jay is found from Europe to South-East Asia and occurs in a variety of forms, all of which boast a colourful patch of blue and black feathers at the bend of the wing, that are favoured by fishermen as hat decorations. Like other members of the family they are notable hoarders and are particularly fond of hiding away autumn acorns as a hedge against hard times to come. Calculations show that, following the last Ice Age, oak forests spread northwards at the amazing rate of a mile a year, a rate that can only be explained by accidental plantings by the hoarding behaviour of these birds.

The jays of North America are predominantly blue or grey in colour. The Blue Jay *Cyanositta cristata* is pale blue above with finely barred blue and black wings and tail. It boasts a blue crest and a white face bordered with a ring of black. Found east of the Rocky Mountains this species has spread into city parks and gardens.

The Magpie *Pica pica* is one of the few species that occurs both in Europe and North America. Its pied plumage gives it its name, but this has been freely applied to many other species that similarly boast long tails, but which completely lack black and white plumage. The Magpie is a solitary bird of woodland that builds a large, domed nest among dense vegetation. The Azure-winged Magpie *Cyanopica cyanus*, while being similar in shape to the Magpie, is a delicately marked pink and blue bird with a black head. Its distribution is quite remarkable, for while it is not uncommon among the cork oaks and forests of Spain and Portugal it breeds otherwise only in China and Japan on the other side of the world. Doubtless these are relics of a once more continuous range.

The two choughs are alpine birds, that live up to the highest altitudes and generally appear in tightly knit flocks. They are excellent fliers and soar and dive in the sky, high against the precipitous cliffs where they nest. While the Red-billed Chough *Pyrrhocorax pyrrhocorax* is found around sea cliffs as well as in mountainous areas, the Yellow-billed *P. graculus* is confined to higher altitudes. Himalayan climbers regularly report these birds around their highest camps in the rarified air of 25,000 feet.

The nutcrackers are among the more specialized members of the Corvidae. They live in coniferous forests and are largely dependent on the seeds of pines for their existence. The boldly spotted Nutcracker *Nucifraga caryocatactes* is replaced in western North America by the grey Clark's Nutcracker *N. columbianus*.

Bibliography

Birdwatching

Alden, Peter, *Finding the Birds in Western Mexico*, Univ. Arizona Press, Tucson, 1969.

Fisher, James, *Watching Birds*, Penguin, Middx, 1941. *The Shell Bird Book*, Ebury Press and Michael Joseph, London, 1966.

Fitter, R.S.R., *Collins Guide to Bird Watching*, Collins, London, 1963.

Gooders, John, *Where to Watch Birds*, Deutsch, London, 1967. *Where to Watch Birds in Europe*, Deutsch, London, 1970. *The Bird-watcher's Book*, David and Charles, Devon, 1974.

Gooders, John, and Alden, Peter, *World Guide to Birds* (in prep.)

Lister M., *The Bird-watcher's Reference Book*, Phoenix, London, 1956.

Peterson, Roger Tory, and Fisher, James, *Wild America*, Collins, London, 1956.

Pettingill, Olin Sewall, *A Guide to Bird Finding*, 2 vols, Oxford Univ. Press, New York, 1951–1953.

Smith, Stuart, *How to Study Birds*, Collins, London, 1945.

Biology and behaviour

Howard, E., *Territory in Bird Life*, Collins Fontana, London, 1964.

Lack, D., *The Life of the Robin*, Witherby, London, 1943. *Enjoying Ornithology*, Methuen, London, 1965. *Population Studies of Birds*, Clarendon, Oxford, 1966.

Lorenz, K.Z., *King Solomon's Ring*, Crowell, New York, 1952.

Meinertzhagen, R., *Pirates and Predators*, Oliver and Boyd, London, 1959.

Selous, E., *Realities of Bird Life*, Constable, London, 1927.

Smith, S., *The Yellow Wagtail*, Collins, London, 1950.

Tinbergen, N., *The Herring Gull's World*, Collins, London, 1953.

Monographs on groups and species

Alexander, W.B., *Birds of the Ocean*, Putnam, London, 1955.

Allen, R.P., *The Roseate Spoonbill*, Nat. Aud. Soc., New York, 1942.

Brown, Leslie, and Amadon, Dean, *Eagles, Hawks and Falcons of the World*, 2 vols, Country Life, London, 1968.

Delacour, Jean, *The Waterfowl of the World*, 4 vols, Country Life, London, 1954–1964.

Fisher, James, *The Fulmar*, Collins, London, 1952.

Fisher, James, and Lockley, R.M., *Seabirds*, Collins, London, 1954.

Forshaw, Joseph M., *Parrots of the World*, Lansdowne, Melbourne, 1973.

Gilliard, E. Thomas, *Birds of Paradise and Bowerbirds*, Weidenfeld and Nicholson, London, 1969.

Goodwin, Derek, *Pigeons and Doves of the World*, Brit. Mus. (Nat. Hist.), London, 1967.

Greenewalt, C.H., *Hummingbirds*, Doubleday, New York, 1960.

World

Austin, Oliver L., Jnr., *Birds of the World*, Hamlyn, London, 1962.

Fisher, James, and Peterson, Roger Tory, *The World of Birds*, MacDonald, London, 1964.

Gooders, John (Editor), *Birds of the World*, 9 vols, IPC, London, 1969–1971.

Peters, James Lee, et al, *Check-list of Birds of the World*, Harvard Univ. Press, 1931–

Thomson, A. Landsborough, *A New Dictionary of Birds*, Nelson, London, 1964.

Vincent, Jack, *Red Data Book – Aves*, IUCN, Morges, 1966.

Europe and Asia

Ali, Salim, and Ripley, Dillon S., *Handbook of the Birds of India and Pakistan*, 10 vols, Oxford Univ. Press, London, 1968–

Bannerman, D.A., and W.M., *Birds of Cyprus*, Oliver and Boyd, London, 1958. *Birds of the Atlantic Islands*, Oliver and Boyd, London, 1963–1968.

Benson, S. Vere, *Birds of Lebanon*, ICBP, London, 1970.

Brunn, Bertel, *The Hamlyn Guide to Birds of Britain and Europe*, Hamlyn, London, 1970.

Dementiev, T.N., et al, *Birds of the Soviet Union*, 6 vols, Israel Program for Scientific Translations, Jerusalem, 1966–1968.

Heinzel, Herman, et al, *The Birds of Britain and Europe*, Collins, London, 1972.

Henry, G.M., *Birds of Ceylon*, Oxford Univ. Press, London, 1955.

Moreau, R.E., *The Palearctic-African Bird Migration Systems*, Academic Press, London, 1972.

Peterson, Roger Tory, et al, *A Field Guide to the Birds of Britain and Europe*, Collins, London, 1954.

Smythies, B.E., *The Birds of Burma*, Oliver and Boyd, London, 1953. *The Birds of Borneo*, Oliver and Boyd, London, 1960.

Vaurie, C., *Birds of the Palearctic Fauna*, 2 vols, Witherby, 1959–1965. *Tibet and its Birds*, Witherby, London, 1972.

Voous, K.H., *Atlas of European Birds*, Nelson, London, 1960.

Witherby, H.F., et al, *Handbook of British Birds*, 5 vols, Witherby, London, 1938–1941.

North America

Bent, A.C., *Life Histories of North American Birds*, Am. Mus. Nat. Hist., New York, 1915–1958.

Godfrey, W. Earl, *The Birds of Canada*, Nat. Mus. Canada, Ottawa, 1966.

Palmer, Ralph S., *Handbook of North American Birds*, Yale, New Haven, 1962.

Peterson, Roger Tory, *A Field Guide to the Birds*, Houghton Mifflin, Boston, 1934. *A Field Guide to Western Birds*, Houghton Mifflin, Boston, 1941. *A Field Guide to the Birds of Texas*, Houghton Mifflin, Boston, 1960.

Robbins, Chandler, et al, *The Golden Guide to Birds*, Golden Press, New York, 1966.

Central and South America

Bond, James, *Birds of the West Indies*, Collins, London, 1960.

De Schauensee, Meyer R., *The Birds of Columbia*, Livingstone, Norberth, Pennsylvania, 1964. *The Birds of South America*, Livingstone, Wynnewood, Pennsylvania, 1970.

Eisenmann, E., *The Species of Middle American Birds*, Trans.Linn. Soc., New York, 1955.

Haverschmidt, F., *Birds of Surinam*, Oliver and Boyd, London, 1968.

Murphy, R.C., *Oceanic Birds of South America*, 2 vols, MacMillan, New York, 1936.

Wetmore, A., *The Birds of the Republic of Panama*, Smithsonian Institute, Washington, 1968.

Australia and Oceania

Cayley, N.W., *What Bird is That?*, Angus and Robertson, Sydney, 1931.

Mayr, E., *Birds of the South-west Pacific*, MacMillan, New York, 1945.

Rand, Austin L., and Gilliard, Thomas E., *Handbook of New Guinea Birds*, Weidenfeld and Nicholson, London, 1967.

Slater, P., et al, *A Field Guide to Australian Birds*, Oliver and Boyd, Edinburgh, 1970.

Africa

Bannerman, D.A., *Birds of West and Equatorial Africa*, 2 vols, Oliver and Boyd, Edinburgh, 1951–1953.

Benson, C.W., et al, *The Birds of Zambia*, Collins, London, 1971.

Cave, F.O., and MacDonald, J.D., *Birds of the Sudan*, Oliver and Boyd, Edinburgh, 1955.

Chapin, James P., *The Birds of the Belgian Congo*, 4 vols, Bull.Am. Mus.Nat.Hist., New York, 1932–1954.

Etchecopar, R.D., and Hüe, F., *The Birds of North Africa*, Oliver and Boyd, London, 1967.

Hall, B.P., and Moreau, R.E., *An Atlas of Speciation in African Passerine Birds*, Brit.Mus.(Nat.Hist.), London, 1970.

Mackworth-Praed, C.W., and Grant, C.H.B., *African Handbook of Birds*, 6 vols, Longmans, London, 1952–1973.

McLachlan, G.R., and Liversidge, R., *Roberts Birds of South Africa*, Trustees John Voeleker Bird Bk.Fd., Cape Town, 1970.

Williams, J.S., *A Field Guide to the Birds of East and Central Africa*, Collins, London, 1963.

Index

347

Acknowledgements

A.F.A: Herbert 161, Tuevo Suominen 99; D.G.ALLAN 207; F.G.H.ALLEN 282 bottom; HEATHER ANGEL 26, 27 top left, 27 bottom left, 123 top; ANTARCTIC SURVEY: Tilbrook 159; ARDEA PHOTOGRAPHICS: 134, 211, F.Balat 287 left, U.Berggren 200, 286 top, Hans Beste 33, 190, 245, B.C.Bevan 272, P.Blasdale 132, R.J.C.Blewitt 145, 293, 294, R.Bloomfield 143, 144, 156 right, 213 top left, 216, 217, 298, 322, J.B. & S.Bottomley 40 top left, 150, 229, 264, G.J.Broekhuysen 96 bottom left, L.H. Brown 51, 76, 96 top left, 154, Donald Burgess 308, Elizabeth Burgess 269, K.J.Carlson 100, 153, 259, 303, G.Chapman 175 top left, 180, 208, 236, 287 right, 333 bottom, 334, I.Curphey 37, W. Curth 21, 192/193, 250, 251, J.S.Dunning 35, 221, 230, 232, 234, 305 top left, M.D.England 102 top left, 110, 127, 135, 138/139, 209 left, 215 top right, 252, 280 top left, 280 bottom, 282 top, 295, 331, K.Fink 228, 231, 242, 243, 300, 339, Clem Haagner 31, Don Hadden 47 top right, 142 top right, Edgar T. Jones 148 bottom, 186/187, 197, Eric Lindgren 178 right, 215 bottom, E.McNamara 246, 286 bottom, 289, 333 top, 335, 336, E.Mickleburgh 44, P.Morris 69 bottom, 194, 196 top, Christopher Mylne 106, 263, R.F.Porter 75, S.Roberts 290, 316, R.T.Smith 292, P.Steyn 210, W.R.Taylor 296, 299, Richard Vaughan 28 bottom right, 270, J.P.Voisin 46 top left, Adrian Warren 59 top, 123 bottom, John S.Wightman 11, 28 top right, 73, 81 top, 84 top, 84 bottom left, 297, 326 top; TOM BANKS 38/39; MICHAEL BARRINGTON-MARTIN 163 top; G.BEVEN 274 top; A.BLOMGREN 262; BRITISH MUSEUM (NATURAL HISTORY) 14 bottom left; BRUCE COLEMAN LTD: Albrecht 304, Des Bartlett 53, 71 top left, 87 top, Beamish 166 top right, Blackburn 268, 273, Jane Burton 307, Dermid 82 top left, 168 top, 312, Francisco Erize 158 top, 222, Fogden 325, M.P.Harris 105 right, 240, 267, 320, D.Hughes 62, Kinne 184 top, Leonard Lee Rue 131, 189, John Markham 183, 202, 225, 277 top, 321, Merton 332 top, D. Middleton 40 bottom, 167, Murton 67, 258, Charles Ott 113, 115 bottom left, J.Pearson 92 bottom right, R.T.Peterson 158 bottom, 172, Pizzey 165, Porter 266, H.Schultz 133 bottom, 224, Vincent Serventy 178 left, 209 right, J.Simon 109, 205, M.F.Soper 34, 49 bottom, 56, 238, 332 bottom, Simon Trevor 72, Joe Van Wormer 87 bottom, 117, 302; PHILIP BURTON, 19, 311; N.CHAFFER 195, 204, 274 bottom, 284; A.CHRISTIANSON 329; JACK COLES 255, 328 top left, 341; COLOUR LIBRARY INTERNATIONAL 22; CONWAY PICTURE LIBRARY 63; JOHN CRANHAM 324; G. CUBITT 10; G.DANGERFIELD 93 bottom, 181 right; EVAN DAVIS 265; HANS DOSSENBACH 128, 140 bottom right, 164 top left; M.P.DRAZIN 111; CRISPIN FISHER 14 top left, 14 top right, 14 bottom right, 15 top left, 15 top right, 15 bottom left; A.D.FORBES-WATSON 277 bottom; C.HILARY FRY 212, 218 right; ROBERT GILLMOR 52, 55, 64; LUTHER GOLDMAN 291, 301; DAVID GOWANS 315; JAN GRAHAN 140 bottom left; P.J.GREEN 13, 16, 17 top left, 17 bottom left, 17 right; PAMELA HARRISON 86 top, 86 bottom right, 152; D.W. HATTON 24, 147 top, 170 right, 227; OLLE HEDVALL 188, 191, 317; GEORGE HOLTON 59 bottom right; ERIC HOSKING 23 bottom right, 41, 45, 46 bottom, 57, 59 bottom left, 68 bottom, 119, 121 left, 155, 157, 160, 164 bottom, 173, 201, 215 top left, 226, 247, 249, 279 left, 340; JEFF HUNT 254 left; A.M. HUTSON 68 top; JACANA: Brosselin 23 top right, 29, 50, 151 top left, 162 top, Chantelat 101 bottom left, Fievet 54 right, Guinion 32 top, C.de Klemm 156 left, Marc Lelo 28 top left, Molinier 162 bottom, Montoya 114, Robert 70, F.Roux 213 bottom, Suinot 36, Summ 103, Varin, 12, 66, 69 top, 77, 146 bottom right, Vicune 146 top, 198, Vienne 54 left, 71 bottom, 101 top, 170 left, 171, Visage 32 bottom, 94, 121 right, 126; E.E.JACKSON 78, 80 bottom, 83, 169; DR. HANS JESSE 218 left; VERNA R. JOHNSTON 90; RUSS KINNE 84 bottom right; C.DE KLEMM 105 left; FRANK W.LANE: Ronald Austing 203, 278, Georg Nystrand 98 top left, H. Schrempp 305 bottom, Zingel 79, 241; E.Laubsche 223 top; KEN LILLY 112, 179, 220; S.D.MACDONALD 115 bottom right 116; H.McSWEENEY 104; OSCAR J.MERNE 115 top; LOUISE METCALFE 239, 309; B. AND J.MORGAN 196 bottom; NATIONAL AUDUBON SOCIETY: John Bourneman 23 left, H.Cruikshank 42, Carl Koford 92 top; NEW ZEALAND HIGH COMMISSION: P.Morrison 30; NEW ZEALAND WILDLIFE SERVICE 177 bottom; N.H.P.A.: Andrew M.Anderson 58, Blackburn 107, 248, D.N.Dalton 175 bottom, Stephen Dalton 27 top right, Brian Hawkes 95 top left, 98 bottom, 319, P.Johnson 102 bottom, 176, 276, K.B.Newman 91, 122, 182, 206, 219, 326 bottom, 328 bottom, 330, Wayne 120; M.A.OGILVIE 80 top; OKAPIA 133 top, 181 left, 337; VIKING OLSSON 318; ORION PRESS: Tahashi Yoshi 74 top; PAUL POPPER 166 bottom right; KLAUS PAYSAN 82 top right; A.N.H.PEACH 260, 271, 279 right, 281, 323; PHOTO RESEARCHERS INCORPORATED: Edmund Appel 74 bottom, Kinne 184 bottom; PICTUREPOINT 49 top, 88; D.G.H.PLOWES 199, 256; RENAULT 60/61; JOHN RIGNALL 237; E.RISDEN 129; W.W.ROBERTS 96/97; N.P. SANFORD 223 bottom; PHILIPPA SCOTT 81 bottom right, 82 bottom, 85 top, 85 bottom; SCOTT-SWEDBERG PHOTOS 95 bottom; NEAL G.SMITH 313; P.O.SWANBERG 147 bottom left, 149, 283; P.SCHWARTZ 306; W.TARBOTON 288; G. TOMISCH 118 bottom; UNIVERSITY OF CANTERBURY, NEW ZEALAND: J.T.KAY 177 top; JAN VAN DE KAM 140 top, 142 bottom, 148 top right, 166 left, 168 bottom right; VERDONK 125; EDWARD WADE 20; C.A.WALKER 28 bottom left; J.WARHAM 47 bottom, 163 bottom, 185; WEHA-PHOTO, BERN 151 bottom; WENZEL 108; M.WHITEHOUSE 254 top right; WORLD WILDLIFE FUND: Noel Simon 81 bottom left; Vollman 93 top left, 118 top left; HERBERT ZETTL 25, 141.

The publishers have made every attempt to contact the owners of the photographs appearing in this book. In the few instances where they have been unsuccessful, they invite the copyright holders to contact them direct.

enjoy

Healthy recipes for family and friends

Easy to cook
and delicious to eat

With best wishes

Arlette 2019

Arlette Haddad-Boutros

enjoy

Healthy recipes for family and friends

Easy to cook
and delicious to eat

Writing and images supplied by Arlette Boutros
unless otherwise stated.

Design, editing and production: Arlette Boutros
Food preparation for photography: Arlette Boutros
Photography: Brian Would

Printed in Lebanon by Raidy Printing Group s.a.l.
ISBN 978-0-9556485-0-2
First edition

This edition © 2007
Publisher: Boutros International
www.boutrosfonts.com

The author is most grateful and wishes to thank Cecil Hourani, Ann Stepien, May Atallah and Conea Rino
for their major contributions and to thank in particular:
Raymond Atallah, Samir Atallah, Krikor Agopian, Mourad, Daniel, Mark, John and Boutros Boutros, Mark Batty, Halim Choueiry,
Dorothy and Jessy Carroll-Connell, Imad Douglas, Martha and Nicole Daw, Antoine Fadel, Huda Husseini , Leslie and David Hawes,
Salma Khan, Claudine Kesrouani, George and Abla Kandalaft, Sharon King, Jackie Maatook, Peter McCree, Samia Nelson,
Ann O'Shaughnessy, Salam Shalhoub, Bella Shapiro, Jacqueline Saleh, Samir Shbatt, Diane Twikkle, Brian Walker
and others whom I may have missed for their contributions and support.

Contents

Intoduction

I started cooking at an early age in Lebanon learning from my mother. Since then I have always enjoyed cooking and providing healthy and appetizing food for my family and friends.

I was trained and work as a graphic and design artist, and I have tried to introduce the creative spirit into the kitchen.

Over the years I have used my imagination to cook dishes based on traditional recipes but with new ingredients or tastes. There are some basic rules of chemistry and common sense which must be followed in the kitchen, but within these rules there is unlimited scope for experiment and innovation.

This book is a collection of recipes from different countries which I like and which are simple and easy to follow and cook. For example I have simplified the traditional presentation of Lebanese 'kibbeh' in two layers and made it into one without altering its taste or appearance. For some dishes traditionally cooked with meat I have substituted chicken or fish, making them lighter and healthier. I have also used olive oil instead of butter or vegetable fats.

Some of the recipes can be adapted for babies in the form of purées with suitable seasonings (which can be frozen for up to 3 months by placing in small containers, then defrosted and reheated). *Milk should be full fat for children.*

Notes

For all recipes: follow one set of measurements only (grams, ounces or cups) and not a mixture.
Standard cups and spoons measurements are level.
When using appropriate cup, shake dry ingredients loosely. Do not tap the cup.
The conversions are approximate only and will not affect the cooking results.

1 Australian standard tablespoon is 20ml. (1 cup= 250ml = 8fl oz)
Cooks in Australia should use 3 teaspoons in place of 1 tablespoon.

Oven and grill (broiler) should be preheated to the specified temperature.
If using a fan assisted oven: follow the manufacturer's instructions for adjusting the time, because fan ovens vary from manufacturer to manufacturer, or set the temperature a bit lower than stated in recipes, the cooking time will be slightly reduced and no-pre-heated is needed.

Conversions

Approx. grams to ounces and ml to cups and ounces

Dry

Metric (grams)	Imperial (ounces)
25-45 g	1-1½ oz
55-70 g	2-2½ oz
85-100 g	3-3½ oz
110-130 g	4-4½ oz (¼ lb)
140-155 g	5-5½ oz
170-185 g	6-6½ oz
198-215 g	7-7½ oz
225-240 g	8-8½ oz (½lb)
250-270 g	9-9½ oz
280-300 g	10-10½ oz
310-330 g	11-11½ oz
340-355 g	12-12½ oz
365-385 g	13-13½ oz
395-415 g	14-14½ oz
425-440 g	15-15½ oz
450-470 g	16-16½ oz (1lb)
500-525 g	18-18½ oz (1lb 2 oz)
1000 g (1 kg)	32 oz (2lb)

Liquids

Metric (millilitres)	Cup	Imperial (ounces)
30 ml		1 fl oz
60 ml	¼ cup	2 fl oz
80 ml	⅓ cup	2¾ fl oz
125 ml	½ cup	4 fl oz
150 ml	⅔ cup	5 fl oz
180 ml	¾ cup	6 fl oz
250 ml	1 cup	8 fl oz
310 ml	1¼ cups	10½ fl oz
375 ml	1½ cups	13 fl oz
430 ml	1¾ cups	15 fl oz
500 ml	2 cups	16 fl oz (1 pint)
625 ml	2½ cups	21 fl oz
700 ml	3 cups	24fl oz
1000 ml (1L)	4 cups	32fl oz
1.25L	5 cups	40fl oz
1.5L	6 cups	48fl oz
1.75L	7 cups	56fl oz
2L	8 cups	64fl oz

4

Mediterranean shopping list

Anise seeds (yansoon)
They come from anise pods and have a sweet taste. Used as well for puddings and pastries as ground anise. The seeds can also be used as tea (for relaxing) and for small children to ease, the teething pains and for digestion.

Aubergine (known also as **eggplant**).

Burghul (burgul) cracked wheat
This is made from wheat which has been boiled, dried and then ground. It is available in a variety of sizes in both brown and white.

Orange-blossom water (mazaher)
Also known as flower water. This fragrant liquid is made from the essence of bitter-orange blossoms and is used in sweet dishes as well as in white coffee by adding 1 teaspoon to 1 cup of boiling water.

Broad (fava) beans (ful-akhdar)
Available in two different varieties, large split and peeled beans and small brown beans, which can be canned or dried.
Using a falafel maker: press down the special lever and scoop out as much paste as you can with the spatula that comes with it and smooth the top carefully, then sprinkle some sesame seeds pressing very gently onto the paste. Drop into the hot oil by releasing the lever and follow as directed in page 90.

Caraway seeds (carawia)
These seeds have a warm taste and can be used ground.

Chickpeas (also known as **garbanzos,** when canned).

Courgette (known also as **zucchini**).

Coriander (known also as **cilantro**).

Mastic
Collected from the Greek pistacias lentiscus tree. It comes as small yellow pale pebbles and needs to be ground before using.

Okra (bamyeh)
Available in different sizes (the small ones are easier to cook). It can be found frozen, canned or fresh.

Pomegranate molasses (dibis al-ruman)
Made from sour pomegranate juice which is boiled until thick. to a thick consistency. Gives a nice flavouring to meat, vegetables, stuffings and sauces.

Rose water (maward)
Another fragrant liquid distilled from rose petals and is used in both savoury and sweet puddings. Use rose water by adding 1 teaspoon to a dish, too much will infuse it with bitter taste, often together with orange-blossom water.

Sumac
Sumac are ground dried berries which have a lemony flavour.

Sesame seeds
Grown in hot countries and used (raw or toasted) in pastries and with different ingredients.

Semolina
The hard part of wheat, sifted out either coarse or fine. Coarse semolina is used to make cakes and fine is used instead of flour to give a lighter texture.

Tahini (sesame paste)
It comes as a thick paste and is made from ground raw sesame seeds. (Stir the oil back to the paste before using.)

Flat wraps (pitta bread)
Available in round shapes and in different sizes. Wraps are thinner than pitta bread. Either can be used. Suitable for freezing.

Vine (grape) leaves (warak enab)
Are available fresh, packed in brine or in airtight jars. They must be cooked in boiling water until they soften.

Pepper (bell) and mushroom omelette

6

Ingredients

8 medium mushrooms, sliced
2 spring (scallions) onions finely chopped
1 green (bell) pepper, seeded and diced
1 red (bell) pepper, seeded and diced
1 medium tomato, peeled and diced
4 medium eggs, beaten with 1 teaspoon
plain (all-purpose) flour
1 tablespoon olive oil
½ teaspoon ground allspice
Salt to taste

Garnish to suit your own taste (optional)

Preparation

1 Sauté the onions and peppers in warm oil in a pan (on medium heat) for 5 minutes. Stir in the mushrooms, tomatoes and seasonings for a further 6-7 minutes or until all tender.

2 Pour in the egg mixture and cook until set and golden on both sides, turning or flipping once. Do not stir.

Note
To remove tomato skin easily: *soak in boiling water for 20-30 seconds before peeling.*

Variations
Replace the peppers with 1 thinly diced courgette.
Add 1-2 tablespoons of grated cheese (of your choice) instead of the flour.

Ideal for children

This dish should be served hot, with pitta or toasted bread

1 cup = 250ml = 8fl oz   1 tablespoon = 15ml   1 teaspoon = 5ml

Scrambled eggs with frankfurters

Ingredients

3 frankfurters, thinly sliced
5 medium eggs, beaten
2 tablespoons olive oil
1 tablespoon chopped fresh basil or thyme
2 tablespoons pine nuts (optional)
½ teaspoon ground allspice
Salt to taste

Garnish to suit your own taste (optional)

Preparation

1 Brown the pine nuts in 2 tablespoons of warm oil in a frying pan (on medium heat) stirring constantly until golden. Remove with a slotted spoon and set aside.

2 In the same pan, Sauté the frankfurters for 1-2 minutes. Stir in the eggs and seasonings until cooked to your liking.

3 Transfer to a platter and sprinkle the pine nuts and basil.

Note
To prepare this dish as an omelette: *whisk the eggs with the seasonings, then pour over the frankfurters and leave to set, turning or flipping once.*

Ideal for children

This dish should be served hot, with green salad or bread

1 cup = 250ml = 8fl oz   1 tablespoon = 15ml   1 teaspoon = 5ml

Calf or chicken liver

10

Ingredients

400g/14oz calf or chicken liver, diced
2 garlic cloves, crushed
2 tablespoons olive oil
½ teaspoon ground allspice
1 tablespoon lemon juice
Salt to taste

Garnish to suit your own taste (optional)

Preparation

1 Sauté the liver together with the seasonings in warm oil in a pan (on medium heat) until cooked to your liking.

2 Stir in the garlic and lemon juice for 10-20 seconds. Do not reheat.

Variations
Stir in 1 tablespoon of pomegranate molasses (page 5) with the garlic mixture.
Marinate the liver with the seasonings and garlic for 1-2 hours, then cook over charcoal and serve hot, adding 1 tablespoon of lemon juice, if desired.

Ideal for children

This dish should be served immediately, with bread

1 cup = 250ml = 8fl oz   *1 tablespoon = 15ml*   *1 teaspoon = 5ml*

Sautéed eggs and potatoes

Ingredients

4 medium potatoes, peeled and finely diced
5 medium eggs, beaten
2 tablespoons olive oil
½ teaspoon ground allspice
Salt to taste

Garnish to suit your own taste (optional)

Preparation

1 Sauté the potatoes in warm oil in a pan (on medium heat) until golden. Simmer, covered, for 15-20 minutes or until cooked but still firm, stirring occasionally.

2 Stir in the eggs and seasonings for 1-2 minutes or to your liking.

Note

To prepare this dish as an omelette: *whisk the eggs with the seasonings, then pour over the potatoes and leave to set, turning or flipping once.*

Ideal for children

This dish should be served hot, with vegetables or bread

1 cup = 250ml = 8fl oz   *1 tablespoon = 15ml*   *1 teaspoon = 5ml*

12

If using a fan assisted oven (page 4)

Tiger prawns (shrimp) in garlic sauce

14

Ingredients

8-12 fresh tiger prawns (shrimp)
1 large tomato, sliced

Dressing
4 tablespoons olive oil
2 tablespoons lemon juice
2 garlic cloves, crushed
Pepper and salt to taste

Garnish to suit your own taste (optional)

Preparation

1 *To clean the prawns:* remove the heads and pull out the black thread along the back by making a slit with a knife.

2 Mix the dressing ingredients together in a bowl. Set aside.

3 Place the prawns in a lightly-greased baking dish. Brush with the dressing and bake in a preheated oven at 200°C/400°F/Gas 6 for 20-30 minutes, brushing and turning occasionally until cooked to your liking. Or grill (broil) under a medium heat for 7-10 minutes.

4 Transfer to a platter and serve with the sliced tomatoes.

Variation
Replace the green leaves with seeded and quartered 1 red and 1 green (bell) pepper by baking or grilling (broiling) together with the prawns until cooked but not burnt.

This dish should be served hot

1 cup = 250ml = 8fl oz   1 tablespoon = 15ml   1 teaspoon = 5ml

If using a fan assisted oven (page 4)

16

Roast duck with honey

Ingredients

3 large duck breasts
4 tablespoons clear honey, mixed with 1 tablespoon dark soy sauce
5 spring onions (scallions), halved widthways, then sliced lenghtways
2 small cucumbers, halved widthways, then cut into thin sticks
10-12 Chinese pancakes, for crispy duck or mini flour tortillas
4 tablespoons dark soy sauce
4 tablespoons hoi-sin or plum sauce

Garnish to suit your own taste (optional)

Preparation

1 Place the duck in a colander and pour over 1 litre (4 cups) of boiling water. Leave in a cool place overnight, covered with kitchen paper.

2 *The next day:* prick the duck in several places with a fork and place on a wire rack in a baking dish with hot water to come half way up the dish without touching the wire rack (or the duck).

3 Bake in a preheated oven at 200°C/400°F/Gas 6 for 30-40 minutes or until cooked in the inside and crisp on the outside, turning occasionally and brushing with honey mixture. (Or cover with kitchen foil, leaving the bottom free and bake at 240°C/475°F/Gas 9 until well done and crisp.) Remove the duck, then cut into strips, discarding the skin and bones.

To serve

Mix the soy and hoi-sin (or plum) sauces together in a serving bowl.
Follow the pancakes pack instructions (or warm in a steamer).
Spread 1-2 teaspoons of the mixed sauce, on each pancake.
Fill with a few duck strips, top with some of the cucumbers and onions.
Roll and serve while still hot.

Note

To make your own pancakes: *Mix 280g/10oz of plain (all-purpose) flour, 1 cup of boiling water and knead into a dough. Cover and leave to stand for 30 minutes. Form into a long sausage roll, then cut into 1 inch (25mm) pieces and form into balls. Take 2 balls at a time and brush one side of one ball with sesame oil and place the oiled side on top of the other ball. Roll together into 5 inch (about 12cm) circle and dry fry in a non-stick hot pan for 5-7 seconds on each side, turning once. Cool, then peel each 2 pancakes apart to make thin ones.*

This dish should be served immediately

1 cup = 250ml = 8fl oz   1 tablespoon = 15ml   1 teaspoon = 5ml

Sesame prawn (shrimp) toasts

Ingredients

1 medium egg, beaten
250g/9oz cooked prawns (shrimp), finely chopped
1 teaspoon cornflour (cornstarch)
4 tablespoons sesame seeds
Cooking oil, for deep frying
4 medium slices wholemeal (or white) bread
Pepper and salt to taste

Garnish to suit your own taste (optional)

18

Preparation

1 Mix the prawns, egg, cornflour, pepper and salt together in a bowl. Spread evenly over the slices of bread, then sprinkle with sesame seeds, pressing with the back of a spoon.

2 Deep fry (prawn mixture side up first) in hot oil (on medium heat). Turn over and cook until golden and crisp on both sides.

3 Drain on kitchen paper. Cut each slice of toast in half, then each half into 3-4 pieces widthways or into 4 triangles.

Variations
Replace the medium bread slices with thin ones.
Replace the prawns with 280g/10oz of very finely chopped chicken breast fillets.

This dish should be served immediately

1 cup = 250ml = 8fl oz   1 tablespoon = 15ml   1 teaspoon = 5ml

Chicken spring rolls

Ingredients

20-25 small spring roll wrappers
200g/7oz chicken breast fillets, finely diced
2 spring (scallions) onions, finely chopped
1 large carrot, finely diced
85g/3oz/¾ cup bean sprouts (optional)
8 small mushrooms, diced
115g/4oz/1 cup shredded green cabbage
200g/7oz can sweetcorn, rinsed and drained
1 teaspoon grated ginger
2 tablespoons dark soy sauce
2 tablespoons hoi-sin sauce
2 tablespoons sesame oil
Cooking oil for deep frying

Garnish to suit your own taste (optional)

20

Preparation

1 Sauté the chicken and onions in hot sesame oil in a pan (on medium heat) for 2 minutes. Stir in the carrots and cabbage for a further 8 minutes.

2 Add the bean sprouts, mushrooms, sweetcorn and seasonings. Simmer, covered for 10-15 minutes or until cooked. Leave to cool.

3 Place 1 heaped tablespoon of the mixture along one edge of each wrapper. Fold in the sides, then roll up to make a sausage shape.

4 Brush the edges with water (or beaten egg) to seal. Carry on with the rest of the rolls. Deep fry in hot oil in batches (on medium heat) until golden.

5 Remove with a slotted spoon and drain on kitchen paper.

Note
If using frozen rolls: *defrost, then cover with kitchen towel and work with 1 roll at a time.*

Variations
Add 55g/2oz/¾ cup of dried fine egg noodles (soaked in boiling water for a few minutes and drained) or broken vermicelli, with the mushroom mixture.
Omit the chicken and serve as a vegetarian dish.

These rolls should be served immediately

1 cup = 250ml = 8fl oz   1 tablespoon = 15ml   1 teaspoon = 5ml

If using a fan assisted oven (page 4)

Chicken wings in honey sauce

22

Ingredients

8 large chicken wings, end parts removed

Sauce
1 spring (scallion) onion chopped (optional)
2 tablespoons tomato ketchup
1 cup fresh pineapple juice
3 tablespoons dark soy sauce
3 tablespoons clear honey
1 teaspoon grated ginger
1 teaspoon cornflour (cornstarch)

Garnish to suit your own taste (optional)

Preparation

1 Mix the sauce ingredients and the chicken wings together in a bowl. Cover and leave to marinate in the refrigerator for 2-4 hours or preferably overnight.

2 Arrange wings in a baking dish and bake in a preheated oven at 200°C/400°F/ Gas 6 for 30-40 minutes or until cooked to your liking, turning occasionally. Or grill (broil) under a medium heat for 12-15 minutes. Do not reheat.

Variations
Replace the chicken wings with drumsticks.
Serve with egg rice as a meal (page 88).

Ideal for children

This dish should be served immediately

1 cup = 250ml = 8fl oz   1 tablespoon = 15ml   1 teaspoon = 5ml

If using a fan assisted oven (page 4)

Feta cheese rolls

24

Ingredients

10 frozen sheets filo (phyllo) pastry, defrost
2-3 tablespoons olive oil
500g/1lb 2oz/2½ cups feta cheese, mashed
2 tablespoons chopped fresh flat-leaf parsley
2 garlic cloves, crushed
Salt to taste

Garnish to suit your own taste (optional)

Preparation

1 Cut each filo sheet into 2 pieces widthways. Cover with a tea towel to prevent from drying out.

2 Mash the cheese in a bowl to a paste and mix together with the parsley and garlic (using a fork). Place 1 heaped tablespoon of the mixture along one edge of each piece. Fold in the sides, then roll up to make a sausage shape.

3 Brush the edges with water (or beaten egg) to seal. Carry on with the rest of the pastries.

4 Brush each roll with a little oil and arrange in a baking dish. Bake in a preheated oven at 190°C/375°F/Gas 5 for 25-30 minutes or until golden and crisp, turning once. Or grill (broil) under a medium heat for 5-8 minutes.

Variations
Replace the feta cheese with 500g/1lb 2oz/2½ cups of strained yogurt or the parsley with 1-2 tablespoons of dried mint, and follow the above instructions.
Alternatively, deep fry in hot cooking oil.
Use small spring roll wrappers instead of the filo pastry.

These rolls should be served immediately

If using a fan assisted oven (page 4)

Chicken satay with peanut butter

Ingredients

400g/14oz skinless chicken breast fillets, cubed
6 tablespoons crunchy peanut butter
1 large onion, quartered
2 garlic cloves, peeled
3 tablespoons coconut cream
1 teaspoon mild curry paste
1 tablespoon clear honey (optional)
1 tablespoon dark soy sauce
2 tablespoons lime juice
1 tablespoon olive oil
Salt to taste

Garnish to suit your own taste (optional)

Preparation

1 Place all the ingredients (except the chicken cubes) in a food processor and blend to a smooth paste.

2 Transfer to a bowl adding the chicken cubes and toss well together. Cover and leave to marinate in the refrigerator for 5-6 hours or overnight.

3 Thread the chicken cubes on to wooden skewers, setting aside the remaining marinade.

4 Skewer, then barbecue or bake in a preheated oven at 200°C/400°F/Gas 6 for 25-30 minutes or until done to your liking, turning and basting with the set aside marinade. Alternatively, grill (broil) under a medium heat for 12-15 minutes.

Variation
Serve with plain (boiled) rice as a meal (page 84), or salad.

Ideal for children

This dish should be served hot

1 cup = 250ml = 8fl oz   1 tablespoon = 15ml   1 teaspoon = 5ml

Chickpeas with olive oil dressing

Ingredients

400g/14oz can chickpeas
2 garlic cloves, crushed
4 tablespoons olive oil or more to taste
1 tablespoon chopped fresh flat-leaf parsley
Salt to taste

28

Preparation

1 Empty the chickpeas in a pan and heat (on medium) for 5 minutes. Remove with a slotted spoon to a serving dish, setting aside the liquid.

2 Mix the oil, garlic, 2-3 tablespoons of the chickpea liquid and salt in a bowl. Pour over the peas and toss gently to coat. Sprinkle with the chopped parsley.

Note
Dried chickpeas have a nicer flavour than canned ones (page 34).

Variation
Empty 400g/14oz mixed can of broad (fava) beans and chickpeas in a pan and heat (on medium) for 5 minutes. Remove with a slotted spoon to a bowl, setting aside the liquid. Add 4 tablespoons of olive oil, 2-3 tablespoons of the set aside liquid, 2 crushed garlic cloves, 4 tablespoons of lemon juice and salt to taste. Toss well to mix and sprinkle with 2 tablespoons of chopped fresh flat-leaf parsley. (Adjust with lemon juice and olive oil, if necessary.)

This dish should be served hot or tepid

1 cup = 250ml = 8fl oz   1 tablespoon = 15ml   1 teaspoon = 5ml

If using a fan assisted oven (page 4)

30

Aubergines (eggplants), yogurt and nuts

Ingredients

2-3 medium aubergines (eggplants)
1 cup natural (plain) yogurt
2 garlic cloves, crushed
3 tablespoons pine nuts
Olive oil
1 teaspoon dried mint (optional)
Salt to taste

Garnish to suit your own taste (optional)

Preparation

1 Peel each aubergine leaving on a few thin black strips. Cut into ½ inch slices widthways and sprinkle with a little salt, then set aside for 10 minutes.

2 Dry with kitchen paper, then brush with oil and sauté in a non-stick hot pan in batches (on medium-low heat) until soft and browned, turning once. Or place in a greased baking dish and bake in a preheated oven at 180°C/350°F/Gas 4. Alternatively, grill (broil) under a medium heat. (Or deep fry in hot cooking oil.) Set aside.

3 Sauté the pine nuts in 2 tablespoons of warm oil in a small pan (on medium heat) stirring constantly until golden. Remove with a slotted spoon and set aside.

To serve
Arrange the aubergine pieces on a platter.
Mix the yogurt with the garlic, then pour over the centre.
Sprinkle with the dried mint and pine nuts.

Variation
Replace the aubergines with sliced cooked beetroot, top with the yogurt mixture and sprinkle with the pine nuts, then drizzle 1 tablespoon of olive oil

This dish should be served at room temperature or chilled

1 cup = 250ml = 8fl oz   1 tablespoon = 15ml   1 teaspoon = 5ml

Stuffed vine (grape) leaves

Ingredients

40-45 vine (grape) leaves (page 5)
2 medium tomatoes, sliced (optional)
2 medium potatoes, sliced (optional)
2 tablespoons olive oil mixed with 2
tablespoons lemon juice (optional)
Pepper and salt to taste

Stuffing
100g/3½oz/2 cups fresh flat-leaf parsley,
chopped
1 teaspoon dried mint or 1 tablespoon
chopped fresh mint leaves
100g/3½oz/½ cup uncooked basmati rice,
rinsed and drained
200g/7oz can chopped tomatoes
1 medium onion, halved and finely chopped
⅓ cup olive oil
⅓ cup lemon juice
½ teaspoon ground allspice
Pepper and salt to taste

Garnish to suit your own taste (optional)

Preparation

1 Drain the vine leaves, if packed in brine and cook in a large pan of boiling water until tender. Remove and place flat on a board (shiny side down). Cut the stems off and set aside the broken leaves.

2 Cover the bottom of a medium-sized pan with the broken leaves, top with the tomatoes, then the potatoes. Set aside.

3 Meanwhile, mix the stuffing ingredients in a bowl. Place 1 heaped teaspoon onto each leaf, then fold both sides (see picture) and roll tightly, squeezing the excess liquid into the bowl.

4 Arrange the rolls side by side in layers over the potatoes (seam side down). Strain the liquid from the left over mixture to cover the rolls. (Add salted boiling water if necessary.)

5 Place a heat-proof small plate on top of the rolls to keep them in position. Bring to the boil, then simmer, covered, for 30-40 minutes. Turn off the heat and remove the plate, Pour in the oil mixture, if desired. Leave to cool.

6 Transfer to a platter (discarding the broken leaves), or turn them over. Use kitchen paper to soak up any excess liquid around the platter. Cover the rolls to prevent from drying out.

This dish should be served at room temperature or cold

1 cup = 250ml = 8fl oz   1 tablespoon = 15ml   1 teaspoon = 5ml

32

Chickpea purée

Hummus

Ingredients

400g/14oz can chickpeas
2 tablespoons tahini (page 5)
⅓ cup lemon juice or more to taste
⅓ cup chickpea liquid or water
2 garlic cloves, peeled
1 tablespoon olive oil
Salt to taste

Garnish to suit your own taste (optional)

Preparation

1 Empty the chickpeas in a pan and heat (on medium) for 5 minutes. Remove with a slotted spoon, setting aside the liquid and place in a food processor with the tahini, lemon, garlic and salt, leaving a few peas to garnish.

2 Process for 1 minute (the sauce will thicken). Gradually add the water or the set aside liquid. Continue processing until a smooth thick paste is formed. (Adjust with lemon juice and water.)

3 Transfer to a serving dish. Arrange the chickpeas in the centre. Drizzle with oil, then garnish with parsley, if desired.

Note

If using dried chickpeas: *place 100g/3½oz/½ cup of chickpeas in a bowl and add 3 cups of cold water with 1 teaspoon bicarbonate of soda (baking soda) and soak overnight. Rinse well and cook in a pan of fresh boiling water (on medium heat) skimming all the foam that forms on the surface, then cover for 30-40 minutes or until cooked.*

34

This dish should be served at room temperature or cold, with pitta bread

1 cup = 250ml = 8fl oz   1 tablespoon = 15ml   1 teaspoon = 5ml

Aubergines (eggplants) with tahini
Baba ghannouj

Ingredients

3 large aubergines (eggplants)
3 tablespoons tahini (page 5)
2 garlic cloves, crushed
4 tablespoons lemon juice or more to taste
Olive oil
Salt to taste

Garnish to suit your own taste (optional)

Preparation

1 Prick the aubergines in several places (to prevent from bursting), then place on kitchen foil and grill (broil) under a medium heat until soft and wrinkled. Or cook over an open fire or gas hob flame, to give a nice smoky flavour.

2 Cut the aubergines in half lengthways and gently scoop out the flesh, discarding the black skin and stalks.

3 Mash with a potato masher and beat in the tahini, garlic, lemon juice and salt until forming a thick and creamy texture. (Adjust with lemon juice and water if necessary.) Drizzle with oil.

Variations

Add 1 tablespoon of plain yogurt with the tahini mixture.
Place the ingredients in a food processor (except the oil and mint). Blend to a paste.
Replace the tahini with 1 finely diced medium tomato and 1 finely chopped medium onion, then mix with the mashed aubergines. Drizzle with 1 tablespoon of olive oil.

36

This dish should be served at room temperature or cold, with pitta bread

1 cup = 250ml = 8fl oz   1 tablespoon = 15ml   1 teaspoon = 5ml

Noodles and sweetcorn soup

Ingredients

85g/3oz/1 cup dried medium egg noodles
400g/14oz can sweetcorn, rinsed and drained
2 large carrots, diced
2 courgettes (zucchini), diced
1 teaspoon fresh ginger, finely chopped
2 spring (scallions) onions chopped
7 cups boiling chicken or vegetable stock (1 cube)
1 tablespoon olive oil
Pepper and salt to taste

Garnish to suit your own taste (optional)

Preparation

1 Sauté the onions, ginger and carrots in warm oil (on medium heat) for 3-4 minutes. Stir in the courgettes for 2-3 minutes.

2 Add the boiling stock, sweetcorn, egg noodles and seasonings. Simmer, covered, for 25-30 minutes or until cooked and the sauce thickens. Serve hot in bowls.

Variations
Replace the olive oil with the same amount of sesame oil.
Add 1 tablespoon of soy or oyster sauce to the mixture for the last 5 minutes of cooking.
Omit the noodles.

Ideal for children (and babies, page 4).

This soup should be served hot, with toasted bread

1 cup = 250ml = 8fl oz   1 tablespoon = 15ml   1 teaspoon = 5ml

38

Red lentil soup

Ingredients

200g/7oz/1 cup red split lentils
2 sticks celery, coarsely chopped
1 large onion, coarsely chopped
2 large carrots, coarsely chopped
3 tablespoons basmati rice, rinsed
2-3 garlic gloves
1-2 tablespoons dried parsley or dried mint
7 cups boiling water
1 tablespoon olive oil
Pepper and salt to taste

40

Preparation

1 Sauté the onion in warm oil in a large pan (on medium heat) for 3 minutes. Stir in the garlic, lentils, celery, carrots and seasonings for 2 minutes.

2 Pour in the boiling water and simmer, covered, for 30-40 minutes or until cooked. Purée with a hand blender or in a food processor.

3 Return to the heat and add the rice. Cook, uncovered (on low heat) for 15-20 minutes or until the rice is cooked and the sauce thickens (stirring regularly). Transfer to bowls and sprinkle with the parsley, if desired

Variations
Replace the dried parsley with 2 tablespoons of finely chopped fresh flat-leaf parsley or fresh mint.

Ideal for children (and babies, page 4).

This soup should be served hot

1 cup = 250ml = 8fl oz   *1 tablespoon = 15ml*   *1 teaspoon = 5ml*

Vegetable soup

Ingredients

1 large onion, quartered
2 courgettes (zucchini), sliced
1 large potato, peeled and quartered
2 large carrots, coarsely chopped
1 large ripe tomato, peeled and quartered
7 cups boiling chicken or vegetable stock
(1 cube)
1 teaspoon plain (all-purpose) flour
dissolved in cold water
1 tablespoon dried basil
Single (light) cream (optional)
3 tablespoons olive oil
½ teaspoon ground allspice
Salt to taste

Garnish to suit your own taste (optional)

Preparation

1 Sauté the onion, courgettes, potato, carrots and tomato in 1 tablespoon of warm oil in a pan (on medium heat) for 5 minutes. Add the seasonings and boiling stock.

2 Simmer, covered, for 30-40 minutes or until tender. Purée in a hand blender or food processor.

3 Return to the heat, stirring in the dissolved flour for 1-2 minutes. Remove, then stir in 2 tablespoons of oil. Serve, drizzled with a little cream, if desired.

Variation
Add 1 celery and 1 leek sticks, coarsely chopped and cook with the other vegetables.

Ideal for children (and babies, page 4).

This soup should be served hot, with toasted bread or croutons

1 cup = 250ml = 8fl oz   1 tablespoon = 15ml   1 teaspoon = 5ml

Chicken or meatball soup

Ingredients

Ball mixture
400g/14oz skinless chicken breast fillets
1 medium onion, halved (optional)
55g/2oz fresh flat-leaf parsley (optional)
½ teaspoon ground allspice
Salt to taste

Sauce
55g/2oz/¼ cup basmati rice, rinsed (optional)
55g/2oz/⅓ cup broken vermicelli
140g/5oz can tomato purée (paste)
1 tablespoon olive oil
7 cups boiling water
3 tablespoons chopped fresh flat-leaf parsley
½ teaspoon ground allspice
Salt to taste

Preparation

1 Place the ball mixture ingredients together in a food processor and blend to a smooth paste. Form into 1 inch balls and sauté in warm oil in a pan (on medium heat) for 5 minutes or until browned.

2 Stir in the tomato purée for 1 minute, then add the boiling water, vermicelli, rice and seasonings.

3 Simmer, covered, for 20-30 minutes or until the sauce thickens, adding the parsley for the last 10 minutes of cooking (leaving 1 tablespoon to garnish, if desired).

Variation
Replace the chicken with 400g/14oz of minced (ground) beef or lamb, and mix in a bowl together with the allspice and salt. Then follow the above instructions.

Ideal for children (and babies, page 4).

44

This soup should be served hot

1 cup = 250ml = 8fl oz   *1 tablespoon = 15ml*   *1 teaspoon = 5ml*

Chicken soup

Ingredients

Chicken mixture
1 medium-sized chicken
1 medium onion, halved
½ teaspoon ground allspice
2 bay leaves (optional)
1 cinnamon stick
Salt to taste

Broth mixture
2 large carrots, sliced (or cubed)
1 courgette (zucchini), sliced (optional)
55g/2oz/⅓ cup broken vermicelli
55g/2oz/¼ cup basmati rice, rinsed (optional)
1 chicken stock cube (optional)

1 tablespoon chopped fresh flat-leaf parsley, to garnish

Preparation

1 Place the chicken in a large pan and add boiling water to cover, the onion, bay leaves and cinnamon stick. Cook (on medium-high heat) skimming all the foam as it forms on the surface. Add the allspice and salt.

2 Simmer, covered, for 1 hour or until tender. Remove the chicken, cutting the flesh into pieces, then place back into the broth, discarding the bones and unwanted pieces.

3 Add the carrots, courgette, rice, vermicelli and stock cube (if using). Bring to the boil, then simmer, covered, for 30- 40 minutes or until cooked. Discard the bay leaves and cinnamon stick. Garnish with the chopped parsley, if desired.

Ideal for children (and babies, page 4).

This soup should be served hot, with toasted bread or croutons

1 cup = 250ml = 8fl oz   1 tablespoon = 15ml   1 teaspoon = 5ml

46

Cabbage and onion soup

Ingredients

450g/1lb/4 cups white or green cabbage
coarsely chopped
2 large onions, coarsely chopped
1 green (bell) pepper, seeded and chopped
1 celery stick, coarsely chopped
400g/14oz can tomatoes
7 cups boiling chicken or vegetable stock
(1 cube)
⅓ teaspoon ground allspice (optional)
1 tabespoon olive oil (optional)
Salt to taste

Garnish to suit your own taste (optional)

Preparation

1 Place all the ingredients (except the tomatoes) in a large pan and cook (on medium heat) for 20 minutes.

2 Add the tomatoes, simmer, covered, for 30 minutes or until all soft.

3 Purée with a hand blender or in a food processor to a smooth paste and transfer back into the pan. Stir in 1 tablespoon of olive oil, if desired.

Note
This soup is ideal for those who like to lose weight.

48

This soup should be served hot

1 cup = 250ml = 8fl oz   1 tablespoon = 15ml   1 teaspoon = 5ml

Lentil and Swiss chard soup

Ingredients

200g/7oz/1 cup large dried green lentils
7 cups boiling water
1 medium potato, peeled and diced
1 bunch Swiss chard, end stalks removed
and coarsely chopped
1 medium onion, halved and finely chopped
3 garlic cloves, crushed
2 tablespoons olive oil
½ teaspoon ground allspice
1 tablespoon sumac (page 5) optional
1 tablespoon pomegranate molasses (page 5)
optional
3 tablespoons lemon juice or more to taste
Salt to taste

Garnish to suit your own taste (optional)

Preparation

1 Sauté the onion in 1 tablespoon of warm oil in a large pan (on medium heat) until golden. Add the lentils, boiling water, allspice and salt.

2 Cook, covered, for 15 minutes. Add the potatoes and cook for a further 20 minutes, followed by the Swiss chard.

3 Simmer for 15-20 minutes or until all cooked and the sauce thickens. Stir in the lemon juice, sumac, pomegranate molasses (if using), 1 tablespoon of oil and garlic for the last 10 minutes of cooking. (Add more water if necessary.)

Variations
Replace the Swiss chard with 225g/8oz of fresh baby leaf spinach.
Use large dried brown lentils instead of the green ones.
Mix 1 teaspoon of plain (all-purpose) flour with a little cold water and stir with the garlic mixture.

Ideal for children (and babies, page 4).

This dish should be served hot or tepid

1 cup = 250ml = 8fl oz   *1 tablespoon = 15ml*   *1 teaspoon = 5ml*

50

Lentil, bean and burghul (bulgur) soup

Ingredients

65g/2¼oz/⅓ cup large dried green lentils
200g/7oz can chickpeas
2 x 400g/(1¾ lb) cans borlotti beans
400g/14oz can butter (lima) beans
55g/2oz/¼ cup burghul (cracked wheat)
6 cups boiling water
1 medium onion, halved and finely chopped
½ teaspoon ground cumin (optional)
2 tablespoons olive oil
½ teaspoon ground allspice
Salt to taste

Garnish to suit your own taste (optional)

52

Preparation

1 Rinse the burghul and drain the beans.

2 Sauté the onion in 1 tablespoon of warm oil in a large pan (on medium heat) until golden. Stir in the lentils and seasonings for 1 minute. Pour in the boiling water and cook, covered for 15 minutes.

3 Add the beans and burghul. Simmer for 20 minutes or until the sauce thickens. Stir in 1 tablespoon of oil, then transfer to bowls. (Add more water if necessary.)

Note
Use fine brown burghul (bulgur) page 5.

Variation
Replace the green lentils with large dried brown ones.

This dish should be served hot or tepid

1 cup = 250ml = 8fl oz   *1 tablespoon = 15ml*   *1 teaspoon = 5ml*

Parsley salad
Tabbouleh

Ingredients

55g/2oz/¼ cup burghul (cracked wheat)
250g/9oz/5 cups fresh flat-leaf parsley finely chopped
3 spring (scallions) onions, finely chopped
3 tablespoons finely chopped fresh mint leaves
5 medium tomatoes, thinly diced
¾ cup olive oil or more to taste
1 teaspoon dried mint
½ cup lemon juice or more to taste
Pepper and salt to taste

Garnish to suit your own taste (optional)

54

Preparation

1 Rinse the burghul under cold water. Drain, squeezing out the excess water, then place in a salad bowl.

2 Wash the parsley under a cold tap, while keeping in a bunch, then shake the water out and dry on kitchen paper. Trim off the end stalks. Tightly hold the bunch and chop very finely.

3 Add the parsley, fresh mint, onions, tomatoes and dried mint with the burghul. Season with pepper and salt.

Just before serving
Pour in the oil and lemon juice, toss well together to coat.

Note
Use fine brown burghul (bulgur) page 5.

Ideal for children

This dish is the most popular Lebanese salad and should be served fresh

1 cup = 250ml = 8fl oz   *1 tablespoon = 15ml*   *1 teaspoon = 5ml*

Mixed vegetable salad with bread
Fattoush

Ingredients

1 loaf of medium flat round pitta bread
150g/5½oz/3 cups fresh flat-leaf parsley, chopped
400g/14oz Romaine lettuce, chopped
4 spring (scallions) onions, finely chopped
1 medium red onion, finely sliced (optional)
5 tablespoons chopped fresh mint leaves
5 medium tomatoes, diced
2 teaspoons dried mint
2 small cucumbers (or ½ large), quartered and diced

Dressing
⅓ cup lemon juice
½ cup olive oil or more to taste
2 garlic cloves, crushed
1-2 teaspoons ground sumac (page 5)
1 tablespoon pomegranate molasses (page 5)
Salt to taste

Lemon slices, to garnish (optional)

Preparation

1 Chop the vegetables coarsely (except both onions) and place in a large salad bowl. Sprinkle with dried mint and salt.

2 Toast the bread (or deep fry in hot cooking oil) until golden and crisp, then break into bite-sized pieces. (Or cut into 1 inch square pieces before toasting or frying.)

Just before serving
Mix the dressing ingredients together in a bowl. Pour over the salad, adding the bread and toss gently to coat. Garnish with lemon slices, if desired.

Note
If using the red onion, rub with a little additional sumac and salt before adding to the other vegetables.

Ideal for children

This dish is a popular Lebanese salad and should be served fresh before the bread gets soggy

56

Lentil salad

Ingredients

100g/3½oz/½ cup large dried green lentils
3 cups boiling water
A small Romaine lettuce, halved widthways
6-8 small tomatoes, halved
½ teaspoon ground cumin (optional)
1 green (bell) pepper, seeded and diced

Dressing
4 tablespoons olive oil or more to taste
3 tablespoons balsamic vinegar
3 garlic cloves, crushed
1 teaspoon mustard
Pepper and salt to taste

Preparation

1 Place the lentils in a pan and add the boiling water, cumin (if using) and salt. Cook (on medium heat) covered, for 30 minutes or until tender, but still firm. Drain and leave to cool.

2 Arrange the lettuce on a salad dish. Add the lentils in the centre, then top with the pepper and tomatoes.

Just before serving
Mix the dressing ingredients together in a bowl. Drizzle gently all over the salad.

Variations
Replace the green lentils with large dried brown ones.
Use 3 tablespoons of lemon juice instead of the vinegar.

58

This salad dish should be served at room temperature

1 cup = 250ml = 8fl oz   1 tablespoon = 15ml   1 teaspoon = 5ml

Yogurt and cucumber salad

Ingredients

2 cups natural (plain) yogurt
1 tablespoon dried mint
2 small cucumbers (or ½ large) thinly sliced
3 garlic cloves, crushed
Salt to taste

Mint sprigs, to garnish (optional)

Preparation

1 Place the yogurt in a salad bowl.

2 Add the garlic, mint and cucumbers and toss well. Serve the same day. Garnish with mint leaves, if desired.

60

This salad dish should be served chilled or cold as a dip

1 cup = 250ml = 8fl oz   1 tablespoon = 15ml   1 teaspoon = 5ml

Green bean and potato salad

Ingredients

*2 x 400g/1¾lb cans green beans, rinsed
and drained
10 small potatoes, peeled and halved
Salt to taste*

Dressing
*3 tablespoons lemon juice
4 tablespoons olive oil or more to taste
1 teaspoon ground sumac (page 5)
2 garlic cloves, crushed
Salt to taste*

Garnish to suit your own taste (optional)

Preparation

1 Cook the potatoes in a medium pan of salted boiling water (on medium heat) covered, for 30 minutes or until tender, but still firm. Remove with a slotted spoon and place in a salad bowl with the green beans.

2 Mix the dressing ingredients together in a bowl. Pour over the potatoes and beans and toss gently to coat.

Note
If using fresh beans: *Trim the ends and halve widthways, then wash and steam until tender.*

Variations
*Omit the sumac.
Use only the beans without the potatoes.*

*This salad can be served
tepid or at room temperature
or even cold*

1 cup = 250ml = 8fl oz   1 tablespoon = 15ml   1 teaspoon = 5ml

Cannellini bean salad

Ingredients

*2 x 400g/1¾lb cans cannellini (or lima)
beans rinsed and drained
2 tablespoons chopped fresh flat-leaf parsley*

Dressing
*4 tablespoons lemon juice
5 tablespoons olive oil or more to taste
2 garlic cloves, crushed
Salt to taste*

Garnish to suit your own taste (optional)

Preparation

1 Place the drained beans in a salad bowl and set aside.

2 Mix the dressing ingredients together in a bowl, then pour over the beans and toss gently to coat. Sprinkle with the parsley.

Note
If using dried beans: *place 200g/7oz/1 cup of beans in a bowl and add 3 cups of cold water. Soak overnight, then rinse well and cook in a pan of fresh boiling water (on medium heat) covered, for 30-40 minutes or until tender. Drain before use.*

Variation
Replace the beans with 4-5 medium-sized peeled potatoes cooked in salted boiling water until tender (but still firm). Leave to cool, then cut into cubes and follow No.2 replacing the parsley with 2 chopped spring (scallions) onions, if desired.

64

**This salad can be served
tepid or at room temperature,
with pitta bread**

1 cup = 250ml = 8fl oz   1 tablespoon = 15ml   1 teaspoon = 5ml

Rocket salad

Ingredients

200g/7oz bunch fresh rocket
1-2 medium onions, halved and thinly sliced
10 cherry tomatoes
1 teaspoon sumac (page 5) optional

Dressing
½ cup olive oil or more to taste
¼ cup lemon juice or balsamic vinegar
3-4 garlic cloves, crushed
Pepper and salt to taste

Preparation

1 Slice the onions, then rub with the sumac (if using).

2 Place the rocket and tomato in a salad dish and sprinkle with the onions.

Just before serving
Mix the dressing ingredients together in a bowl. Drizzle gently all over the salad.

*This salad goes well
with any grilled meat*

1 cup = 250ml = 8fl oz   1 tablespoon = 15ml   1 teaspoon = 5ml

Feta cheese salad

Ingredients

225g/8oz Romaine lettuce, coarsely chopped
2 medium tomatoes, thinly sliced
1 green (bell) pepper, seeded and cut into
thin strips
1 red (bell) pepper, seeded and cut into
thin strips
3-5 fresh basil leaves, finely chopped
200g/7oz/1⅓ cup feta cheese, cubed
10 black olives, pitted (stoned)

Dressing
4 tablespoons lemon juice
5 tablespoons olive oil or more to taste
2 garlic cloves, crushed
Pepper and salt to taste

Garnish to suit your own taste (optional)

Preparation

Arrange the lettuce in a salad dish. Top with the peppers and tomatoes, followed by the olives, feta and basil.

Just before serving
Mix the dressing ingredients together in a bowl. Drizzle gently all over the salad.

Variation
Replace the lemon juice with 2 tablespoons of balsamic vinegar.

68

This salad goes well with grilled chicken

1 cup = 250ml = 8fl oz   *1 tablespoon = 15ml*   *1 teaspoon = 5ml*

Spinach, cheese and avocado salad

Ingredients

225g/8oz fresh baby leaf spinach
6 large slices mozzarella cheese
1 medium ripe avocados, skinned and sliced
4 medium tomatoes, sliced or cut into wedges
6-8 black olives, pitted (stoned)
4 fresh basil leaves

<u>*Dressing*</u>
2 tablespoons white wine vinegar
4 tablespoons olive oil or more to taste
2 garlic cloves, crushed
1 teaspoon mustard
Pepper and salt to taste

Preparation

1 Arrange the spinach, tomatoes, avocado, cheese, basil and olives in a large dish.

2 Mix the dressing ingredients together in a bowl. Drizzle gently all over the salad.

Note
If not serving immediately: *rub the avocado with a little lemon juice to prevent from discolouring.*

Variations
Sprinkle 1-2 tablespoons of toasted pine nuts.
Replace the vinegar with 2 tablespoons of lemon juice.

70

This salad should be served immediately

1 cup = 250ml = 8fl oz   1 tablespoon = 15ml   1 teaspoon = 5ml

Sweetcorn and avocado salad

Ingredients

1 large ripe avocado, sliced
340g/12oz can sweetcorn, rinsed and
drained
1 small iceberg lettuce, coarsely chopped
3 medium tomatoes, sliced
2 small cucumbers (or ½ large) diced or sliced
1 teaspoon dried mint

Dressing
3 tablespoons white wine vinegar
4 tablespoons olive oil or more to taste
2 garlic cloves, crushed (optional)
Pepper and salt to taste

Preparation

1 Place the lettuce in a salad bowl and top with the other vegetables.

2 Mix the dressing ingredients together in a bowl. Pour over the salad and toss gently to coat. Sprinkle with the mint.

Note
If not serving immediately: *rub the avocado with a little lemon juice to prevent from discolouring.*

Variation
Replace the vinegar with 3 tablespoons of lemon juice.

Ideal for children

72

This salad should be served immediately

1 cup = 250ml = 8fl oz   1 tablespoon = 15ml   1 teaspoon = 5ml

Spinach salad with croutons

Ingredients

225g/8oz fresh baby leaf spinach
A handful of croutons
4 tablespoons blanched almonds, toasted
2 tablespoons olive oil, for the almonds
2 teaspoons sesame seeds (preferably toasted)

Dressing
3 tablespoons lemon juice
4 tablespoons olive oil or more to taste
3 garlic cloves, crushed
Pepper and salt to taste

Preparation

1 Sauté the almonds in 2 tablespoons of warm oil in a small pan (on medium heat) stirring constantly until golden. Remove with a slotted spoon and set aside.

2 Arrange the spinach, croutons and almonds in a salad dish. Sprinkle with sesame seeds, if desired. Set aside.

3 Mix the dressing ingredients together in a bowl. Drizzle gently over the salad.

Variation
Replace the lemon juice with 2 tablespoons of balsamic vinegar.

74

This salad should be served fresh

1 cup = 250ml = 8fl oz   1 tablespoon = 15ml   1 teaspoon = 5ml

Garlic dip

Ingredients

*1 medium bulb garlic, cloves separated and
peeled
1½ cups olive (or vegetable) oil
2 tablespoons lemon juice
1 medium egg white
Salt to taste*

1 small potato, peeled and boiled (optional)

Preparation

1 Place the garlic in a food processor and blend until mashed. (Stop the blender processor often to scrape down the sides.)

2 Add the egg and continue blending until mixed with the garlic. Pour in the oil in a thin stream while is still running until a thick white mayonnaise consistency is formed, adding salt and half of the lemon juice in the middle of processing and leaving the other half until the last minute.

3 If the mixture is too strong for your taste: add more oil.

Note
*Will keep in the refrigerator (in a glass container) for up to 4-5 days.
To keep longer in the refrigerator, replace the egg white with 1 small boiled and well drained, cooled potato.*
If the paste curdles: *Strain and place in a bowl, stirring with a fork until you get the desired consistency. (Or use an electric mixer.)*

Variations *(for a smaller amount)*
Place 4-5 crushed garlic cloves in a bowl with salt and mix well. Slowly add ½ cup of oil, stirring with a fork until the oil runs out, then stir in 2 tablespoons of mayonnaise. (Or replace the mayonnaise with 1 medium peeled, then boiled and mashed potato.)

This dish can be served at room temperature or cold, with grilled meat

1 cup = 250ml = 8fl oz   1 tablespoon = 15ml   1 teaspoon = 5ml

Tahini dip (sesame paste)
Tarator

Ingredients

½ cup tahini (page 5)
2 garlic cloves, crushed
½ cup lemon juice or more to taste
⅓ cup water or more
1 tablespoon chopped fresh flat-leaf parsley
Salt to taste

Garnish to suit your own taste (optional)

Preparation

1 Place the tahini, lemon juice, garlic and salt in a bowl and mix well together. (The sauce will thicken.)

2 Gradually add the water stirring until it reaches the consistency of gravy. Adjust with lemon juice and water, then sprinkle the parsley.

Note
Will keep in the refrigerator for up to 2 weeks.

This dish could be served at room temperature, with falafel and baked fish

1 cup = 250ml = 8fl oz   1 tablespoon = 15ml   1 teaspoon = 5ml

78

Pesto (basil) sauce

Ingredients

150g/5½oz bunch fresh basil leaves
2-3 garlic cloves, peeled
3-4 tablespoons pine nuts or pistachio nuts
½ cup olive oil
5 tablespoons grated Parmesan cheese
Salt to taste

Preparation

1 Place all the ingredients in a food processor (except the oil) and blend to a smooth paste.

2 Gradually add the oil and continue blending until the desired consistency is produced.

This dish should be served tepid or at room temperature for pasta and spaghetti

1 cup = 250ml = 8fl oz   *1 tablespoon = 15ml*   *1 teaspoon = 5ml*

Mashed potatoes with milk

Ingredients

4 large potatoes, peeled and quartered
½ cup milk
1 teaspoon butter or margarine
Salt to taste

Garnish to suit your own taste (optional)

Preparation

1 Cook the potatoes in a large pan of salted boiling water (on medium heat) covered, for 30 minutes or until tender. Remove with a slotted spoon, and mash, adding the butter while still hot.

2 Stir in the milk to produce a thick creamy mixture. Season with more salt.

Variation
Replace the butter with 1 tablespoon of olive oil.

Ideal for children (and babies, page 4).

**This dish can be served
hot or tepid.
Goes with meat dishes**

1 cup = 250ml = 8fl oz   1 tablespoon = 15ml   1 teaspoon = 5ml

Vermicelli rice

Ingredients

200g/7oz/1 cup basmati rice, rinsed and
drained
55g/2oz/⅓ cup broken vermicelli
1 tablespoon olive oil
2 cups boiling chicken or vegetable stock
(1 cube)
Salt to taste

Garnish to suit your own taste (optional)

Preparation

1 Sauté the vermicelli in warm oil in a pan (on medium heat) stirring constantly until golden. Stir in the rice for a few seconds, then add the boiling stock, (or replace with salted boiling water).

2 Simmer, covered, for 15-20 minutes or until the rice is cooked and the water is absorbed.

Note

If serving with plain (boiled) rice: *place the rice in a pan and add the boiling stock (or replace with salted boiling water). Simmer, covered, for 15-20 minutes or until cooked and the water is absorbed. Add salt if necessary.*

Variation

Soak the rinsed rice in cold water for 10 minutes, then drain before cooking.

Ideal for children (and babies, page 4).

84

This rice dish can be served hot or tepid, with plain yogurt and with most stewed dishes

1 cup = 250ml = 8fl oz   1 tablespoon = 15ml   1 teaspoon = 5ml

Couscous

Ingredients

170g/6oz/1 cup couscous, rinsed and drained
1 cup salted boiling water
1 tablespoons olive oil

Garnish to suit your own taste (optional)

Preparation

1 Place the drained couscous in a large bowl and mix well with the oil.

2 Pour in the salted boiling water (or replace with chicken or vegetable stock, using 1 cube) and set aside for 15 minutes or until the couscous is tender and the water is absorbed. Stir with a fork to separate the grains.

Variations

Cook the couscous in a steamer by placing above the stew, stirring occasionally.
Place the couscous in a strainer and pour 2-3 cups of boiling water all over. Drain and sauté in 1 tablespoon of warm olive oil in a pan (on medium-low heat) for 1 minute, stirring constantly. Gradually add ½ cup of salted boiling water, or stock. Simmer, covered, for 10 minutes or until cooked and the water is absorbed, stirring regularly and gently with a fork to separate the grains.

Ideal for children (and babies, page 4).

This dish should be served hot. Goes with tagine and many main dishes

1 cup = 250ml = 8fl oz   1 tablespoon = 15ml   1 teaspoon = 5ml

Egg rice

Ingredients

200g/7oz/1 cup basmati rice, rinsed and drained
2 cups salted boiling water
1 medium egg, whisked
1 tablespoon olive oil
Salt to taste

Garnish to suit your own taste (optional)

Preparation

1 Place the rice in a pan and add the salted boiling water (or replace with chicken or vegetable stock, using 1 cube). Simmer, covered, for 15-20 minutes or until cooked and the water is absorbed.

2 Fry the egg in warm oil until set. Break into small pieces with a wooden spoon, then stir into the rice.

Variations
Fry the egg until set and break into pieces. Stir in the drained rice, adding the salted boiling water (or the stock), bring to the boil, then simmer, covered, for 15-20 minutes or until cooked and the water is absorbed.
Soak the rinsed rice in cold water for 10 minutes, then drain before cooking.

Ideal for children (and babies, page 4).

**This dish should be served hot.
Goes with most
Chinese dishes**

1 cup = 250ml = 8fl oz   1 tablespoon = 15ml   1 teaspoon = 5ml

Falafel

Ingredients

200g/7oz/1 cup split dried broad (fava) beans
100g/3½oz/½ cup dried chickpeas
20g/¾oz fresh coriander (cilantro)
5-6 tablespoons sesame seeds, (optional)
1 medium onion, peeled and halved
5 large garlic gloves
1 teaspoon ground falafel spices
1 teaspoon ground coriander
⅓ teaspoon ground cumin (optional)
1½ teaspoon bicarbonate of soda (baking soda)
Cooking oil, for deep frying
Pepper and salt to taste

Preparation

1 Place the broad beans (page 5) and chickpeas in a large bowl with 5 cups of cold water and ½ teaspoon of bicarbonate of soda and soak overnight.

2 Rinse and drain, then place in a food processor with all the ingredients (except the bicarbonate of soda, sesame seeds and oil) and blend to a smooth paste.

3 *Before cooking:* mix the paste with 1 teaspoon of bicarbonate of soda and leave to rest for 20 minutes, then form gently into 1¾ inch balls, using the palms of your hands. Roll each ball in the sesame seeds (if using) and place on a plate.

4 Deep fry balls in batches in hot oil (on medium-high heat) for 2-3 minutes or until cooked on the inside and light brown on the outside, turning once. Remove and drain on kitchen paper.

To serve
Place the falafel on a platter with pitta bread and mixed salad of (fresh parsley, fresh mint, tomatoes, radish, lettuce and cucumbers) and a bowl of tahini (page 78).
Or serve as a wrap by placing the falafel in pitta bread, top with the mixed vegetables and drizzle with tahini.

Notes
Use falafel spices, available from Mediterranean shops (or mix together 1 teaspoon of allspice and ½ teaspoon of nutmeg.
If frozen: defrost then mix with the bicarbonate of soda.
For using falafel maker (page 5).

90

This dish can be served as a wrap in pitta bread

1 cup = 250ml = 8fl oz   1 tablespoon = 15ml   1 teaspoon = 5ml

Lentil purée

Ingredients

200g/7oz/1 cup dried large green lentils
5 cups boiling water
1 medium onion, halved and finely chopped
2 tablespoons basmati rice, rinsed
2 tablespoons olive oil
½ teaspoon ground allspice (optional)
Salt to taste

Medium flat round pitta bread, toasted
(optional)

Preparation

1 Place the lentils in a pan and add the boiling water. Cook (on medium heat) covered, for 30-40 minutes or until tender. Purée with a hand blender or in a food processor to a smooth paste and set aside.

2 Sauté the onion in 1 tablespoon of warm oil (on medium heat) until golden. Stir in the lentil purée, rice and seasonings. Simmer, covered, for 15-20 minutes or until the rice is cooked, stirring regularly to prevent sticking. (Add more water if necessary.)

3 Stir in 1 tablespoon of oil and transfer to a bowl. Leave to cool and serve with toasted pitta bread, if desired.

Notes
This dish can be made into a hot soup by adding an extra cup of boiling water.
If serving with toasted pitta bread (page 56 No.2).

Ideal for children (and babies, page 4).

92

This dish should be served
at room temperature or chilled,
with salad or pitta bread

1 cup = 250ml = 8fl oz   1 tablespoon = 15ml   1 teaspoon = 5ml

Chickpeas with yogurt and nuts

Ingredients

2 x 400g/1¾ lb cans chickpeas
1 cup natural (plain) yogurt
1 loaf of medium flat round pitta bread
4 garlic cloves, crushed
1 teaspoon dried mint (optional)
5 tablespoons pine nuts
6 tablespoons olive oil
Cooking oil, for the bread (optional)
Salt to taste

Garnish to suit your own taste (optional)

Preparation

1 Sauté the pine nuts in 2 tablespoons of warm oil in a small pan (on medium heat) stirring constantly until golden. Remove with a slotted spoon and set aside.

2 Toast the bread (or deep fry in hot cooking oil) until golden and crisp, then break into bite-sized pieces. (Or cut into 1 inch square pieces before toasting or frying.)

3 Empty the canned chickpeas in a pan and heat (on medium) for 4 minutes, setting aside the liquid. Remove to a bowl with a slotted spoon. Add 4 tablespoons of oil, 4 tablespoons of the set aside liquid and salt, mixing well together.

To serve
Arrange the bread in the bottom of a serving dish.
Spread the chickpea mixture over.
Sprinkle the dried mint (if using) and top with the yogurt and pine nuts.

Variations
Use dried chickpeas instead of canned (page 34).
Omit the bread.

Ideal for children

94

This dish should be served
immediately

1 cup = 250ml = 8fl oz   1 tablespoon = 15ml   1 teaspoon = 5ml

Aubergines (eggplants) in tomato sauce

Ingredients

2 large aubergines (eggplants)
115g/4oz can chickpeas, rinsed and drained
1 medium onion, halved and thinly sliced
6 garlic cloves, peeled (optional)
1 tablespoon dried mint
400g/14oz can chopped tomatoes
Olive oil
½ teaspoon ground allspice
Salt to taste

Garnish to suit your own taste (optional)

Preparation

1 Peel the aubergines leaving a few thin black strips. Quarter lengthways and cut into large pieces. Sprinkle with a little salt, then set aside for 10 minutes. Dry with kitchen paper and brush with a little oil. Sauté in a non-stick hot pan in batches (on medium-low heat) until just tender and browned on all sides. Or place in a greased baking dish and bake in a preheated oven at 200°C/400°F/Gas 6. Alternatively, grill (broil) under a medium heat.

2 Sauté the onion and garlic (if using) in 1 tablespoon oil in a pan (on medium heat) for 2-3 minutes or until soft. Add the chickpeas, dried mint and seasonings and cook for a further minute.

3 Stir in the aubergine pieces , then pour in the tomatoes and bring to the boil. Simmer, covered, for 20-25 minutes or until cooked and the sauce thickens.

Variation
Use dried chickpeas instead of canned (page 20).

96

This dish should be served tepid or at room temperature, with pitta bread

1 cup = 250ml = 8fl oz   1 tablespoon = 15ml   1 teaspoon = 5ml

Chickpea and potato curry

Ingredients

1 medium onion, halved and finely chopped
10-12 small potatoes, peeled and half boiled
400g/14oz can chickpeas, rinsed and drained
3 tablespoons olive oil
200g/7oz can chopped tomatoes
1 tablespoon tomato purée (paste)
1 teaspoon finely chopped fresh ginger
5 garlic cloves, crushed
Boiling water
1 teaspoon mild (or hot) chilli powder
1 teaspoon ground coriander
5 black cloves
10 whole black peppers
2 cinnamon sticks
2 bay leaves
Salt to taste

Preparation

1 Sauté the onion in 1 tablespoon of warm oil in a pan (on medium heat) until golden. Stir in the garlic, ginger, tomato purée and the remaining oil for 1 minute.

2 Add the seasonings, bay leaves and tomatoes. Bring to the boil. Simmer, covered, until the oil rises to the surface. Add the potatoes, chickpeas and boiling water to cover the potato mixture.

3 Simmer, covered, for 30-40 minutes or until the potatoes are cooked (but still firm) and the sauce thickens..

Variations

Replace the chickpeas with 400g/14oz of frozen garden peas.
Omit the potatoes and chickpeas. Instead, sauté 6-8 skinned chicken thighs with the onion in 1 tablespoon of warm olive oil until golden before adding the seasonings and other ingredients.

This dish should be served hot, with plain (boiled) rice (page 84) or naan bread

1 cup = 250ml = 8fl oz   1 tablespoon = 15ml   1 teaspoon = 5ml

Green beans in tomato sauce

Ingredients

500g/1lb 2oz frozen green beans, defrosted
400g/14oz can chopped tomatoes
1 medium onion, halved and finely chopped
6 garlic cloves, peeled
2 tablespoons olive oil
½ teaspoon ground allspice
Salt to taste

Preparation

1 Sauté the onion and garlic in 1 tablespoon of warm oil in a pan (on medium-low heat) for 1 minute. Add the beans, remaining oil and seasonings. Cook, covered, for 20-30 minutes or until tender, stirring regularly.

2 Pour in the tomatoes and bring to the boil. Simmer, covered, for 20 minutes or until the sauce thickens.

Note
If using fresh beans: *Trim the ends and halve widthways, wash and steam, then stir with the onion mixture for 2-3 minutes and follow No.2, stirring regularly.*

Ideal for children (and babies, page 4).

100

This dish should be served tepid or cold, with green salad or pitta bread

1 cup = 250ml = 8fl oz   1 tablespoon = 15ml   1 teaspoon = 5ml

Sautéed potatoes and vegetables

Ingredients

4 medium potatoes, peeled and diced
30g/1oz/¾ cup fresh coriander (cilantro),
chopped
1 red (bell) pepper, seeded and finely diced
1 green (bell) pepper, seeded and finely diced
2 garlic cloves, crushed
1-2 tablespoons olive oil
1 tablespoon lemon juice (optional)
½ teaspoon mild (or hot) chilli powder
½ teaspoon ground allspice
Pepper and salt to taste

Garnish to suit your own taste (optional)

Preparation

1 Sauté the potatoes in warm oil in a pan (on medium-low heat) for 10 minutes. Stir in the peppers for 8 minutes.

2 Add the coriander, garlic, seasonings and lemon juice (if using). Cook, covered, for a further 10 minutes or until all tender. (The potatoes should be cooked but still firm.)

This dish can be served tepid or at room temperature, with green salad or pitta bread

1 cup = 250ml = 8fl oz   1 tablespoon = 15ml   1 teaspoon = 5ml

Borlotti beans in tomato sauce

Ingredients

*2 x 400g/1¾ lb cans borlotti beans, rinsed
and drained
140g/5oz can tomato purée (paste)
4 cups boiling water
1 medium onion, halved and finely chopped
1 carrot, thinly sliced or diced (optional)
1 tablespoon olive oil
½ teaspoon ground allspice
Salt to taste*

Garnish to suit your own taste (optional)

Preparation

1 Sauté the onion in warm oil in a pan (on medium heat) until golden. Stir in the carrot for 2 minutes (if using), followed by the tomato purée for a further minute.

2 Add the beans, boiling water and seasonings and allow to boil, then simmer, covered, for 25 minutes or until the carrots are tender and the sauce thickens.

Variations
*Omit the carrot.
Use dried beans instead of canned (page 64).
Serve with vermicelli or plain (boiled) rice (page 84).*

Ideal for children (and babies, page 4).

104

*This dish can be served
hot or tepid, with salad
or pitta bread*

1 cup = 250ml = 8fl oz   1 tablespoon = 15ml   1 teaspoon = 5ml

If using a fan assisted oven (page 4)

Spinach in filo (phyllo) pastry

Ingredients

8 frozen sheets filo (phyllo) pastry, defrost
225g/8oz fresh baby leaf spinach
2 medium onions, halved and finely chopped
1 medium ripe tomato, finely diced
4 tablespoons pine nuts
¼ cup lemon juice or to taste
¼ cup olive oil or more to taste
3 tablespoons olive oil, for brushing
1 teaspoon ground allspice
1 teaspoon ground sumac (page 5) optional
1 tablespoon pomegranate molasses (page 5) optional
Pepper and salt to taste

Garnish to suit your own taste (optional)

Preparation

1 Mix all the ingredients together in a bowl (except the filo pastry).

2 Place half the filo sheets in a lightly-greased ovenproof dish and brush each with a little oil. Spread the spinach mixture on top, then cover with the remaining sheets, folding the overhanging edges inwards.

3 Bake in a preheated oven at 180°C/350°F/Gas 4 for 15-20 minutes or until golden.

This dish can be served hot or at room temperature, with salad

1 cup = 250ml = 8fl oz   1 tablespoon = 15ml   1 teaspoon = 5ml

If using a fan assisted oven (page 4)

Spaghetti with milk sauce

Ingredients

500g/1lb 2oz dried spaghetti, broken in half
1 tablespoon olive oil
4 tablespoons plain (all-purpose) flour
3 cups milk
1 tablespoon margarine or butter
½ teaspoon of nutmeg
6 tablespoons breadcrumbs
Salt to taste

Garnish to suit your own taste (optional)

Preparation

1 Cook the spaghetti in a large pan of salted boiling water (on medium heat) for 15 minutes, adding the oil to prevent sticking, (or according to the packet instructions). Drain and rinse under cold water and set aside.

2 Arrange the spaghetti in a lightly-greased baking dish and set aside.

3 In a pan, dissolve the flour in the cold milk and sprinkle the nutmeg and salt. Bring to the boil, stirring constantly until the sauce thickens. Stir in the butter while still hot.

4 Pour the mixture over the spaghetti and top with the breadcrumbs. Bake in a preheated oven at 180°C/350°F for 20 minutes or until golden. Or grill (broil) under a medium heat for 5-8 minutes.

Variations
Add 3-4 finely diced smoked ham slices with the milk mixture.
Replace the breadcrumbs with 115g/4oz/1 cup of mozzarella or Parmesan cheese.

Ideal for children (and babies, page 4).

108

This dish should be served immediately

1 cup = 250ml = 8fl oz   1 tablespoon = 15ml   1 teaspoon = 5ml

Spaghetti with tomatoes and basil

Ingredients

500g/1lb 2oz dried spaghetti, broken in half
400g/14oz can chopped tomatoes
2 spring (scallions) onions, finely chopped
3 garlic cloves, crushed
1 tablespoon tomato purée (paste)
½ teaspoon allspice (optional)
2 tablespoons olive oil
1-2 teaspoons dried basil (or use basil sauce, page 80)
Pepper and salt to taste

Preparation

1 Cook the spaghetti in a large pan of salted boiling water (on medium heat) for 15 minutes, adding the oil to prevent sticking, (or according to the packet instructions). Drain and rinse under cold water and set aside.

2 Sauté the onions and garlic in 1 tablespoon of warm oil (on medium heat) for 2 minutes. Stir in the tomato purée for a further minute.

3 Add the tomatoes, (basil sauce if using) and seasonings. Bring to the boil, then simmer, covered, for 15-20 minutes or until the sauce thickens.

Just before serving
Place the spaghetti with the tomato mixture, stirring together (on medium heat) for 1-2 minutes. Transfer to a platter and sprinkle with the dried basil (if not using the sauce).

Variations
During stage 1, add 2 crushed garlic cloves and sprinkle with grated Parmesan cheese. Stir (on medium heat) for 1-2 minutes and serve immediately.

Ideal for children (and babies, page 4).

110

This dish should be served hot

1 cup = 250ml = 8fl oz   1 tablespoon = 15ml   1 teaspoon = 5ml

If using a fan assisted oven (page 4)

Spanish omelette

Ingredients

2 courgettes (zucchini), finely diced
1 spring (scallion) onion, finely chopped
200g/7oz frozen peas, defrosted
1 green (bell) pepper, seeded and finely diced
1 large potato, peeled and finely diced
5 medium eggs, beaten with 1 tablespoon plain (all-purpose) flour
1 tablespoon olive oil
½ teaspoon allspice (optional)
Pepper and salt to taste

Garnish to suit your own taste (optional)

Preparation

1 Sauté the onion in warm oil in a pan (on medium-low heat) for 1 minute. Stir in the potato and peas for 15 minutes. Add the pepper and courgettes. Simmer, covered, for a further 20 minutes or until all just tender.

2 Spread the vegetables evenly in a lightly-greased baking dish and top with the egg mixture, after beating well with the seasonings.

3 Bake in a preheated oven at 180°C/350°F/Gas 4 for 20 minutes or until set and golden.

Ideal for children (and babies, page 4).

112

This dish should be served hot or tepid, with salad

1 cup = 250ml = 8fl oz   1 tablespoon = 15ml   1 teaspoon = 5ml

If using a fan assisted oven (page 4)

Broccoli and cauliflower gratin

Ingredients

1 medium cauliflower, separated into florets
1 medium broccoli, separated into florets
2 cups (cold) milk
3 tablespoons plain (all-purpose) flour
1 tablespoon butter or margarine
115g/4oz/1 cup grated mozzarella cheese
½ teaspoon ground nutmeg
Salt to taste

Preparation

1 Cook the cauliflower and broccoli in a pan of boiling water (on medium heat) for 15-20 minutes or until tender. Drain and arrange in a lightly-greased oven-proof dish.

2 In a pan, dissolve the flour in the (cold) milk and sprinkle the nutmeg and salt. Bring to the boil, stirring constantly until the sauce thickens. Stir in the butter while still hot. (Add more milk if necessary.)

3 Pour the milk mixture over the vegetables and sprinkle with the cheese. Bake in a preheated oven at 180°C/350°F/Gas 4 for 20 minutes or until the cheese melts and turns golden. Or grill (broil) under a medium heat for 7-10 minutes.

Variations
Replace the cauliflower and broccoli with 4 courgettes and 3 aubergines, cut into ½ inch slices widthways, (then sprinkle only the aubergine with a little salt, leaving aside for 10 minutes and dry with kitchen paper). Brush both with a little olive oil and sauté in batches (on medium-low heat) until soft and golden, then arrange in a lightly-greased ovenproof dish and follow the above instructions from No.2.
Deep fry the cauliflower in hot cooking oil in batches (on medium heat) until browned. Remove with a slotted spoon and drain on kitchen paper. Season with salt and serve with Mediterranean salad.

Ideal for children (and babies, page 4).

114

This dish should be served immediately. Goes well with salad

1 cup = 250ml = 8fl oz   1 tablespoon = 15ml   1 teaspoon = 5ml

If using a fan assisted oven (page 4)

Baked vegetables with cheese

Ingredients

2 spring (scallions) onions, finely chopped
3 medium potatoes, peeled and diced
1 large aubergine (eggplant), diced
2 courgettes (zucchini), diced
6-8 small mushrooms, sliced
400g/14oz can chopped tomatoes
1 tablespoon tomato purée (paste)
1 tablespoon chopped fresh coriander
(cilantro)
1-2 tablespoons olive oil
½ cup boiling water
3 garlic cloves, crushed
170g/6oz/1½ cups grated mozzarella cheese
1 teaspoon dried thyme
½ teaspoon ground allspice
Pepper and salt to taste

Garnish to suit your own taste (optional)

Preparation

1 Dice the aubergine and sprinkle with a little salt, then set aside for 10 minutes. Dry with kitchen paper.

2 Sauté the onions, garlic and potatoes in warm oil in a pan (on medium-low heat) for 5 minutes. Stir in the aubergine, courgettes and mushrooms for 3 minutes, followed by the tomato purée for a further minute.

3 Add the tomatoes, boiling water, coriander and seasonings. Bring to the boil, then simmer, covered, for 20-30 minutes or until cooked.

4 Transfer to a lightly-greased baking dish. Top with the cheese and bake in a preheated oven at 180°C/350°F/Gas 4 for 20 minutes or until the cheese melts and turns golden. Or grill (broil) under a medium heat for 5-8 minutes.

Variations
Replace the potatoes with 1 green and 1 red diced seeded (bell) pepper.
Replace the mozzarella cheese with grated Parmesan.

Ideal for children (and babies, page 4).

116

This dish should be served immediately.
Goes well with salad

1 cup = 250ml = 8fl oz   1 tablespoon = 15ml   1 teaspoon = 5ml

Okra in tomato sauce

Ingredients

500g/1lb 2oz frozen large or medium-sized okra
1 medium onion, halved and finely chopped
2 garlic cloves, crushed
2 tablespoons lemon juice or to taste
1 tablespoon pomegranate molasses (page 5), optional
400g/14oz) can chopped tomatoes
30g/1oz/¾ cup fresh coriander (cilantro), chopped
1 tablespoon olive oil
½ teaspoon ground allspice
Salt to taste

Garnish to suit your own taste (optional)

Preparation

1 Defrost the okra, then drain on kitchen paper and set aside.

2 Sauté the onions in warm oil in a pan (on medium heat) for 3 minutes. Stir in the okra for 5 minutes. Add the coriander and garlic, stirring together for a further minute.

3 Add the tomatoes, lemon juice, pomegranate molasses (if using), and seasonings. Bring to the boil, then simmer, covered, for 20-30 minutes or until tender and the sauce thickens. Serve with couscous (page 86), rice (page 84), or pitta bread.

Ideal for children (and babies, page 4).

This dish can be served tepid or at room temperature

1 cup = 250ml = 8fl oz   *1 tablespoon = 15ml*   *1 teaspoon = 5ml*

*If using a fan assisted
oven (page 4)*

Pumpkin kibbeh

Ingredients

Pumpkin mixture
*450g/1lb small pumpkin
200g/7oz/1 cup fine brown burghul
(bulgur) page 5
30g/1oz fresh coriander (cilantro)
1 large onion, quartered
1 tablespoon plain (all-purpose) flour
1 teaspoon ground coriander
Grated zest of 1 orange or lemon
½ teaspoon ground allspice
Salt to taste*

Stuffing
*2 medium onions, halved and thinly sliced
5 tablespoons halved blanched almonds
5 tablespoons pine nuts
1 tablespoon crushed walnuts
4 tablespoons olive oil
½ teaspoon ground allspice
½ teaspoon ground coriander
Salt to taste*

Garnish to suit your own taste (optional)

**This dish should be served hot
or tepid, with salad**

Preparation

1 Rinse the burghul under cold water. Drain and set aside.

2 Cook the pumpkin in a large pan of boiling water (on medium heat) until tender. Drain and remove the skin, squeezing out any excess water. Place in a food processor with the onion, coriander, zest and seasonings. Blend to a smooth paste. Tranfer to a bowl and knead well with the burghul, dipping your hand in cold water, then return to the food processor in batches and pulse a few times. (Add the flour if necessary.)

3 Sauté the pine nuts and almonds separately in 2 tablespoons of warm oil in a pan (on medium heat) stirring constantly until golden. Remove with a slotted spoon and set aside

4 In the same pan, stir in the onions and seasonings (on medium heat) until soft. Add the walnuts, almonds and pine nuts, mixing well together. Place in a medium-sized baking dish, topped with the pumpkin mixture paste. Smooth evenly using the back of a spoon dipped in water, oil or flour.

5 Brush with 2 tablespoons of oil and run a knife around the edges. Bake in a preheated oven at 200°C/400°F/Gas 6 for 20-25 minutes or until browned. Cut as desired. Transfer gently to a platter, turning it over.

Variations
*Stir 1 tablespoon of pomegranate molasses (page 5) into the onions (after softened).
Add 2 tablespoons of crushed canned chickpeas with the walnut mixture.*

1 cup = 250ml = 8fl oz   1 tablespoon = 15ml   1 teaspoon = 5ml

120

Lentils and rice

Ingredients

200g/7oz/1 cup large dried green lentils
5 cups boiling water
1 medium onion, finely chopped
2 medium onions, halved and thinly sliced (optional)
55g/2oz/¼ cup basmati rice, rinsed and drained
2 tablespoons olive oil
½ teaspoon ground allspice
Salt to taste
Cooking oil for deep frying

Garnish to suit your own taste (optional)

Preparation

1 Deep fry the sliced onions (if using) in hot cooking oil until browned. Remove with a slotted spoon and drain on kitchen paper. Set aside.

2 Sauté the chopped onion in 1 tablespoon of warm oil in a pan (on medium heat) until golden. Stir in the lentils, boiling water and seasonings. Cook (on medium heat) covered, for 20 minutes or until tender. (The lentils should still be firm.)

3 Add the rice, then simmer for 15-20 minutes or until the rice is cooked and the water is absorbed, stirring regularly. (Add more water if necessary.)

4 Stir in 1 tablespoon of oil. Transfer to a shallow dish and leave to cool. Top with the sliced onions, if desired.

Variations
Replace the green lentils with large dried brown ones.
Omit the deep fried onions.

122

This dish should be served at room temperature, with salad or plain yogurt

1 cup = 250ml = 8fl oz　　　　*1 tablespoon = 15ml*　　　　*1 teaspoon = 5ml*

Spinach with rice and pine nuts

Ingredients

1 medium onion, halved and very thinly sliced
2 garlic cloves, crushed
450g/1lb fresh baby leaf spinach
200g/7oz/1 cup basmati rice, rinsed and drained
4-5 tablespoons pine nuts
2 cups boiling chicken or vegetable stock (1 cube)
2 tablespoons olive oil
½ teaspoon ground allspice
Salt to taste

Preparation

1 Sauté the pine nuts in warm oil in a pan (on medium heat) stirring constantly until golden. Remove half and set aside.

2 Stir in the onion (on medium-low heat) until soft. Add the rice, garlic, spinach in batches and seasonings and cook for 1-2 minutes.

3 Pour in the boiling stock and simmer, covered, for 15-20 minutes or until the rice is cooked and the water is absorbed.

4 Serve, sprinkled with the remaining pine nuts.

Variations
Replace the onion with 2 finely chopped spring (scallions) onions.
Soak the rinsed rice in cold water for 10 minutes, then drain before cooking.

This dish can be served hot or tepid, with salad

1 cup = 250ml = 8fl oz   1 tablespoon = 15ml   1 teaspoon = 5ml

Rice with peas

Ingredients

200g/7oz/1 cup basmati rice, rinsed and drained
400g/14oz can peas, rinsed and drained
1 spring (scallion) onion, finely chopped
2 cups boiling chicken or vegetable stock (1 cube)
1 tablespoon olive oil
Pepper and salt to taste

Garnish to suit your own taste (optional)

Preparation

1 Sauté the onion in warm oil in a pan (on medium heat) for 1 minute. Stir in the rice for 30-40 seconds. Add the boiling stock and seasonings.

2 Simmer, covered, for 15-20 minutes or until the rice is cooked and the water is absorbed. Stir in the peas for the last 2-3 minutes of cooking.

Variations

Replace the canned peas with frozen ones and cook with the onion (on medium-low heat) until half cooked before adding the rice.
Omit the spring onion, if serving with yogurt.
Soak the rinsed rice in cold water for 10 minutes, then drain before cooking.

Ideal for children (and babies, page 4).

126

This dish can be served hot or tepid, with salad or plain yogurt

1 cup = 250ml = 8fl oz   1 tablespoon = 15ml   1 teaspoon = 5ml

Spinach curry with chickpeas

Ingredients

450g/1lb fresh baby leaf spinach
30g/1oz/¾ cup fresh coriander (cilantro),
chopped
2 spring (scallions) onions, finely chopped
200g/7oz/1 cup can chickpeas, rinsed and
drained
1 red (bell) pepper, seeded and chopped
1 large ripe tomato, peeled and finely diced
2 garlic cloves, crushed
½ cup boiling chicken or vegetable stock
(1 cube)
1 tablespoon olive oil
½ teaspoon ground cumin (optional)
½ teaspoon ground turmeric
1 teaspoon mild curry paste
Salt to taste

Garnish to suit your own taste (optional)

128

Preparation

1 Sauté the onions, garlic and pepper in warm oil in a pan (on medium heat) for 3 minutes. Stir in the tomatoes and chickpeas for 2 minutes.

2 Add the spinach in batches, covered, until nearly wilted. Stir in the coriander, seasonings and boiling stock, then simmer, covered, for 10-15 minutes or until the sauce thickens.

*This dish can be served hot
or at room temperature,
with plain (boiled) rice (page 84)*

1 cup = 250ml = 8fl oz   1 tablespoon = 15ml   1 teaspoon = 5ml

Rice with sweetcorn

Ingredients

200g/7oz/1 cup basmati rice, rinsed and drained
400g/14oz can sweetcorn, rinsed and drained
1 spring (scallion) onion, finely chopped
2 cups boiling chicken or vegetable stock (1 cube)
½ teaspoon ground turmeric (optional)
1 tablespoon olive oil
Pepper and salt to taste

Garnish to suit your own taste (optional)

Preparation

1 Sauté the onion in warm oil in a pan (on medium heat) for 1 minute. Stir in the rice for 30-40 seconds. Add the boiling stock and seasonings.

2 Simmer, covered, for 15-20 minutes or until the rice is cooked and the water is absorbed. Stir in the sweet corn for the last 2-3 minutes of cooking.

Variations
Slice 8 small mushrooms and stir with the rice before adding the stock (and 1 teaspoon of ground turmeric, if desired).
Omit the spring onion, if serving with yogurt.
Soak the rinsed rice in cold water for 10 minutes, then drain before cooking.

Ideal for children (and babies, page 4).

This dish can be served hot or tepid, with salad or plain yogurt

1 cup = 250ml = 8fl oz   1 tablespoon = 15ml   1 teaspoon = 5ml

Peas and carrots with meat stew

Ingredients

500g/1lb 2oz diced beef or lamb shoulder
3 medium carrots, thinly sliced
500g/1lb 2oz frozen peas, defrosted
1 medium onion, halved and finely chopped
140g/5oz can tomato purée (paste)
5 cups boiling water
1 tablespoon olive oil
1 teaspoon ground allspice
Salt to taste

Preparation

1 Dry fry the meat in a non-stick hot pan (on medium-low heat) for 3 minutes. Stir in the onion, oil and seasonings for 5 minutes.

2 Add the tomato purée, stirring for 1 minute, then pour in the boiling water. Simmer, covered until half cooked. (Time depends on the meat you use.)

3 Add the carrots and peas. Cook for 30-40 minutes or until tender and the sauce thickens.

Note
If using canned peas: add for the last 15 minutes of cooking.

Variation
Sauté 280g/10oz of minced (ground) beef or lamb with the onion and seasonings in 1 tablespoon of warm olive oil in a pan (on medium heat) for 5 minutes. Add the carrots and peas and cook for 5 minutes. Stir in the tomato purée before adding the boiling water, then simmer, covered, until tender and the sauce thickens.

Ideal for children (and babies, page 4).

This dish should be served hot, with vermicelli or plain (boiled) rice (page 84)

1 cup = 250ml = 8fl oz   1 tablespoon = 15ml   1 teaspoon = 5ml

Butter (lima) bean and meat stew

Ingredients

*2 x 400g (1¾ lb) cans butter (lima) beans,
rinsed and drained
500g/1lb 2oz diced beef or lamb shoulder
5 cups boiling water
1 medium onion, halved and finely chopped
140g/5oz can tomato purée (paste)
1 tablespoon olive oil
1 teaspoon ground allspice
Salt to taste*

Garnish to suit your own taste (optional)

Preparation

1 Strain the beans and set aside.

2 Dry fry the meat in a non-stick hot pan (on medium-low heat) for 3 minutes. Stir in the onion, oil and seasonings for 5 minutes.

3 Add the tomato purée, stirring for 1 minute, then pour in the boiling water. Simmer, covered, until nearly tender. (Time depends on the meat you use.)

4 Add the beans and cook for 20-30 minutes or until the sauce thickens.

Note
Can be dried beans instead of canned (page 64).

Variation
Sauté 280g/10oz of minced (ground) beef or lamb with the onion and seasonings in 1 tablespoon of warm olive oil in a pan (on medium heat) for 5 minutes. Stir in the tomato purée before adding the boiling water and follow No.4.

Ideal for children (and babies, page 4).

134

*This dish should be served hot,
with vermicelli or
plain (boiled) rice (page 84)*

1 cup　=　250ml　=　8fl oz　　　　　*1 tablespoon　=　15ml*　　　　*1 teaspoon　=　5ml*

Courgette (zucchini), potato and meat stew

Ingredients

4 courgettes (zucchini), sliced
280g/10oz minced (ground) beef or lamb
3 medium potatoes, peeled and cut into bite-sized pieces
5 cups boiling water
1 medium onion, halved and finely chopped
140g/5oz can tomato purée (paste)
1 tablespoon olive oil
1 teaspoon ground allspice
Salt to taste

Preparation

1 Sauté the onion, meat and seasonings in warm oil in a pan (on medium heat) for 2-3 minutes. Stir in the potatoes for 8 minutes, followed by the courgettes for a further 2 minutes.

2 Add the tomato purée, stirring for 1 minute, then pour in the boiling water.

3 Simmer, covered, for 20-30 minutes or until cooked and the sauce thickens. (The courgettes and the potatoes should be cooked but still firm.)

Variations
Use diced beef or lamb shoulder (page 134, No.2 and 3). Stir in the potatoes for 8 minutes, then the courgettes for 2 minutes and follow the above No.3. (Add more water if necessary.)
Omit the potatoes.
For vegetarians, omit the meat.

Ideal for children (and babies, page 4).

This dish should be served hot, with vermicelli or plain (boiled) rice (page 84)

1 cup = 250ml = 8fl oz   1 tablespoon = 15ml   1 teaspoon = 5ml

Runner bean and meat stew

Ingredients

*500g/1lb 2oz frozen sliced (or whole)
runner beans, defrosted*
500g/1lb 2oz diced beef or lamb shoulder
140g/5oz can tomato purée (paste)
1 medium onion, halved and finely chopped
5 cups boiling water
1 tablespoon olive oil
1 teaspoon ground allspice
6 garlic cloves, peeled
Salt to taste

Garnish to suit your own taste (optional)

Preparation

1 Dry fry the meat in a non-stick hot pan (on medium-low heat) for 3 minutes. Stir in the onion, garlic, oil and seasonings for a further 5 minutes.

2 Add the tomato purée, stirring for 1 minute, then pour in the boiling water. Simmer, covered, until half cooked. (Time depends on the meat you use.)

3 Add the beans and cook together for 30-40 minutes or until all tender and the sauce thickens. stirring occasionally.

Note
If using fresh beans: Trim the ends and halve widthways, wash and steam. Cook the meat until tender before adding the beans, then simmer, covered for 20 minutes or until the sauce thickens.

Variations
Sauté 280g/10oz of minced (ground) beef or lamb with the onion and seasonings in 1 tablespoon of warm olive oil in a pan (on medium heat) for 5 minutes. Stir in the tomato purée and beans for 1-2 minutes before adding the boiling water. Simmer, covered, for 30-40 minutes or until cooked and the sauce thickens.

Ideal for children (and babies, page 4).

138

This dish should be served hot, with vermicelli or plain (boiled) rice (page 84)

1 cup = 250ml = 8fl oz　　　　1 tablespoon = 15ml　　　　1 teaspoon = 5ml

Okra and meat stew

Ingredients

500g/1lb 2oz frozen medium-sized okra
500g/1lb 2oz diced beef or lamb shoulder
1 medium onion, halved and finely chopped
2 garlic cloves, crushed
30g/1oz/¾ cup fresh coriander (cilantro), chopped
140g/5oz can tomato purée (paste)
1 tablespoon pomegranate molasses (page 5), optional
5 cups boiling water
1 tablespoon olive oil
1 teaspoon ground allspice
Salt to taste

Garnish to suit your own taste (optional)

Preparation

1 Defrost the okra, then drain on kitchen paper and set aside.

2 Dry fry the meat in a non-stick hot pan (on medium-low heat) for 3 minutes. Stir in the onion, garlic, oil and seasonings for a further 5 minutes.

3 Add the tomato purée, stirring for 1 minute, then pour in the boiling water. Simmer, covered, until nearly tender. (Time depends on the meat you use.)

4 Stir in the okra, coriander, pomegranate molasses (if using) and lemon juice. Cook for 20-30 minutes or until cooked and the sauce thickens.

Variation
Replace the meat with 500g/1lb 2oz of diced chicken breast fillets.

Ideal for children (and babies, page 4).

This dish should be served hot, with vermicelli rice (page 84) or couscous (page 86)

1 cup = 250ml = 8fl oz　　　1 tablespoon = 15ml　　　1 teaspoon = 5ml

Spinach and meat stew

Ingredients

900g/2 lb fresh baby leaf spinach
280g/10oz minced (ground) beef or lamb
1 medium onion, halved and finely chopped
4 tablespoons pine nuts
3 tablespoons lemon juice or to taste
2 tablespoons olive oil
1 cup boiling water
1 teaspoon ground allspice
Salt to taste

Preparation

1 Sauté the pine nuts in warm oil in a large pan (on medium heat) stirring constantly until golden. Stir in the meat, onion and seasonings for 5 minutes.

2 Add the spinach in batches (on medium-low heat) covered, for 4-6 minutes or until wilted. Pour in the boiling water, then add the lemon juice and cook (on low heat) for a further 10 minutes.

Variations

Replace the minced (ground) meat with 500g/1lb 2oz of diced beef or lamb shoulder and dry fry in a non-stick hot pan (on medium heat) for 3 minutes, then stir in the onion, 1 tablespoon of olive oil and seasonings for 5 minutes. Pour in 1 cup of boiling water and cook until tender. (Time depends on the meat you use.) Add the spinach and follow No.2, by adding the sautéed pine nuts for the last 2 minutes of cooking.
Reserve half of the pine nuts to garnish.
Omit the yogurt.
For vegetarians, omit the meat.

Ideal for children (and babies, page 4).

142

This dish should be served hot, with vermicelli or plain (boiled) rice (page 84)

1 cup = 250ml = 8fl oz   1 tablespoon = 15ml   1 teaspoon = 5ml

If using a fan assisted oven (page 4)

Aubergine (eggplant) and meat stew

Ingredients

3 medium aubergines (eggplants), end stalks removed
280/10oz minced (ground) beef or lamb
1 medium onion, halved and finely chopped
400g/14oz can chopped tomatoes
4 tablespoons pine nuts
1 tablespoon tomato purée (paste) diluted with ½ cup boiling water
Olive oil
1 teaspoon ground allspice
1 tablespoon of pomegranate molasses (page 5), optional
Salt to taste

Garnish to suit your own taste (optional)

Preparation

1 Peel the aubergines leaving a few thin black strips. Cut into 4 pieces lengthways (or into 1 inch slices widthways) and sprinkle with a little salt, then set aside for 10 minutes. Dry with kitchen paper and brush with oil. Sauté in a non-stick hot pan in batches (on medium heat) until just tender and browned on all sides. Or place in a greased baking dish and bake in a preheated oven at 200°C/400°F/Gas 6. Alternatively, grill (broil) under a medium heat.

2 Sauté the pine nuts in 1 tablespoon warm oil in a pan (on medium heat) stirring constantly until golden. Stir in the meat, onion and seasonings for 2-3 minutes. Add the aubergines, followed by the tomatoes and the diluted tomato purée, mixed with the pomegranate molasses (if using).

3 Bring to the boil. Simmer, covered, for 20 minutes or until the sauce thickens. Remove gently to a serving dish. (Or arrange the aubergines in a slightly-greased ovenproof dish, topped with the tomato mixture, then bake in a preheated oven at 180°C/350°F/Gas 4 for 20-25 minutes or until cooked and the sauce thickens.

Variations
Deep fry the aubergine pieces in hot cooking oil.
Cut the aubergines into a small cubes and follow the above instructions.
Replace the tomato sauce with the white sauce and cheese (page 168 No.4 and 5, without the spinach) by using the small aubergine cubes. Bake in a preheated oven at 180°C/350°F/Gas 4 for 20 minutes or until the cheese melts and turns golden.

Ideal for children (and babies, page 4).

144

This dish should be served hot, with vermicelli rice (page 84) or couscous (page 86)

1 cup = 250ml = 8fl oz   1 tablespoon = 15ml   1 teaspoon = 5ml

Cooked yogurt and meat stew

Ingredients

500g/1lb 2oz diced beef or lamb shoulder
1 medium onion, halved and thinly sliced
2 cups boiling water, for the meat
2 cups natural (plain) yogurt
4 garlic cloves, crushed
2 tablespoons dried mint
1 medium egg, beaten
1 tablespoon cornflour (cornstarch), dissolved
in 3½ cups cold water
2 tablespoons olive oil
1 teaspoon ground allspice
Salt to taste

Garnish to suit your own taste (optional)

Preparation

1 Dry fry the meat in a non-stick hot pan (on medium-low heat) for 3 minutes. Stir in the onion, 1 tablespoon oil and seasonings for 5 minutes. Pour in the boiling water and simmer, covered, until tender. (Time depends on the meat you use.)

2 In another pan, blend the yogurt, cornflour mixture, egg and salt. Bring to the boil, stirring constantly in the same direction (to prevent curdling).

3 Add the meat and 1 cup of its broth to the yogurt mixture. Simmer, covered, for 7-10 minutes, stirring occasionally.

4 Sauté the garlic and the dried mint in 1 tablespoon of warm oil in a small pan (on low heat) for 1 minute, then stir in with the mixture for a further 1-2 minutes.

Variations
Omit the meat and follow No.2 and 4.
Brown small sausage-shaped chicken (or meat) kafta in 1 tablespoon of warm olive oil (page 156, No.1, first line only) then add to the cooked yogurt (No.2) and cook together (on low heat) for 7-10 minutes, then follow No.4.

Ideal for children (and babies, page 4).

146

This dish should be served hot, with vermicelli or plain (boiled) rice (page 84)

1 cup = 250ml = 8fl oz   *1 tablespoon = 15ml*   *1 teaspoon = 5ml*

Potato and meat stew

Ingredients

500g/1lb 2oz diced beef or lamb shoulder
5 cups boiling water
6 medium potatoes, peeled and cut into bite-sized pieces
1 medium onion, halved and finely chopped
140g/5oz can tomato purée (paste)
1 tablespoon olive oil
1 tablespoon balsamic vinegar (optional)
1 teaspoon ground allspice
Salt to taste

Garnish to suit your own taste (optional)

Preparation

1 Dry fry the meat in a hot non-stick pan (on medium-low heat) for 3 minutes. Stir in the onion, oil and seasonings for a further 5 minutes.

2 Add the tomato purée, stirring for 1 minute, then pour in the boiling water. Simmer, covered, until nearly tender. (Time depends on the meat you use.)

3 Stir in the potatoes for 6 minutes, then add the vinegar (if using) and cook (on low heat) for 20-30 minutes or until cooked and the sauce thickens. (The potatoes should still be firm.)

Variations

Sauté 280g/10oz of minced (ground) beef or lamb in 1 tablespoon of olive oil with the onion for 2 minutes. Stir in the potatoes for 6 minutes, followed by the tomato purée for a further minute before adding the boiling water.
Replace the diced meat with 500g/1lb 2oz of diced chicken breast fillets.

Ideal for children (and babies, page 4).

148

This dish should be served hot, with vermicelli or plain (boiled) rice (page 84)

1 cup = 250ml = 8fl oz   1 tablespoon = 15ml   1 teaspoon = 5ml

If using a fan assisted oven (page 4)

Potato and meat pie

Ingredients

8 medium potatoes, peeled and halved
280g/10oz minced (ground) beef or lamb
1 medium onion, halved and finely chopped
5 tablespoons pine nuts
½ teaspoon ground allspice
4-6 tablespoons breadcrumbs
4 tablespoons olive oil
Salt to taste

Preparation

1 Cook the potatoes in a large pan of salted boiling water (on medium heat) covered, for 30 minutes or until tender. Remove with a slotted spoon and mash while still hot. Set aside.

2 Sauté the pine nuts in 2 tablespoons of warm oil in a pan (on medium heat) stirring constantly until golden. Stir in the meat, onion and seasonings for 5 minutes or until cooked.

3 Place half of the mashed potatoes in the bottom of a lightly-greased 10 inch (about 25cm) round or square baking dish. Smooth evenly, using the back of a spoon dipped in water or milk. Spread the meat mixture over and cover with the remaining half.

4 Brush with 2 tablespoons of oil and sprinkle with the breadcrumbs. Run a knife around the edges and bake in a preheated oven at 180°C/350°F/Gas 4 for 20 minutes or until golden. Or grill (broil) under a medium heat for 5-8 minutes. Cut as desired.

Variations
Stir 1 tablespoon of pomegranate molasses (page 5) into the meat mixture during the last minute of cooking.
For vegetarians: omit the meat and use 2 medium sliced onions instead of chopped.

Ideal for children (and babies, page 4).

150

This dish should be served hot or tepid, with green salad

Spaghetti with meat and pine nuts

Ingredients

500g/1lb 2oz dried spaghetti, broken in half
280g/10oz minced (ground) beef or lamb
1 medium onion, halved and finely chopped
5 tablespoons pine nuts (optional)
140g/5oz can tomato purée (paste))
2 cups boiling water
3 tablespoons olive oil
1 teaspoon lemon juice (optional)
½ teaspoon ground allspice
Pepper and salt to taste

Garnish to suit your own taste (optional)

Preparation

1 Cook the spaghetti in a large pan of salted boiling water (on medium heat) for 15 minutes, adding the oil to prevent sticking, (or according to the packet instructions). Drain and rinse under cold water and set aside.

2 In the same pan, sauté the pine nuts (if using) in 2 tablespoons of warm oil (on medium heat) stirring constantly until golden. Stir in the meat, onion and seasonings for 5 minutes, followed by the tomato purée for a further minute.

3 Pour in the boiling water and lemon juice (if using). Simmer, covered, for 20 minutes or until the sauce thickens. Add the spaghetti a few minutes before serving, tossing well together to coat.

Variations
Stir 1 tablespoon of pomegranate molasses (page 5) into the meat mixture during the last minute of cooking.
Sprinkle 1-2 tablespoons of grated Parmesan cheese for each serving.
Replace the spaghetti with any pasta.

Ideal for children (and babies, page 4).

152

This dish should be served hot

Courgettes (zucchini) stuffed with meat

Ingredients

12-18 small courgettes (zucchini), trimmed
280g/10oz/minced (ground) beef or lamb
4-6 lamb chops (optional)
100g/7oz/1 cup basmati rice, rinsed and drained
2 tablespoons tomato purée (paste), diluted with boiling water, to cover the courgettes
2 tablespoons olive oil
1 tablespoon dried mint
2 tablespoons lemon juice
4 garlic cloves, crushed
½ teaspoon ground allspice
Salt to taste

Garnish to suit your own taste (optional)

Preparation

1 Core the courgettes gently from the stem end with an apple corer, leaving a wide hollow while making sure the root end remains intact.

2 Mix the rice, meat and seasonings and stuff each courgette three-quarters full, leaving room for the rice to expand.

3 In a pan, sauté the chops (if using) in 1 tablespoon of warm oil (on medium heat) for 1 minute on both sides. Arrange the courgettes on top. Cover with the diluted tomato purée and salt. Simmer, covered, for 40-50 minutes or until cooked and the sauce thickens.

4 Sauté the garlic and dried mint in 1 tablespoon of warm oil in a small pan (on low heat) for 1 minute, then add to the tomato purée mixture, followed by the lemon juice, for the last 8-10 minutes of cooking.

Variations
Add 200g/7oz can chopped tomatoes to the stuffing.
Mix the garlic, mint and lemon juice in a bowl (omit the oil) and add to the tomato purée mixture (No.4).

Ideal for children (and babies, page 4).

154

This dish should be served hot, with salad or plain yogurt

1 cup = 250ml = 8fl oz   1 tablespoon = 15ml   1 teaspoon = 5ml

*If using a fan assisted
oven (page 4)*

Baked vegetables with kafta meat

Ingredients

Kafta
*400g/14oz diced beef or lamb (from shoulder
or leg)
1 medium onion, halved
1 teaspoon ground allspice
40g/1½oz fresh flat-leaf parsley
Salt to taste*

Potato mixture
*4 medium potatoes, peeled and cut into
½ inch slices widthways
4 medium ripe tomatoes, thinly sliced
2 medium aubergines (eggplants), cut into
½ inch slices widthways
3 tablespoons tomato purée (paste), diluted
with boiling water to cover the vegetables
½ teaspoon ground allspice
Olive oil
Salt to taste*

Garnish to suit your own taste (optional)

156

*This dish can be served hot,
with green salad, vermicelli or
plain (boiled) rice (page 84)*

Preparation

1 Place all the kafta ingredients in a food processor and blend to a smooth paste. Flatten in the bottom of a lightly-greased baking dish and smooth evenly with the back of a spoon dipped in water or in oil. Set aside.

2 Half-cook the sliced potatoes in a large pan of boiling water (on medium heat). Drain and set aside.

3 Peel each aubergine leaving on a few thin black strips, then slice and sprinkle with a little salt. Set aside for 10 minutes. Dry with kitchen paper and brush with oil. Sauté in a non-stick hot pan in batches (on medium heat) until just tender and browned, turning once. Or place in a greased baking dish and bake in a preheated oven at 200°C/400°F/Gas 6. Alternatively, grill (broil) under a medium heat. (Or deep fry in hot cooking oil.)

4 Arrange the aubergines over the kafta, cover with the potatoes, followed by the sliced tomatoes. Add the diluted tomato purée, mixed with the seasonings.

5 Bake in a preheated oven at 180°C/350°F/Gas 4 for 30-40 minutes or until cooked and the sauce thickens. (Or cover with kitchen foil and bake at 230°C/450°F/Gas 8 for 50-60 minutes.)

Variations
*Omit either the aubergines or the potatoes.
Replace the diced meat with diced chicken breast fillets.*

Ideal for children (and babies, page 4).

1 cup = 250ml = 8fl oz   1 tablespoon = 15ml   1 teaspoon = 5ml

If using a fan assisted oven (page 4)

Artichoke hearts stuffed with meat

Ingredients

10-12 frozen large artichoke hearts, defrosted
280g/10oz minced (ground) beef or lamb
4 tablespoons pine nuts
1 medium onion, finely chopped
400g/14oz can chopped tomatoes
1 tablespoon tomato purée (paste), diluted
with 1 cup boiling water
4-5 tablespoons olive oil
1 tablespoon lemon juice
½ teaspoon ground allspice
Pepper and salt to taste

Garnish to suit your own taste (optional)

Preparation

1 Drain the artichokes and dry on kitchen paper. Brush each one with a little oil and sauté in a non-stick hot pan in batches (on medium-low heat) for 2 minutes on each side. Arrange in a lightly-greased baking dish. Set aside.

2 Sauté the pine nuts in 2 tablespoons of warm oil in a pan (on medium heat) stirring constantly until nearly golden. Stir in the meat, onion and seasonings for 5 minutes. Place 1 heaped tablespoon of the filling on each artichoke.

3 Mix the tomatoes, diluted tomato purée, lemon juice, pepper and salt in a bowl. Pour evenly over the artichokes.

4 Bake in a preheated oven at 180°C/350°F/Gas 4 for 30-40 minutes or until tender and the sauce thickens. (Or cover with kitchen foil and bake at 230°C/450°F/Gas 8 for 40-50 minutes.)

Variations
Stir 1 tablespoon of pomegranate molasses (page 5) into the meat mixture during the last minute of cooking.
Replace the tomatoes with a white sauce. *Dissolve 3 tablespoons of plain (all-purpose) flour in 3 cups of chicken stock (1 cube), stirring constantly until the sauce thickens. Add 2-3 tablespoons of lemon juice and cook for a further minute. Pour over the stuffed artichokes. Cover with kitchen foil and bake as in No.4, for 20-25 minutes.*

158

This dish should be served hot, with vermicelli or plain (boiled) rice (page 84)

1 cup = 250ml = 8fl oz   1 tablespoon = 15ml   1 teaspoon = 5ml

Meatballs in tomato sauce

Ingredients

500g/5lb 2oz minced (ground) beef or lamb
1 medium onion, quartered
1 medium onion, halved and thinly sliced
1 tablespoon lemon juice (optional)
4 cups boiling chicken or vegetable stock (1 cube)
1 tablespoon plain (all-purpose) flour, dissolved in a little cold water
140g/5oz can tomato purée (paste)
1 tablespoon pomegranate molasses (page 5), optional
2 tablespoons olive oil
1 tablespoon ground allspice
Pepper and salt to taste

1 tablespoon chopped fresh flat-leaf parsley, to garnish (optional)

Preparation

1 Place the quartered onion in a food processor and pulse a few times. Add the meat and half of the seasonings. Blend to a smooth paste.

2 Form into golf-ball sized and sauté in warm oil in a pan (on medium heat) for 5 minutes or until browned. Remove with a slotted spoon and set aside.

3 In the same pan, sauté the sliced onions (on medium-low heat) until soft. Stir in the meat balls, remaining seasonings and the tomato purée for a further minute.

4 Add the boiling stock (or replace with salted boiling water) and dissolved flour. Bring to the boil, then simmer, covered, for 20 minutes or until the sauce thickens, stirring in the lemon juice and the pomegranate molasses (if using).

5 Transfer to a platter and sprinkle with the parsley, if desired.

Variations
Brown 4 tablespoons of pine nuts in 2 tablespoons of warm olive oil in a pan (on medium heat) stirring constantly until golden. Drain and sprinkle over the mixture.
Replace the minced meat with 400g/14oz of minced chicken breast fillets.
Omit the sliced onions.

Ideal for children (and babies, page 4).

160

This dish should be served hot, with rice (page 84) or with mashed potatoes (page 82)

Lamb tajine

Ingredients

500g/1lb 2oz diced beef or lamb shoulder
1 medium onion, halved and finely sliced
3 courgettes (zucchini), quartered and cut into large pieces
Boiling water
3 carrots, halved and cut into large pieces
1 sweet potato, cut into large pieces
1 medium tomato, quartered
400g/14oz can chickpeas, rinsed and drained
225g/8oz green (or white) cabbage, thinly sliced
1 tablespoon olive oil
2 garlic cloves, crushed
1 tablespoon ground turmeric
1 tablespoon ground allspice
½ teaspoon ground cumin (optional)
1 teaspoon ground coriander
Pepper and salt to taste

Preparation

1 Dry fry the meat in a hot non-stick large pan (on medium-low heat) for 3 minutes. Stir in the onion, tomato, garlic, oil and seasonings for 5 minutes.

2 Pour in 1 cup of boiling water and simmer, covered, until the meat is nearly tender. (Time depends on the meat you use.) Add the potatoes and carrots and cook (on medium-low heat) covered, for 10 minutes, followed by the cabbage, courgettes and chickpeas for a further 3 minutes, stirring occasionally.

3 Cover with boiling water. Simmer again for 20-30 minutes or until the sauce thickens. (The courgettes and the potatoes should be cooked but still firm.)

Variations
Replace the meat with chicken drumsticks or boneless, skinless thighs.
Add 2 large-sliced aubergines (eggplants) with the courgettes and chickpeas.
Omit the cabbage and replace the turmeric with 3 tablespoons of tomato purée (paste) by stirring with the onion mixture for 1 minute before adding the boiling water.

Ideal for children

162

This dish should be served hot, with couscous (page 86)

1 cup = 250ml = 8fl oz   1 tablespoon = 15ml   1 teaspoon = 5ml

If using a fan assisted oven (page 4)

Beef fillet steaks in tomato sauce

Ingredients

500g/1lb 2oz beef fillet steaks, thinly sliced
2 large carrots, diagonally sliced
2 tablespoons tomato purée (paste)
2 cups boiling water
⅓ cup dry white wine or balsamic vinegar (optional)
3 garlic cloves, thinly sliced
1-2 tablespoons olive oil
½ teaspoon ground allspice
Salt to taste

Garnish to suit your own taste (optional)

Preparation

1 Sauté the steaks in warm oil in a pan (on medium heat) for 3 minutes. Stir in the carrots and garlic, tomato purée and seasonings for a further minute.

2 Add the wine (if using) and the boiling water. Simmer, covered, for 20-30 minutes or until cooked and the sauce thickens. Serve with steamed or sautéed vegetables, if desired.

Notes
If serving with mashed potatoes (page 82).
If serving with sautéed potatoes: *cook new (small) potatoes in a pan of salted boiling water (on medium heat) covered, until just tender. Drain and sauté in 1 tablespoon of warm olive oil in a deep frying pan until well cooked (but still firm) and golden on all sides, turning occasionally. (Or drain and brush with a little olive oil, then bake in a preheated oven at 190°C/375°F/Gas 5 for 20-30 minutes.) Remove and sprinkle with 1 tablespoon of dried parsley, oregano or rosemary.*

Ideal for children

164

This dish should be served hot, with mashed or sautéed potatoes and vegetables to your liking

1 cup = 250ml = 8fl oz   1 tablespoon = 15ml   1 teaspoon = 5ml

If using a fan assisted oven (page 4)

Lasagne in red and white sauce

Ingredients

10-12 lasagne sheets
280g/10oz minced (ground) beef or lamb
2 spring (scallions) onions, finely chopped
400g/14oz can chopped tomatoes
1 tablespoon tomato purée (paste)
2 garlic cloves, crushed
2 tablespoons olive oil
½ teaspoon allspice
1 tablespoon margarine or butter
3 tablespoons plain (all-purpose) flour
2 cups (cold) milk
225g/8oz fresh baby leaf spinach
1 tablespoon basil sauce (page 82) or dried
1 teaspoon dried oregano (optional)
115g/4oz/1 cup grated mozzarella cheese
½ teaspoon ground nutmeg
Salt to taste

Garnish to suit your own taste (optional)

Preparation

1 Cook the lasagne in a large pan of salted boiling water until nearly tender, adding 1 tablespoon of oil and one sheet at a time. Separate under cold water, then drain and set aside.

2 Sauté the meat and onions in warm oil in a pan (on medium heat) for 5 minutes. Stir in the garlic, basil, oregano, tomato purée and seasonings for 1 minute. Add the tomatoes. Simmer, covered, for 10-15 minutes or until the sauce thickens.

3 Place half of the lasagne sheets in a lightly-greased baking dish. Cover with the meat mixture and top with the remaining sheets. Set aside.

4 In a pan, dissolve the flour in the (cold) milk and sprinkle the nutmeg and salt. Bring to the boil, stirring constantly until the sauce thickens. Simmer, stirring in the butter and the spinach for 1-2 minutes.

5 Spread the spinach mixture on top of the lasagne. Sprinkle with the cheese and bake in a preheated oven at 180°C/350°F/Gas 4 for 20-30 minutes or until the cheese melts and turns golden.

Variations
Replace the spinach with 8 sliced small mushrooms and cook with the garlic mixture. Omit the meat and serve as a vegetarian dish.

Ideal for children (and babies, page 4).

This dish should be served immediately

166

1 cup = 250ml = 8fl oz　　　1 tablespoon = 15ml　　　1 teaspoon = 5ml

*If using a fan assisted
oven (page 4)*

Baked aubergines (eggplants) with meat

Ingredients

*280g/10oz minced (ground) beef or lamb
3 large aubergines (eggplants), cut into ½
inch slices widthways
115g/4oz/1 cup grated mozzarella cheese
225g/8oz fresh baby spinach leaf (optional)
2 cups (cold) milk
3 tablespoons plain (all-purpose) flour
1 tablespoon butter or margarine
2 spring (scallions) onions finely chopped
2 garlic cloves, crushed
8 small mushrooms, sliced (optional)
Olive oil
1 tablespoon tomato purée (paste)
1 cup boiling water
1 teaspoon dried oregano or basil
½ teaspoon ground nutmeg
½ teaspoon allspice
Pepper and salt to taste*

Garnish to suit your own taste (optional)

Preparation

1 Peel each aubergine leaving on a few thin black strips, then slice and sprinkle with a little salt. Set aside for 10 minutes. Dry with kitchen paper and brush with oil. Sauté in a non-stick hot pan in batches (on medium heat) until tender and browned, turning once. Or place in a greased baking dish and bake in a preheated oven at 200°C/400°F/Gas 6. Alternatively, grill (broil) under a medium heat. (Or deep fry in hot cooking oil.) Set aside.

2 Sauté the meat, onions, garlic, allspice, oregano, pepper and salt in 1 tablespoon of warm oil in a pan (on medium heat) for 4-5 minutes. Stir in the mushrooms (if using) for 2 minutes, followed by the tomato purée for a further minute.

3 Pour in the boiling water and simmer, covered, for 15 minutes or until the sauce thickens. Arrange half of the aubergine slices in a baking dish. Spread the meat mixture over, then top with the remaining slices. Set aside.

4 In a pan, dissolve the flour in the (cold) milk and sprinkle the nutmeg and salt. Bring to the boil, stirring constantly until the sauce thickens. Simmer, stirring in the butter and the spinach (if using) for 1-2 minutes, then pour over the aubergine pieces. Sprinkle with the cheese.

5 Bake in a preheated oven at 180°C/350°F/Gas 4 for 20 minutes or until the cheese melts and turns golden. Or grill (broil) under a medium heat for 7-10 minutes.

Variation
Omit the meat or the white sauce and replace with more red sauce.

Ideal for children (and babies, page 4).

*This dish should be served
immediately, on its own or
with salad*

1 cup = 250ml = 8fl oz   1 tablespoon = 15ml   1 teaspoon = 5ml

Rice, chickpea and meat stew

Ingredients

280g/10oz minced (ground) beef or lamb
4 medium onions, halved and thinly sliced
400g/14oz can chickpeas, rinsed and drained
200g/7oz/1 cup basmati rice, rinsed and drained
2 cups boiling chicken or vegetable stock (1 cube)
2 tablespoons olive oil
½ teaspoon cinnamon (optional)
1 tablespoon ground turmeric
½ teaspoon allspice
Salt to taste

Garnish to suit your own taste (optional)

Preparation

1 Sauté the meat in warm oil in a pan (on medium heat) for 3-5 minutes.

2 Stir in the onions (on medium-low heat) until soft and transparent. Add the chickpeas, rice and seasonings, stirring together for a further 1-2 minutes.

3 Pour in the boiling stock (or replace with salted boiling water) and simmer, covered, for 15-20 minutes or until the rice is cooked and the water is absorbed.

Variations
Use dried chickpeas instead of canned (page 34).
Soak the rinsed rice in cold water for 10 minutes, then drain before cooking.

Ideal for children (and babies, page 4).

This dish should be served hot, with green salad

1 cup = 250ml = 8fl oz   1 tablespoon = 15ml   1 teaspoon = 5ml

Meat rolls with eggs and wine

Ingredients

675g/1½lb beef or lamb from leg, cubed
1 medium onion, quartered
5-6 fresh mint leaves
2 tablespoons olive oil
1 teaspoon ground allspice
Pepper and salt to taste
2 medium eggs, boiled and sliced
5 garlic cloves, sliced (optional)
1 medium ripe tomato, sliced
3-4 tablespoons plain (all-purpose) flour
3 tablespoons dry red wine (optional)

Garnish to suit your own taste (optional)

Preparation

1 Place the meat, onion, mint, allspice, pepper and salt in a food processor and blend to a smooth paste.

2 Make 3 medium-sized balls, tossing with flour to prevent sticking and flatten into thin circles on a piece of foil.

3 Arrange some egg slices or garlic in a line down the centre. Fold and roll, pressing to seal the edges. Sauté in warm oil in a large pan (on medium-low heat) until browned.

4 Add the tomato. Simmer, covered, for 10 minutes, then pour in the wine (if using) and cook for a further 5 minutes. Remove, then cut into ¾ inch thick slices. (Mash the sauce and set aside.)

5 Mix 1 tablespoon of gravy with 1 cup of cold water and add to the set aside sauce. Bring to the boil, stirring constantly.

Note
If serving with mashed potatoes (page 82).

Ideal for children

172

This dish should be served hot, with gravy, mashed potatoes and vegetables of your choice

1 cup = 250ml = 8fl oz   *1 tablespoon = 15ml*   *1 teaspoon = 5ml*

Cabbage, rice and meat stew

Ingredients

280g/10oz minced (ground) beef or lamb
100g/7oz/1 cup basmati rice, rinsed and drained
2 cups salted boiling water, for cooking the rice
3 garlic cloves, crushed
1 tablespoon dried mint
4 tablespoons lemon juice
340g/12oz white or green cabbage
½ teaspoon ground allspice
1 tablespoon olive oil
Pepper and salt to taste

Garnish to suit your own taste (optional)

Preparation

1 Cut the cabbage in half and separate the leaves gently. Cook in a large pan of boiling water (on medium heat) until nearly soft. Remove with a slotted spoon. Cool and chop coarsely, setting aside a few large leaves to garnish (optional).

2 Sauté the meat, rice and seasonings in warm oil in a pan (on medium heat) for 5 minutes, stir in the chopped cabbage for 1 minute. Pour in the salted boiling water and simmer, covered, for 15-20 minutes or until the rice is cooked and the water is absorbed.

3 Blend the lemon juice, garlic and mint together in a bowl and add to the rice mixture for the last 10 minutes of cooking.

4 Transfer to a platter. Arrange the set aside large leaves around it, if desired.

Variation
Soak the rinsed rice in cold water for 10 minutes, then drain before cooking.

Ideal for children *(with plain yogurt).*

174

This dish should be served hot or tepid, with salad or plain yogurt

1 cup = 250ml = 8fl oz   1 tablespoon = 15ml   1 teaspoon = 5ml

Chicken kafta with peas and potatoes

Ingredients

Kafta
400g/14oz diced chicken breast fillets
1 medium onion, halved
1 teaspoon ground allspice
40g/1½oz fresh flat-leaf parsley
Salt to taste

Peas mixture
500g/1lb 2oz frozen peas, defrosted
3 medium potatoes, peeled and cut into
bite-sized pieces
1-2 tablespoons olive oil
3 tablespoons tomato purée (paste)
5 cups boiling water
½ teaspoon ground allspice
Salt to taste

Garnish to suit your own taste (optional)

Preparation

1 Place all the kafta ingredients in a food processor and blend to a smooth paste. Flatten into small burgers and brown in warm oil (on medium heat). Remove with a slotted spoon and set aside.

2 In the same pan, sauté the potatoes and peas for 10 minutes, then stir in the tomato purée for 1 minute. Add the kafta burgers, boiling water and seasonings.

3 Simmer, covered, for 20-30 minutes or until cooked and the sauce thickens. (The potatoes should be cooked but still firm.)

Variations
Replace the chicken with 400g/14oz of diced beef or lamb (from shoulder or leg) and form into small sausages.
Omit the potatoes.

Ideal for children (and babies, page 4).

176

**This dish should be served hot,
with vermicelli or
plain (boiled) rice (page 84)**

1 cup = 250ml = 8fl oz   *1 tablespoon = 15ml*   *1 teaspoon = 5ml*

If using a fan assisted oven (page 4)

Chicken kebabs and meat kafta

Ingredients

Chicken mixture

400g/14oz skinless chicken breast fillets, cubed
8-10 cherry tomatoes
6-8 small onions, peeled
1 teaspoon ground allspice
1 tablespoon plain yogurt (optional)
1 teaspoon tomato ketchup
3 garlic cloves, crushed
1 tablespoon olive oil
Salt to taste

Kafta

400g/14oz diced beef or lamb (from shoulder or leg)
1 medium onion, halved
1 teaspoon ground allspice
40g/1½oz fresh flat-leaf parsley
Salt to taste

Garnish to suit your own taste (optional)

Preparation

1 Place the chicken ingredients in a bowl and leave to marinate in the refrigerator for 2-4 hours or overnight.

2 Place the kafta ingredients in a food processor and blend to a smooth paste. Form into large sausages.

3 Skewer both chicken and kafta, then barbecue, bake in a preheated oven at 200°C/400°F/Gas 6 for 25-30 minutes or until done to your liking, turning once or twice. Alternatively, grill (broil) under a medium heat for 12-15 minutes.

Note
To prevent the kafta from falling off the skewers while cooking, place in-between a double-sided barbecue griller.

Variations
Use cubed lamb shoulder or monkfish, instead of the chicken for No.1.
Serve with 1 thinly-sliced large onion mixed with 30g/1oz of fresh flat-leaf parsley (finely chopped) and 1 teaspoon of sumac (page 5).

Ideal for children

This dish should be served hot, with hummus or garlic dip, salad and pitta bread

178

1 cup = 250ml = 8fl oz   *1 tablespoon = 15ml*   *1 teaspoon = 5ml*

*If using a fan assisted
oven (page 4)*

Chicken kibbeh

Ingredients

Chicken mixture

400g/14oz diced chicken breast, fillets
400g/14oz/2 cups fine brown burghul
(bulgur) page 5
1 medium onion, quartered
1 teaspoon dried mint
½ teaspoon ground allspice
Salt to taste

Stuffing

2 medium onions, halved and thinly sliced
4 tablespoons olive oil
5 tablespoons pine nuts
½ tablespoon ground allspice
Salt to taste

Preparation

1 Rinse the burghul under cold water. Drain and set aside. Place the chicken mixture ingredients in a food processor (except the burghul) and blend to a smooth paste. Tranfer to a bowl and knead well with the burghul, dipping your hand in cold water, then return to the food processor in batches and pulse a few times.

2 Place in a lightly-greased 15 inch (about 30cm) wide round baking dish and smooth evenly using the back of a spoon dipped in water or in oil. Brush with 2 tablespoons of oil and run a knife around the edges.

3 Bake in a preheated oven at 200°C/400°F/Gas 6 for 25-30 minutes or until browned.

4 Meanwhile, sauté the pine nuts in 2 tablespoons of warm oil in a pan (on medium-low heat) stirring constantly until golden. Stir in the onions and seasonings until soft and transparent. Spread evenly over the paste, then return to the oven for a further 1-2 minutes. Cut as desired.

Variations

Stir 1 tablespoon of pomegranate molasses (page 5) into the onion mixture during the last minute of cooking.
Replace the chicken with 400g/14oz of diced beef or lamb (from shoulder or leg).
Use the chicken paste only.
Spread the onion mixture in the bottom of the baking dish and top with the paste, then brush with 2 tablespoons of olive oil and score the paste vertically and horizontally with a knife running it around the edges and follow the above No.3.

180

This dish should be served hot or tepid, with salad, plain yogurt, or hummus (page 34)

1 cup = 250ml = 8fl oz   1 tablespoon = 15ml   1 teaspoon = 5ml

If using a fan assisted oven (page 4)

Baked chicken with honey

Ingredients

1 large chicken
1 medium onion, quartered
2 sweet potatoes, peeled and cubed
3 carrots, peeled and sliced
Boiling water
2 oranges, sliced (1 to garnish, optional)
4 tablespoons clear honey
1 tablespoon olive oil
1 teaspoon ground turmeric
1 teaspoon ground allspice
1 cinnamon stick
2 bay leaves
Pepper and salt to taste

Garnish to suit your own taste (optional)

Preparation

1 Mix the allspice and turmeric together in a bowl. Rub the chicken with half of the mixture amount (setting aside the other half).

2 Sauté the chicken in warm oil in a large pan (on medium heat), turning occasionally until golden. Cover with boiling water, skimming all the foam as it forms on the surface. Add the carrots, sweet potatoes, set aside seasonings, onion, bay leaves, cinnamon stick, pepper and salt. Simmer, covered for 20 minutes.

3 Remove with a slotted spoon and transfer to a baking dish. Drizzle with the honey and pour in 2 cups of the chicken broth (discarding the onion, bay leaves and cinnamon stick).

4 Arrange the orange slices over the top and around the chicken with the sweet potatoes and carrots. Bake in a preheated oven at 200°C/400°F/Gas 6 for 30 minutes or until cooked and browned, basting once or twice.

5 Discard the cooked oranges and transfer to a platter, then replace with uncooked orange slices, if desired. Serve with the left over chicken mixture honey sauce.

Variation
Replace the sweet potatoes with (half-boiled) normal potatoes.

Ideal for children

This dish should be served hot, with salad

1 cup = 250ml = 8fl oz   *1 tablespoon = 15ml*   *1 teaspoon = 5ml*

If using a fan assisted oven (page 4)

Baked chicken and potatoes

Ingredients

4-6 large chicken drumsticks or 8-12 thighs
4-6 medium potatoes, peeled and sliced
⅓ cup olive oil
3 garlic cloves, crushed
½ cup lemon juice
½ teaspoon ground allspice
Pepper and salt to taste

Preparation

1 Mix the lemon juice, oil, garlic and seasonings together in a bowl and toss well with the chicken and potatoes, then place in an ovenproof dish.

2 Bake in a preheated oven at 180°C/350°F/Gas 4 for 1 hour or until cooked and browned on all sides, turning and basting once or twice. (Or cover with kitchen foil and cook at 230°C/450°F/Gas 8.) Brush or drizzle with more lemon juice and oil, if necessary.

Note
The potatoes should be cooked but still firm.

Ideal for children

This dish should be served hot, with salad, garlic dip (page 76) or hummus (page 34)

1 cup = 250ml = 8fl oz   1 tablespoon = 15ml   1 teaspoon = 5ml

*If using a fan assisted
oven (page 4)*

Chicken shawarma

Ingredients

*675g/1½lb skinless chicken breast fillets,
halved widthways and cut into strips
1 teaspoon kutchup (optional)
1 teaspoon olive oil
2 garlic cloves, crushed
2 teaspoons dry white wine (optional)
2 teaspoons white vinegar
1 teaspoon ground allspice
½ teaspoon ground nutmeg
1 teaspoon ground cardamom (optional)
Pepper and salt to taste*

Garnish to suit your own taste (optional)

Preparation

1 Mix all the ingredients in a bowl. Add the chicken and toss well together. Leave to marinate for 2-4 hours or overnight in the refrigerator.

2 Place in a lightly-greased baking dish and bake in a preheated oven at 200°C/400°F/Gas 6 for 20-30 minutes or until tender and browned on all sides, turning once and separate. Or grill (broil) under a medium heat for 12-15 minutes.

3 Serve hot with flat round pitta bread, salad and tahini dip (page 78).

Variations
*Replace the tahini dip with the garlic dip (page 76).
Add ⅓ teaspoon of crushed mastic (page 5) with the marinade.
Replace the chicken with 675g/1½lb of lamb (from shouder or leg) or beef fillet, cut into strips.*

**This dish should be served
with tahini dip (page 78)
and salad**

1 cup = 250ml = 8fl oz   1 tablespoon = 15ml   1 teaspoon = 5ml

Chicken with meat, rice and nuts

Ingredients

Chicken mixture
1 medium chicken
1 medium onion, halved
1 cinnamon stick
½-1 teaspoon ground allspice
2 bay leaves (optional)
1-2 tablespoons olive oil
Salt to taste

Rice mixture
140g/5oz minced (ground) beef or lamb
200g/7oz/1 cup basmati rice, rinsed and drained
1 chicken stock cube
5 tablespoons pine nuts
5 tablespoons blanched almonds
3 tablespoons olive oil
½ teaspoon ground allspice
Salt to taste

Garnish to suit your own taste (optional)

Preparation

1 Sauté the chicken in 1 tablespoon of warm oil in a large pan (on medium heat) until browned on all sides, adding the onion, bay leaves and cinnamon stick. Cover with boiling water, skimming all the foam as it forms on the surface. Add the allspice and salt. Simmer, covered, for 1 hour or until tender.

2 Brown the pine nuts and almonds separately in 2 tablespoons of warm oil in a pan (on medium heat) stirring constantly until golden. Remove half to garnish, then stir in the meat and seasonings with the remaining half for 5 minutes.

3 Add the rice and stir with the meat mixture for 1 minute. Pour in 2 cups of the boiling broth, adding the stock cube. Return to the boil. Simmer, covered, for 15-20 minutes or until the rice is cooked and the broth is absorbed.

To serve
Transfer the rice mixture to a platter.
Remove the hot chicken and cut the flesh into large pieces, discarding the bones and skin, then place on top of the rice. Sprinkle with the remaining nuts.

Variations
Omit either the meat or the chicken.
If using the meat, add 2 cups of boiling chicken stock (1 cube).
Soak the rinsed rice in cold water for 10 minutes, then drain before cooking.

Ideal for children (and babies, page 4).
With plain yogurt.

188

This dish should be served hot, with salad, hummus (page 34) or garlic dip (page 76)

1 cup = 250ml = 8fl oz   1 tablespoon = 15ml   1 teaspoon = 5ml

If using a fan assisted oven (page 4)

Baked chicken in pitta bread

Ingredients

8-10 boneless, skinless chicken thighs
4-5 flat round pitta bread
2 medium onions, halved and thinly sliced
½ teaspoon ground allspice
½ teaspoon ground coriander
2-3 tablespoons sumac
1 tablespoon lemon juice, for brushing
2-3 tablespoons olive oil
Salt to taste

Garnish to suit your own taste (optional)

Preparation

1 Mix the chicken thighs in a bowl together with 1 tablespoon of oil, allspice, coriander and salt, then transfer to a lightly greased ovenproof dish and bake in a preheated oven at 180°C/350°F/Gas 4 for 20-30 minutes or until nearly tender, turning once or twice.

2 Sauté the onions in 1-2 tablespoons of warm oil in a pan (on medium- low heat) for 5 minutes or until soft.

3 Open up the bread and place some of the onions on one half and sprinkle with a little sumac, then top with enough chicken mixture, setting aside the sauce. Cover with more onions and sumac.

4 Brush the other half with the set aside sauce and return to the oven. Bake for 10-15 minutes. Continue brushing the chicken mixture with the sauce or lemon juice to prevent from drying out. Close each wrap before serving.

This dish should be served hot, with salad or hummus (page 34)

1 cup = 250ml = 8fl oz   1 tablespoon = 15ml   1 teaspoon = 5ml

If using a fan assisted oven (page 4)

Chicken burgers

Ingredients

400g/14oz diced chicken breast fillets
4 large sesame rolls
115g/4oz/1 cup grated mozzarella cheese
1 large onion, quartered
1 tablespoon fresh thyme or oregano
1 tablespoon plain yogurt (optional)
1 medium egg, beaten (optional)
½ teaspoon ground mild paprika (optional)
Lettuce leaves (optional)
4 tablespoons breadcrumbs
2 tablespoons olive oil
Pepper and salt to taste

Garnish to suit your own taste (optional)

Preparation

1 Place the chicken and onion in a food processor and blend to a smooth paste. Add the egg, yogurt, paprika (if using) thyme and salt, pulsing a few times.

2 Flatten into burgers or patties (tossing in flour if necessary), then coat well with the breadcrumbs. Brush with a little oil and sauté in a non-stick hot pan (on medium-low heat) until cooked and golden, turning once. Or place in a lightly-greased baking dish and bake in a preheated oven at 200°C/400°F/Gas 6 for 20-30 minutes. Alternatively, grill (broil) under a medium heat for 12-15 minutes.

4 Open up the sesame rolls adding a few lettuce leaves in each roll, top with the burgers and sprinkle with the cheese. Return to the grill (broiler) under a medium heat until the cheese melts. Close together before serving.

Variations
Replace the sesame rolls with sautéed potatoes (page 164) or mashed (page 82) and omit the cheese. Or serve with salad or oven cooked chips.
Use grated Parmesan cheese instead of the mozzarella.

Ideal for children

192

This dish should be served hot

1 cup = 250ml = 8fl oz   1 tablespoon = 15ml   1 teaspoon = 5ml

If using a fan assisted oven (page 4)

Chicken rissoles

Ingredients

500g/1lb 2oz chicken breast fillets, cubed
6 tablespoons breadcrumbs
1 medium egg, beaten (optional)
½ teaspoon ground allspice
1 tablespoon plain yogurt (optional)
Olive oil
Salt to taste

Garnish to suit your own taste (optional)

Preparation

1 Mix the egg and yogurt (if using) with the seasonings in a bowl and toss the chicken cubes in the mixture. Leave to marinate for 1-2 hours.

2 Coat each cube in the breadcrumbs and place in a lightly-greased baking dish. Bake in a preheated oven at 200°C/400°F/Gas 6 for 20-30 minutes or until cooked and browned, turning once. Or grill (broil) under a medium heat for 12-15 minutes.

3 Drizzle with a little oil or lemon juice during cooking to prevent from drying out. Serve immediately.

Variations
Sauté the chicken cubes in 2 tablespoons of warm olive oil in a pan (on medium-low heat) until cooked and browned.
Replace the egg and yogurt with 1 tablespoon of olive oil.

Ideal for children
Serve the rissoles in round rolls with a few lettuce and a little mayonnaise.

194

This dish should be served hot, with baked beans or mashed potatoes (page 82)

1 cup = 250ml = 8fl oz   *1 tablespoon = 15ml*   *1 teaspoon = 5ml*

Cream chicken with spaghetti

Ingredients

1 large chicken, skinned and cut into pieces
500g/1lb 2oz dried spaghetti, broken in half
2 spring (scallions) onions, finely chopped
3 tablespoons olive oil
12 medium mushrooms, sliced
2 garlic cloves, crushed
2 tablespoons fresh chopped flat-leaf parsley
⅓ cup dry white wine
½ teaspoon ground nutmeg
1 cup fresh single (light) cream
Pepper and salt to taste

Garnish to suit your own taste (optional)

Preparation

1 Sauté the chicken pieces in 1 tablespoon of warm oil in a large pan (on medium-low heat) until golden. Stir in the onions, garlic, mushrooms and seasonings for 3 minutes.

2 Add the wine and parsley. Simmer, covered, for 20 minutes or until the chicken is tender. Add the cream and cook for 10 minutes or until the sauce thickens.

3 Meanwhile, cook the spaghetti in another large pan of salted boiling water (on medium heat) for 15 minutes, adding 1 tablespoon of oil to prevent sticking, (or according to the packet instructions). Drain and toss with the remaining oil.

4 Arrange the spaghetti in a large dish, top with the chicken mixture.

Variations
Replace the cream with 1 tablespoon of plain (all-purpose) flour dissolved in 1 cup of cold water.
Omit the spaghetti and serve with mashed potatoes (page 82).

196

This dish should be served immediately

1 cup = 250ml = 8fl oz   1 tablespoon = 15ml   1 teaspoon = 5ml

Chicken and mushrooms with rice

Ingredients

8 boneless, skinless chicken thighs, halved
10 small mushrooms, sliced (optional)
12 new (small) potatoes, peeled and halved
200g/7oz/1 cup basmati rice, rinsed and drained
1 cooking apple, peeled and cubed (optional)
2 garlic cloves, crushed
5 tablespoons blanched almonds, toasted
5 cups boiling chicken stock (1 cube)
3 tablespoons olive oil
1 teaspoon mild curry powder
1 teaspoons ground coriander
Salt to taste

Garnish to suit your own taste (optional)

Preparation

1 Brown the blanched almonds in 2 tablespoons of warm oil in a small pan (on medium heat) stirring constantly until golden. Remove with a slotted spoon and set aside.

2 Sauté the thighs in 1 tablespoon of warm oil (on medium-low heat) until soft. Stir in the potatoes for 5 minutes, followed by the apple, mushrooms, garlic and seasonings for a further 3 minutes.

3 Pour in the boiling stock and simmer, covered, for 20 minutes or until all cooked. (The potatoes should still be firm).

4 In another pan, place the rice, adding 2 cups of the boiling stock (No.3). Simmer, covered, for 15-20 minutes or until the rice is cooked and the stock is absorbed.

5 Transfer the rice to a platter, top with the chicken mixture and sprinkle with the almonds.

Variations
Replace the thighs with small drumsticks (or diced chicken breast fillets) and the curry powder with ground turmeric.
Use sweet potatoes (cut into cubes) instead of the new (small) potatoes.
Replace the almonds with 3-4 tablespoons of sultanas (raisins) by stiring with the chicken mixture for the last 1-2 minutes of cooking.
Soak the rinsed rice in cold water for 10 minutes, then drain before cooking.

198

This dish should be served hot, with salad

1 cup = 250ml = 8fl oz   1 tablespoon = 15ml   1 teaspoon = 5ml

Chicken with spinach and yogurt

Ingredients

400g/14oz diced chicken breast fillets
2 spring ((scallions) onions, finely chopped
900g/2 lb fresh baby leaf spinach
½ cup natural (plain) yogurt
5 tablespoons pine nuts
2 tablespoons olive oil
½-1 tablespoon ground mild curry powder
Salt to taste

Preparation

1 Sauté the pine nuts in warm oil in a pan (on medium heat) stirring constantly until golden. Remove half to garnish, if desired.

2 Stir in the onions, chicken and seasonings (on medium-low heat) for 8 minutes. Add the spinach in batches and cook covered, until wilted.

3 Remove from heat, then add the yogurt and mix well. Sprinkle the remaining pine nuts and serve immediately.

Variations
Omit the yogurt.
Replace the curry powder with ½-1 teaspoon of ground turmeric.

Ideal for children

200

This dish should be served hot, with vermicelli or plain (boiled) rice (page 84)

1 cup = 250ml = 8fl oz   1 tablespoon = 15ml   1 teaspoon = 5ml

Chicken in red wine sauce

Ingredients

8-9 boneless and skinless chicken thighs
200g/7oz can chopped tomatoes (optional)
4 medium potatoes, washed and sliced
8 medium mushrooms, sliced
1 tablespoon tomato purée (paste)
½ cup fresh orange or pineapple juice
30g/1oz/¾ cup fresh coriander (cilantro)
chopped
⅓ cup dry white wine
4 tablespoons dark soy sauce
3 garlic cloves, crushed
1 tablespoon olive oil
1 teaspoon ground turmeric
1 teaspoon ground paprika
Salt to taste

Preparation

1 Slice the potatoes into ¾ inch widthways (with the skins on) and cook in a pan of salted boiling water (on medium heat) covered, for 15 minutes or until half-cooked. Set aside.

2 Sauté the chicken thighs and seasonings in warm oil in a pan (on medium heat) for 5 minutes. Stir in the mushrooms, garlic, tomato purée and coriander for a further minute.

3 Add the tomatoes, soy sauce, wine, juice and ¼ cup of boiling water and bring to the boil. Simmer, covered, for 10 minutes.

4 Add the potatoes and cook for a further 15-20 minutes or until all cooked and the sauce thickens. (The potatoes should be cooked but still firm.)

Variations
Replace the chicken thighs with drumsticks.
Omit the potatoes and serve with plain (boiled) rice (page 88) or mashed potatoes (page 82).

This dish should be served hot

1 cup = 250ml = 8fl oz   1 tablespoon = 15ml   1 teaspoon = 5ml

Mexican chicken with rice

Ingredients

Chicken mixture
1 medium chicken
1 medium onion, halved
½-1 teaspoon ground allspice
2 bay leaves and 1 cinnamon stick (optional)
1-2 tablespoons olive oil
Salt to taste

Rice mixture
200g/7oz/1 cup basmati rice, rinsed and drained
1 medium ripe tomato, finely diced
1 green (bell) pepper, seeded and diced
1 spring (scallion) onion, finely chopped
5-6 tablespoons pine nuts
1 chicken stock cube
5 tablespoons blanched split almonds
3 tablespoons olive oil
1 teaspoon ground nutmeg
1 teaspoon mild (or hot) ground paprika
Salt to taste

Garnish to suit your own taste (optional)

Preparation

1 Sauté the chicken in 1 tablespoon of warm oil in a large pan (on medium heat) until browned on all sides, adding the onion, bay leaves and cinnamon stick. Cover with boiling water, skimming all the foam as it forms on the surface. Add the allspice and salt. Simmer, covered, for 1 hour or until tender.

2 When the chicken is half-cooked, brown the pine nuts and almonds (separately) in 2 tablespoons of warm oil in a small pan (on medium heat) stirring constantly until golden. Remove with a slotted spoon and set aside.

3 Sauté the onion, pepper and tomato in 1 tablespoon of warm oil in a pan (on medium-low heat) for 10-15 minutes. Stir in the rice, followed by 2 cups of the boiling chicken broth, stock cube and seasonings.

4 Bring to the boil. Simmer, covered for 15-20 minutes or until the rice is cooked and the water is absorbed.

To serve
Transfer the rice mixture to a platter.
Remove the hot chicken and cut into large pieces, discarding the bones and skin, then place on top of the rice. Sprinkle with the pine nuts and almonds.

Variations
Replace the paprika with mild or hot chilli powder.
Omit the spring onion.

This dish should be served hot, with salad

204

1 cup = 250ml = 8fl oz   1 tablespoon = 15ml   1 teaspoon = 5ml

Chicken in tortilla wraps

Ingredients

4-6 tortilla wraps
400g/14oz diced chicken breast fillets
1 cup of tortilla sauce
1 red and 2 green (bell) peppers, seeded
1 large tomato, peeled and sliced
115g/4oz/1 cup grated mozzarella
Olive oil and salt to taste

Avocado dip
1 medium avocado and 1 onion, quartered
1 medium tomato, peeled and salt to taste

Cheese dip
400g/14oz/2 cups Philadelphia cheese,
cut into pieces
4 tablespoons plain yogurt and salt to taste

Salsa dip
2 medium tomatoes, peeled and chopped
1 green (bell) pepper, seeded and diced
1 tablespoon tomato purée (paste)
1 teaspoon chilli or mild curry paste
1 tablespoon olive oil and ⅓ cup water
1 teaspoon dried oregano and salt to taste

Preparation

1 Sauté the chicken in 1 tablespoon of warm oil in a pan (on medium heat) for 3 minutes. Stir in the peppers and tomato for a further 5 minutes.

2 Add the tortilla sauce and seasonings. Simmer, covered, for 10-15 minutes or until the sauce thickens.

To prepare the dips
Place the avocado dip ingredients in a food processor and blend to a paste. Repeat the same for the cheese and salsa dips.

To serve
Add some of the chicken mixture in the centre of each tortilla and cover with cheese.
Grill (broil) the open tortilla under a medium heat until the cheese melts.
Top with the dip of your choice.
Roll up and serve as a wrap. Garnish to suit your own taste.

Note
You could serve this meal with ready-made dips (available in most shops).

Variation
Omit the chicken and serve as a vegetarian dish.
Replace the mozzarella cheese with grated cheddar cheese.

This dish should be served immediately

1 cup = 250ml = 8fl oz   1 tablespoon = 15ml   1 teaspoon = 5ml

Chicken, peppers (bell) and baby corn cobs

Ingredients

400g/14oz chicken breast fillets
1 courgette (zucchini), cut into strips
1 green (bell) pepper, seeded and cut into strips
1 red (bell) pepper, seeded and cut into strips
10 small mushrooms, thinly sliced
1 spring (scallion) onion, finely chopped
6-8 baby corn cobs, halved lengthways
½ cup chicken stock (1 cube)
1 teaspoon cornflour (cornstarch), dissolved in ½ cup cold water
2 garlic cloves, crushed
2 tablespoons dark soy sauce
1 tablespoon oyster sauce
1 teaspoon brown sugar or clear honey
1 tablespoon sesame (or olive) oil
1 teaspoon grated fresh ginger

Garnish to suit your own taste (optional)

Preparation

1 Cut the chicken into large pieces (or strips) and sauté with the onion, garlic and ginger in warm oil in a pan (on medium heat) for 3 minutes. Stir in the peppers and baby corn cobs for 5 minutes, followed by the courgette and mushrooms for a further 2 minutes.

2 Stir in the dissolved cornflour, sugar, oyster and soy sauces. Bring to the boil, then simmer, covered, for 15-20 minutes.

Variation
Replace the mushrooms with 10 mangetout (snow peas).

This dish should be served hot, with plain (boiled) rice (page 84) or dried egg noodles (page 210)

1 cup = 250ml = 8fl oz   1 tablespoon = 15ml   1 teaspoon = 5ml

Chicken with mangetout (snow peas)

Ingredients

400g/14oz diced chicken breast fillets
400g/14oz mangetout (snow peas)
10 medium mushrooms, thinly sliced
1 spring (scallion) onion, finely chopped
6 tablespoons roasted cashew nuts
½ cup boiling chicken stock (1 cube)
⅓ cup dry white wine
1 teaspoon cornflour (cornstarch), dissolved
in a little cold water
4 tablespoons dark soy sauce
1 tablespoon sesame (or olive) oil
1 teaspoon finely chopped ginger,
1-2 teaspoons brown sugar

Garnish to suit your own taste (optional)

Preparation

1 Sauté the chicken, onion and ginger in tablespoon of warm oil in a pan (on medium heat) for 4 minutes. Stir in the mangetout for 5 minutes, followed by the mushrooms for a further 2 minutes.

2 Add the wine, soy sauce, dissolved cornflour, boiling stock and sugar. Bring to the boil, then simmer, covered, for 15-20 minutes or until tender and the sauce thickens. Remove, then stir in the cashew nuts.

Notes

If serving with medium (or thin) dried egg noodles: *cook 250g/9oz of noodle in a large pan of salted boiling water (on medium heat) for 2-3 minutes, (or according to the packet instructions). Drain and toss with 1 tablespoon of sesame (or olive) oil. Separate gently with a fork.*

If using untoasted cashew nuts: *sauté in 2 tablespoons of warm olive oil in a small pan (on medium heat) stirring constantly until golden. Remove with a slotted spoon and set aside.*

This dish should be served hot, with egg rice (page 88) or dried egg noodles

1 cup = 250ml = 8fl oz   1 tablespoon = 15ml   1 teaspoon = 5ml

Chicken with peanut butter

Ingredients

400g/14oz diced chicken breast fillets
2 courgettes (zucchini), halved widthways
and sliced
12-15 small mushrooms, halved
1 spring onion (scallion) finely chopped
½ cup boiling water
5-6 tablespoons toasted cashew nuts
2 tablespoons dark soy sauce
2 tablespoons smooth peanut butter
2-3 tablespoons sesame (or olive) oil
1 tablespoon lemon juice
1 teaspoon finely chopped ginger
200g/7oz/1 cup basmati rice, rinsed and
drained
2 cups chicken or vegetable stock (1 cube) for
cooking the rice

Garnish to suit your own taste (optional)

Preparation

1 Cut the chicken into long strips and halve, then sauté with the onion and ginger in 1 tablespoon of warm oil in a pan (on medium heat) for 3 minutes. Stir in the mushrooms and courgettes for a further 4-5 minutes.

2 Mix the peanut butter, ½ cup of boiling water, soy sauce, lemon juice together in a bowl and add to the chicken mixture. Bring to the boil, then simmer, covered, for 12-15 minutes. (The courgettes should be cooked but still firm.)

3 Meanwhile, place the rice in a pan and add the boiling stock (or replace with salted boiling water). Simmer, covered, for 15-20 minutes or until cooked and the water is absorbed, then place in a serving dish. Top with the chicken mixture and sprinkle with the cashew nuts.

Note

If using untoasted cashew nuts: sauté in 2 tablespoons of warm olive oil in a small pan (on medium heat) stirring constantly until golden. Remove with a slotted spoon and set aside.

**This dish should be served hot,
with plain (boiled) rice
or dried egg noodles (page 210)**

1 cup = 250ml = 8fl oz   1 tablespoon = 15ml   1 teaspoon = 5ml

Chicken and peppers (bell) with honey

Ingredients

Sauce
2 tablespoons tomato ketchup
1 cup fresh pineapple juice
4 tablespoons dark soy sauce
3 tablespoons clear honey
1 teaspoon cornflour (cornstarch)

Chicken mixture
400g/14oz diced chicken fillets
5-6 tablespoons toasted cashew nuts
1-2 tablespoons sesame (or olive) oil
2 green (bell) peppers, seeded and diced
2 red (bell) peppers, seeded and diced
1 yellow (bell) pepper, seeded and diced
(optional)
2 medium onions, quartered and separated
1 teaspoon finely chopped ginger

Garnish to suit your own taste (optional)

Preparation

1 Mix the sauce ingredients together in a bowl, using a fork. Set aside.

2 Sauté the chicken in warm oil in a pan (on medium heat) for 3 minutes. Stir in the onions, ginger and peppers for 8-10 minutes.

3 Mix the sauce ingredients together, then pour over the chicken mixture. Bring to the boil, then simmer, covered, for 10-15 minutes or until the sauce thickens. Stir in the cashew nuts for the last 1-2 minutes of cooking.

Note
If using untoasted cashew nuts: *sauté in 2 tablespoons of warm olive oil in a small pan (on medium heat) stirring constantly until golden. Remove with a slotted spoon and set aside.*

This dish should be served hot, with plain (boiled) rice (page 84) or dried egg noodles (page 210)

1 cup = 250ml = 8fl oz   1 tablespoon = 15ml   1 teaspoon = 5ml

Chicken korma in tomato sauce

Ingredients

8-12 boneless, skinless chicken thighs
1 medium onion, halved and thinly sliced
2 tablespoons tomato purée (paste)
3 garlic cloves, crushed
½ cup natural (plain) yogurt or soya milk
⅔ cup coconut cream
1 teaspoon grated ginger
2-3 tablespoons olive oil
4-5 tablespoons blanched almonds (optional)
1 teaspoon ground cumin (optional)
1 tablespoon ground coriander
1 tablespoon ground turmeric
6 cloves
6 cardamoms
Salt to taste

Garnish with chopped coriander (cilantro)
and sliced red (bell) pepper (optional)

Preparation

1 Mix the chicken together with the ginger, turmeric, ground coriander, yogurt (or soya milk), cumin and coconut cream. Leave to marinate for 1-2 hours or overnight in the refrigerator.

2 Brown the almonds in 2 tablespoons of warm oil in a small pan (on medium heat) stirring constantly until golden. Remove with a slotted spoon and set aside.

3 Sauté the onion in 1 tablespoon of warm oil in a pan (on medium heat) for 3 minutes. Stir in the garlic and tomato purée for 1 minute, then add the marinated chicken, cinnamon stick, cloves and cardamoms, stirring together for 2-3 minutes.

4 Bring to the boil, simmer, covered, for 30-40 minutes or until cooked and the sauce thickens. (Add more yogurt or coconut cream if necessary.)

5 Transfer to a dish and sprinkle with the almonds. Garnish with 1 tablespoon of chopped fresh coriander and a few slices of red pepper, (or to suit your own taste).

Variations
Replace the thighs with a whole chicken, skinned and cut into 8 pieces or drumsticks (and the coconut cream with 2 tablespoons of desiccated coconut).
Replace the yogurt or the soya milk with single (light) cream and omit the tomato purée.
Half-boil peeled new (small) potatoes and cook with the chicken mixture. (The potatoes should be cooked but still firm.)

This dish should be served hot, with plain (boiled) rice (page 84) or naan bread

1 cup = 250ml = 8fl oz   *1 tablespoon = 15ml*   *1 teaspoon = 5ml*

If using a fan assisted oven (page 4)

Fish kibbeh

Ingredients

Fish mixture
400g/14oz skinless white fish fillets
200g/7oz/1 cup burghul (cracked wheat)
40g/1½oz fresh coriander (cilantro)
2 medium onions, quartered
1 tablespoon plain (all-purpose) flour
½ teaspoon ground cumin (optional)
1 grated zest of orange or lemon
½ teaspoon ground allspice
Salt to taste

Stuffing
2 medium onions, halved and thinly sliced
3 tablespoons chopped fresh coriander (cilantro)
4-5 tablespoons pine nuts
2-3 tablespoons olive oil
½ teaspoon ground allspice
½ teaspoon ground cumin (optional)
Salt to taste

Garnish to suit your own taste (optional)

Preparation

1 Rinse the burghul under cold water. Drain and set aside.

2 Place the fish mixture ingredients (except the burghul and flour) in a food processor and blend to a smooth paste. Tranfer to a bowl and knead well with the burghul and flour, dipping your hand in cold water, then return to the food processor in batches and pulse a few times.

3 Sauté the pine nuts in 2 tablespoons of warm oil in a pan (on medium heat) stirring constantly until nearly golden. Stir in the onions and seasonings until the onions are softened.

4 Place the pine nuts mixture in a medium-sized baking dish, topped with the fish mixture paste. Smooth evenly using the back of a spoon dipped in water or in oil. Score the paste vertically and horizontally with a knife running it around the edges. Drizzle with oil all over the paste.

5 Bake in a preheated oven at 200°C/400°F/Gas 6 for 20-25 minutes or until browned. Cut as desired. Transfer gently to a platter, turning it over.

Note
Use fine brown burghul (bulgur) page 5.

Variation
Serve only the fish mixture paste and omit the stuffing.

218

This dish should be served hot, or tepid with green salad

1 cup = 250ml = 8fl oz   *1 tablespoon = 15ml*   *1 teaspoon = 5ml*

*If using a fan assisted
oven (page 4)*

Baked fish with tahini sauce

Ingredients

*675g/1½lb skinless white fish fillets
½ cup tahini (page 5)
30g/1oz/¾cup finely chopped fresh
coriander (cilantro)
4 garlic cloves, crushed
1 lemon, sliced
2 tablespoons olive oil
4 tablespoons pine nuts
4 tablespoons blanched almonds
2 tablespoons shelled walnuts, crushed
½ teaspoon mild or hot paprika
½ cup water
½ cup lemon juice
½ teaspoon ground allspice
Pepper and salt to taste*

Garnish to suit your own taste (optional)

Preparation

1 Place the fish in a lightly-greased ovenproof dish. Sprinkle with pepper and salt. Arrange the sliced lemon over the top and bake in a preheated oven at 180°C/350°F/Gas 4 for 20-30 minutes or until cooked. Or grill (broil) under a medium heat for 12-15 minutes.

2 Meanwhile, brown the pine nuts and almonds separately in warm oil in a small pan (on medium heat) stirring constantly until golden. Remove with a slotted spoon and set aside.

3 Mix the tahini and lemon juice in a pan. (The tahini will thicken). Gradually add the water, stirring until it reaches the consistency of gravy. Add the garlic, and coriander (setting aside 1 tablespoon to garnish, if desired).

4 Bring to the boil, stirring constantly. Simmer for 1-2 minutes, then add the seasonings and walnuts. (Adjust with more water and lemon juice if necessary.)

5 Arrange the fish in an ovenproof serving dish. Top evenly with the tahini mixture and return to the oven. Bake or grill (broil) for 1-2 minutes. Remove and sprinkle with the nuts and almonds. Garnish with the set aside coriander.

Variation
Serve with plain (boiled) rice (page 84).

220

*This dish can be served hot,
tepid or cold, with toasted pitta
bread (page 56 No.2)*

1 cup = 250ml = 8fl oz   1 tablespoon = 15ml   1 teaspoon = 5ml

If using a fan assisted oven (page 4)

Baked fish with vegetables

Ingredients

1 large or 2 medium- sized fresh sea bass, cleaned
1 lemon, sliced
1-2 tablespoons olive oil
1 tablespoon chopped fresh flat-leaf parsley or fennel sprigs
½ teaspoon ground allspice
1 teaspoon ground coriander
Pepper and salt to taste

Garnish to suit your own taste (optional)

Preparation

1 Place the fish in a lightly-greased ovenproof dish. Sprinkle with the seasonings and parsley (or fennel), then top with the sliced lemon.

2 Bake in a preheated oven at 180°C/350°F/Gas 4 for 20-30 minutes or until cooked. (Or cover with kitchen foil and bake at 230°C/450°F/Gas 8 for 30-40.) Do not reheat.

3 Serve hot with mashed potatoes (page 82) or sautéed potatoes (page 164) and vegetables of your choice.

Ideal for children

222

This dish should be served immediately, with steamed, baked or sautéed vegetables

1 cup = 250ml = 8fl oz   *1 tablespoon = 15ml*   *1 teaspoon = 5ml*

If using a fan assisted
oven (page 4)

Baked fish with spinach and cheese

Ingredients

500g/1lb 2oz skinless fresh white fish fillets
450g/1lb fresh baby leaf spinach
115g/4oz/1 cup grated mozzarella cheese
1 lemon, sliced
1 tablespoon butter or margarine
2 tablespoons plain (all-purpose) flour
1 cup (cold) milk
1 teaspoon ground nutmeg
Pepper and salt to taste

Garnish to suit your own taste (optional)

Preparation

1 Cut the fish into large pieces and place in a lightly-greased baking dish. Sprinkle with pepper and salt, then arrange the sliced lemon on top.

2 Bake in a preheated oven at 180°C/350°F/Gas 4 for 20-30 minutes or until cooked, turning once. Or grill (broil) under a medium heat for 12-15 minutes. Remove the lemon slices and set aside.

3 In a pan, dissolve the flour in the (cold) milk and sprinkle the nutmeg and salt. Bring to the boil, stirring constantly until the sauce thickens. Simmer, stirring in the butter and the spinach for 1-2 minutes. Pour the mixture evenly over the fish and top with the cheese.

4 Return to the oven and bake for 20 minutes or until the cheese melts and turns golden. Or grill (broil) under a medium heat for 7-10 minutes.

Variations
Replace the cheese with 4-5 tablespoons of breadcrumbs.
Omit the butter, flour and milk, adding only the uncooked spinach over the baked fish and cook until wilted, then cover with the cheese and follow No.4.
Replace the fish with 500g/1lb 2oz of diced chicken breast fillets and sauté in 1 tablespoon of warm olive oil in a pan (on medium heat) for 10 minutes, adding 1 chopped spring (scallion) onion, 1 teaspoon allspice and salt, then place in a lightly-greased baking dish and follow No.3 and 4.

This dish should be served
immediately, with steamed, baked
or sautéed potatoes (page 164)

1 cup = 250ml = 8fl oz   1 tablespoon = 15ml   1 teaspoon = 5ml

If using a fan assisted oven (page 4)

Grilled fish with saffron rice

Ingredients

500g/1lb 2oz skinless fresh white fish fillets
200g/7oz/1 cup basmati rice, rinsed and drained
1 small onion, halved and very finely sliced
2 cups boiling chicken stock (1 cube) for the rice
½ teaspoon saffron threads, soaked in 1 tablespoon boiling water
3-4 tablespoons sultanas (raisins), soaked
½ lemon, sliced
2-3 tablespoons olive oil
Pepper and salt to taste

Garnish to suit your own taste (optional)

Preparation

1 Place the saffron threads in a small bowl with the boiling water, leaving to soak for 15-20 minutes.

2 Place the fish in a lightly-greased baking dish. Sprinkle with salt and top with the lemon slices. Bake in a preheated oven at 180°C/350°F/Gas 4 for 20-30 minutes or until cooked. Or grill (broil) under a medium heat for 12-15 minutes.

3 Meanwhile, sauté the onion in 1 tablespoon of warm oil in a pan (on medium heat) until soft. Stir in the rice for 30-40 seconds. Add the boiling stock (or replace with boiling water), saffron mixture, pepper and salt.

4 Bring to the boil, simmer, covered for 15-20 minutes or until the rice is cooked and the water is absorbed.

5 Transfer to a platter. Spread the hot fish (broken into large pieces) and sprinkle with the sultanas (after being soaked in hot water for 5 minutes and drained).

Variations
Omit the saffron and replace with chicken or fish stock (1 cube).
Replace the sultanas with 4-5 tablespoons blanched toasted almonds.

Ideal for children

This dish should be served immediately, with salad

1 cup = 250ml = 8fl oz   *1 tablespoon = 15ml*   *1 teaspoon = 5ml*

If using a fan assisted oven (page 4)

Fish burgers with vegetables

Ingredients

500g/1lb 2oz skinless fresh white fish fillets
1 medium onion, quartered
30g/1oz fresh coriander (cilantro)
2 garlic cloves, crushed
1 tablespoon zest of lemon or orange
1 tablespoon lime juice
1 tablespoon plain (all-purpose) flour
1 teaspoon thyme or fennel
½ teaspoon ground paprika (optional)
1-2 tablespoons olive oil
Salt to taste

Garnish to suit your own taste (optional)

Preparation

1 Mix the ingredients in a food processor (except the oil) and blend to a smooth paste.

2 Take a little amount of the paste (tossing in flour if necessary) and form into a large burger or sausage shape. Repeat with the rest of the paste.

3 Sauté in batches in 1-2 tablespoons of warm oil in a pan (on medium-low heat) until cooked and browned on both sides, turning once.

Note
If serving with mashed potatoes (page 82), or sautéed (page 164).

Variations
Brush the burgers with a little olive oil and barbecue over charcoal, or place in a lightly-greased ovenproof dish and grill (broil) under a medium heat until cooked and browned on both sides, turning once.
Replace the coriander with fresh flat-leaf parsley.

Ideal for children

This dish should be served hot, with steamed (or sautéed) potatoes and vegetables

1 cup = 250ml = 8fl oz   1 tablespoon = 15ml   1 teaspoon = 5ml

Cream spaghetti with prawns (shrimp)

Ingredients

400g/14 dried spaghetti, broken in half
12-16 tiger prawns (shrimp) cleaned
1 cup single (light) cream or more
10 small mushrooms, sliced
1-2 spring (scallions) onions, finely chopped
30g/1oz/¾ cup fresh coriander (cilantro),
chopped
3 garlic cloves, crushed
2 tablespoons olive oil
½ teaspoon ground nutmeg
Pepper and salt to taste

Preparation

1 Cook the spaghetti in a large pan of salted boiling water (on medium heat) for 10 minutes or until nearly tender, adding 1 tablespoon oil to prevent sticking. (or according to the packet instructions). Drain and rinse under cold water. Set aside.

2 In the same pan, sauté the onions, garlic and mushrooms in 1 tablespoon of warm oil (on medium heat) for 1 minute. Stir in the spaghetti and coriander (setting aside 1 tablespoon to garnish, if desired), followed by the cream and seasonings.

3 Bring to the boil. Simmer, covered for 8-10 minutes or until the spaghetti is tender and the sauce is absorbed. (Add more cream if necessary.)

4 Stir in the prawns for 1 minute. Serve, sprinkled with the set aside coriander.

Variations
Replace the coriander with fresh flat-leaf parsley.
Use fresh crab instead of the prawns.
Top with 2-3 tablespoons of grated Parmesan cheese.
Omit the prawns and serve as a vegetarian dish.

Ideal for children

This dish should be served immediately

1 cup = 250ml = 8fl oz   *1 tablespoon = 15ml*   *1 teaspoon = 5ml*

Prawns (shrimp) with vegetables

Ingredients

10-15 tiger or large prawns (shrimp)
200g/7oz can sweetcorn
30-40 broccoli florets
1 large carrot, finely sliced
1 spring (scallion) onion, finely chopped
55g/2oz/½ cup bean sprouts (optional)
2 tablespoons oyster or black bean sauce
2 tablespoons dry sherry (optional)
2 garlic cloves, crushed
3 tablespoons dark soy sauce
1 teaspoon cornflour (cornstarch) dissolved in
¼ cup cold water
1 tablespoon clear honey or brown sugar
2-3 tablespoons sesame (or olive) oil
1 teaspoon fresh ginger, grated
250g/9oz dried fine egg noodles

Preparation

1 Sauté the prawns and onion in 1 tablespoon of warm oil in a pan (on medium heat) for 1 minute. Add the broccoli and carrot and cook , covered, for 10 minutes.

2 Stir in the sweetcorn, bean sprouts, garlic and ginger for 2 minutes. Add the honey, sherry, oyster (or black bean sauce) and soy sauce, mixing well together.

3 Pour in the dissolved cornflour, then simmer, covered, for 8-12 minutes.

4 Meanwhile, cook the noodles in a pan of salted boiling water for 2-3 minutes or until tender, then drain and toss with 1 tablespoon of sesame (or olive) oil. Separate gently with a fork. (Or use ready cooked ones by following the packet instructions.)

5 Arrange the noodles in a serving dish, topped with the prawn mixture.

Variations

Replace the prawns with 400g/14oz of diced chicken breast fillets, and the broccoli with 10-15 mangetout, Chinese separated leaves or 1 sliced courgette (zucchini). Before serving, sprinkle 2 tablespoons of toasted sesame seeds.

232

This dish should be served hot, with thin noodles or plain (boiled) rice (page 84)

1 cup = 250ml = 8fl oz   1 tablespoon = 15ml   1 teaspoon = 5ml

Rice and caraway pudding

Ingredients

170g/6oz/1 cup ground rice
7 cups water
2 tablespoons ground caraway
1 tablespoon ground cinnamon
1 teaspoon ground anise
200g/7oz/1 cup caster (superfine) sugar
7-8 tablespoons ground coconut
4 tablespoons pine nuts, soaked in cold water
4 tablespoons blanched almonds, soaked in cold water
4 tablespoons walnuts, soaked in cold water

Preparation

1 Soak the nuts in a bowl in cold water. Drain before serving.

2 Place the rice, water, cinnamon, anise, caraway and sugar in a large pan, mixing well together and bring to the boil, stirring constantly.

3 Reduce the heat to medium and continue cooking and stirring for 15-20 minutes or until the mixture thickens.

4 Serve in individual bowls, at room temperature or chilled from the refrigerator.

To serve
Sprinkle with a layer of coconut and garnish with the pine nuts, almonds and walnuts.

Notes
This dish will keep in the refrigerator for one week, including the soaked nuts. (Replace with fresh water once a day).
To remove the skin: *blanche the almonds in boiling water and drain.*

Ideal for children

This pudding is prepared to celebrate the birth of a baby

1 cup = 250ml = 8fl oz　　　　1 tablespoon = 15ml　　　　1 teaspoon = 5ml

Milk and cream pudding

Ingredients

2 cups milk
1 cup single (light) cream
3 tablespoons cornflour (cornstarch),
dissolved in a little cold water
5 tablespoons caster (superfine) sugar or
more to taste
½ tablespoon rose water (page 5)
½ tablespoon orange-blossom water (page 5)
1 teaspoon crushed mastic (page 5) optional

4-5 tablespoons coarsely ground pistachio nuts

Preparation

1 Place the milk, cream, dissolved cornflour, and sugar in a pan, mixing well together and bring to the boil, stirring constantly.

2 Simmer, adding the mastic, rose and orange-blossom water. Continue stirring for 5-7 minutes or until the mixture thickens.

3 Serve in individual bowls and leave to cool before garnishing with the pistachio nuts, if desired.

Variations

Drizzle a little clear honey for each serving.
Replace the cream with milk.
Omit the rose and blossom water.

Ideal for children (and babies, page 4).

This pudding should be served at room temperature or chilled

1 cup = 250ml = 8fl oz   *1 tablespoon = 15ml*   *1 teaspoon = 5ml*

Chocolate custard with biscuits

Ingredients

First layer
2 cups milk
2 tablespoons custard powder
4 tablespoons caster (superfine) sugar
8 digestive biscuits

Second layer
2 cups milk
2 tablespoons custard powder
1-2 tablespoons unsweetened cocoa powder
4 tablespoons brown sugar

Preparation

1 Place the first layer ingredients (except the biscuits) in a pan and mix well together. Bring to the boil, stirring constantly. Make sure not to leave any lumps.

2 Pour evenly into a deep medium-sized serving dish and leave to set for 2-3 minutes.

3 Arrange the biscuits over the top. Set aside.

4 In a clean pan, mix the second layer ingredients, following the same instructions as in No.1. Then pour evenly over the biscuits and flatten immediately with the back of a spoon, if necessary.

Ideal for children

This pudding should be served chilled

1 cup = 250ml = 8fl oz   1 tablespoon = 15ml   1 teaspoon = 5ml

*If using a fan assisted
oven (page 4)*

Semolina cake with almonds

Ingredients

Syrup
*½ cup water
400g/14oz/2 cups caster (superfine) sugar
2 tablespoons unsalted butter
1 teaspoon lemon juice
1 tablespoon rose water (page 5) optional
1 tablespoon orange-blossom water (page 5)
(optional)*

Cake
*430g/15oz/2½ cups coarse semolina (page 5)
200g/7oz/1 cup caster (superfine) sugar
¾ cup whole milk, warmed
1 tablespoon baking powder
130g/4½oz/½ cup unsalted butter, melted
1 tablespoon tahini (page 5) for greasing
Blanched almonds
2 tablespoons desiccated coconut (optional)*

Garnish to suit your own taste (optional)

Preparation

To prepare the syrup
Mix the water and sugar in a pan, stirring until the sugar dissolves. Bring to the boil and continue to boil for 2-3 minutes. Simmer, then stir in the lemon juice for 1-2 minutes. Remove from heat and stir in the butter, rose and orange-blossom water. Leave to cool.

1 Place the semolina and sugar in a bowl. Add the warmed milk, melted butter, coconut (if using) and baking powder, mixing well together.

2 Spread the mixture evenly into a deep 23cm (9 inch) square lightly-greased baking dish and leave to rest for 30 minutes. Then score the cake with a knife into 5cm (2 inch) squares or diamond shapes. Press one almond in the centre of each portion.

3 Run a knife around the edges and bake in a preheated oven at 160°C /325°F/ Gas 3 for 40-50 minutes or until golden. Remove from heat and pour the syrup all over the cake while still hot.

If serving with camomile tea (or any herbal tea)
*Place a handful of the herbs in a large pot, adding boiling water. Leave to stand for 4-5 minutes before serving.
Alternatively, place the herbs in a pan with boiling water and boil for 1-2 minutes.*

This cake should be served at room temperature or chilled

1 cup = 250ml = 8fl oz   1 tablespoon = 15ml   1 teaspoon = 5ml

If using a fan assisted oven (page 4)

Flour and turmeric cake

Ingredients

375g/13oz/3 cups plain (all-purpose) flour
200g/7oz/1 cup caster (superfine) sugar
1 teaspoon anise seeds
1 teaspoon vanilla essence (extract)
1 whole nutmeg, grated
1 cup milk
1 tablespoon baking powder
1 tablespoon ground turmeric (optional)
1 cup olive oil
1 tablespoon unsalted butter, softened
20-25 almonds, blanched

Garnish to suit your own taste (optional)

Preparation

1 Mix the flour, sugar, anise seeds, turmeric, vanilla and nutmeg in a bowl. Add the oil, butter and baking powder and mix well together, while slowly adding the milk.

2 Spread the mixture evenly into a deep 23cm (9 inch) square lightly-greased baking dish. Score with a knife into 5cm (2 inch) squares or diamond shapes and press one almond in the centre of each portion.

3 Run a knife around the edges and bake in a preheated oven at 160°C 325°F/Gas 3 for 30-40 minutes or until golden.

If serving with anise seed tea
Place 2 tablespoons of the seeds in a large pot, adding boiling water. Leave to stand for 4-5 minutes before serving.
Alternatively, place the seeds in a pan with boiling water and boil for 1-2 minutes.

This cake should be served at room temperature or chilled

1 cup = 250ml = 8fl oz   *1 tablespoon = 15ml*   *1 teaspoon = 5ml*

*If using a fan assisted
oven (page 4)*

Chocolate cake topped with coconut

Ingredients

375g/13oz/3 cups self-raising flour
250g/9oz/1 cup unsalted butter
600g/1⅓lb/3 cups caster (superfine) sugar
5 medium eggs
1 teaspoon baking powder
2 teaspoons vanilla essence (extract)
4 tablespoons unsweetened cocoa powder
1 tablespoon ground almonds
*170g/6oz/1 cup semi-sweet dark chocolate,
broken into pieces*
4-6 tablespoons desiccated coconut (optional)
200g/7oz/1 cup chocolate smarties (optional)

Garnish to suit your own taste (optional)

Preparation

1 Melt the butter and chocolate pieces (on medium heat) in a pan.

2 Place the flour, sugar, almonds, cocoa, vanilla and baking powder in a large bowl and blend with an electric mixer until creamy. Add 1 egg at a time, beating well between additions. Pour in the melted chocolate mixture and mix all together.

3 Pour into a deep lightly-greased 20cm (about 8 inch) round cake tin and bake in a preheated oven at 160°C/325°F/Gas 3 for 40-50 minutes or until risen and a skewer comes away clean after being inserted in the centre.

4 Remove and cover with coconut. Decorate with chocolate smarties, if desired.

Variation
Replace the coconut with chocolate spread.

244

*This cake should be served
at room temperature
or chilled*

1 cup = 250ml = 8fl oz   *1 tablespoon = 15ml*   *1 teaspoon = 5ml*

If using a fan assisted oven (page 4)

Ricotta cheesecake with apricots

Ingredients

8 sheets filo (phyllo) pastry, brushed with melted butter
85g/3oz/⅓ cup unsalted butter, melted
200g/7oz/1 cup caster (superfine) sugar
65g/2¼oz/½ cup plain (all-purpose) flour
2 cups milk
2 tablespoons ground pistachio nuts
500g/1lb 2oz/2½ cups ricotta cheese, mashed
5 medium eggs
200g/7oz can prunes, drained (or chopped dates)
8-10 dried apricots (optional)
400g/14oz can apricots, reserving the liquid
1 teaspoon grated orange zest

Preparation

1 Brush 4 of the filo sheets with some of the melted butter and layer together in a lightly-greased medium-sized ovenproof dish. Cut the overhanging pieces (or fold inwards).

2 Place the sugar, milk, flour and pistachio nuts in a pan and bring to the boil (on medium heat), stirring constantly until the mixture thickens. Leave to cool.

3 Transfer the mixture to a bowl adding the eggs, cheese, 2 tablespoons of the canned apricot liquid and the zest. Blend together with an electric mixer until smooth.

4 Stir in the prunes (or dates) and the dried apricots. Pour evenly over the prepared pastry and layer with the remaining sheets (brushing each with the remaining melted butter). Cut the overhanging pieces (or fold inwards).

5 Bake in a preheated oven at 160°C/325°F/Gas 3 for 40-50 minutes or until golden. Leave to cool.

Just before serving
Drain the canned apricots, then arrange on top of the cake. Serve immediately.

This cake should be served at room temperature or chilled

1 cup = 250ml = 8fl oz   1 tablespoon = 15ml   1 teaspoon = 5ml

If using a fan assisted oven (page 4)

Cheese and creme caramel puddings

Ingredients

Syrup
200g/7oz/1 cup caster (superfine) sugar
½ cup water

Pudding
1 cup milk
200g/7oz/1 cup caster (superfine) sugar
500g/1lb 2oz/2½ cups ricotta cheese, mashed
5 medium eggs
1 teaspoon lemon zest
Few drops vanilla essence (extract)

Garnish to suit your own taste (optional)

Preparation

1 Mix the syrup ingredients in a pan. Stir (on low heat) until the sugar dissolves, then bring to the boil, uncovered (without stirring) and boil until the mixture turns golden brown. Pour the caramel into a deep 20cm (about 8 inch) round ovenproof dish, swirling to coat the base and sides evenly. Leave to set in the freezer for 10-15 minutes.

2 Stir the milk and 1 cup of sugar in a pan (on low heat) until the sugar dissolves without boiling and set aside.

3 Place the cheese in a large bowl and blend with an electric mixer until smooth, slowly add the warm milk mixture, followed by the lemon zest, vanilla and 1 egg at a time (beating well between additions).

4 Pour the mixture over the caramel and place the dish inside a roasting tin and add enough hot water to come two third of the way up the dish (bain Marie).

5 Bake in a preheated oven at 160°C/325°F/Gas 3 for 1-1⅓ hours or until a skewer inserted in the centre comes out clean. Cool, then leave in the refrigerator for 6-7 hours or overnight before turning it over.

Variation (creme caramel)
Prepare the caramel as in No.1, then, blend together 7 tablespoons of sugar and 5 eggs (1 at a time). Add 3½ cups of warm milk, 1 zest of lemon and a few drops of vanilla and mix well before pouring into the caramel dish and follow No.4 and 5.

These puddings should be served chilled or cold

1 cup = 250ml = 8fl oz   1 tablespoon = 15ml   1 teaspoon = 5ml

Custard and banana sponge cake

Ingredients

2 large round sponge cakes
5 medium bananas, sliced
Lemon juice, for tossing the bananas
4 medium-sized apples, peeled and sliced
3 tablespoons custard powder
3 cups milk
4 tablespoons caster sugar

To garnish, hundreds and thousands

Preparation

1 Place the apples and 1 tablespoon of sugar in a pan. Stir (on low heat) until softened. Add the bananas (after tossing with a little lemon juice, to prevent from discolouring), stirring and mashing well together.

2 Divide the fruit mixture equally between both sponges. Set aside.

3 Place the custard, 3 tablespoons of sugar and the milk in a pan. Stir constantly (on medium heat) until it starts to bubble and thicken. Make sure not to leave any lumps.

4 Pour the custard mixture evenly over the fruit mixture, then sandwich the sponges together. Sprinkle with hundreds and thousands (or any decoration) over the top, if desired.

Ideal for children

250

This cake should be served immediately before it gets soggy

1 cup = 250ml = 8fl oz   1 tablespoon = 15ml   1 teaspoon = 5ml

*If using a fan assisted
oven (page 4)*

Marble cake

Ingredients

250g/9oz/2 cups self-raising flour
250g/9oz/1 cup unsalted butter
250g/9oz/1½ cup caster (superfine) sugar
6 medium eggs
1 teaspoon baking powder
2 teaspoons vanilla essence (extract)
1-2 tablespoons unsweetened cocoa powder

Garnish to suit your own taste (optional)

Preparation

1 Place all the ingredients in a large bowl (except the cocoa) and blend to a smooth paste, using an electric mixer.

2 Pour ¾ of the mixture into a deep 20cm (about 8 inch) round lightly-greased baking dish. Then beat the cocoa into the remaining mixture and drizzle gently over the top of the cake without stirring.

3 Bake in a preheated oven at 160°C/325°F/Gas 3 for 45-50 minutes or until risen and browned.

Variations
Add 3 tablespoons of desiccated coconut with the mixture (No.1).
Omit the cocoa.

If serving with mint tea
Place a handful of fresh mint sprigs in a large teapot and add boiling water. Leave to stand for 4-5 minutes before serving.
Alternatively, add 1 sachet of English breakfast tea with the mint.

**This cake should be served
at room temperature**

1 cup = 250ml = 8fl oz   1 tablespoon = 15ml   1 teaspoon = 5ml

If using a fan assisted
oven (page 4)

Chocolate cookies

Ingredients

340g/12oz/2¾ cups plain (all-purpose) flour
250g/9oz/1 cup unsalted butter, melted
150g/5½oz/¾ cup caster (superfine) sugar
2 medium eggs
170g/6oz/1 cup milk chocolate chips
1 teaspoon vanilla essence (extract)
⅓ teaspoon of salt
1 teaspoon bicarbonate of soda (baking soda)

Garnish to suit your own taste (optional)

Preparation

1 Place all the ingredients in a bowl and mix well together with a fork, then leave to rest for 30 minutes.

2 Form gently into golf-ball sized without pressing (or flatten into thin patties) and place in a lightly-greased baking dish, leaving space between each one.

3 Bake in a preheated oven at 160°C/325°F/Gas 3 for 30-40 minutes or until risen and browned.

Variation
Add 1 tablespoon of cocoa powder to the mixture.

These cookies should be served
at room temperature

1 cup = 250ml = 8fl oz   1 tablespoon = 15ml   1 teaspoon = 5ml

Banana and Strawberry pancakes

Ingredients

Pancakes

4 tablespoons plain (all-purpose) flour
3 cups milk
4 medium eggs
1 zest of lemon and orange
3 tablespoons brown or caster (surperfine) sugar
⅓ teaspoon of salt

Filling

4-5 bananas, peeled and sliced
24-26 strawberries, each cut into 3 pieces
12-16 strawberries, halved (for decoration)
250g/9oz/1 cup chocolate sauce (ready-made)
4-5 tablespoons clear honey (optional)

Garnish to suit your own taste (optional)

Preparation

1 Place the pancake ingredients in a bowl and blend well together with a fork.

2 Pour 1 ladle of the mixture into a hot lightly-greased 14cm (5½ inch) frying pan and swirl it around. Cook (on medium heat) until set and golden on both sides, flipping or turning gently once.

3 Remove and leave to cool. Repeat until all the mixture is used.

Just before serving
Arrange half of the pancakes in a platter and top each one with some banana and strawberry slices, then cover with the remaining pancakes, strawberries and bananas (leaving a few banana slices and the halved strawberries for decoration, if desired). Drizzle with the chocolate sauce or honey.

Variation (for home-made chocolate sauce)
Mix 250g/9oz/1 cup of dark chocolate (broken into pieces) with 2 tablespoons of unsalted butter and 1-2 tablespoons of caster sugar in a pan, stirring together (on medium-low heat) until melted.

Ideal for children

These pancakes should be served at room temperature

1 cup = 250ml = 8fl oz   1 tablespoon = 15ml   1 teaspoon = 5ml

*If using a fan assisted
oven (page 4)*

Chocolate layer cake

Ingredients

Cake
250g/9oz/2 cups self-raising flour
250g/9oz/1 cup unsalted butter
250g/9oz/1½ cup caster (superfine) sugar
6 medium eggs
1 teaspoon baking powder
2 teaspoons vanilla essence (extract)
3-4 tablespoons unsweetened cocoa powder

Filling
1 cup strong cold expresso coffee
150g/7oz/1 cup unsweetened chocolate,
broken into pieces
250g/9oz/1 cup unsalted butter
5 medium eggs
1 teaspoon vanilla essence (extract)
250g/9oz/1 cup mascarpone
200g/7oz/1 cup caster (superfine) sugar
1 tablespoon brandy (optional)

Garnish
170g/6oz/1 cup chocolate chips (optional)

Preparation

1 Place the cake ingredients in a large bowl and blend with an electric mixer until smooth paste. Pour into a deep 20cm (about 8 inch) round lightly-greased baking dish.

2 Bake in a preheated oven at 160°C/325°F/Gas 3 for 45-50 minutes until set and a skewer inserted in the centre comes out clean. Remove and leave to cool.

3 Meanwhile, melt the butter and chocolate in a pan (on medium heat). Transfer to a bowl and allow to cool. Add the sugar, eggs, mascarpone, vanilla, expresso coffee and brandy and mix well together, using an electric mixer.

4 Carefully cut the cake in half. Cover with half the amount of the filling (No.3), then sandwich the halves together. Top with the remaining filling and garnish with the chocolate chips (or ½ cup of whipping cream), if desired.

258

*This cake should be served
chilled or cold. Goes well with
ice cream*

1 cup = 250ml = 8fl oz   1 tablespoon = 15ml   1 teaspoon = 5ml

Mango and chocolate ice cream

Ingredients

Mango ice cream
4-5 fresh mango, peeled
200g/7oz/1 cup caster (superfine) sugar
1 tablespoon lime juice
2 cups whole milk
1 cup double (thick/heavy) cream, whipped
5 egg whites
1 tablespoon vanilla essence (extract)
1 teaspoon crushed mastic (optional)

Chocolate ice cream
1 cup whole milk
1 cup single (light) cream
2 cups double (thick/heavy) cream, whipped
5 egg whites

150g/7oz/1 cup dark chocolate, broken into pieces
200g/7oz/1 cup caster (superfine) sugar
1 teaspoon crushed mastic (optional)

Garnish to suit your own taste (optional)

Preparation

Mango ice cream
1 Purée the mangos in a blender until smooth. Transfer to a bowl and set aside. Whisk the eggs and sugar until thick and creamy, using an electric mixer. Set aside.

2 Heat the milk in a pan (on medium heat) until hot, without boiling. Pour it slowly over the egg mixture, stirring constantly until well mixed.

3 Transfer the egg mixture to the pan. Stir (on low heat) until thickens, without boiling. Pour over the mango purée, adding lime juice and vanilla. Mix well together and leave to cool.

4 Gently fold the whipped cream into the mixture. Place into a container and freeze until half-frozen. Remove and stir with a fork, then freeze again until totally frozen.

Chocolate ice cream
1 Whisk the eggs and sugar until thick and creamy, using an electric mixer. Set aside.

2 Heat the milk and single cream in a pan (on medium heat) until hot, without boiling. Pour it slowly over the egg mixture, stirring constantly until well mixed.

3 Transfer the mixture to the pan. Add the chocolate, stirring (on medium heat) until melts and the mixture thickens (without boiling). Leave to cool, then follow the same as No.4 above.

Notes
Remove from freezer ½ hour before serving.
Replace the sugar with 3 tablespoons of clear honey.

These ice creams can be served, with chocolate flakes and smarties for children

1 cup = 250ml = 8fl oz   *1 tablespoon = 15ml*   *1 teaspoon = 5ml*

Index

263

raidy@raidy.com | www.raidy.com

MEMORIES

MEMORIES

with photographs by

GEMMA LEVINE

EBURY PRESS
LONDON

DEDICATION
To my mother, Mae Josephs

First published in 1998

3 5 7 9 10 8 6 4

Photographs © 1998 Gemma Levine

Text © 1998 the contributors to this book

First published in the United Kingdom in 1998 by
Ebury Press, Random House, 20 Vauxhall Bridge Road,
London SW1V 2SA

Random House Australia (Pty) Limited
20 Alfred Street, Milsons Point, Sydney, New South Wales 2061,
Australia

Random House New Zealand Limited
18 Poland Road, Glenfield, Auckland 10, New Zealand

Random House South Africa (Pty) Limited
Endulini, 5a Jubilee Road, Parktown 2193, South Africa

Random House UK Limited Reg. No. 954009

Papers used by Ebury Press are natural, recyclable products made
from wood grown in sustainable forests.

A CIP catalogue record for this book is available from the British
Library.

ISBN 0 09 18607 3

Printed and bound in Italy by New Interlitho S.p.a Milan

The Alzheimer's Disease Society
Gordon House
10 Greencoat Place
London SW1P 1PH

Telephone: 0171 306 0606
Helpline: 0845 300 0336

The Alzheimer's Disease Society is a registered charity, number 296645

CONTENTS

◆

FOREWORD

◆

A photograph captures a moment, a second in someone's life that is preserved for ever. A mere glimpse of a holiday snapshot may conjure up memories of relaxation, new experiences and enjoyment – or the opposite – shared with acquaintances and loved ones. And the sight of a rediscovered school or family photo may remind us of those to whom we were once close but who no longer feature in our lives, for whatever reason. Similarly, while a professional portrait may trigger very personal memories in the sitter and the photographer, quite different thoughts and recollections will be stirred in the minds of others.

From the moment we are born, we store in our memories an infinite cornucopia of knowledge – sometimes vital, sometimes trivial: language and numerical skills, melodies, tastes, smells, how to differentiate colour, or tell the time. We discover that people can be our friends or our enemies, and that mistakes can be rectified and actions forgiven. The list is endless.

Our memories shape our lives, they make us who we are; above all, our memories are personal. They are integral to our sense of self and to our shared experience of others. As we grow older, our memories become selective and when we are without our memories we cannot help but become different people.

Loss of memory is a symptom of Alzheimer's disease, which robs people of both their past and their future. It viciously attacks not only those experiencing its effects but also the family, friends and loved ones who watch helplessly as this most cruel of terminal illnesses takes health,

strength, dignity and ultimately self from the afflicted person.

For the person who has Alzheimer's, the suffering is of a singular and devastating nature. Before the disease has taken hold, the individual may realise that his or her mind is in the grip of a relentless and irreversible force. Until oblivion descends, the person must face the sensation of being dragged into a bottomless pit – a little further every day.

The Alzheimer's Disease Society provides care for people with dementia and their families, and also funds. vital research into the cause and treatment of this disease. Additional funds are always needed, so my thanks to Gemma for creating this memorable book and to all those who have contributed to it, and who took time to send in a sample memory that is important to them. Some have related childhood memories; others have remembered highlights of their careers, poignant moments of inspiration, pride, humour and triumph. There are also heartfelt tributes to others, and memories of happiness, sadness and loss.

All these memories of the past serve as a reminder that the Alzheimer's Disease Society needs support now and for the future. We should be thankful for our memories and not forget the thousands who have been robbed of theirs through no fault of their own.

Dr Jonathan Miller CBE
President, The Alzheimer's Disease Society

ALAN BATES

A TRIBUTE TO HARRY ANDREWS

◆

When I think of Harry, I now think of someone who signified a great deal to me, although I was not aware of this at the time. In retrospect, I can say that Harry was the first person in my career who represented stability, security in himself, self-awareness – a man who knew where he was, and had no false ideas about anything. We meet only a few people like this in our lives, and we do not always realise until too late just how significant they have been.

I wish I had known the first half of Harry's career, which was obviously spectacular when I talk to his friends and contemporaries. After starting at the Liverpool Rep in 1933, John Gielgud took him to New York in his *Hamlet* of 1935; when they returned he appeared in the West End in various plays, and then Gielgud took him up again for his own company.

Subsequently, Harry joined Laurence Olivier's Old Vic Company. It is at this point that his roles seem to increase in importance and stature.

Then came ten glorious years with the Stratford Memorial Theatre, where he established himself as one of our finest actors, and was described by Tynan as 'the backbone of British theatre'. Harry himself said something like 'I don't want to be a star – I want to be a good actor in good parts'. Well, he was what he wanted to be, but he was more. He could not help his charisma making him a star. His physical presence and voice made him unforgettable, and his subtlety and sensitivity made him, to my mind, great.

Harry always found it difficult to learn lines, and I think it is only fair to mention his great courage in taking on important parts, knowing that he had a handicap with his memory – later in his career he played increasingly smaller roles. This, of course, was a huge bonus for everyone else because it gave them a rare opportunity of working with a great actor in a minor part.

When I worked with him in the early 1980s in *A Patriot For Me*, the whole company adored him, not just because of his humour and his splendour as a character, but because at his late age in life he was so interested in the rest of us and played no games of hierarchy. His company spirit was tremendously evident when Ron Eyre, the director, asked for volunteers to take part in the famous drag ball sequence. Ron said, 'We simply haven't got enough people, so we need anyone who has got time for a quick change in this scene.' Harry was the first to volunteer. Ron took me aside and said, 'I think this is a rather rash request on my part – what drag costume exists that could possibly disguise Harry Andrews?' In the end, they settled on a huge kaftan and a yashmak, made him a fortune teller, sat him down and surrounded him with a lot of other people in elaborate costumes. Harry's commitment really was 100 per cent.

Fortunately, his memory problem did not prevent his continuing his career in the cinema, and there are great performances on film right up to, and including, his last two or three years, with beautiful performances from him on screen.

Harry loved nothing more than to make a wicked remark, but one always laughed because you knew that he had a huge affection for the person he was talking about, and it was only his affection which made him mischievous. He was one of the great ones – never to be forgotten.

ALAN YENTOB

◆

My journey in television started in radio. Armed with a law degree, I entered the revolving doors of Bush House as a BBC general trainee. Just across the road, at the London School of Economics, dangerous agitators like the student leader Jack Straw were busy rousing the rabble and manning the barricades, in support of the partisans of Paris.

Bush House seemed just as much of a hotbed. The place was abuzz, twenty-four hours a day, in pursuit of knowledge and ideas.

At the age of twenty, I felt the world was at my fingertips. In the morning, I'd phone the French student leader Danny Cohn-Bendit for an interview – or give Idi Amin a ring (he returned my call, incidentally). In the afternoon, I'd get Harold Pinter in for a programme, or Noel Coward. At the weekend, I would set off with my tape recorder to gather impressions of Grimethorpe Colliery for my listeners in Bali and Bangalore.

Radio was a wonderfully supple medium. You could be researcher, recordist, sound editor, producer, presenter – all in one. You had a blood intimacy with your material – literally in my case, as I stood over the tape machine, a blunt razor blade in hand, my fingers as hacked to pieces as the tape.

I found my vocation in broadcasting. The BBC had the questing, plural atmosphere of a very open university. It was full of presenters sharing skills and ideas – full of dreamers and doers.

ALBERT & MICHEL ROUX

◆

We have so many memories of the first years after we opened Le Gavroche – some more amusing than others.

Our most abiding memory sums up the great affection we had for one another. We had a nightly ritual: at seven o'clock, before the evening service, one of us (we took it in turns) would change from his chef's whites into a dinner jacket before taking the orders in the restaurant. The other stayed in the basement kitchen, where the temperature could soar to 40° or 50° centigrade (he had to endure this session in the 'sauna' for four hours).

Once in a while, at about 11.30pm, after around eighty customers had been served, the panic was over and tensions between the kitchen and the restaurant had passed danger point and begun to subside, the brother who had been on duty in the restaurant would carry a glass of champagne down to his sibling in the kitchen. In return, the one in the kitchen would send up to the restaurant a lovingly prepared dish for his brother, who would sit in a corner of the dining room to eat it, watched by the customers, whose eyes were fixed enviously on his plate.

While one of us whetted his whistle, the other tickled his tastebuds. Once again, the ties of brotherhood had bound us together.

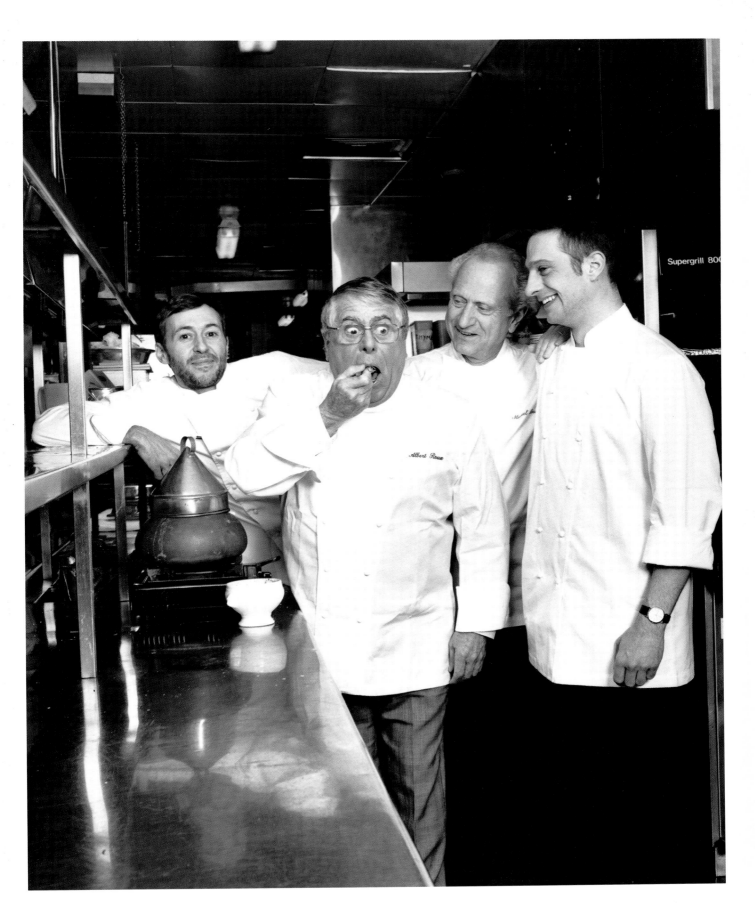

ANNE ROBINSON

♦

My earliest memories are of summers spent in the south of France. An annual, magical escape in July and August from the dreariness of Liverpool to the Carlton Hotel in Cannes.

The travel allowance in the early 1950s was about £25 a head, which barely covered a couple of days on the beach. So at some point my ever-resourceful mother, the family breadwinner, would have a clandestine meeting with the hotel manager and arrangements were made for the bill to be paid back in London.

We were a magnificent example of post-war new money; fair skinned, unwisely sunburnt, and unselfconsciously British. Not for us horrid food. The dining-room staff were under clear instructions to replace with ham or egg any bit of the menu that still sounded suspiciously French after it had been haltingly translated by the Maître d'.

But food was not the feast. The excitement was our fellow guests. The Carlton was awash with celebrities: ex-King Farouk, Tyrone Power, Merle Oberon, Bette Davis, Sugar Ray Robinson and the Dockers with their gold-plated Bentley and famous yacht, *The Shamara*. My brother and I would tuck ourselves into a corner of the hotel foyer and watch them climb into limousines for a night at the casino.

Looking back, it was a remarkable achievement to have spent a decent part of one's formative years in a foreign country and to have remained so untouched by its culture. It was also remarkably imaginative for my mother to have thought such ridiculously extravagant holidays were, as she put it, 'important for your education'.

She was like that – eccentric, funny, beautiful, with a razor-sharp brain, and a talent for business. Plus an unashamed love of shopping. Emptying Bond Street was her most regular hobby. I'm glad I remember her beauty and her brilliance. Because sadly both disappeared as the harsh, unforgiving disease of Alzheimer's took over. But she left a wonderful legacy. 'Seize the moment,' she would command. We've tried, Mum. But nobody did it quite like you.

BEN KINGSLEY

◆

I have been staring at this blank sheet of paper for too long. All my life. That is to say that I've never committed any memory to paper. My childhood memories are few; but then to me that is hardly surprising.

I was barely into my first few steps, walking down a slope of lawn in bright, warm sunshine, towards a bed of roses. One rose was very bright, pulsing with yellow and pink in the sun. I walked towards the flower and stood with it level to my face. I reached out to touch the rose and the moment was shattered by a male voice bawling, 'Don't touch it! Don't touch it!! DON'T TOUCH IT!!!'

It was his garden, his rose, my moment.

The screen goes blank, swirls with grey dots and goes blank.

I now have a lawn that slopes, and roses of my own. No thanks to that cruel old bastard.

BERNARD LEVIN

PEDIGREE, WHAT PEDIGREE?

◆

To start with, let me give you an idea of the difficulty I would face if I embarked on an expedition to trace my ancestors; one item will, I think, suffice. When my mother's parents made the trek from the Pale – their home village was Nezhin, some 40 miles from Kiev – they fetched up in Szczecin (né Stettin), from which the great diaspora sailed. Where they were sailing to was for them of no consequence; the only thing they knew was that they were going somewhere where there were no pogroms, no Cossacks, no restrictions as to where they might live, no tiny list of trades they were allowed to practise.

My grandparents boarded the next ship; it was going to the United States. (I cannot break myself of the habit of wondering what sort of life I would have had if I had been American.) Just before the ship sailed, my grandmother fell ill and could not go; she, and her young husband, disembarked. Her illness was found to be nothing serious, and she recovered in a few days, but the ship that was going to New York had sailed. No matter; where was the next one going? England, they were told. That left them no wiser, because they had never heard of England.

More astonishment; my grandmother could neither read nor write in any language; my grandfather could read Hebrew, and struggled with just about enough English to read a newspaper, but not enough to read a book. I used to read to them, though few books were simple enough for my boobah. (But she bore one of the world's most beautiful names: Bathsheba.) I am not sure but I think I remember my grandfather signing something with a cross.

Now then; with that background, would anyone expect documents, family Bibles, genealogical tables going back to the Pale and all the other family impedimenta of those who can trace their ancestors through a settled life in a settled community?

No documents, but much reminiscence. As a child, I sat hypnotised as my grandparents spun the stories of life in the Pale – real stories, that is, with real characters, real tragedies and real comedies, real brutality and real comforting. What is the calm of a family archive to the thunder of Cossack hooves, for all that I have not a scrap of paper to back up my memories?

Apart from the clothes they stood up in, my grandparents brought only two things from Nezhin: the samovar and the mortar-and-pestle. The latter was a fine bronze one, wielded with effortless skill by my grandmother; but the samovar was the great prize of the family. My grandmother polished it weekly; it now adorns my sister's home.

Yet the pull of the Pale was stronger than I could have guessed. In the Second World War, Nezhin was mentioned in Stalin's Order of the Day; the retreating Germans had left it. My grandmother, who, I recollect, made a form of cherry brandy (presumably in an illicit still) broached her finest vat and the family had to toast the very place from which they had fled because of her persecution. By then, my grandparents had been living in Britain for something like sixty years, yet the ties that bind proved astoundingly strong.

What is there in me of my forefathers? … Perhaps it is not in me to answer that question.

BETTY BOOTHROYD

◆

I encountered the most surprising couturier on the River Nile near Esna. With a party of friends we were all sunning ourselves on the top deck of a cruise boat. Down below on the bank, about three yards from the cruiser, a line of boys arrived from the local market. In their elegant jellabahs, they leaped about, shouting, laughing, gesticulating and brandishing all kinds of clothes. (Anyone who has cruised between Luxor and Aswan will recognise this scene.)

My eye caught one little black number with sparkles around the neck and down the front. The salesman's eye swiftly noticed my interest. He threw the garment up to me in a knotted plastic bag. I missed the catch and it fell into the river. He jumped in, fished it out, put it in another bag and threw it up again. This time it landed at my feet.

I tried it on immediately over my swimsuit and it was a perfect fit. Pure thick black cotton, full length, larded with brilliant glass beads, sequins, gold, silver, amber, ruby. 'How much?' I shouted at the smiling face. He threw both hands in the air, fingers spread widely and gestured twice, indicating 20 Egyptian pounds.

Always ready to bargain, I shook my head. 'Too much,' I said and offered 10 pounds. We bargained away in good humour counting fingers and thumbs and eventually settled for 15 pounds. I put the money in the bag and tossed it across the water for him to catch. Huge smiles and waves. It was a great sale for him and a bargain for me.

Resisting the temptation to wear it in the Chair on my return to London, it was christened in the Dining Room of Speaker's House when I hosted an official dinner for the Speaker of the Egyptian Parliament. It was much admired and is still worn from time to time.

Thank you, my couturier in the wet jellabah.

BRYAN ADAMS

◆

It looked like I was going to be late for my concert in New York City on 14 September, 1985. I was having a Japanese dinner when I realised how time had zoomed by, so I dashed out to the street to look for a cab but it was one of those nights when neither love nor money could find you a taxi. So it was down to the subway instead, and on to the uptown train, in the hopes that I would find Madison Square Garden.

One thing I hadn't counted on was the train being packed with fans going to the concert, so I pulled my hat down and pointed my face at the floor, hoping that I wouldn't get spotted. Occasionally I looked up to see where I was, and noted that two fans sitting in the seats across from me were stealing glances and shaking their heads as if to say 'impossible'. I decided to follow them off the train, as it seemed like the best way to get to the venue on time. I think we disembarked around 34th Street, but when I reached the top of the stairs they had disappeared, so the question was: should I go left or right?

I felt momentarily stranded, with only fifteen minutes left before showtime. Suddenly the two fans came running up and said, 'Hey, Bryan. Was that really you on the train? We're in Row 7, Blue Section!' I explained I was late and didn't know where the hall was, and asked for directions. They pointed down the street and said. 'IT'S THIS WAY! WE'LL SHOW YA!' So we walked briskly together to the show, with them giggling all the way.

Nice folks, New Yorkers.

CECIL PARKINSON

◆

One of the strangest and most memorable days of my life was the day I took my seat in the House of Commons in November 1970. Having been elected in a by-election at Enfield West following the death of the Chancellor of the Exchequer, Iain Macleod, I had never set foot in the Chamber of the House of Commons until the day I took my seat – and the whole place was a mystery to me. I arrived with my wife, Ann, and my three daughters, Mary, Emma and Jo, and the Deputy Chief Whip, Jack Weatherill, entertained us all to lunch in the Stranger's Dining Room. The girls were very small and very excited, and, for a short time, I thought they were going to run riot, but they soon settled down and Jack Wetherill was absolutely charming to them.

At the end of lunch he took me off to introduce me to Francis Pym, then Chief Whip. We were joined by James Allason (my own MP), and in the corridor outside the Chief Whip's Office we rehearsed the procedure of taking one's seat. Both James and Francis were military men and they insisted that we had to carry out the Introduction Ceremony with military precision. Francis Pym was 5' 6" and weighed about 11 stone and James was about 6' 3" and weighed about 16 stone. When they both leaned on me, James's extra weight made the three of us tilt so I imagine we must have looked like the walking Tower of Pisa.

After walking up and down the corridor and bowing as one would have to do in the Chamber, I was told I could relax and wait until the end of the Prime Minister's Questions when we would meet in the Bar of the House and go through the procedure we had been rehearsing.

In due course, the Speaker called out 'Introduction of New Members', and the three of us stood at the Bar of the House, bowed to the Speaker, marched three paces, bowed again and they then escorted me to the Speaker's table, where the Clerk of the House administered the Oath of Allegiance. At that point my sponsors disappeared and the Speaker stood smiling and held his hand out for me to shake.

During the whole of this time, a sort of mumbling noise filled the Chamber. It was my first acquaintance with that strange 'yer, yer, yer, yer' noise which passes in Parliament for a sign of approval. Having shaken the Speaker's hand, I found myself behind the Chair without the slightest idea of what to do.

At that point the Chamber started to empty and the Prime Minister, Ted Heath, and the leading members of the Cabinet walked past and wished me luck. Having stood around for a few minutes and not knowing quite what I should do next, I then approached a very senior and knowledgeable-looking Member of Parliament, who had just left the Conservative Benches, and asked him if he could tell me the way back to the Members' Lobby.

He later became a very good friend and admitted to me that he had only been in the House for a few days and scarcely knew his own way round, but we subsequently went back to the Members' Lobby where I rejoined my family. We all had tea and I then put them in a taxi home.

Later that evening, John Eden, a very senior backbencher, approached me and asked if I was free for dinner. He took me into the Members' Dining Room, and introduced me to eight or nine Members who were sitting at a table. They all made me feel extremely welcome. Only at that point did I begin to feel that I was a real Member of Parliament.

CHARLES FORTE

◆

I remember clearly back to a time when I had a friend who was much older than me. Carlo Micallef was nearly sixty. His name was of Maltese origin, but he was a Florentine and one of the most elegant men I have ever known. He had his suits made at Kilgour & French, his shoes came from Lobb, his hats from Lock. He had an elegant house just off Portland Place in Mansfield Street; he had come to England when he was about thirty and had done well.

One evening I was having dinner with him when he said, 'I think it's time you got married old boy.'

'So my father and mother keep telling me. Don't you start.'

A day or two later, Micallef rang up: 'I would like you specially to come to dinner.'

'Where?' I asked. 'At your place?'

No, I am giving a little dinner party at the Hungaria in Lower Regent Street.'

About a dozen people sat round the table in a private room downstairs. I had been placed next to a young girl called Irene. But it so happened that I had already seen Irene before, in her mother's delicatessen in Soho. I had walked in one day and saw a girl behind the counter in a neat white overall. She was young, fresh, unspoilt looking with a lovely smile. She was translating a letter into English from Italian for a very old man standing at the counter. I waited for

a while, admiring the grace and gentleness with which the girl addressed the old man, who also happened to be slightly deaf.

Eventually I interrupted to ask if I could buy some prosciutto. She replied, 'If I had any prosciutto I'd eat it myself. Don't you know there's a war on?'

I was delighted to see her at the dinner party and we got on very well. I knew her surname was Chierico, not a common Italian name. I found her even more attractive on closer acquaintance. She was twenty-one and I was thirty-three. We laughed all evening. Towards the end of the dinner, I said to her, 'What are you doing tomorrow evening?'

'I have a date.'

'Well, cancel it.'

'I can't do that.'

Next morning I phoned her. 'Are we going out this evening?' She said yes – she had cancelled her date. I took her out the following evening and a week later, when we were dining in the Savoy restaurant, I proposed to her. She accepted immediately. I always tell her that I had hardly got the words out of my mouth before she said yes. We went to the Embassy Club in Bond Street to celebrate and danced all night. We married a few months later.

It was the happiest and most fortunate thing that has ever happened to me.

CHARLIE WILSON

◆

I remember Charles Douglas-Home as the bravest man I ever knew. In early 1982 he was appointed Editor of *The Times* and less than a year later he literally by accident discovered he was suffering from myeloma, cancer of the bone marrow.

From the beginning he knew that the prognosis was not good. He had broken his thigh in a fall and the X-ray showed the condition was advanced. His friends were conscious that this was the most grotesque irony. His career ambition had been to edit *The Times*. Now it was to be taken from him with a brutality that no newspaper proprietor could equal.

Editing any national newspaper is a fearsome test not only of intellectual robustness but of physical endurance. Most people would have accepted that myeloma and editorship are incompatible and found more comfortable ways of spending their final days. Charlie One, as the staff called him, took a different view. He used *The Times* as his therapy, his inspiration, his reason for living. Despite the pain, the incapacity, and the sureness of his impending death, he attacked the job with all the mental and physical effort he could muster.

As the months went by, he grew weaker but he refused to compromise. The disease took its malignant inexorable toll and he slipped from one walking stick to two sticks, to a zimmer frame, and then a motorised wheelchair. With the support of his exceptional wife and two equally remarkable sons he laughed and joked about his condition and did not cease to direct *The Times* strategically and tactically. Charlie wrote a Leader every publishing day, sometimes dictated while he was lying flat on his back in a hospital ward.

The severity of his treatment, and the pernicious false hope that temporary regression brings, took him in and out of hospital many times. As his Deputy Editor – the staff called me Charlie Two – my job was to make sure that the paper came out whether Charlie was there or not. In truth, he was always there. He had a squawk-box by his hospital bed on which he conducted Leader conferences and with which he kept in open-line touch.

As the inevitable grew closer, management and staff began discussing succession. As Deputy, I was one of those mentioned. Charlie was a man I had always admired and respected and who respected me. His courage and demeanour during his 31-month reign took my friendship and regard for him to a higher plane. But just as for him, so for me the editorship of *The Times* was a career pinnacle. I recall sitting for most of one night alone with a bottle of whisky and the stark understanding that for me to realise my life's ambition, Charlie One had to die.

When Charlie did die, I was appointed Editor of *The Times*. I still remember the dichotomy of emotion and the feeling of guilt that I should be glad as well as sad.

Cherie Booth

◆

My best memories are of people rather than events and particularly my grandma, who taught me how important it is to remember.

I was six weeks old when I went to live with my father's family, and it was my grandma who looked after my sister and me, while my mum went to work. My earliest memories are of the stories grandma told me about herself and our family history. She had a phenomenal memory and a huge store of old family photographs. She was a formidable woman who had left school at the age of fourteen and was determined that we should do better ourselves.

The Courts fascinated her and she used to tell us how she would go and listen to Rose Heilbron, one of the first women QCs, in court in Liverpool. I don't think any of us felt then that it would be possible that someone from our family would end up in a similar position. She was there when I was called to the Bar but she died in 1987 and so missed the day in April 1995 when I became a Queen's Counsel myself. I know that she would have loved all the pomp and ceremony of that day, and the fact that the whole family was there to share it.

At the end of her life, my grandma became confused and would often forget things, but she never lost her ability to tell a tale and her stories of her early life were as vivid as ever.

I remember her every day and, by bringing to mind my memories of her, I try to pass on to my children all the things she taught me.

CHRIS MOON

◆

Memory

1. the faculty by which things are recalled or kept in the mind.

2. *a)* this faculty in an individual (my memory is beginning to fail).

2. *b)* one's store of things remembered (buried deep in my memory).

3. a recollection or remembrance (as in the remembrance of better times).

As stated in *The Concise Oxford Dictionary Ninth Edition* (if I remember correctly).

Memory 1

When I was seventeen I participated in a voluntary service programme organised by the school. I thought I'd be cutting grass for old ladies or helping paint a youth centre or something similar. It was a surprise when two of us were sent to the local mental hospital. We made tea on the geriatric ward. Many of the patients had Alzheimer's disease. They were sometimes agitated and violent, sometimes confused, sometimes very pleasant and sometimes vacant empty shells. They could no longer recognise the people they loved. Their spirits had gone and they had ceased to be themselves.

A ninety-year-old man talked endlessly about how hard it was to drive his men 'over the top' in the First World War. He sometimes recognised me and one day confided he wasn't the hard son of unmarried parents his men thought he was. 'Oh, no,' he said. 'I just wanted to go home to my mum like the rest of them, but I couldn't give in because I had responsibility.'

He couldn't remember the present, just the distant past. I used to read to a well-spoken blind lady who didn't look that old. I was surprised to see how many Alzheimer's sufferers weren't ancient. I read her *The Keys of the Kingdom* by A.J. Cronin. I am very lucky to be able to remember the book was an excellent read.

Memory 2

I remember standing in the scorching sun of the dry season in Phnom Penh, Cambodia. By chance I had just met Neil, who was in my platoon at the Royal Military Academy, Sandhurst. Thanks to a quirk of fate we were working for de-mining agencies in Cambodia at the same time. I hadn't seen him for a while and it was good to talk to him. I had been engrossed in conversation for several minutes when I felt someone touching and gently pushing me. The smell told me it was a beggar. I was surprised the beggar had come so close and invaded my personal space. I took a step backwards and carried on talking. The beggar put his head in front of my face and kept nodding at the Land Rover. I took another step backwards and was shocked to see he had no arms, just six-inch bony stumps.

Neil explained that he could see 'mine clearance' written in Khmer on the side of the vehicle and that he was trying to tell us what had happened to him. I was embarrassed because I didn't have any money to give him. Neil generously put some dollars in the man's top pocket. He walked away bowing his head and saying thank you.

DAVID SEAMAN

◆

One of my greatest memories is of Euro '96.

The tremendous honour of playing for my country, hearing the National Anthem being sung by 70,000 Englishmen, the hairs on the back of my neck standing up and, of course, that song – 'Football's Coming Home'.

From beating Scotland, and the Dutch, to saving the deciding penalty against Spain.

We once again met Germany in the semi-final. Even though we lost on penalties, the nation became one and football really had come home.

Then I remember the standing ovation from the Centre Court at Wimbledon, and receiving the ultimate of honours, the MBE from the Queen.

Truly magical memories!

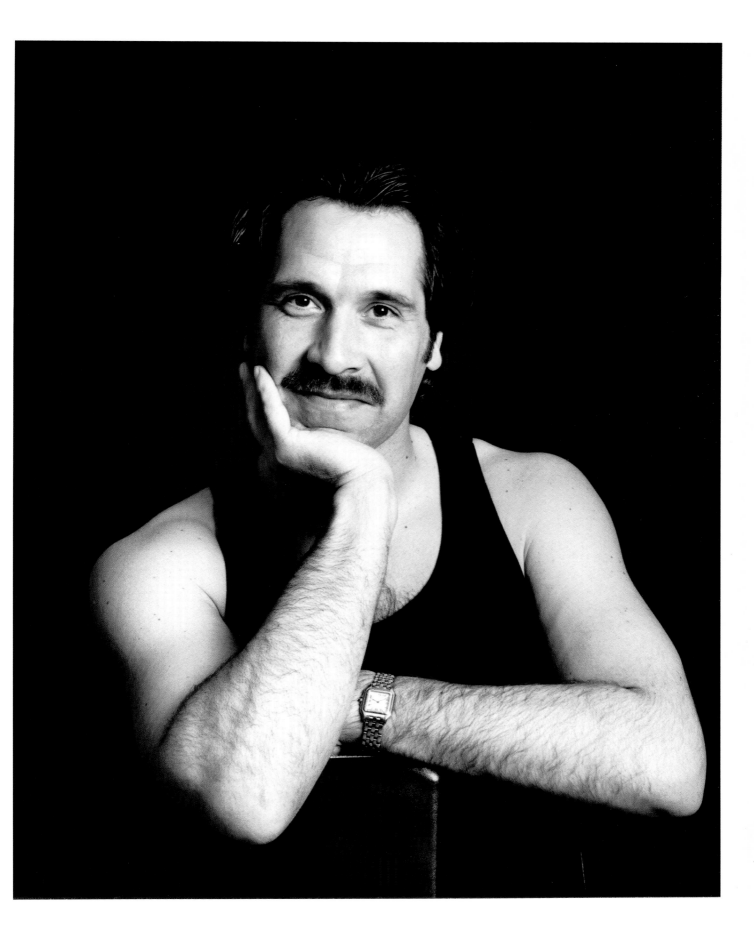

DAVID SUCHET

◆

My memory is a recollection when I thank God for giving me a 'memory'.

Summer 1973, The Royal Shakespeare Company. It was my first season and all was going well. I was due to play Oliver in *As You Like It* and Tybalt in *Romeo and Juliet*. In three days we were due to open *As You Like It*. *Romeo and Juliet* was already on. So was *Richard II*, and *As You Like It* was the third play to open.

I was the understudy to John Abbott as Hotspur in *Richard II*, Bernard Lloyd as Orlando in *As You Like It* and Bernard Lloyd as Mercutio in *Romeo and Juliet*.

Three days before opening *As You Like It*, Bernard Lloyd got injured. I had three days to learn Orlando. I had four days to learn Mercutio and the same amount of time to learn Hotspur – simultaneously.

At that time, my wife was miles away at the Liverpool Theatre and she rang me, once an hour, every hour, day and night for three days and three nights to check on my progress. It worked!

Thank God for my memory.

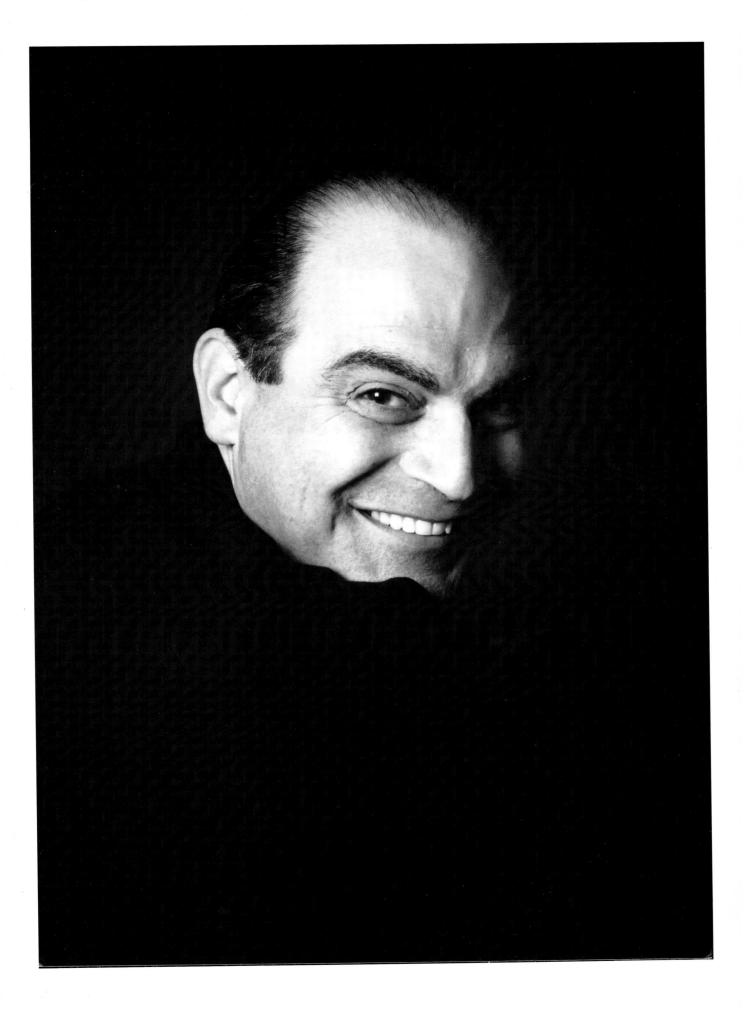

ELAINE PAIGE

◆

In 1981, I was fortunate enough to appear in the premiere production of *Cats* at the New London Theatre playing the role of Grizabella and singing Andrew Lloyd Webber's wonderful song 'Memory'. It was the culmination of a rather unusual sequence of events which I remember very vividly because fate definitely seemed to be playing a hand.

I was driving home late one night to my home in Barnes, southwest London, listening to the news at midnight. Just after this a melody by Andrew Lloyd Webber was introduced. It was as yet without lyrics, and as I approached my house I stopped the car and ran in to set the tape recorder so that I could have another listen to this magnificent and haunting tune, entitled 'Memory'.

As I did so, I nearly tripped over a thin, bedraggled black cat that was lurking at my front door. She gracefully crossed my path and then followed me in as I set about my task of retrieving a tape in double-quick time. I was determined to find out more about the melody and resolved to do so the next day. Meanwhile the cat was making herself at home after a very welcome bowl of milk.

The following morning I was awoken with a call from Cameron Mackintosh, the producer of *Cats*, asking me if I would step into the role of Grizabella at short notice, a cameo role with one great song. My sympathy was with Judi Dench who had damaged her ankle and couldn't perform but when I heard that I would be singing a song called 'Memory' I flew at the chance.

We only had a few days of rehearsals. Then we went into previews and during this time the lyrics were changed each day. By the opening night they were finally settled and what should be the first word of the song but 'midnight' – that witching hour when I first heard the hauntingly beautiful melody and was adopted by my black alley cat.

EMMA NICHOLSON

◆

My father had gone late, bruised and miserable to bed. He was in pain from a severe hunting fall in Yorkshire, of such ferocity that the local hunt fraternity, of which the Master was a fellow Parliamentarian, had deemed it to be terminal and, acting according to normal hunting practice, had doffed their hats and caps, stopped pursuing the fox and, calling in the hounds, returned sombrely across the fields to mourn a fellow huntsman's death. Meanwhile, my father, very much alive, had pulled his horse to its feet, remounted and was bouncing along merrily to resume the chase.

My mother had not seen the joke. When he recounted this merry tale, expecting a good audience response, my mother in reply had laid down her domestic law. He was not to hunt again; it was too much for her to countenance and remain comfortable about his welfare. From now on, hunting was out of bounds.

My father's continued bravery in many fields of physical endeavour, that only trained athletes would normally tackle, stemmed from his year of illness when, as a schoolboy, he was bed-bound and very sick indeed. He was a victim of the 1917 cerebral influenza which swept across Europe towards the end of the First World War. He had been lucky to survive but rose from his bed, physically damaged in terms of loss of complete mobility, but determined to put it all behind him and to resume life as if he had no physical problems of any nature. He took up horse racing and mountaineering shortly afterwards. Much later on, at an age beyond normal recruitment, he joined the army while in the House of Commons at the outbreak of the Second World War and took grave risks in occupied France. He was a native French speaker

from his mother's Huguenot ancestry. By the time he was approaching his sixth decade, when he took his Yorkshire tumble, hunting remained an occasional activity alongside regular physical work on Sunday afternoons away from the constituency in his Berkshire woodland. To be forbidden hunting was a bitter blow.

The following morning we assembled for breakfast. I expected my father to come in with a sad face despite the fact that it was his sixtieth birthday and that, as a family, we celebrated birthdays heartily. My mother's hand was raised, pouring her first cup of coffee, as the dining-room door opened. My father entered, his purposefulness restored, eyes bright, stance happy and determined – a different person from the one last seen sadly on his way to bed.

Something was afoot. He sat down and, hand reaching out for *The Times*, said nonchalantly, 'I've had an idea.' The table froze. My mother's coffee cup was returned to its saucer. 'What now?' she asked. 'I am going to take up parachuting,' he replied jauntily, stretched for his coffee, opened *The Times*, and that was that.

He became an honorary Red Beret (the Parachute Regiment's Association), regularly parachuting for fifteen years; went up in the first hot-air balloon flight in the UK; crashed and destroyed the electricity supply for ten German villages in a later hot-air ballooning competition in the Alps, and founded the Parascending Club. He continued his airborne activities until his eightieth birthday, when he took flying lessons in the hopes of getting his private pilot's licence.

I often felt my mother would have done better in terms of saving herself personal worry if she had allowed him to fall off strange horses from time to time.

Evelyn Glennie

◆

While I was in the first year at Ellon Academy (16 miles north of Aberdeen), there was a stream of regular musical performances, including Music for a Summer's Evening and Music for Christmas and the twice yearly shows in conjunction with the Drama Department. Musicals such as *Guys and Dolls* and *My Fair Lady*, and pantomimes. I very quickly became involved in these events, as a performer on piano and percussion.

I particularly remember some fun we had with *Aladdin*, which we staged at Christmas 1980. I was by now an old hand in front of an audience and untroubled by demands made on me by the run of performances, which always included matinées for the local senior citizens and schools as well as evening presentations for mums and dads and anyone else who was interested.

On this particular occasion, we had given an afternoon show to the old folks; everything had gone extremely well and at the end a rather sweet old lady stood up to give us a vote of thanks. She spoke for some minutes and then seemed to stop. Thinking that she had completed her address I began to play on the piano one of the numbers from the show to keep the audience in a jolly mood as they filed out of the hall.

Unfortunately, the spokeswoman had only been catching her breath before continuing with her congratulations, and my fortissimo rendering of 'You Can Make Magic' drowned her kind remarks, to the hysteria of the cast and the Ellon Academy Music Department. No doubt on this occasion my hearing aids would have been found on top of the piano, which was increasingly their position when I was playing music, and my euphoria at the audience's enthusiasm may have prevented me from paying quite as much attention to the old lady's speech as I should have done.

FELICITY KENDAL

◆

After a fitful night in a shuddering bed (my basement room in a cheap Earl's Court hotel was practically in the underground train tunnel), I set off for Waterloo. I was hours too early for the audition for Olivier's season at the Old Vic, but at least I was there. I walked up and down the river going over my lines. Eventually, I knocked on the door of the Nissan huts that were office and rehearsal rooms for the Vic.

The casting lady led me to meet the great man. He was charming, dressed in cord shirt and braces and much taller than I had imagined. His two hands shaking mine were warm and reassuring. He introduced me to Kenneth Tynan, dapper, thin and smoking hard – I had no idea who he was. The casting lady said a few nice things about me, then they all sat down.

I might have worked on stages all over India from the age of nine but I was totally unprepared for the trauma of auditioning and not fitted out with the required emotional nerve. I launched into Ophelia's madness with a sinking heart, then swept straight into Saint Joan. The sun was shining through the windows of the hut and, in the bright daylight, standing only a few feet away from one of the gods of the theatre, I felt gawky and vulnerable. My legs began to shake uncontrollably inside my bell-bottoms and, by the time I got to Viola, my voice (once quite strong but weakened by lack of practice) had deteriorated into a high-pitched squeak.

I got to the end. I knew that I had failed miserably. Olivier thanked me, as if I had been perfectly wonderful; Tynan stuttered something witty, told me how much he had liked my recent film and wished me great success in the future. They were so nice, but I walked out of the Nissan huts certain that I had failed yet again. With my tail tucked firmly between my legs, I got the next train back to Olton.

I later discovered that Kenneth Tynan *had* reviewed *Shakespeare Wallah* for the *Observer*. He loved the film, describing me as Buckingham's daughter, 'Also their Ophelia is charmingly played by the dumpling-faced Felicity Kendal.'

FELICITY LOTT

◆

Memory is a curious phenomenon: I have little to show for the years spent studying French and Latin literature, and couldn't tell you the name of the book I read last week, but I could sing you hundreds of songs in French or German at the drop of a hat, and perform a handful of operas by Strauss or Mozart with minimal warning. Of course. one wouldn't ideally choose those circumstances to make a début at one of the world's most prestigious opera houses, but …

One morning in the summer of 1992, the phone rang at 7am – not a good time (it usually denoted family illness). This was not family, but the Countess in the new Salzburg production of *The Marriage of Figaro*. She was ill, and had been forced to pull out of that evening's premiere. Would I take over? I live in a tiny Sussex village; I never fly and sing on the same day; I hadn't sung *Figaro* for ages … 'If we sent you a private jet?' 'Well, maybe our family-together-day could be spent jet-setting to Salzburg rather than driving to Beachy Head?'

Gatwick was a delight: no queues, no check-in, no customs – and then a plane just big enough for my husband and our eight-year-old daughter, plus a couple of pilots and a large silver platter piled high with smoked salmon sandwiches. We bounced across the clouds and when we arrived Gabriel and Emily 'did' Salzburg in the rain, while I was whisked to the Opera House, where frazzled dressmakers achieved miracles and let down every hem. Then I rushed to a rehearsal room to be shown the basics of the production.

By that time, Act One was beginning (the Countess doesn't appear until Act Two, which opens with her alone on stage singing a sad aria. Gradually, I was joined by friends – Thomas Allen, Robert Tear, and Sylvia McNair. Bernard Haitink was conducting, so help was all round. My husband and daughter swear I didn't look under-rehearsed, and the producer kindly told me that I made him feel redundant! (They had been rehearsing for six weeks.)

In the big set-piece arias, as long as you remember the words and music, don't bump into the furniture or try to exit up the chimney, you can't do too much damage to the production. But in Act Four of *Figaro* things get very complicated. The Countess disguises herself as her maid, Susannah, and flirts with her own husband, who can't tell that the six-foot blonde he is embracing isn't the petite brunette he's been lusting after for the past three Acts. In Salzburg, at least, and uniquely in my experience, the Susannah (Sylvia McNair) was almost as tall as I am, so I didn't have to do all the dodging in and out of pergolas and summerhouses with my knees bent. Otherwise I remember nothing of the performance.

We went back to London the next day, slumming it in Club Class, on a plane with other people. 'Ah, well,' I said, 'we were Royalty for a day.' Our daughter was less impressed. 'Economy Class Royalty,' she said. 'That silver salver was plastic covered in foil.' But she admitted to enjoying the smoked salmon sandwiches.

GEORG SOLTI

12 OCTOBER 1912 – 5 SEPTEMBER 1997

◆

Everything he did, both in his professional and private life, was imbued, indeed overflowed with enthusiasm and *joie de vivre*. Solti's philosophy was that life was precious and every moment of God's gift had to be used to the full.

He loved to share his enjoyments in life. Disliking parties and social life, he was happiest at home surrounded by friends and fellow musicians. Whatever his favourite experience – his greatest joy was to share it with those around him – eating fresh ripe cherries, apricots and strawberries; the taste of a newly discovered brand of malt whisky, or a home-made Hungarian salami. There were early morning visits to art galleries; reading and sharing books – particularly Thomas Mann. And there was sport: watching athletics or football on television; riding his bicycle in Italy; swimming in the Mediterranean; or lying in the sun on the beach, preferably surrounded by young and beautiful girls. Most of all, there was his music. When he was working on a new score he would call me or anyone who was nearby, to come and look at a special theme or passage in the score – either tapping out the rhythm or whistling the main theme – remarking, 'What a miracle – a genius of invention. Doesn't it thrill you?'

His happiest moments were undoubtedly working with his beloved Chicago Symphony Orchestra, or with young musicians, always inspiring everyone round him to give of their best. The greatest pleasure I think he ever had was the one concert with his dream orchestra – a personally hand-picked ensemble of seventy-five star players from forty world orchestras – twenty of whom were principal players within their own orchestras. There were musicians from the Vienna and Berlin Philharmonics, the great American orchestras (Chicago, Cleveland, Philadelphia, New York, San Francisco) and from Denmark, Hong Kong, South Africa, Italy, Sweden, Finland and Holland – as well as representatives from four British orchestras. He called this virtuoso ensemble 'The World Orchestra for Peace' – it was created to celebrate the fiftieth anniversary of the United Nations.

When the chattering masses heard about the project, they expressed doubts about the viability of such an orchestra made up of players with such varying styles and whether they would be able to produce anything except cacophony. With the short rehearsal time available, the feeling was that there would be no cohesion or ensemble playing, and undoubtedly there would be jealousies between all those leaders. The doubters regarded it as a crazy and expensive idea for one performance only – it was Solti's most risky enterprise.

The concert took place in Geneva at the Victoria Hall. At the first rehearsal the tensions were high – both players, onlookers and the Maestro held their breath – he gave the downbeat for the 'William Tell Overture', which starts with the cellos. What followed was the most glorious orchestral playing any of us had ever heard – it was undoubtedly the most joyful moment of Solti's professional life. He whispered to the orchestra, 'Listen hard, my dears. You have never heard anything like this before and you will never hear it again.' He turned to us in the auditorium and shouted out, 'Sounds good?' 'Sounds brilliant,' we replied.

GEORGE CAREY

◆

I did my National Service as one of a small band of wireless operators based at Shaibah, in Iraq. Our small signals hut was three miles out in the desert, often in temperatures reaching 120° Fahrenheit. During duty periods, I occasionally strolled in the beauty of the desert, sometimes chatting with the Bedouin travellers and giving them much-needed water.

Once, I went further than I had intended, and got completely lost. I recall the panic welling up as I told myself to be calm. 'Use logic,' I told myself. 'If you look for clues, you'll get back soon.' But logic did not help. The surrounding desert looked the same in every direction. 'Boy, are you in trouble,' I thought. 'You won't be missed until tonight's relief takes over. In that time you could be well and truly dead.' I started to pray as I frantically looked for clues. If only I could see an aircraft, or smoke from the oil wells. But there was nothing.

After an hour, I was very tired and thirsty; no longer panicked but resigned. I needed to conserve my energy so I could shout for help.

And then I saw a little spot of red and white that seemed to dance before my eyes. As the spot moved closer, I saw it was a Bedouin girl who I had seen on occasions with her friendly parents and goats. She bounded towards me and looked puzzled by my obvious distress. Her family arrived a few minutes later. I gesticulated that I was lost. They understood at once and thrust a water bottle into my hands. They led me back to my hut and to the welcome tedium of my duties.

Embarrassed but content, I bade them goodbye. The times I had given them hospitality had paid off a thousandfold through their generosity. 'Allah be with you.' 'Allah,' the cry of the desert, was the last thing I heard them say. For me, it marked the grateful realisation that all things are dependent on God and when we wander from him we all need help and directions to get safely back home.

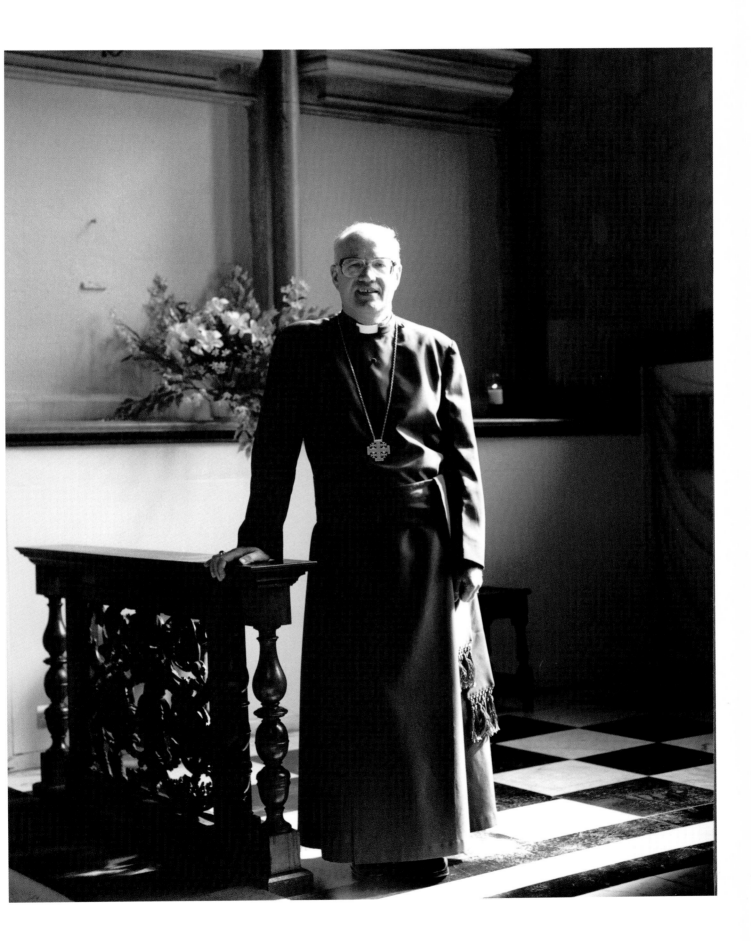

GERRY ROBINSON

◆

When he was eighty-two years old, my father, never having seen the inside of a hospital in all his life, failed to make a full recovery after a minor operation. Having gone in with 'all his marbles', he emerged a confused and lost old man, singing half-remembered Irish rebel songs to the embarrassed amusement of the (mainly Irish) nursing staff. I felt ashamed, hurt, angry, and overwhelmingly sad all at the same time. He didn't recognise me but, when I was left alone with him, I hugged him for the first time in my life. It was a bitter pill to discover that I loved him at the moment of losing him.

In rude health he was terrifying; a big man, hugely unpredictable, angry, passionate and impulsive. In thirty-five years I had only once seen his soft inner break through to the surface. His son and my brother, Eddie, drowned while swimming in the sea on a warm July day in Donegal. He was fourteen years old. My mother was in England and my father was in charge. He felt the responsibility sorely. He crumpled in front of us shedding big, raw tears that became anxious and fretful, worrying about where we were and what we were doing. His own terror made it even more difficult to get close to him.

My father lived for two years after the operation and, in his confused and befuddled world, I grew close to him. In his rare lucid moments, we talked together in a way that we'd never managed before. When his mind slipped into childhood, he wouldn't recognise me but we talked of events and people long past that were real at that moment.

He fought mightily against being helped to use the toilet, a child again but with a man's sensibilities, angry and embarrassed. There were moments of wry humour in his conviction that the young nurses were 'after him' and they humoured him in his youthful advances. I would have happily taken the brunt of his anger again to see him as his old self – but it was never to be. The loss of his dignity was, I know, humiliating to him even in his demented ramblings.

Two weeks after he entered a nursing home, he died. I had spent most of the previous day with him and had felt closer to him than at any other time in our lives. My sense of loss of him was, and indeed remains, far more powerful than I could ever have imagined.

GINNY ELLIOTT

◆

When I was asked to write about the most memorable moment of my career in horse trials, I thought 'no problem'. But in twenty years there have been too many that are special, so I decided to list them all.

◆ Winning the Junior Europeans on Dubonnet in the early 1970s started my career. Dubonnet was an unlikely candidate for Three-Day Eventing – heavily built, small and lacking good breeding, but he proved his worth and silenced his critics.

◆ My mother selling her precious dining-room table to finance two new horses.

◆ My wheelchair-bound father somehow getting to the ringside at a prize-giving so he could wave a miniature bottle of champagne and share in the celebrations.

◆ My first win at Burghley on Priceless in the 1980s – we had made the big time!

◆ Competing in my first senior team and working with 'The Greats' whom I had previously only admired from afar.

◆ Representing my country at my first Olympics in Los Angeles. The experience was everything and more than I had anticipated.

◆ Winning my first senior European title with Priceless and then the ultimate – the world championships with the same horse.

◆ Sharing the highs and lows with my family, helpers and sponsors. My sport is all about teamwork – without the ground crew's efficiency, nothing functions.

Finally, my retirement was the toughest decision I've had to make. I have no regrets, just deep gratitude and wonderful memories of the people and horses that helped me during my career in a great sport.

GREG RUSEDSKI

◆

Wednesday 28 June 1995. My first appearance on Wimbledon Centre Court is a cherished memory. All the emotion and excitement of the enormous reception during the measured walk across the lush green carpet. An occasion I had always dreamed about. Seven games in just eighteen minutes against the seeded Frenchman but only one of them mine and the dream was becoming a nightmare …

But then later, in the warm sunshine of the glorious afternoon, I can still hear the prolonged cheers echoing around that hallowed stadium, still picture my leap into the air, still recall so many smiling faces as headband, shirt and racquet were propelled one by one into the crowd. I knew then that only the Wimbledon trophy could ever taste sweeter.

HAROLD PINTER

◆

In the trial scene in *The Merchant of Venice*, one night I said to Anew McMaster (as Bassiano) instead of 'For thy three thousand ducats here is six', quite involuntarily, 'For thy three thousand *buckets* here is six'. He replied quietly and with emphasis: 'If every *bucket* in six thousand *buckets* were in six parts, and every part a *bucket* I would not draw them – I would have my bond.' I could not continue. The other members of the court scene and I turned upstage. Some walked into the wings. But Mac stood, remorseless, grave, like an eagle waiting for my reply.

HELEN SHARMAN

◆

We often used to look out at the Earth spinning below us. The oceans are a gorgeous deep blue, the clouds so brilliantly white it hurts your eyes to look at them for long and the deserts are crossed with long, sandy-coloured roads that seem to have neither beginnings nor ends. As my last night on the Space Station approached, I wanted to make the most of it, knowing that I might not have that view of the world again. I positioned my sleeping bag by a window and snuggled in, hoping to stay awake until it was time to start preparations for our return to Earth.

The next day would probably be the most dangerous of my life. There was a small but marked chance that I would die and I was surprised to find that I was not worried. I understood the systems, I knew how to cope in any number of emergencies – before the launch I had rationalised life's inherent risks, but all that was a logical process. Why weren't my emotions telling me to be scared?

It had been an eventful few days. There had been problems throughout the mission with technical failures, the most significant of which became apparent as our tiny Soyuz spacecraft made its final approach to the Space Station.

Our automatic docking system was not working properly so we had to take manual control. Each of us had individual jobs to do: I had a periscopic television camera to operate, Sergei worked out which information was reliable, and Tole operated the rocket engines to steer us to our goal. We trusted our lives to each other and when we finally docked with the Station we were rewarded with an elated feeling of closeness and companionship. We had done it and we were still alive!

Now, looking back at the Earth for maybe the last time, I felt a warm glow inside me as the Station moved over parts of the world where there were people I knew. I remembered the times we had spent together, the laughs and the tears. Looking back, the significant part of my life involved other people. It had been good. Maybe that's why I wasn't scared.

Being in space makes you realise how insignificant we are; yet in any one life it is the people around us who are more important than anything else. We might be a backward form of life on a tiny planet by a puny star, but to other people you can make a difference. In the end, it's people that count. That is a memory I hope never to forget.

Ian McLaurin

◆

As the new chairman of the England and Wales Cricket Board, I attended all the Test Matches in 1997 and saw at first hand the highs and lows of international cricket. The season started wonderfully well for the England side when we won all three one-day internationals.

We then won the first Test Match and hopes were high of us regaining the Ashes from the Australians. Sadly for the English team, the match at Lords was drawn and we suffered with very bad weather. We then lost three matches running – Old Trafford, Headingley and Trent Bridge. The excellent Australian side retained the Ashes and we played the final Test Match at the Oval. The England side completed a most exciting victory within three days.

So ended a most wonderful season of international cricket. But my lasting memory of the summer is of both teams sitting in the Australian dressing room at the Oval drinking beer and chatting about the series. Between the rival teams, friendships were cemented. And despite all the pressures of the season, the players clearly appreciated and enjoyed each other's company – a wonderful advertisement for sport played in the very best spirit.

JOANNA LUMLEY

A CARGO FOR POLAND

◆

The big spare bedroom in my parents' house had been turned into a kind of wardrobe/workshop. The beds were piled high with clothes; an ironing board was set up; tissue paper in neat piles waited for the packing; big black plastic bags billowed and slithered off every surface.

One of my mother's friends, a Polish doctor, was planning to drive a lorry over to Częstochowa, north of Kraków, filled with provisions for the needy people there. Everyone in the village knew about the scheme, and each day another collection of goodies was delivered.

Everything was to be in the best possible condition, so the first job was to throw away the frankly unwearable and completely moth-eaten garments. Then anything that needed cleaning was sent off to Tenterden; other things were sponged and inspected. All buttons were to be sewn on neatly, broken zips replaced, belts found and attached.

Incredible changes took place: crumpled, unfashionable blouses began to bloom again under the hissing steam iron, and ludicrously old-fashioned coats became attractive and even desirable, as though they had regained a former dignity. My favourites were the children's clothes: tiny trousers and home-made cardigans took such a short time to repair and press; and we found ways of packing things together if we thought they shouldn't be separated, so in one's mind's eye one could see a Polish toddler in *this* checked shirt with *those* dungarees.

The children from the village school sent little parcels of soap (then a great luxury in Poland), each wrapped in a note from the child, written in Polish, saying 'love from Annie' and 'love from Kevin'. These we placed in every pocket we could find.

How strange fashion is! As I ironed scarves that had been sent to us as outcasts because of their colour or design, I could imagine them becoming noble once they were worn by a handsome Polish woman. Perhaps that big skirt covered with mauve roses would look superb when teamed up with the beige pullover and elasticated snakeskin belt.

Would the people of Częstochowa like what we'd sent? Would they know we cared? We filled every shoe and pocket with more soap, and added needles, pins, hooks and eyes, elastic and paper handkerchiefs. On Thursday the lorry backed into the drive and we hurriedly loaded the bulging black bags, stowed tightly beside boxes of medical equipment and a second-hand wheelchair. Then in the August sun the great vehicle slowly set off, brushing against the rhododendron leaves in Kent, taking our ironed clothes and our love to Poland.

JOANNA TROLLOPE

◆

In the attics of the rectory where I was born, there was a dressing-up box. It was, in fact, a trunk, a huge battered black ball-dress trunk, lined in torn striped ticking, with a tray let into the top. The tray held shoes and feathers; Turkish slippers and Dutch clogs, and dyed ostrich plumes with quills as thick as pencils.

Underneath the tray, the clothes lay jumbled, as they had lain for at least two generations of children before my brother and sister and me. The Joan of Arc tunic with its faded gold fleur-de-lis, the muslin shepherdess dress hitched up over a pink quilted petticoat, the red and yellow jester's tabard jingling with tarnished bells, the leopard cub outfit complete with ears and pin-on tail, the satin dandies' coats and brocade waistcoats. All these had been worn by our mother and uncles and aunt, and, before that, by our grandmother and her siblings.

Indeed, some of them had dropped something of their own lives into the trunk from time to time – a tin helmet from the Great War, an Edwardian evening shawl of black net heavy with tiny jet beads, a robe-like Moroccan dressing gown the colours of a stained-glass window, gloves and canes and sashes and hats – from a tasselled fez to a cavalry officer's bowler.

The trunk was a toy of infinite possibility. There were shrieks and tears over favourites and splendid opportunities for unselfconscious cross dressing. After hours of primping and preening and changing our minds, in which the old sweetish musty air of the attic had sifted into every corner of our lungs, came the superb moment of clattering and stumbling and sweeping downstairs in our heels and plumes and swords to parade about on the broad grass terraces of the rectory garden.

I have the trunk still. It sits in my attic now, the contents dustier and frailer, but as powerfully characterful as ever. And I only have to lift the lid and take a breath to see, in my mind's eye, a disordered procession of children, solemnly trailing their tattered and eccentric finery across a Gloucestershire garden before an indifferent audience of my grandmother's hens.

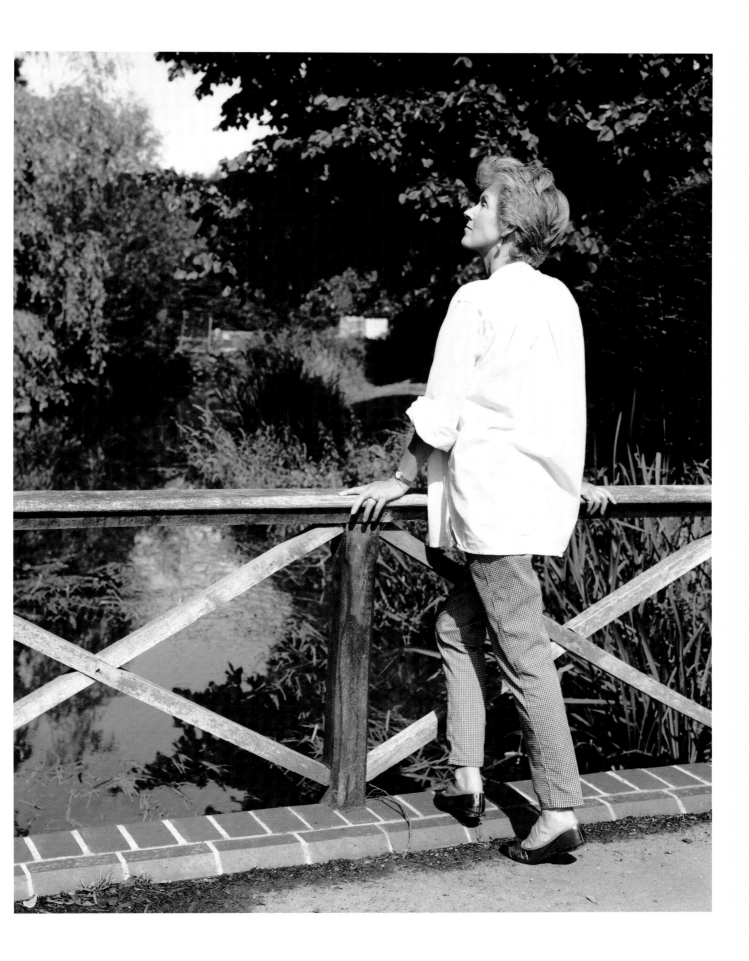

JOHN GIELGUD

◆

MEMORY LANE
A few hints for those advancing years.

Don't forget to
       Answer that letter
       Accept or refuse that invitation
       Check locks, shutters and windows
       Feed dogs, cats, fishes

Turn off
       Hearing aid
       Mobile phone
       Radio
       Television

Check
       Address book
       Post code

Retire to bed

Don't be unduly disturbed by failing
to remember certain names, addresses,
first lines of poems and familiar
quotations. If you manage to relax
and think of other things completely,
the word you're seeking for so
desperately will probably flash
back into your mind at some
unexpected moment – either
quite a short time, minutes
or even hours later!

JOHN HARVEY-JONES

◆

One of the greatest gifts I have enjoyed throughout my business life has been a healthy cynicism about technology and the chance of it working. I think I can trace this tendency to 'only believe it when you see it' to a very early and rather shattering experience.

The first time I saw action in my chosen career of the Royal Navy, I was a midshipman in charge of the quarter deck aboard a destroyer. We were operating in the Mediterranean and, together with another ship, became engaged by the enemy. As tends to happen in these matters, the enemy had the range on us and we spent quite a time enduring showers of shells – most of which, apart from frightening us and drenching us with water, did no actual harm as we strove to get within effective firing range of the guns. Needless to say, we were all tensed up and eager

for the great moment when we would start fighting back. Eventually we were judged to be within range and the firing gong went, followed by a thunderous explosion.

Whilst we were reloading, I peered round the side of the gun shield to see where our shots had landed. The enemy at the time was about five miles away and we were firing at a pretty well extreme range. I was therefore rather shaken when I saw that a shell which had been fired from the gun above us had landed on the quarter deck and was rolling around a few feet away from our gun. It seemed to me there was a considerable shortfall between the five feet that our shell had gone and the five miles that were needed.

Ever since, I have had a wholesome disregard for the probability of any mechanical device working as predicted.

JOHN MAJOR

A MEMORY OF CHRISTMAS IN NIGERIA

◆

In 1965 I went to work in Nigeria for the Standard Bank of West Africa. The Biafran War had begun in Nigeria, but I was posted to Jos – far away from the fighting and on a plateau with a beautiful climate. I was allocated a Bank flat with another young bachelor, Richard Cochram, a Liverpudlian who, unlike me, was a permanent member of the overseas staff. I was simply on short-term secondment.

As Christmas approached, Richard bought a large chicken (no turkeys available) for our Christmas dinner. The electricity supply was erratic and refrigeration almost non-existent, so he bought a live chicken and tethered it in a small pen for the day or so before Christmas.

Christmas Day dawned and Richard and I sat on our terrace in the warm sun and awaited lunch, which was being prepared by our steward, Moses. The smell of roast lunches from the flats below us wafted upwards appetisingly. We became ever more hungry.

But lunch did not appear. There was no sign of it. Nor was there any sign of activity in the kitchen apart from the ever-present insects. Richard summoned Moses and demanded to know – where was the chicken?

'Downstairs,' he was told. Richard, unpersuaded, wanted to see it. Moses was gone some time and returned with the chicken. It was led into the room with a piece of string round its neck and it walked around perkily.

Richard was dumbfounded. He was literally speechless. He then exploded. I don't recall all that he said because I was laughing too much, but the essence was that he wanted to eat the chicken and not take it for walks.

Moses' defence was impeccable. No one had told him that, he insisted. He was handed a live chicken and no one had ever said it was to be cooked. The chicken preened itself merrily and strolled from the room on its lead.

Days later we had chicken sandwiches for supper. And, ever after, instructions from Richard to Moses were very precise.

JOHN MORTIMER

◆

Childhood is a great time for lying. Later in life you may be able to boast of some real achievement or some extraordinary adventure; in childhood all must be supplied from the imagination. So I told my friend that I was the son of a Russian aristocrat, smuggled out of Moscow during the revolution, and had kindly been taken in by the simple English lawyer with whom I happened to live.

I had a long story, a rare sporting fantasy, about walking along the towpath at Hammersmith when the cox of the Oxford crew had a heart attack and, being then of the appropriate weight, steering the eight to victory in the Boat Race.

More consistently, I pretended that my parents never stopped going to cocktail parties, bickering, throwing 'White Ladies' and 'Manhattans' into each other's faces, and would soon be getting a divorce. If I had one clear ambition during those years it was to be the child of a broken home.

JOHN SUCHET

◆

It was a defining moment in our history. People no longer ask, 'Where were you when you learned President Kennedy had been shot?' They ask, 'How did you hear about Princess Diana's death?'

I was with my wife in Poitiers in France, on the way down to Gascony for our summer holiday. A waitress at breakfast told us. 'Lady Di est morte,' she said, using the old title the French have always used. We took the first available flight home. We were not the only ones. My programme editor, in Majorca, was told all flights to London were full. He explained why he had to get back and a seat was immediately made available for him.

The next week was the most difficult I have had in a quarter of a century of working in television news. And providing the commentary for the Princess's funeral at the end of it will never be surpassed in the uniqueness of the demands that it put on me. How to put into words what the nation felt?

The pictures took my breath – and my voice – away. We did not expect crowds like it. We did not expect the silence, broken only by the applause. We did not expect the flowers. We did not expect the emotion.

There is a rule in television news broadcasting. When the pictures are powerful, no words are needed. That was my guiding principle in what were the most emotional and difficult hours I have ever spent in a television studio, and am ever likely to again. So I said as little as I could. But for the rest of my life I will be pleased that I was there and that I was involved. Journalism, someone once said, is the first draft of history. I participated in history being made, and I will always remember it.

JONATHAN SACHS

◆

When I think back to my childhood, almost my first memory is of seder night, the first evening of Passover. We would gather round the table in my grandparents' house – a vast, extended family of uncles, aunts, cousins and distant relatives, and always some strangers, whose names I never knew.

There, in the musty Victorian house with its chiming clocks and oak bookcases, we would tell the ancient story of how, long ago, the Israelites were slaves in Egypt, and how with the help of God they made their way to freedom.

It was different, and fun, and I never forgot it. There were songs and stories and intriguing rituals. The idea was not just to tell the story of the past but to enter into it as if it were happening now. So we ate the *matzah*, the unleavened 'bread of affliction'. We tasted the *maror*, the 'bitter herbs' of slavery. We drank four cups of wine, each celebrating a stage on the way to freedom.

As the youngest child – I must have been three or four – I was given the starring role. It was my task to ask the four questions, beginning 'Why is this night different from all other nights?' and

that set the whole narrative in motion. It was not until many years later that I realised what was happening, that year and every year. I was being inducted into a people and its memories. I was learning its past and making it my own. I was part of a story that had begun more than three thousand years earlier and had been handed on from generation to generation ever since.

More than most, Jews have reflected on the power of memory to shape identity. The Hebrew Bible is full of commands to remember. We carry our past with us, and it helps to make us who we are. We never forgot the bread of affliction nor the long road to freedom, and they gave us hope, knowing that we are still part of that journey whose destination is a world of justice, compassion and peace.

We are what we remember. That is why Alzheimer's disease is so devastating. It robs us of our memory, our past, our sense of who we are, the story of which we are a part, our sense of connectedness to others and the world. Caring for those who suffer from it, and for their carers, has become one of the great imperatives of our time.

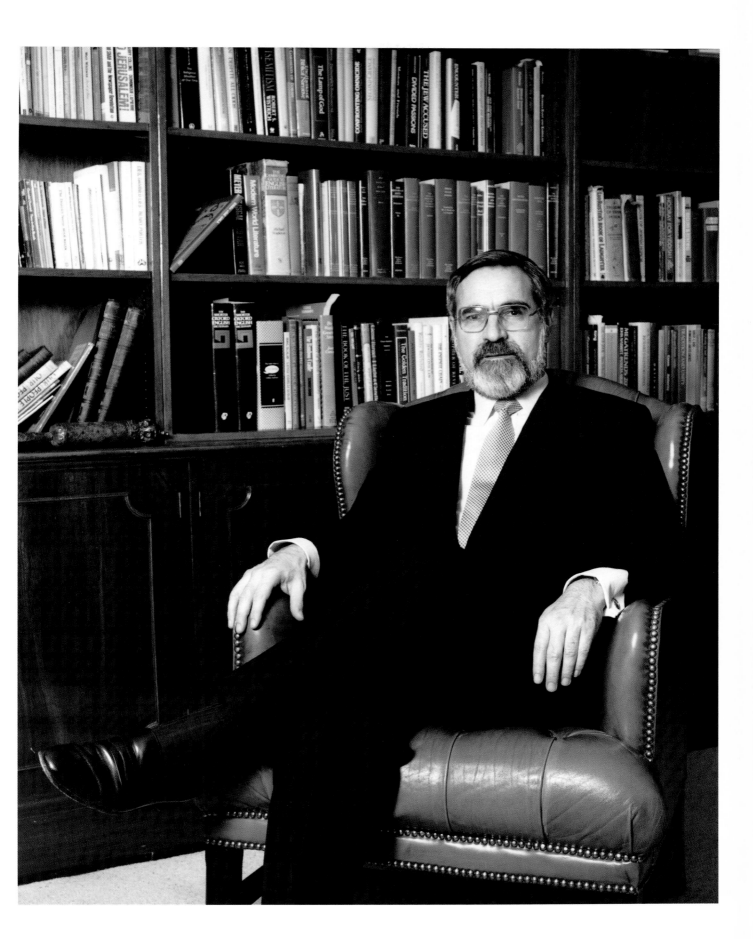

JUDI DENCH

◆

One of my earliest memories is during wartime and of being very young and at home with a baby-sitter while my parents had gone with my brother to his school concert. I remember thinking of the baby-sitter as being very old and grown-up, but she was probably only in her teens. During the evening, the air-raid sirens went. We had been told to go to the cellar if this happened. However, the baby-sitter insisted on our sitting at the top of the cellar steps, although I didn't know why, and this is where my parents found us when they returned a short time later. It wasn't until years afterwards that I discovered that she was more afraid of going down into the cellar than she was of the bombs!

Failing memory is often associated with old age, except for those people who develop Alzheimer's disease, and it is often a case of remembering far distant things but not what happened yesterday, or even five minutes ago. We should cherish our memories and enjoy them while we can.

LAURENCE MARKS & MAURICE GRAN

◆

Despite accepted belief we are not joined at the hip. We are sometimes joined at the brain. We are two distinct personalities. We are Laurence and Maurice, not 'LoandMo'. Therefore to recall a memory of mutual euphoria is certainly not effortless.

Yet our memory is as one when we recall the afternoon and evening of Thursday 22 November, 1990. We remember sharing the same relish and delight. We had just 'de-planed', as the Virgin girlies are wont to say, at Gatwick airport. Our driver was there to collect us, and there he stood with a grin on his face the size of an Oxford college.

'Have you heard?'

'We've been in the air for eleven hours,' said Maurice.

'We are dehydrated. Take us home,' said Laurence. 'Heard what?'

'She's gone. She's resigned. Announced her resignation at half past ten this morning,' said the driver, without once considering that we might have no idea who 'She' might be.

'She didn't have the backing of the Cabinet, did She. Felt She had to stand down. After eleven years, we had at long last seen the back of Margaret Thatcher.

The unadulterated thrill, the superlative joy, the uncontaminated excitement that we both felt as the driver took us into London, seeing people in poorer suburbs of our capital city in a state of celebration; a memory we shall never forget. We knew this day was special, of course we did. No longer would we have to listen to the tirades of this blonde-coiffed woman, with the funny teeth and the affected voice that sounded as though she had inhaled whatever is the opposite of helium.

The woman, who made Laurence and Maurice much the richer, had also made so many others much the poorer. The woman who encouraged the selfish society. The woman who smashed the mining communities. The woman whose politics were responsible for a society where 'love thy neighbour' went out of the window ... and straight into the cardboard box that was now the home for so many of Thatcher's children.

And now she had gone.

We had known nights of celebration. God knows we had! We had won an Emmy. We had won a British Academy Award. We would win the ultimate Academy Award, the Writers' Award, two years later. We had seen Arsenal win two championships in three years. We would soon see Arsenal win the European Cup Winners' Cup. Maurice had seen the birth of his two children, and Laurence had seen the back of his mother. We had made 15 million people laugh in a single half hour, but none of these events, not a singular one of them, could come close to the elation of knowing that 'The Iron Lady' wasn't made of iron at all, rather a soft waxy substance. She was fallible. She had fallen.

That evening we opened a bottle of 1979 Krug. 1979! Was that ironic or what? The very year that Thatcher became our Prime Minister. We were saving that bottle for some occasion of monumental celebration and we could hardly have envisaged a greater one than this.

The only fly in the ointment was we had written two episodes of our new series of *The New Statesman*, and now all our Thatcher references and jokes and plots would have to be changed, but that was an infinitesimal price to pay for having arrived home from Hollywood to find 'She' had gone. For ever? We did hope so.

Laurence (above) and Maurice

LILIAN HOCHHAUSER

◆

Since the day Stalin died in 1953, and doors opened to the Soviet Union, Victor and I have been closely associated with almost all of the legendary Russian artists.

The great composer Dmitri Shostakovich, our guest here on many occasions, the two musicians of genius for whom he wrote some of his finest works, David Oistrakh and Mstislav Rostropovich, Evgeni Mravinsky and the Leningrad Philharmonic Orchestra, Emil Gilels, Gennady Rozhdestvensky – the list is endless. From the world of ballet, Galina Ulanova, Rudolf Nureyev, Vasiliev, Baryshnikov, Pilsetskaya and all the great dancers of the Kirov and Bolshoi Ballets have appeared under our banner, becoming our friends during the devastating years of the Soviet regime.

But the most complex was undoubtedly Sviatoslav Richter, one of the greatest pianists of all time with whom we worked from 1961 until he died in 1997. Unable to travel to the West until 1960, he was at once hailed as a phenomenal pianist.

He was much more; an intellectual, a painter of distinction, passionate about literature and creatively involved in the theatre with ideas about all forms of art that were so original and breathtaking that he was a constant inspiration.

He never spoke on the telephone and only flew if absolutely necessary. For instance, he did not find it necessary to fly to Japan but would set off by car from Moscow and spend several weeks *en route* playing in towns and villages across Russia, Georgia, Armenia and Uzbekistan until reaching Vladivostok, and then crossing by sea to Japan. Everywhere the crowds filled the halls whether he played in the morning or at midnight.

All my plans with him had to be made in person and I followed him around the world simply to hear the last word on a particular programme. In Italy, when he played at the festival in Stresa, he would stay on the tiny Isola da Pescatori in the middle of Lake Maggiore. We would settle everything sailing to and from the mainland, his sense of humour inevitably provoking great hilarity.

Continuously plagued by ill health, he was forced to cancel on many occasions, sometimes only a few hours before a concert. His public, though, never tired of him and came back time after time to hear playing of a virtuosity that was inspired, deeply felt and mysterious – the sound and memory of which would remain with them for ever.

MARGARET THATCHER

◆

When we first met, it was clear to me at once that Denis was an exceptional man. He knew at least as much about politics as I did and a good deal more about economics. His professional interest in paint and mine in plastics may seem an unromantic foundation for friendship, but it also enabled us right away to establish a joint interest in science. I soon discovered that his views were no-nonsense Conservatism.

From then on, we met from time to time at constituency functions, and began to see more of each other outside the constituency. Denis had a certain dash and style. He had a penchant for fast cars and drove a Jaguar and, being ten years older, he simply knew more of the world than I did. At first our meetings revolved around political discussion. But as we saw more of each other, we started going to the occasional play and had dinner together.

When Denis asked me to be his wife, I thought long and hard about it. I had so much set my heart on politics that I really hadn't figured marriage in my plans. I suppose I pushed it to the back of my mind and simply assumed that it would occur of its own accord at some time in the future. I know that Denis, too, because a war-time marriage had ended in divorce, only asked me to be his wife after much reflection. But the more I considered, the surer I was. There was only one possible answer. More than forty years later I know that my decision to say 'yes' was one of the best I ever made.

MARK BIRLEY

◆

I had a great stroke of luck just before opening Annabel's in June 1963. Louis, who was then the manager of the most fashionable restaurant in London, the Mirabelle, called me to ask if I was looking for someone to take charge of the place. This amazed me as the club had not yet opened and few people were giving it much of a chance anyway. Louis thus joined me and set about assembling the staff. The first few weeks of Annabel's were pretty chaotic but the reassuring presence of Louis brought about some semblance of professionalism, something which I sadly lacked. In all our thirty or so years together, I don't think we ever had a row. Disagreements, yes, but his benign presence made the difference between success and failure.

The first evening I tried to do as I was told. 'Good evening,' I said cheerfully to the couple in the middle of their dinner. 'I hope everything is all right and that you are being taken care of?' After finishing the remains of his asparagus, the man pointed to his plate – 'Cold and disgusting,' he said while his wife nodded in agreement. The

next table was even worse. 'Whoever is doing the cooking here should be shot. Just look at this Steak Diane.' 'Oh dear. I'll get this changed immediately.' After another earful at the third table I gave up. 'For heaven's sake get me the bill – we're leaving.'

Under pressure Louis would rise to great heights. In fact, he positively enjoyed over-bookings and irate customers demanding tables that didn't exist. Those were the early days and no matter what disaster struck, I always felt that Louis and I would win through. Our two marvellous barmen, George Hobart and Sidney Seymour, were extraordinary anchormen, who always had time for a joke or for a discussion about that day's racing at Sandown.

In retrospect it was all great fun. Serious but light hearted at the same time. That is all about thirty-five years ago. Louis and Freddie, his assistant, have retired and George and Sidney are sadly no longer with us, but their legacy is a tradition of service and hospitality which continues to this day.

MARTIN GILBERT

◆

My strangest memory is of my first visit to the man who was to become my first boss – Randolph Churchill. I had been summoned by telegram to visit him at his home in Suffolk ('I am nearly always here,' the telegram informed me). It was the eve of my twenty-fifth birthday. Friends warned me that Randolph would be impossible, even for an evening. When I finally screwed up the courage to go, I was dreading the encounter.

To my surprise, I was met in the late afternoon at Randolph's local station (Maningtree) by a smartly dressed man whom I took to be his driver. In fact, he was the head of Randolph's research team on the biography of Sir Winston Churchill. I remember being so in awe of the whole set-up that I assumed throughout the entire evening that he was a super valet/ chauffeur. As to Randolph, he could not have been more mellifluous, though he was surprised to discover that I had never before eaten either of the first two dishes that were produced for dinner: hare pâté and gulls' eggs. I remember how, towards midnight, I was left alone with him by the other researchers (a technique of disappearance I was soon to perfect myself) and

then faced a barrage of questions about where I stood in the appeasement debate. He asked whether I was against 'the Coroner' (Neville Chamberlain)? Did I have a high opinion of Duff Cooper, who had resigned from the Cabinet after Munich. 'How I loved that man,' Randolph declared.

At some point, long after I was used to being in bed, I said something about French government policy at the time of Munich. This led him to criticise me harshly, after which he declaimed, in stentorian tones (as if to a crowded debating chamber): 'The only thing that interests me is the truth.' The word 'truth' was shouted out so loudly I thought it would wake the whole village. He then offered me a nightcap (a 1911 brandy, if my memory still serves) and told me to 'get a little shut-eye before morning'.

When morning came – the morning of my twenty-fifth birthday – I found him in a dressing gown, wandering about downstairs. He asked me to come out into his garden with him (it was a nippy October day). He then, to my amazement, offered me a job as one of his team.

Five years (and two sackings later), I was still on his payroll.

MAURICE SAATCHI

A TRIBUTE TO IRIS MURDOCH

◆

Iris Murdoch is a uniquely beautiful woman. Conventional wisdom characterises beauty as the exclusive domain of the artist. But in Iris's case her beauty spans both art and science.

If you wanted to pick one area of 'art' in which you could say the term 'science' might apply, it would surely be to Iris's writing, whether in her novels or her works of philosophy – a developed carefulness and attention to detail; a habit of being clear; a sceptical perusal of alleged facts; and a tireless curiosity about the possible meanings, their bearings on other facts or notions; the requirement for orderliness; the ethic of scholarship.

I once asked Iris to explain her understanding of the meaning of the word 'truth'. Her answer was to describe that moment of revelation you experience in an art gallery when you stand in front of a particularly beautiful masterpiece and understand its meaning for the first time.

All Iris's writing achieves such truths, through a method for which there is no more appropriate word than 'scientific' – observation, deduction, experimentation, rejection. Iris has always searched and searched to provide her readers with 'the only possible words in the only possible order'. Because Iris knows that beauty in writing is the outcome of technical subtlety – the goal not the starting point.

All those capable of judging say that the theory of quantum electrodynamics is 'beautiful' – a favourite term, I am told, of theoreticians' praise. And I am told that nearly all physicists believe as a matter of intuition or faith that there must in the very long run be elegance and harmony in nature.

Iris Murdoch has devoted her life to the rigorous and disciplined pursuit of elegance and harmony in writing. Scientists say that each person's Iris is unique and unchanging through their lives. That is certainly true of my Iris. Iris Murdoch's elegance and harmony has always been plain to see.

MICHAEL LEVY

◆

One of my most powerful memories in recent years was when I first visited the Sam Beckman Special Day Centre in northwest London. This is an amazing day care resource for people with Alzheimer's disease run by Jewish Care, the organisation of which I am currently President.

Among the first people I met was Charles, who I had known many years ago. He was a university Professor of Mathematics and a leading member of his synagogue. He was a few years older than me and I assumed he was a volunteer at the centre. I asked him about his wife and son and about some of our mutual friends. He didn't appear to know me or be able to respond to my questions. Instead he took me by the hand and insisted I meet his mother, who I knew had been dead for many years.

It took me a while to come to terms with the fact that Charles had Alzheimer's disease and his brilliant mind could no longer recognise his family let alone his friends. Yet I felt that the

Beckman Centre was a place of hope. It looked at positives and built upon what the members *could* do rather than what they had left behind.

The reminiscence therapy sparked old memories and it was very moving to hear from those who could accurately describe their past, often from the East End of London, evoking laughter and tears as special events were remembered. The arts and crafts room was full of people discovering new skills; their paintings were bright, bold splashes of colour evoking the Jewish festival which still meant so much to them.

Alzheimer's is a terrible, debilitating disease. It is stressful for family and friends to see a loved one change into a person unrecognisable from their former self.

I was and continue to be deeply moved by the work that Jewish Care does for the sufferers and their families – providing special Centres that give their members dignity, care and love.

MICHAEL PORTILLO

◆

When my father died, it was as though a curtain had been thrown back and I could see him once more. During the last seven years of his life he suffered from Alzheimer's disease and I watched him by degrees forget everything – including, most painfully, how to speak.

My father had written poetry, not professionally but continually. At any idle moment you could see him tapping out rhythms with his fingers on his skull. Many people commented that they had never met a man with such an extensive vocabulary. His poems were full of words that most others had never met. My father loved words and lived by them. You could not imagine anything crueller than that he should forget them all. I was reminded of that line from *Hamlet*: 'What a noble mind is here o'erthrown.'

But when he died memory played a second trick. I discovered that, for the years he had Alzheimer's, it was as though a veil had descended in my mind, preventing me from seeing through his illness to what he had been before. And when he died, suddenly I found him again, my father talking. How he could talk! He told me stories of his life, the Spanish Civil War, from dramatic verbal confrontations of the pre-war period, to his own suffering from illness at the front. Not that he bore arms himself. His

brothers were on the other side and he lived in fear of killing them in war. But there he was at the front, running messages and getting ill.

He told me of plots of plays and operas and films and, of course, the stories of El Cid and Don Quixote. His eyes would fill with tears as he told me the tales, not necessarily from sadness, but from the sheer passion of the drama. We became opera and theatre-going companions, most often in the eight-shilling seats at the Old Vic. He loved music, and even when his mind began to go, he would respond to a familiar aria.

And to photographs. Of animals, for instance. He had a talent for taking a piece of paper and freehand, with a pair of scissors, cutting out a cow or a pig or a sheep. Imagine how we loved that as children. They even stood up. And then he loved pictures of Spain, of his adoptive city of Salamanca, where before the Civil War and his exile he had taught. The saddest thing I ever heard was from a friend who met my father one night, when he already knew his mind was going, walking along the streets of the city in tears. 'What's wrong?' she asked him. 'I am saying goodbye to Salamanca,' he told her.

Now we have said goodbye to him. But in our memories he lives still. His mind is whole and he can speak.

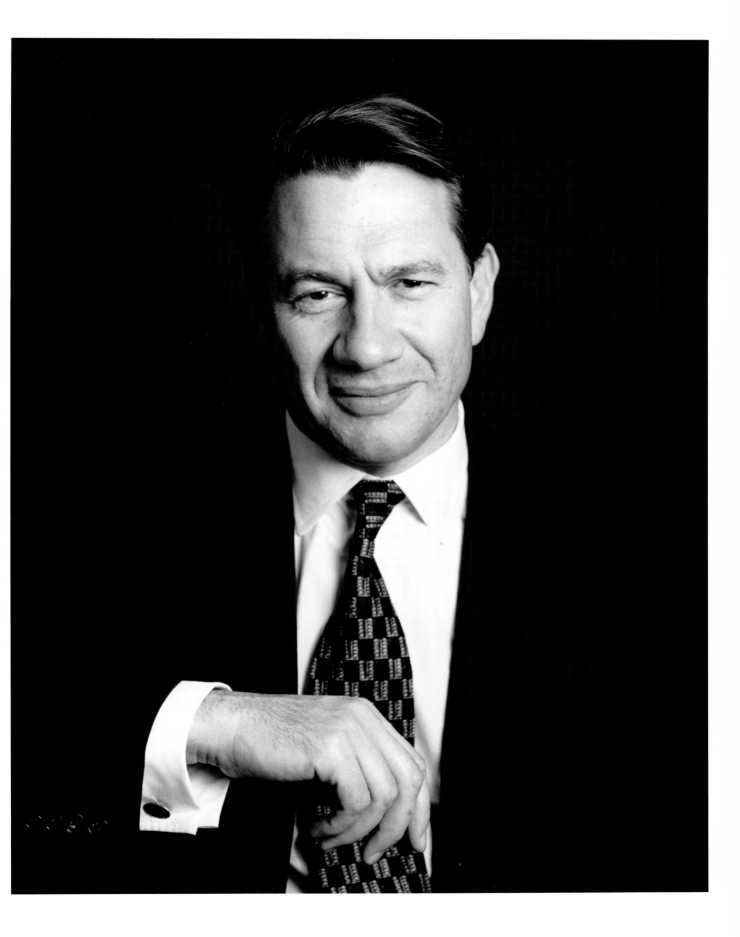

MIRIAM STOPPARD

◆

I was quite unprepared for mother love in all its manifestations but none so much as that engendered at the Junior Colts Mini-rugby 3rd team at Caldicott School eighteen years ago.

As a new pupil my son had been murmuring vaguely all week about clean football boots and games strip for the coming Saturday afternoon and, realising this meant something extra-curricular, surmised he must be involved in an inter-schools fixture, though he demurred when I suggested he might be representing the school.

I duly turned up at the playing fields to find a mêlée of neatly kitted-out little boys engaged in very serious warm-up exercises. At the shrill 'pip' of the headmaster's whistle, the Brownian movement resolved itself into half a dozen teams on the pitches, one of which held my son.

It is my introduction to schoolboy rugby and it is love at first sight. Only a few moments into the game and I hold my breath as my son is tackled and brought to the ground with a fierce thump. He struggles up, all his team-mates' eyes on him, mine too. He is clearly hurt. The ref runs over to him and from the distance I'm watching I can only make out the mime.

'Are you hurt, Stoppard?'
Nod of assent.
'Where does it hurt?'
Points to left thigh. From my spot on the touchline, I can sense the tears welling up.
'Do you want to go off?'
Hesitation, shake of head.
'Will you play on?'
Hesitation, nod of head.
Sound of distant clapping from the rest of the appreciative house team.
Play is resumed.

My brave eight-year-old! At that sentimental moment, it seemed to me the little enactment on the rugby pitch presaged a microcosm of his adult life. He'd find no grown-up decision or action any harder.

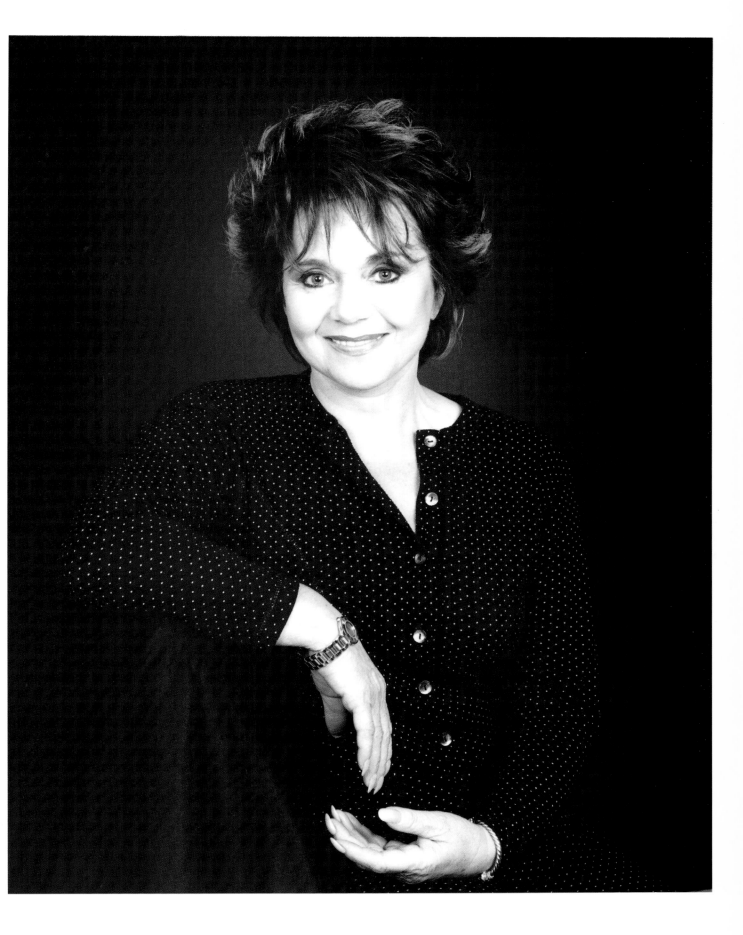

NED SHERRIN

◆

Very little that is worth being dignified as anecdotal has happened to me. I am more a picker up of unconsidered trifles that star others. I did hear, at second hand, of Denis Quilley's problem when Dr Jonathan Miller cast him, against type, as the witty, bitchy gossip, Sir Benjamin Backbite, in the Good Doctor's production of Sheridan's *A School for Scandal* at the National Theatre. Denis, a fine, honest, upstanding actor and man, could find no clue to the character until finally, in desperation, he sought advice from his director. 'Have you ever met Ned Sherrin?' Jonathan offered. Denis understood instantly. I have always found Miller limited as a *metteur en scène* and irresistible as a performer; but here he does seem to have given a perfect, helpful note.

If I carry no anecdotal baggage, I have an even clearer sheet when it comes to experiences of the supernatural. Or nearly. Nothing goes bump in my night (an increasing occasion for regret). Chills do not run up and down my spine. The hair does not stand up on the back of my neck.

Ghostly visitations have always given me a miss except, perhaps, in this story: but, even here, maybe I am being fanciful in claiming the experience as supernatural. In New York for a couple of days I was staying on the Upper West Side in the apartment of my friend Glen Roven, a dazzling composer-lyricist in the line of Cole Porter and Stephen Sondheim. I christen the spare rooms of my friends when I stay in them often enough 'The Grace Poole Suite', after the madwoman shut away in a wing in *Jane Eyre*, and

I present them with a plaque saying 'Grace Poole Suite'. I was lodged in this Grace Poole Suite – but I lunched, on the second day, at the extraordinary borscht-coloured Russian Tea Rooms. No visit to New York was enjoyed without such a visit. Now they are being revamped. I suspend judgement.

One of the most regular lunchers there – virtually a fixture – was a whimsical old theatre producer, Harry Rigby. Harry was a man who revived *No, No Nanette*, *Irene*, *Good News* and also *Sugar Babies*. At about 12.30pm, I watched Harry pass down the other side of the restaurant. I made a mental note to say hello before I left the room.

Lunch over, I looked around. I could not find Harry, so thinking no more of it, I went back up town to be met by a very glum Glen. He was a great friend and indeed a protégé of Harry's who had engaged him at a very young age to be the musical director of *Sugar Babies*, which meant handling the demanding stars – Anne Miller and Mickey Rooney – and a lot of dancers and aged comics.

'Harry died,' he greeted me. 'He had a lunch date at the Russian Tea Rooms. When he didn't show they called his apartment. And when they got no reply the janitor went in and found him. He died about 12.30pm.' Did I see Harry passing through his favourite watering hole *en route* to a more celebrated destination? Or was it some other distinguished-looking Broadway luncher?

I like to think I saw Harry.

NICOLA HORLICK

◆

Even the most organised events can go wrong when you least expect them to. In the City, lunch time is an opportunity to entertain clients, prospective clients and other business associates. Most firms have smart dining rooms and the smell of furniture wax, flowers and exotic culinary dishes mingle together as you approach. The food is served by well-groomed staff with a butler, probably trained at a royal palace, in charge. Getting the right chef is very important as it is essential that guests go away hoping that they will be invited again and soon.

In 1992, I was appointed Managing Director of Morgan Grenfell Investment Management, the firm's UK pension fund business. During my first six months in the job, I made it my mission to meet all of the 102 pension fund clients. One of our clients was a family-owned building company and the widow of the founder was a trustee of the pension fund. She was eighty years old, but was still interested in the company's affairs and joined me at our offices one day with the other trustees for lunch. I welcomed all our guests to the principal dining room.

When they had all arrived, we exchanged pleasantries over drinks and our marvellous butler, Kevin, attended to their every need. When I thought we were ready to sit down, I gave Kevin the nod and he went to tell the chef that we were ready. As I assigned our guests to their seats, there was a scratching noise above my head. Something fell from above into my glass which, thankfully, was empty. It took me a moment to realise what it was. It was not a piece of plaster nor a light fitting ... it was a mouse.

I have never been afraid of snakes, spiders, or lizards, but I must admit that the sight of an unwanted rodent fills me with horror. I managed not to scream, but was frozen with fright, as was my aged female guest. I was praying that she did not suffer from a heart condition.

As we all stood in suspended animation, Kevin came back into the room, saw the mouse in the glass, calmly placed a side plate over it and exited from the room. There was a huge sigh of relief and much hilarity although I did notice the odd glance upwards from my guests as we ate our lunch. No doubt they were wondering whether there was a nest of mice in the ceiling.

A couple of months later, Martin Taylor, Chief Executive of Barclays Bank, joined me for lunch in the same dining room. I happily recounted the 'mouse' story to him. He wrote to me afterwards saying how delicious the lunch had been and how pleased he was that he had not had to face chicken à la souris!

NIGEL HAWTHORNE

◆

Actors are always being asked, 'How on earth do you remember all those lines?' The simple answer is that you sit down and learn them. Once they are 'in', the great problem is keeping them there so that they come out at the right time and preferably in the right order.

I first met the late and great Gwen Ffrangcon-Davies when she was in her mid-nineties and we became friends. Producer David Spenser suggested I do a radio programme encouraging her to perform her favourite Shakespearean speeches. There was no hope of her reading her lines as her sight was appalling.

At the recording she sailed through word perfect. David then asked whether perhaps she remembered any of Queen Katharine from *Henry VIII*. 'Oh, darling, that was ages ago,' she chortled. 'I took over from Edith Evans in 1951. I only played her for six weeks. Yes, I can remember.' And she did. She'd kept the words in her head all those years and out they came – in the right order.

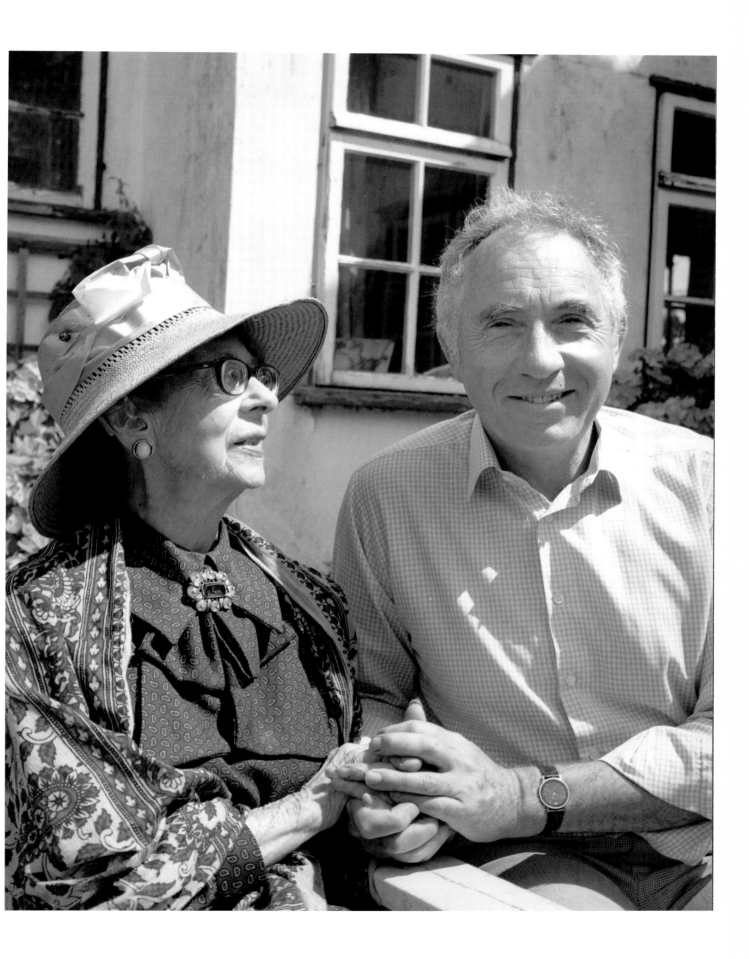

Norman Foster

◆

Memories are the only link with those loved ones who are no longer alive – for me, such memories are the most precious, personal and private. I think a great deal about my mother and father, who both died a long time ago. A few years back, in a quest to find out more about my mother, I contacted a cousin – the only person it seemed who might be able to help.

We met for lunch and reminisced over the way in which our lives had crossed as children in Manchester; his recollections of my mother confirmed and sharpened some of my hazier thoughts from the past. Inevitably, the conversation led to his own parents. I was surprised and delighted to hear that his father was still alive and living in a nursing home in Australia. Although my mother had been adopted, his father had been very close to her for many years as her favourite brother. Now I had the opportunity to ask so many of the questions that I wished I had raised when she was still alive.

It was late November and by the end of the lunch I had agreed to go to Melbourne with my cousin early in the New Year which was his next planned visit. But in the days that followed I became uneasy – intuitively I felt a sense of urgency, a feeling that my visit could not wait until the following month. So I flew to Australia, stopping only long enough for a brief lunch in Hong Kong. It was one of the few days that I could not get a direct flight to Melbourne so I stayed overnight in Sydney.

The next morning I called the nursing home to ask about my uncle and to agree when I might see him. The lady in charge, the matron, said that two days earlier she had gone with him to a tea shop and he talked all the time about my visit.

But she went on to say that there was now a problem, possibly the result of a severe heat wave in the area. Apparently my uncle was affected by it and I was not to be disappointed if, when I arrived that evening, he was unable to communicate very well.

That afternoon I flew to Melbourne, pausing at the hotel to drop off my bag and carrying on to the nursing home, which was nearly an hour's drive from the city. By the time I arrived everyone had gone to bed except my uncle. When we met, the gap of forty years evaporated – he was so recognisably the same person that I remembered from my early teens. But sadly it was virtually a one-way communication – an occasional nod or flicker of his eyes were the only signals that he was aware of my presence and of my words which took us to a past of long ago and far away.

The matron came back and suggested that it was time for my uncle to retire to bed. On the way out she was full of reassurances, saying that it was normal at his age to be physically down one day and back to normal the next. She was sure that by tomorrow morning, after breakfast, we would be able to talk together.

The next day I ordered a cab and I was just leaving the hotel room when the phone rang. It was the matron and I knew immediately from her voice that something was wrong. It seemed that after my visit my uncle was quite cheerful with the staff and even managed to convey how happy he had been to see me – they left him that night in high spirits.

But the news was that he never woke up again; when they checked his room at 2.30am he was no longer alive. In a state of shock, I departed the same day on a flight back to London.

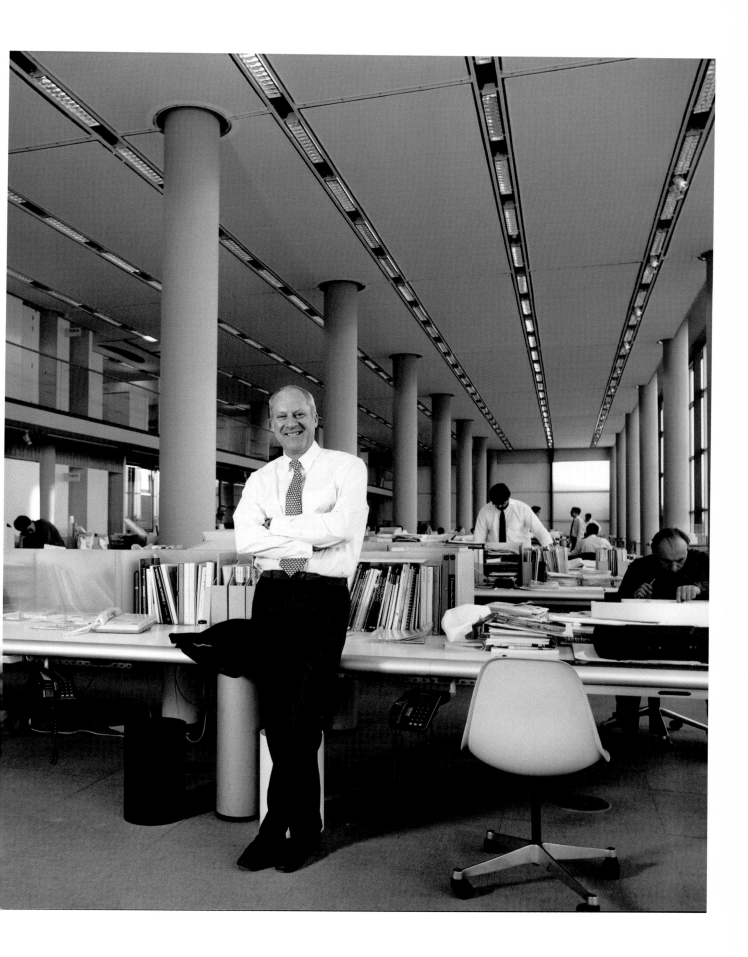

P D JAMES

◆

My personal memory is a mixture of great happiness and high anxiety: the birth of my second daughter in Queen Charlotte's Hospital on 14 July 1944 at the height of the bombardment of London by Hitler's doodlebugs. These were the pilotless planes which flew low with a deafening and terrifying rattle and a flaming tail. The moment when the engine stopped was followed by a silence which seemed both unnaturally quiet and prolonged while we waited for the explosion. And then came relief which was quickly tempered by the realisation that we had been lucky this time, but that someone close had not.

It is difficult to understand now why I stayed in London in the last weeks of pregnancy, but it seemed perfectly reasonable at the time, perhaps because we had become inured to enemy action. For a few weeks before I went into labour I lived with friends in Hampstead, Dr and Mrs Lindsay Batten and their family. They took the view that children didn't become frightened if their parents showed no fear, and both Dr and Mrs Batten had a healthy disregard for bombs of any type and stayed comfortably in their beds throughout the war. But they did feel that a pregnant visitor should receive protection, so I slept in the cellar with their two youngest children for company.

The nights were hardly restful as the anti-aircraft guns kept up an almost continual barrage. My consolation was reading Jane Austen by torch-light. There can be no greater solace in times of danger than her calm, measured, ironic voice. After my daughter was born, I named her Jane – not fashionable then, as

the Registrar for some reason reminded me.

Life was equally exciting in hospital after the birth. We had our babies beside us in cots and would place a pillow over the baby's head to provide some small protection against falling debris or flying glass. I can remember the matron, a formidable lady, visiting the ward when enemy activity was at its height. She was a cheerful reassuring figure, particularly when she appeared at night wearing a Jaeger dressing gown and with her pigtail flying. Freshly laundered bed linen was very short at the time and our ward sister would rifle the linen cupboard to ensure her ward had a supply, hiding the clean sheets under our pillows or in our lockers. Sisters from neighbouring wards, aware of the stratagem, would make periodic raids, triumphantly bearing off their spoils. We the patients co-operated in these skirmishes and became ingenious in concealing freshly laundered sheets. Clean linen was important to comfort. In those days, the usual stay after childbirth was about two weeks.

At night the babies were taken underground and our beds wheeled against the corridor wall for greater protection. I can remember praying. 'Oh God, if you let me come out of hospital alive with my baby I will never complain again,' a prayer which has haunted me at all whingeing moments ever since. But it was, in fact, answered, and I can remember with what relief I boarded the train with Jane to join her sister Clare and my parents-in-law in South Wales, where my father-in-law, a major in the RAMC, was stationed. I remember Queen Charlotte's Hospital with gratitude and, in retrospect, my memories of July 1944 are of happiness rather than terror.

PADDY ASHDOWN

◆

This is a brief extract from the diary I wrote when I visited Bosnia in 1992. The day was Tuesday, 11 August.

I was unprepared for what I met. An indescribable sight of squalor. Perhaps 3,000 people, mostly Muslims. Absolutely no facilities. They had taken over an old school and had camped out on the playground. The Red Cross were visiting them when we arrived and were getting them to fill in Red Cross identification forms in return for packets of cigarettes. I was taken into the medical area and met the doctors who were simply overwhelmed.

Outside were a few wounded lying on filthy fly-blown mattresses. In the playing field was camped a miserable heap of humanity. People who had come with almost nothing and, in some cases, literally nothing. Some were lying out in the sun, others under makeshift awnings, suitable for shade but hopeless when it rained. I stopped and talked to some of them, getting increasingly depressed.

In the sleeping areas were men, women, children and some young babies. I spoke to one man who was an economist but now made equal with all the others in his misery. A nice man. Again, I could hardly speak for emotion. Some cooking was going on, largely a sort of dreadful stew with noodles which came, I am told, chiefly from money for the Red Cross. Why had the UN not set up protected havens for these wretched people? They had nowhere to go, being turned back from Croatia and terrorised by the Serbs. In fact, such was the pitiable nature of their condition that some Serbs had actually protected the area themselves from the deprivations of the Serb extremists who came in at night, robbing, beating and raping the women.

PATRICK LICHFIELD

◆

On our seventh Unipart shoot, we pushed into the centre of Bali and discovered some astonishing landscapes. View after magnificent view unfolded one after the other as our minibus drove on through the mountains, transfixing me but leaving the model beside me completely cold; she spent the entire journey with her nose in a paperback romance.

We came back with some beautiful shots, using the distant semi-naked figures as elements in a series of almost orientally balanced compositions, a deeply sensitive approach that was none too subtly sabotaged on the calendar itself by the inclusion of additional steamy close-ups inserted at the foot of each page. (I simply cut off the lower six inches from every month; I lost the dates as well, of course, but who looks at a calendar for the date?)

Our eighth and final shoot scaled new heights of ambition for no better reason than that we finally discovered the one place where we could be guaranteed to be almost alone: Death Valley at the peak of summer. Accompanied by Jilly Super-Trooper Cooper (whose presence alone made the trip a total delight), we drove over a hundred miles each day, worked from four in the morning until ten at night, sweated off pounds and produced the best calendar, indeed

the best pictures, that I think I have ever taken. The nudes were seen in their proper perspective, tiny flesh-coloured daubs dwarfed by the immense spaces around them, figures in a landscape at last.

One shot demanded a minuscule model poised perilously on the knife-edged summit of an immense sand dune twice as high as a house. As she stood there in the far distance, glowing in the viewfinder like a garnet on a field of gold, I saw her stretch out her arm, open her hand and let drop a single sheet of brilliant pink Kleenex. There is no way to remove a piece of unwanted tissue from the middle of a vast expanse of pristine desert without leaving tracks. So we all stood there, watching the little pink relic blow first this way, then that way, up the dune and down the dune and up the dune again until finally, as the light faded, it scuttled out of shot.

The model, who had to remain teetering in the sun whilst we waited, suffered more than most for her foolishness and, understandably, was still a little bit shaky at breakfast next morning. Preparing to sketch a perfunctory apology, I rather brusquely asked her what was wrong. 'The trouble with you,' she cried, 'is you don't have to work with people like you.' I wished, in a way, she was right.

PAUL BURRELL

A MEMORY OF BOSNIA

◆

While in Bosnia in July 1997, a typical day for the Princess of Wales and myself began armed with only a bottle of water, a cheese sandwich and a piece of fruit. Long journeys lay ahead. We travelled in four-wheel-drive vehicles along hot and dusty, primitive tracks, through simple and sometimes derelict villages, to seek out those people most touched by the war in Bosnia, those innocents affected by hidden tragedy – unmarked fields filled with landmines.

We travelled in a group of five. Three men sat in the back: Ken Rutherford, Jerry White and myself. The driver and the Princess sat up front. The first thing the Princess would do was lean into the back and say, 'Take your legs off boys.' Ken and Jerry were both survivors of the hidden evil. We had three legs between the three of us, and as I had two of them I constantly felt greedy. Legs dismantled, the journey was more comfortable. No one was offended – it seemed the natural thing to do.

During the trip we visited landmine survivors in their war-torn homes. They showed overwhelming hospitality. They gave everything despite having nothing. 'We never thought we would ever meet a princess,' they said. She certainly brought a new light into their lives.

On one occasion, barely weeks before that fatal crash, we visited makeshift homes on a hillside overlooking Sarajevo. There we met a fifteen-year-old girl who had been injured by a landmine. She lived with her family including several sisters and brothers. Unbeknown to us at this stage, her youngest sister was severely handicapped.

While the press was busily interviewing this bewildered girl, the Princess and I wandered into a dark, curtained back room where we were met by the sight of the girl's emaciated four-year-old sister. Instinctively, the Princess picked her up from her soiled bed where she had clearly been lying for days. She cuddled her wasted arms and legs and spoke softly to her, making eye contact. The little girl responded to what was obviously a rare moment of attention. I could see that she was trying to focus her eyes, although she was almost blind.

For me that was a very moving and spiritual moment. I could not contain my emotion. I realised that I was witnessing the innocence and purity of unconditional love. There were no photographers or journalists in the room to record the moment – but it is a memory that will remain with me for ever.

PETER PARKER

◆

These days, when I hear talk of the privatisation of the railways, I have a flashback to long ago, the day before I became Chairman of British Railways in September 1976. Alone on a very early Oxford train, the carriage empty, I was enjoying the quiet moment, the end of summer landscape, solemn, darkening green. My mind as blank as possible, I was trying to stay loose, like a boxer stepping into the ring.

Then a grizzled guard came in to check my ticket. I held out my gold pass – this was the medallion's first outing – and I kept looking out of the window to avoid conversation; after all, this was going to be my last easy ride for a long, long time. But I felt the pass taken from my palm. I turned to see the guard scrutinising it thoroughly, even the temporary plastic label (made in Hong Kong) tagged to it with my surname typed on.

'So you're Parker.' 'That's right.' He moved a step towards me, his hand outstretched to shake mine, saying, 'And the best of luck.'

As we shook hands, glancing at each other, something happened which I later found happened quite often when I was 'on the rails'. Eyes would meet over a handshake and something seemed to click wordlessly – a railway connection. And the stranger's left hand would come over to reinforce the handshake. Then inevitably the stranger would go on to say, as the guard did … 'And I'll tell you what's wrong. The problem with British Rail is …'.

I asked the guard for mercy. I had a few days still before the awful truths were sure to dawn or, more likely, blaze around my head. 'My real problem at this moment is to see that I don't lose this gold medallion.'

We discussed a number of merry suggestions before agreeing that the safest thing was to hang it around my private parts. Chuckling, the guard slid the door shut; then, face straight, he slid the door open again.

'Of course, in your job, you could lose those too.' Privatisation in its earliest, crudest form …

PRUE LEITH

◆

My worst experience as a cookery writer was when I wrote a recipe for Oxford Marmalade, the dark one with a couple of tablespoons in it. In those days I wrote by hand and I failed to cross the 't' in 'tablespoons', so you got 2 lbs instead of 2 tbs black treacle.

You would not believe how many people believe the written word. The *Daily Mail* switchboard went red hot with people complaining about the coal black, rock-hard caramel they had made. We had to give them all 80p, the cost of the ingredients. Then one woman rang up and said, 'Look, I know I've made a complete boo-boo here, but how many oranges and how much sugar do I have to add to get the proportions right again?' I thought great; we'll save a lot of money from now on, and just encourage people to make a few years' marmalade at once. We worked out that she'd end up with 160 lbs of marmalade. So we gave her 80p.

Next day I found a letter bomb on my desk. I thought, I know it's a bit rough screwing up the marmalade recipe but I don't deserve this. I knew it was a bomb because it was during the first IRA letter bomb campaign and we'd been given bomb training. I could feel a squashy bit in the middle of the envelope and wires protruding from each end. So I called the post room, who called the bomb squad, who sent a nice copper in a flak jacket who disappeared with my letter and returned five minutes later with the letter opened. Inside was a lump of marmalade toffee embedded into which was a wire dental brace with two teeth attached. Also enclosed was a large orthodontist's bill!

QUENTIN CREWE

◆

The unjust thing about memories is the whimsical nature of the selections the mind makes. While I struggle to remember names and faces, my mind is cluttered up with quite useless and absurd things. Many of them come from childhood. I can recite the six tributaries of the Yorkshire Ouse – Swale, Ure, Nid, Wharf, Aire and Calder. Miss Davies, the geography mistress of my prep school, fixed the mnemonic SUNWAC in my memory.

Similarly I remember the order of the planets by the phrase 'Many Very Early Men Journey Swiftly Up North'. This ignores Pluto, but a young friend tells me his phrase contains them all – 'My Very Easy Method, Just Set Up Nine Planets'.

An even earlier memory is of an Italian tongue-twister: Apelle, figlio d'Apollo faceva una palla di pelle di pollo. Tutti i pesce vengono a gala per vedere la palla di pelle di pollo fato d'Apelle, figlio d'Apollo. What use is that to me? But I can never get rid of it, anymore than I can throw out being able to recite π to thirty-six places of decimals.

It aggravates me as well that I have stored away such an abundance of information that I will never need – the routes round the different places that I have lived over the years. What I am asking for is a kind of 'mind Hoover' similar to the devices that can clear up a lot of junk on one's computer. Equally, there should be another device that could fix something ineradically so that one could always retrieve it.

A further improvement might be the ability to leave one's children knowledge that would save their having to learn, say, their way around London, or the capitals of the world etc.

If we believe Darwin, I would have thought that such elementary evolutionary improvements should have happened automatically.

RICHARD BRANSON

◆

My attempt in January 1997 to circumnavigate the globe in a balloon, *Virgin Challenger*, with Per Lindstrand and Alex Ritchie (who joined us at extremely short notice and has since tragically died in a parachuting accident) is firmly lodged in my memory. Here is an extract from the diary I wrote before, during and after our flight.

7 January: Launch

08.45 My first glimpse of the balloon. An awesome sight, towering above the city.

10.15 It is hard to say goodbye to Dad whose eyes are filled with tears. He is seventy-nine. Mother, as usual, is strong as an ox but presses into my hand a letter to open six days into the flight. She is being sentimental at last. Holly is as ever smiling and happy. Sam is enthralled. At last they are old enough to understand and enjoy my adventures. Then Sam breaks down. It is one of the hardest moments.

11.19 Per begins the countdown. 'Ten, nine, eight' – I barely hear him say 'one' as the explosive bolts are released. The whole thing shakes and twists. It feels like it is going incredibly fast. This is the most dangerous time.

11.23 1,000 ft, 2,000 ft. I look out of the hatch door which is still open. The snow-capped Atlas Mountains are rising up to greet us. At 10,000 ft we shut the hatch. We are on our own.

12.35 Per sinks into a fit of depression. He passes me a message from the ground. It's the first mistake. We cannot release the six one-tonne propane gas tanks. If the balloon does not work at nightfall we will plummet with no way of dropping the fuel tanks.

15.30 The second shock. We are heading for restricted air space near Béchar in Algeria.

16.40 Fantastic news. A new fax. We can transit Béchar air space. The Algerians wish us luck.

19.10 We begin dumping ballast. We are working fast. But we are falling faster, not slower.

19.12 We are falling at 2,000 ft a minute. At this rate we will hit the ground in minutes.

19.15 At 12,000 ft we depressurise and manage to open the glass-topped hatch. Something is terribly wrong. Our supplies are gone. The dream is over. I just want to get us out of this.

19.20 I push Alex up on to the roof at 8,500 ft to release the couplings on the gas cylinders. He turns the locking device off, on, and off again. He turns to the next one. He knows what he is doing. Per shouts, 'Get back inside. We've got 90 seconds.' We throw ourselves in our seats. We are hurtling down. There are only seconds left. One tank drops away. We soar into the air. What a wonderful feeling. I put my hand on Alex's shoulder. 'Thank God you're with us Alex.'

January 8

01.15 Send a message to base: 'Had a serious problem. Will have to abort flight.'

06.30 We have cleared the mountains into Algeria as the sun rises. The scenery is breathtaking. We are dropping at 300 ft a minute. I don't want it to end.

07.19 We come in with a bump at 250 ft a minute. It was a solid bone-shaking landing. The second we hit the ground, Per releases the bolts and the balloon wafts into the air. Alex is screaming with joy. We throw our arms around each other. We feel like we have landed on the moon. We dance arm in arm around the capsule.

RONNIE MASSARELLA

◆

I have a very fond memory of being at the Royal Dublin Horse Show in the late 1950s, with my Uncle Andrew and cousin John. Horse show week is famous for its show jumping and hunter classes, but for many visitors the horse sales are the highlights.

The first morning, as we walked into the show through the iron gates, we saw an old farmer coming towards us. He was leading a chestnut horse with a white face and four white legs (there is an old superstition among horse dealers that horses with four white legs are taboo). For the next two mornings this was the horse near the entrance when we arrived. On the fourth morning, my uncle said. 'The first thing we see will be the chestnut horse', and lo and behold there he was.

Some while later, John was riding and jumping a horse with a view to buy but my uncle's attention was diverted to three farmers trying to get this chestnut, with no rider, to go over a pole about 18 inches high. They had him on a lunge line but this horse would not jump. Suddenly they made him try again and one of the farmers threw a bundled-up raincoat at his hind quarters as he came to the pole. The horse put in a terrific leap and jumped about 5 feet over it. Within minutes my uncle and cousin had bought the horse for the princely sum of £370.

The new acquisition (Foxhound) was shipped over to the Massarella farm at Bentley, South Yorkshire, to begin training for show jumping. His first few outings were inauspicious and there was still doubt about him. He was ridden by a young lad named Bobby Beilby and started to win small competitions. When we moved him to the next grade, he began to show signs of being very good, and we renamed him Mister Softee,

after an ice-cream made by the family business. Mister Softee was soon ready for a higher grade of jumping and David Barker, who had ridden at the Rome Olympics in 1960, became his rider.

This partnership was successful and before too long Mister Softee was selected to represent Great Britain in the European Championships at White City in London, where he won the Gold Medal. He then went on to represent Great Britain in a number of Nations Cups around Europe. He also toured the United States, winning the Puissance in Washington, the prestigious Grand Prix of New York, and the Maple Leaf Stakes in Toronto.

Incidentally, after the Grand Prix, an American offered me about £47,000 for Mister Softee (a lot of money in the 1960s and especially for a horse). But in a transatlantic phone call, my cousin John said, 'We'll keep him for his Queen and country. Bring him home.'

By now the horse was in line to be selected for the Olympics in Tokyo. He was short-listed and started trials, but was withdrawn after developing a slight leg problem. Riders changed again and he was taken over by David Broome, a superb show-jumping rider.

They were immediately successful, winning in one year the four top UK events – the King George V Cup, the Hickstead Derby, the British Olympic Trial and the Victor Ludorum at Wembley. Mister Softee's success continued μthrough to the Mexico Olympics where he won a Bronze. He was a great horse that gave more than 100 per cent; everyone loved to watch him. A real character, a flashy looking animal and, when I sit at home and think about how he was purchased and his wonderful performances, I feel so lucky to have been involved with him.

SEBASTIAN COE

◆

Sport doesn't always get it right. There are few fans of our national sports that can't at some stage recall some shabby episodes, whether administrative shortcomings or competitive excess. My old sport, track and field, is not exempt from this. But in September 1995 my sport did get it right.

Sarajevo, for so long providing war-torn images and the human anguish that always accompanies them, for one day became host to an international athletics event. The International Olympic Committee and the International Amateur Athletics Federation together donated over $1,000,000 to rebuild the Kosovo Stadium in Sarajevo as part of the peace process. I flew into Sarajevo, a city that I visited eleven years earlier, to watch the Winter Olympic Games and I was stunned.

I recognise that people of my generation have led relatively sheltered lives and, apart from our armed services, have rarely witnessed the effects of civil war. I never thought that I would visit a war-torn city within three hours' flying time from London. The indoor stadium where Torvill and Dean elevated their sport into an art form was burnt out and left an ugly tangle of twisted steel. The International Broadcast Centre which sent to all corners of the globe the television pictures of these phenomenal competitions had also been razed to the ground. By lunch time on the day of the competition, a steady stream of people made their way by foot (a few lucky ones made use of the one working tram) to the new stadium.

The athletes competing had set aside their appearance fees and had endured a difficult journey by military planes from NATO airfields in Italy. After an intimate opening ceremony, competition got under way and 50,000 enthusiasts forgot about their depressing daily existence. For a few hours they enjoyed a sporting festival that would have been considered relatively commonplace anywhere else in the world.

I have long believed that sport has a real ability to foster international friendship and understanding. Never have I witnessed a more profound example of this than on that day.

SHERIDAN MORLEY

◆

It is about 1956, and we are in Rome. Robert, my father, was then much in demand for mad emperors and kings of France in MGM epics being made in Italy, which was where you could still get cheap actors to fill out the battle scenes. If you couldn't get Charles Laughton then you got Robert, and if he wasn't available then you went for Peter Ustinov.

Robert and I were nearly always late and on this particular morning had been in the hotel bar talking to Graham Greene, a recent convert to Catholicism who, like many, had become so devout that when he finally met the Pope they had a half-hour conversation at the end of which the Pope said, 'Oh, Mr Greene, I do so understand your point of view; you see I, too, am a Catholic.'

On this occasion, Pa and I had been invited after the day's shooting to a 'papal audience'; Graham to his chagrin had not, but made us promise to return to the hotel that evening with a detailed account. The day started badly enough. 'Quickly!' we said to the wonderfully caparisoned hotel doorman. 'Get us taxi to studio.' 'Alas I cannot,' he replied, 'and for two reasons; there is today a taxi strike in Rome, and I am Papal Nuncio to the Vatican.'

Somehow we got there, and then to the 'private audience' which simply meant standing with several thousand others under the Basilica of St Peter's, as a little man in white was carried through the far distance. Still, we could hardly disappoint Graham who was eagerly awaiting us at the bar.

'It was wonderful,' Pa told him. 'His Holiness spoke fluent English, invited us into his private study, asked all about the British film industry and especially Anna Neagle.' Graham accepted this unquestioningly, until as usual Pa went just too far: 'And then of course the wife came in,' he added, 'offered us a drink and asked us to stay to lunch.' Graham never spoke to us again.

SIMON CALLOW

◆

Galas are useful things, popular and effective in raising money. There is a pleasant bonus, too, for the performers: individual ego is entirely subordinate both to the cause in question, and to the seemingly impossible task of getting the cumbersome great things on stage. Actors who might not normally work with or see each other for years thus get together for a few hours in a very intimate atmosphere: we're all clinging to each other for dear life.

I have an especially vivid memory of an Amnesty Gala in aid of imprisoned writers held one Sunday in 1982 at the Duke of York's Theatre under the firm – not to say stern – leadership of Harold Pinter. There was a particularly distinguished line-up on that occasion: Eileen Atkins, Tim West, Prunella Scales, Alan Bates, Edward Fox, Clare Bloom, Michael Bryant, Vanessa Redgrave, John Gielgud.

In the afternoon, we ran through the individual items making up the first half; last to appear before the interval was Sir John, with Richard II's great soliloquy from the final act of the play. We all slipped out into the stalls to watch him speak the lines he had first spoken on stage more than half a century before, and which he had made so very much his own. It was a kind of quintessence of Gielgud. He stood in the centre of the stage, very simply, in his street clothes, and out of him poured, in a seamless lyrical thread, the great aria: 'I have been studying how I may compare/This prison where I live unto the world:/And, for because the world is populous,/And here is not a creature but myself,/I cannot do it.'

Violas, oboes, bassoons in his voice, his heart brimming up through his eyes. 'Music do I hear?/Ha, ha! keep time: – how sour sweet music is/When time is broke and no proportion kept!' We sat there in the empty theatre – seasoned actors, leaders of the profession – like children, transfixed, tears trickling down our faces, knowing that no one would ever again speak these words with such spontaneous artistry, direct from his generous heart. 'Yet blessing on his heart that gives it me!/For 'tis a sign of love; and love to Richard/Is a strange brooch in this all-hating world.'

There was perfect silence as he finished. Harold got up. 'Very good, John,' he said. 'Bit sentimental.' 'Quite right,' said Sir John. 'I always cry too much. Never stop telling me if I do.' His performance that night was indeed on a tighter rein, and all the more powerful in the context of all the many cries of pain from prisoners past and present. But that still Sunday afternoon in the stalls of the Duke of York's Theatre is the single most intimate moment I have ever shared with my fellow actors.

SOPHIE RYDER

◆

When I was ten years old, I was walking along the banks of the River Thames with a friend when we came across a man at his easel, painting a watercolour. I approached and asked if I could have a look. He stood back for me to see and I remember thinking that his picture was rather dull. He asked me what I wanted to be when I grew up. I said, 'I already am what I want to be – an Artist,' and when we then said that we were going to look around the shops he replied, 'If you were a *real* artist, you would be spending this lovely Saturday morning drawing or painting.' I have never forgotten that remark and because of it I feel guilty every time I go shopping.

Years before this, when I was about four, I used to sit for hours filling sketchbook after sketchbook. I remember drawing families of fish and bumblebees. It was a kind of obsession, drawing and constructing anything – from cardboard sculpture to mobiles and jewellery.

Now that I have children of my own, I am fascinated to see the way in which they draw and construct things. I try not to intervene or even help. I think it's better to let them develop in their own way. They are very interested in my work and love spending time in the studio. Like me when I was young, they too spend hours folding and cutting, making fantastical constructions. My eldest daughter, Maud, when six, asked why she had to go to school and work when I was at home having fun in my studio!

STANLEY KALMS

◆

I have pressed the 'It can't be happening to me'
button on my memory bank and four thoughts
flash up:

◆ My first solo flight in a Chipmunk. Am I out
of my mind? All alone, my life in my own hands
– controlled by a joystick – and with only
fourteen hours of lessons. Defying gravity, single
engine, travelling at 180mph and only a thin
piece of concrete on which to return to safety.

◆ Then across the Atlantic and making a short
walk in a New York snowstorm across town to
visit my son, and getting caught in a massive
snowdrift in the middle of Park Avenue – the
widest boulevard in New York. Freezing cold as
only a New York canyon can be – wearing
inappropriate city clothes and shoes – I am
three-quarters buried in a mini-avalanche and
starting to panic and visualise the next day's
headlines ... 'Tycoon freezes to death in the
middle of the road'. Not a person in sight, no
traffic – it could have been Siberia. Luckily only
the good die young!

◆ Then I am kneeling on a pedestal and this
distinguished looking lady advances towards me
brandishing a sword. Is it all over? Not quite as,
deftly missing my head, she tapped me on each
shoulder and 'mister' disappeared out of my life.

◆ And the most long-lasting and memorable –
when the most desirable lady in the world said
'yes' to a tentative suggestion I had put to her
regarding our future legal relationship.

STEPHEN TUMIM

◆

In the Spring of 1996 I was in Uganda, looking at the criminal justice system and, in particular, at the prisons, so as to see where funding was most needed. The prisoners in Uganda are not held in cells but in large sheds with tin roofs and little lighting. Their blankets (they have no beds) line the walls, and at the far end there are the remains of lavatories, holes in the ground and sometimes buckets of water.

I stood alone one morning outside one of the sheds when a large group of half-naked prisoners called to me to follow them and look in the shed. I peered into the dark, where many bodies appeared to be standing or lying about. 'Pull-pull, pull-pull,' they called to me and I was invited, partly pushed, further into the gloom. I was moved right through the shed. There was no lighting but much calling out: 'pull-pull, pull-pull.' I found myself at the back of the shed where there was a small window in the tin roof, and the lavatory holes were likely to be.

As everywhere in Uganda, there was a minimum of smell, and a surprising amount of cleanliness considering the lack of soap and water. I looked up and for the first time in the shed was able to pick out some colour. There was a battered red tin box, eight feet up the wall and there was a string hanging from it. 'Pull-pull,' they cried. I pulled the string, and there was a tiny flush of water below. The prisoners clapped and cheered. It was the first and only time when I found a flushing lavatory in a Ugandan prison.

I have had three careers. I was a barrister and a County Court judge. I was her Majesty's Chief Inspector of Prisons, and I was Principal of St Edmund Hall, Oxford. As a lawyer I met many prisoners, but was never invited to pull a plug. As a prison inspector, one of my main concerns had been with sanitation. At the Hall, we had both sanitation and undergraduates as polite and cheerful as Ugandan prisoners. My journey through that shed was the time when my various careers seemed to come together.

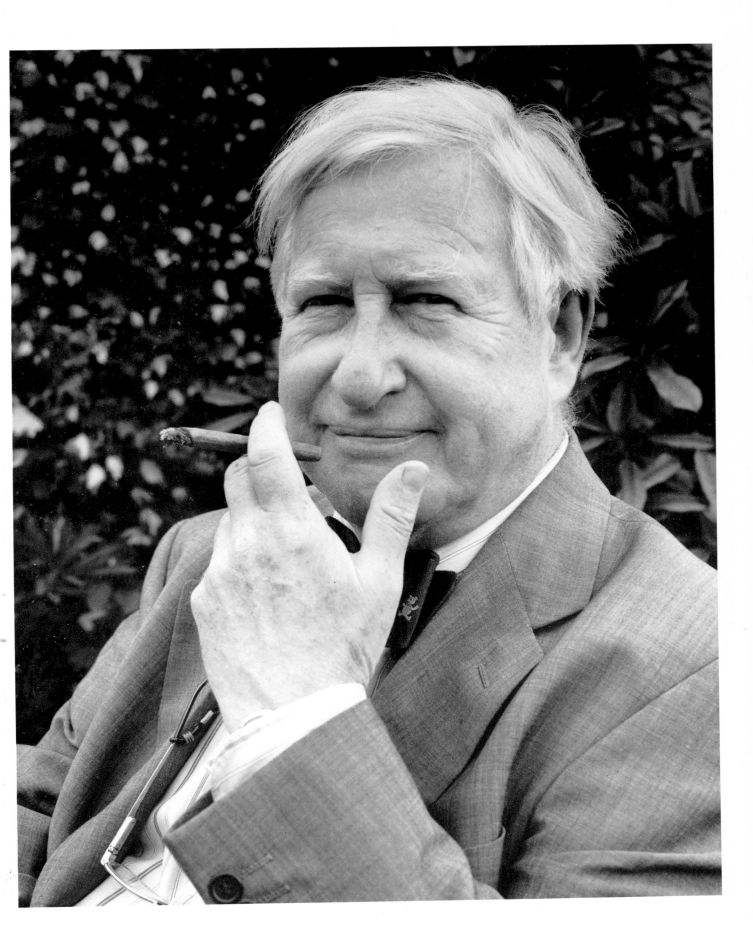

STEVE McFADDEN

◆

At the age of twenty-five I decided to become an actor. I auditioned at any drama school that would let me. One of those auditions was at Manchester Polytechnic where they did a combined degree/acting course.

On Monday I went along for the audition, watched others perform and did my own audition speeches. At the end of the audition, as is customary, certain people were asked to stay behind. I was one of those lucky few. A couple of people went in before me and came out saying that they were starting in the next academic year. I said, with my thumb up in the air, see you in September.

I went in to meet the head of the drama department and he said to me that he had asked people to stay behind for two reasons; firstly to offer students a place and to start next September, and secondly to advise others that it was not worth their while pursuing a career in the theatre and that, unfortunately, I fell into the latter category. I didn't know whether to laugh or cry or punch him. On Wednesday of the same week, I auditioned at RADA and got in.

STEVEN ISSERLIS

◆

Perhaps it is because our father comes from Russia that my sisters, Annette and Rachel, and I are incurably (and mostly unashamedly) nostalgic. We are constantly harking back to our childhood. Memories which, while richly unamusing for others, keep us happy for hours.

Until her late teens, Rachel insisted (every so often) on buying and consuming tins of baby food (an improvement on her diet as a toddler when she would swap meals with her cat – perhaps that in itself was nostalgia for an earlier feline existence). We all love to surprise each other at Christmas and on birthdays with little relics from our childhood – out-of-print books or long-forgotten games or toys.

I can't explain why these memories are so fascinating for us; maybe it is because it gives us a sense of continuity. It is true that when we remember how we all felt as youngsters, we realise that not much has changed.

Several years ago, I became friends with Nigel Kennedy, and invited him to my parents' house for a meal. Once there, he dutifully turned his dessert bowl upside down, sending his chocolate pudding cascading to the floor (he claimed that he wanted to see if it would stick). My sisters reminded me that my friends always behaved like that. At an earlier birthday party, my friend

Bakewell had done exactly the same, probably for pretty much the same reason. I'd blurted out 'Frankie's my best friend – and I hate him.'

Today, in the midst of a heated chamber music rehearsal with my nearest and dearest colleagues, all too often I feel exactly the same emotions surging within. And even musically. When I was two years old, I composed my first deathless masterpiece, 'Banana Custard for Pudding'. The music (which Annette claims to have composed although I have my doubts about this – it has not yet become a legal issue between us) consists of a series of descending triads spanning a minor seventh, falling by steps a tone apart. The words (which I definitely composed) were: 'Banana custard for pudding, banana custard for pudding, banana custard for pudding, banana custard for pudding' etc, until it got too low for me to sing – a very early example of minimalism.

When, in the late 1980s, John Tavener wrote for me his monumental work for cello and strings 'The Protecting Veil', inspired by the ecstatic music of the Russian Orthodox Church, I felt at first a little bemused by this unfamiliar style. But then I noticed, on the first page, a very familiar theme – a series of descending triads spanning a minor seventh. Suddenly the meaning of the music became clear.

TERRY WAITE

◆

There was a time in my life when I spent many years totally alone in a dark room. For a long time I had nothing to read nor was I ever given a pen or pencil. It was during these long years that I drew on memory. In some respects the experience was similar to an ageing process. I found that I had difficulty remembering recent events but childhood memories came flooding back. I was able to use my memory actively so that as I trod down the corridor of ages I talked to the people I met along the way; felt the warmth of a childhood sun and savoured the smell of freshly baked bread. By using imagination, I was able to keep my mind alive and meet many old friends, together with some not so friendly faces.

There is one memory of those solitary days that lingers in my mind. One night as I was sleeping on the floor of my cell I had a dream. I dreamed that I was walking alone along a deserted beach. Suddenly I felt fear. I was lost. I peered into the distance and to my relief saw a figure walking towards me. This person took my hand and guided me to the nearest town. Then I woke up and realised that the person who had helped me was my youngest daughter. I felt a deep sense of peace.

Years later when I was finally released I was taken to hospital. There I met my family for the first time in years. My youngest daughter took my hand and said to me, 'Daddy, take all the help that will be given to you here.' It was then that I remembered the dream.

Tim Rice

Both my parents were literary rather than musical; in fact both were more or less tone deaf. They did, however, read prodigiously – fact and fiction, ancient and modern, heavy and light. The house was full of books (mainly sixpenny Penguins) and magazines, when a fraction of the number published today existed. There are still many cubic feet of *Punch* and *The Aeroplane* in my mother's attic. They loved the radio, and the *Radio Times* became one of my favourite journals – a magical cornucopia of dates, times, numbers, people and places.

And it really was the radio times that mattered – the television listings were a tiny footnote to those of the Light Programme, Home Service and Third Programme and, having no television, we had no need of them anyway. My father's general knowledge was voluminous. Every car journey was like an up-market game show with quizzes, and facts and figures about every subject under the sun. I am still unbeatable on British cars from 1946 to 1956 – a foreign car was a major event and about a 1 in 200 shot on the English country lanes back then. And I still like to be asked to name all the states of America in under two minutes.

TONY BLAIR

◆

It was eight o'clock on Wednesday night when I knocked on John Burton's door to see if it was possible to get the Trimdon Village nomination for the new seat of Sedgefield in County Durham. The general election of 1983 had just been called, and I was not feeling very cheerful because I had no seat to fight. Sedgefield had suddenly become available at the last moment. It was the last constituency in the country to select a Labour candidate. It was my last chance.

I had already spent a fruitless week there trying to get a nomination from other branches, and without a nomination I couldn't even get on the short list. It seemed a hopeless quest. I hadn't been married very long so by the Tuesday thoughts of Cherie were uppermost in my mind. I had even thought about ringing John and cancelling our meeting. But when I phoned him to make the appointment, there had been something about his voice on the phone, something about the conversation we had. It was nothing I could put my finger on but I knew I had to go and see him.

When I entered his sitting room there were five of them – John, Terry Ward, Peter Brookes, Simon Hoban and Paul Trippett. There were also numerous cans of beer, a wine box, and Aberdeen *v* Real Madrid on the television. John

said, 'Grab a can and sit down. We're watching the final of the European Cup Winners' Cup, and we'll have a chat when it's finished.'

During the game there was a lot of laughter and good-humoured banter, and although this was the first time I had met them, I felt a part of the group and knew there was something special about them. But I was nervous and the match seemed to last for ever. It was a draw at half time, still a draw at extra time, and finally Aberdeen won on penalties. I thought the game would never end.

Finally, the questioning began. They wanted to know about my political beliefs, why I wanted the Sedgefield seat and what I intended to do to change the Labour Party to make it more in tune with the ordinary man and woman in the street. It was 1983, a small village in County Durham, yet these five young people knew that the Labour Party had to change, and we discovered that we had many similar ideas as to how this could be achieved.

That was what had drawn me there that night, and when they said they would get me the nomination, and do everything they could to get me selected and then elected, I really believed they could do it.

And they did.

TREVOR MCDONALD

◆

Memories have an intrinsic value in the trade of journalism. They can form part of the journalist's armour, the side which he or she displays to the non-media world. They come in a variety of shapes and sizes but among the better known are those recalled to prove the worth, the integrity or the bravery of the story-teller.

The memory of which I am most proud has little to do with either journalistic enterprise or bravery. I remember it for an entirely different reason. I think of it as one of the few occasions when in the course of my journalism I was able to do something transparently useful.

Several years ago, I was filming in Hong Kong on the influx of refugees from Vietnam. As part of the exercise, we were taken offshore in a coastguard cutter to see the latest batch of arrivals who had been kept, for health reasons, on a sort of floating platform. They were a pathetic lot, sixty or seventy of them squatting in silence as we approached noisily. At that moment when I first saw them, they looked the most forlorn people in the world, floating in a void off the mainland, clinging to the edge of civilisation.

The coastguard cutter tied up alongside, and we climbed aboard. None of the refugees moved. No one said a word. They spoke only when spoken to. Otherwise they simply stared into the middle distance. I did a number of fairly routine interviews with the assistance of one of their number who spoke good English, and heard in low, flat, dissonant voices the heart-rending tales of their crossing to Hong Kong. It had been a journey of true desperation – a journey which had broken too many families.

When our interviews were done, I sat next to the man who had acted as my interpreter and asked him what on earth had made him decide to make the hazardous journey in cramped, half-seaworthy boats, only to face the ghastly prospect of incarceration in an overcrowded refugee camp. He told me a most amazing story. He said that he had come to Hong Kong to escape the regime in Vietnam and to try to connect up with his brother in America. 'How will you do that from here?' I asked, incredulous. Before he could answer, I volunteered to try to contact his brother if he had the address. He did and I sped back to my hotel and to my old typewriter.

I left Hong Kong soon after my encounter with the refugees and travelled back to London. Some four months later, I received a letter from a man in Los Angeles chiding me for getting his address wrong, but thanking me for finding his brother.

For many days afterwards, I found it impossible to hide my joy.

TREVOR NUNN

◆

The build-up to the first night of Andrew Lloyd Webber's musical *Cats* had been gruellingly longer than planned. Judi Dench had broken her Achilles tendon mid-rehearsal so the preview period was extended in the belief that with a delayed opening she might recover sufficiently to appear. When finally all hopes of Judi's return were dashed by a second injury, Elaine Paige came into the show at the kind of short notice that myths are made of. She sang her role, building up to her impassioned aria 'Memory', with extraordinary emotional commitment while still largely unaware of the overall story of which she was a climactic part.

At long last, the production played its press night and for some, who had found utterly risible the very idea of a group of adults imitating pussy cats in the service of a small collection of children's poems, the wait had clearly been almost unbearable. A sort of whispering sniggering curiosity was in the air (according to the feline sixth sense which I had by then developed) and most people I knew had an unmistakable tone of commiseration in their greeting.

The show was designed with thrilling originality by John Napier, playing games with our sense of scale, and thrillingly choreographed by Gillian Lynne, who had taken her phenomenally fit, double-jointed company beyond the pain barrier in terms of both stamina and daring. Improvisational techniques ensured that the cast established a mercurial interactive relationship with the celebrity audience, sharing confidences, offering endearments and yet playing treacherously with disdain and aloof superiority.

The grip began to exert itself, the cheering got louder as the evening progressed. Elaine Paige stopped the show with her eleven o'clock number, and finally the company burst into the first part of their curtain call. What would have happened thereafter we shall never know.

Brian Blessed strode in a most unfeline manner to stage centre, and when his gesturing failed to achieve silence he took off (horror of horrors) his flowing guruesque Old Deuteronomy wig. This man had a problem. A hush descended, into which Brian dropped the information that since the theatre had been informed that there was a bomb in the auditorium, it would be advisable for everybody to leave in an orderly fashion.

The tension and fear replacing what had been so ecstatic only moments before was as cruel as it was palpable. The police instruction applied to backstage as well as front, and a few minutes after completing a no-holds-barred performance which had taken from them every last ounce of energy and drop of emotion, the cast were wandering in the street outside, still in costume, still garishly made up, shivering in the night air, confused, tearful, grim, robbed. A number of audience members draped their coats around the stunned performers, as sniffer dogs entered the building and the crowds were urged to move further away. It is extraordinary to think that a show with such an unpromising beginning and which seemed fated not to succeed should still be running in the same theatre a generation later.

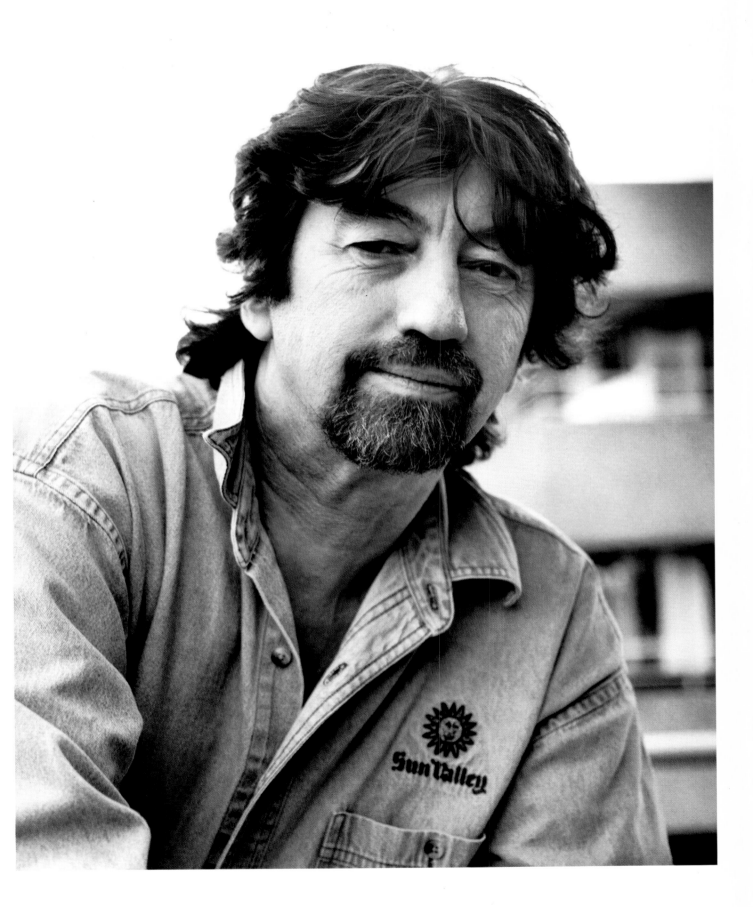

URI GELLER

◆

My most notable moment was when I glimpsed a girl, caught through thick mist about two years ago. And I've thought about this moment so much, it has changed my life. The tale would be more dramatic if I had seen her in a blaze of lightning, with thunder shattering my senses. But the reality is I saw her only when the clouds parted for a second, and the impact of the vision did not strike me for a long, long time.

I was having my picture taken in Bristol. The event was a book promotion, and a newspaper wanted shots of me on Brunel's suspension bridge. 'Don't bend it,' they said. Yeah, sure, like I'd want the bridge to give a sudden twist when it's the only thing between me and a plunge 300 feet into the gorge.

I pulled on a sheepskin jacket for the shoot, and still wasn't warm enough. The photographer couldn't get his flash to work – I warn people that technology gets temperamental around me. So I started pacing on the bridge, to pass the time and keep the shivers away, and as I turned for the third time I saw the girl.

She had not been there a moment earlier. She stood at the centre of the span, with the cloud blowing around her, and for all I could see she might have been floating. Her hair was long, waist-length, and of a blondeness so bright it could have been polished silver. For just one instant, I thought she was my daughter Natalie (they looked about the same age) but Nat doesn't have hair like that.

The next thought to hit me was fear. What was she doing, on the middle of the bridge, wearing no coat on a cold, wet evening? The bridge is a notorious spot for suicides. Surely she wasn't … 'Are you OK?' I yelled out, and when she didn't look at me I twisted round to call for Martin, the

photographer. I turned back, and she was gone.

I ran across the bridge, hoping that a burst of cloud had come down and I would bump into her. But I didn't. So I prayed. Please God, please, please don't let her have jumped. Let her be a figment of the light. Say my mind was playing tricks. I'll even believe she was a ghost. But don't let her be a suicide.

When I was warm and dry, and my wife had talked some sense into me, things seemed better. She was probably just out for a walk. Maybe there was a boyfriend two steps behind, invisible in the mist. Maybe she heard me yelling, and decided she'd better head back home sharpish. At any rate, no body like hers has been pulled from the Avon (I asked my cuttings agency to check). So I am thankful my prayers were heard.

But since that night, I haven't stopped thinking about her. I gave her a name, Ella, because in Hebrew it means Girl of God. It seemed to fit. And I gave her a family that might provoke a teenage girl into long, cold, mysterious walks on wet nights. I told myself stories about her – how she possessed paranormal powers like mine, how she was bullied and abused and treated like a freak. In the end, I wrote a novel, just to get the glimpse out of my system.

But she's still there, like a taste of the truth while we make gluttons of ourselves with lies all our lives. The truth always is that way. For a few moments, we see it clearly. The mist rolls back and our senses lock onto the vivid image. Afterwards, we doubt those senses. We accuse them of fabrication. We prefer to linger in our comfortable mists, and reject the sensational, inconvenient instants of clarity. Perhaps we are too feeble to look at the truth. Except through mists, and from the corners of our eyes.

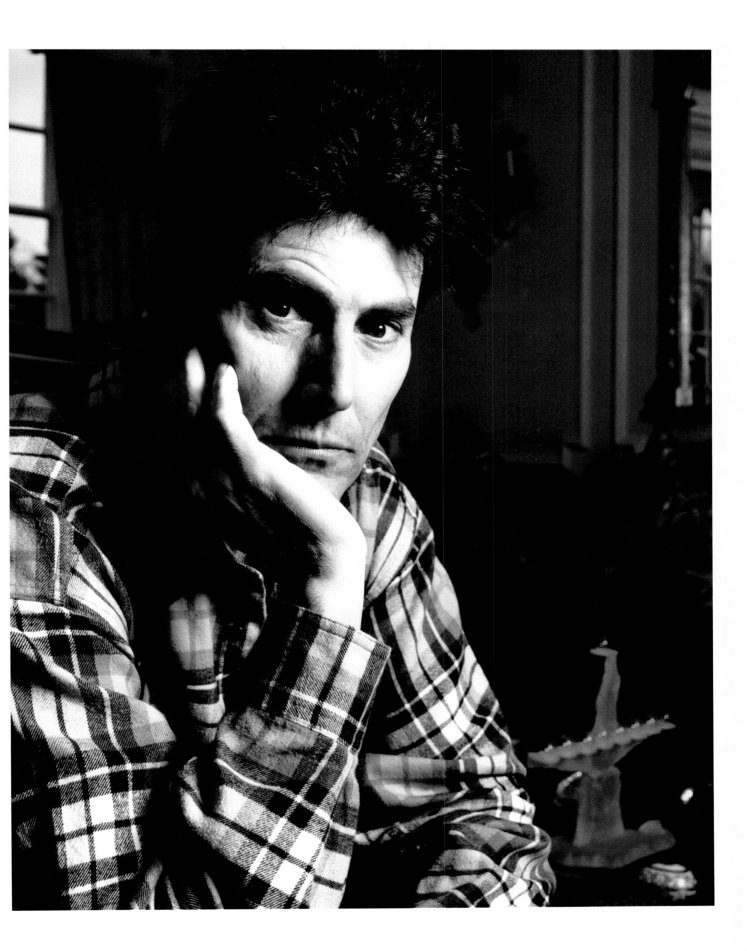

VIVIANA DURANTE

◆

For me, my return in 1998 to the Teatro dell' Opera di Roma with the *Sleeping Beauty* was like closing a big chapter of my life. I left Rome with the same ballet when I was ten – dancing the White Cat – and returned to it with Aurora. It was a real awakening for me to find myself in my country, triumphant and amongst my friends and loved ones.

All the suffering and hard work suddenly made sense and gave me a further reason to continue. Subconsciously I was waiting for the moment when I could show my fondest gratitude to my parents for everything they have done for me. It seemed the best way to do this was publicly to dedicate these performances to them. And so this is what I did.

WILLIAM HAGUE

◆

Some of my strongest memories are associated with places. I remember as a young boy the first time I visited my father's factory in Rotherham and being entranced by the whirring machinery.

But not all my memories are of visiting places for the first time. We can all walk through a familiar landscape a dozen times and think nothing of it, and then walk through it again and see it in a wholly new light.

I have a vivid memory of just such a moment five years ago. It came towards the end of a 120-mile walk from the west coast of England to my home near Catterick in North Yorkshire.

It was late afternoon, and I had already covered 20 miles that day. I was looking forward to a good dinner and a pint in Keld. Suddenly, I came over the hill and found myself at the top of Swaledale in the Yorkshire Dales, looking out at the most breathtaking scene of hills and valleys bathed in the golden light of the sunset. Swaledale is close to my home. Sandwiched between Wensleydale and Arkengarthdale, it is one of the most striking of the Dales, and is in the heart of 'Herriot country'.

I must have driven through Swaledale a hundred times before and since then. And the walk along the Swale Gorge from Keld to Muker is one of my favourite walks. But for some reason, that day it was as though I had never seen Swaledale before. Its astonishing beauty and grandeur struck me like a revelation. The River Swale glistened like a ribbon of silver in the valley below. As the sun started to set, I became conscious of something I suppose I had always instinctively known: that I am fortunate to live in the most beautiful corner of the earth.

ZOË WANAMAKER

◆

It was very early on Sunday morning, 1 June 1997, that I decided to test the acoustics of the Globe Theatre without anybody there – no visitors, no workmen, no fellow actors. I drove to Southwark to go through the opening speech of *Henry V* privately, the first line being 'Oh, for a muse of fire ...'. These were going to be the official first words of Shakespeare that would herald the beginning of the Globe's new life, the first words spoken by an actor. Although I had resisted the request I felt that it would be fitting I said them.

The nightwatchman, who I knew well, had said he would meet me at eight o'clock before he left for home. It was a beautiful morning, the sun was shining and I walked into the empty theatre. It was quiet and seemingly a vast space. It took me a while to summon up the courage to open my mouth – I was lacking in confidence and felt shy and strangely embarrassed. I wandered around the stage looking to see where was the best place to stand, and gradually each time I went through the speech my confidence grew with the knowledge that I knew the words.

After the third time of speaking it full out, looking out at the empty seats, imagining the Queen and Prince Philip on my left, imagining the people standing looking up at me and being able to look back at them, I gained my confidence and 'performed'. At the end, I gave a bow and from nowhere came applause. Two policemen and three security guards had been listening and came forward, and as they did so the sun came up and blinded me and filled the whole stage with light.

I am not a believer but this was a very moving experience. I feel that perhaps my father was present, along with Shakespeare.

ACKNOWLEDGEMENTS

◆

I would like to express my personal gratitude to the following sponsors. Without their generous support, this book would never have materialised. In particular

Sir Stanley Kalms, Dixons Foundation
Sir Harry Solomon
Greg Hutchings, Tomkins Plc
Lord Hamlyn
Michael and Debra Edison
Eisai-Pfizer Ltd

Also
Ronald Cohen (Apax Partners & Co)
Sir Richard Greenbury (Marks & Spencer Plc)
Graham Kirkham (DFS Furniture Co Plc)
David Pomson (Western Foil)
John Ritblat (The British Land Co Ltd)
Melanie R Sabelhaus, USA

Sir David Alliance, Jarvis Astaire,
David Brecher, Michael Bullman,
Stanley Cohen, Geoffrey Counsell, Lord Forte,
DJ Freeman, Pat Froomberg, Ian Gibson,
Andrew Harriman, Maurice Hatter,
Henman's Solicitors, Sir Christopher Hogg,
Henry Knobil, Ervin Landau, GJ Lipton,
Sir Peter Parker, Stephen Rubin,
Ibram Shalam, Sir Sigmund Sternberg,
Dr Miriam Stoppard, Tom Stoppard

My thanks to colleagues and friends
Gordon Bishop Laboratories
Hasselblad UK Ltd
Peter Osborne of The Berkeley Square Gallery
Rob Carter
Valerie Long
Lorna Duckworth
Mr Print
Nina Bialoguski
Nicky Thompson *and* Christine Wood *for their editorial and design work respectively*

A special mention for Harry Cayton, Executive Director, Martin Horwood *and their team at the Alzheimer's Disease Society whose support and enthusiasm were greatly appreciated*

My personal thanks and apologies also go to those who generously gave me their time and a memory for this book, but who have not been included because of the limited number of pages

Finally, a special word of gratitude to Matron and all the wonderful staff at 'Westmount', who care for the elderly and those with Alzheimer's disease and dementia